My Little Pony

Friends Forever

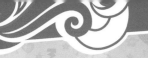

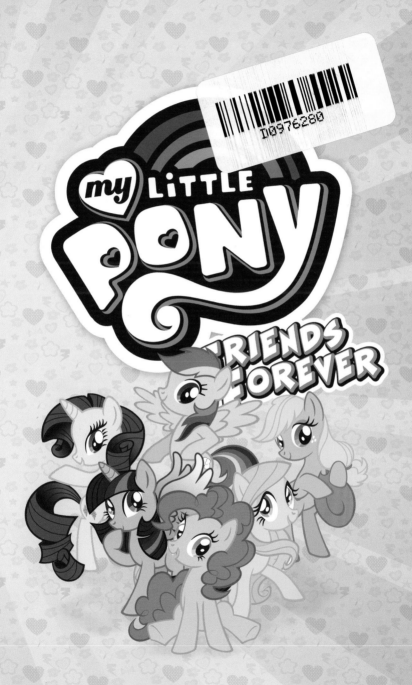

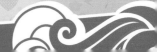

Rarity & Babs

Written by **Jeremy Whitley**
Art by **Agnes Garbowska**
Color Assist by **Lauren Perry**

Spike & Princess Luna

Written by **Jeremy Whitley**
Art by **Agnes Garbowska**
Color Assist by **Lauren Perry**

Applejack & Mayor Mare

Written by **Bobby Curnow**
Art by **Brenda Hickey**
Colors by **Heather Breckel**

Silver Spoon & Diamond Tiara

Written by **Jeremy Whitley**
Art by **Jenn Blake**
Colors by **Heather Breckel**

Twilight Sparkle & Big Mac

Written by **Ted Anderson**
Art by **Brenda Hickey**
Colors by **Heather Breckel**

Letters by **Neil Uyetake**
Series Edits by **Bobby Curnow**

Cover Art by **Jay Fosgitt**
Collection Edits by **Justin Eisinger & Alonzo Simon**
Collection Design by **Neil Uyetake**
Publisher: **Ted Adams**

Licensed By: Hasbro

www.IDWPUBLISHING.com

ISBN: 978-1-63140-882-3

20 19 18 17   1 2 3 4

Special thanks to Meghan McCarthy, Eliza Hart, Ed Lane, Beth Artale, and Michael Kelly.   For international rights, contact licensing@idwpublishing.com

Ted Adams, CEO & Publisher • **Greg Goldstein,** President & COO • **Robbie Robbins,** EVP/Sr. Graphic Artist • **Chris Ryall,** Chief Creative Officer • **David Hedgecock,** Editor-in-Chief • **Laurie Windrow,** Senior Vice President of Sales & Marketing • **Matthew Ruzicka,** CPA, Chief Financial Officer • **Lorelei Bunjes,** VP of Digital Services • **Jerry Bennington,** VP of New Product Development

Facebook: facebook.com/idwpublishing • Twitter: @idwpublishing • YouTube: youtube.com/idwpublishing
Tumblr: tumblr.idwpublishing.com • Instagram: instagram.com/idwpublishing

Rainbow Dash & Fluttershy

Written by **Christina Rice**
Art by **Jay Fosgitt**
Colors by **Heather Breckel**

Rarity & The Cakes

Written by **Christina Rice**
Art by **Brenda Hickey**
Colors by **Heather Breckel**

Princess Luna & Discord

Written by **Jeremy Whitley**
Art by **Brenda Hickey**
Colors by **Heather Breckel**

Zecora & Spike

Written by **Ted Anderson**
Art by **Agnes Garbowska**
Color Assist by **Lauren Perry**

Princess Celestia & Pinkie Pie

Written by **Christina Rice**
Art by **Jay Fosgitt**
Colors by **Heather Breckel**

Fluttershy & Applejack

Written by **Ted Anderson**
Art by **Tony Fleecs**
Colors by **Heather Breckel**

Rarity & Gilda

Written by **Georgia Ball**
Art by **Jay Fosgitt**
Colors by **Heather Breckel**

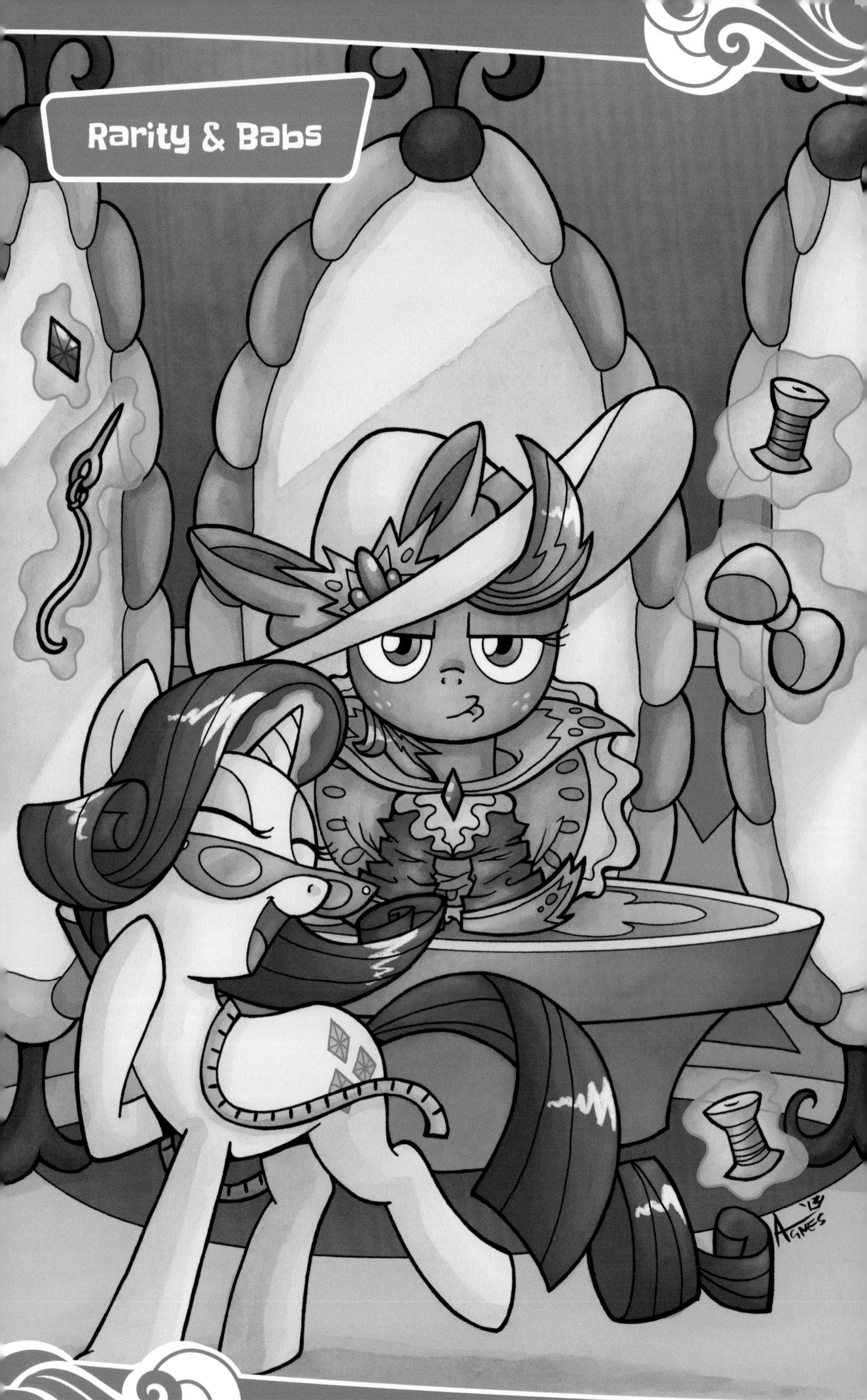
Rarity & Babs
Agnes '13

art by AGNES GARBOWSKA

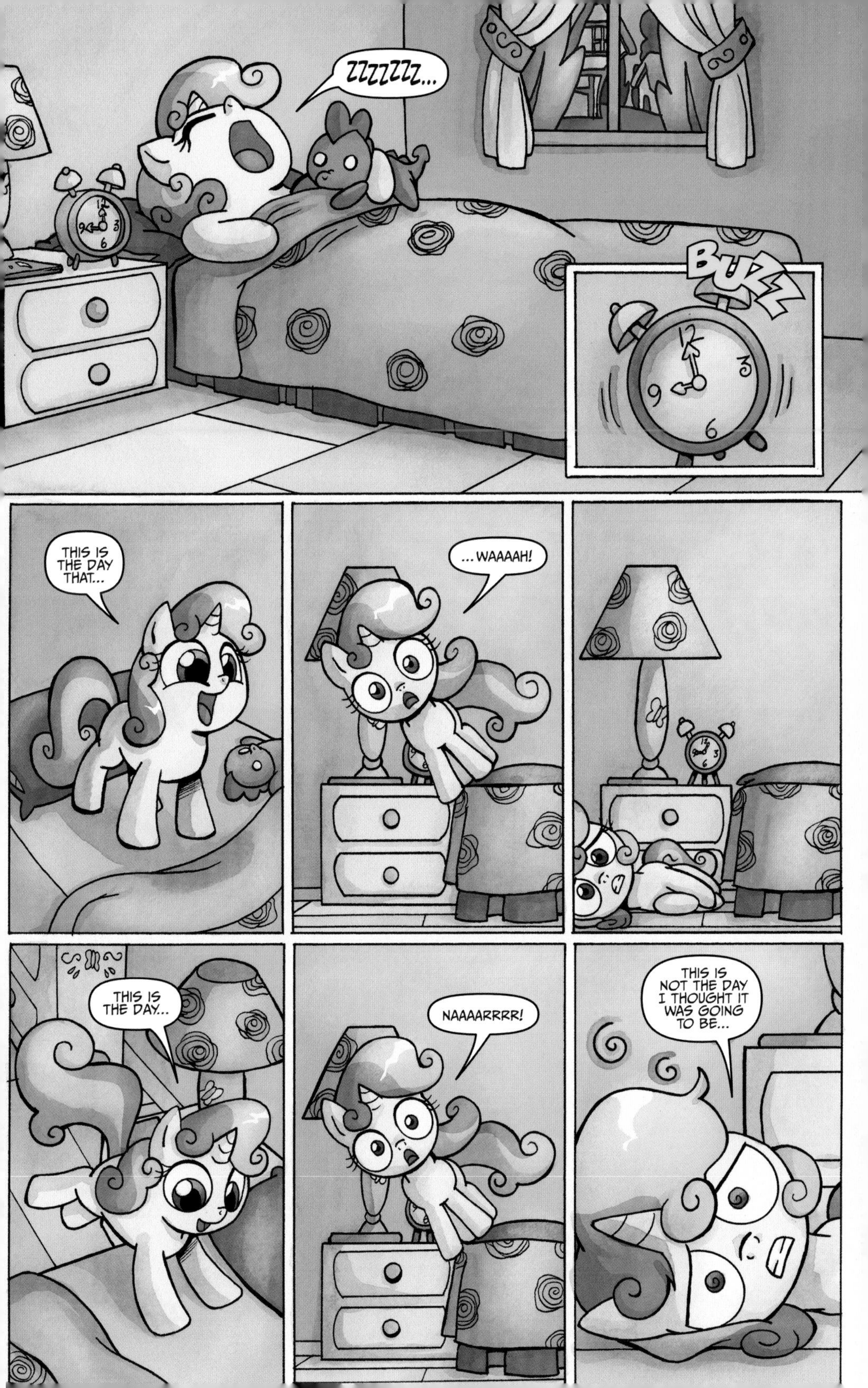
ZZZZZZZ...
BUZZ
THIS IS THE DAY THAT...
...WAAAAH!
THIS IS THE DAY...
NAAAARRRR!
THIS IS NOT THE DAY I THOUGHT IT WAS GOING TO BE...

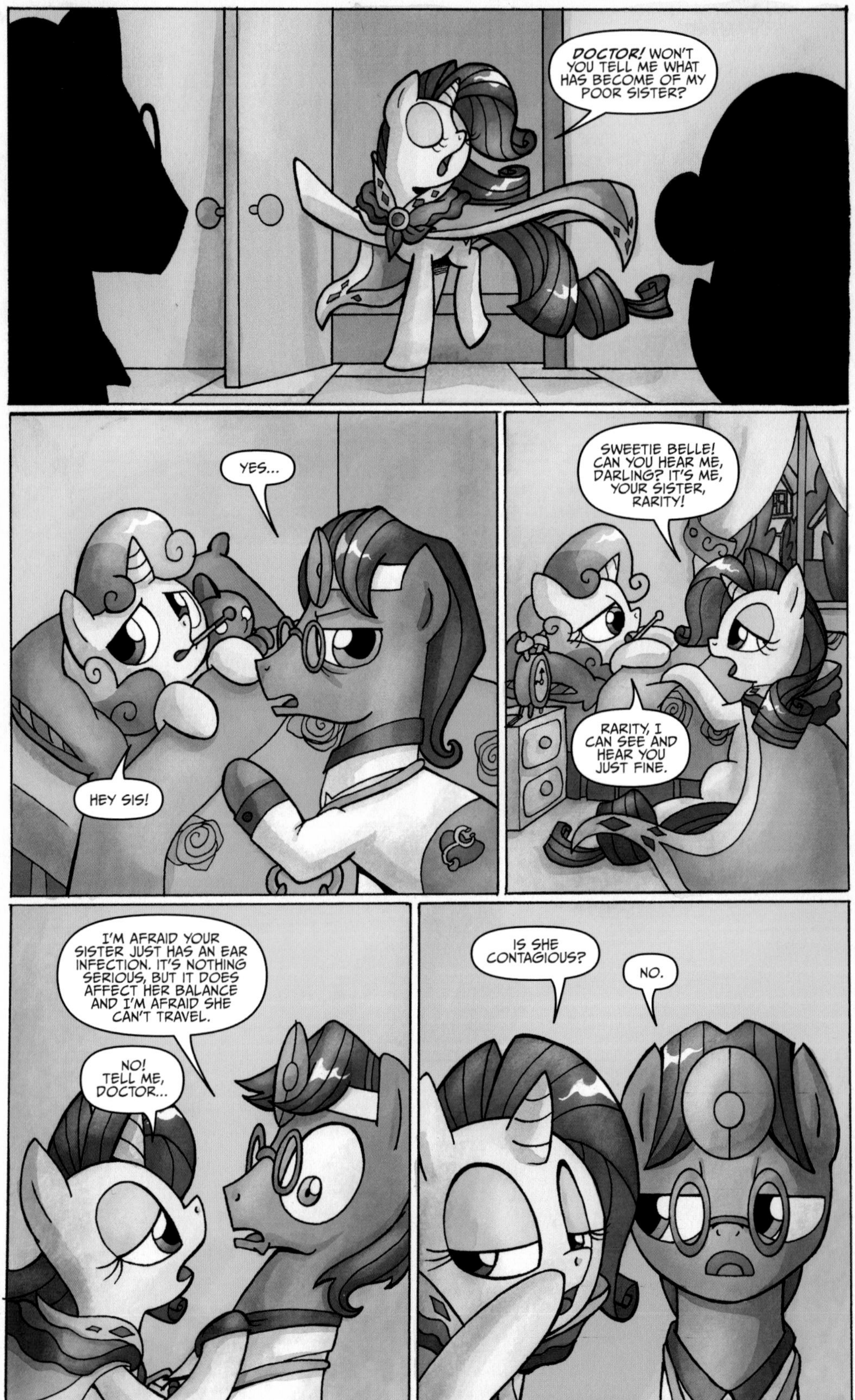
DOCTOR! WON'T YOU TELL ME WHAT HAS BECOME OF MY POOR SISTER?
YES...
HEY SIS!
SWEETIE BELLE! CAN YOU HEAR ME, DARLING? IT'S ME, YOUR SISTER, RARITY!
RARITY, I CAN SEE AND HEAR YOU JUST FINE.
I'M AFRAID YOUR SISTER JUST HAS AN EAR INFECTION. IT'S NOTHING SERIOUS, BUT IT DOES AFFECT HER BALANCE AND I'M AFRAID SHE CAN'T TRAVEL.
NO! TELL ME, DOCTOR...
IS SHE CONTAGIOUS?
NO.

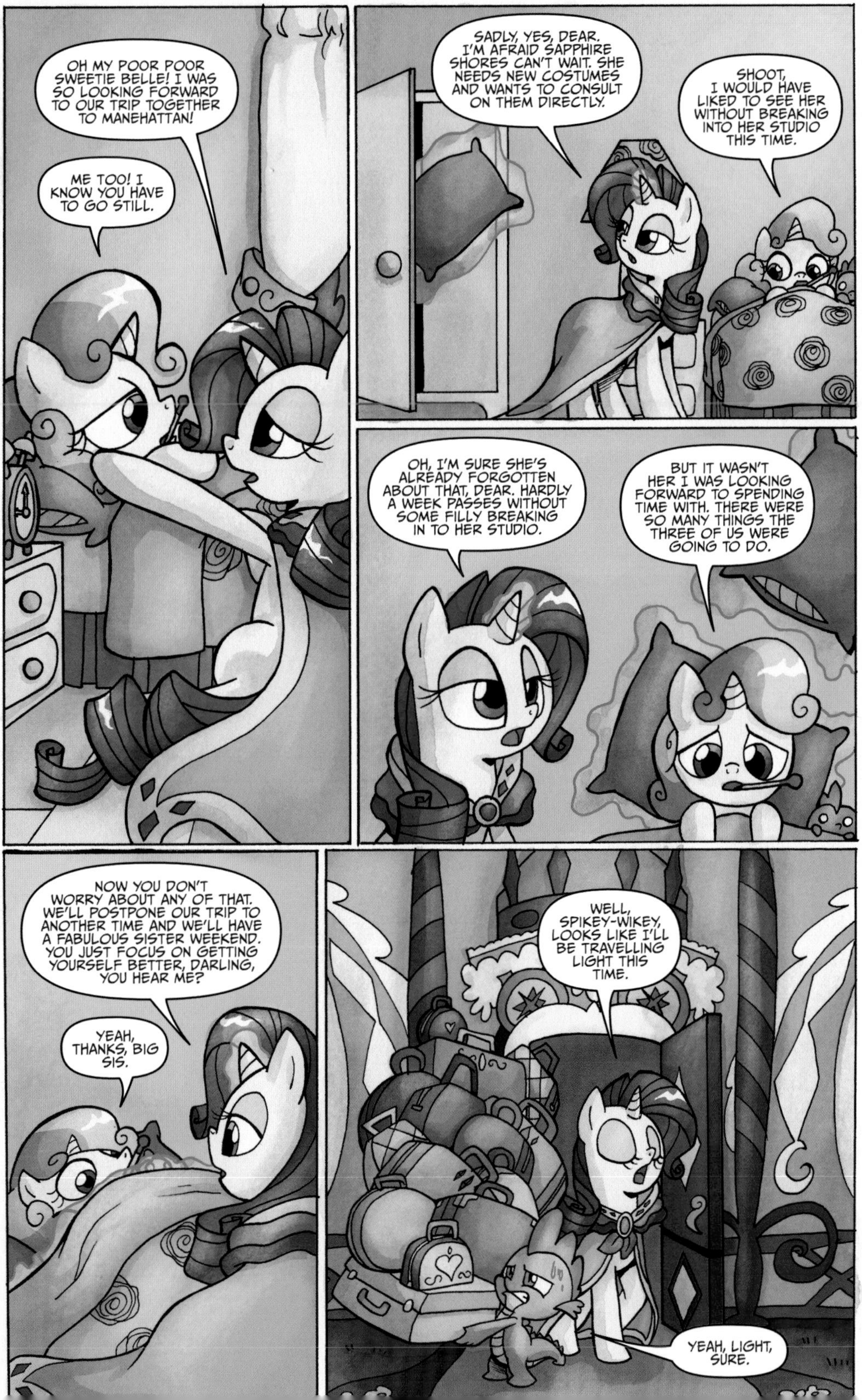
OH MY POOR POOR SWEETIE BELLE! I WAS SO LOOKING FORWARD TO OUR TRIP TOGETHER TO MANEHATTAN!
ME TOO! I KNOW YOU HAVE TO GO STILL.
SADLY, YES, DEAR. I'M AFRAID SAPPHIRE SHORES CAN'T WAIT. SHE NEEDS NEW COSTUMES AND WANTS TO CONSULT ON THEM DIRECTLY.
SHOOT, I WOULD HAVE LIKED TO SEE HER WITHOUT BREAKING INTO HER STUDIO THIS TIME.
OH, I'M SURE SHE'S ALREADY FORGOTTEN ABOUT THAT, DEAR. HARDLY A WEEK PASSES WITHOUT SOME FILLY BREAKING IN TO HER STUDIO.
BUT IT WASN'T HER I WAS LOOKING FORWARD TO SPENDING TIME WITH. THERE WERE SO MANY THINGS THE THREE OF US WERE GOING TO DO.
NOW YOU DON'T WORRY ABOUT ANY OF THAT. WE'LL POSTPONE OUR TRIP TO ANOTHER TIME AND WE'LL HAVE A FABULOUS SISTER WEEKEND. YOU JUST FOCUS ON GETTING YOURSELF BETTER, DARLING, YOU HEAR ME?
YEAH, THANKS, BIG SIS.
WELL, SPIKEY-WIKEY, LOOKS LIKE I'LL BE TRAVELLING LIGHT THIS TIME.
YEAH, LIGHT, SURE.

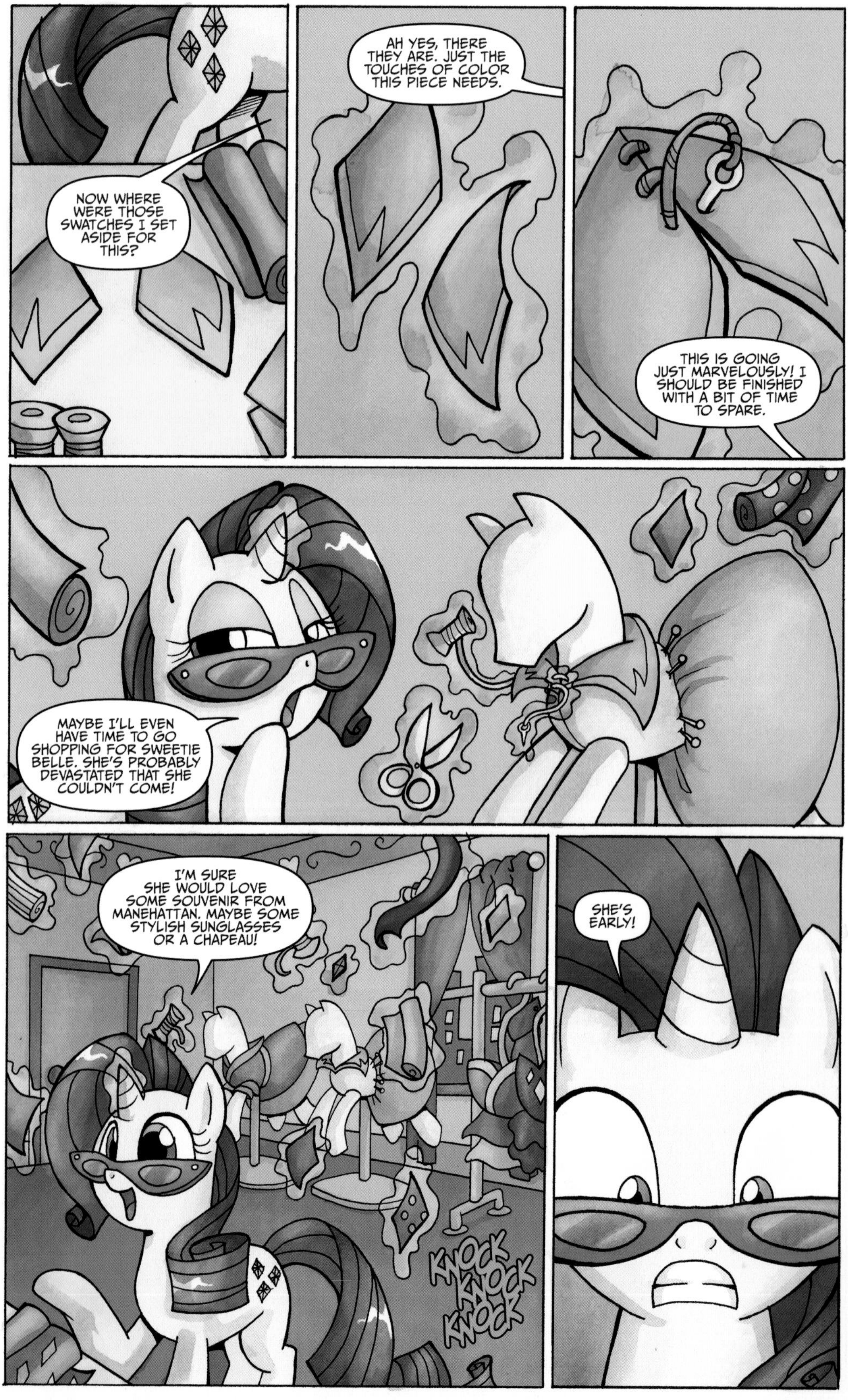
NOW WHERE WERE THOSE SWATCHES I SET ASIDE FOR THIS?
AH YES, THERE THEY ARE. JUST THE TOUCHES OF COLOR THIS PIECE NEEDS.
THIS IS GOING JUST MARVELOUSLY! I SHOULD BE FINISHED WITH A BIT OF TIME TO SPARE.
MAYBE I'LL EVEN HAVE TIME TO GO SHOPPING FOR SWEETIE BELLE. SHE'S PROBABLY DEVASTATED THAT SHE COULDN'T COME!
I'M SURE SHE WOULD LOVE SOME SOUVENIR FROM MANEHATTAN. MAYBE SOME STYLISH SUNGLASSES OR A CHAPEAU!
KNOCK KNOCK KNOCK
SHE'S EARLY!

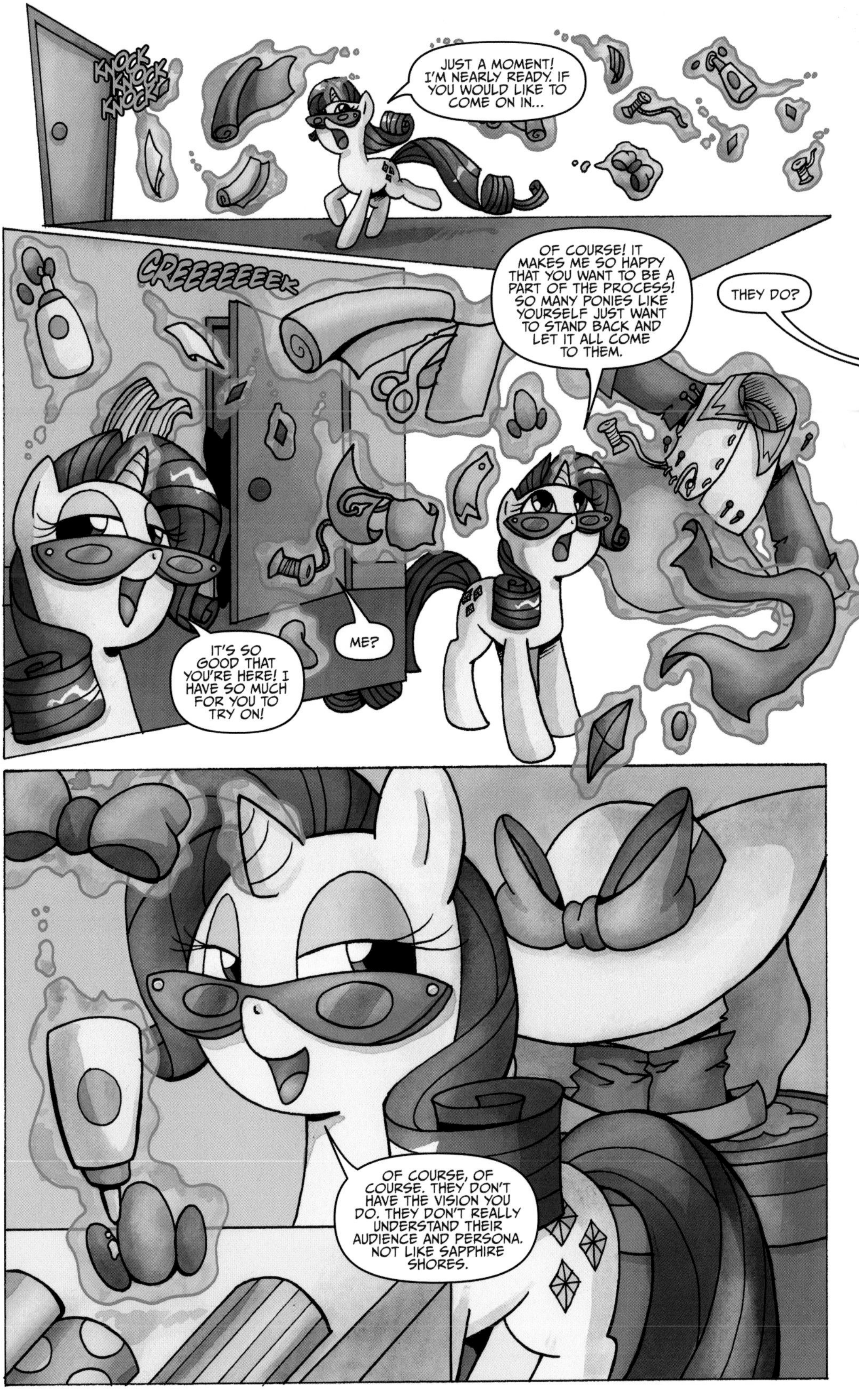
KNOCK KNOCK KNOCK
JUST A MOMENT! I'M NEARLY READY. IF YOU WOULD LIKE TO COME ON IN...
CREEEEEEEK
IT'S SO GOOD THAT YOU'RE HERE! I HAVE SO MUCH FOR YOU TO TRY ON!
ME?
OF COURSE! IT MAKES ME SO HAPPY THAT YOU WANT TO BE A PART OF THE PROCESS! SO MANY PONIES LIKE YOURSELF JUST WANT TO STAND BACK AND LET IT ALL COME TO THEM.
THEY DO?
OF COURSE, OF COURSE. THEY DON'T HAVE THE VISION YOU DO. THEY DON'T REALLY UNDERSTAND THEIR AUDIENCE AND PERSONA. NOT LIKE SAPPHIRE SHORES.

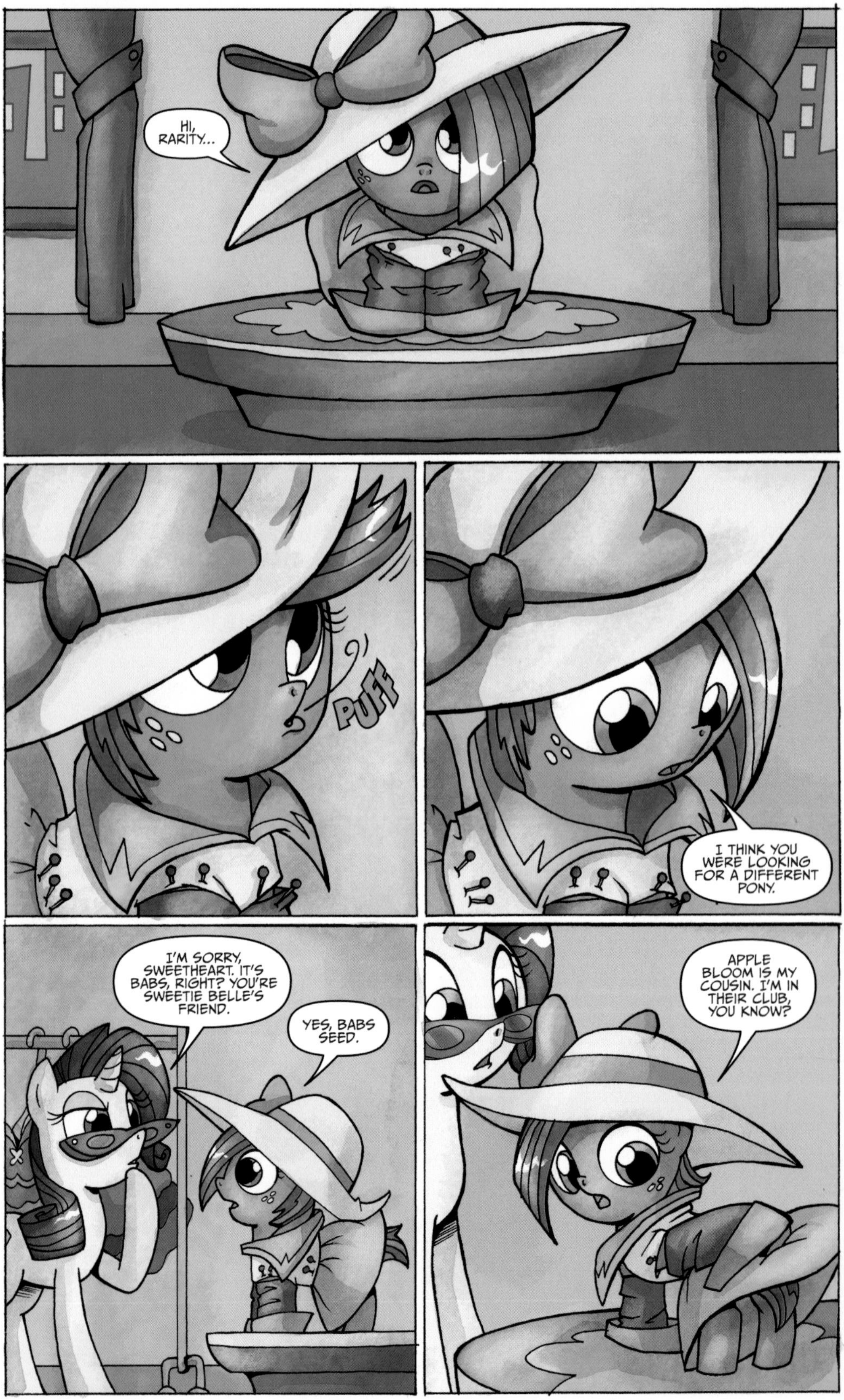
HI, RARITY...
PUFF
I THINK YOU WERE LOOKING FOR A DIFFERENT PONY.
I'M SORRY, SWEETHEART. IT'S BABS, RIGHT? YOU'RE SWEETIE BELLE'S FRIEND.
YES, BABS SEED.
APPLE BLOOM IS MY COUSIN. I'M IN THEIR CLUB, YOU KNOW?

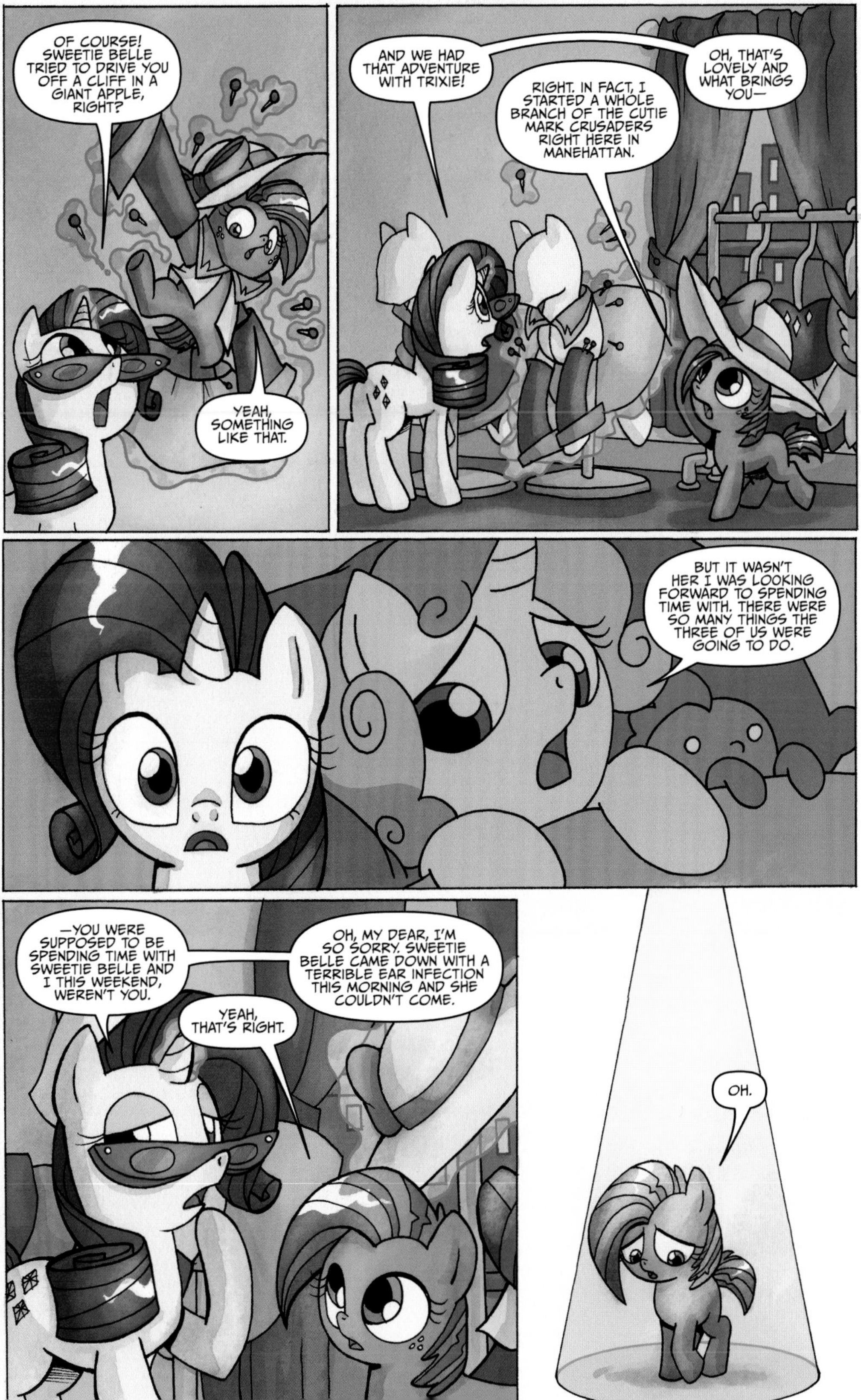
OF COURSE! SWEETIE BELLE TRIED TO DRIVE YOU OFF A CLIFF IN A GIANT APPLE, RIGHT?
YEAH, SOMETHING LIKE THAT.
AND WE HAD THAT ADVENTURE WITH TRIXIE!
RIGHT. IN FACT, I STARTED A WHOLE BRANCH OF THE CUTIE MARK CRUSADERS RIGHT HERE IN MANEHATTAN.
OH, THAT'S LOVELY AND WHAT BRINGS YOU—
BUT IT WASN'T HER I WAS LOOKING FORWARD TO SPENDING TIME WITH. THERE WERE SO MANY THINGS THE THREE OF US WERE GOING TO DO.
—YOU WERE SUPPOSED TO BE SPENDING TIME WITH SWEETIE BELLE AND I THIS WEEKEND, WEREN'T YOU.
YEAH, THAT'S RIGHT.
OH, MY DEAR, I'M SO SORRY. SWEETIE BELLE CAME DOWN WITH A TERRIBLE EAR INFECTION THIS MORNING AND SHE COULDN'T COME.
OH.

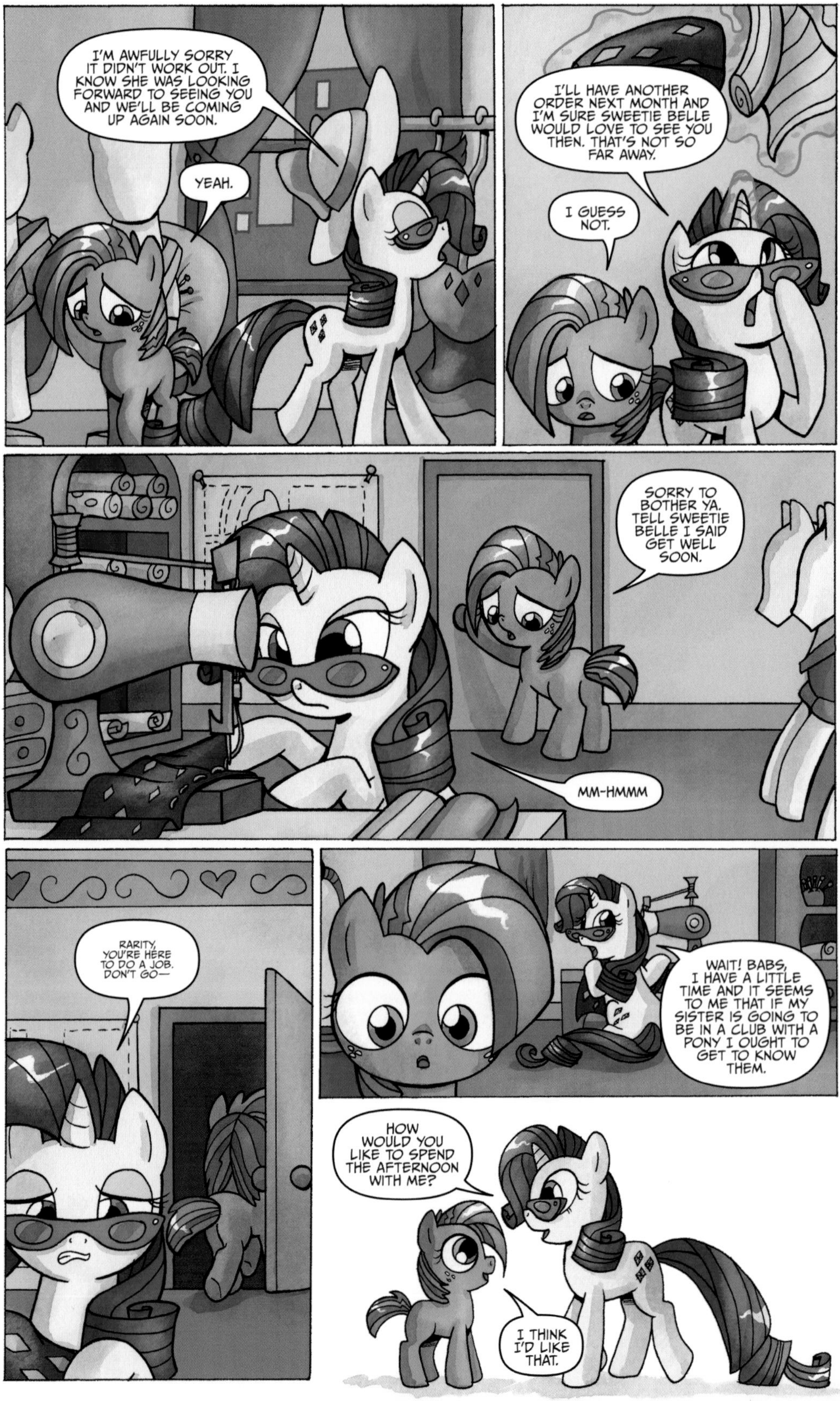
I'M AWFULLY SORRY IT DIDN'T WORK OUT. I KNOW SHE WAS LOOKING FORWARD TO SEEING YOU AND WE'LL BE COMING UP AGAIN SOON.
YEAH.
I'LL HAVE ANOTHER ORDER NEXT MONTH AND I'M SURE SWEETIE BELLE WOULD LOVE TO SEE YOU THEN. THAT'S NOT SO FAR AWAY.
I GUESS NOT.
SORRY TO BOTHER YA. TELL SWEETIE BELLE I SAID GET WELL SOON.
MM-HMMM
RARITY, YOU'RE HERE TO DO A JOB. DON'T GO—
WAIT! BABS, I HAVE A LITTLE TIME AND IT SEEMS TO ME THAT IF MY SISTER IS GOING TO BE IN A CLUB WITH A PONY I OUGHT TO GET TO KNOW THEM.
HOW WOULD YOU LIKE TO SPEND THE AFTERNOON WITH ME?
I THINK I'D LIKE THAT.

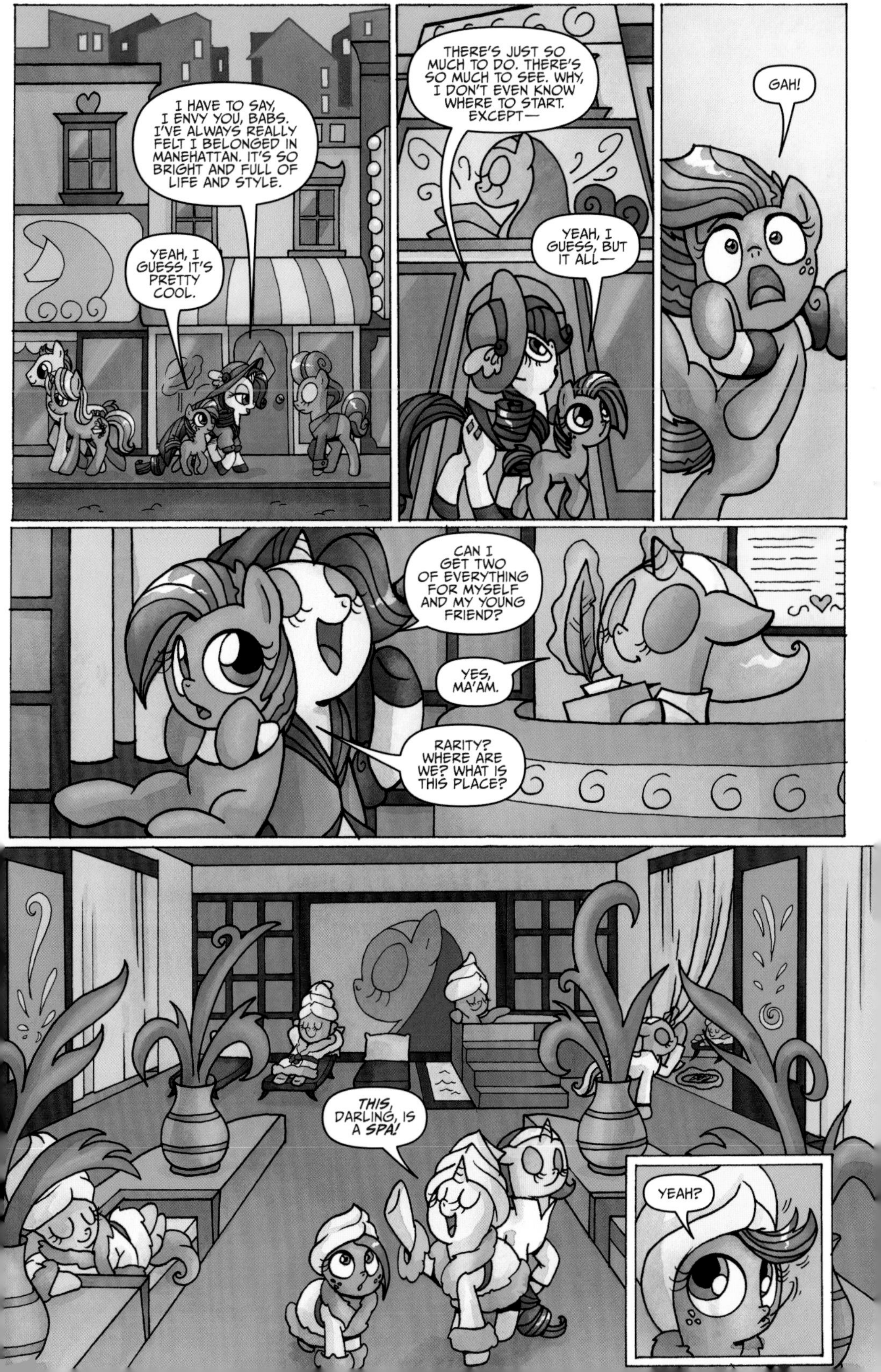
I HAVE TO SAY, I ENVY YOU, BABS. I'VE ALWAYS REALLY FELT I BELONGED IN MANEHATTAN. IT'S SO BRIGHT AND FULL OF LIFE AND STYLE.
YEAH, I GUESS IT'S PRETTY COOL.
THERE'S JUST SO MUCH TO DO. THERE'S SO MUCH TO SEE. WHY, I DON'T EVEN KNOW WHERE TO START. EXCEPT—
YEAH, I GUESS, BUT IT ALL—
GAH!
CAN I GET TWO OF EVERYTHING FOR MYSELF AND MY YOUNG FRIEND?
YES, MA'AM.
RARITY? WHERE ARE WE? WHAT IS THIS PLACE?
THIS, DARLING, IS A *SPA!*
YEAH?

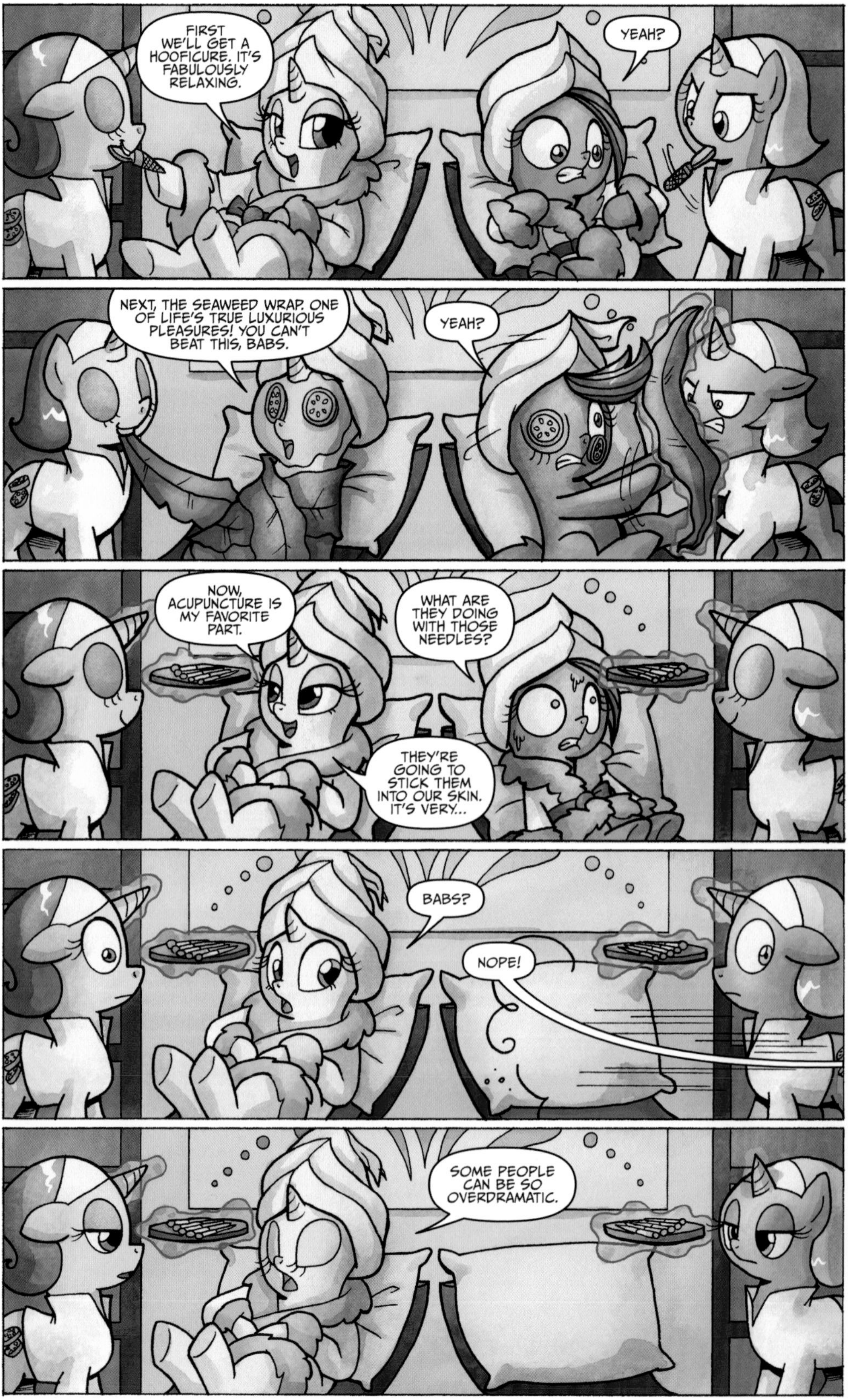
FIRST WE'LL GET A HOOFICURE. IT'S FABULOUSLY RELAXING.
YEAH?
NEXT, THE SEAWEED WRAP. ONE OF LIFE'S TRUE LUXURIOUS PLEASURES! YOU CAN'T BEAT THIS, BABS.
YEAH?
NOW, ACUPUNCTURE IS MY FAVORITE PART.
WHAT ARE THEY DOING WITH THOSE NEEDLES?
THEY'RE GOING TO STICK THEM INTO OUR SKIN. IT'S VERY...
BABS?
NOPE!
SOME PEOPLE CAN BE SO OVERDRAMATIC.

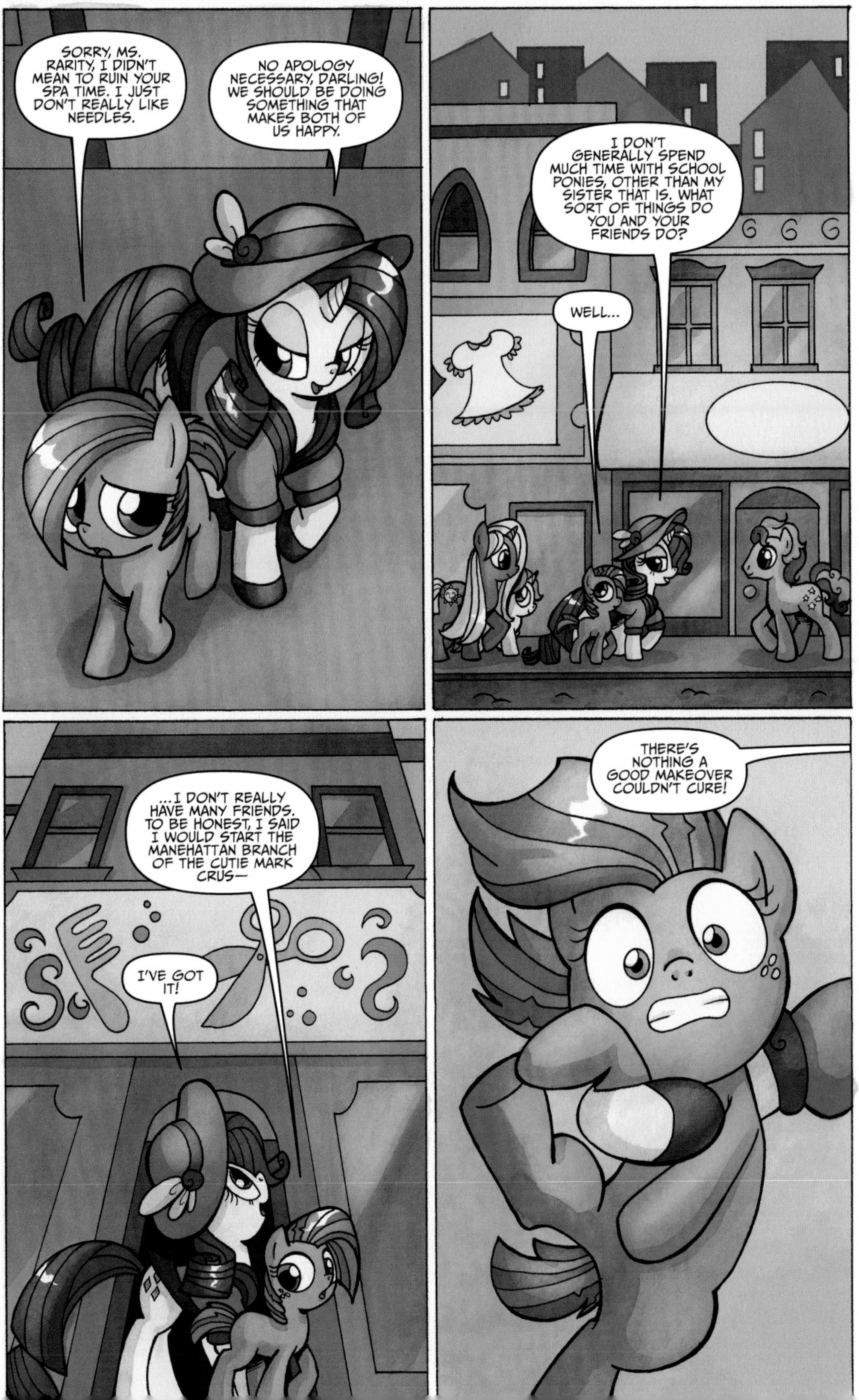
SORRY, MS. RARITY, I DIDN'T MEAN TO RUIN YOUR SPA TIME. I JUST DON'T REALLY LIKE NEEDLES.
NO APOLOGY NECESSARY, DARLING! WE SHOULD BE DOING SOMETHING THAT MAKES BOTH OF US HAPPY.
I DON'T GENERALLY SPEND MUCH TIME WITH SCHOOL PONIES, OTHER THAN MY SISTER THAT IS. WHAT SORT OF THINGS DO YOU AND YOUR FRIENDS DO?
WELL...
...I DON'T REALLY HAVE MANY FRIENDS. TO BE HONEST, I SAID I WOULD START THE MANEHATTAN BRANCH OF THE CUTIE MARK CRUS—
I'VE GOT IT!
THERE'S NOTHING A GOOD MAKEOVER COULDN'T CURE!

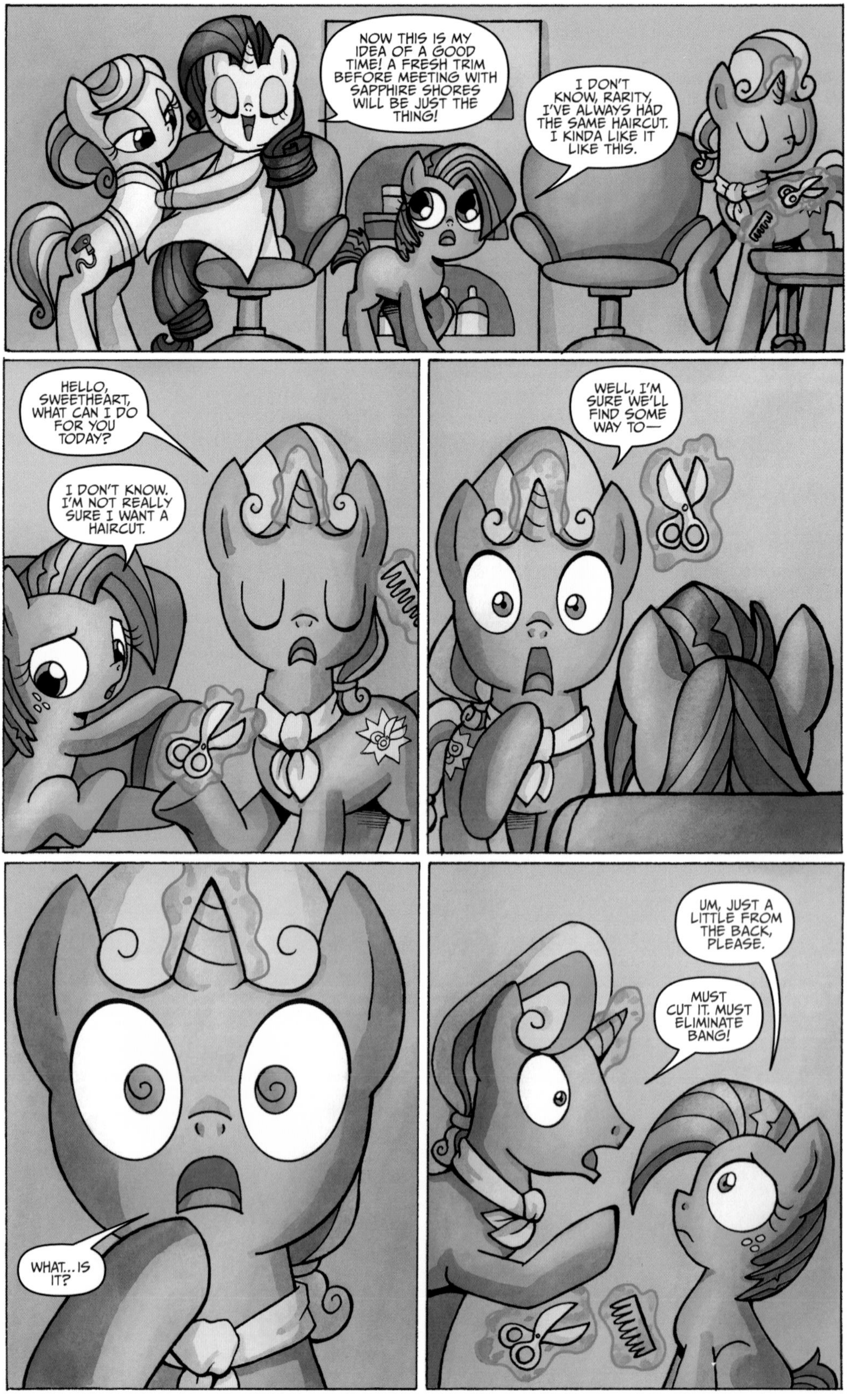
NOW THIS IS MY IDEA OF A GOOD TIME! A FRESH TRIM BEFORE MEETING WITH SAPPHIRE SHORES WILL BE JUST THE THING!
I DON'T KNOW, RARITY, I'VE ALWAYS HAD THE SAME HAIRCUT. I KINDA LIKE IT LIKE THIS.
HELLO, SWEETHEART, WHAT CAN I DO FOR YOU TODAY?
I DON'T KNOW. I'M NOT REALLY SURE I WANT A HAIRCUT.
WELL, I'M SURE WE'LL FIND SOME WAY TO—
WHAT… IS IT?
UM, JUST A LITTLE FROM THE BACK, PLEASE.
MUST CUT IT. MUST ELIMINATE BANG!

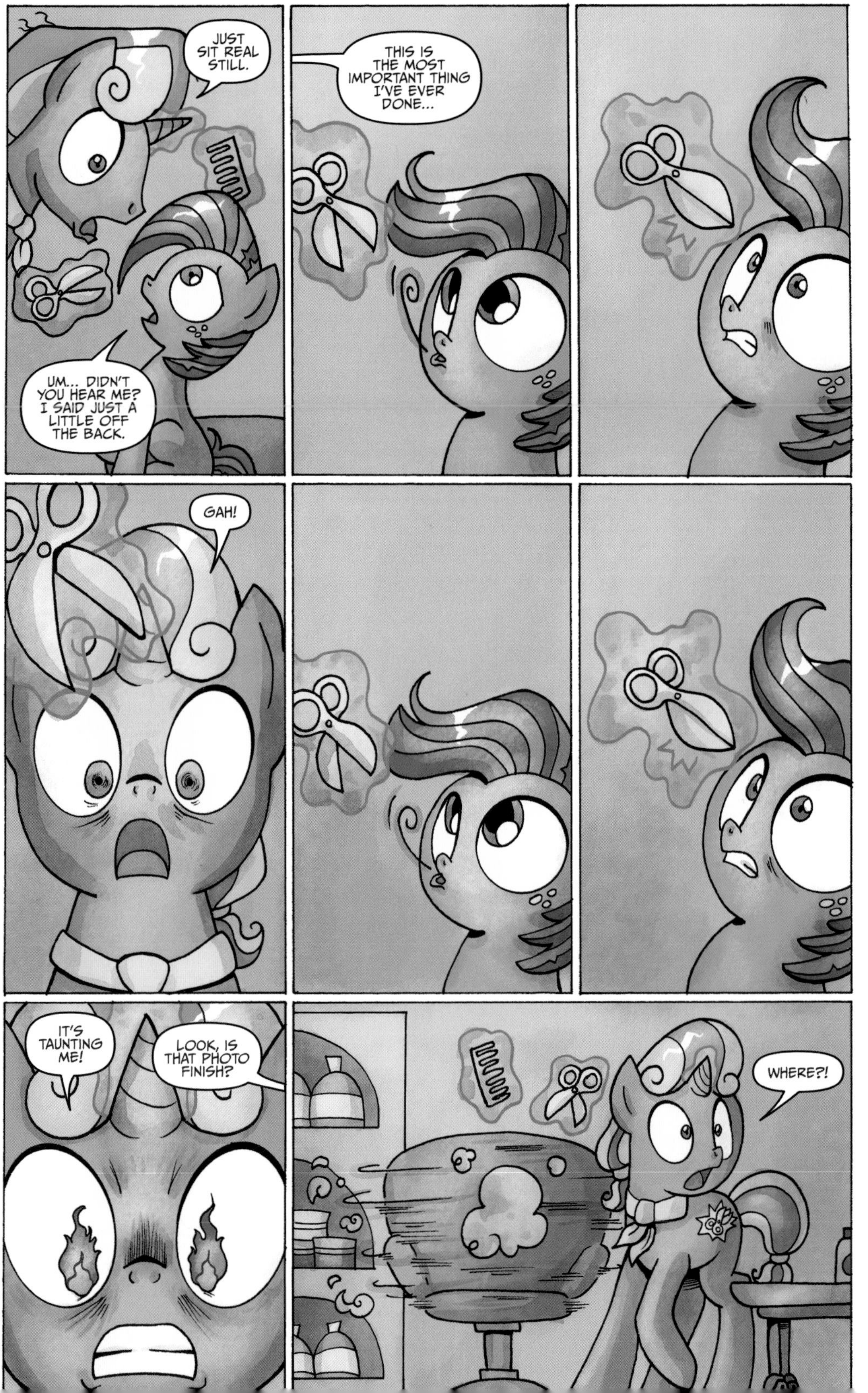
JUST SIT REAL STILL.
UM... DIDN'T YOU HEAR ME? I SAID JUST A LITTLE OFF THE BACK.
THIS IS THE MOST IMPORTANT THING I'VE EVER DONE...
GAH!
IT'S TAUNTING ME!
LOOK, IS THAT PHOTO FINISH?
WHERE?!

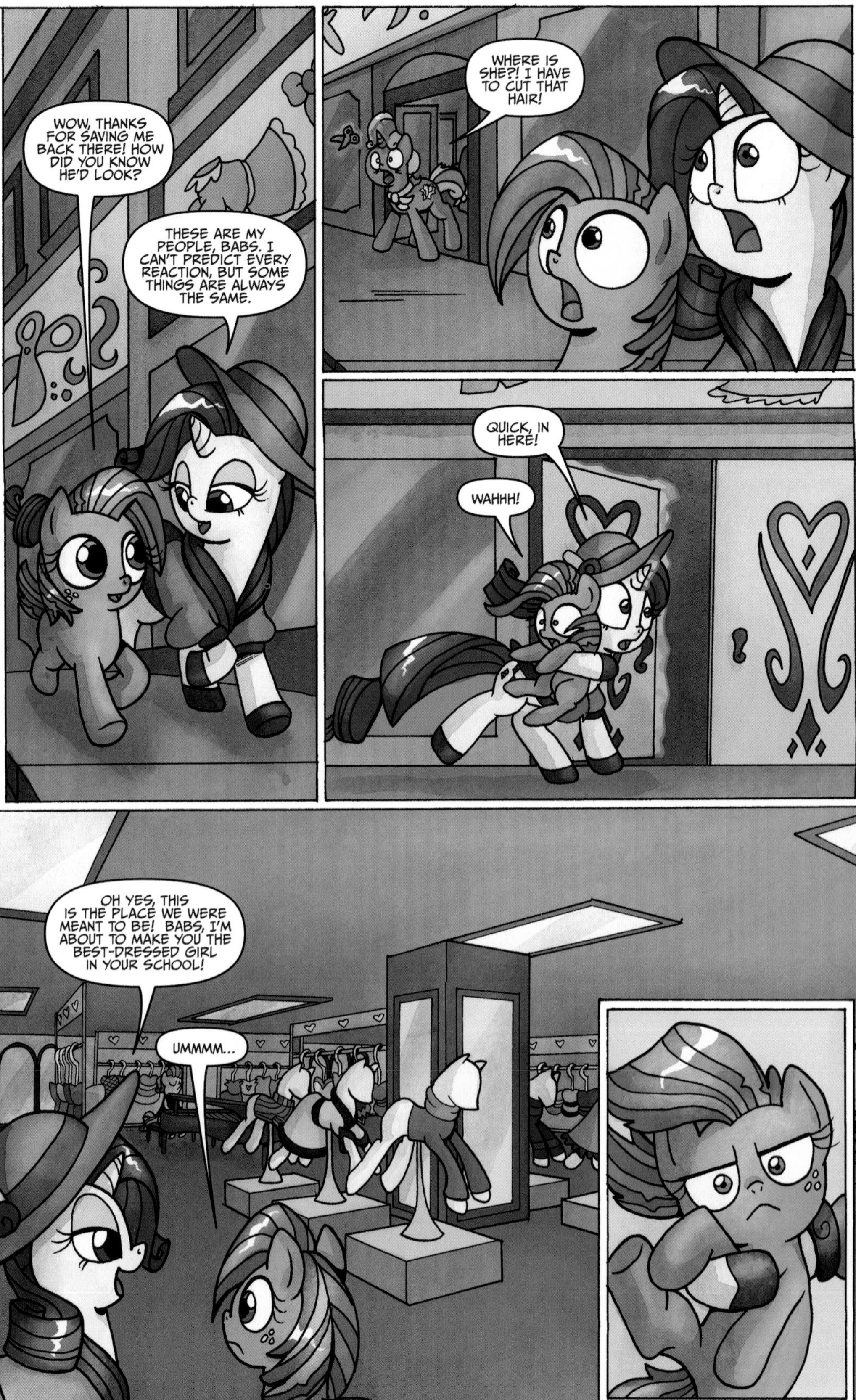
WOW, THANKS FOR SAVING ME BACK THERE! HOW DID YOU KNOW HE'D LOOK?
THESE ARE MY PEOPLE, BABS. I CAN'T PREDICT EVERY REACTION, BUT SOME THINGS ARE ALWAYS THE SAME.
WHERE IS SHE?! I HAVE TO CUT THAT HAIR!
QUICK, IN HERE!
WAHHH!
OH YES, THIS IS THE PLACE WE WERE MEANT TO BE! BABS, I'M ABOUT TO MAKE YOU THE BEST-DRESSED GIRL IN YOUR SCHOOL!
UMMMM...

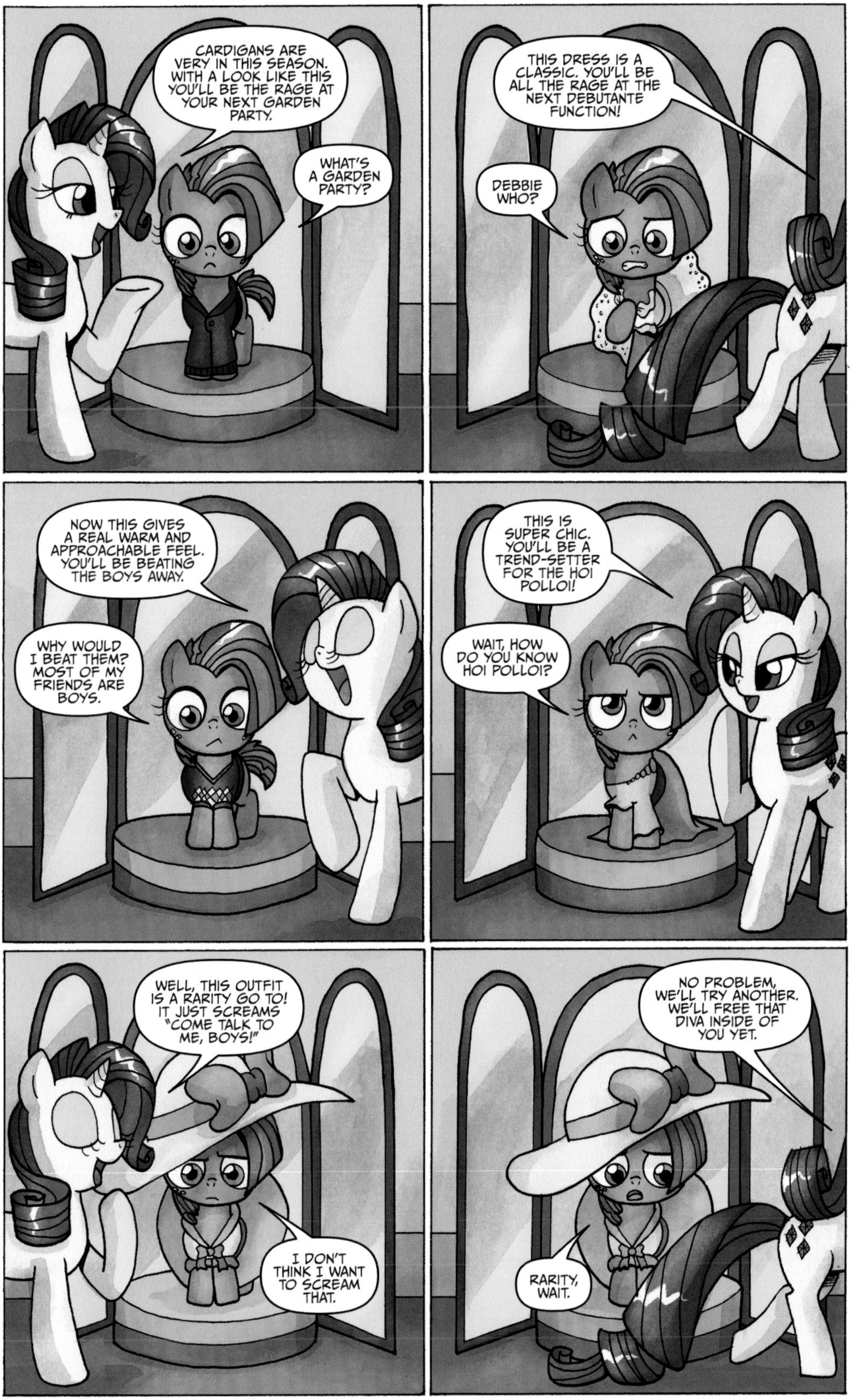
CARDIGANS ARE VERY IN THIS SEASON. WITH A LOOK LIKE THIS YOU'LL BE THE RAGE AT YOUR NEXT GARDEN PARTY.
WHAT'S A GARDEN PARTY?
THIS DRESS IS A CLASSIC. YOU'LL BE ALL THE RAGE AT THE NEXT DEBUTANTE FUNCTION!
DEBBIE WHO?
NOW THIS GIVES A REAL WARM AND APPROACHABLE FEEL. YOU'LL BE BEATING THE BOYS AWAY.
WHY WOULD I BEAT THEM? MOST OF MY FRIENDS ARE BOYS.
THIS IS SUPER CHIC. YOU'LL BE A TREND-SETTER FOR THE HOI POLLOI!
WAIT, HOW DO YOU KNOW HOI POLLOI?
WELL, THIS OUTFIT IS A RARITY GO TO! IT JUST SCREAMS "COME TALK TO ME, BOYS!"
I DON'T THINK I WANT TO SCREAM THAT.
NO PROBLEM, WE'LL TRY ANOTHER. WE'LL FREE THAT DIVA INSIDE OF YOU YET.
RARITY, WAIT.

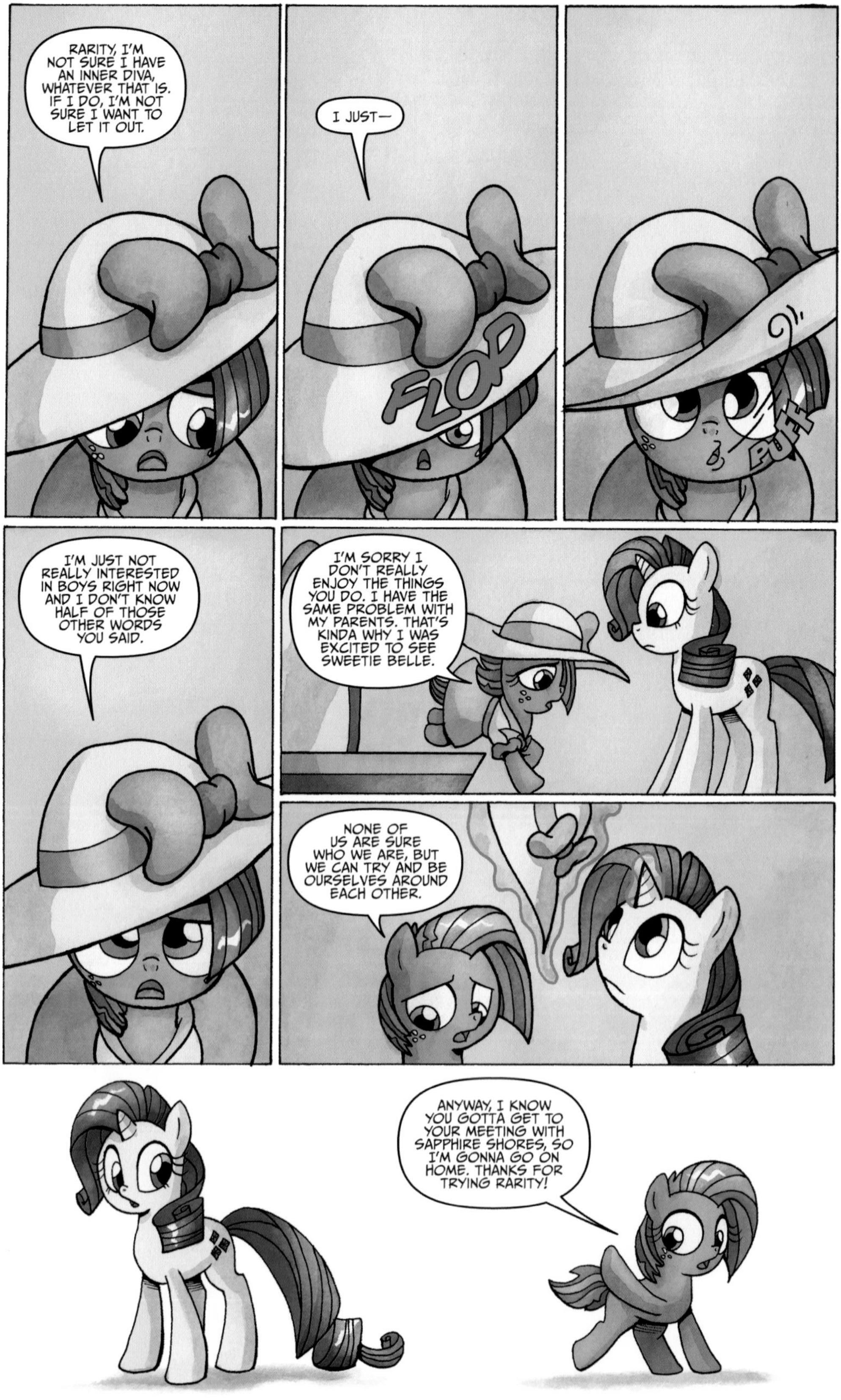
RARITY, I'M NOT SURE I HAVE AN INNER DIVA, WHATEVER THAT IS. IF I DO, I'M NOT SURE I WANT TO LET IT OUT.
I JUST—
FLOP
PUFF
I'M JUST NOT REALLY INTERESTED IN BOYS RIGHT NOW AND I DON'T KNOW HALF OF THOSE OTHER WORDS YOU SAID.
I'M SORRY I DON'T REALLY ENJOY THE THINGS YOU DO. I HAVE THE SAME PROBLEM WITH MY PARENTS. THAT'S KINDA WHY I WAS EXCITED TO SEE SWEETIE BELLE.
NONE OF US ARE SURE WHO WE ARE, BUT WE CAN TRY AND BE OURSELVES AROUND EACH OTHER.
ANYWAY, I KNOW YOU GOTTA GET TO YOUR MEETING WITH SAPPHIRE SHORES, SO I'M GONNA GO ON HOME. THANKS FOR TRYING RARITY!

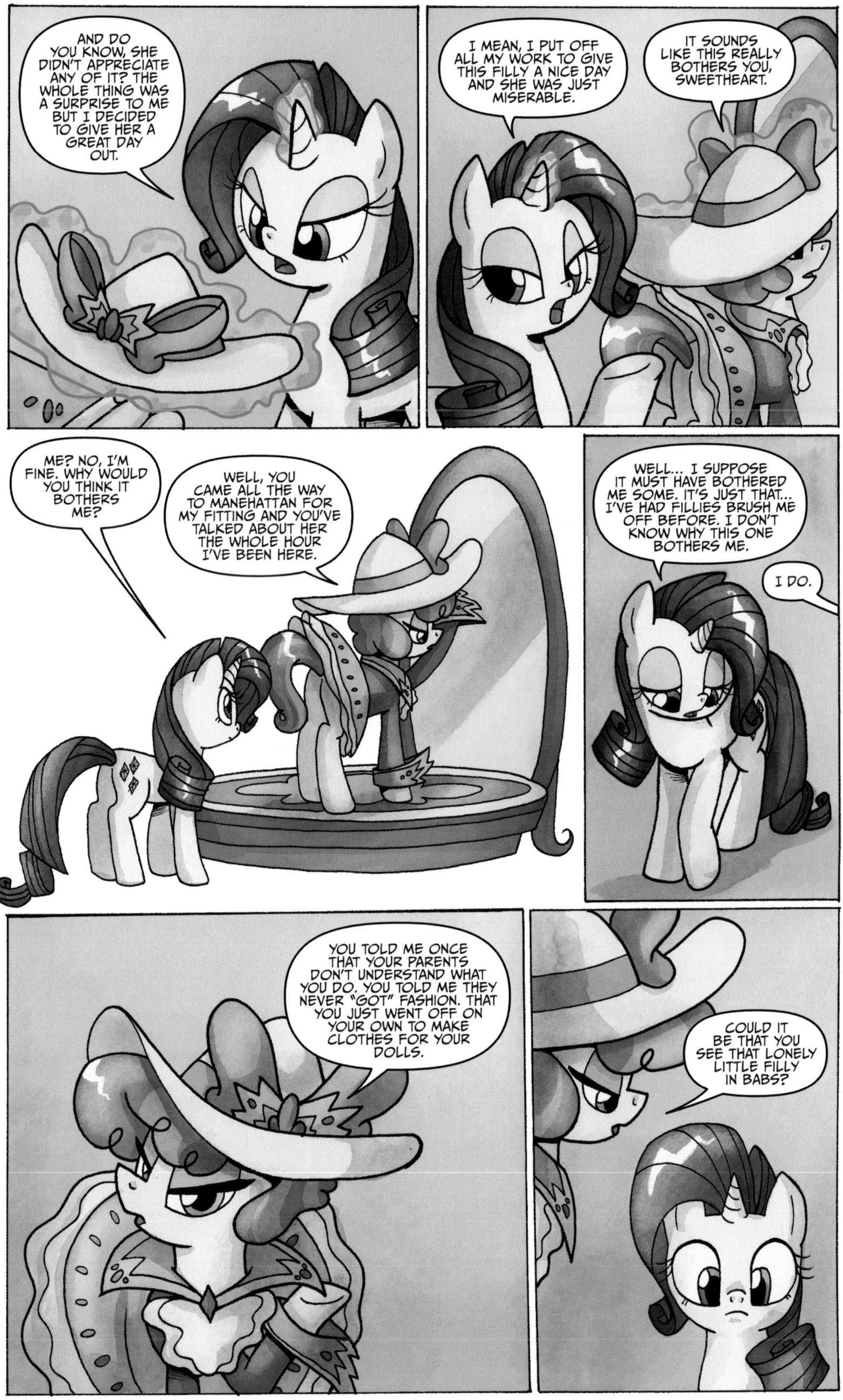
AND DO YOU KNOW, SHE DIDN'T APPRECIATE ANY OF IT? THE WHOLE THING WAS A SURPRISE TO ME BUT I DECIDED TO GIVE HER A GREAT DAY OUT.
I MEAN, I PUT OFF ALL MY WORK TO GIVE THIS FILLY A NICE DAY AND SHE WAS JUST MISERABLE.
IT SOUNDS LIKE THIS REALLY BOTHERS YOU, SWEETHEART.
ME? NO, I'M FINE. WHY WOULD YOU THINK IT BOTHERS ME?
WELL, YOU CAME ALL THE WAY TO MANEHATTAN FOR MY FITTING AND YOU'VE TALKED ABOUT HER THE WHOLE HOUR I'VE BEEN HERE.
WELL... I SUPPOSE IT MUST HAVE BOTHERED ME SOME. IT'S JUST THAT... I'VE HAD FILLIES BRUSH ME OFF BEFORE. I DON'T KNOW WHY THIS ONE BOTHERS ME.
I DO.
YOU TOLD ME ONCE THAT YOUR PARENTS DON'T UNDERSTAND WHAT YOU DO. YOU TOLD ME THEY NEVER "GOT" FASHION. THAT YOU JUST WENT OFF ON YOUR OWN TO MAKE CLOTHES FOR YOUR DOLLS.
COULD IT BE THAT YOU SEE THAT LONELY LITTLE FILLY IN BABS?

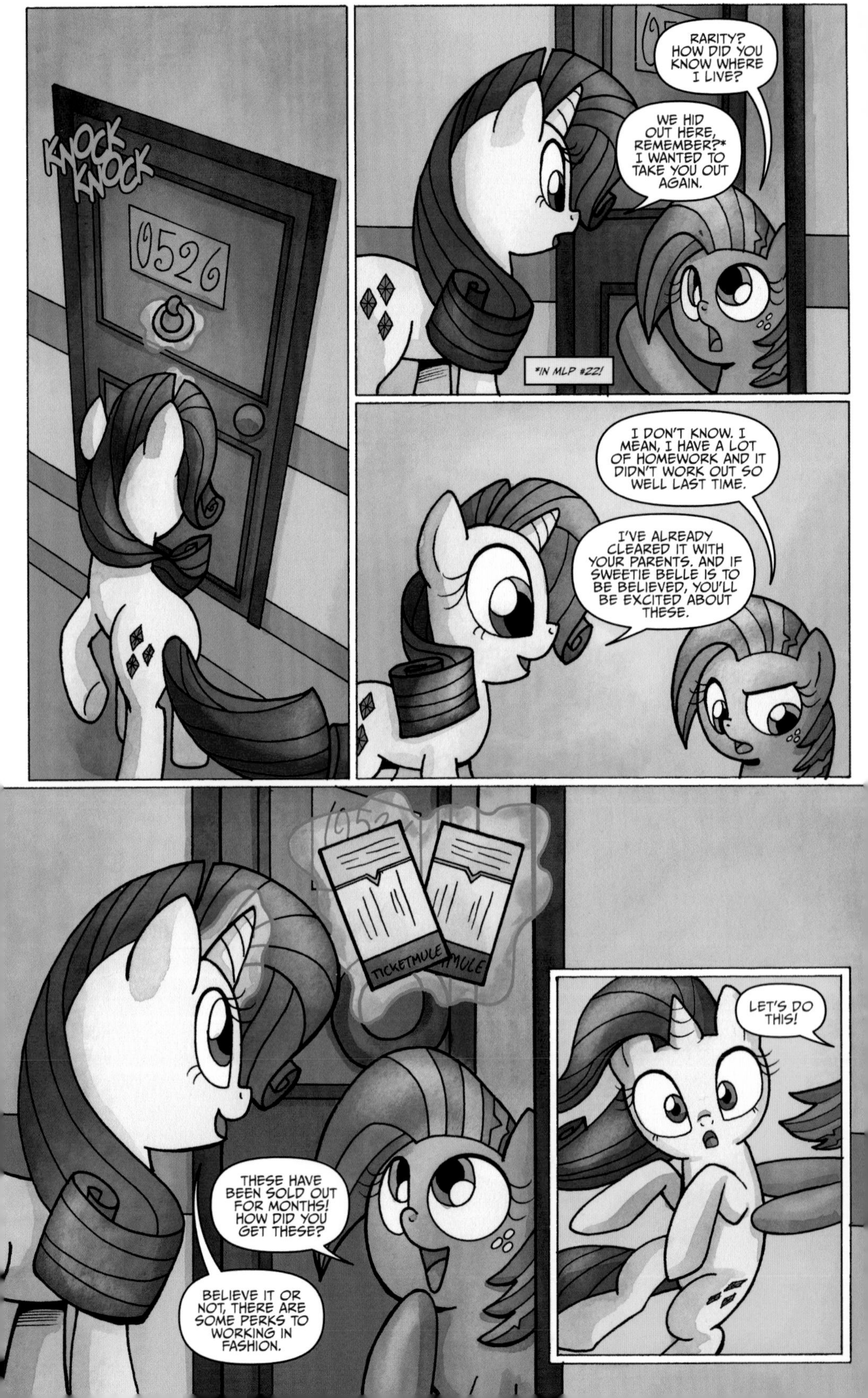
KNOCK KNOCK
0526
RARITY? HOW DID YOU KNOW WHERE I LIVE?
WE HID OUT HERE, REMEMBER?* I WANTED TO TAKE YOU OUT AGAIN.
*IN MLP #22!
I DON'T KNOW. I MEAN, I HAVE A LOT OF HOMEWORK AND IT DIDN'T WORK OUT SO WELL LAST TIME.
I'VE ALREADY CLEARED IT WITH YOUR PARENTS. AND IF SWEETIE BELLE IS TO BE BELIEVED, YOU'LL BE EXCITED ABOUT THESE.
TICKETMULE
THESE HAVE BEEN SOLD OUT FOR MONTHS! HOW DID YOU GET THESE?
BELIEVE IT OR NOT, THERE ARE SOME PERKS TO WORKING IN FASHION.
LET'S DO THIS!

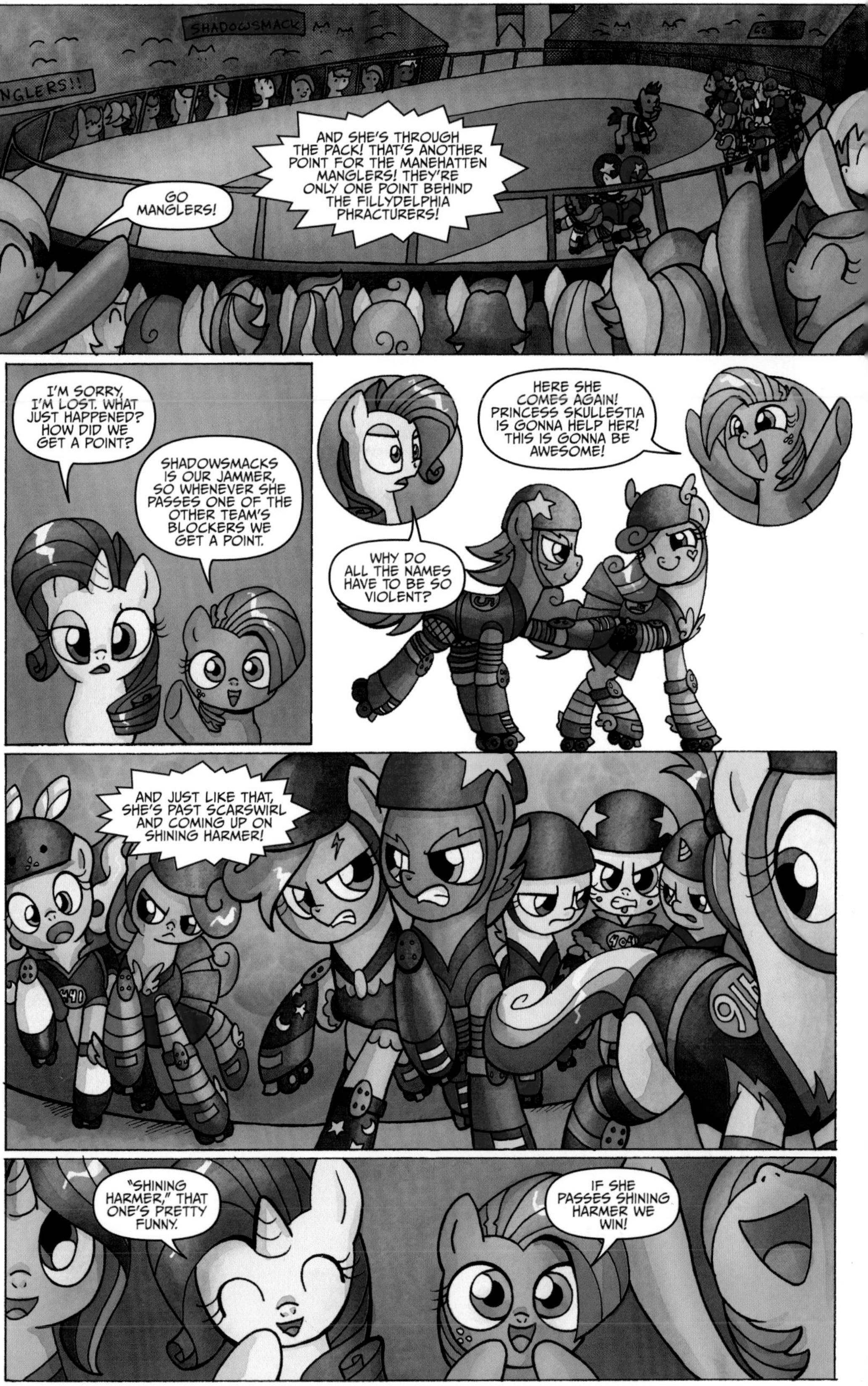
SHADOWSMACK
NGLERS!!
AND SHE'S THROUGH THE PACK! THAT'S ANOTHER POINT FOR THE MANEHATTEN MANGLERS! THEY'RE ONLY ONE POINT BEHIND THE FILLYDELPHIA PHRACTURERS!
GO MANGLERS!
I'M SORRY, I'M LOST. WHAT JUST HAPPENED? HOW DID WE GET A POINT?
SHADOWSMACKS IS OUR JAMMER, SO WHENEVER SHE PASSES ONE OF THE OTHER TEAM'S BLOCKERS WE GET A POINT.
HERE SHE COMES AGAIN! PRINCESS SKULLESTIA IS GONNA HELP HER! THIS IS GONNA BE AWESOME!
WHY DO ALL THE NAMES HAVE TO BE SO VIOLENT?
AND JUST LIKE THAT, SHE'S PAST SCARSWIRL AND COMING UP ON SHINING HARMER!
"SHINING HARMER," THAT ONE'S PRETTY FUNNY.
IF SHE PASSES SHINING HARMER WE WIN!

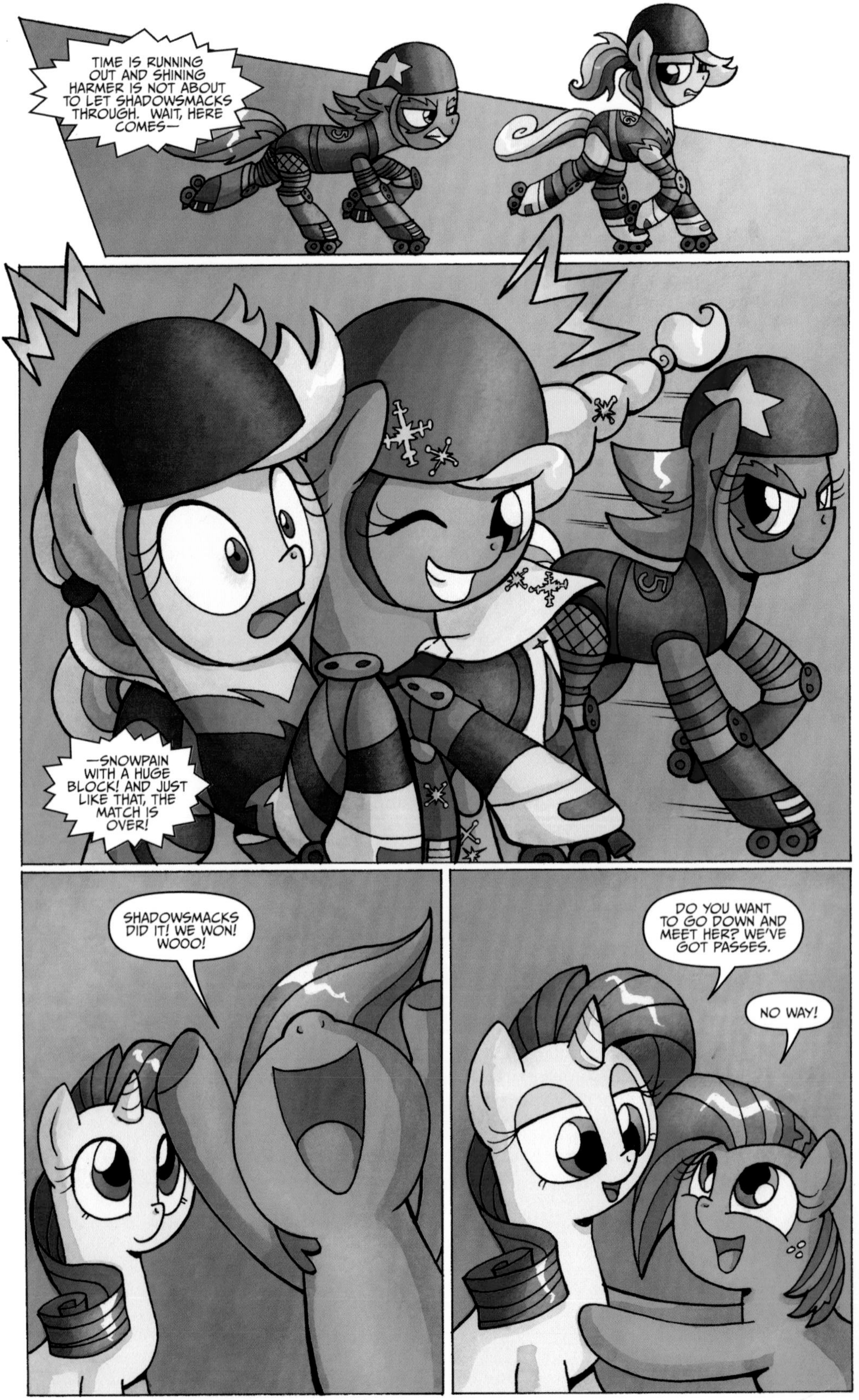
TIME IS RUNNING OUT AND SHINING HARMER IS NOT ABOUT TO LET SHADOWSMACKS THROUGH. WAIT, HERE COMES—
—SNOWPAIN WITH A HUGE BLOCK! AND JUST LIKE THAT, THE MATCH IS OVER!
SHADOWSMACKS DID IT! WE WON! WOOO!
DO YOU WANT TO GO DOWN AND MEET HER? WE'VE GOT PASSES.
NO WAY!

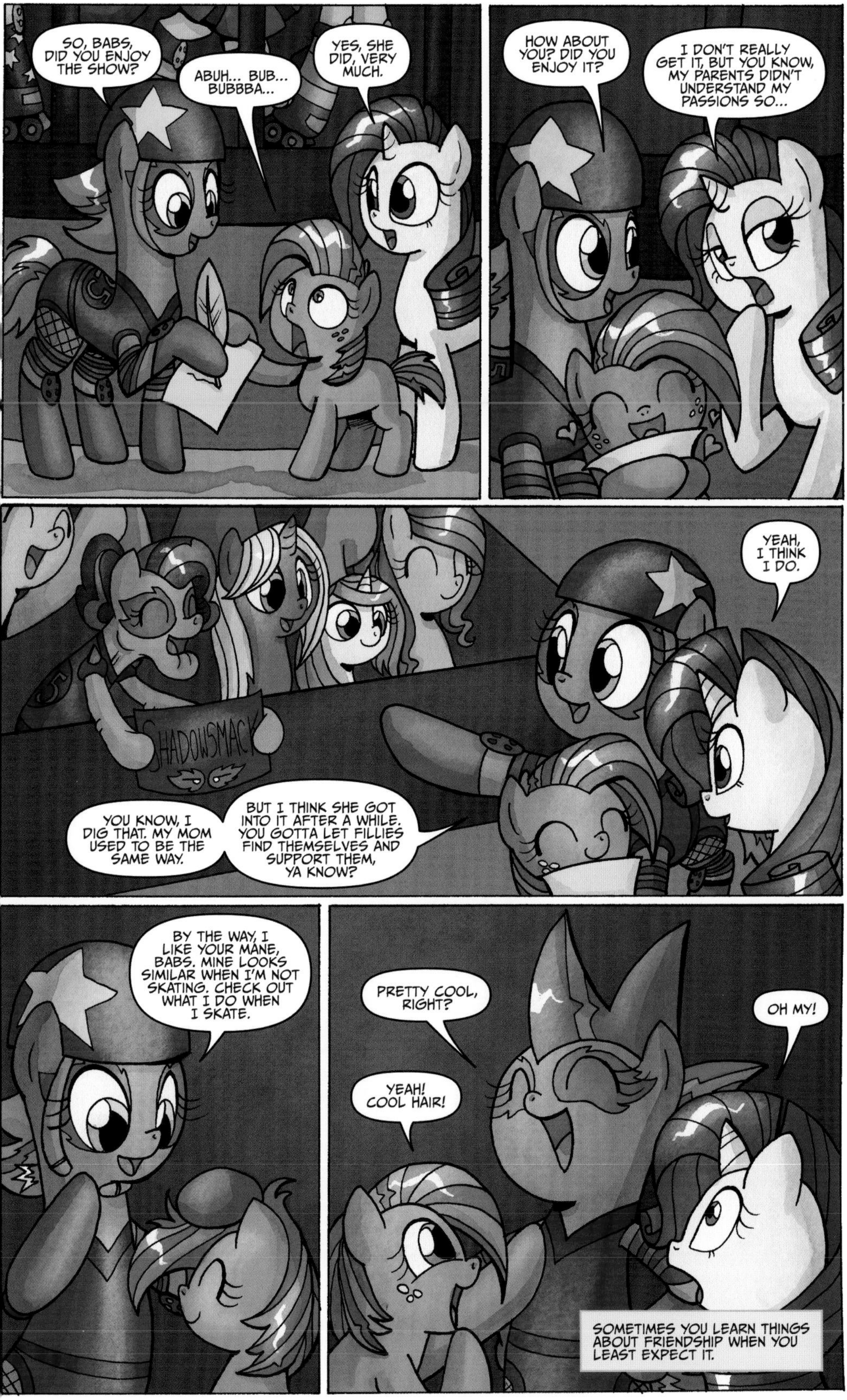
SO, BABS, DID YOU ENJOY THE SHOW?
ABUH... BUB... BUBBBA...
YES, SHE DID, VERY MUCH.
HOW ABOUT YOU? DID YOU ENJOY IT?
I DON'T REALLY GET IT, BUT YOU KNOW, MY PARENTS DIDN'T UNDERSTAND MY PASSIONS SO...
YEAH, I THINK I DO.
SHADOWSMACK
YOU KNOW, I DIG THAT. MY MOM USED TO BE THE SAME WAY.
BUT I THINK SHE GOT INTO IT AFTER A WHILE. YOU GOTTA LET FILLIES FIND THEMSELVES AND SUPPORT THEM, YA KNOW?
BY THE WAY, I LIKE YOUR MANE, BABS. MINE LOOKS SIMILAR WHEN I'M NOT SKATING. CHECK OUT WHAT I DO WHEN I SKATE.
PRETTY COOL, RIGHT?
OH MY!
YEAH! COOL HAIR!
SOMETIMES YOU LEARN THINGS ABOUT FRIENDSHIP WHEN YOU LEAST EXPECT IT.

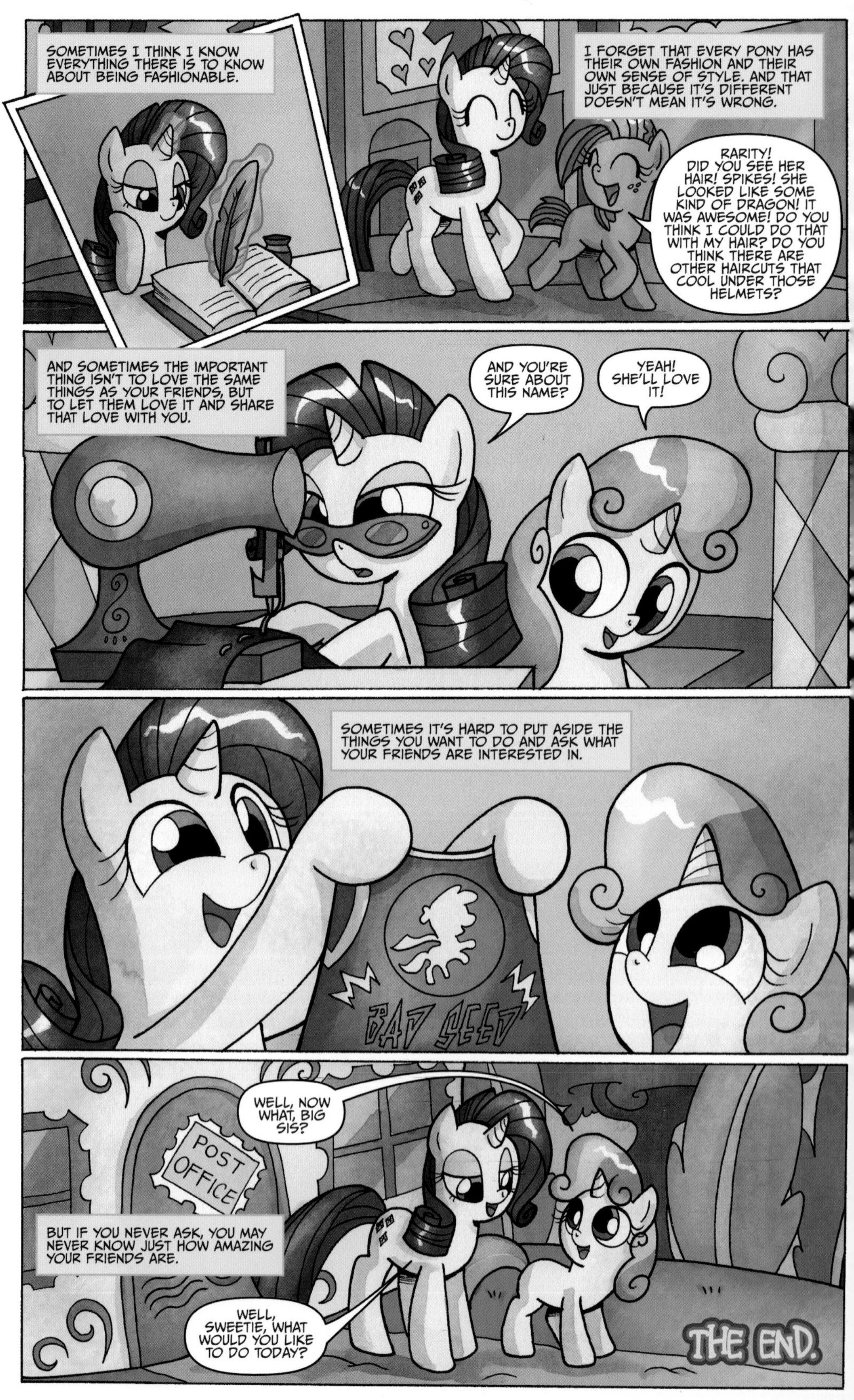

SOMETIMES I THINK I KNOW EVERYTHING THERE IS TO KNOW ABOUT BEING FASHIONABLE.
I FORGET THAT EVERY PONY HAS THEIR OWN FASHION AND THEIR OWN SENSE OF STYLE. AND THAT JUST BECAUSE IT'S DIFFERENT DOESN'T MEAN IT'S WRONG.
RARITY! DID YOU SEE HER HAIR! SPIKES! SHE LOOKED LIKE SOME KIND OF DRAGON! IT WAS AWESOME! DO YOU THINK I COULD DO THAT WITH MY HAIR? DO YOU THINK THERE ARE OTHER HAIRCUTS THAT COOL UNDER THOSE HELMETS?
AND SOMETIMES THE IMPORTANT THING ISN'T TO LOVE THE SAME THINGS AS YOUR FRIENDS, BUT TO LET THEM LOVE IT AND SHARE THAT LOVE WITH YOU.
AND YOU'RE SURE ABOUT THIS NAME?
YEAH! SHE'LL LOVE IT!
SOMETIMES IT'S HARD TO PUT ASIDE THE THINGS YOU WANT TO DO AND ASK WHAT YOUR FRIENDS ARE INTERESTED IN.
BAD SEED
WELL, NOW WHAT, BIG SIS?
POST OFFICE
BUT IF YOU NEVER ASK, YOU MAY NEVER KNOW JUST HOW AMAZING YOUR FRIENDS ARE.
WELL, SWEETIE, WHAT WOULD YOU LIKE TO DO TODAY?
THE END.

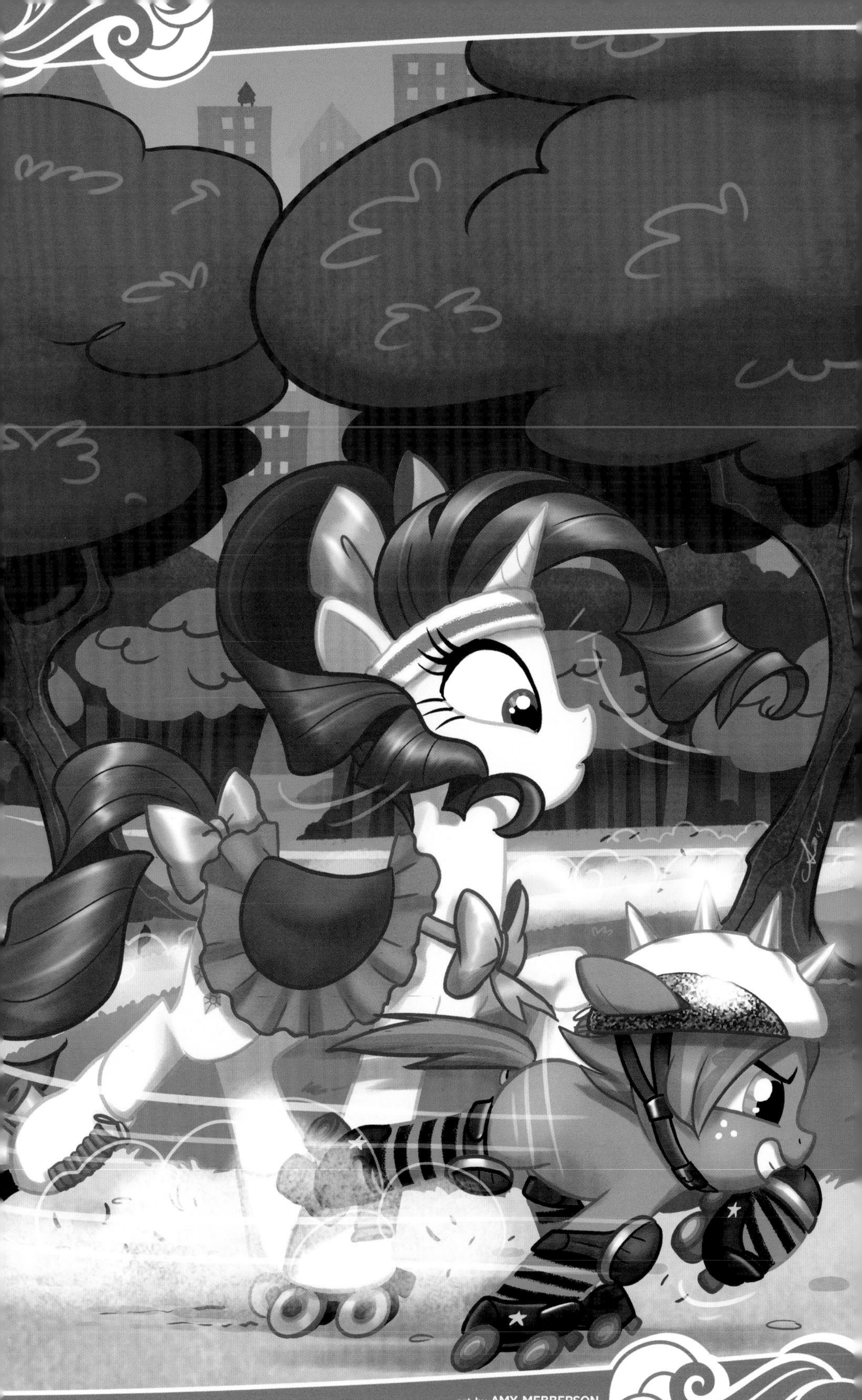

art by AMY MEBBERSON

Spike & Princess Luna

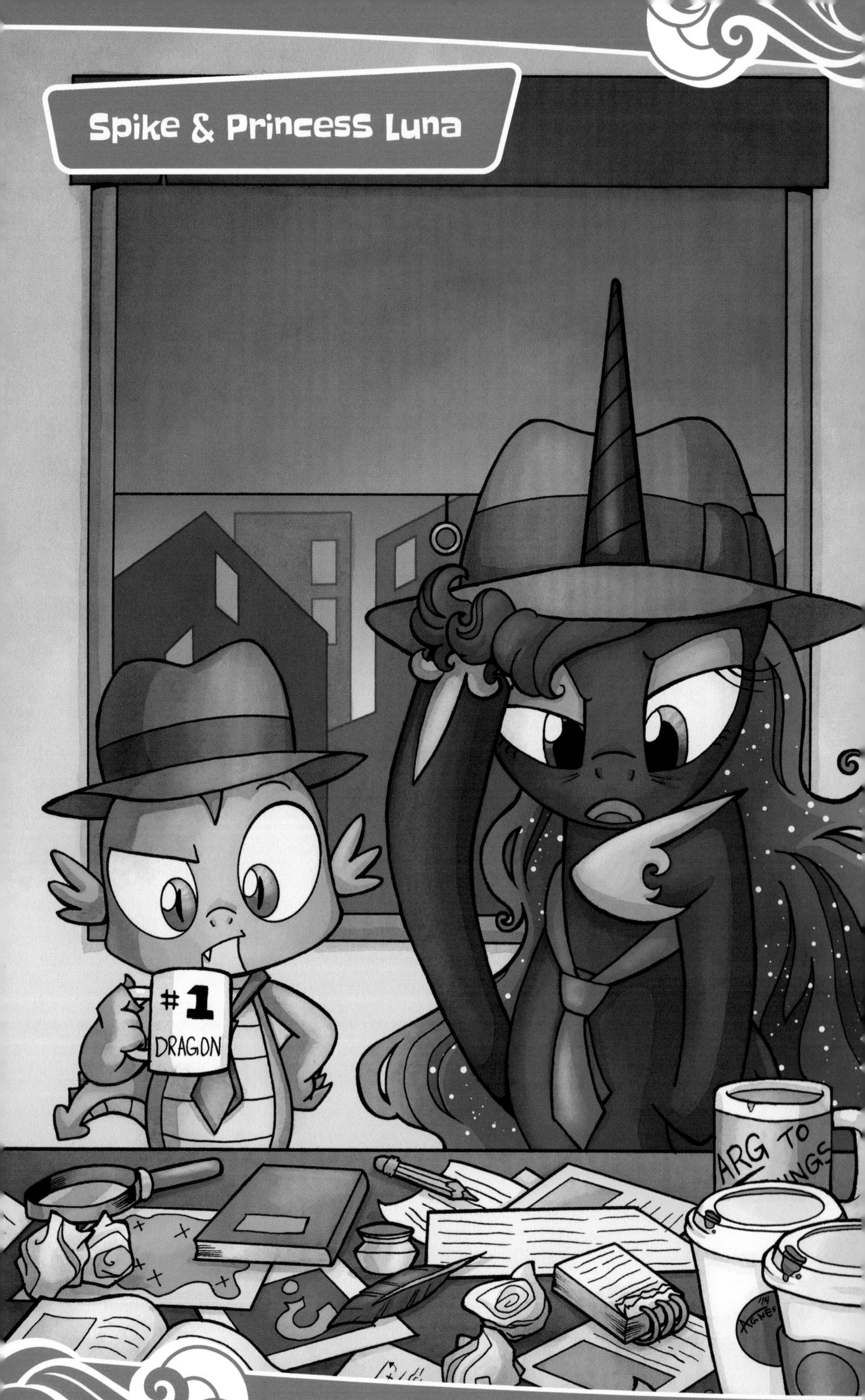
#1
DRAGON

art by AGNES GARBOWSKA

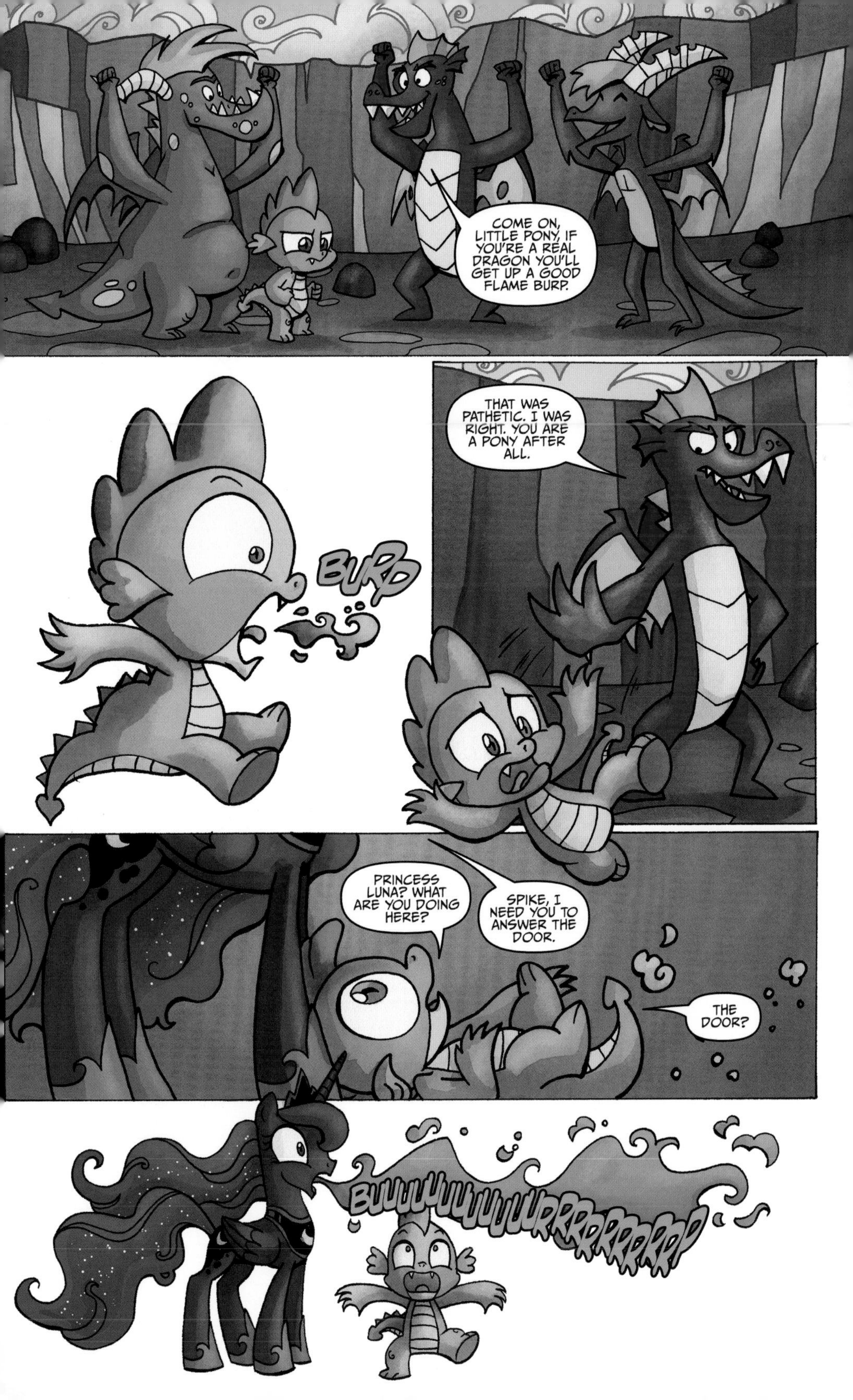
COME ON, LITTLE PONY, IF YOU'RE A REAL DRAGON YOU'LL GET UP A GOOD FLAME BURP.
BURP
THAT WAS PATHETIC. I WAS RIGHT. YOU ARE A PONY AFTER ALL.
PRINCESS LUNA? WHAT ARE YOU DOING HERE?
SPIKE, I NEED YOU TO ANSWER THE DOOR.
THE DOOR?
BUUUUUUUUUUUURRRRRRRRRP

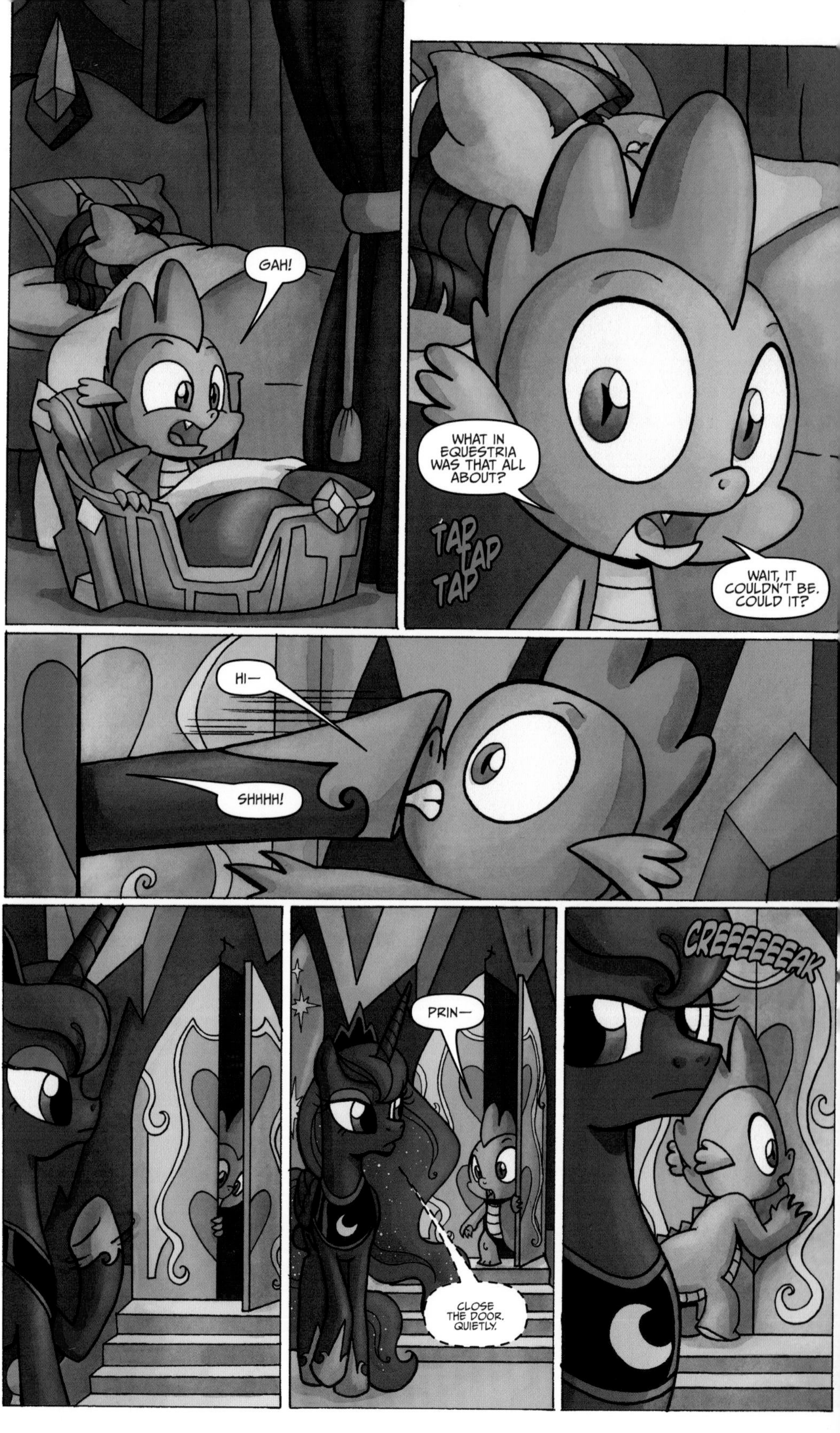
GAH!
WHAT IN EQUESTRIA WAS THAT ALL ABOUT?
TAP TAP TAP
WAIT, IT COULDN'T BE. COULD IT?
HI—
SHHHH!
PRIN—
CLOSE THE DOOR. QUIETLY.
CREEEEEEEAK

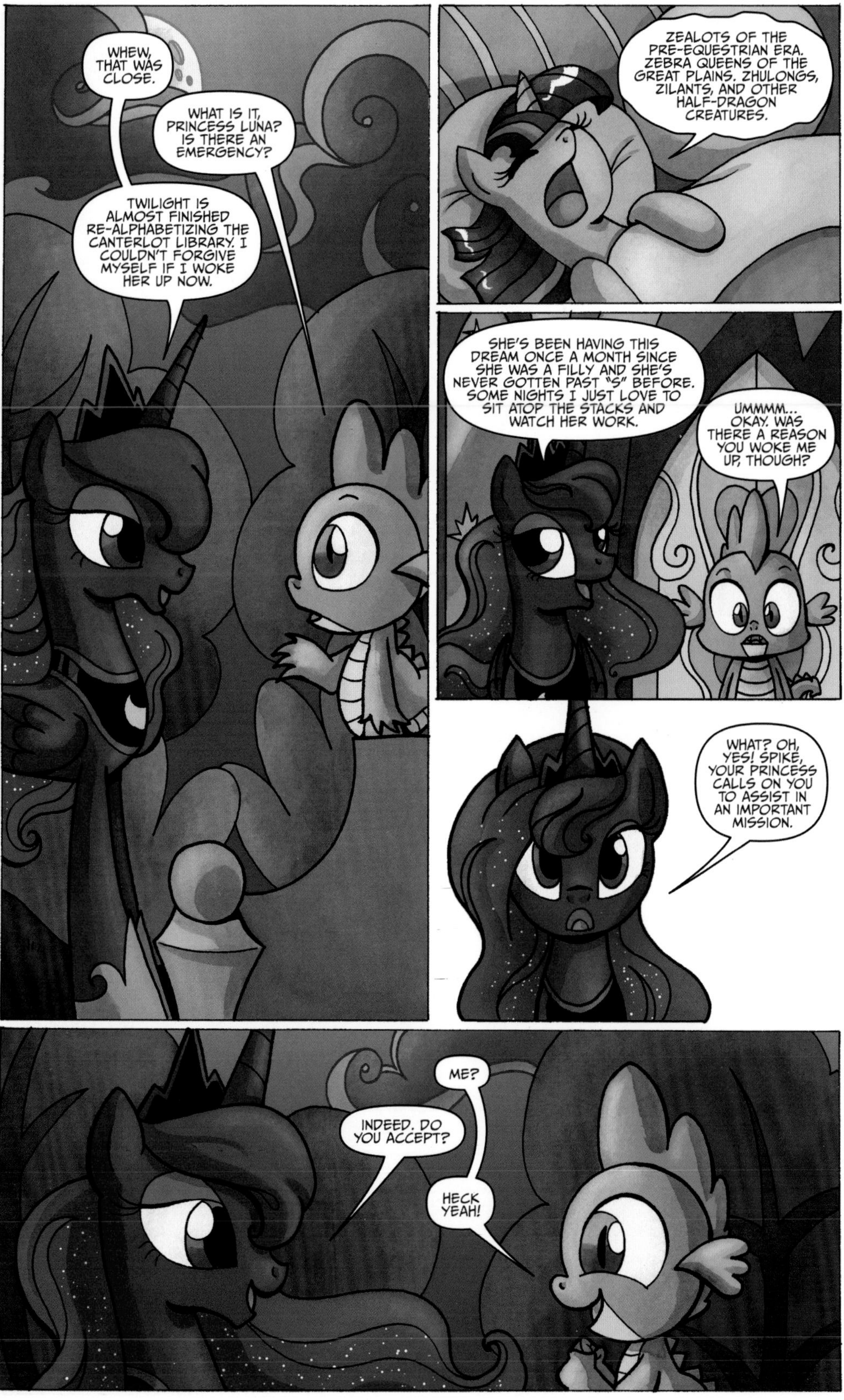
WHEW, THAT WAS CLOSE.
WHAT IS IT, PRINCESS LUNA? IS THERE AN EMERGENCY?
TWILIGHT IS ALMOST FINISHED RE-ALPHABETIZING THE CANTERLOT LIBRARY. I COULDN'T FORGIVE MYSELF IF I WOKE HER UP NOW.
ZEALOTS OF THE PRE-EQUESTRIAN ERA. ZEBRA QUEENS OF THE GREAT PLAINS. ZHULONGS, ZILANTS, AND OTHER HALF-DRAGON CREATURES.
SHE'S BEEN HAVING THIS DREAM ONCE A MONTH SINCE SHE WAS A FILLY AND SHE'S NEVER GOTTEN PAST "S" BEFORE. SOME NIGHTS I JUST LOVE TO SIT ATOP THE STACKS AND WATCH HER WORK.
UMMMM... OKAY. WAS THERE A REASON YOU WOKE ME UP, THOUGH?
WHAT? OH, YES! SPIKE, YOUR PRINCESS CALLS ON YOU TO ASSIST IN AN IMPORTANT MISSION.
ME?
INDEED. DO YOU ACCEPT?
HECK YEAH!

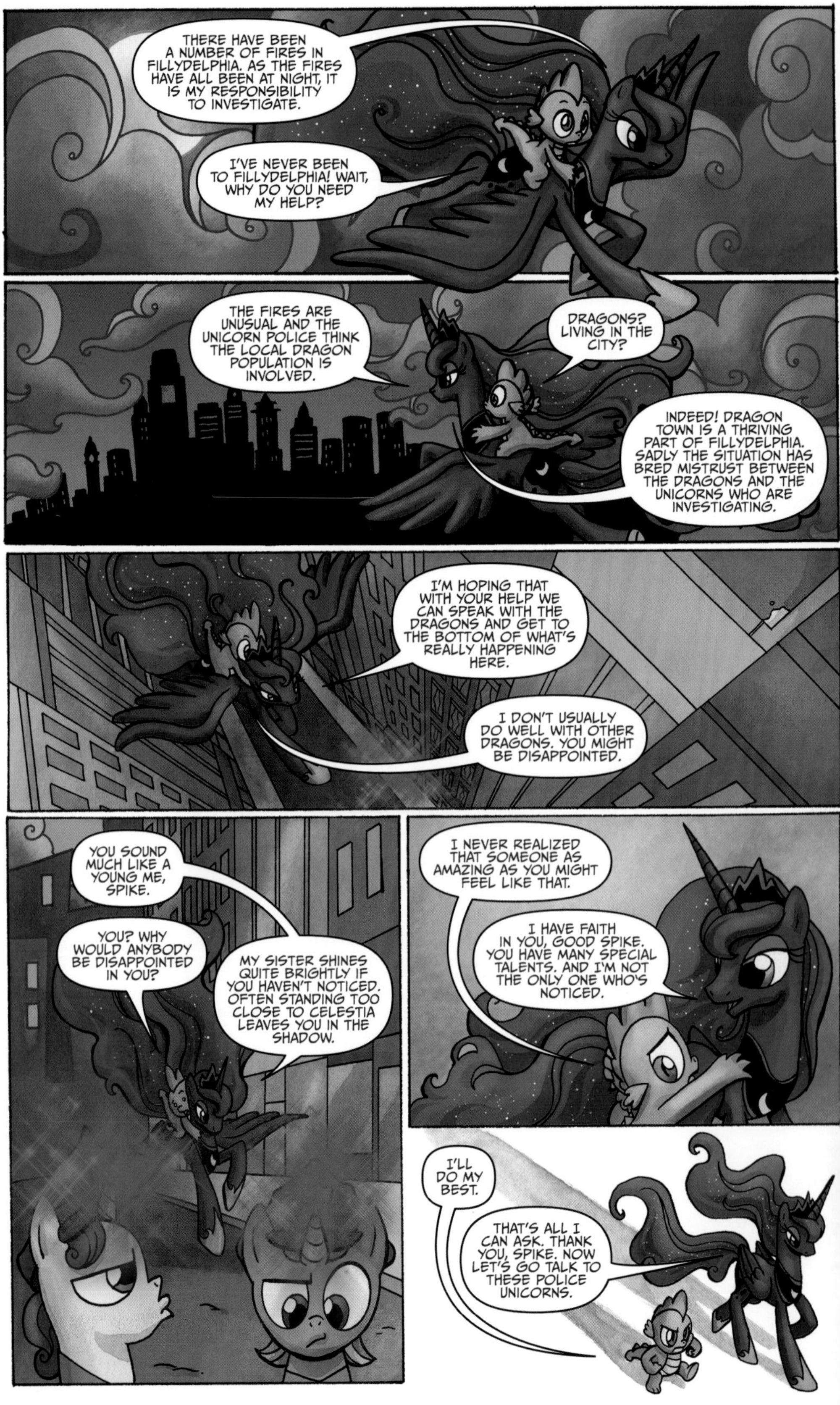
THERE HAVE BEEN A NUMBER OF FIRES IN FILLYDELPHIA. AS THE FIRES HAVE ALL BEEN AT NIGHT, IT IS MY RESPONSIBILITY TO INVESTIGATE.
I'VE NEVER BEEN TO FILLYDELPHIA! WAIT, WHY DO YOU NEED MY HELP?
THE FIRES ARE UNUSUAL AND THE UNICORN POLICE THINK THE LOCAL DRAGON POPULATION IS INVOLVED.
DRAGONS? LIVING IN THE CITY?
INDEED! DRAGON TOWN IS A THRIVING PART OF FILLYDELPHIA. SADLY THE SITUATION HAS BRED MISTRUST BETWEEN THE DRAGONS AND THE UNICORNS WHO ARE INVESTIGATING.
I'M HOPING THAT WITH YOUR HELP WE CAN SPEAK WITH THE DRAGONS AND GET TO THE BOTTOM OF WHAT'S REALLY HAPPENING HERE.
I DON'T USUALLY DO WELL WITH OTHER DRAGONS. YOU MIGHT BE DISAPPOINTED.
YOU SOUND MUCH LIKE A YOUNG ME, SPIKE.
YOU? WHY WOULD ANYBODY BE DISAPPOINTED IN YOU?
MY SISTER SHINES QUITE BRIGHTLY IF YOU HAVEN'T NOTICED. OFTEN STANDING TOO CLOSE TO CELESTIA LEAVES YOU IN THE SHADOW.
I NEVER REALIZED THAT SOMEONE AS AMAZING AS YOU MIGHT FEEL LIKE THAT.
I HAVE FAITH IN YOU, GOOD SPIKE. YOU HAVE MANY SPECIAL TALENTS. AND I'M NOT THE ONLY ONE WHO'S NOTICED.
I'LL DO MY BEST.
THAT'S ALL I CAN ASK. THANK YOU, SPIKE. NOW LET'S GO TALK TO THESE POLICE UNICORNS.

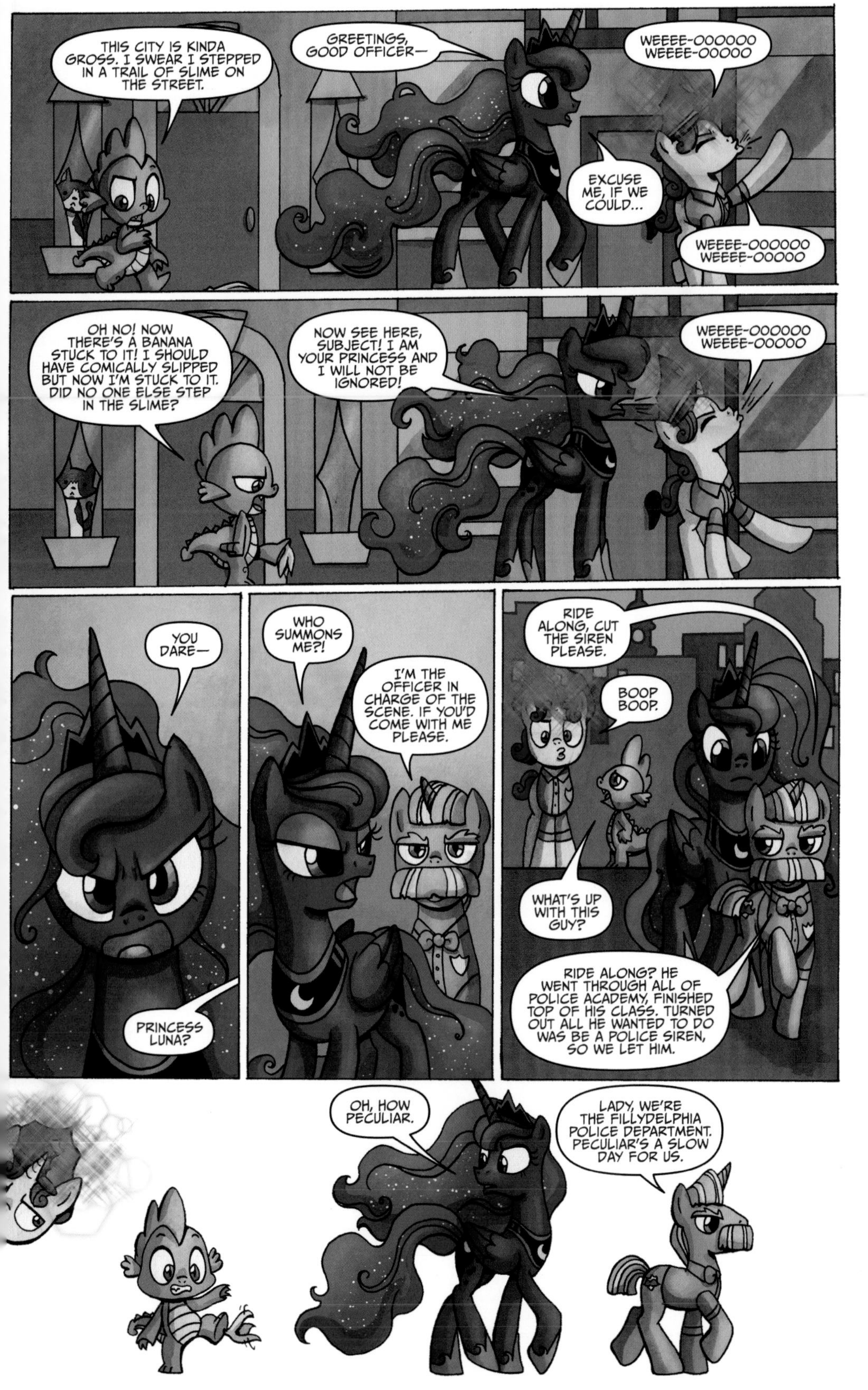
THIS CITY IS KINDA GROSS. I SWEAR I STEPPED IN A TRAIL OF SLIME ON THE STREET.
GREETINGS, GOOD OFFICER—
WEEEE-OOOOOO WEEEE-OOOOO
EXCUSE ME, IF WE COULD...
WEEEE-OOOOOO WEEEE-OOOOO
OH NO! NOW THERE'S A BANANA STUCK TO IT! I SHOULD HAVE COMICALLY SLIPPED BUT NOW I'M STUCK TO IT. DID NO ONE ELSE STEP IN THE SLIME?
NOW SEE HERE, SUBJECT! I AM YOUR PRINCESS AND I WILL NOT BE IGNORED!
WEEEE-OOOOOO WEEEE-OOOOO
YOU DARE—
PRINCESS LUNA?
WHO SUMMONS ME?!
I'M THE OFFICER IN CHARGE OF THE SCENE. IF YOU'D COME WITH ME PLEASE.
RIDE ALONG, CUT THE SIREN PLEASE.
BOOP BOOP.
WHAT'S UP WITH THIS GUY?
RIDE ALONG? HE WENT THROUGH ALL OF POLICE ACADEMY, FINISHED TOP OF HIS CLASS. TURNED OUT ALL HE WANTED TO DO WAS BE A POLICE SIREN, SO WE LET HIM.
OH, HOW PECULIAR.
LADY, WE'RE THE FILLYDELPHIA POLICE DEPARTMENT. PECULIAR'S A SLOW DAY FOR US.

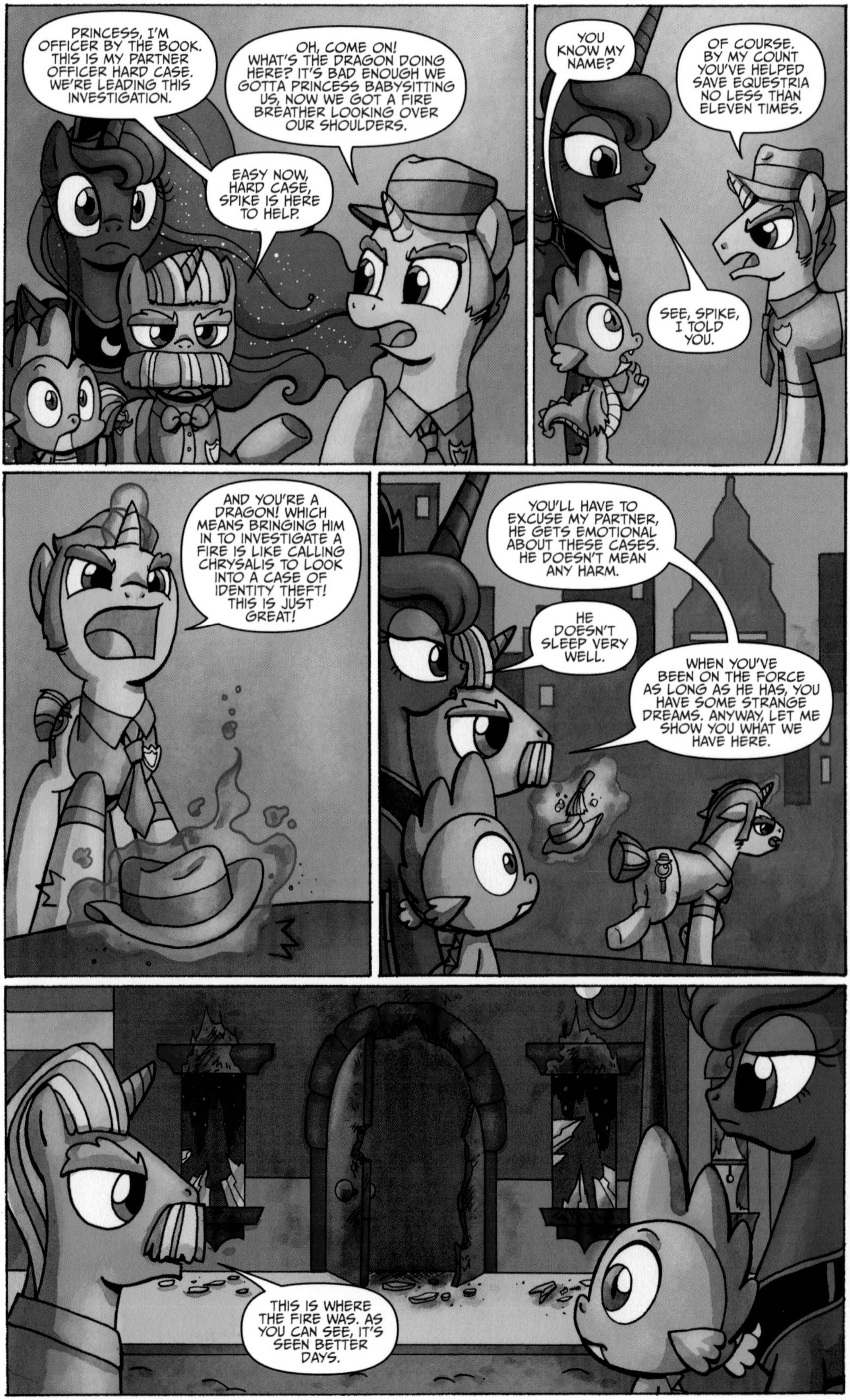
PRINCESS, I'M OFFICER BY THE BOOK. THIS IS MY PARTNER OFFICER HARD CASE. WE'RE LEADING THIS INVESTIGATION.
OH, COME ON! WHAT'S THE DRAGON DOING HERE? IT'S BAD ENOUGH WE GOTTA PRINCESS BABYSITTING US, NOW WE GOT A FIRE BREATHER LOOKING OVER OUR SHOULDERS.
EASY NOW, HARD CASE, SPIKE IS HERE TO HELP.
YOU KNOW MY NAME?
OF COURSE. BY MY COUNT YOU'VE HELPED SAVE EQUESTRIA NO LESS THAN ELEVEN TIMES.
SEE, SPIKE, I TOLD YOU.
AND YOU'RE A DRAGON! WHICH MEANS BRINGING HIM IN TO INVESTIGATE A FIRE IS LIKE CALLING CHRYSALIS TO LOOK INTO A CASE OF IDENTITY THEFT! THIS IS JUST GREAT!
YOU'LL HAVE TO EXCUSE MY PARTNER, HE GETS EMOTIONAL ABOUT THESE CASES. HE DOESN'T MEAN ANY HARM.
HE DOESN'T SLEEP VERY WELL.
WHEN YOU'VE BEEN ON THE FORCE AS LONG AS HE HAS, YOU HAVE SOME STRANGE DREAMS. ANYWAY, LET ME SHOW YOU WHAT WE HAVE HERE.
THIS IS WHERE THE FIRE WAS. AS YOU CAN SEE, IT'S SEEN BETTER DAYS.

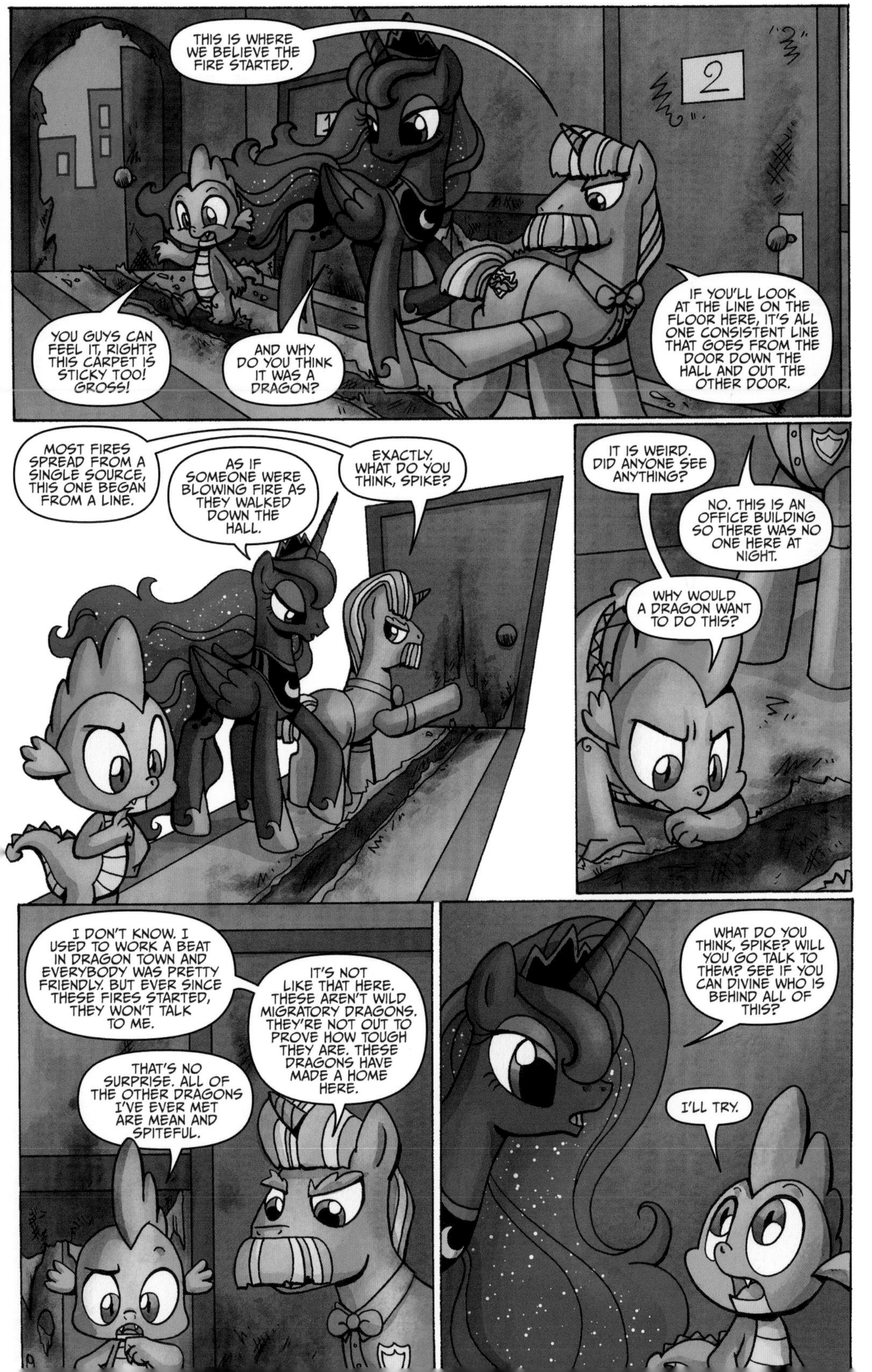
THIS IS WHERE WE BELIEVE THE FIRE STARTED.
2
YOU GUYS CAN FEEL IT, RIGHT? THIS CARPET IS STICKY TOO! GROSS!
AND WHY DO YOU THINK IT WAS A DRAGON?
IF YOU'LL LOOK AT THE LINE ON THE FLOOR HERE, IT'S ALL ONE CONSISTENT LINE THAT GOES FROM THE DOOR DOWN THE HALL AND OUT THE OTHER DOOR.
MOST FIRES SPREAD FROM A SINGLE SOURCE, THIS ONE BEGAN FROM A LINE.
AS IF SOMEONE WERE BLOWING FIRE AS THEY WALKED DOWN THE HALL.
EXACTLY. WHAT DO YOU THINK, SPIKE?
IT IS WEIRD. DID ANYONE SEE ANYTHING?
NO. THIS IS AN OFFICE BUILDING SO THERE WAS NO ONE HERE AT NIGHT.
WHY WOULD A DRAGON WANT TO DO THIS?
I DON'T KNOW. I USED TO WORK A BEAT IN DRAGON TOWN AND EVERYBODY WAS PRETTY FRIENDLY. BUT EVER SINCE THESE FIRES STARTED, THEY WON'T TALK TO ME.
IT'S NOT LIKE THAT HERE. THESE AREN'T WILD MIGRATORY DRAGONS. THEY'RE NOT OUT TO PROVE HOW TOUGH THEY ARE. THESE DRAGONS HAVE MADE A HOME HERE.
THAT'S NO SURPRISE. ALL OF THE OTHER DRAGONS I'VE EVER MET ARE MEAN AND SPITEFUL.
WHAT DO YOU THINK, SPIKE? WILL YOU GO TALK TO THEM? SEE IF YOU CAN DIVINE WHO IS BEHIND ALL OF THIS?
I'LL TRY.

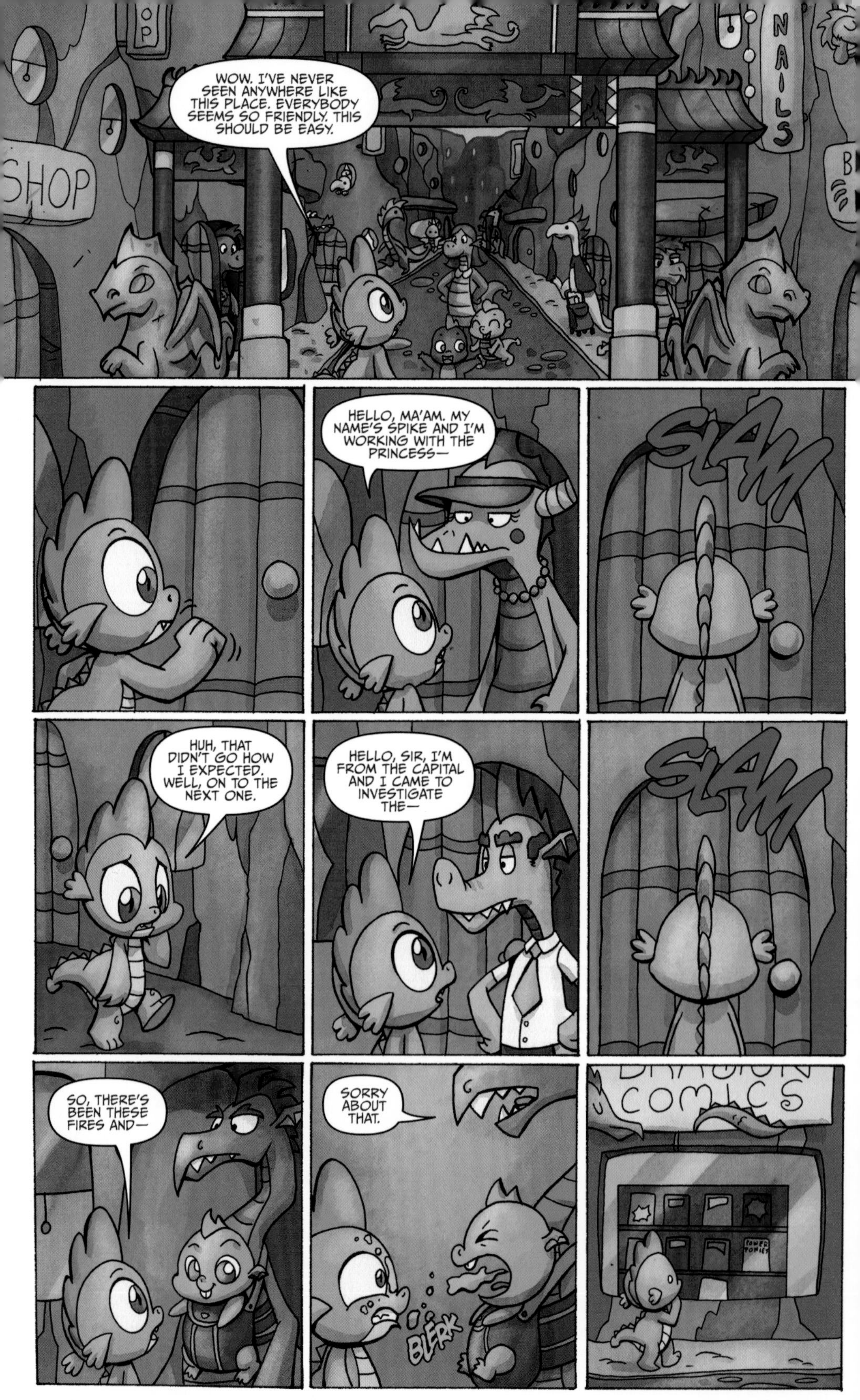
OP
NAILS
SHOP
WOW. I'VE NEVER SEEN ANYWHERE LIKE THIS PLACE. EVERYBODY SEEMS SO FRIENDLY. THIS SHOULD BE EASY.
HELLO, MA'AM. MY NAME'S SPIKE AND I'M WORKING WITH THE PRINCESS—
SLAM
HUH, THAT DIDN'T GO HOW I EXPECTED. WELL, ON TO THE NEXT ONE.
HELLO, SIR, I'M FROM THE CAPITAL AND I CAME TO INVESTIGATE THE—
SLAM
SO, THERE'S BEEN THESE FIRES AND—
SORRY ABOUT THAT.
BLERK
COMICS

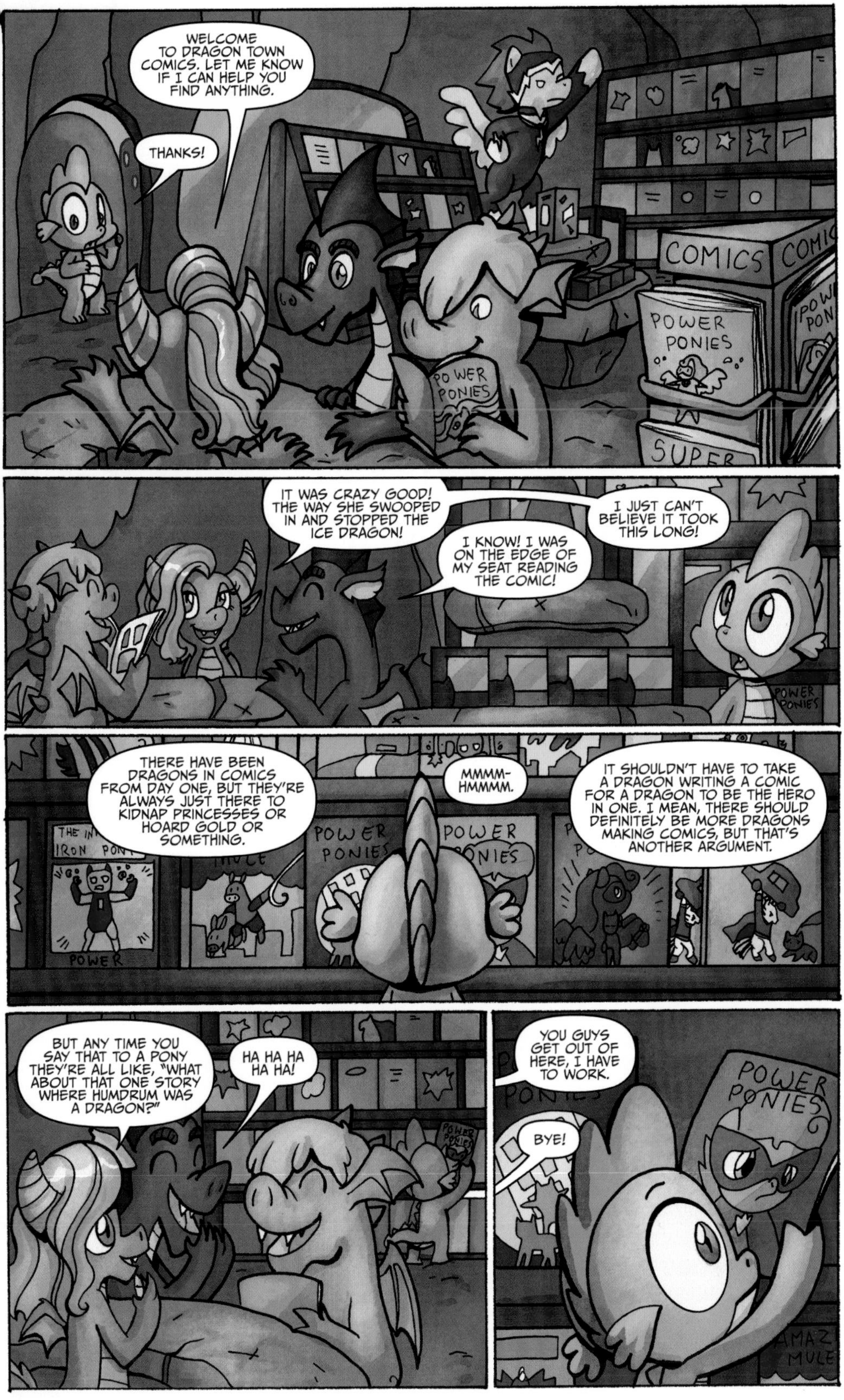
WELCOME TO DRAGON TOWN COMICS. LET ME KNOW IF I CAN HELP YOU FIND ANYTHING.
THANKS!
COMICS
POWER PONIES
IT WAS CRAZY GOOD! THE WAY SHE SWOOPED IN AND STOPPED THE ICE DRAGON!
I KNOW! I WAS ON THE EDGE OF MY SEAT READING THE COMIC!
I JUST CAN'T BELIEVE IT TOOK THIS LONG!
THERE HAVE BEEN DRAGONS IN COMICS FROM DAY ONE, BUT THEY'RE ALWAYS JUST THERE TO KIDNAP PRINCESSES OR HOARD GOLD OR SOMETHING.
MMMM-HMMMM.
IT SHOULDN'T HAVE TO TAKE A DRAGON WRITING A COMIC FOR A DRAGON TO BE THE HERO IN ONE. I MEAN, THERE SHOULD DEFINITELY BE MORE DRAGONS MAKING COMICS, BUT THAT'S ANOTHER ARGUMENT.
POWER PONIES
BUT ANY TIME YOU SAY THAT TO A PONY THEY'RE ALL LIKE, "WHAT ABOUT THAT ONE STORY WHERE HUMDRUM WAS A DRAGON?"
HA HA HA HA HA!
YOU GUYS GET OUT OF HERE, I HAVE TO WORK.
BYE!
POWER PONIES

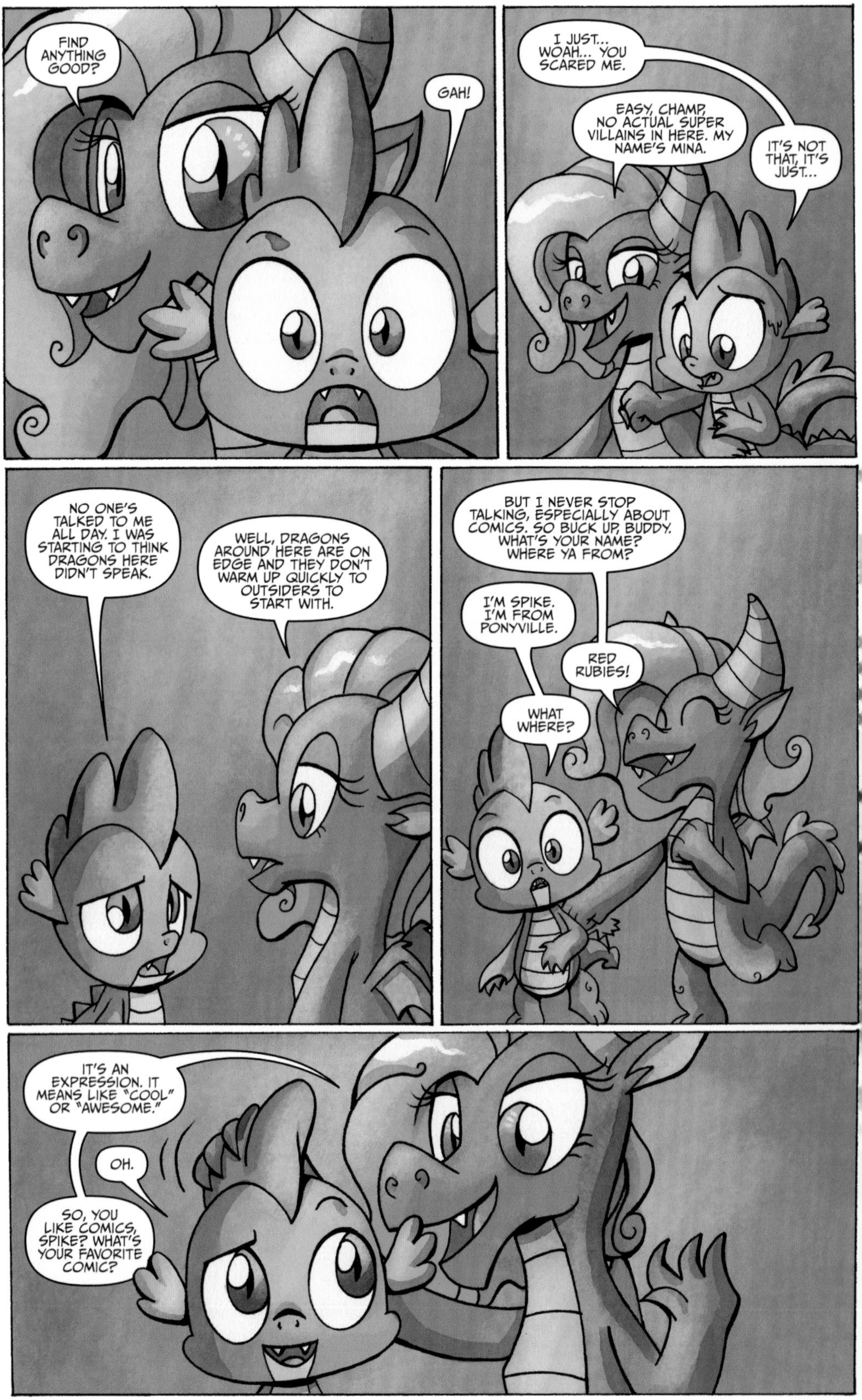

FIND ANYTHING GOOD?
GAH!
I JUST... WOAH... YOU SCARED ME.
EASY, CHAMP, NO ACTUAL SUPER VILLAINS IN HERE. MY NAME'S MINA.
IT'S NOT THAT, IT'S JUST...
NO ONE'S TALKED TO ME ALL DAY. I WAS STARTING TO THINK DRAGONS HERE DIDN'T SPEAK.
WELL, DRAGONS AROUND HERE ARE ON EDGE AND THEY DON'T WARM UP QUICKLY TO OUTSIDERS TO START WITH.
BUT I NEVER STOP TALKING, ESPECIALLY ABOUT COMICS. SO BUCK UP, BUDDY. WHAT'S YOUR NAME? WHERE YA FROM?
I'M SPIKE. I'M FROM PONYVILLE.
RED RUBIES!
WHAT WHERE?
IT'S AN EXPRESSION. IT MEANS LIKE "COOL" OR "AWESOME."
OH.
SO, YOU LIKE COMICS, SPIKE? WHAT'S YOUR FAVORITE COMIC?

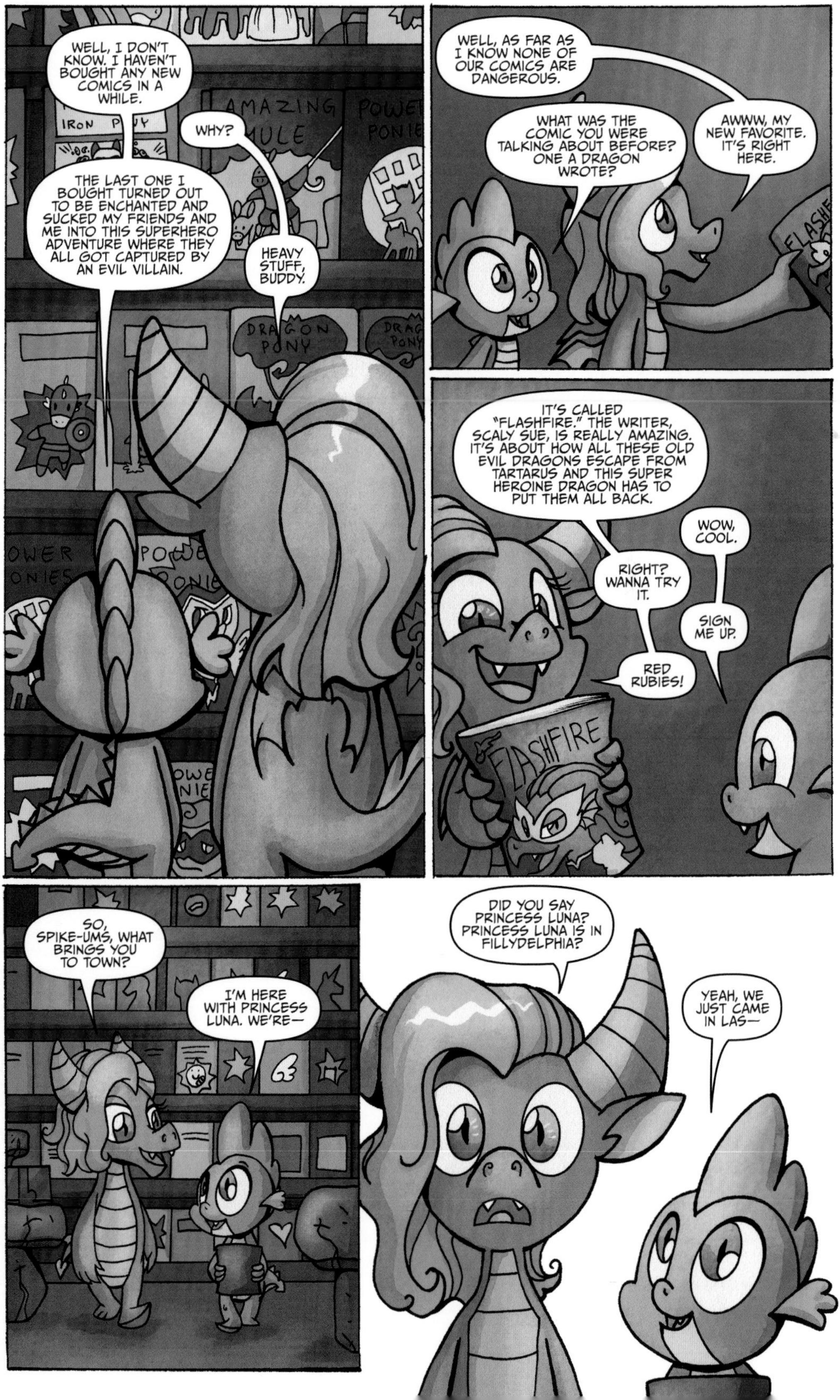
WELL, I DON'T KNOW. I HAVEN'T BOUGHT ANY NEW COMICS IN A WHILE.
THE LAST ONE I BOUGHT TURNED OUT TO BE ENCHANTED AND SUCKED MY FRIENDS AND ME INTO THIS SUPERHERO ADVENTURE WHERE THEY ALL GOT CAPTURED BY AN EVIL VILLAIN.
WHY?
HEAVY STUFF, BUDDY.
IRON PONY
AMAZING MULE
POWER PONIES
DRAGON PONY
WELL, AS FAR AS I KNOW NONE OF OUR COMICS ARE DANGEROUS.
WHAT WAS THE COMIC YOU WERE TALKING ABOUT BEFORE? ONE A DRAGON WROTE?
AWWW, MY NEW FAVORITE. IT'S RIGHT HERE.
IT'S CALLED "FLASHFIRE." THE WRITER, SCALY SUE, IS REALLY AMAZING. IT'S ABOUT HOW ALL THESE OLD EVIL DRAGONS ESCAPE FROM TARTARUS AND THIS SUPER HEROINE DRAGON HAS TO PUT THEM ALL BACK.
WOW, COOL.
RIGHT? WANNA TRY IT.
SIGN ME UP.
RED RUBIES!
FLASHFIRE
SO, SPIKE-UMS, WHAT BRINGS YOU TO TOWN?
I'M HERE WITH PRINCESS LUNA. WE'RE—
DID YOU SAY PRINCESS LUNA? PRINCESS LUNA IS IN FILLYDELPHIA?
YEAH, WE JUST CAME IN LAS—

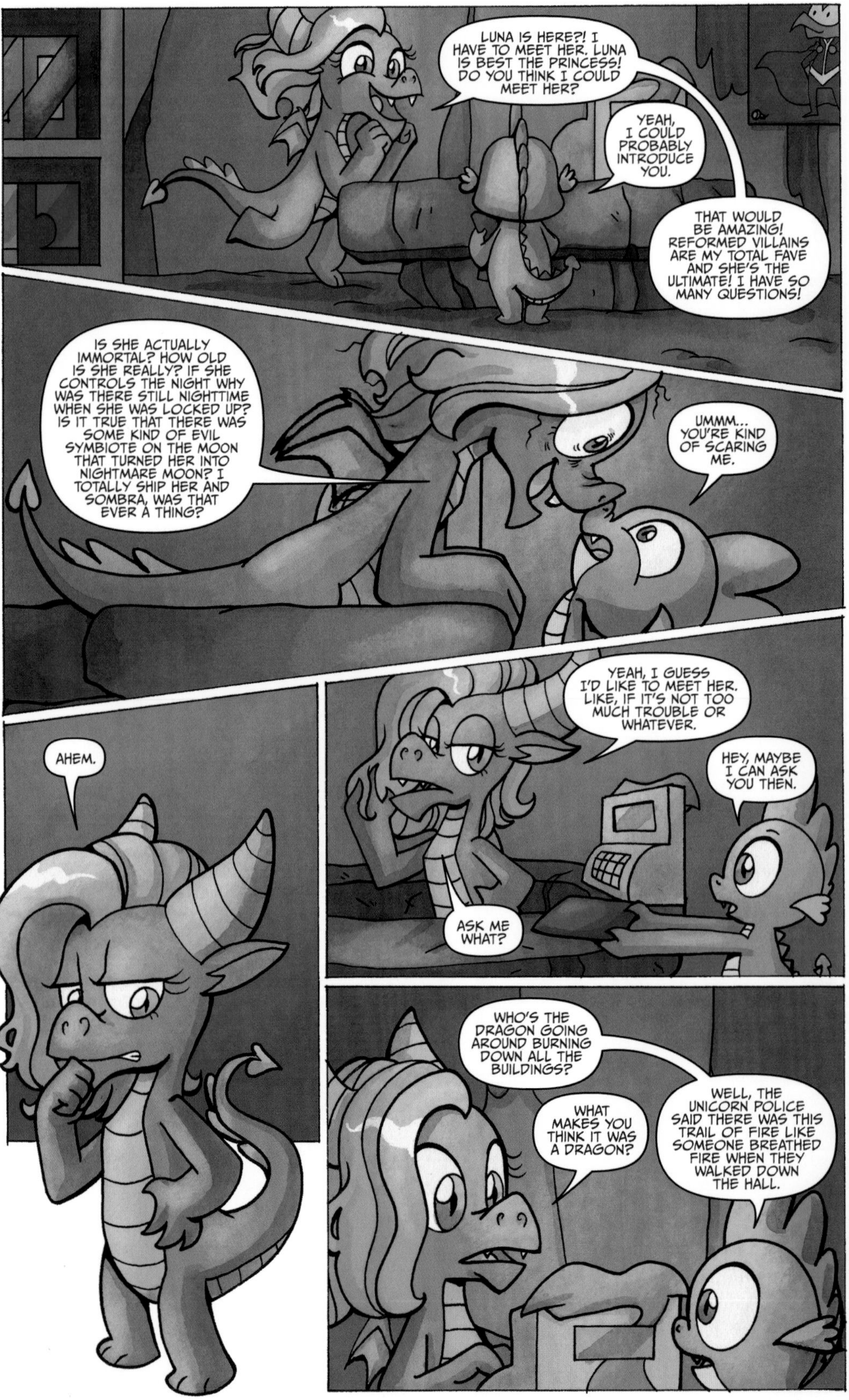
LUNA IS HERE?! I HAVE TO MEET HER. LUNA IS BEST THE PRINCESS! DO YOU THINK I COULD MEET HER?
YEAH, I COULD PROBABLY INTRODUCE YOU.
THAT WOULD BE AMAZING! REFORMED VILLAINS ARE MY TOTAL FAVE AND SHE'S THE ULTIMATE! I HAVE SO MANY QUESTIONS!
IS SHE ACTUALLY IMMORTAL? HOW OLD IS SHE REALLY? IF SHE CONTROLS THE NIGHT WHY WAS THERE STILL NIGHTTIME WHEN SHE WAS LOCKED UP? IS IT TRUE THAT THERE WAS SOME KIND OF EVIL SYMBIOTE ON THE MOON THAT TURNED HER INTO NIGHTMARE MOON? I TOTALLY SHIP HER AND SOMBRA, WAS THAT EVER A THING?
UMMM... YOU'RE KIND OF SCARING ME.
AHEM.
YEAH, I GUESS I'D LIKE TO MEET HER. LIKE, IF IT'S NOT TOO MUCH TROUBLE OR WHATEVER.
HEY, MAYBE I CAN ASK YOU THEN.
ASK ME WHAT?
WHO'S THE DRAGON GOING AROUND BURNING DOWN ALL THE BUILDINGS?
WHAT MAKES YOU THINK IT WAS A DRAGON?
WELL, THE UNICORN POLICE SAID THERE WAS THIS TRAIL OF FIRE LIKE SOMEONE BREATHED FIRE WHEN THEY WALKED DOWN THE HALL.

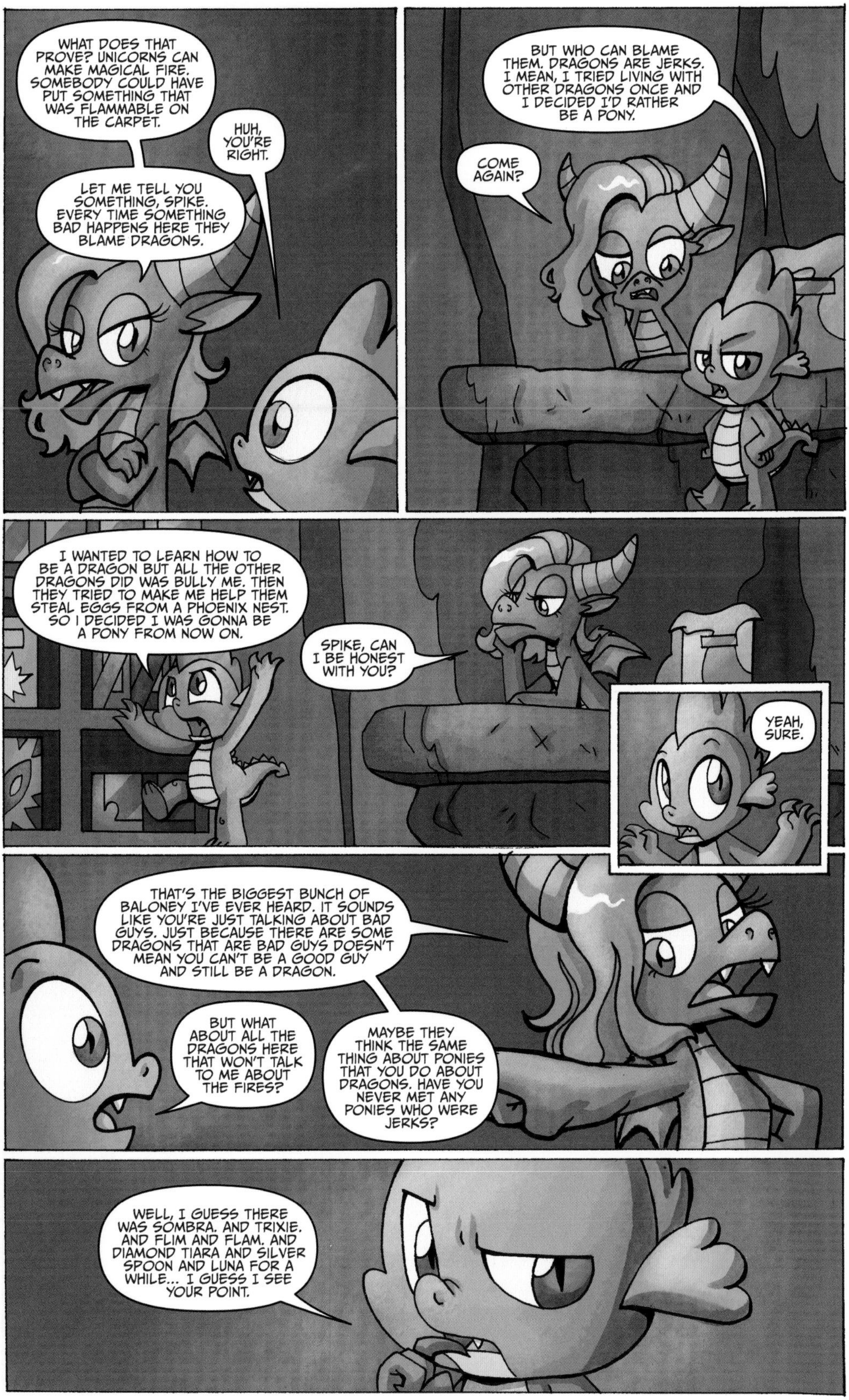
WHAT DOES THAT PROVE? UNICORNS CAN MAKE MAGICAL FIRE. SOMEBODY COULD HAVE PUT SOMETHING THAT WAS FLAMMABLE ON THE CARPET.
HUH, YOU'RE RIGHT.
LET ME TELL YOU SOMETHING, SPIKE. EVERY TIME SOMETHING BAD HAPPENS HERE THEY BLAME DRAGONS.
BUT WHO CAN BLAME THEM. DRAGONS ARE JERKS. I MEAN, I TRIED LIVING WITH OTHER DRAGONS ONCE AND I DECIDED I'D RATHER BE A PONY.
COME AGAIN?
I WANTED TO LEARN HOW TO BE A DRAGON BUT ALL THE OTHER DRAGONS DID WAS BULLY ME. THEN THEY TRIED TO MAKE ME HELP THEM STEAL EGGS FROM A PHOENIX NEST. SO I DECIDED I WAS GONNA BE A PONY FROM NOW ON.
SPIKE, CAN I BE HONEST WITH YOU?
YEAH, SURE.
THAT'S THE BIGGEST BUNCH OF BALONEY I'VE EVER HEARD. IT SOUNDS LIKE YOU'RE JUST TALKING ABOUT BAD GUYS. JUST BECAUSE THERE ARE SOME DRAGONS THAT ARE BAD GUYS DOESN'T MEAN YOU CAN'T BE A GOOD GUY AND STILL BE A DRAGON.
BUT WHAT ABOUT ALL THE DRAGONS HERE THAT WON'T TALK TO ME ABOUT THE FIRES?
MAYBE THEY THINK THE SAME THING ABOUT PONIES THAT YOU DO ABOUT DRAGONS. HAVE YOU NEVER MET ANY PONIES WHO WERE JERKS?
WELL, I GUESS THERE WAS SOMBRA. AND TRIXIE. AND FLIM AND FLAM. AND DIAMOND TIARA AND SILVER SPOON AND LUNA FOR A WHILE... I GUESS I SEE YOUR POINT.

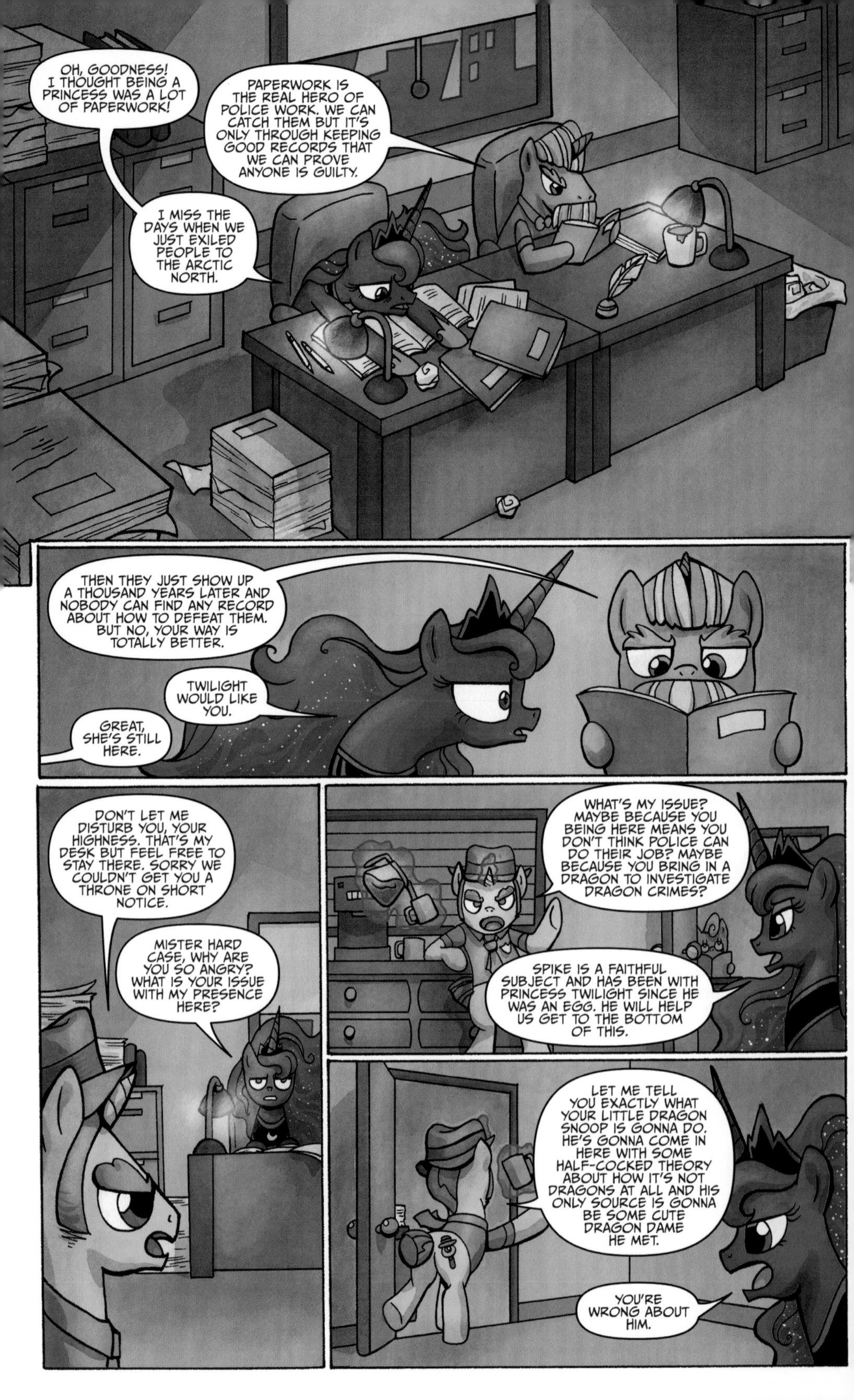
OH, GOODNESS! I THOUGHT BEING A PRINCESS WAS A LOT OF PAPERWORK!
PAPERWORK IS THE REAL HERO OF POLICE WORK. WE CAN CATCH THEM BUT IT'S ONLY THROUGH KEEPING GOOD RECORDS THAT WE CAN PROVE ANYONE IS GUILTY.
I MISS THE DAYS WHEN WE JUST EXILED PEOPLE TO THE ARCTIC NORTH.
THEN THEY JUST SHOW UP A THOUSAND YEARS LATER AND NOBODY CAN FIND ANY RECORD ABOUT HOW TO DEFEAT THEM. BUT NO, YOUR WAY IS TOTALLY BETTER.
TWILIGHT WOULD LIKE YOU.
GREAT, SHE'S STILL HERE.
DON'T LET ME DISTURB YOU, YOUR HIGHNESS. THAT'S MY DESK BUT FEEL FREE TO STAY THERE. SORRY WE COULDN'T GET YOU A THRONE ON SHORT NOTICE.
MISTER HARD CASE, WHY ARE YOU SO ANGRY? WHAT IS YOUR ISSUE WITH MY PRESENCE HERE?
WHAT'S MY ISSUE? MAYBE BECAUSE YOU BEING HERE MEANS YOU DON'T THINK POLICE CAN DO THEIR JOB? MAYBE BECAUSE YOU BRING IN A DRAGON TO INVESTIGATE DRAGON CRIMES?
SPIKE IS A FAITHFUL SUBJECT AND HAS BEEN WITH PRINCESS TWILIGHT SINCE HE WAS AN EGG. HE WILL HELP US GET TO THE BOTTOM OF THIS.
LET ME TELL YOU EXACTLY WHAT YOUR LITTLE DRAGON SNOOP IS GONNA DO. HE'S GONNA COME IN HERE WITH SOME HALF-COCKED THEORY ABOUT HOW IT'S NOT DRAGONS AT ALL AND HIS ONLY SOURCE IS GONNA BE SOME CUTE DRAGON DAME HE MET.
YOU'RE WRONG ABOUT HIM.

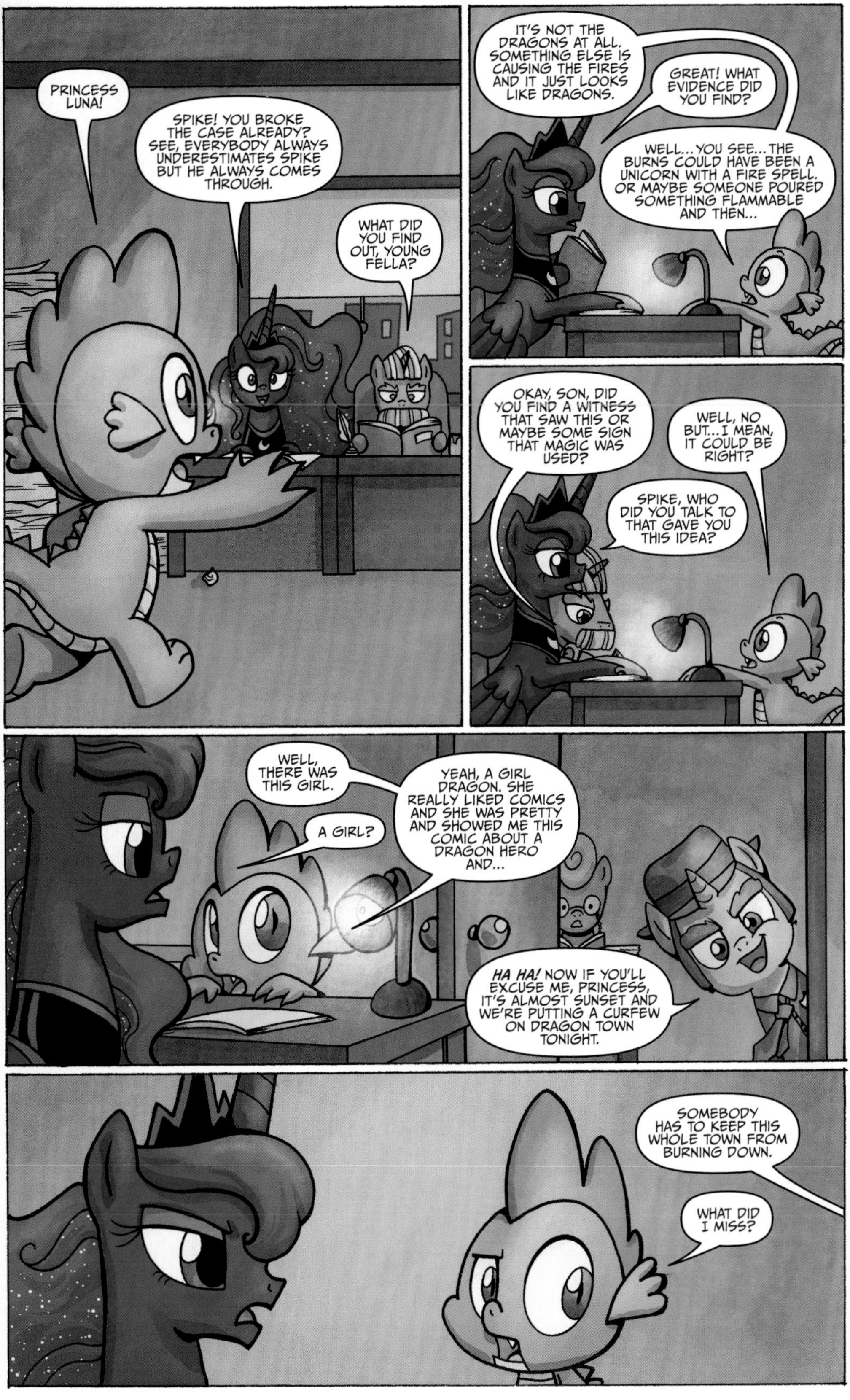
PRINCESS LUNA!
SPIKE! YOU BROKE THE CASE ALREADY? SEE, EVERYBODY ALWAYS UNDERESTIMATES SPIKE BUT HE ALWAYS COMES THROUGH.
WHAT DID YOU FIND OUT, YOUNG FELLA?
IT'S NOT THE DRAGONS AT ALL. SOMETHING ELSE IS CAUSING THE FIRES AND IT JUST LOOKS LIKE DRAGONS.
GREAT! WHAT EVIDENCE DID YOU FIND?
WELL... YOU SEE... THE BURNS COULD HAVE BEEN A UNICORN WITH A FIRE SPELL. OR MAYBE SOMEONE POURED SOMETHING FLAMMABLE AND THEN...
OKAY, SON, DID YOU FIND A WITNESS THAT SAW THIS OR MAYBE SOME SIGN THAT MAGIC WAS USED?
WELL, NO BUT... I MEAN, IT COULD BE RIGHT?
SPIKE, WHO DID YOU TALK TO THAT GAVE YOU THIS IDEA?
WELL, THERE WAS THIS GIRL.
A GIRL?
YEAH, A GIRL DRAGON. SHE REALLY LIKED COMICS AND SHE WAS PRETTY AND SHOWED ME THIS COMIC ABOUT A DRAGON HERO AND...
HA HA! NOW IF YOU'LL EXCUSE ME, PRINCESS, IT'S ALMOST SUNSET AND WE'RE PUTTING A CURFEW ON DRAGON TOWN TONIGHT.
SOMEBODY HAS TO KEEP THIS WHOLE TOWN FROM BURNING DOWN.
WHAT DID I MISS?

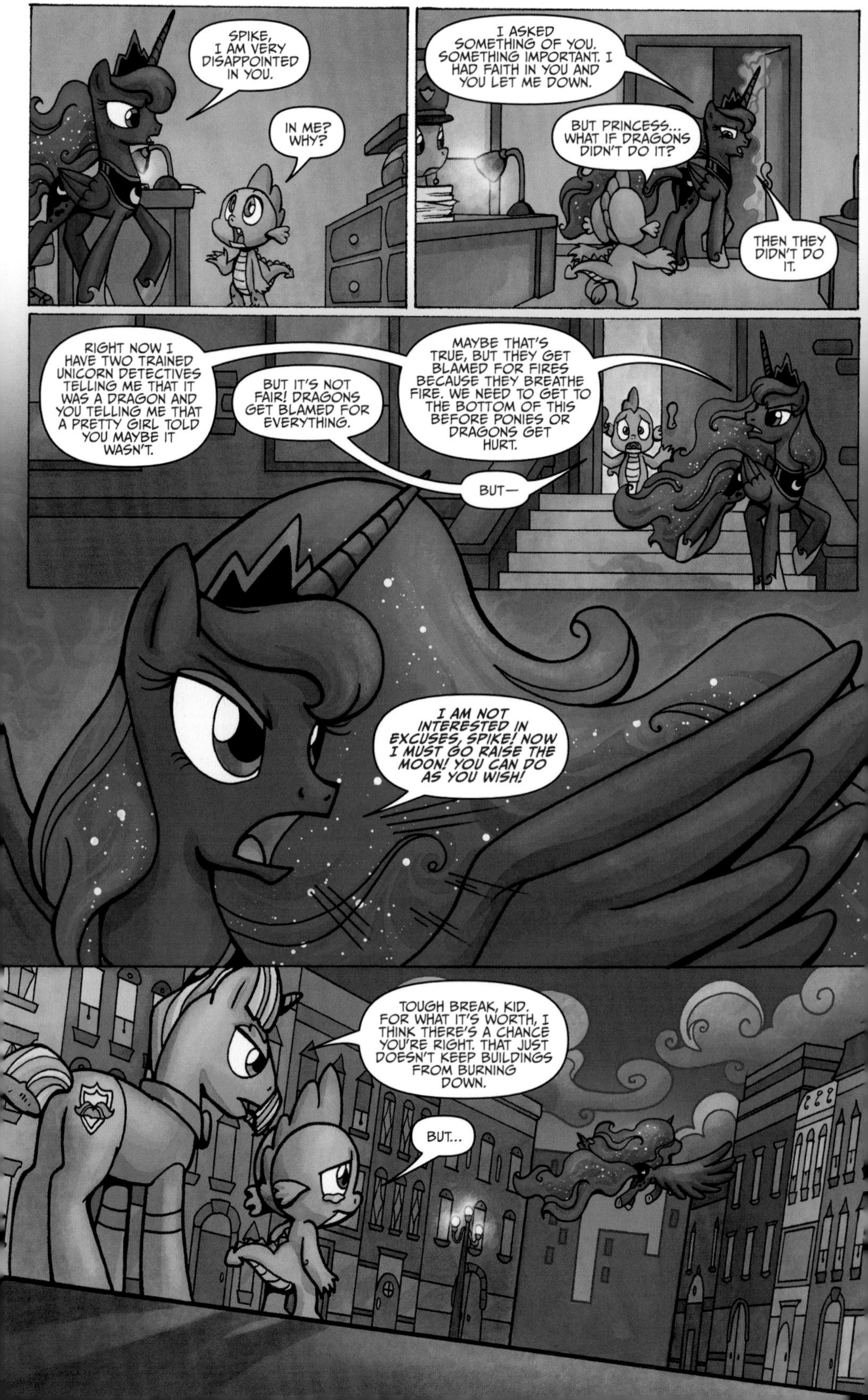
SPIKE, I AM VERY DISAPPOINTED IN YOU.
IN ME? WHY?
I ASKED SOMETHING OF YOU. SOMETHING IMPORTANT. I HAD FAITH IN YOU AND YOU LET ME DOWN.
BUT PRINCESS... WHAT IF DRAGONS DIDN'T DO IT?
THEN THEY DIDN'T DO IT.
RIGHT NOW I HAVE TWO TRAINED UNICORN DETECTIVES TELLING ME THAT IT WAS A DRAGON AND YOU TELLING ME THAT A PRETTY GIRL TOLD YOU MAYBE IT WASN'T.
BUT IT'S NOT FAIR! DRAGONS GET BLAMED FOR EVERYTHING.
MAYBE THAT'S TRUE, BUT THEY GET BLAMED FOR FIRES BECAUSE THEY BREATHE FIRE. WE NEED TO GET TO THE BOTTOM OF THIS BEFORE PONIES OR DRAGONS GET HURT.
BUT—
I AM NOT INTERESTED IN EXCUSES, SPIKE! NOW I MUST GO RAISE THE MOON! YOU CAN DO AS YOU WISH!
TOUGH BREAK, KID. FOR WHAT IT'S WORTH, I THINK THERE'S A CHANCE YOU'RE RIGHT. THAT JUST DOESN'T KEEP BUILDINGS FROM BURNING DOWN.
BUT...

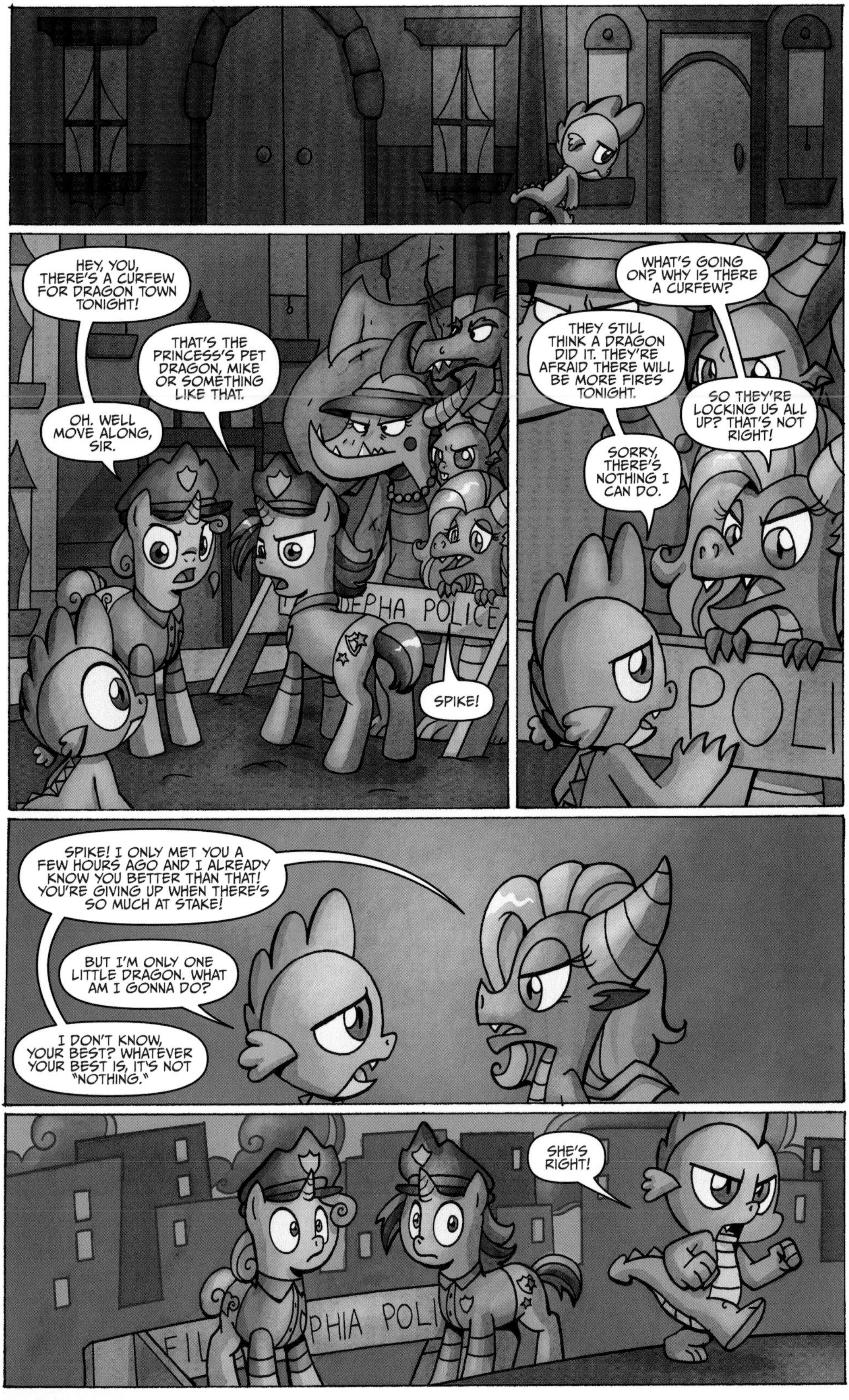
HEY, YOU, THERE'S A CURFEW FOR DRAGON TOWN TONIGHT!
THAT'S THE PRINCESS'S PET DRAGON, MIKE OR SOMETHING LIKE THAT.
OH. WELL MOVE ALONG, SIR.
PHA POLICE
SPIKE!
WHAT'S GOING ON? WHY IS THERE A CURFEW?
THEY STILL THINK A DRAGON DID IT. THEY'RE AFRAID THERE WILL BE MORE FIRES TONIGHT.
SO THEY'RE LOCKING US ALL UP? THAT'S NOT RIGHT!
SORRY, THERE'S NOTHING I CAN DO.
POLI
SPIKE! I ONLY MET YOU A FEW HOURS AGO AND I ALREADY KNOW YOU BETTER THAN THAT! YOU'RE GIVING UP WHEN THERE'S SO MUCH AT STAKE!
BUT I'M ONLY ONE LITTLE DRAGON. WHAT AM I GONNA DO?
I DON'T KNOW, YOUR BEST? WHATEVER YOUR BEST IS, IT'S NOT "NOTHING."
SHE'S RIGHT!
FIL PHIA POLI

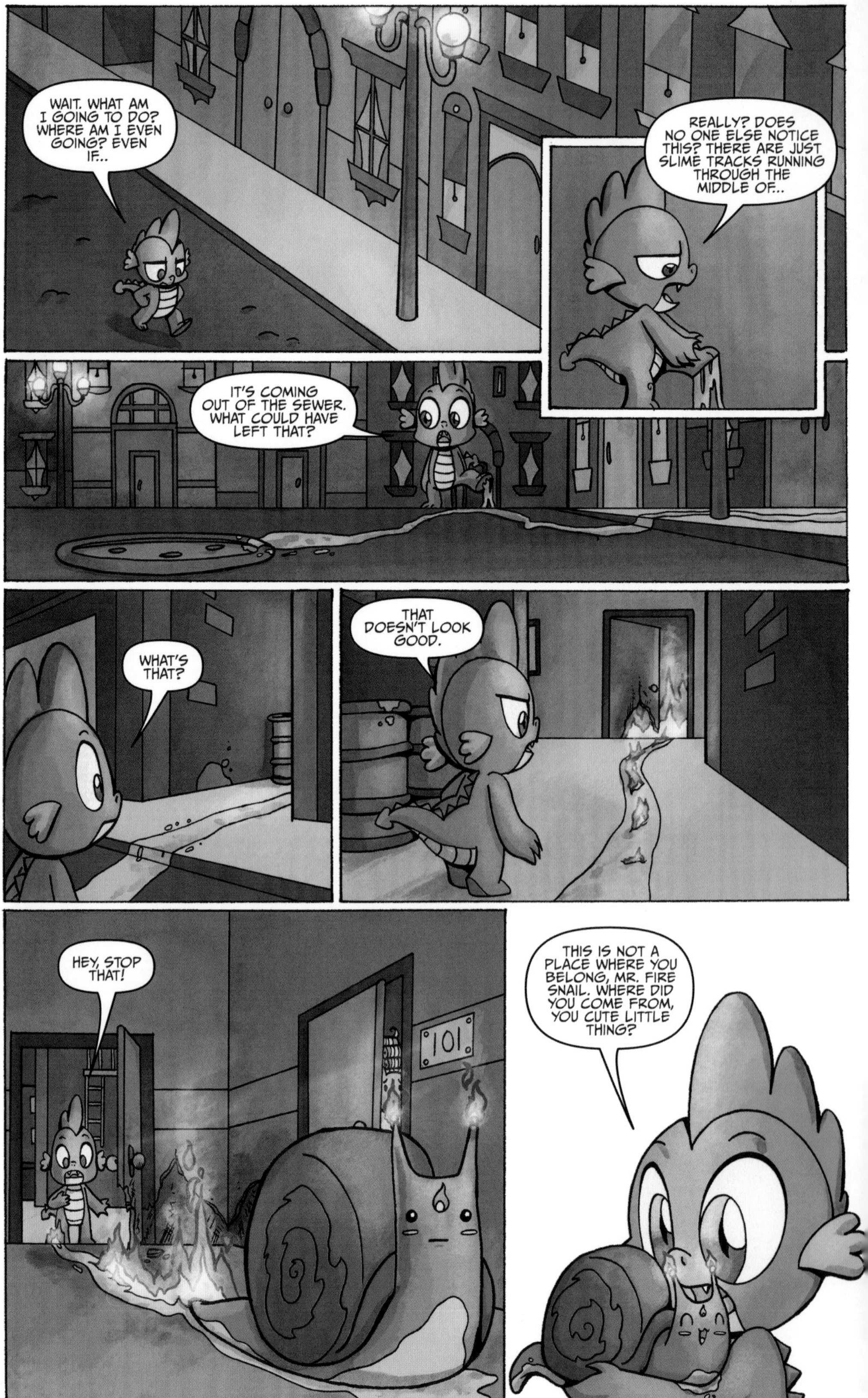
WAIT. WHAT AM I GOING TO DO? WHERE AM I EVEN GOING? EVEN IF...
REALLY? DOES NO ONE ELSE NOTICE THIS? THERE ARE JUST SLIME TRACKS RUNNING THROUGH THE MIDDLE OF...
IT'S COMING OUT OF THE SEWER. WHAT COULD HAVE LEFT THAT?
WHAT'S THAT?
THAT DOESN'T LOOK GOOD.
HEY, STOP THAT!
101
THIS IS NOT A PLACE WHERE YOU BELONG, MR. FIRE SNAIL. WHERE DID YOU COME FROM, YOU CUTE LITTLE THING?

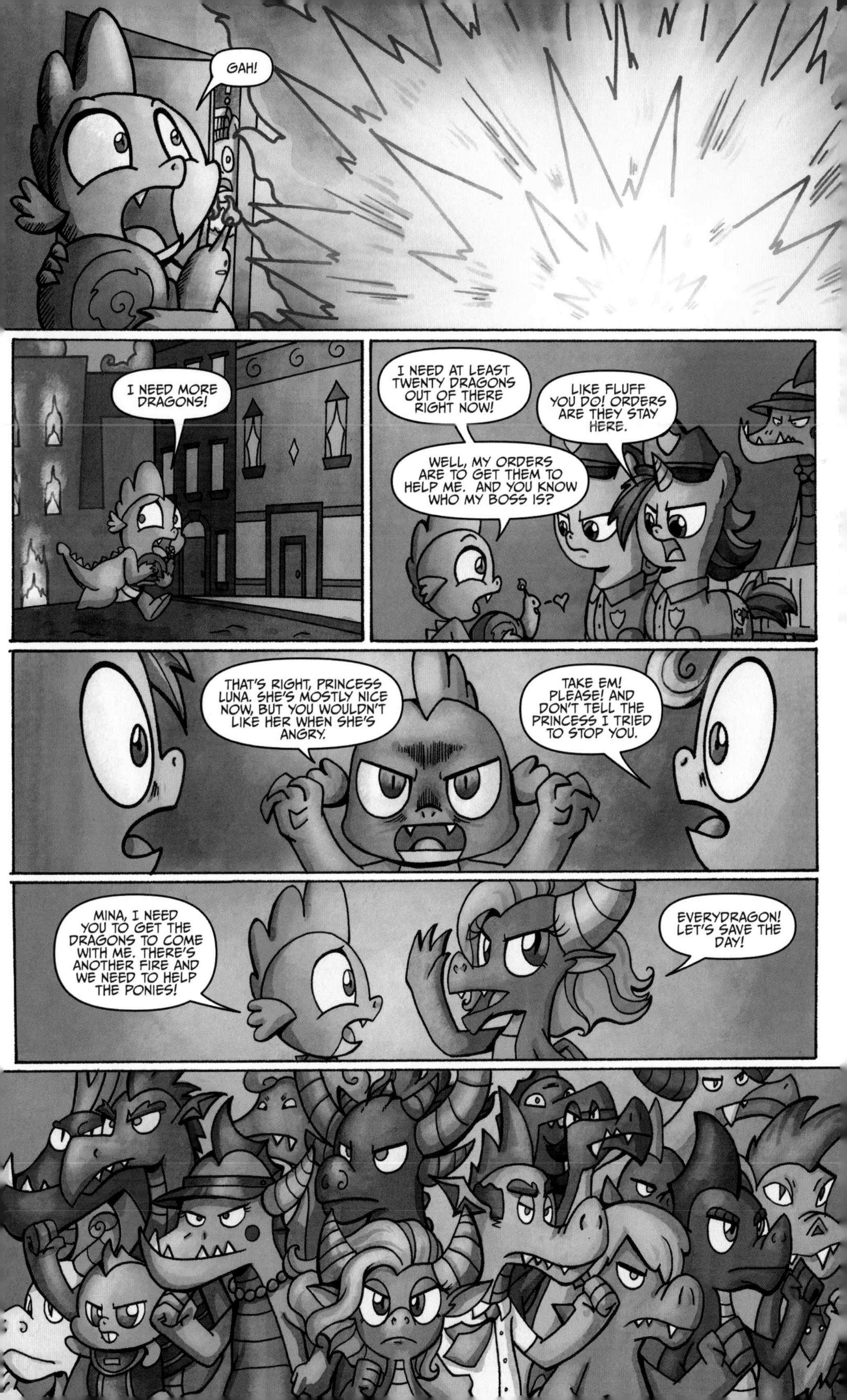
GAH!
I NEED MORE DRAGONS!
I NEED AT LEAST TWENTY DRAGONS OUT OF THERE RIGHT NOW!
LIKE FLUFF YOU DO! ORDERS ARE THEY STAY HERE.
WELL, MY ORDERS ARE TO GET THEM TO HELP ME. AND YOU KNOW WHO MY BOSS IS?
THAT'S RIGHT, PRINCESS LUNA. SHE'S MOSTLY NICE NOW, BUT YOU WOULDN'T LIKE HER WHEN SHE'S ANGRY.
TAKE EM! PLEASE! AND DON'T TELL THE PRINCESS I TRIED TO STOP YOU.
MINA, I NEED YOU TO GET THE DRAGONS TO COME WITH ME. THERE'S ANOTHER FIRE AND WE NEED TO HELP THE PONIES!
EVERYDRAGON! LET'S SAVE THE DAY!

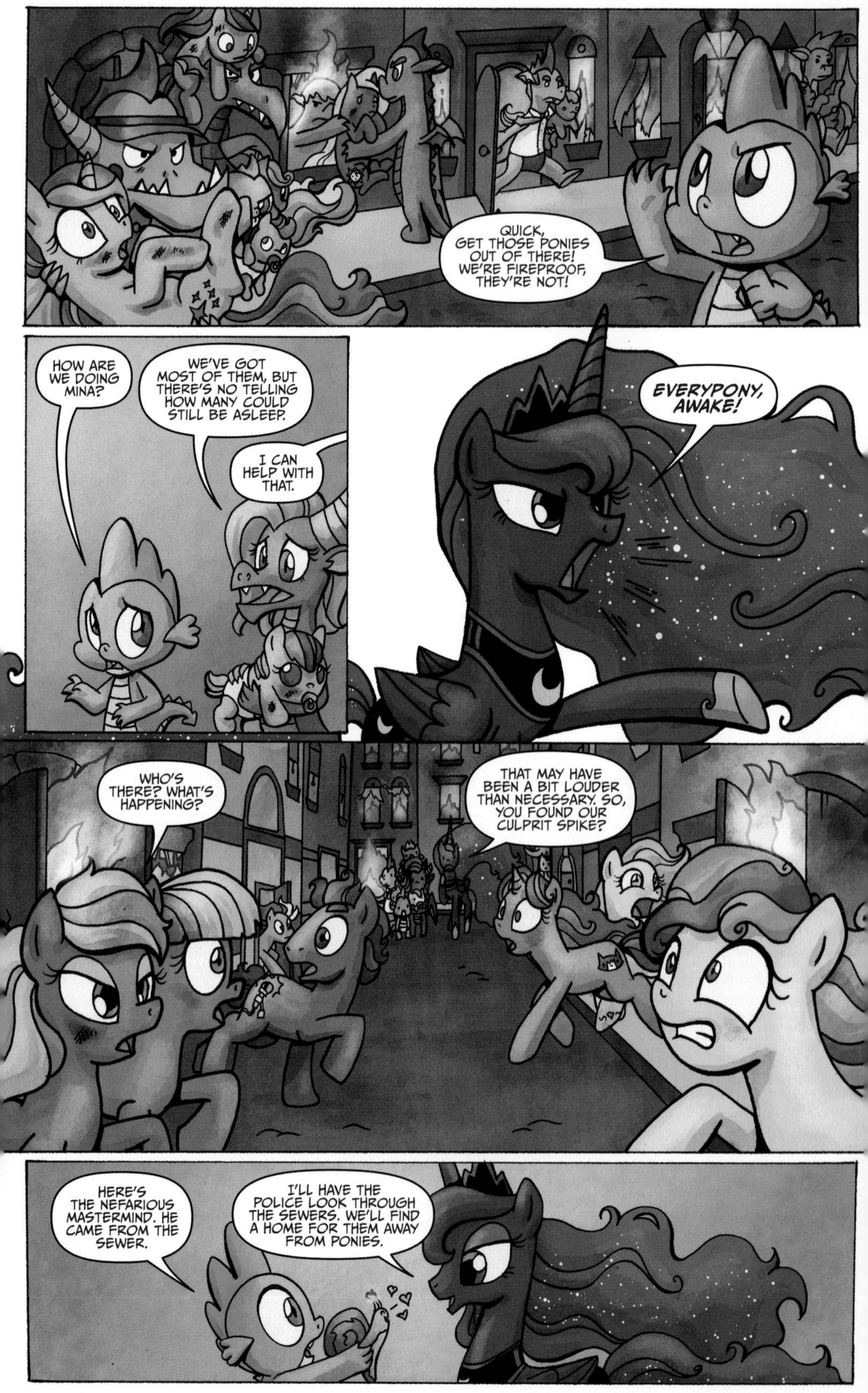
QUICK, GET THOSE PONIES OUT OF THERE! WE'RE FIREPROOF, THEY'RE NOT!
HOW ARE WE DOING MINA?
WE'VE GOT MOST OF THEM, BUT THERE'S NO TELLING HOW MANY COULD STILL BE ASLEEP.
I CAN HELP WITH THAT.
EVERYPONY, AWAKE!
WHO'S THERE? WHAT'S HAPPENING?
THAT MAY HAVE BEEN A BIT LOUDER THAN NECESSARY. SO, YOU FOUND OUR CULPRIT SPIKE?
HERE'S THE NEFARIOUS MASTERMIND. HE CAME FROM THE SEWER.
I'LL HAVE THE POLICE LOOK THROUGH THE SEWERS. WE'LL FIND A HOME FOR THEM AWAY FROM PONIES.

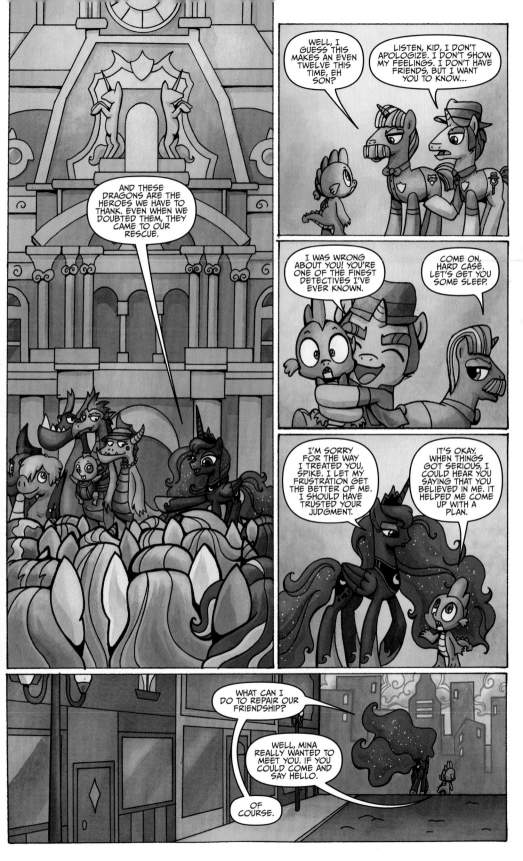

AND THESE DRAGONS ARE THE HEROES WE HAVE TO THANK. EVEN WHEN WE DOUBTED THEM, THEY CAME TO OUR RESCUE.

WELL, I GUESS THIS MAKES AN EVEN TWELVE THIS TIME, EH SON?

LISTEN, KID, I DON'T APOLOGIZE. I DON'T SHOW MY FEELINGS. I DON'T HAVE FRIENDS, BUT I WANT YOU TO KNOW...

I WAS WRONG ABOUT YOU! YOU'RE ONE OF THE FINEST DETECTIVES I'VE EVER KNOWN.

COME ON, HARD CASE. LET'S GET YOU SOME SLEEP.

I'M SORRY FOR THE WAY I TREATED YOU, SPIKE. I LET MY FRUSTRATION GET THE BETTER OF ME. I SHOULD HAVE TRUSTED YOUR JUDGMENT.

IT'S OKAY. WHEN THINGS GOT SERIOUS, I COULD HEAR YOU SAYING THAT YOU BELIEVED IN ME. IT HELPED ME COME UP WITH A PLAN.

WHAT CAN I DO TO REPAIR OUR FRIENDSHIP?

WELL, MINA REALLY WANTED TO MEET YOU. IF YOU COULD COME AND SAY HELLO.

OF COURSE.

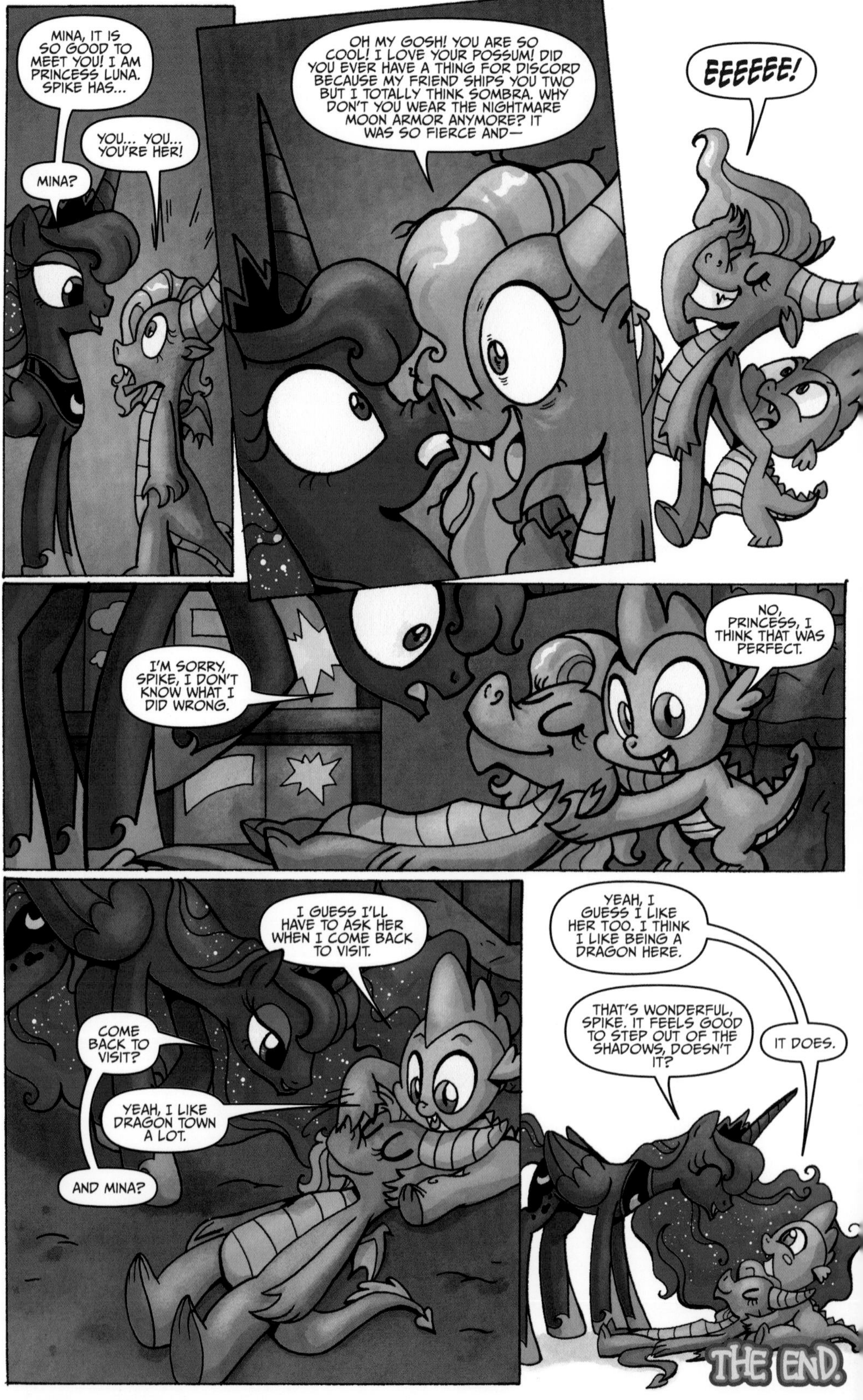
MINA, IT IS SO GOOD TO MEET YOU! I AM PRINCESS LUNA. SPIKE HAS...
YOU... YOU... YOU'RE HER!
MINA?
OH MY GOSH! YOU ARE SO COOL! I LOVE YOUR POSSUM! DID YOU EVER HAVE A THING FOR DISCORD BECAUSE MY FRIEND SHIPS YOU TWO BUT I TOTALLY THINK SOMBRA. WHY DON'T YOU WEAR THE NIGHTMARE MOON ARMOR ANYMORE? IT WAS SO FIERCE AND—
EEEEEE!
I'M SORRY, SPIKE, I DON'T KNOW WHAT I DID WRONG.
NO, PRINCESS, I THINK THAT WAS PERFECT.
I GUESS I'LL HAVE TO ASK HER WHEN I COME BACK TO VISIT.
COME BACK TO VISIT?
YEAH, I LIKE DRAGON TOWN A LOT.
AND MINA?
YEAH, I GUESS I LIKE HER TOO. I THINK I LIKE BEING A DRAGON HERE.
THAT'S WONDERFUL, SPIKE. IT FEELS GOOD TO STEP OUT OF THE SHADOWS, DOESN'T IT?
IT DOES.
THE END.

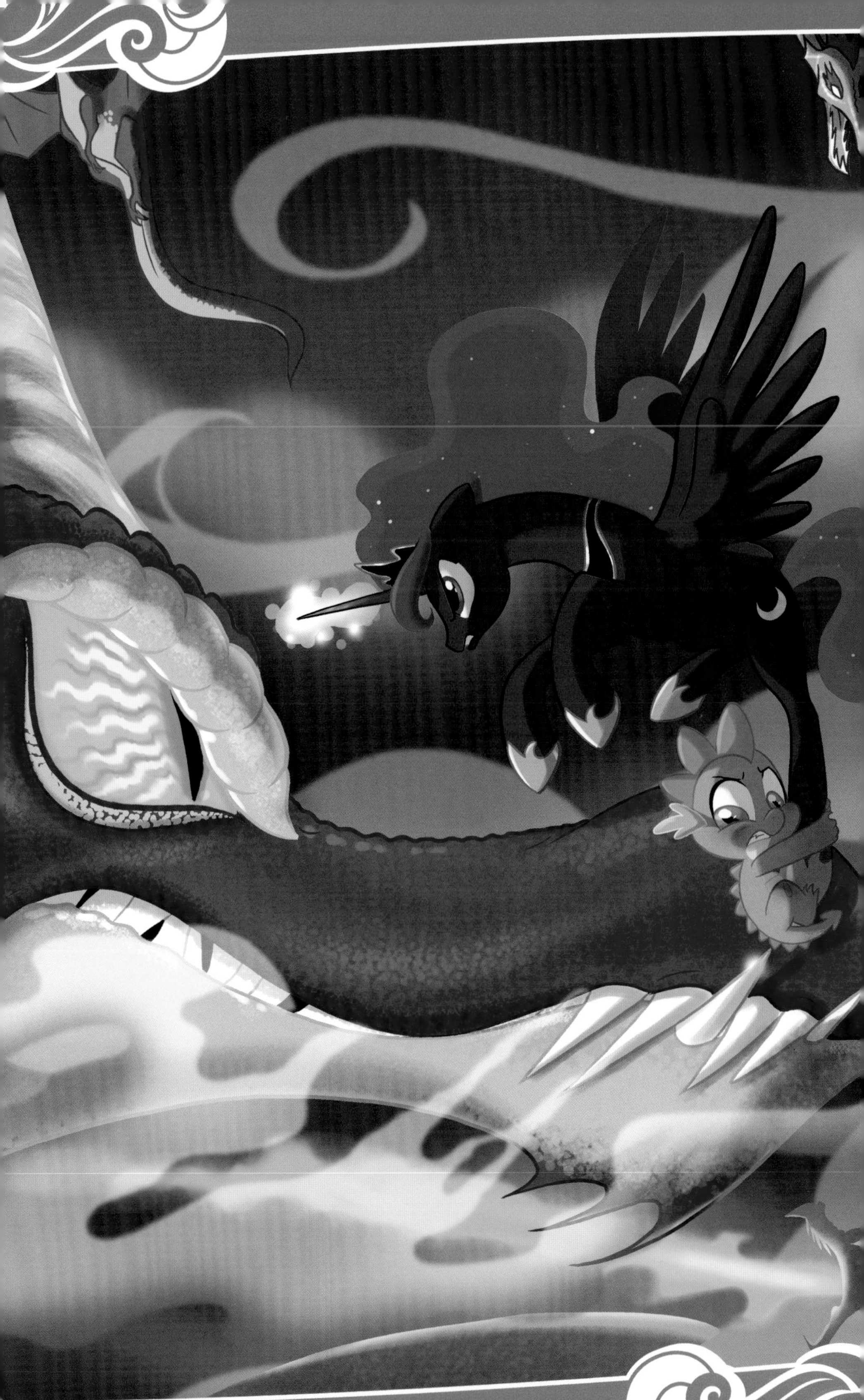

art by AMY MEBBERSON

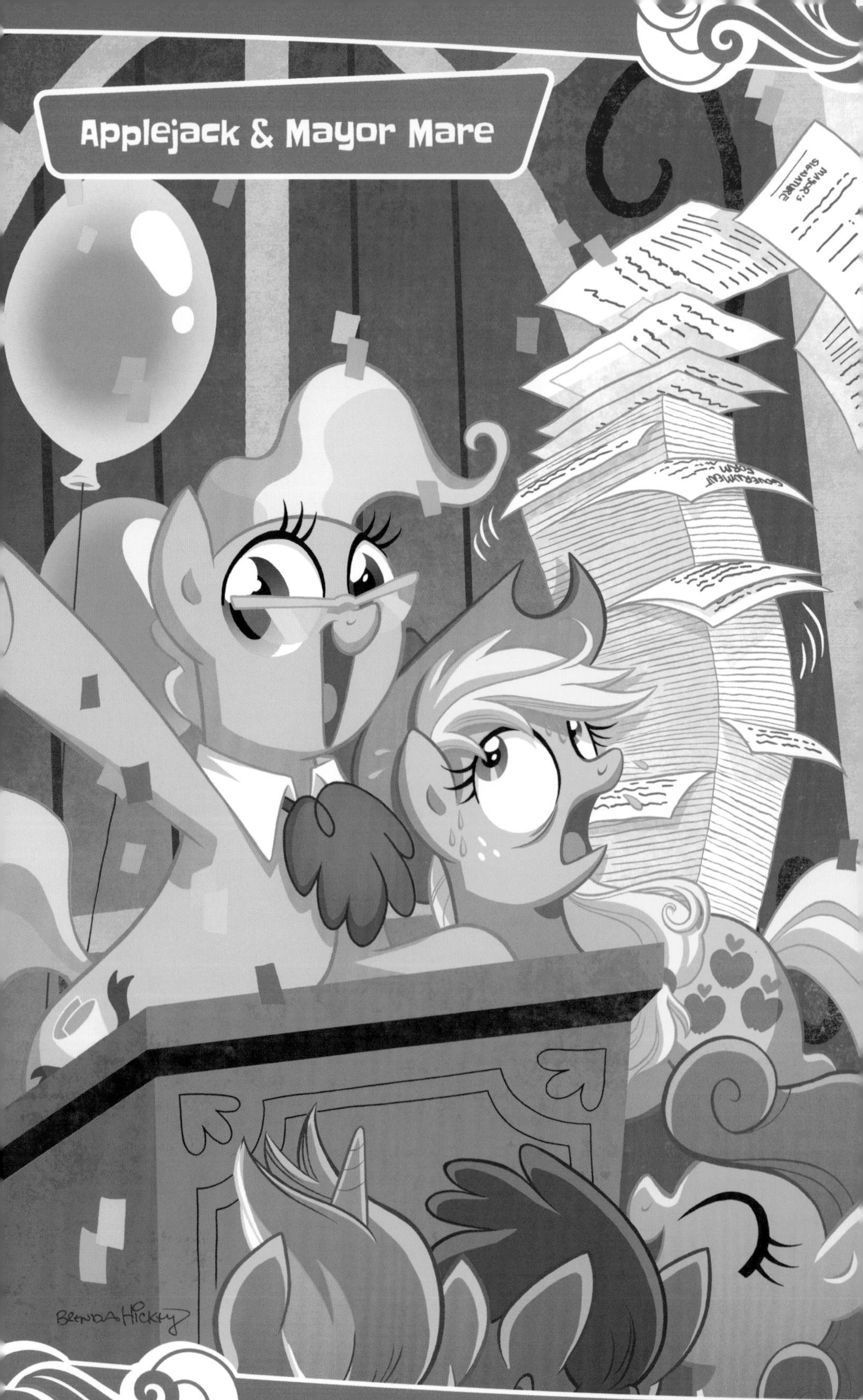
Applejack & Mayor Mare
MAYOR'S SIGNATURE
GOVERNMENT FORM
BRENDA HICKEY

art by BRENDA HICKEY

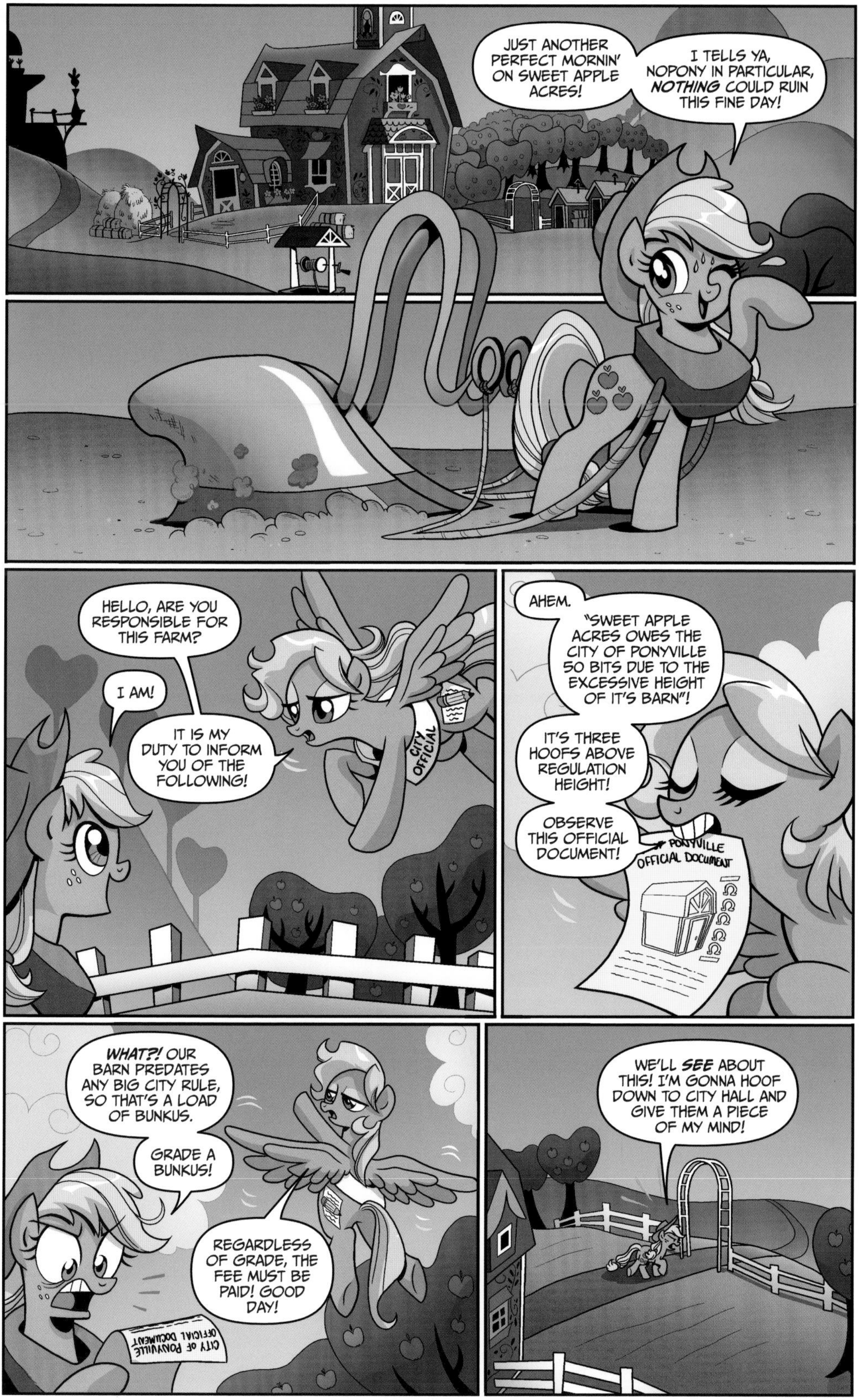
JUST ANOTHER PERFECT MORNIN' ON SWEET APPLE ACRES!
I TELLS YA, NOPONY IN PARTICULAR, *NOTHING* COULD RUIN THIS FINE DAY!
HELLO, ARE YOU RESPONSIBLE FOR THIS FARM?
I AM!
IT IS MY DUTY TO INFORM YOU OF THE FOLLOWING!
CITY OFFICIAL
AHEM.
"SWEET APPLE ACRES OWES THE CITY OF PONYVILLE 50 BITS DUE TO THE EXCESSIVE HEIGHT OF IT'S BARN"!
IT'S THREE HOOFS ABOVE REGULATION HEIGHT!
OBSERVE THIS OFFICIAL DOCUMENT!
PONYVILLE OFFICIAL DOCUMENT
WHAT?! OUR BARN PREDATES ANY BIG CITY RULE, SO THAT'S A LOAD OF BUNKUS.
GRADE A BUNKUS!
REGARDLESS OF GRADE, THE FEE MUST BE PAID! GOOD DAY!
CITY OF PONYVILLE OFFICIAL DOCUMENT
WE'LL *SEE* ABOUT THIS! I'M GONNA HOOF DOWN TO CITY HALL AND GIVE THEM A PIECE OF MY MIND!

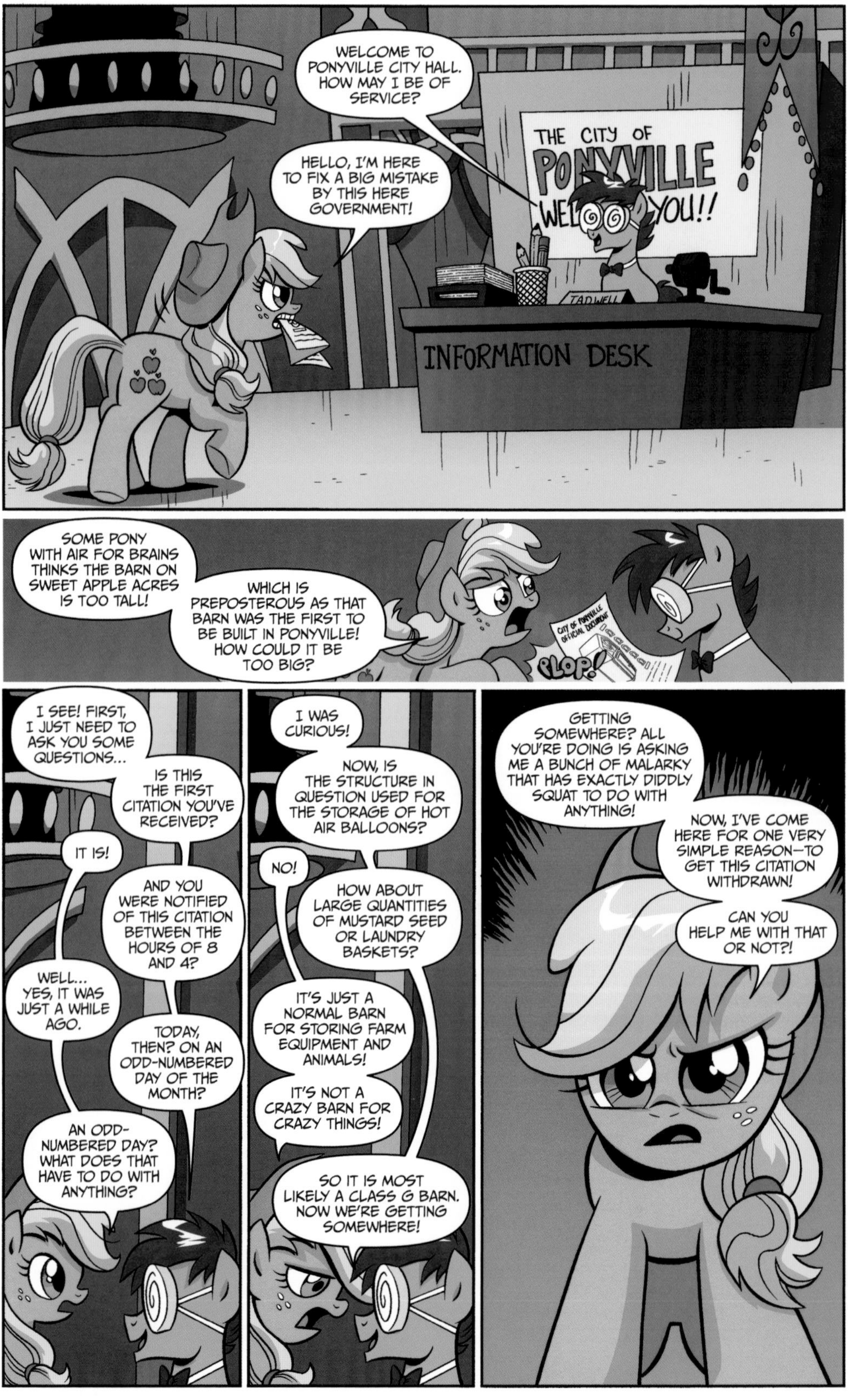
WELCOME TO PONYVILLE CITY HALL. HOW MAY I BE OF SERVICE?
HELLO, I'M HERE TO FIX A BIG MISTAKE BY THIS HERE GOVERNMENT!
THE CITY OF PONYVILLE WEL YOU!!
TADWELL
INFORMATION DESK
SOME PONY WITH AIR FOR BRAINS THINKS THE BARN ON SWEET APPLE ACRES IS TOO TALL!
WHICH IS PREPOSTEROUS AS THAT BARN WAS THE FIRST TO BE BUILT IN PONYVILLE! HOW COULD IT BE TOO BIG?
CITY OF PONYVILLE OFFICIAL DOCUMENT
PLOP!
I SEE! FIRST, I JUST NEED TO ASK YOU SOME QUESTIONS...
IS THIS THE FIRST CITATION YOU'VE RECEIVED?
IT IS!
AND YOU WERE NOTIFIED OF THIS CITATION BETWEEN THE HOURS OF 8 AND 4?
WELL... YES, IT WAS JUST A WHILE AGO.
TODAY, THEN? ON AN ODD-NUMBERED DAY OF THE MONTH?
AN ODD-NUMBERED DAY? WHAT DOES THAT HAVE TO DO WITH ANYTHING?
I WAS CURIOUS!
NOW, IS THE STRUCTURE IN QUESTION USED FOR THE STORAGE OF HOT AIR BALLOONS?
NO!
HOW ABOUT LARGE QUANTITIES OF MUSTARD SEED OR LAUNDRY BASKETS?
IT'S JUST A NORMAL BARN FOR STORING FARM EQUIPMENT AND ANIMALS!
IT'S NOT A CRAZY BARN FOR CRAZY THINGS!
SO IT IS MOST LIKELY A CLASS G BARN. NOW WE'RE GETTING SOMEWHERE!
GETTING SOMEWHERE? ALL YOU'RE DOING IS ASKING ME A BUNCH OF MALARKY THAT HAS EXACTLY DIDDLY SQUAT TO DO WITH ANYTHING!
NOW, I'VE COME HERE FOR ONE VERY SIMPLE REASON—TO GET THIS CITATION WITHDRAWN!
CAN YOU HELP ME WITH THAT OR NOT?!

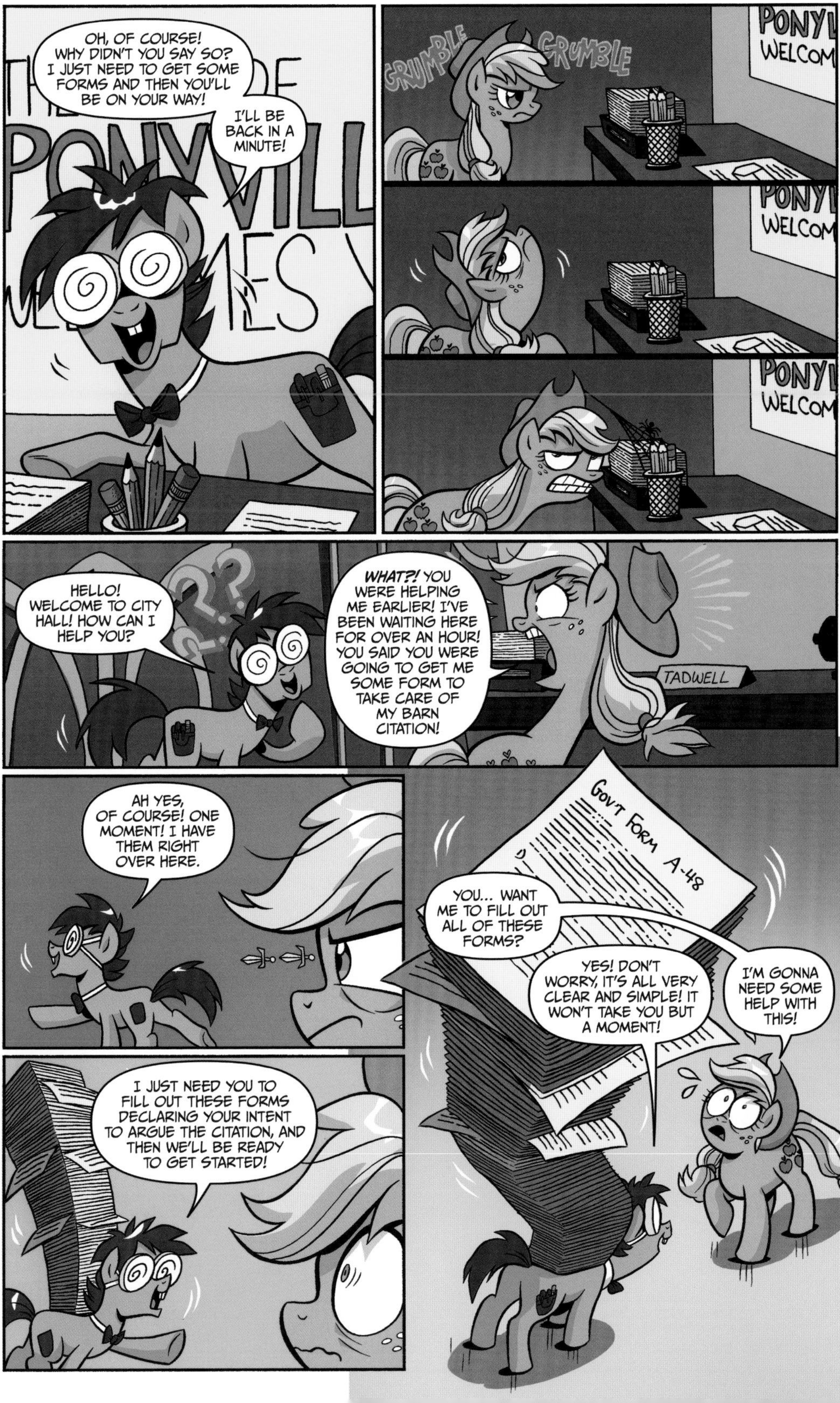
OH, OF COURSE! WHY DIDN'T YOU SAY SO? I JUST NEED TO GET SOME FORMS AND THEN YOU'LL BE ON YOUR WAY!
I'LL BE BACK IN A MINUTE!
GRUMBLE
GRUMBLE
PONYV
WELCOM
HELLO! WELCOME TO CITY HALL! HOW CAN I HELP YOU?
WHAT?! YOU WERE HELPING ME EARLIER! I'VE BEEN WAITING HERE FOR OVER AN HOUR! YOU SAID YOU WERE GOING TO GET ME SOME FORM TO TAKE CARE OF MY BARN CITATION!
TADWELL
AH YES, OF COURSE! ONE MOMENT! I HAVE THEM RIGHT OVER HERE.
I JUST NEED YOU TO FILL OUT THESE FORMS DECLARING YOUR INTENT TO ARGUE THE CITATION, AND THEN WE'LL BE READY TO GET STARTED!
GOV'T FORM A-48
YOU... WANT ME TO FILL OUT ALL OF THESE FORMS?
YES! DON'T WORRY, IT'S ALL VERY CLEAR AND SIMPLE! IT WON'T TAKE YOU BUT A MOMENT!
I'M GONNA NEED SOME HELP WITH THIS!

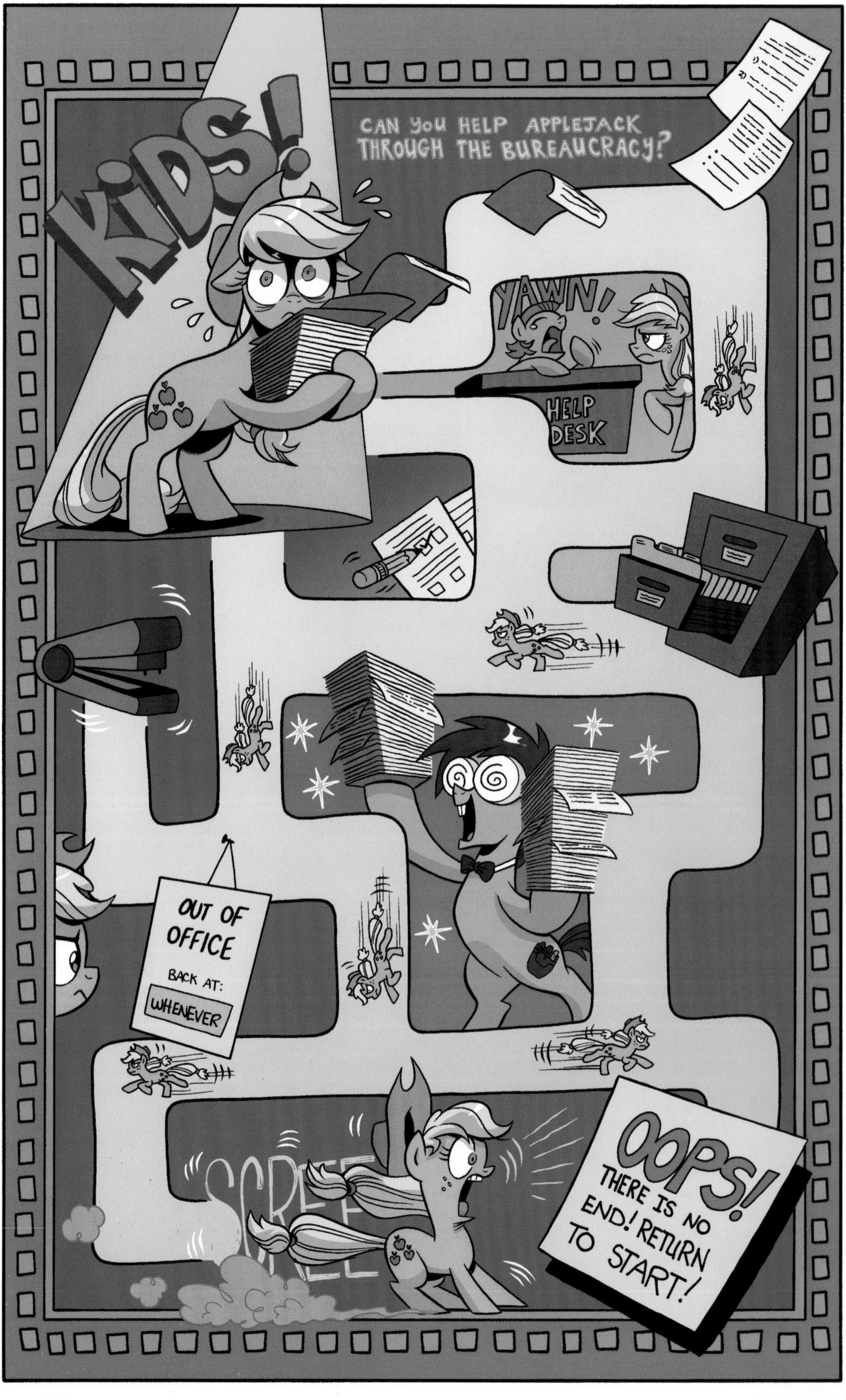
KIDS!
CAN YOU HELP APPLEJACK THROUGH THE BUREAUCRACY?
YAWN!
HELP DESK
OUT OF OFFICE
BACK AT:
WHENEVER
SCREEE
OOPS! THERE IS NO END! RETURN TO START!

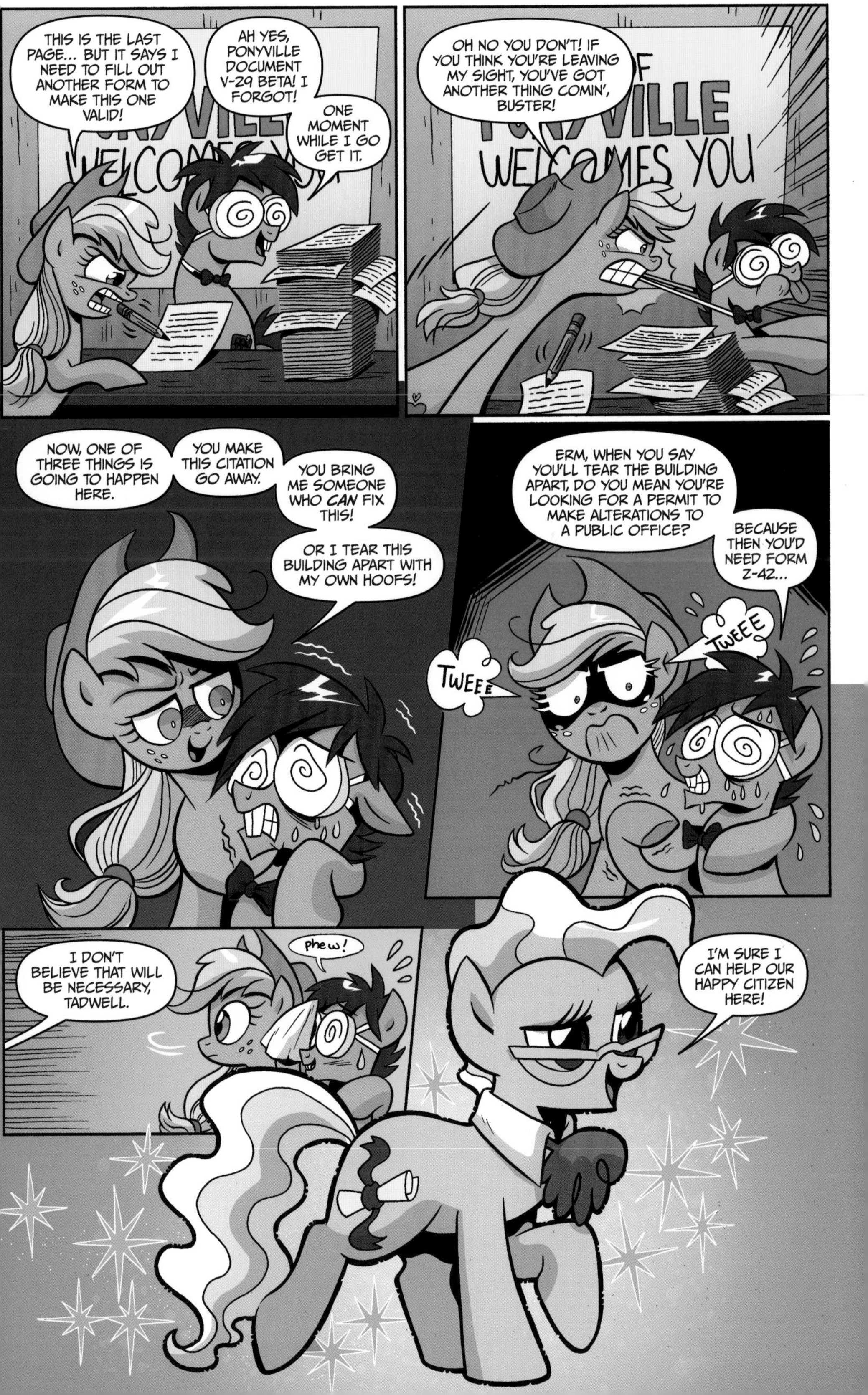
THIS IS THE LAST PAGE... BUT IT SAYS I NEED TO FILL OUT ANOTHER FORM TO MAKE THIS ONE VALID!
AH YES, PONYVILLE DOCUMENT V-29 BETA! I FORGOT!
ONE MOMENT WHILE I GO GET IT.
OH NO YOU DON'T! IF YOU THINK YOU'RE LEAVING MY SIGHT, YOU'VE GOT ANOTHER THING COMIN', BUSTER!
PONYVILLE WELCOMES YOU
NOW, ONE OF THREE THINGS IS GOING TO HAPPEN HERE.
YOU MAKE THIS CITATION GO AWAY.
YOU BRING ME SOMEONE WHO *CAN* FIX THIS!
OR I TEAR THIS BUILDING APART WITH MY OWN HOOFS!
ERM, WHEN YOU SAY YOU'LL TEAR THE BUILDING APART, DO YOU MEAN YOU'RE LOOKING FOR A PERMIT TO MAKE ALTERATIONS TO A PUBLIC OFFICE?
BECAUSE THEN YOU'D NEED FORM Z-42...
TWEEE
TWEEE
I DON'T BELIEVE THAT WILL BE NECESSARY, TADWELL.
phew!
I'M SURE I CAN HELP OUR HAPPY CITIZEN HERE!

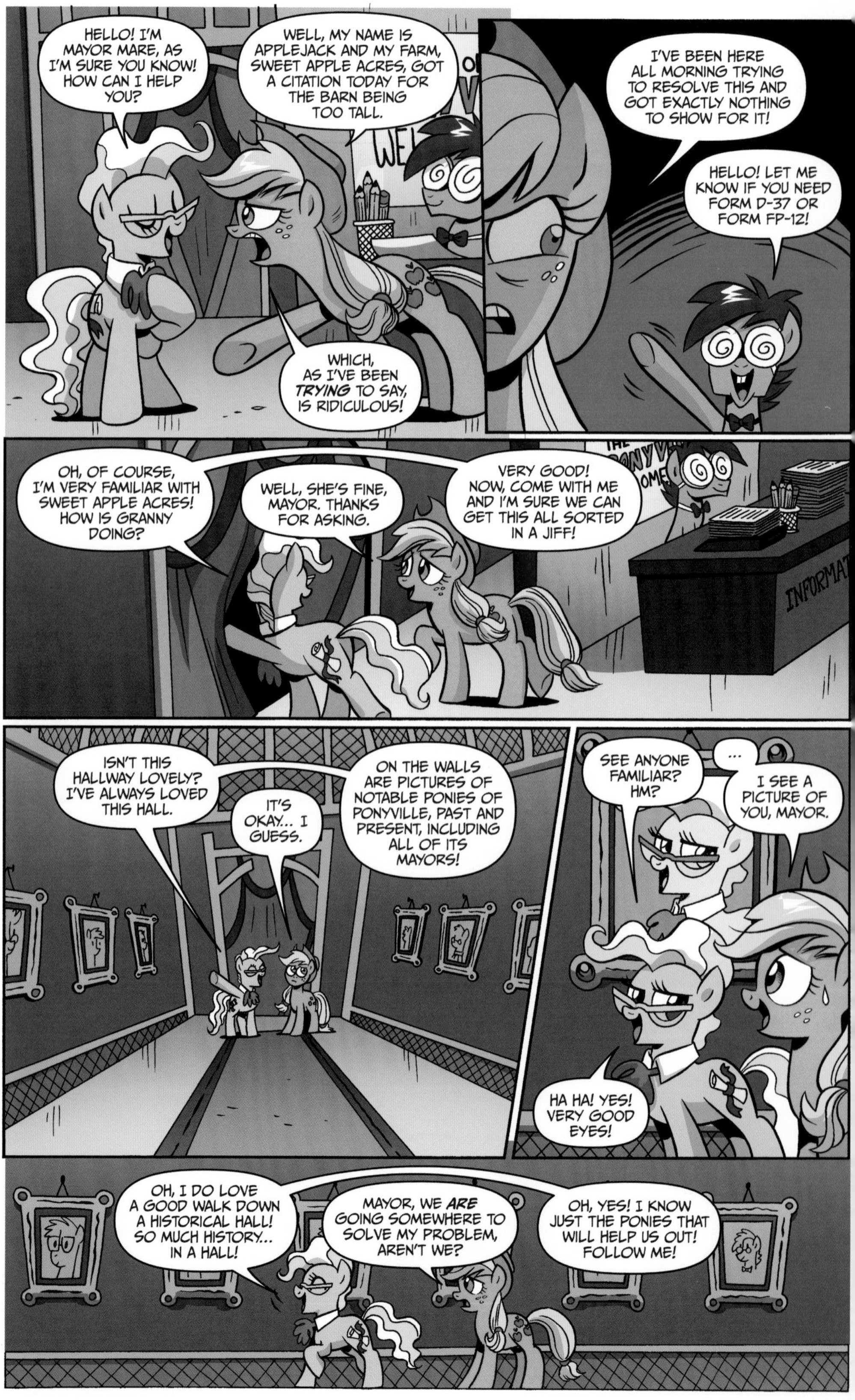
HELLO! I'M MAYOR MARE, AS I'M SURE YOU KNOW! HOW CAN I HELP YOU?
WELL, MY NAME IS APPLEJACK AND MY FARM, SWEET APPLE ACRES, GOT A CITATION TODAY FOR THE BARN BEING TOO TALL.
WHICH, AS I'VE BEEN TRYING TO SAY, IS RIDICULOUS!
I'VE BEEN HERE ALL MORNING TRYING TO RESOLVE THIS AND GOT EXACTLY NOTHING TO SHOW FOR IT!
HELLO! LET ME KNOW IF YOU NEED FORM D-37 OR FORM FP-12!
OH, OF COURSE, I'M VERY FAMILIAR WITH SWEET APPLE ACRES! HOW IS GRANNY DOING?
WELL, SHE'S FINE, MAYOR. THANKS FOR ASKING.
VERY GOOD! NOW, COME WITH ME AND I'M SURE WE CAN GET THIS ALL SORTED IN A JIFF!
INFORMAT
ISN'T THIS HALLWAY LOVELY? I'VE ALWAYS LOVED THIS HALL.
IT'S OKAY... I GUESS.
ON THE WALLS ARE PICTURES OF NOTABLE PONIES OF PONYVILLE, PAST AND PRESENT, INCLUDING ALL OF ITS MAYORS!
SEE ANYONE FAMILIAR? HM?
...
I SEE A PICTURE OF YOU, MAYOR.
HA HA! YES! VERY GOOD EYES!
OH, I DO LOVE A GOOD WALK DOWN A HISTORICAL HALL! SO MUCH HISTORY... IN A HALL!
MAYOR, WE ARE GOING SOMEWHERE TO SOLVE MY PROBLEM, AREN'T WE?
OH, YES! I KNOW JUST THE PONIES THAT WILL HELP US OUT! FOLLOW ME!

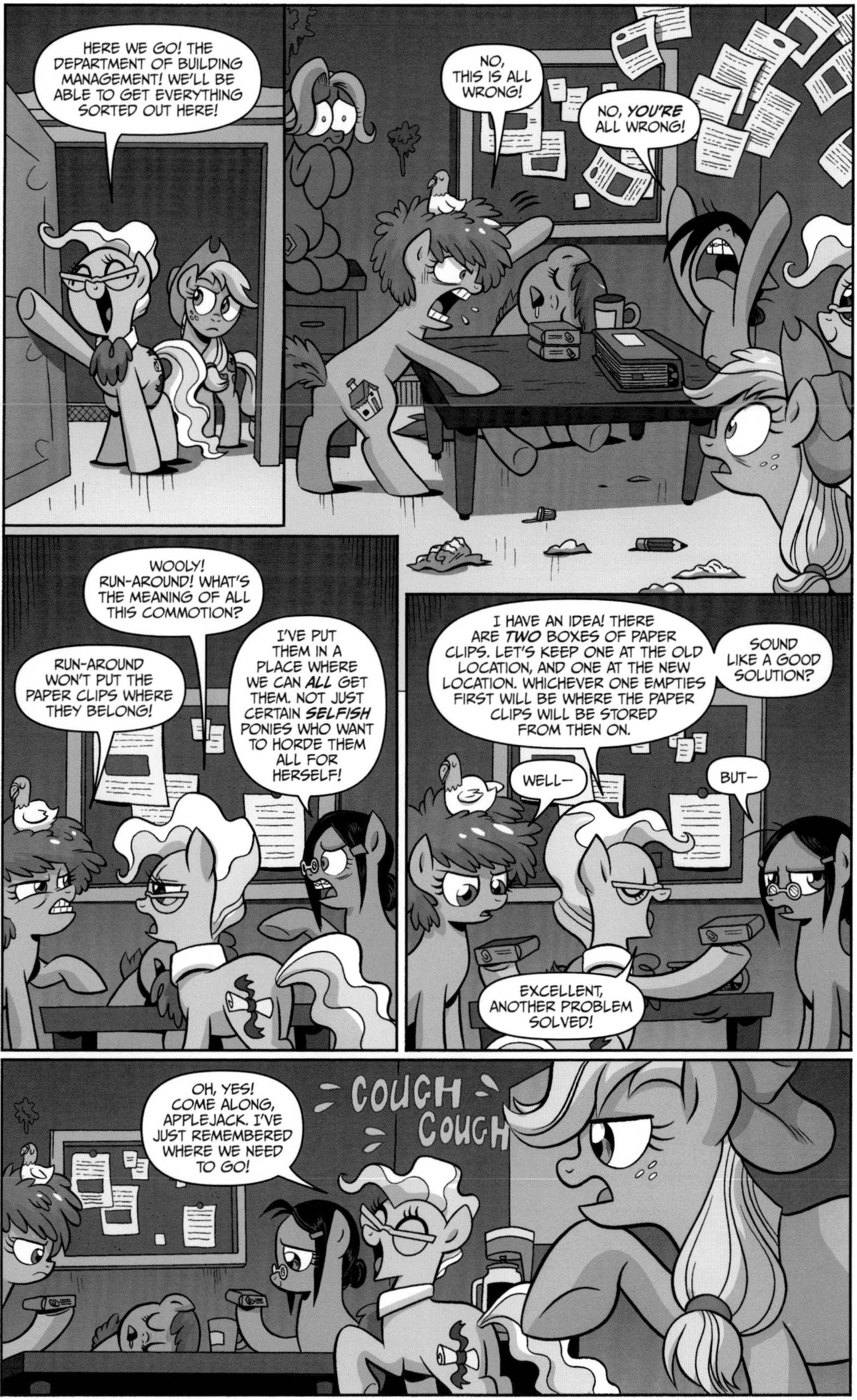
HERE WE GO! THE DEPARTMENT OF BUILDING MANAGEMENT! WE'LL BE ABLE TO GET EVERYTHING SORTED OUT HERE!
NO, THIS IS ALL WRONG!
NO, YOU'RE ALL WRONG!
WOOLY! RUN-AROUND! WHAT'S THE MEANING OF ALL THIS COMMOTION?
RUN-AROUND WON'T PUT THE PAPER CLIPS WHERE THEY BELONG!
I'VE PUT THEM IN A PLACE WHERE WE CAN ALL GET THEM. NOT JUST CERTAIN SELFISH PONIES WHO WANT TO HORDE THEM ALL FOR HERSELF!
I HAVE AN IDEA! THERE ARE TWO BOXES OF PAPER CLIPS. LET'S KEEP ONE AT THE OLD LOCATION, AND ONE AT THE NEW LOCATION. WHICHEVER ONE EMPTIES FIRST WILL BE WHERE THE PAPER CLIPS WILL BE STORED FROM THEN ON.
SOUND LIKE A GOOD SOLUTION?
WELL-
BUT-
EXCELLENT, ANOTHER PROBLEM SOLVED!
COUGH
COUGH
OH, YES! COME ALONG, APPLEJACK. I'VE JUST REMEMBERED WHERE WE NEED TO GO!

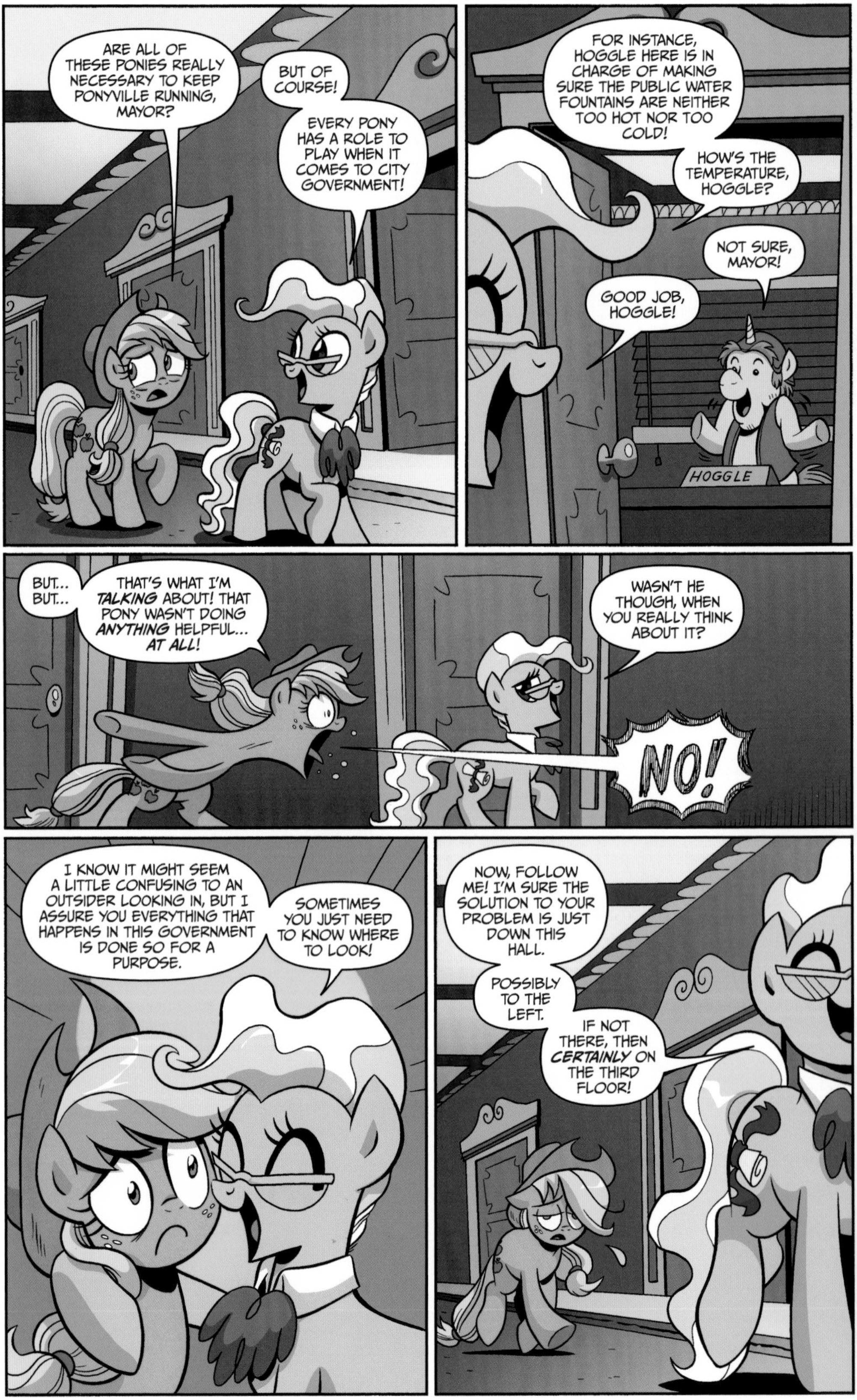
ARE ALL OF THESE PONIES REALLY NECESSARY TO KEEP PONYVILLE RUNNING, MAYOR?
BUT OF COURSE!
EVERY PONY HAS A ROLE TO PLAY WHEN IT COMES TO CITY GOVERNMENT!
FOR INSTANCE, HOGGLE HERE IS IN CHARGE OF MAKING SURE THE PUBLIC WATER FOUNTAINS ARE NEITHER TOO HOT NOR TOO COLD!
HOW'S THE TEMPERATURE, HOGGLE?
NOT SURE, MAYOR!
GOOD JOB, HOGGLE!
HOGGLE
BUT... BUT...
THAT'S WHAT I'M *TALKING* ABOUT! THAT PONY WASN'T DOING *ANYTHING* HELPFUL... *AT ALL!*
WASN'T HE THOUGH, WHEN YOU REALLY THINK ABOUT IT?
NO!
I KNOW IT MIGHT SEEM A LITTLE CONFUSING TO AN OUTSIDER LOOKING IN, BUT I ASSURE YOU EVERYTHING THAT HAPPENS IN THIS GOVERNMENT IS DONE SO FOR A PURPOSE.
SOMETIMES YOU JUST NEED TO KNOW WHERE TO LOOK!
NOW, FOLLOW ME! I'M SURE THE SOLUTION TO YOUR PROBLEM IS JUST DOWN THIS HALL.
POSSIBLY TO THE LEFT.
IF NOT THERE, THEN *CERTAINLY* ON THE THIRD FLOOR!

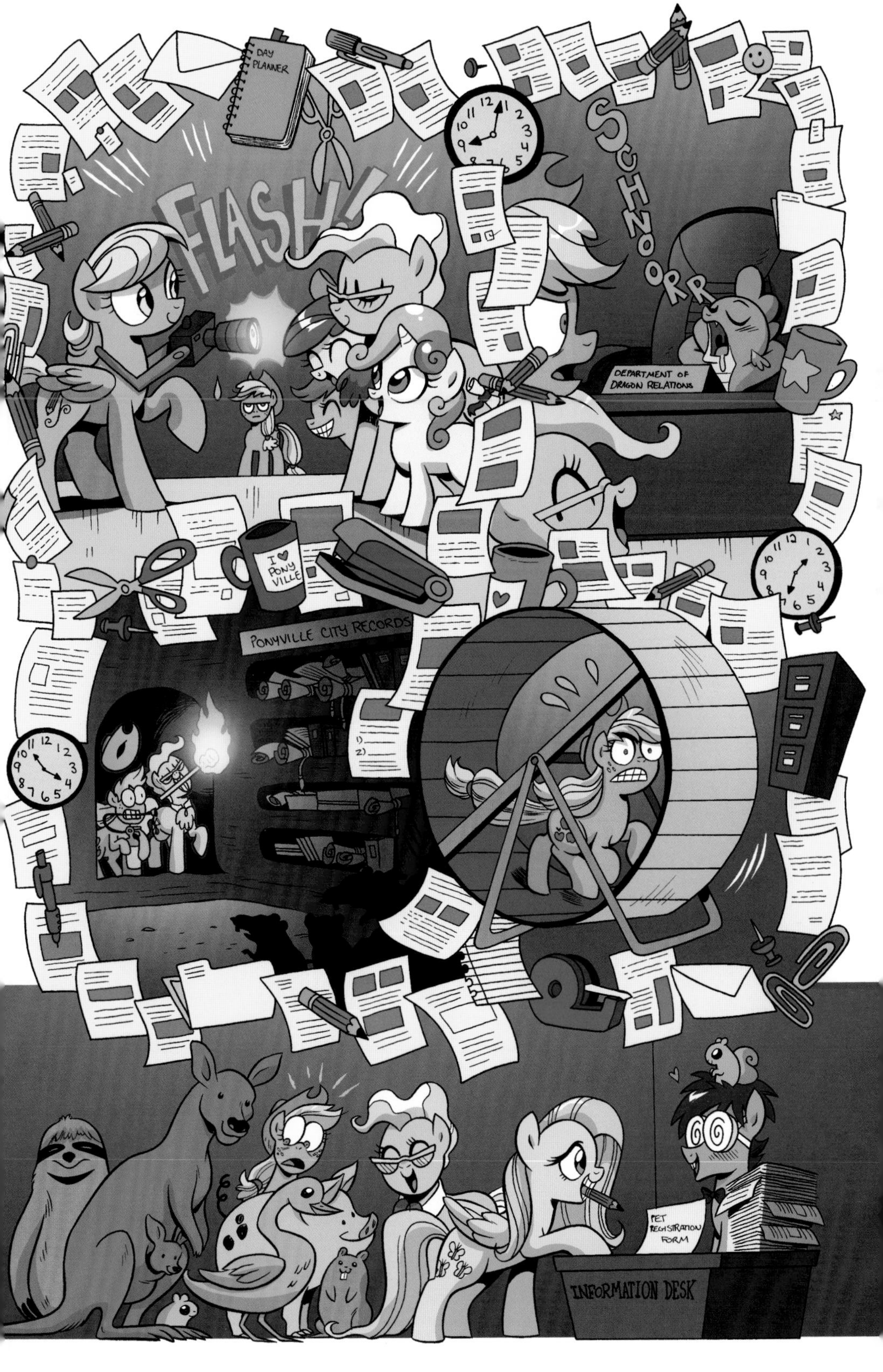
DAY PLANNER
FLASH!
SCHNOORR
DEPARTMENT OF DRAGON RELATIONS
I ♥ PONYVILLE
PONYVILLE CITY RECORDS
PET REGISTRATION FORM
INFORMATION DESK

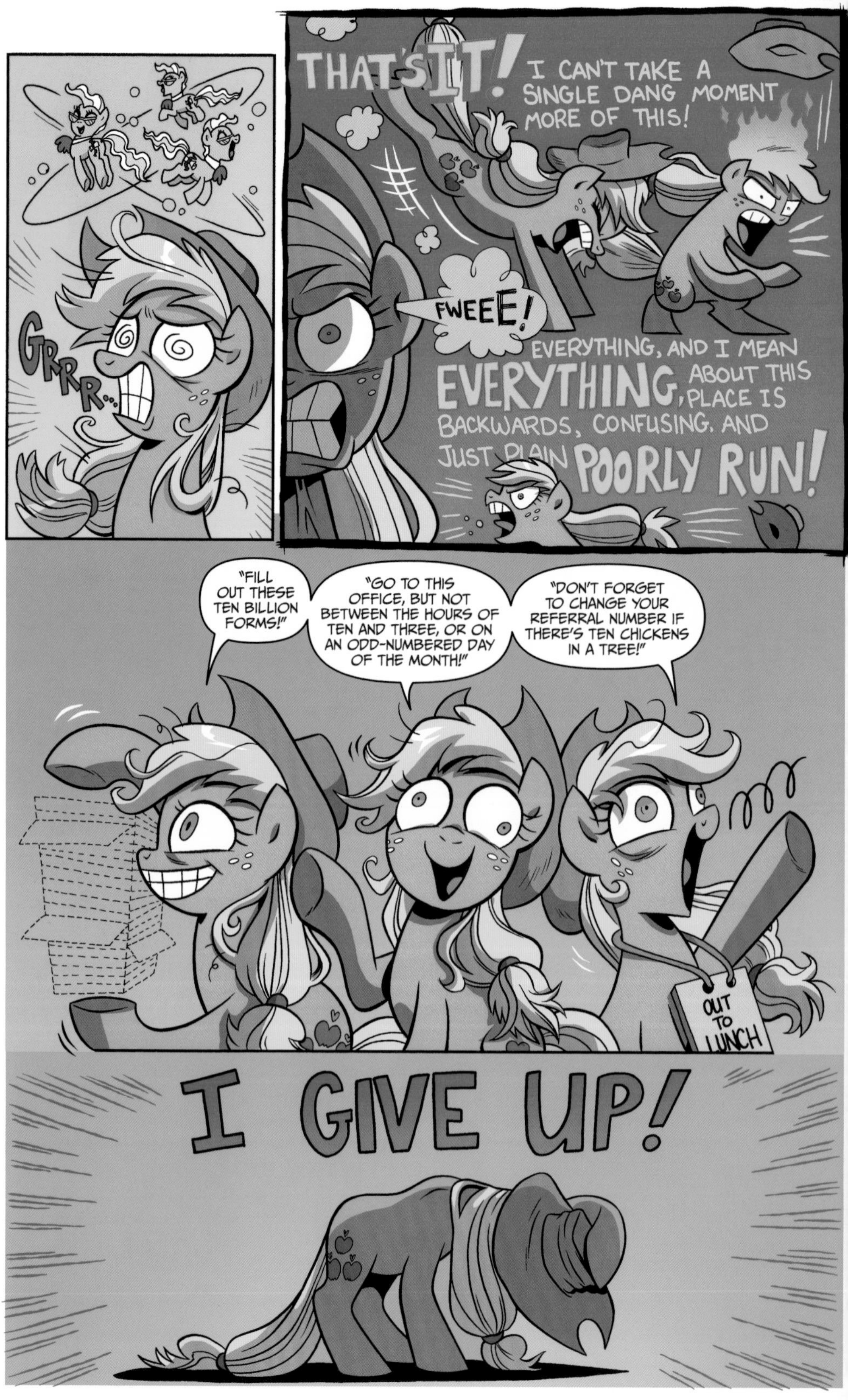
GRRRR...
THAT'S IT! I CAN'T TAKE A SINGLE DANG MOMENT MORE OF THIS!
FWEEE!
EVERYTHING, AND I MEAN EVERYTHING, ABOUT THIS PLACE IS BACKWARDS, CONFUSING, AND JUST PLAIN POORLY RUN!
"FILL OUT THESE TEN BILLION FORMS!"
"GO TO THIS OFFICE, BUT NOT BETWEEN THE HOURS OF TEN AND THREE, OR ON AN ODD-NUMBERED DAY OF THE MONTH!"
"DON'T FORGET TO CHANGE YOUR REFERRAL NUMBER IF THERE'S TEN CHICKENS IN A TREE!"
OUT TO LUNCH
I GIVE UP!

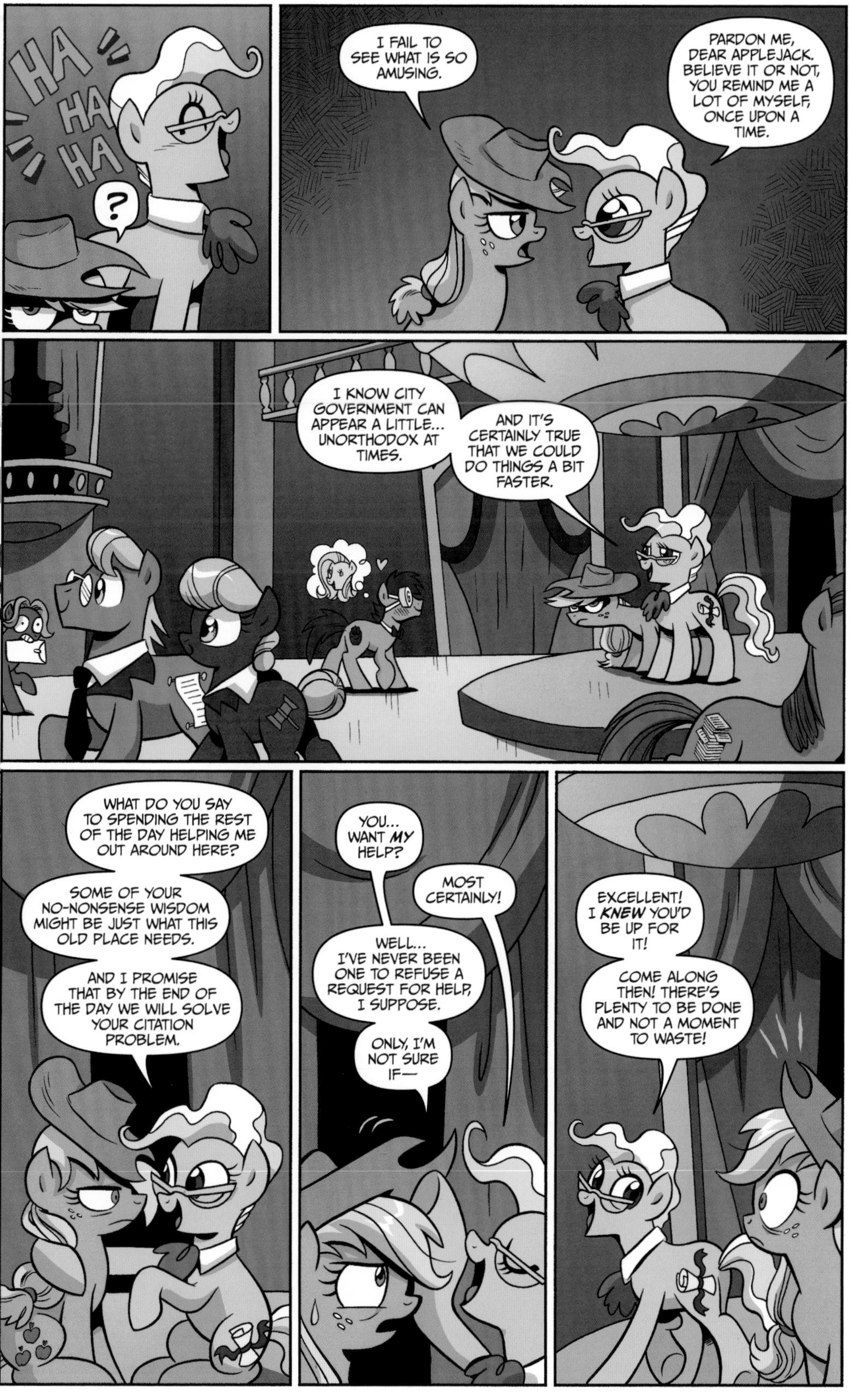
HA HA HA HA
?
I FAIL TO SEE WHAT IS SO AMUSING.
PARDON ME, DEAR APPLEJACK. BELIEVE IT OR NOT, YOU REMIND ME A LOT OF MYSELF, ONCE UPON A TIME.
I KNOW CITY GOVERNMENT CAN APPEAR A LITTLE... UNORTHODOX AT TIMES.
AND IT'S CERTAINLY TRUE THAT WE COULD DO THINGS A BIT FASTER.
WHAT DO YOU SAY TO SPENDING THE REST OF THE DAY HELPING ME OUT AROUND HERE?
SOME OF YOUR NO-NONSENSE WISDOM MIGHT BE JUST WHAT THIS OLD PLACE NEEDS.
AND I PROMISE THAT BY THE END OF THE DAY WE WILL SOLVE YOUR CITATION PROBLEM.
YOU... WANT *MY* HELP?
MOST CERTAINLY!
WELL... I'VE NEVER BEEN ONE TO REFUSE A REQUEST FOR HELP, I SUPPOSE.
ONLY, I'M NOT SURE IF—
EXCELLENT! I *KNEW* YOU'D BE UP FOR IT!
COME ALONG THEN! THERE'S PLENTY TO BE DONE AND NOT A MOMENT TO WASTE!

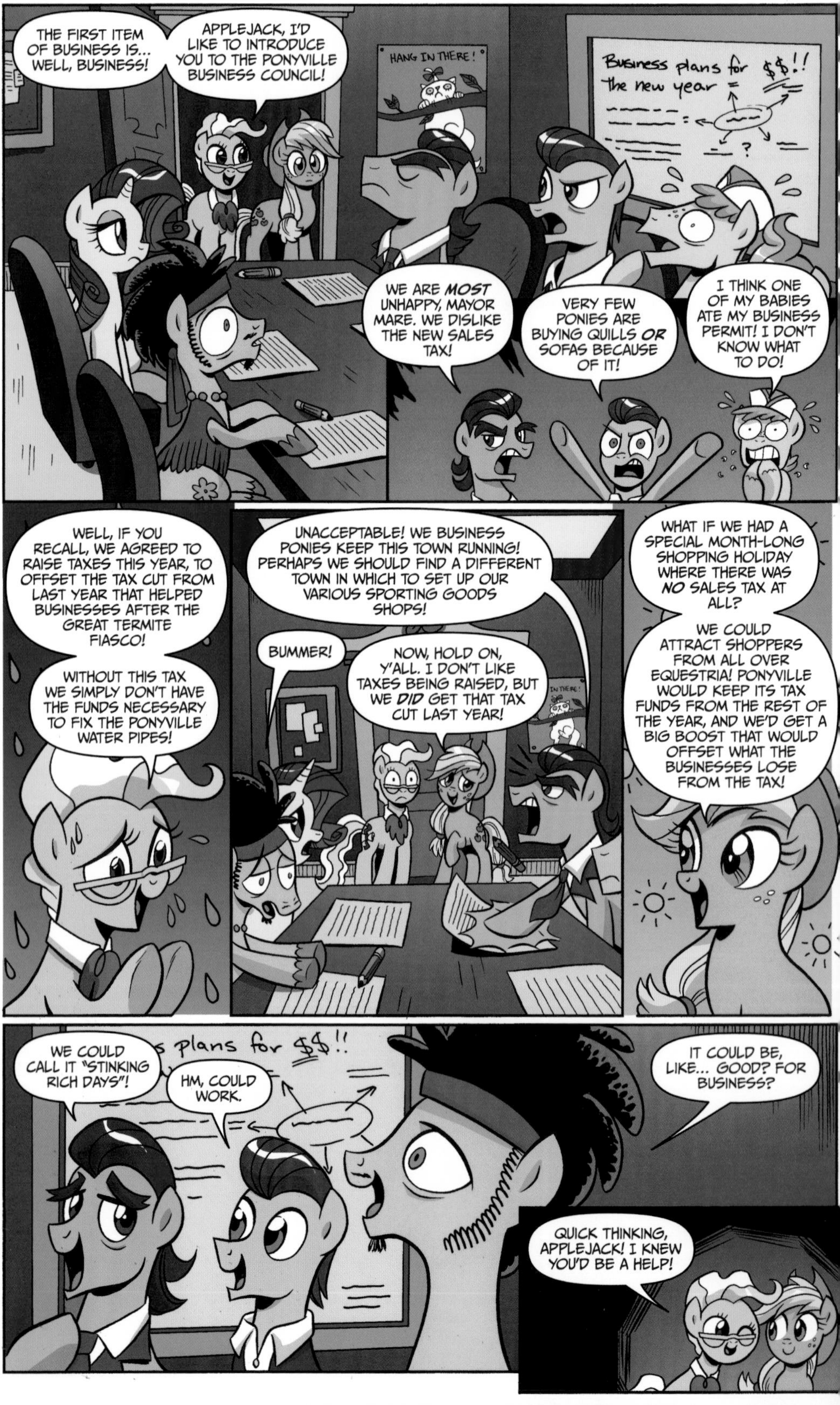
THE FIRST ITEM OF BUSINESS IS... WELL, BUSINESS!
APPLEJACK, I'D LIKE TO INTRODUCE YOU TO THE PONYVILLE BUSINESS COUNCIL!
HANG IN THERE!
Business plans for $$!! the new year =
WE ARE MOST UNHAPPY, MAYOR MARE. WE DISLIKE THE NEW SALES TAX!
VERY FEW PONIES ARE BUYING QUILLS OR SOFAS BECAUSE OF IT!
I THINK ONE OF MY BABIES ATE MY BUSINESS PERMIT! I DON'T KNOW WHAT TO DO!
WELL, IF YOU RECALL, WE AGREED TO RAISE TAXES THIS YEAR, TO OFFSET THE TAX CUT FROM LAST YEAR THAT HELPED BUSINESSES AFTER THE GREAT TERMITE FIASCO!
WITHOUT THIS TAX WE SIMPLY DON'T HAVE THE FUNDS NECESSARY TO FIX THE PONYVILLE WATER PIPES!
UNACCEPTABLE! WE BUSINESS PONIES KEEP THIS TOWN RUNNING! PERHAPS WE SHOULD FIND A DIFFERENT TOWN IN WHICH TO SET UP OUR VARIOUS SPORTING GOODS SHOPS!
BUMMER!
NOW, HOLD ON, Y'ALL. I DON'T LIKE TAXES BEING RAISED, BUT WE DID GET THAT TAX CUT LAST YEAR!
WHAT IF WE HAD A SPECIAL MONTH-LONG SHOPPING HOLIDAY WHERE THERE WAS NO SALES TAX AT ALL?
WE COULD ATTRACT SHOPPERS FROM ALL OVER EQUESTRIA! PONYVILLE WOULD KEEP ITS TAX FUNDS FROM THE REST OF THE YEAR, AND WE'D GET A BIG BOOST THAT WOULD OFFSET WHAT THE BUSINESSES LOSE FROM THE TAX!
WE COULD CALL IT "STINKING RICH DAYS"!
HM, COULD WORK.
IT COULD BE, LIKE... GOOD? FOR BUSINESS?
QUICK THINKING, APPLEJACK! I KNEW YOU'D BE A HELP!

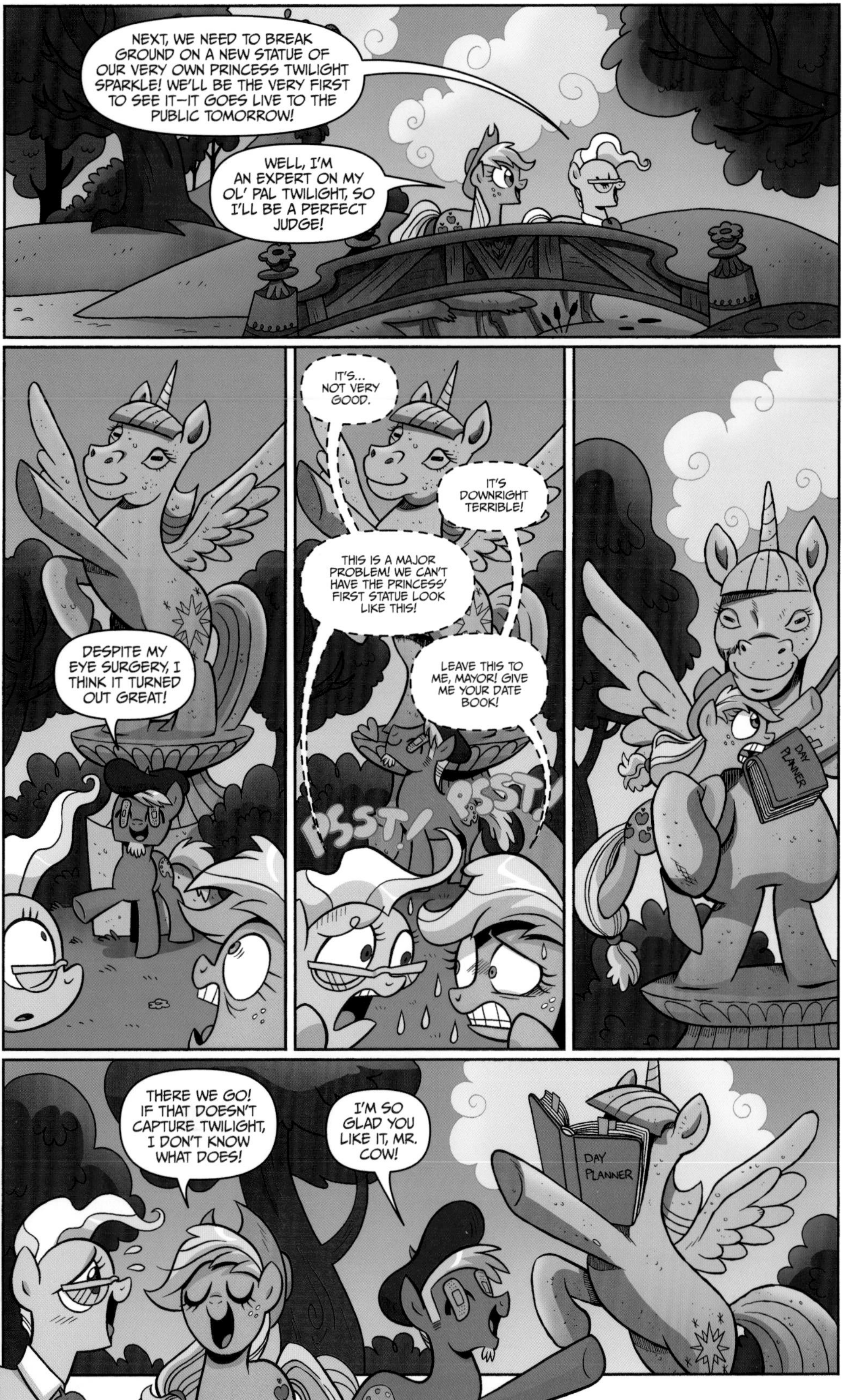
NEXT, WE NEED TO BREAK GROUND ON A NEW STATUE OF OUR VERY OWN PRINCESS TWILIGHT SPARKLE! WE'LL BE THE VERY FIRST TO SEE IT—IT GOES LIVE TO THE PUBLIC TOMORROW!
WELL, I'M AN EXPERT ON MY OL' PAL TWILIGHT, SO I'LL BE A PERFECT JUDGE!
DESPITE MY EYE SURGERY, I THINK IT TURNED OUT GREAT!
IT'S... NOT VERY GOOD.
IT'S DOWNRIGHT TERRIBLE!
THIS IS A MAJOR PROBLEM! WE CAN'T HAVE THE PRINCESS' FIRST STATUE LOOK LIKE THIS!
LEAVE THIS TO ME, MAYOR! GIVE ME YOUR DATE BOOK!
PSST!
PSST!
DAY PLANNER
THERE WE GO! IF THAT DOESN'T CAPTURE TWILIGHT, I DON'T KNOW WHAT DOES!
I'M SO GLAD YOU LIKE IT, MR. COW!
DAY PLANNER

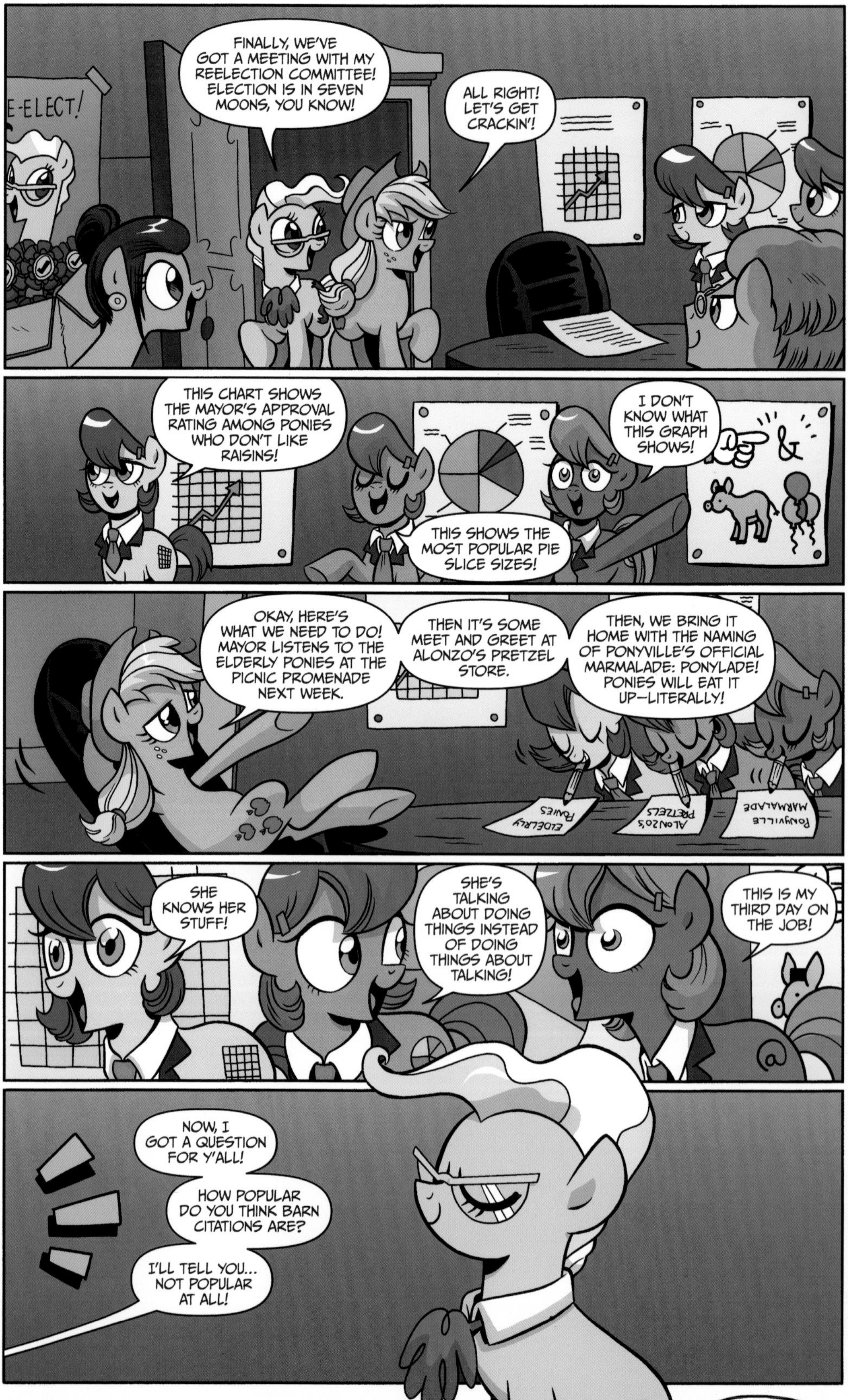
E-ELECT!
FINALLY, WE'VE GOT A MEETING WITH MY REELECTION COMMITTEE! ELECTION IS IN SEVEN MOONS, YOU KNOW!
ALL RIGHT! LET'S GET CRACKIN'!
THIS CHART SHOWS THE MAYOR'S APPROVAL RATING AMONG PONIES WHO DON'T LIKE RAISINS!
THIS SHOWS THE MOST POPULAR PIE SLICE SIZES!
I DON'T KNOW WHAT THIS GRAPH SHOWS!
&
OKAY, HERE'S WHAT WE NEED TO DO! MAYOR LISTENS TO THE ELDERLY PONIES AT THE PICNIC PROMENADE NEXT WEEK.
THEN IT'S SOME MEET AND GREET AT ALONZO'S PRETZEL STORE.
THEN, WE BRING IT HOME WITH THE NAMING OF PONYVILLE'S OFFICIAL MARMALADE: PONYLADE! PONIES WILL EAT IT UP—LITERALLY!
ELDERLY PONIES
ALONZO'S PRETZELS
PONYVILLE MARMALADE
SHE KNOWS HER STUFF!
SHE'S TALKING ABOUT DOING THINGS INSTEAD OF DOING THINGS ABOUT TALKING!
THIS IS MY THIRD DAY ON THE JOB!
NOW, I GOT A QUESTION FOR Y'ALL!
HOW POPULAR DO YOU THINK BARN CITATIONS ARE?
I'LL TELL YOU... NOT POPULAR AT ALL!

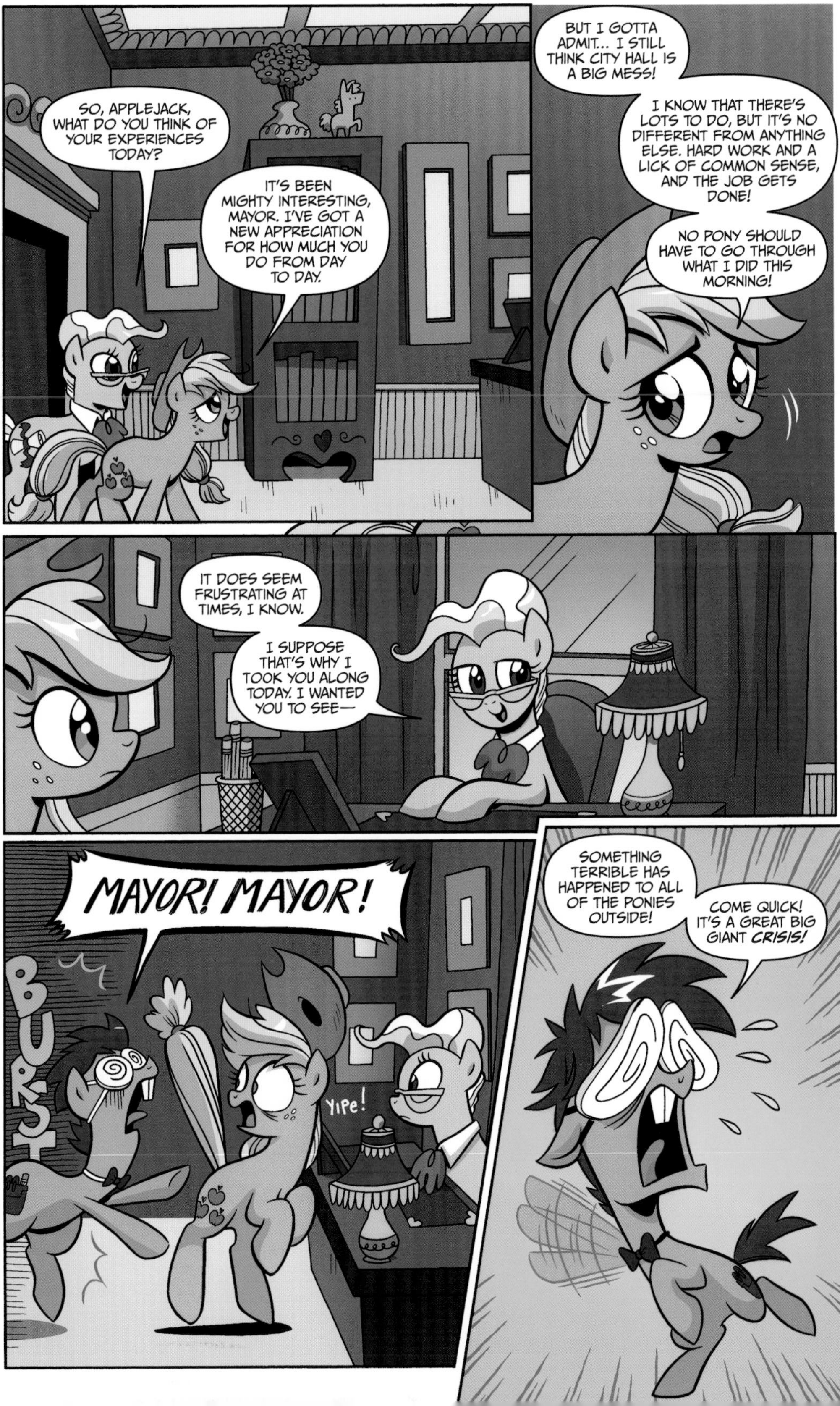

SO, APPLEJACK, WHAT DO YOU THINK OF YOUR EXPERIENCES TODAY?
IT'S BEEN MIGHTY INTERESTING, MAYOR. I'VE GOT A NEW APPRECIATION FOR HOW MUCH YOU DO FROM DAY TO DAY.
BUT I GOTTA ADMIT... I STILL THINK CITY HALL IS A BIG MESS!
I KNOW THAT THERE'S LOTS TO DO, BUT IT'S NO DIFFERENT FROM ANYTHING ELSE. HARD WORK AND A LICK OF COMMON SENSE, AND THE JOB GETS DONE!
NO PONY SHOULD HAVE TO GO THROUGH WHAT I DID THIS MORNING!
IT DOES SEEM FRUSTRATING AT TIMES, I KNOW.
I SUPPOSE THAT'S WHY I TOOK YOU ALONG TODAY. I WANTED YOU TO SEE—
MAYOR! MAYOR!
BURST
YIPE!
SOMETHING TERRIBLE HAS HAPPENED TO ALL OF THE PONIES OUTSIDE!
COME QUICK! IT'S A GREAT BIG GIANT *CRISIS!*

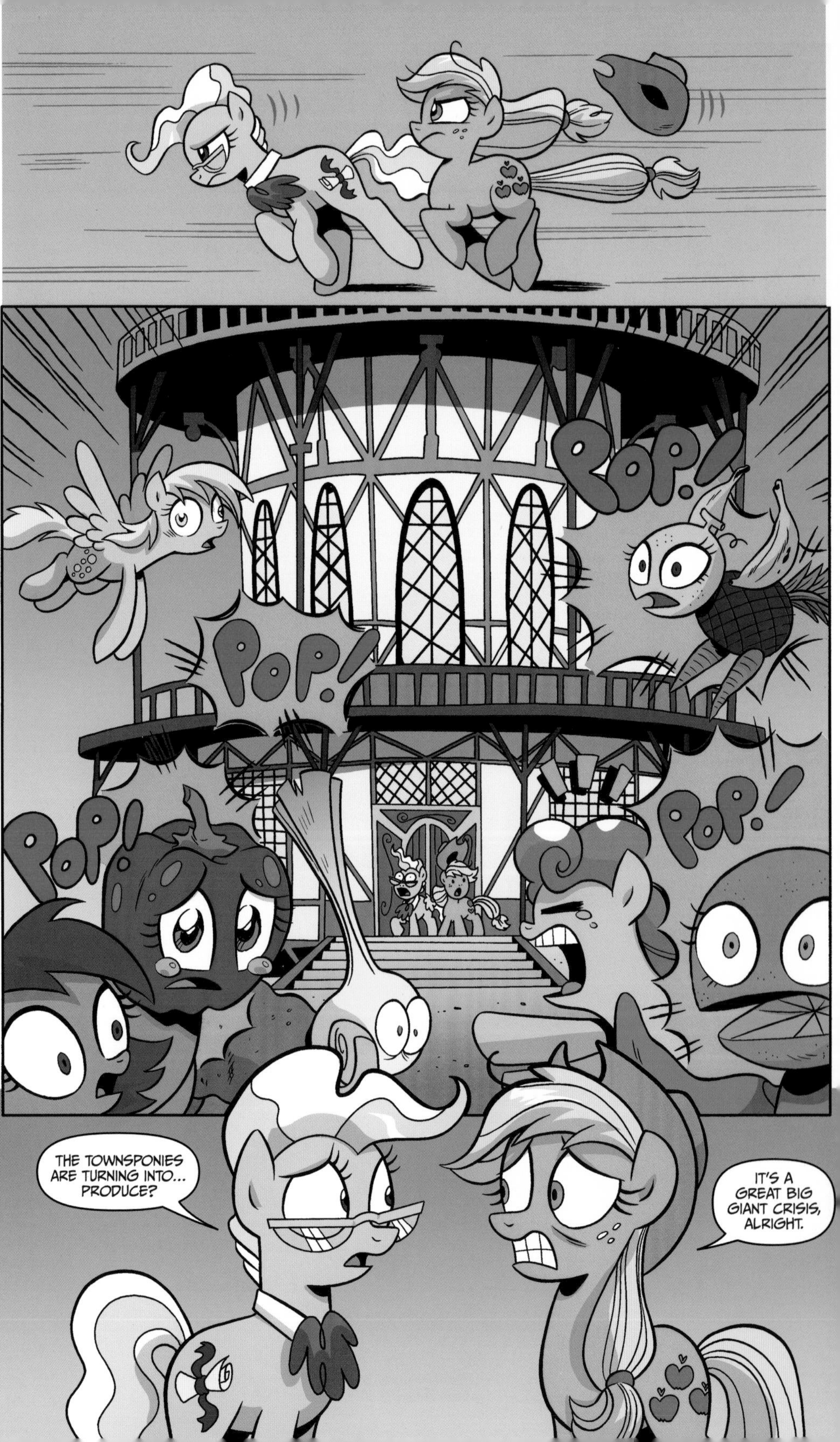
POP!
POP!
POP!
POP!
THE TOWNSPONIES ARE TURNING INTO... PRODUCE?
IT'S A GREAT BIG GIANT CRISIS, ALRIGHT.

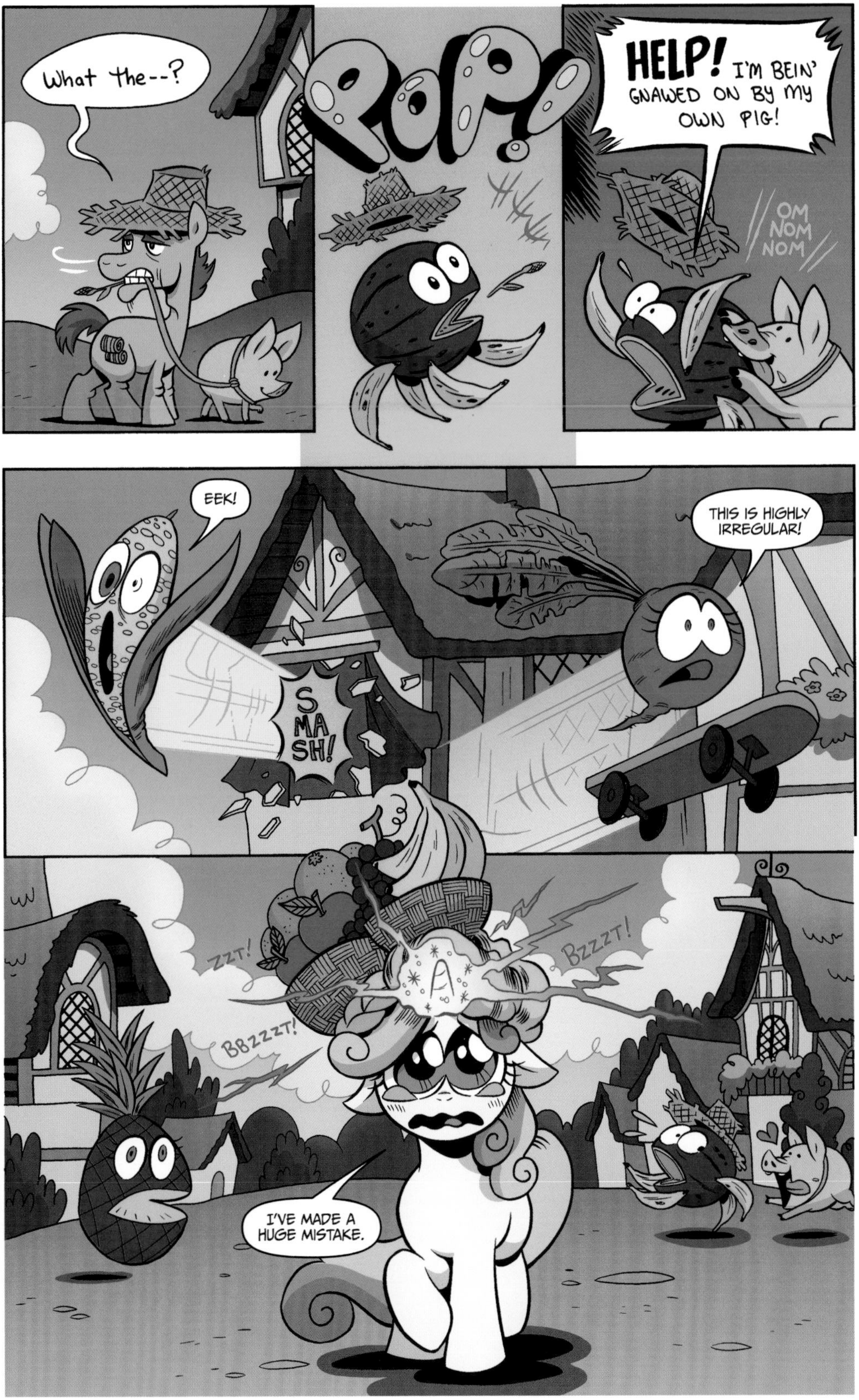
What the--?
POP!
HELP! I'M BEIN' GNAWED ON BY MY OWN PIG!
OM NOM NOM
EEK!
THIS IS HIGHLY IRREGULAR!
SMASH!
ZZT!
BZZZT!
BBZZZT!
I'VE MADE A HUGE MISTAKE.

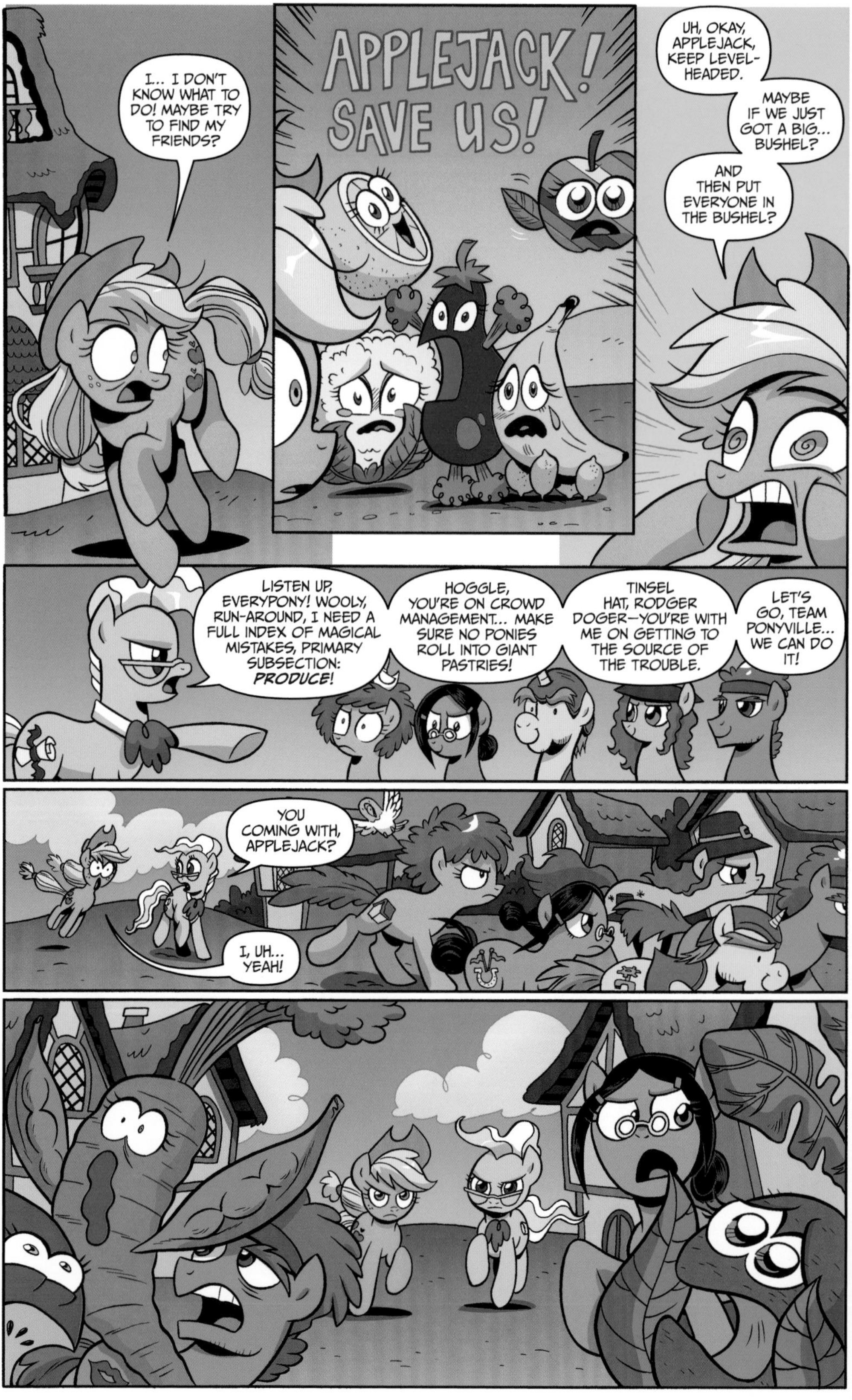
I... I DON'T KNOW WHAT TO DO! MAYBE TRY TO FIND MY FRIENDS?
APPLEJACK! SAVE US!
UH, OKAY, APPLEJACK, KEEP LEVEL-HEADED.
MAYBE IF WE JUST GOT A BIG... BUSHEL?
AND THEN PUT EVERYONE IN THE BUSHEL?
LISTEN UP, EVERYPONY! WOOLY, RUN-AROUND, I NEED A FULL INDEX OF MAGICAL MISTAKES, PRIMARY SUBSECTION: PRODUCE!
HOGGLE, YOU'RE ON CROWD MANAGEMENT... MAKE SURE NO PONIES ROLL INTO GIANT PASTRIES!
TINSEL HAT, RODGER DOGER—YOU'RE WITH ME ON GETTING TO THE SOURCE OF THE TROUBLE.
LET'S GO, TEAM PONYVILLE... WE CAN DO IT!
YOU COMING WITH, APPLEJACK?
I, UH... YEAH!

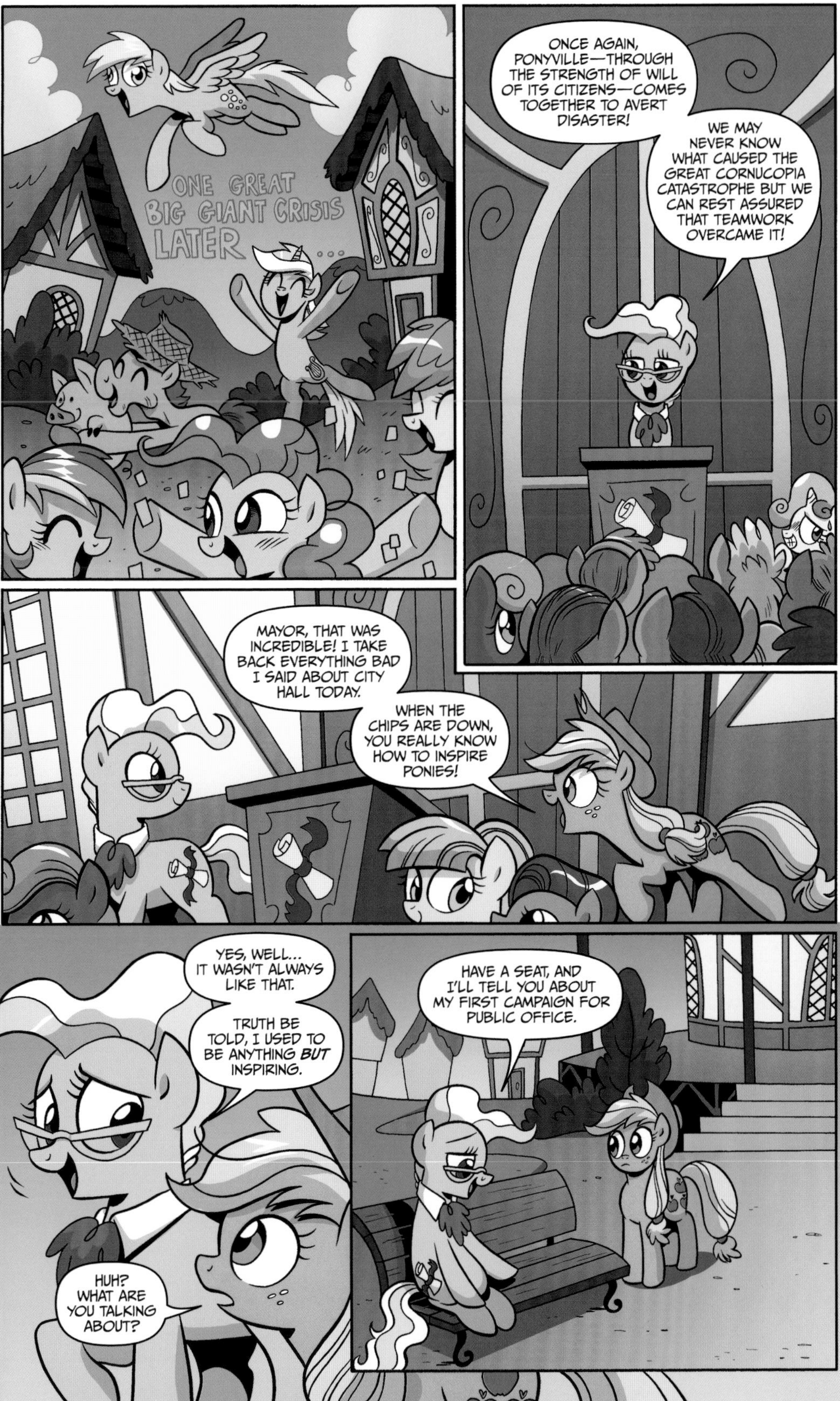
ONE GREAT BIG GIANT CRISIS LATER . . .
ONCE AGAIN, PONYVILLE—THROUGH THE STRENGTH OF WILL OF ITS CITIZENS—COMES TOGETHER TO AVERT DISASTER!
WE MAY NEVER KNOW WHAT CAUSED THE GREAT CORNUCOPIA CATASTROPHE BUT WE CAN REST ASSURED THAT TEAMWORK OVERCAME IT!
MAYOR, THAT WAS INCREDIBLE! I TAKE BACK EVERYTHING BAD I SAID ABOUT CITY HALL TODAY.
WHEN THE CHIPS ARE DOWN, YOU REALLY KNOW HOW TO INSPIRE PONIES!
YES, WELL... IT WASN'T ALWAYS LIKE THAT.
TRUTH BE TOLD, I USED TO BE ANYTHING *BUT* INSPIRING.
HUH? WHAT ARE YOU TALKING ABOUT?
HAVE A SEAT, AND I'LL TELL YOU ABOUT MY FIRST CAMPAIGN FOR PUBLIC OFFICE.

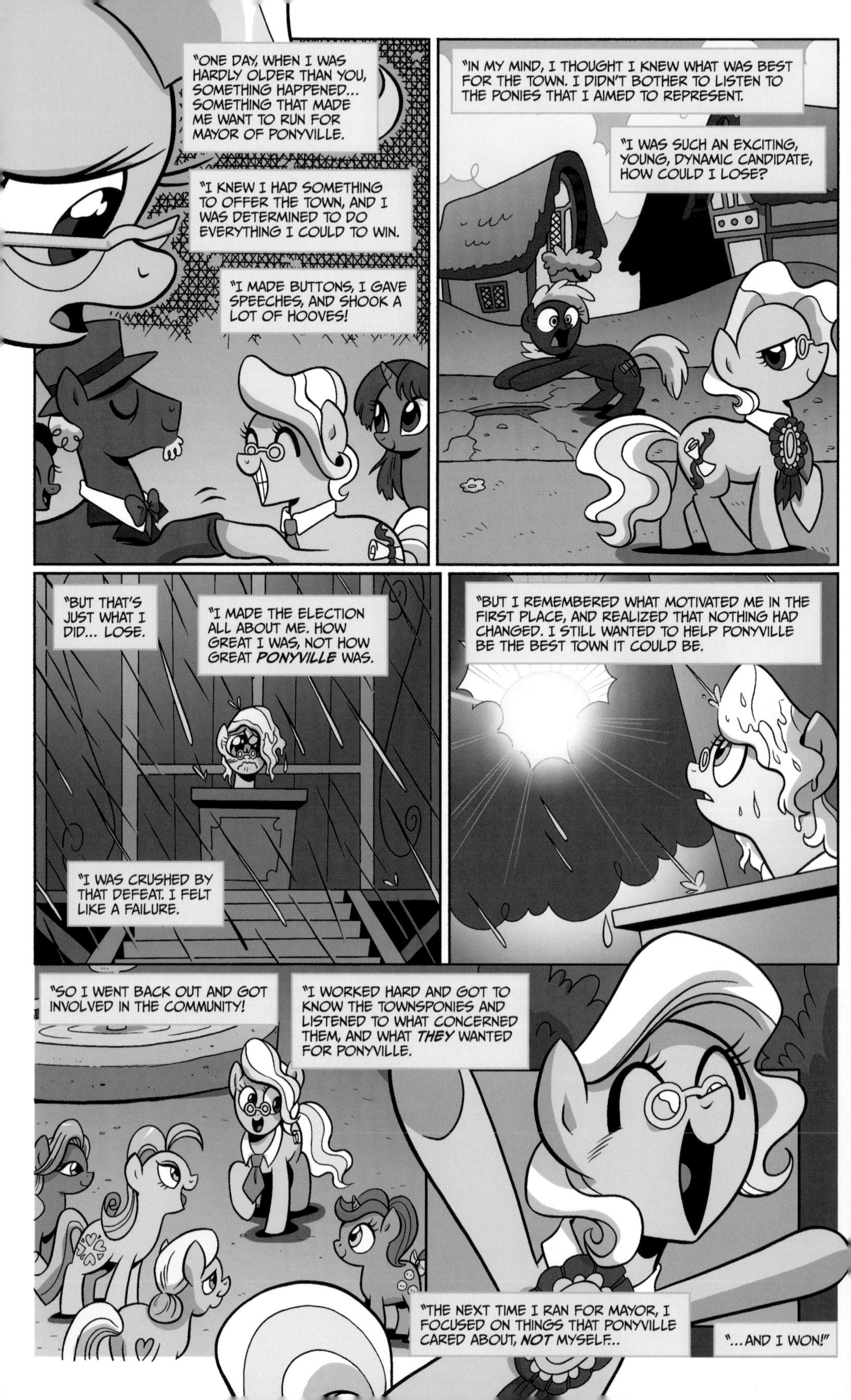
"ONE DAY, WHEN I WAS HARDLY OLDER THAN YOU, SOMETHING HAPPENED... SOMETHING THAT MADE ME WANT TO RUN FOR MAYOR OF PONYVILLE.
"I KNEW I HAD SOMETHING TO OFFER THE TOWN, AND I WAS DETERMINED TO DO EVERYTHING I COULD TO WIN.
"I MADE BUTTONS, I GAVE SPEECHES, AND SHOOK A LOT OF HOOVES!
"IN MY MIND, I THOUGHT I KNEW WHAT WAS BEST FOR THE TOWN. I DIDN'T BOTHER TO LISTEN TO THE PONIES THAT I AIMED TO REPRESENT.
"I WAS SUCH AN EXCITING, YOUNG, DYNAMIC CANDIDATE, HOW COULD I LOSE?
"BUT THAT'S JUST WHAT I DID... LOSE.
"I MADE THE ELECTION ALL ABOUT ME. HOW GREAT I WAS, NOT HOW GREAT *PONYVILLE* WAS.
"I WAS CRUSHED BY THAT DEFEAT. I FELT LIKE A FAILURE.
"BUT I REMEMBERED WHAT MOTIVATED ME IN THE FIRST PLACE, AND REALIZED THAT NOTHING HAD CHANGED. I STILL WANTED TO HELP PONYVILLE BE THE BEST TOWN IT COULD BE.
"SO I WENT BACK OUT AND GOT INVOLVED IN THE COMMUNITY!
"I WORKED HARD AND GOT TO KNOW THE TOWNSPONIES AND LISTENED TO WHAT CONCERNED THEM, AND WHAT *THEY* WANTED FOR PONYVILLE.
"THE NEXT TIME I RAN FOR MAYOR, I FOCUSED ON THINGS THAT PONYVILLE CARED ABOUT, *NOT* MYSELF...
"...AND I WON!"

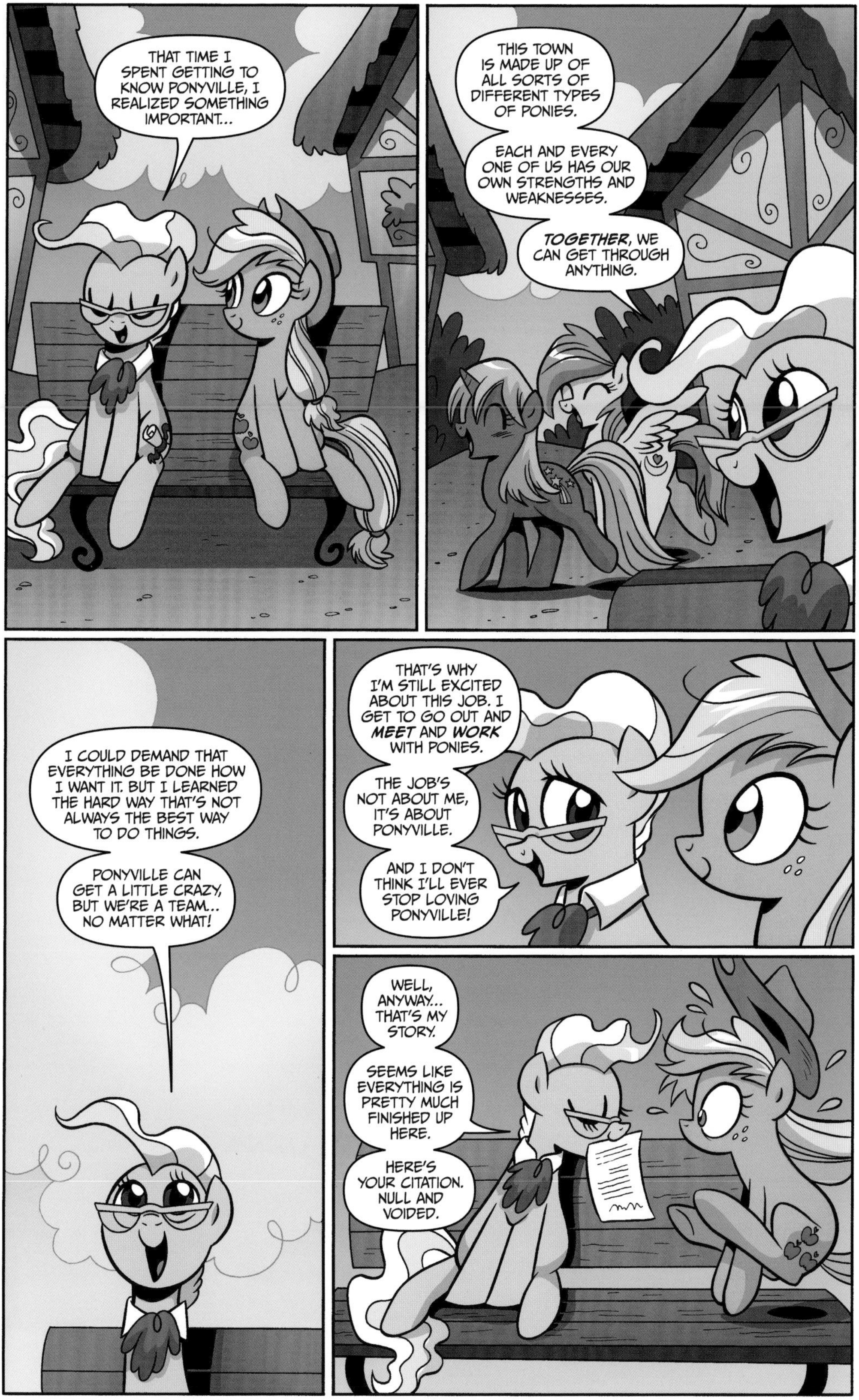
THAT TIME I SPENT GETTING TO KNOW PONYVILLE, I REALIZED SOMETHING IMPORTANT...
THIS TOWN IS MADE UP OF ALL SORTS OF DIFFERENT TYPES OF PONIES.
EACH AND EVERY ONE OF US HAS OUR OWN STRENGTHS AND WEAKNESSES.
TOGETHER, WE CAN GET THROUGH ANYTHING.
I COULD DEMAND THAT EVERYTHING BE DONE HOW I WANT IT. BUT I LEARNED THE HARD WAY THAT'S NOT ALWAYS THE BEST WAY TO DO THINGS.
PONYVILLE CAN GET A LITTLE CRAZY, BUT WE'RE A TEAM... NO MATTER WHAT!
THAT'S WHY I'M STILL EXCITED ABOUT THIS JOB. I GET TO GO OUT AND *MEET* AND *WORK* WITH PONIES.
THE JOB'S NOT ABOUT ME, IT'S ABOUT PONYVILLE.
AND I DON'T THINK I'LL EVER STOP LOVING PONYVILLE!
WELL, ANYWAY... THAT'S MY STORY.
SEEMS LIKE EVERYTHING IS PRETTY MUCH FINISHED UP HERE.
HERE'S YOUR CITATION. NULL AND VOIDED.

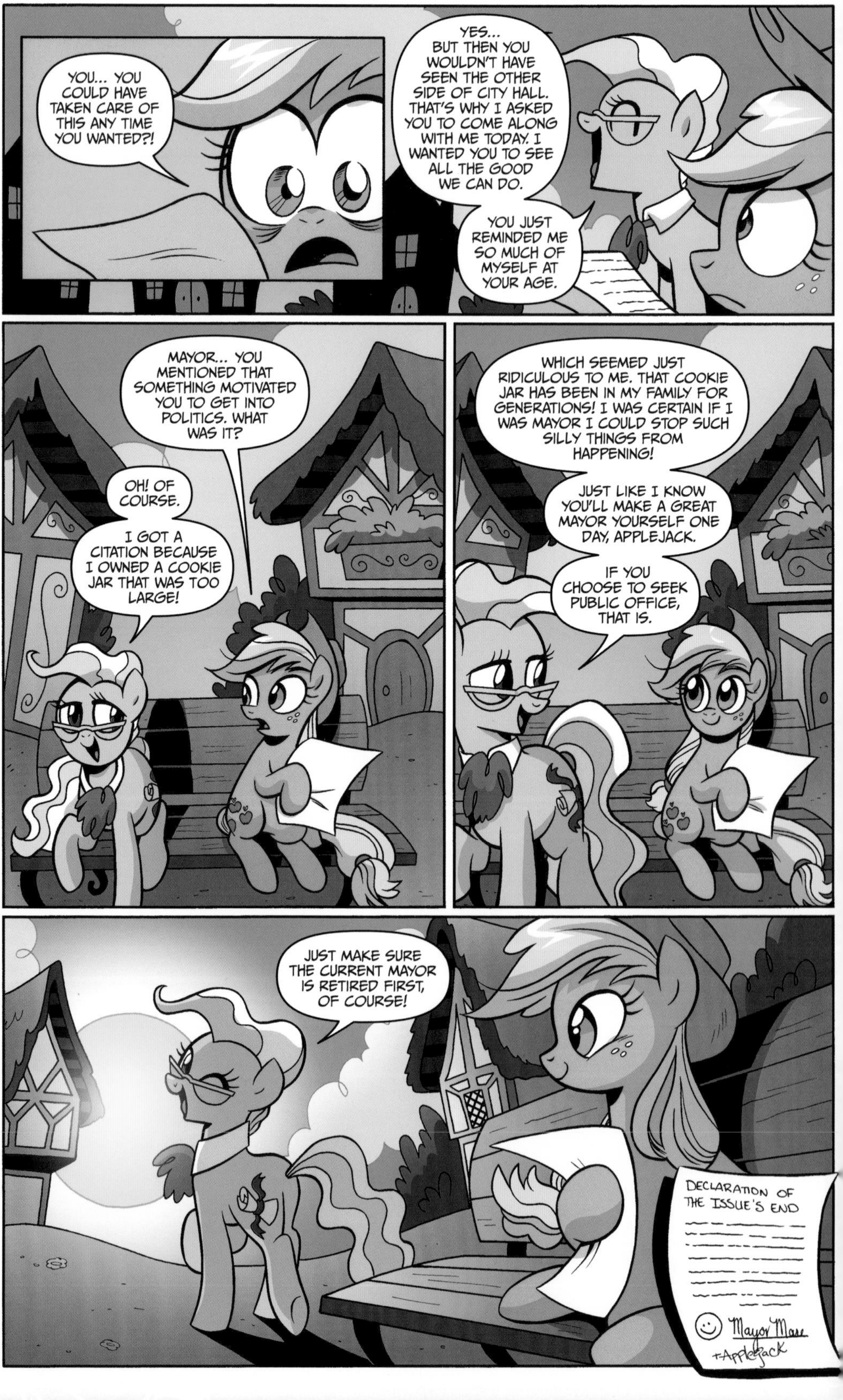

YOU... YOU COULD HAVE TAKEN CARE OF THIS ANY TIME YOU WANTED?!
YES... BUT THEN YOU WOULDN'T HAVE SEEN THE OTHER SIDE OF CITY HALL. THAT'S WHY I ASKED YOU TO COME ALONG WITH ME TODAY. I WANTED YOU TO SEE ALL THE GOOD WE CAN DO.
YOU JUST REMINDED ME SO MUCH OF MYSELF AT YOUR AGE.
MAYOR... YOU MENTIONED THAT SOMETHING MOTIVATED YOU TO GET INTO POLITICS. WHAT WAS IT?
OH! OF COURSE.
I GOT A CITATION BECAUSE I OWNED A COOKIE JAR THAT WAS TOO LARGE!
WHICH SEEMED JUST RIDICULOUS TO ME. THAT COOKIE JAR HAS BEEN IN MY FAMILY FOR GENERATIONS! I WAS CERTAIN IF I WAS MAYOR I COULD STOP SUCH SILLY THINGS FROM HAPPENING!
JUST LIKE I KNOW YOU'LL MAKE A GREAT MAYOR YOURSELF ONE DAY, APPLEJACK.
IF YOU CHOOSE TO SEEK PUBLIC OFFICE, THAT IS.
JUST MAKE SURE THE CURRENT MAYOR IS RETIRED FIRST, OF COURSE!
DECLARATION OF THE ISSUE'S END
Mayor Mare
+Applejack

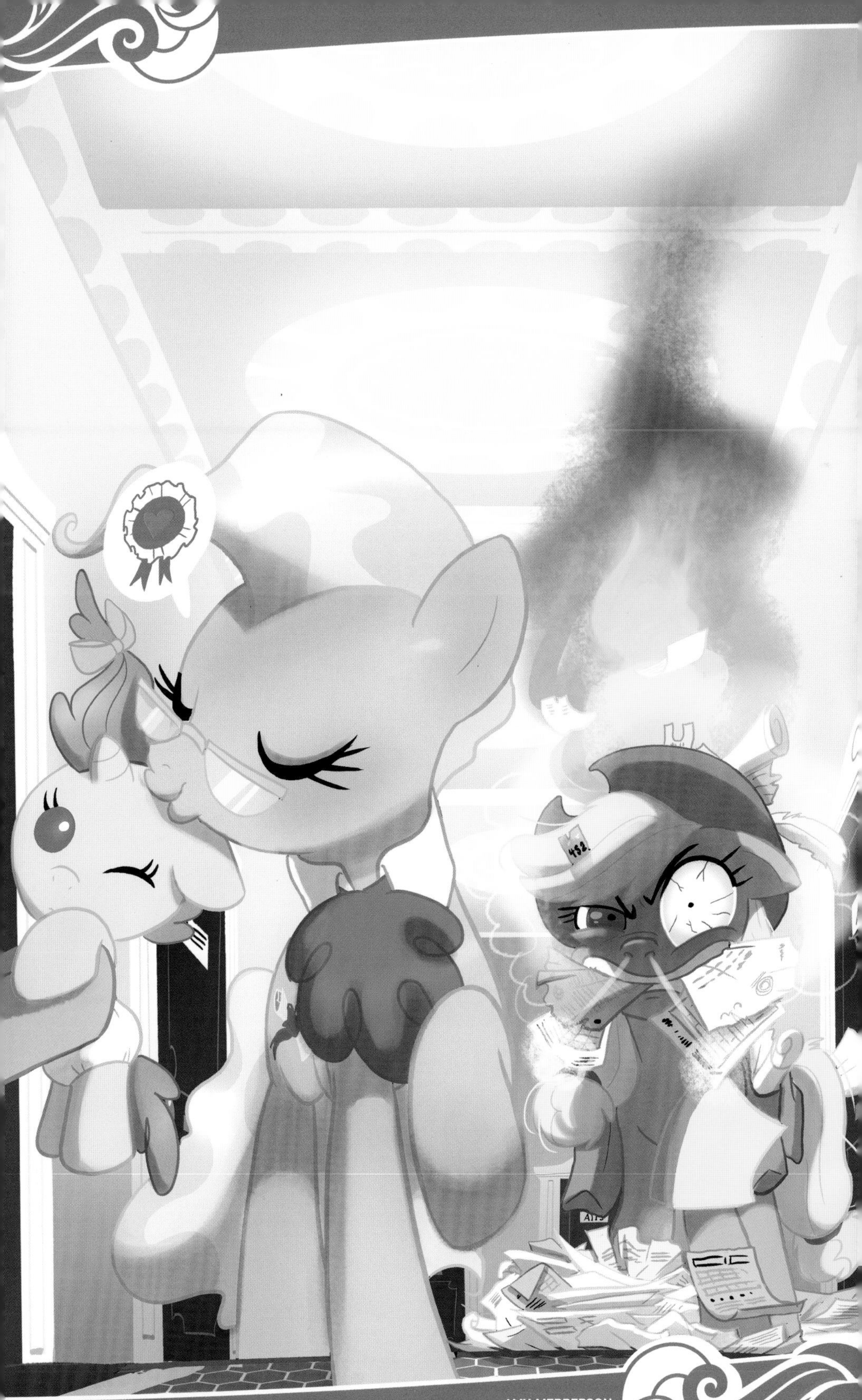

art by AMY MEBBERSON

Silver Spoon & Diamond Tiara

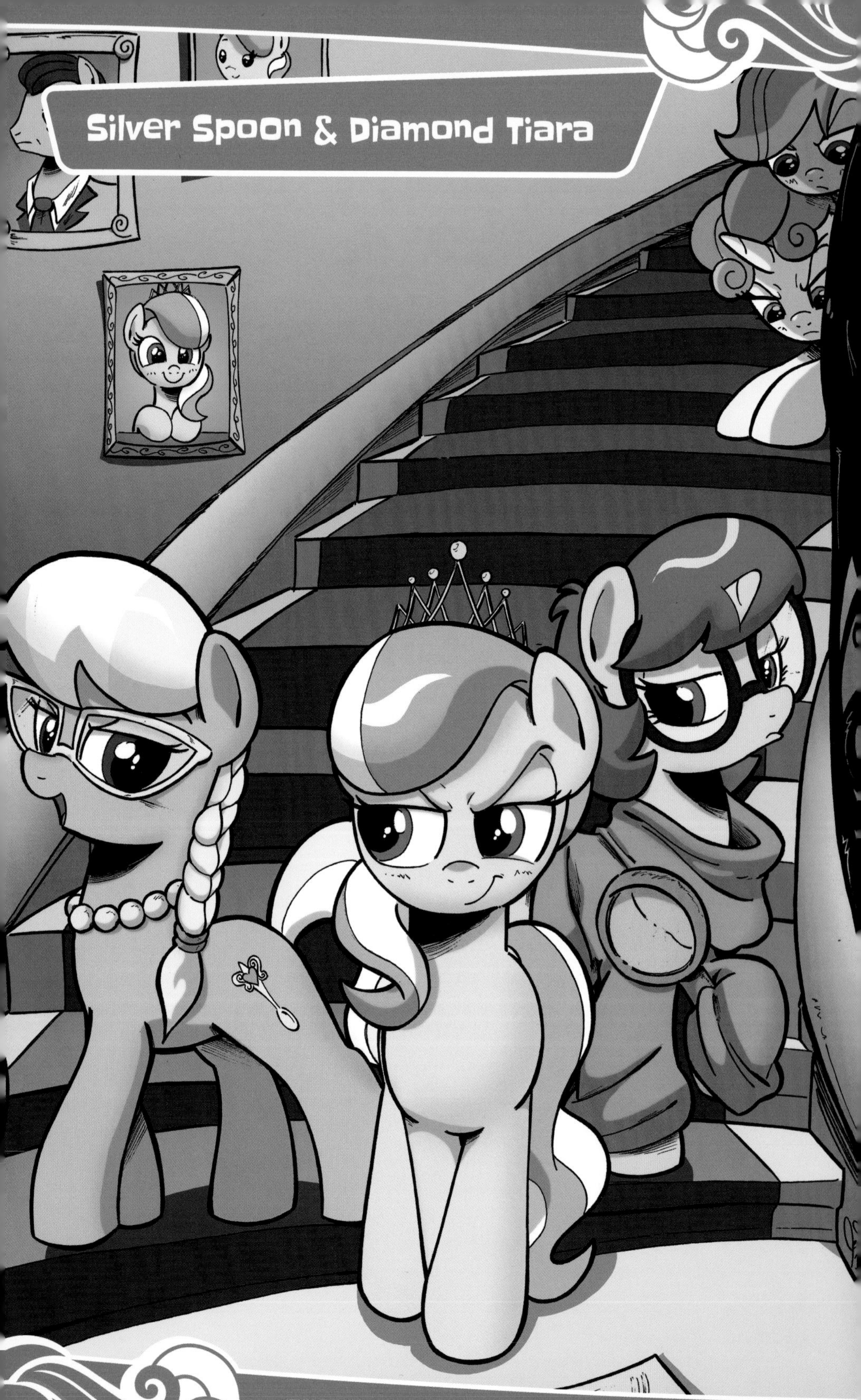

art by JENN BLAKE

"ONCE UPON A TIME THERE WAS A RINKY-DINK LITTLE BACKWATER TOWN CALLED PONYVILLE."

"IT WAS A TOWN SO FULL OF TOTAL LOSERS AND CHUMPS THAT IT WAS AMAZING THE BUILDINGS EVEN STAYED STANDING. THE KIND OF TOWN THAT MOST PONIES ONLY EVEN COME TO IF THEY GET LOST. A TOWN SO..."

"MOVE ON WITH THE STORY, PLEASE!"

"BUT IN THIS DULL HUM-DRUM TOWN FULL OF NOBODIES, THERE WERE A FEW VERY SPECIAL PONIES. PONIES WHO SHINED ABOVE THE REST. THEY WERE PONIES THAT EVERYBODY LOVED AND OTHER LITTLE PONIES WANTED TO BE LIKE. AND OTHER PONIES KNEW THEY WERE COMING BY THEIR CALL."

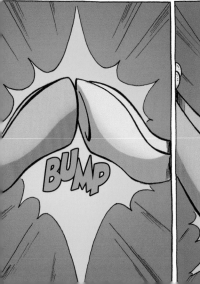

BUMP

BUMP

BUMP

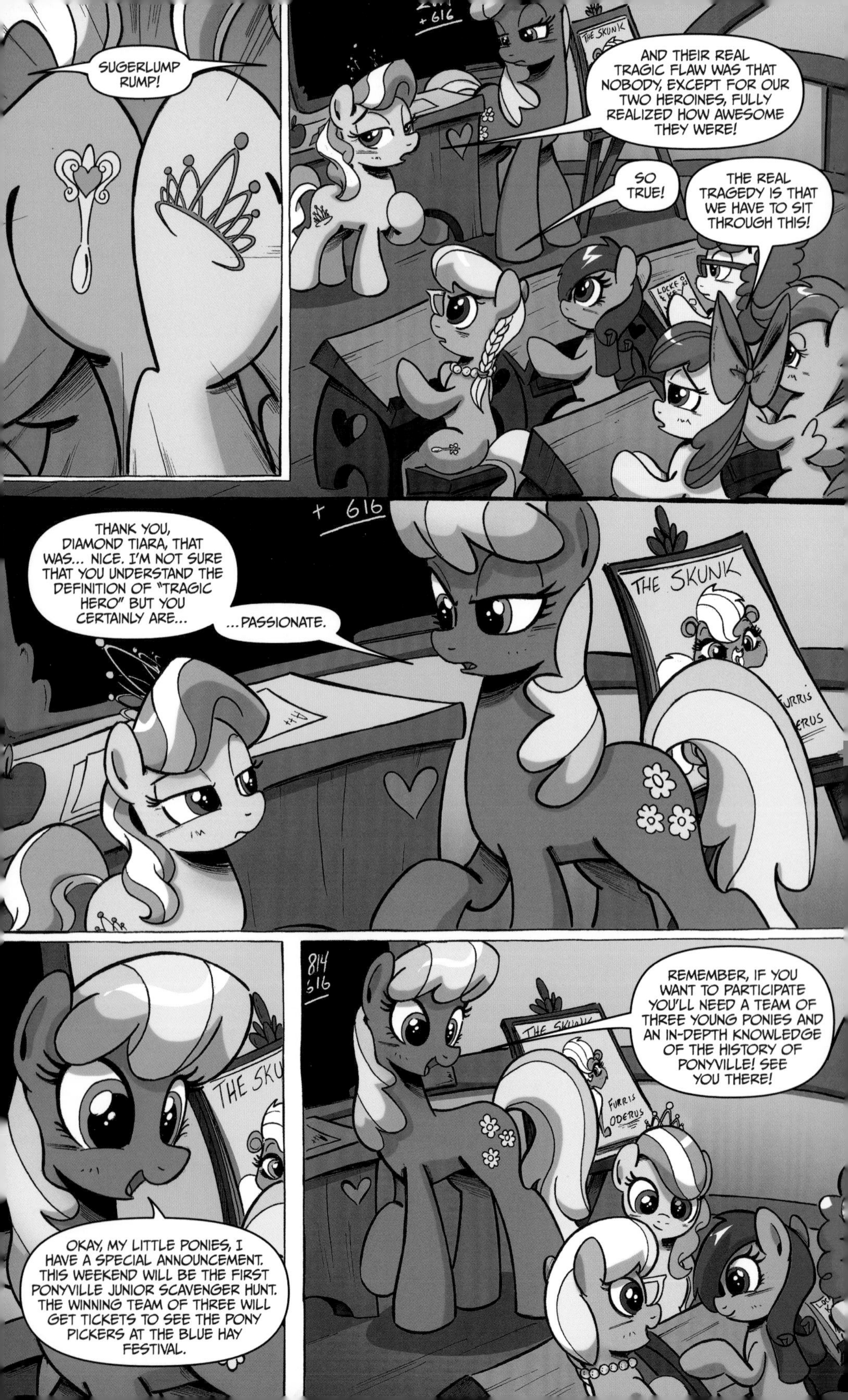
SUGERLUMP RUMP!
AND THEIR REAL TRAGIC FLAW WAS THAT NOBODY, EXCEPT FOR OUR TWO HEROINES, FULLY REALIZED HOW AWESOME THEY WERE!
SO TRUE!
THE REAL TRAGEDY IS THAT WE HAVE TO SIT THROUGH THIS!
+ 616
THANK YOU, DIAMOND TIARA, THAT WAS... NICE. I'M NOT SURE THAT YOU UNDERSTAND THE DEFINITION OF "TRAGIC HERO" BUT YOU CERTAINLY ARE...
...PASSIONATE.
THE SKUNK
OKAY, MY LITTLE PONIES, I HAVE A SPECIAL ANNOUNCEMENT. THIS WEEKEND WILL BE THE FIRST PONYVILLE JUNIOR SCAVENGER HUNT. THE WINNING TEAM OF THREE WILL GET TICKETS TO SEE THE PONY PICKERS AT THE BLUE HAY FESTIVAL.
814
616
REMEMBER, IF YOU WANT TO PARTICIPATE YOU'LL NEED A TEAM OF THREE YOUNG PONIES AND AN IN-DEPTH KNOWLEDGE OF THE HISTORY OF PONYVILLE! SEE YOU THERE!
FURRIS ODERUS

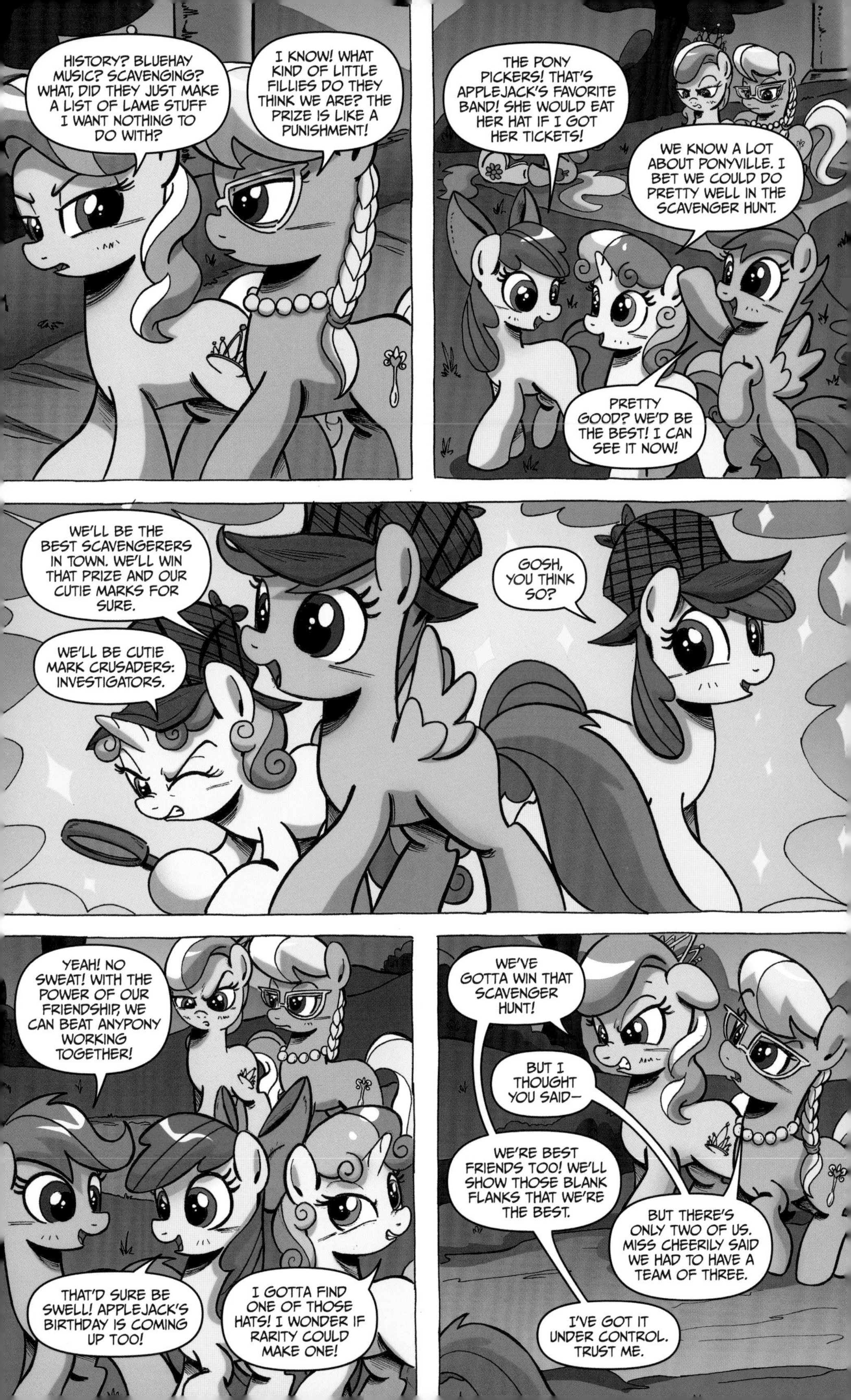
HISTORY? BLUEHAY MUSIC? SCAVENGING? WHAT, DID THEY JUST MAKE A LIST OF LAME STUFF I WANT NOTHING TO DO WITH?
I KNOW! WHAT KIND OF LITTLE FILLIES DO THEY THINK WE ARE? THE PRIZE IS LIKE A PUNISHMENT!
THE PONY PICKERS! THAT'S APPLEJACK'S FAVORITE BAND! SHE WOULD EAT HER HAT IF I GOT HER TICKETS!
WE KNOW A LOT ABOUT PONYVILLE. I BET WE COULD DO PRETTY WELL IN THE SCAVENGER HUNT.
PRETTY GOOD? WE'D BE THE BEST! I CAN SEE IT NOW!
WE'LL BE THE BEST SCAVENGERERS IN TOWN. WE'LL WIN THAT PRIZE AND OUR CUTIE MARKS FOR SURE.
WE'LL BE CUTIE MARK CRUSADERS: INVESTIGATORS.
GOSH, YOU THINK SO?
YEAH! NO SWEAT! WITH THE POWER OF OUR FRIENDSHIP, WE CAN BEAT ANYPONY WORKING TOGETHER!
THAT'D SURE BE SWELL! APPLEJACK'S BIRTHDAY IS COMING UP TOO!
I GOTTA FIND ONE OF THOSE HATS! I WONDER IF RARITY COULD MAKE ONE!
WE'VE GOTTA WIN THAT SCAVENGER HUNT!
BUT I THOUGHT YOU SAID—
WE'RE BEST FRIENDS TOO! WE'LL SHOW THOSE BLANK FLANKS THAT WE'RE THE BEST.
BUT THERE'S ONLY TWO OF US. MISS CHEERILY SAID WE HAD TO HAVE A TEAM OF THREE.
I'VE GOT IT UNDER CONTROL. TRUST ME.

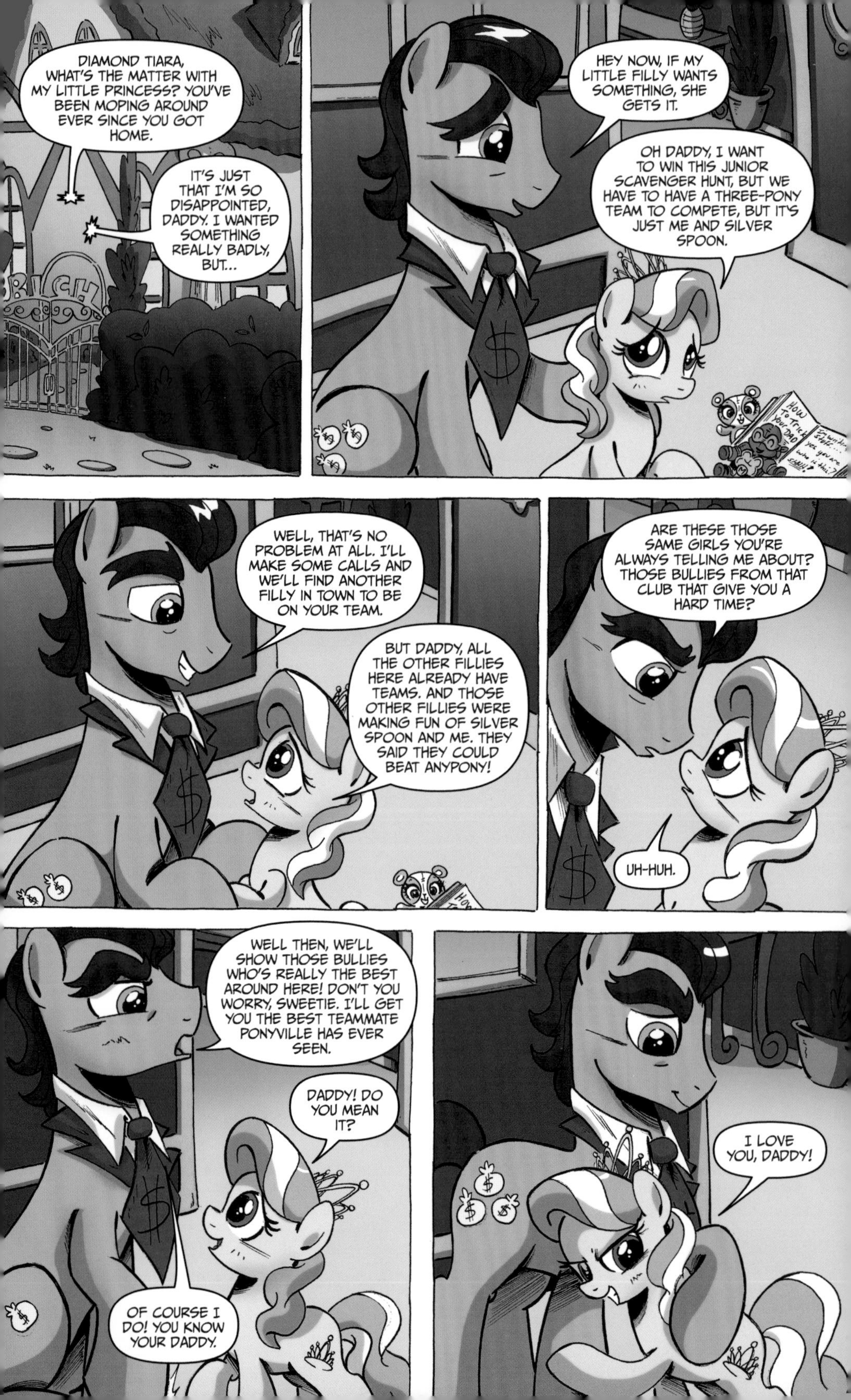
DIAMOND TIARA, WHAT'S THE MATTER WITH MY LITTLE PRINCESS? YOU'VE BEEN MOPING AROUND EVER SINCE YOU GOT HOME.
IT'S JUST THAT I'M SO DISAPPOINTED, DADDY. I WANTED SOMETHING REALLY BADLY, BUT...
RICH
HEY NOW, IF MY LITTLE FILLY WANTS SOMETHING, SHE GETS IT.
OH DADDY, I WANT TO WIN THIS JUNIOR SCAVENGER HUNT, BUT WE HAVE TO HAVE A THREE-PONY TEAM TO COMPETE, BUT IT'S JUST ME AND SILVER SPOON.
HOW To Trick Your DAD
WELL, THAT'S NO PROBLEM AT ALL. I'LL MAKE SOME CALLS AND WE'LL FIND ANOTHER FILLY IN TOWN TO BE ON YOUR TEAM.
BUT DADDY, ALL THE OTHER FILLIES HERE ALREADY HAVE TEAMS. AND THOSE OTHER FILLIES WERE MAKING FUN OF SILVER SPOON AND ME. THEY SAID THEY COULD BEAT ANYPONY!
ARE THESE THOSE SAME GIRLS YOU'RE ALWAYS TELLING ME ABOUT? THOSE BULLIES FROM THAT CLUB THAT GIVE YOU A HARD TIME?
UH-HUH.
WELL THEN, WE'LL SHOW THOSE BULLIES WHO'S REALLY THE BEST AROUND HERE! DON'T YOU WORRY, SWEETIE. I'LL GET YOU THE BEST TEAMMATE PONYVILLE HAS EVER SEEN.
DADDY! DO YOU MEAN IT?
OF COURSE I DO! YOU KNOW YOUR DADDY.
I LOVE YOU, DADDY!

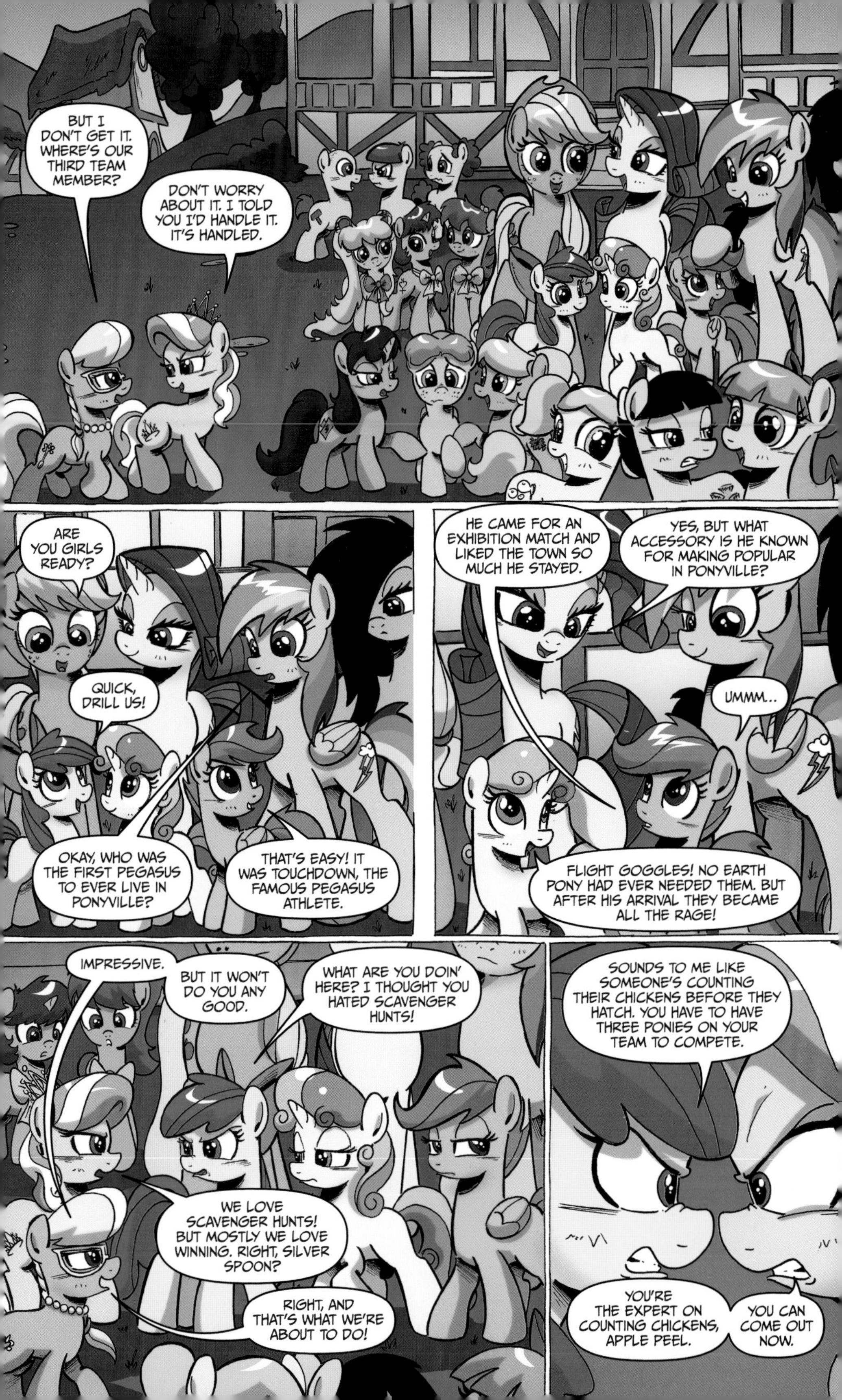
BUT I DON'T GET IT. WHERE'S OUR THIRD TEAM MEMBER?
DON'T WORRY ABOUT IT. I TOLD YOU I'D HANDLE IT. IT'S HANDLED.
ARE YOU GIRLS READY?
QUICK, DRILL US!
OKAY, WHO WAS THE FIRST PEGASUS TO EVER LIVE IN PONYVILLE?
THAT'S EASY! IT WAS TOUCHDOWN, THE FAMOUS PEGASUS ATHLETE.
HE CAME FOR AN EXHIBITION MATCH AND LIKED THE TOWN SO MUCH HE STAYED.
YES, BUT WHAT ACCESSORY IS HE KNOWN FOR MAKING POPULAR IN PONYVILLE?
UMMM...
FLIGHT GOGGLES! NO EARTH PONY HAD EVER NEEDED THEM. BUT AFTER HIS ARRIVAL THEY BECAME ALL THE RAGE!
IMPRESSIVE.
BUT IT WON'T DO YOU ANY GOOD.
WHAT ARE YOU DOIN' HERE? I THOUGHT YOU HATED SCAVENGER HUNTS!
WE LOVE SCAVENGER HUNTS! BUT MOSTLY WE LOVE WINNING. RIGHT, SILVER SPOON?
RIGHT, AND THAT'S WHAT WE'RE ABOUT TO DO!
SOUNDS TO ME LIKE SOMEONE'S COUNTING THEIR CHICKENS BEFORE THEY HATCH. YOU HAVE TO HAVE THREE PONIES ON YOUR TEAM TO COMPETE.
YOU'RE THE EXPERT ON COUNTING CHICKENS, APPLE PEEL.
YOU CAN COME OUT NOW.

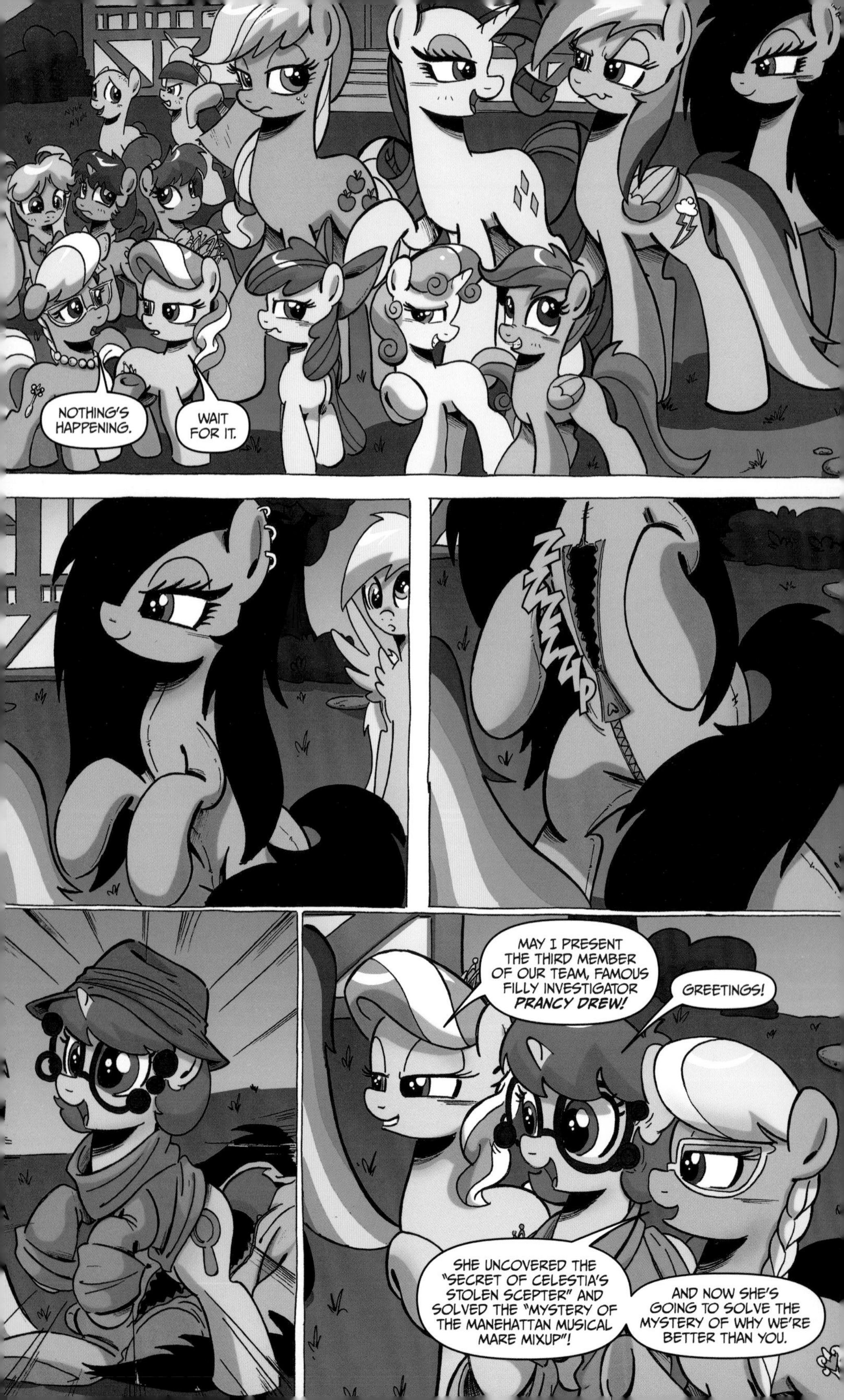
NYUK NYUK
NOTHING'S HAPPENING.
WAIT FOR IT.
MAY I PRESENT THE THIRD MEMBER OF OUR TEAM, FAMOUS FILLY INVESTIGATOR *PRANCY DREW!*
GREETINGS!
SHE UNCOVERED THE "SECRET OF CELESTIA'S STOLEN SCEPTER" AND SOLVED THE "MYSTERY OF THE MANEHATTAN MUSICAL MARE MIXUP"!
AND NOW SHE'S GOING TO SOLVE THE MYSTERY OF WHY WE'RE BETTER THAN YOU.

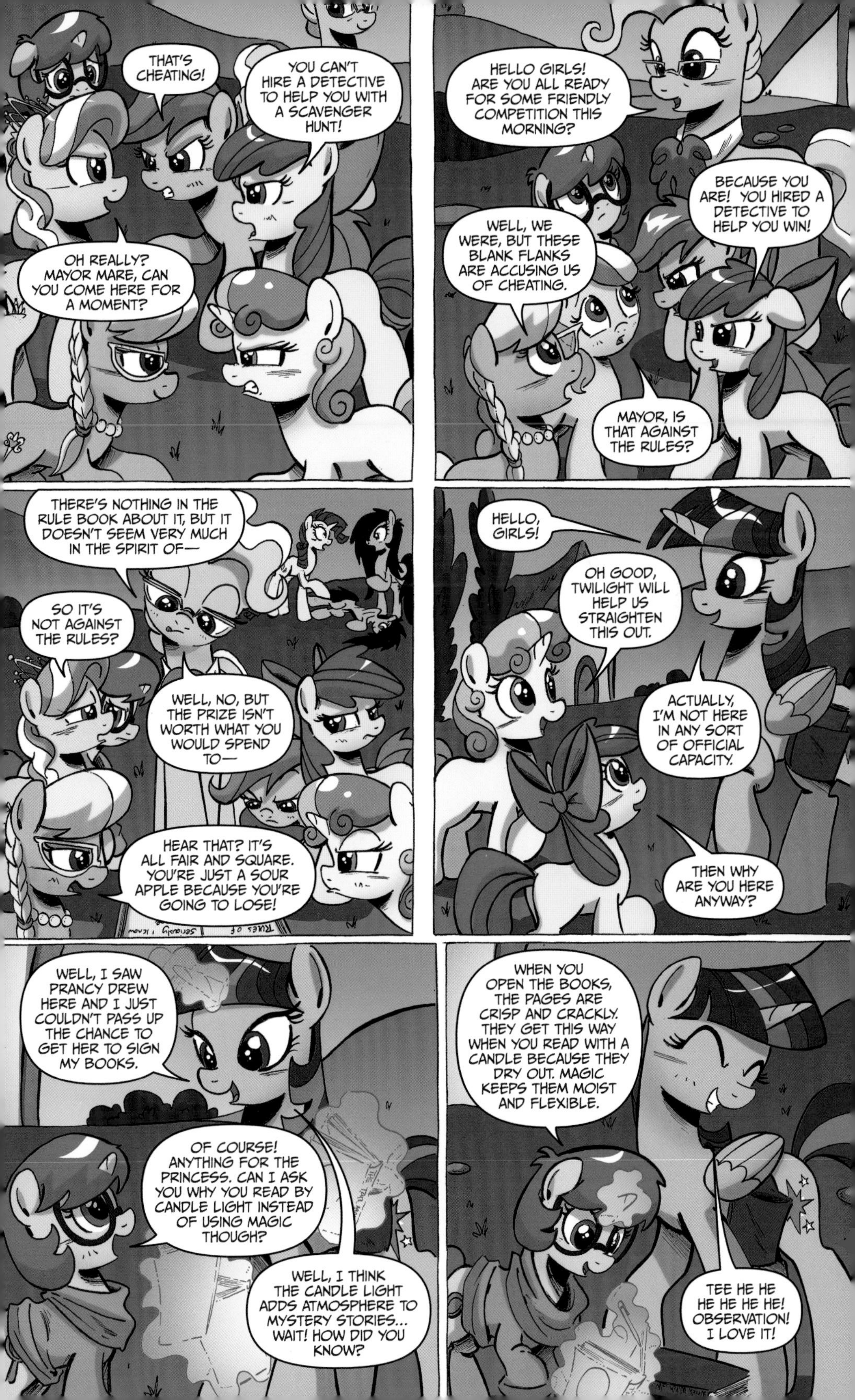
THAT'S CHEATING!
YOU CAN'T HIRE A DETECTIVE TO HELP YOU WITH A SCAVENGER HUNT!
OH REALLY? MAYOR MARE, CAN YOU COME HERE FOR A MOMENT?
HELLO GIRLS! ARE YOU ALL READY FOR SOME FRIENDLY COMPETITION THIS MORNING?
WELL, WE WERE, BUT THESE BLANK FLANKS ARE ACCUSING US OF CHEATING.
BECAUSE YOU ARE! YOU HIRED A DETECTIVE TO HELP YOU WIN!
MAYOR, IS THAT AGAINST THE RULES?
THERE'S NOTHING IN THE RULE BOOK ABOUT IT, BUT IT DOESN'T SEEM VERY MUCH IN THE SPIRIT OF—
SO IT'S NOT AGAINST THE RULES?
WELL, NO, BUT THE PRIZE ISN'T WORTH WHAT YOU WOULD SPEND TO—
HEAR THAT? IT'S ALL FAIR AND SQUARE. YOU'RE JUST A SOUR APPLE BECAUSE YOU'RE GOING TO LOSE!
HELLO, GIRLS!
OH GOOD, TWILIGHT WILL HELP US STRAIGHTEN THIS OUT.
ACTUALLY, I'M NOT HERE IN ANY SORT OF OFFICIAL CAPACITY.
THEN WHY ARE YOU HERE ANYWAY?
WELL, I SAW PRANCY DREW HERE AND I JUST COULDN'T PASS UP THE CHANCE TO GET HER TO SIGN MY BOOKS.
OF COURSE! ANYTHING FOR THE PRINCESS. CAN I ASK YOU WHY YOU READ BY CANDLE LIGHT INSTEAD OF USING MAGIC THOUGH?
WELL, I THINK THE CANDLE LIGHT ADDS ATMOSPHERE TO MYSTERY STORIES... WAIT! HOW DID YOU KNOW?
WHEN YOU OPEN THE BOOKS, THE PAGES ARE CRISP AND CRACKLY. THEY GET THIS WAY WHEN YOU READ WITH A CANDLE BECAUSE THEY DRY OUT. MAGIC KEEPS THEM MOIST AND FLEXIBLE.
TEE HE HE HE HE HE HE! OBSERVATION! I LOVE IT!

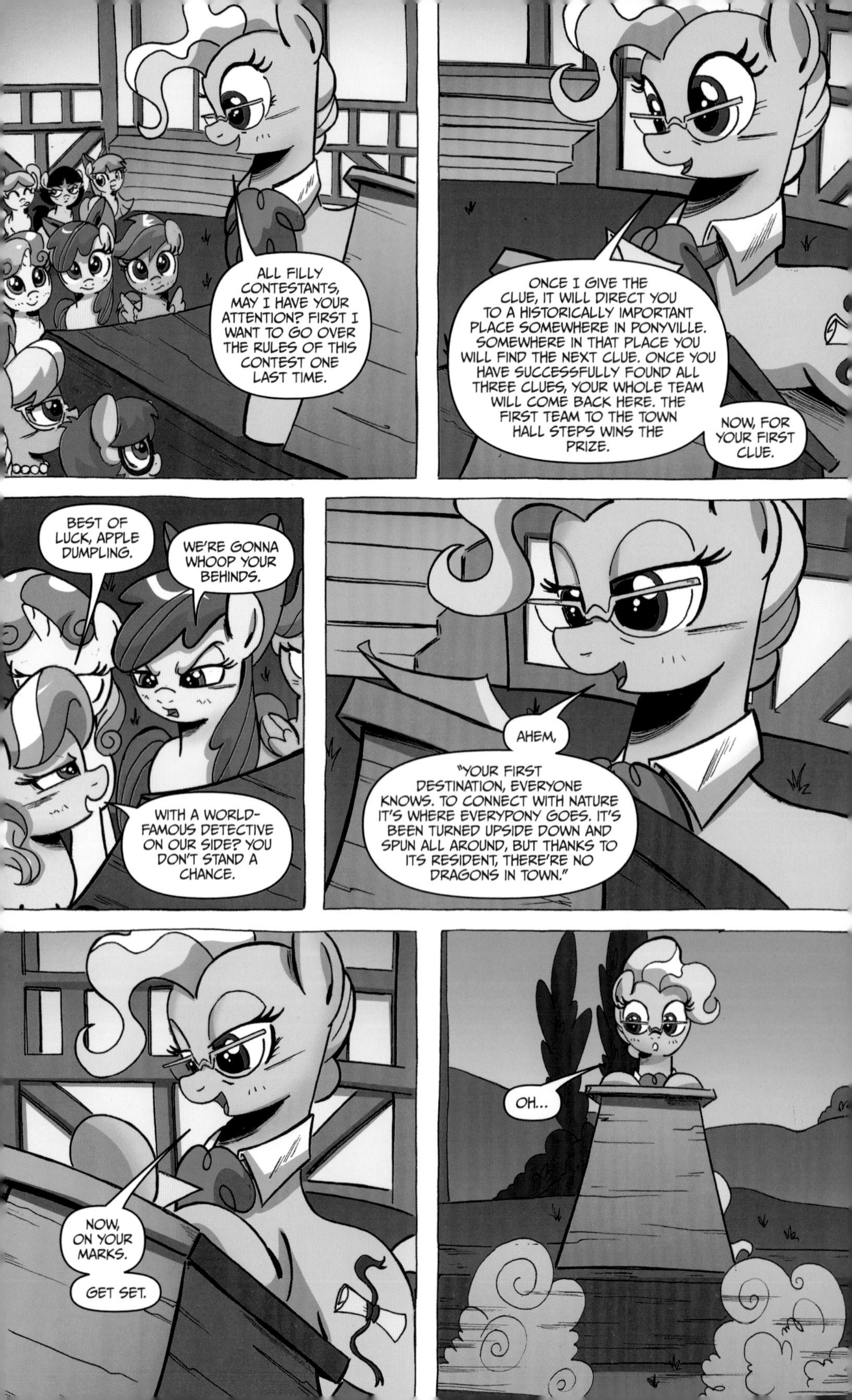

ALL FILLY CONTESTANTS, MAY I HAVE YOUR ATTENTION? FIRST I WANT TO GO OVER THE RULES OF THIS CONTEST ONE LAST TIME.
ONCE I GIVE THE CLUE, IT WILL DIRECT YOU TO A HISTORICALLY IMPORTANT PLACE SOMEWHERE IN PONYVILLE. SOMEWHERE IN THAT PLACE YOU WILL FIND THE NEXT CLUE. ONCE YOU HAVE SUCCESSFULLY FOUND ALL THREE CLUES, YOUR WHOLE TEAM WILL COME BACK HERE. THE FIRST TEAM TO THE TOWN HALL STEPS WINS THE PRIZE.
NOW, FOR YOUR FIRST CLUE.
BEST OF LUCK, APPLE DUMPLING.
WE'RE GONNA WHOOP YOUR BEHINDS.
WITH A WORLD-FAMOUS DETECTIVE ON OUR SIDE? YOU DON'T STAND A CHANCE.
AHEM,
"YOUR FIRST DESTINATION, EVERYONE KNOWS. TO CONNECT WITH NATURE IT'S WHERE EVERYPONY GOES. IT'S BEEN TURNED UPSIDE DOWN AND SPUN ALL AROUND, BUT THANKS TO ITS RESIDENT, THERE'RE NO DRAGONS IN TOWN."
NOW, ON YOUR MARKS.
GET SET.
OH...

I DON'T KNOW WHAT THAT CLUE EVEN MEANS!

WELL, IT SAID THE PLACE WAS SPUN ALL AROUND. THE WINDMILL IS THE ONLY PLACE I CAN THINK OF THAT SPINS AROUND.

OF COURSE! GOOD THINKING, SWEETIE BELLE.

THE BLANK FLANKS ARE GOING TO THE WINDMILL, BECAUSE IT SPINS AROUND.

GOOD SPYING, SILVER SPOON! THEY FIGURED IT OUT ALREADY! WHY DIDN'T YOU THINK OF THAT, PRANCY?

I DID. I SIMPLY DEDUCED THAT THEIR ANSWER WAS INCORRECT.

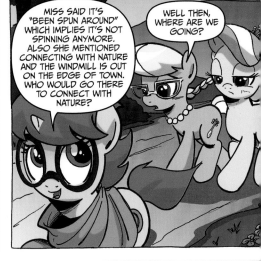

MISS SAID IT'S "BEEN SPUN AROUND" WHICH IMPLIES IT'S NOT SPINNING ANYMORE. ALSO SHE MENTIONED CONNECTING WITH NATURE AND THE WINDMILL IS OUT ON THE EDGE OF TOWN. WHO WOULD GO THERE TO CONNECT WITH NATURE?

WELL THEN, WHERE ARE WE GOING?

THINK! WHO DO YOU ALL KNOW WHO'S DRIVEN OFF A DRAGON FROM PONYVILLE?

THERE WAS THAT TIME THAT RARITY YELLED AT SPIKE AND...

SPIKE IS STILL HERE. WHO ELSE?

I GOT IT!

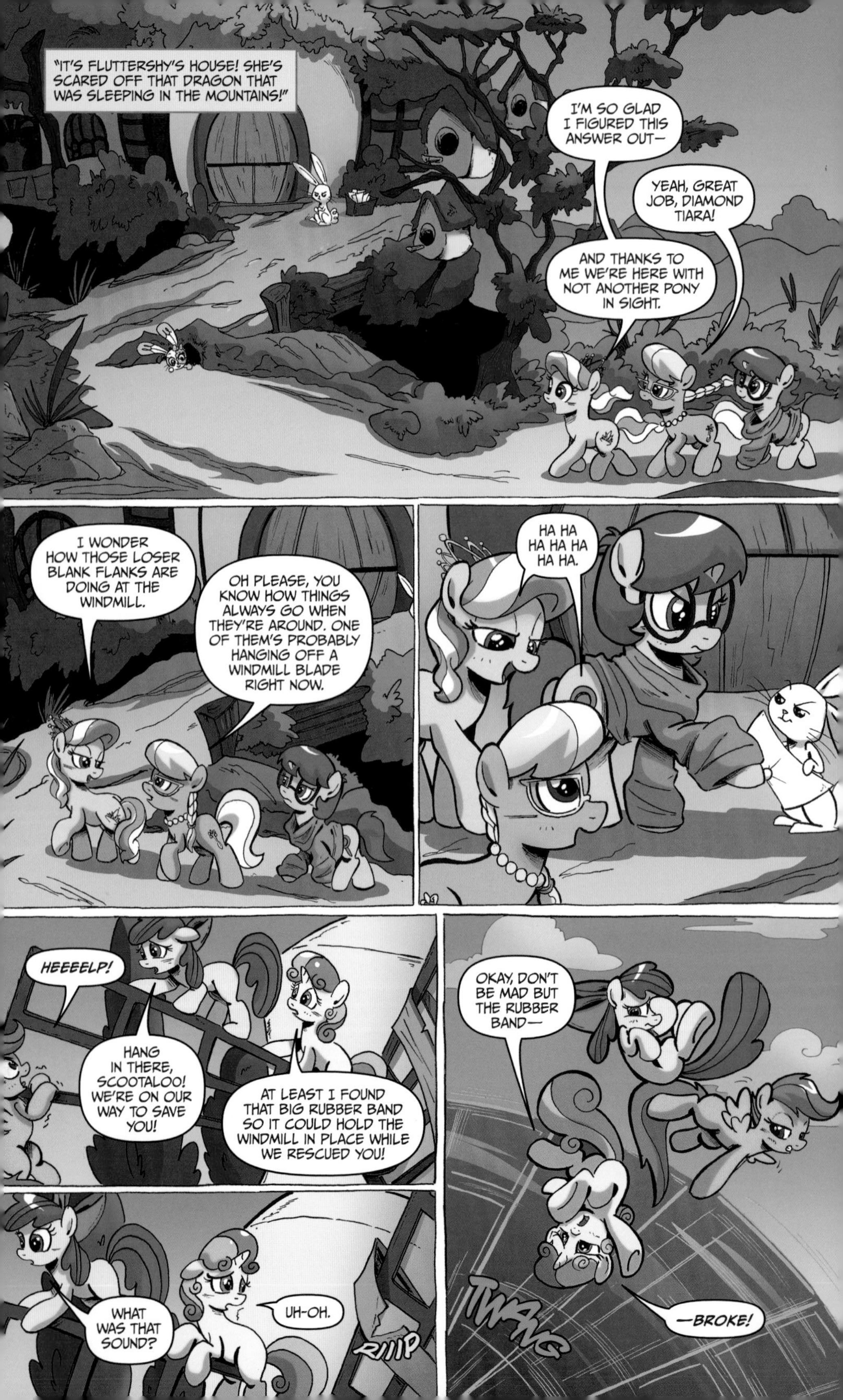
"IT'S FLUTTERSHY'S HOUSE! SHE'S SCARED OFF THAT DRAGON THAT WAS SLEEPING IN THE MOUNTAINS!"
I'M SO GLAD I FIGURED THIS ANSWER OUT—
YEAH, GREAT JOB, DIAMOND TIARA!
AND THANKS TO ME WE'RE HERE WITH NOT ANOTHER PONY IN SIGHT.
I WONDER HOW THOSE LOSER BLANK FLANKS ARE DOING AT THE WINDMILL.
OH PLEASE, YOU KNOW HOW THINGS ALWAYS GO WHEN THEY'RE AROUND. ONE OF THEM'S PROBABLY HANGING OFF A WINDMILL BLADE RIGHT NOW.
HA HA HA HA HA HA HA.
HEEEELP!
HANG IN THERE, SCOOTALOO! WE'RE ON OUR WAY TO SAVE YOU!
AT LEAST I FOUND THAT BIG RUBBER BAND SO IT COULD HOLD THE WINDMILL IN PLACE WHILE WE RESCUED YOU!
WHAT WAS THAT SOUND?
UH-OH.
RIIIP
OKAY, DON'T BE MAD BUT THE RUBBER BAND—
TWANG
—BROKE!

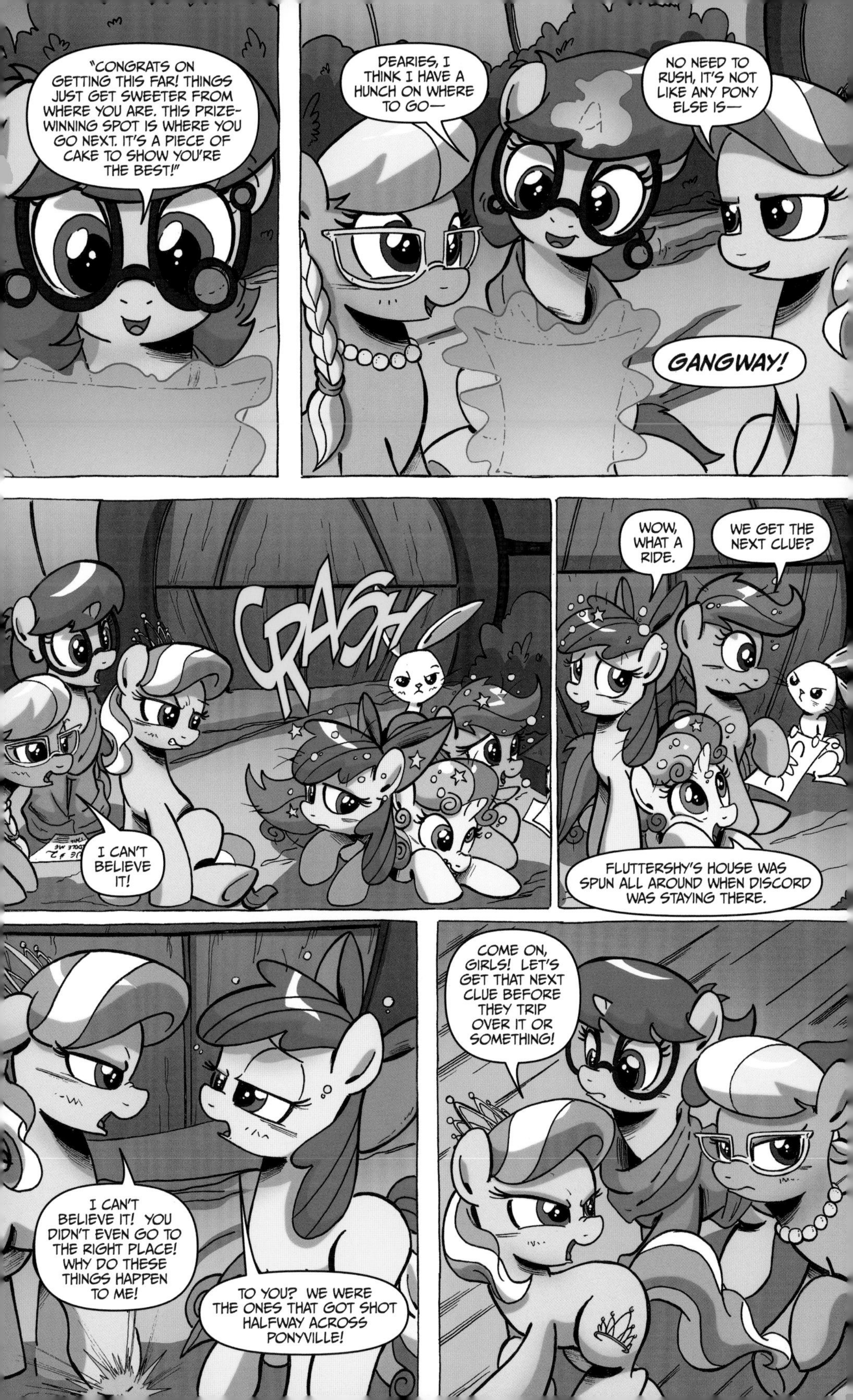
"CONGRATS ON GETTING THIS FAR! THINGS JUST GET SWEETER FROM WHERE YOU ARE. THIS PRIZE-WINNING SPOT IS WHERE YOU GO NEXT. IT'S A PIECE OF CAKE TO SHOW YOU'RE THE BEST!"
DEARIES, I THINK I HAVE A HUNCH ON WHERE TO GO—
NO NEED TO RUSH, IT'S NOT LIKE ANY PONY ELSE IS—
GANGWAY!
CRASH
I CAN'T BELIEVE IT!
WOW, WHAT A RIDE.
WE GET THE NEXT CLUE?
FLUTTERSHY'S HOUSE WAS SPUN ALL AROUND WHEN DISCORD WAS STAYING THERE.
I CAN'T BELIEVE IT! YOU DIDN'T EVEN GO TO THE RIGHT PLACE! WHY DO THESE THINGS HAPPEN TO ME!
TO YOU? WE WERE THE ONES THAT GOT SHOT HALFWAY ACROSS PONYVILLE!
COME ON, GIRLS! LET'S GET THAT NEXT CLUE BEFORE THEY TRIP OVER IT OR SOMETHING!

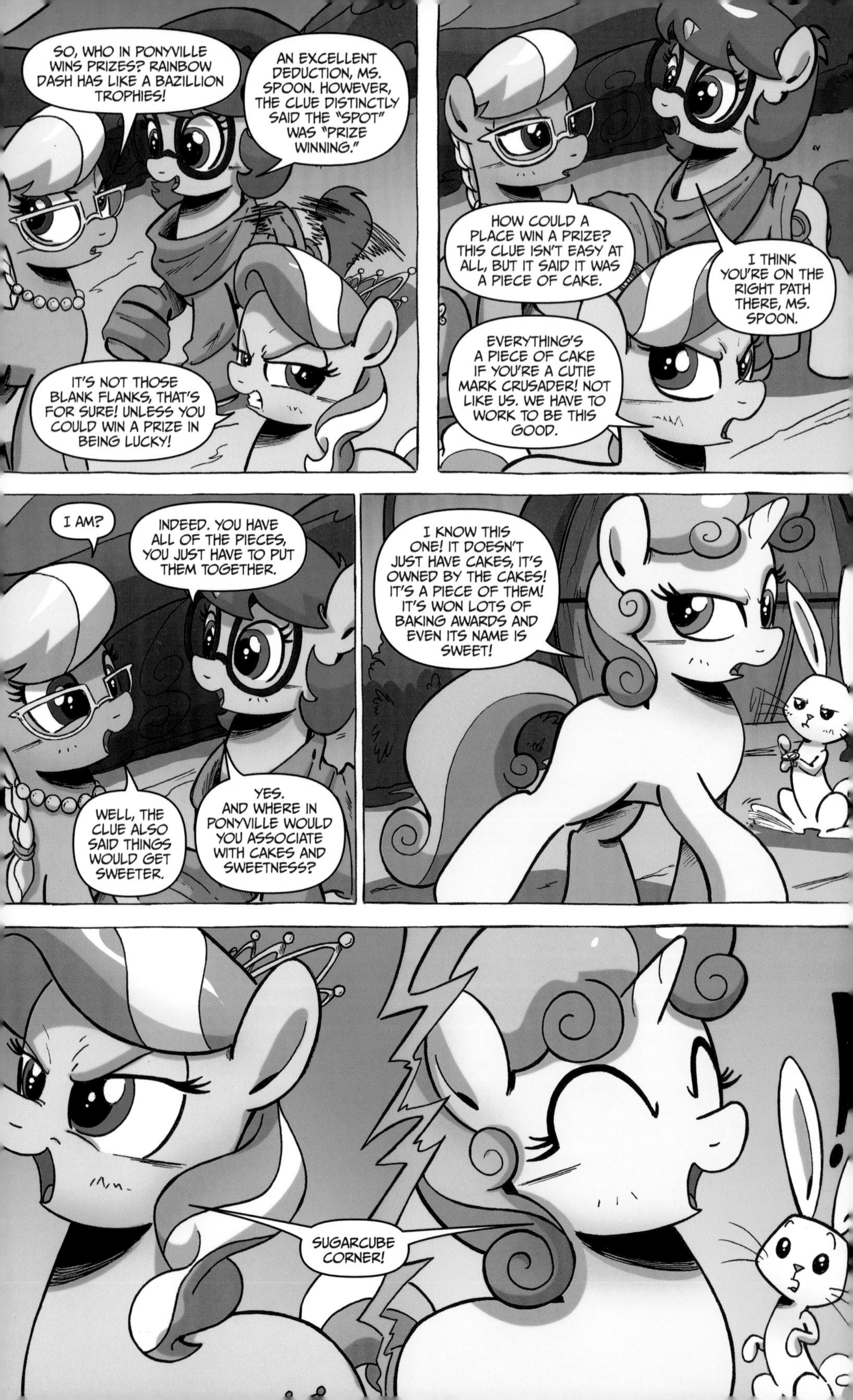
SO, WHO IN PONYVILLE WINS PRIZES? RAINBOW DASH HAS LIKE A BAZILLION TROPHIES!
AN EXCELLENT DEDUCTION, MS. SPOON. HOWEVER, THE CLUE DISTINCTLY SAID THE "SPOT" WAS "PRIZE WINNING."
IT'S NOT THOSE BLANK FLANKS, THAT'S FOR SURE! UNLESS YOU COULD WIN A PRIZE IN BEING LUCKY!
HOW COULD A PLACE WIN A PRIZE? THIS CLUE ISN'T EASY AT ALL, BUT IT SAID IT WAS A PIECE OF CAKE.
I THINK YOU'RE ON THE RIGHT PATH THERE, MS. SPOON.
EVERYTHING'S A PIECE OF CAKE IF YOU'RE A CUTIE MARK CRUSADER! NOT LIKE US. WE HAVE TO WORK TO BE THIS GOOD.
I AM?
INDEED. YOU HAVE ALL OF THE PIECES, YOU JUST HAVE TO PUT THEM TOGETHER.
WELL, THE CLUE ALSO SAID THINGS WOULD GET SWEETER.
YES. AND WHERE IN PONYVILLE WOULD YOU ASSOCIATE WITH CAKES AND SWEETNESS?
I KNOW THIS ONE! IT DOESN'T JUST HAVE CAKES, IT'S OWNED BY THE CAKES! IT'S A PIECE OF THEM! IT'S WON LOTS OF BAKING AWARDS AND EVEN ITS NAME IS SWEET!
SUGARCUBE CORNER!

HEEEEEEEEEYA GIRLS!

WHAT'S GOING ON IN HERE?

WELL, THE CAKES MADE A CHOCOLATE FOUNTAIN. AAAAND... THAT GOT ME THINKING THAT IF YOU CAN HAVE A CHOCOLATE FOUNTAIN, COULD YOU HAVE A CHOCOLATE WATERFALL? NOW MY CHOCOLATE WATERFALL HAS MADE A CHOCOLATE *RIVER!*

WE DON'T HAVE TIME FOR THIS NONSENSE! DO YOU HAVE THE CLUES FOR THE SCAVENGER HUNT OR NOT?

HUH? OH YEAH! THEY'RE AROUND TWO KNOTS OFF THE STARBOARD BOW.

HUH?

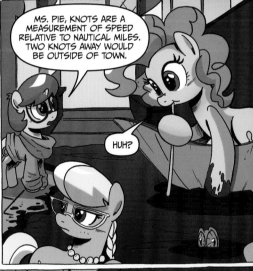

MS. PIE, KNOTS ARE A MEASUREMENT OF SPEED RELATIVE TO NAUTICAL MILES. TWO KNOTS AWAY WOULD BE OUTSIDE OF TOWN.

HUH?

NO, SILLY. IT'S OVER THERE BY THOSE TWO KNOTS.

OH. MY MISTAKE, I SUPPOSE?

IT'S OKAY! YOU'RE STILL YOUNG. YOU'LL LEARN A LOT MORE ABOUT CHOCOLATE NAVIGATION WHEN YOU GROW UP!

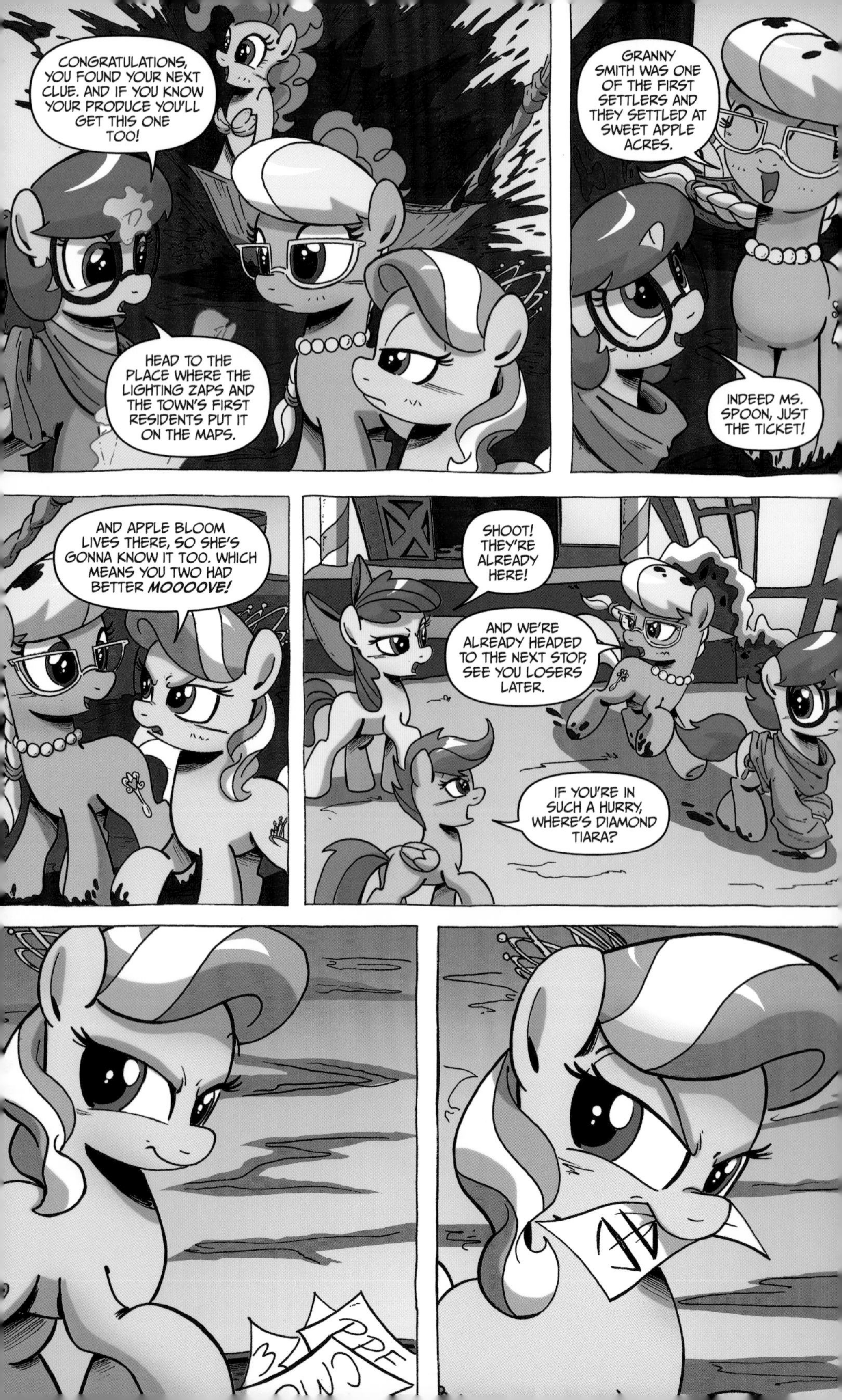
CONGRATULATIONS, YOU FOUND YOUR NEXT CLUE. AND IF YOU KNOW YOUR PRODUCE YOU'LL GET THIS ONE TOO!
HEAD TO THE PLACE WHERE THE LIGHTING ZAPS AND THE TOWN'S FIRST RESIDENTS PUT IT ON THE MAPS.
GRANNY SMITH WAS ONE OF THE FIRST SETTLERS AND THEY SETTLED AT SWEET APPLE ACRES.
INDEED MS. SPOON, JUST THE TICKET!
AND APPLE BLOOM LIVES THERE, SO SHE'S GONNA KNOW IT TOO. WHICH MEANS YOU TWO HAD BETTER *MOOOOVE!*
SHOOT! THEY'RE ALREADY HERE!
AND WE'RE ALREADY HEADED TO THE NEXT STOP, SEE YOU LOSERS LATER.
IF YOU'RE IN SUCH A HURRY, WHERE'S DIAMOND TIARA?

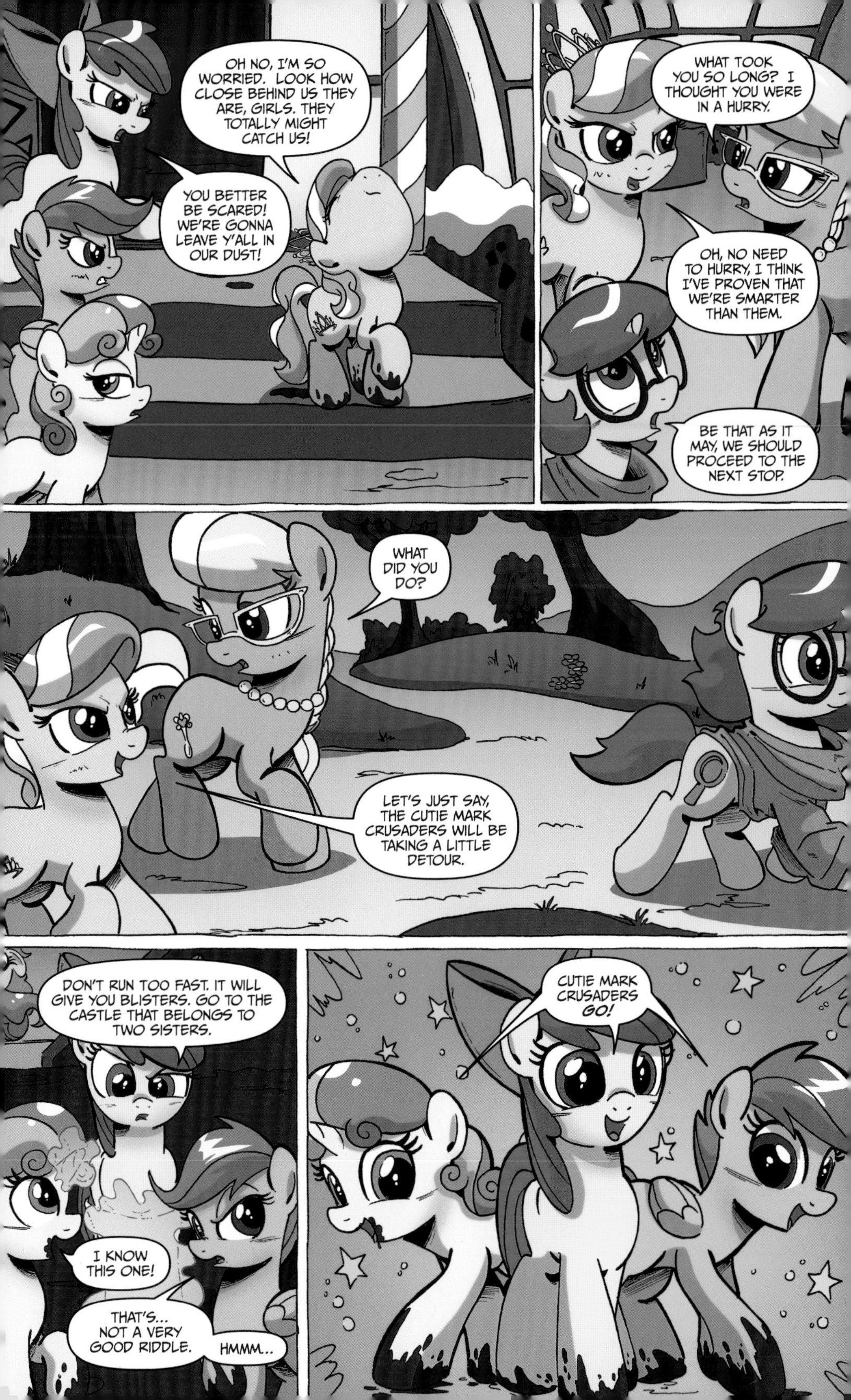
OH NO, I'M SO WORRIED. LOOK HOW CLOSE BEHIND US THEY ARE, GIRLS. THEY TOTALLY MIGHT CATCH US!
YOU BETTER BE SCARED! WE'RE GONNA LEAVE Y'ALL IN OUR DUST!
WHAT TOOK YOU SO LONG? I THOUGHT YOU WERE IN A HURRY.
OH, NO NEED TO HURRY, I THINK I'VE PROVEN THAT WE'RE SMARTER THAN THEM.
BE THAT AS IT MAY, WE SHOULD PROCEED TO THE NEXT STOP.
WHAT DID YOU DO?
LET'S JUST SAY, THE CUTIE MARK CRUSADERS WILL BE TAKING A LITTLE DETOUR.
DON'T RUN TOO FAST. IT WILL GIVE YOU BLISTERS. GO TO THE CASTLE THAT BELONGS TO TWO SISTERS.
I KNOW THIS ONE!
THAT'S... NOT A VERY GOOD RIDDLE.
HMMM...
CUTIE MARK CRUSADERS *GO!*

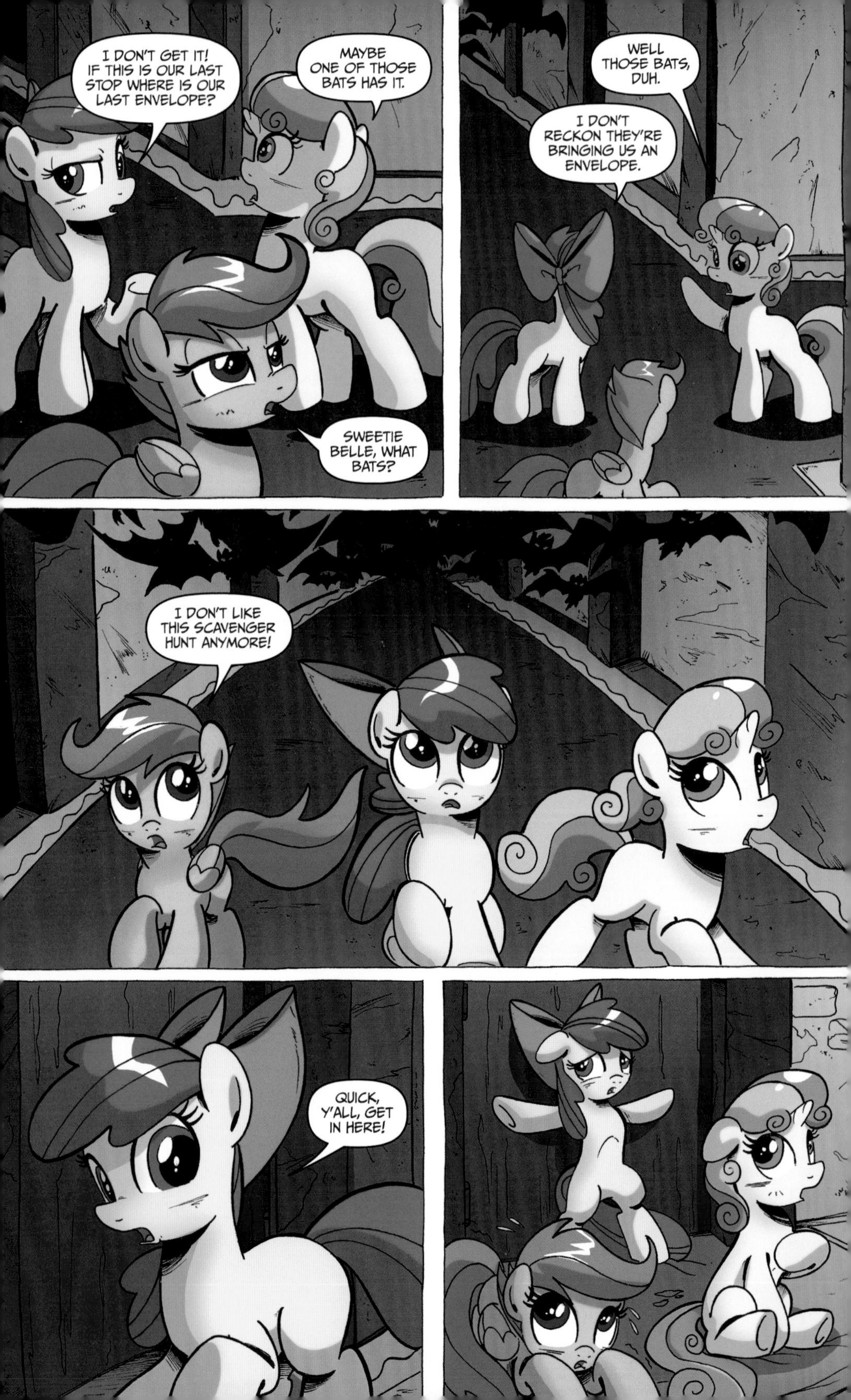
I DON'T GET IT! IF THIS IS OUR LAST STOP WHERE IS OUR LAST ENVELOPE?
MAYBE ONE OF THOSE BATS HAS IT.
SWEETIE BELLE, WHAT BATS?
WELL THOSE BATS, DUH.
I DON'T RECKON THEY'RE BRINGING US AN ENVELOPE.
I DON'T LIKE THIS SCAVENGER HUNT ANYMORE!
QUICK, Y'ALL, GET IN HERE!

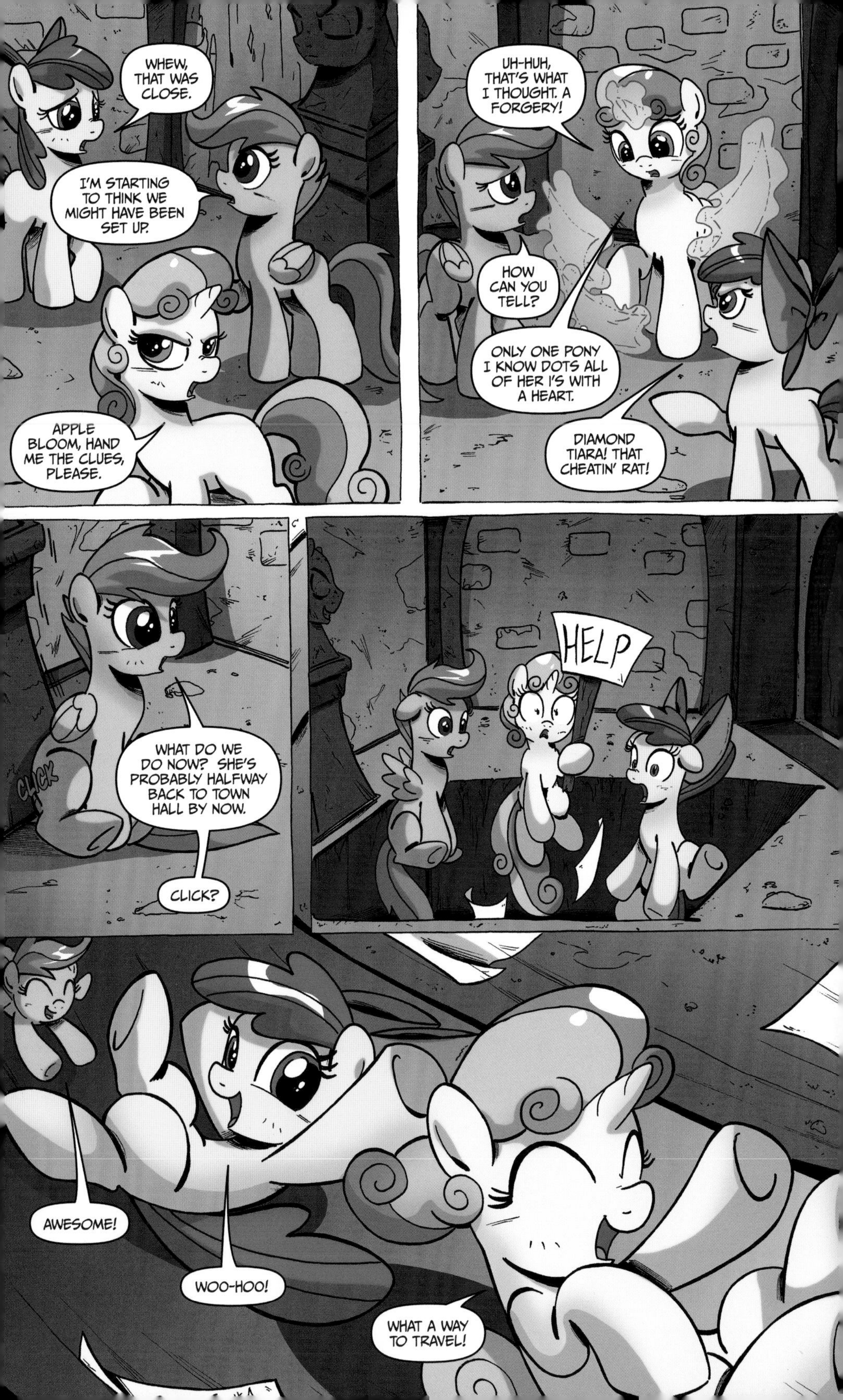
WHEW, THAT WAS CLOSE.
I'M STARTING TO THINK WE MIGHT HAVE BEEN SET UP.
APPLE BLOOM, HAND ME THE CLUES, PLEASE.
UH-HUH, THAT'S WHAT I THOUGHT. A FORGERY!
HOW CAN YOU TELL?
ONLY ONE PONY I KNOW DOTS ALL OF HER I'S WITH A HEART.
DIAMOND TIARA! THAT CHEATIN' RAT!
CLICK
WHAT DO WE DO NOW? SHE'S PROBABLY HALFWAY BACK TO TOWN HALL BY NOW.
CLICK?
HELP
AWESOME!
WOO-HOO!
WHAT A WAY TO TRAVEL!

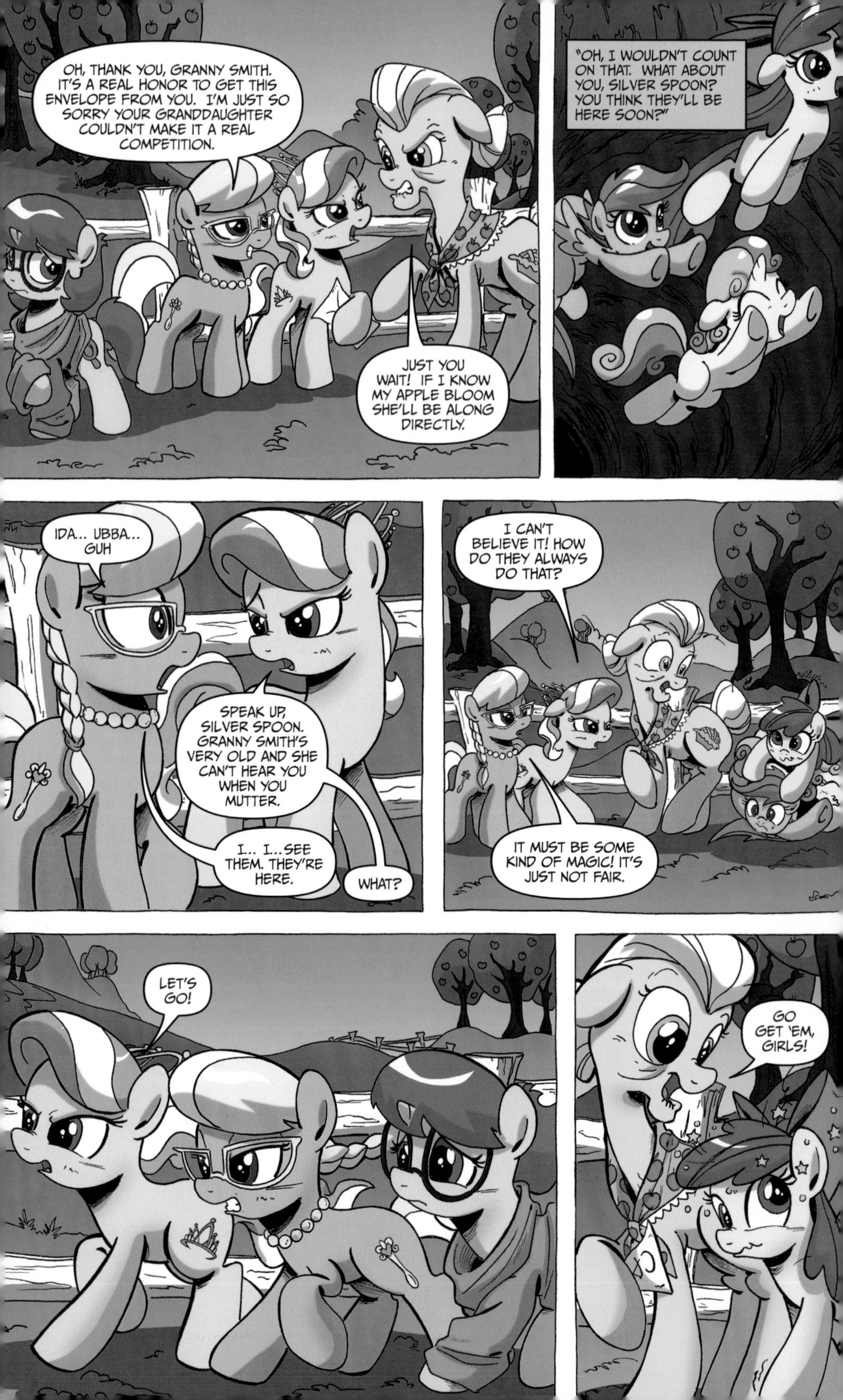
OH, THANK YOU, GRANNY SMITH. IT'S A REAL HONOR TO GET THIS ENVELOPE FROM YOU. I'M JUST SO SORRY YOUR GRANDDAUGHTER COULDN'T MAKE IT A REAL COMPETITION.
JUST YOU WAIT! IF I KNOW MY APPLE BLOOM SHE'LL BE ALONG DIRECTLY.
"OH, I WOULDN'T COUNT ON THAT. WHAT ABOUT YOU, SILVER SPOON? YOU THINK THEY'LL BE HERE SOON?"
IDA... UBBA... GUH
SPEAK UP, SILVER SPOON. GRANNY SMITH'S VERY OLD AND SHE CAN'T HEAR YOU WHEN YOU MUTTER.
I... I...SEE THEM. THEY'RE HERE.
WHAT?
I CAN'T BELIEVE IT! HOW DO THEY ALWAYS DO THAT?
IT MUST BE SOME KIND OF MAGIC! IT'S JUST NOT FAIR.
LET'S GO!
GO GET 'EM, GIRLS!

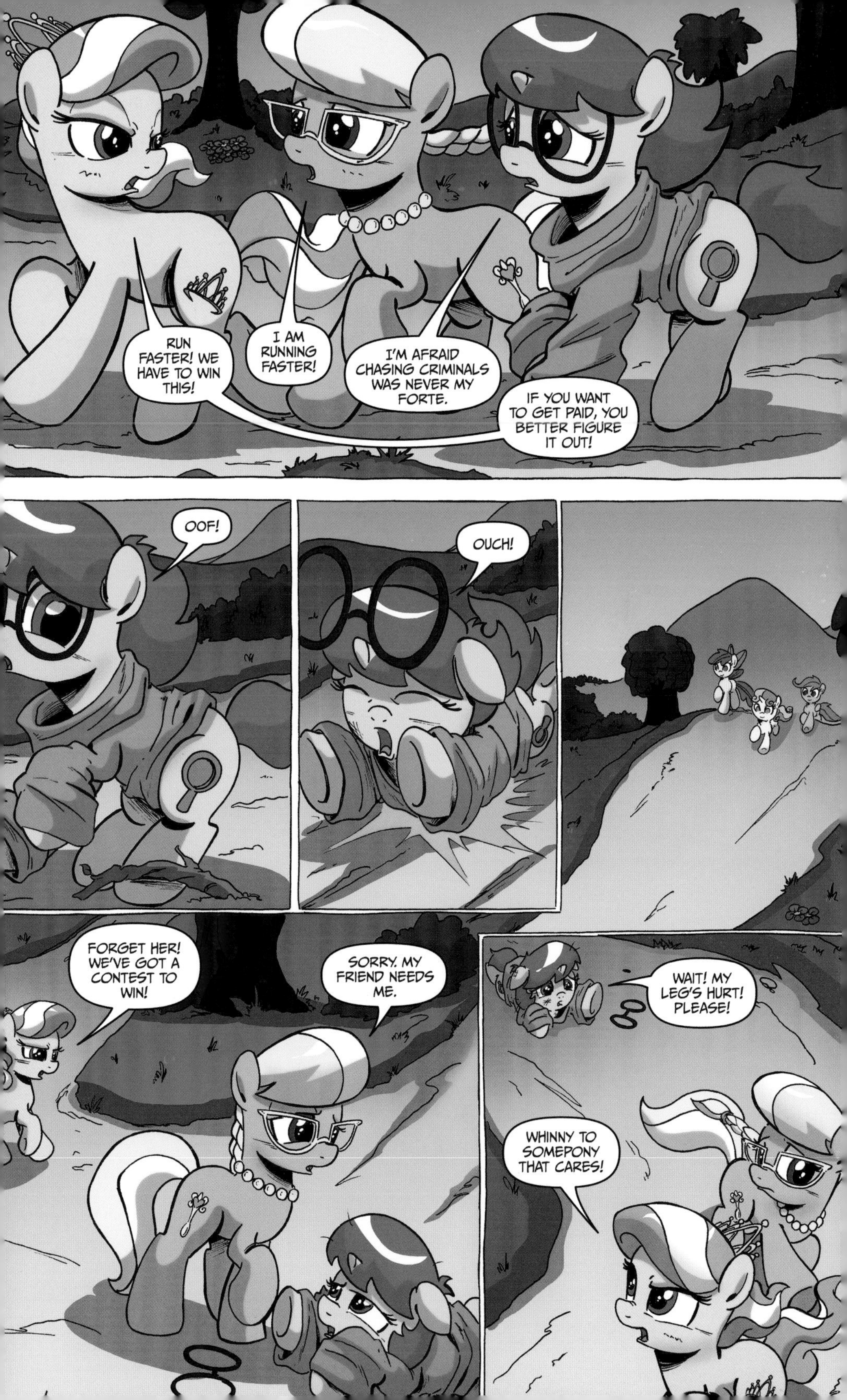
RUN FASTER! WE HAVE TO WIN THIS!
I AM RUNNING FASTER!
I'M AFRAID CHASING CRIMINALS WAS NEVER MY FORTE.
IF YOU WANT TO GET PAID, YOU BETTER FIGURE IT OUT!
OOF!
OUCH!
FORGET HER! WE'VE GOT A CONTEST TO WIN!
SORRY. MY FRIEND NEEDS ME.
WAIT! MY LEG'S HURT! PLEASE!
WHINNY TO SOMEPONY THAT CARES!

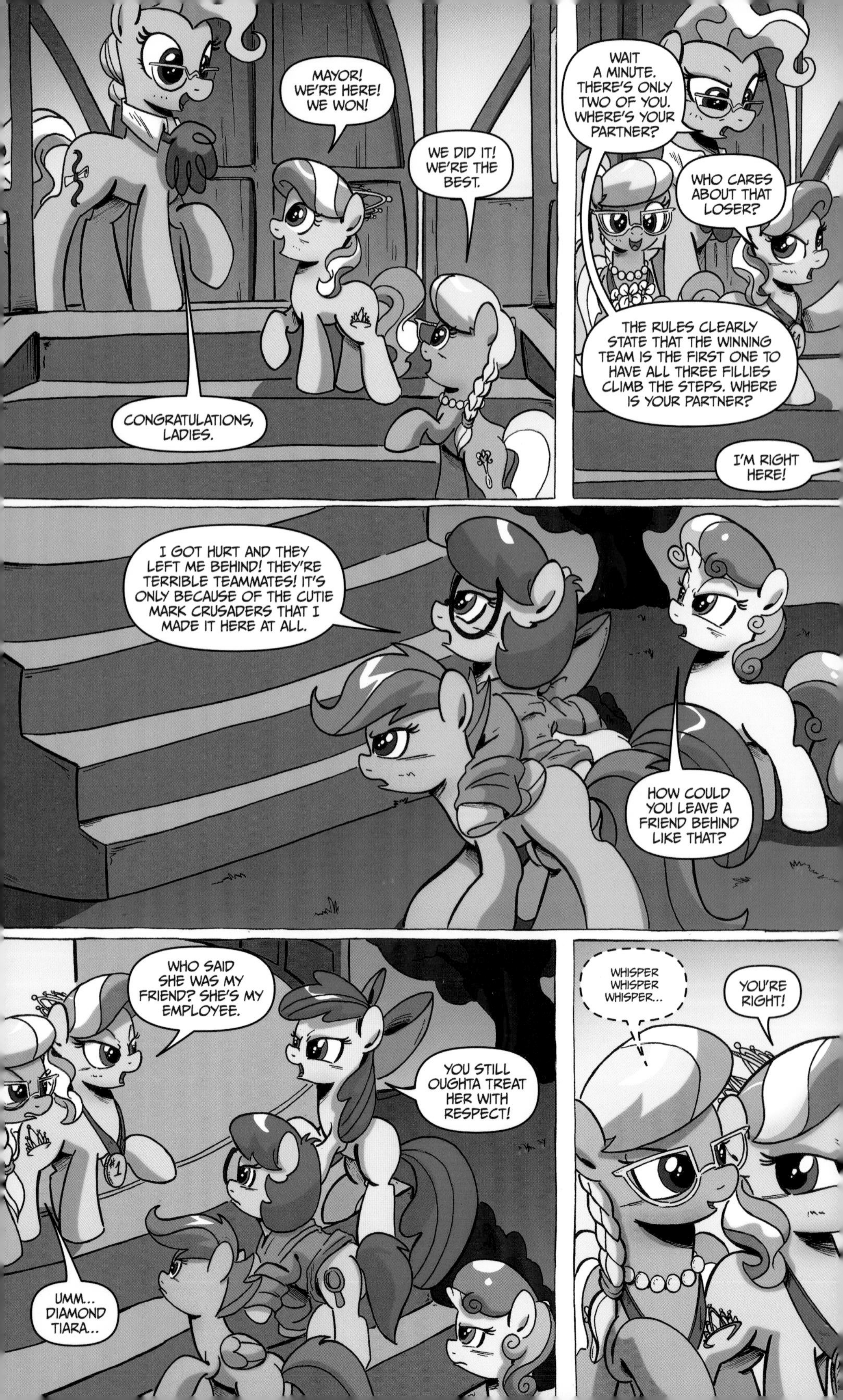
MAYOR! WE'RE HERE! WE WON!
WE DID IT! WE'RE THE BEST.
CONGRATULATIONS, LADIES.
WAIT A MINUTE. THERE'S ONLY TWO OF YOU. WHERE'S YOUR PARTNER?
WHO CARES ABOUT THAT LOSER?
THE RULES CLEARLY STATE THAT THE WINNING TEAM IS THE FIRST ONE TO HAVE ALL THREE FILLIES CLIMB THE STEPS. WHERE IS YOUR PARTNER?
I'M RIGHT HERE!
I GOT HURT AND THEY LEFT ME BEHIND! THEY'RE TERRIBLE TEAMMATES! IT'S ONLY BECAUSE OF THE CUTIE MARK CRUSADERS THAT I MADE IT HERE AT ALL.
HOW COULD YOU LEAVE A FRIEND BEHIND LIKE THAT?
WHO SAID SHE WAS MY FRIEND? SHE'S MY EMPLOYEE.
YOU STILL OUGHTA TREAT HER WITH RESPECT!
UMM... DIAMOND TIARA...
WHISPER WHISPER WHISPER...
YOU'RE RIGHT!

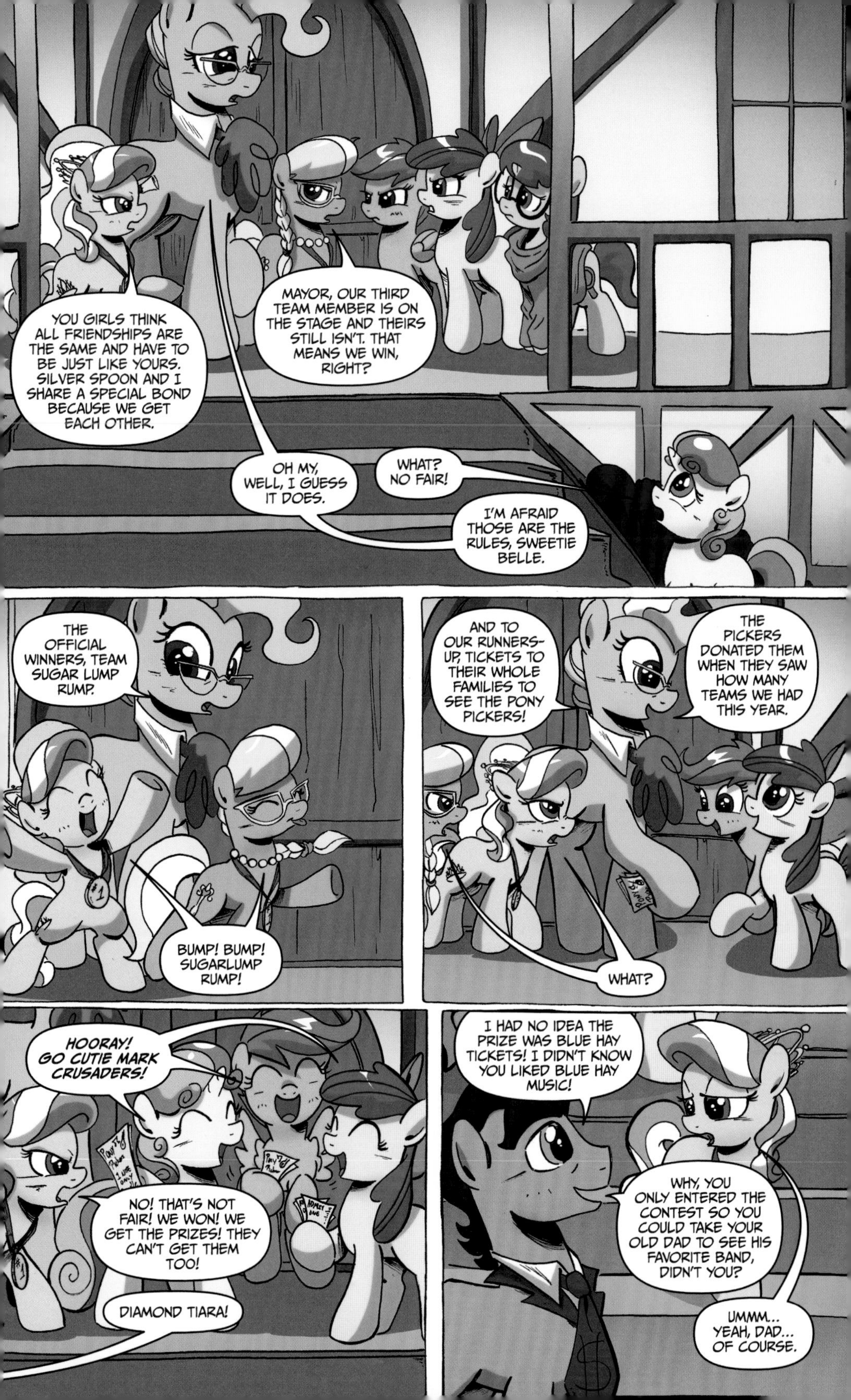
YOU GIRLS THINK ALL FRIENDSHIPS ARE THE SAME AND HAVE TO BE JUST LIKE YOURS. SILVER SPOON AND I SHARE A SPECIAL BOND BECAUSE WE GET EACH OTHER.
MAYOR, OUR THIRD TEAM MEMBER IS ON THE STAGE AND THEIRS STILL ISN'T. THAT MEANS WE WIN, RIGHT?
OH MY, WELL, I GUESS IT DOES.
WHAT? NO FAIR!
I'M AFRAID THOSE ARE THE RULES, SWEETIE BELLE.
THE OFFICIAL WINNERS, TEAM SUGAR LUMP RUMP.
BUMP! BUMP! SUGARLUMP RUMP!
AND TO OUR RUNNERS-UP, TICKETS TO THEIR WHOLE FAMILIES TO SEE THE PONY PICKERS!
THE PICKERS DONATED THEM WHEN THEY SAW HOW MANY TEAMS WE HAD THIS YEAR.
WHAT?
HOORAY! GO CUTIE MARK CRUSADERS!
NO! THAT'S NOT FAIR! WE WON! WE GET THE PRIZES! THEY CAN'T GET THEM TOO!
DIAMOND TIARA!
I HAD NO IDEA THE PRIZE WAS BLUE HAY TICKETS! I DIDN'T KNOW YOU LIKED BLUE HAY MUSIC!
WHY, YOU ONLY ENTERED THE CONTEST SO YOU COULD TAKE YOUR OLD DAD TO SEE HIS FAVORITE BAND, DIDN'T YOU?
UMMM.. YEAH, DAD... OF COURSE.

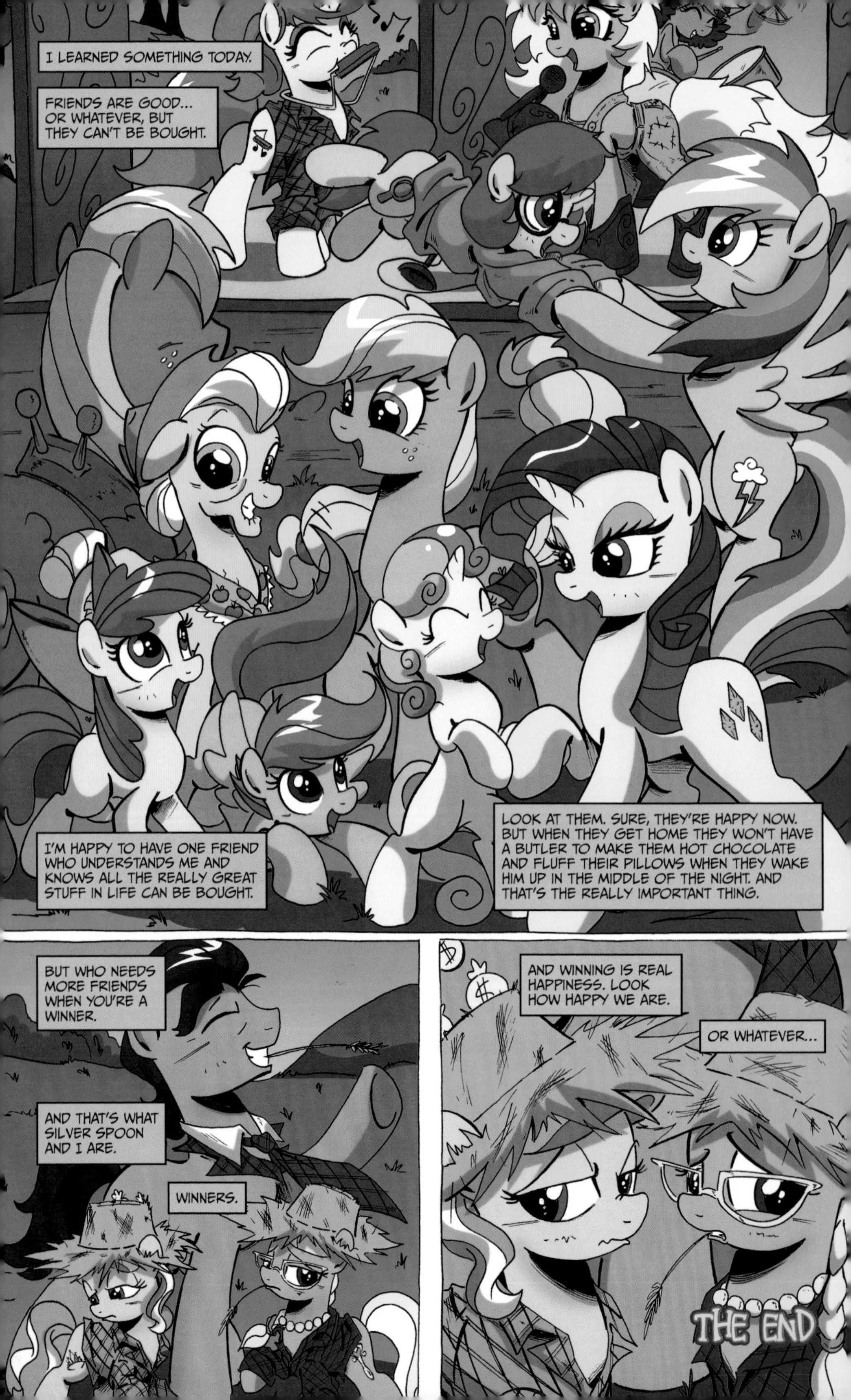
I LEARNED SOMETHING TODAY.
FRIENDS ARE GOOD... OR WHATEVER, BUT THEY CAN'T BE BOUGHT.
I'M HAPPY TO HAVE ONE FRIEND WHO UNDERSTANDS ME AND KNOWS ALL THE REALLY GREAT STUFF IN LIFE CAN BE BOUGHT.
LOOK AT THEM. SURE, THEY'RE HAPPY NOW. BUT WHEN THEY GET HOME THEY WON'T HAVE A BUTLER TO MAKE THEM HOT CHOCOLATE AND FLUFF THEIR PILLOWS WHEN THEY WAKE HIM UP IN THE MIDDLE OF THE NIGHT. AND THAT'S THE REALLY IMPORTANT THING.
BUT WHO NEEDS MORE FRIENDS WHEN YOU'RE A WINNER.
AND THAT'S WHAT SILVER SPOON AND I ARE.
WINNERS.
AND WINNING IS REAL HAPPINESS. LOOK HOW HAPPY WE ARE.
OR WHATEVER...
THE END

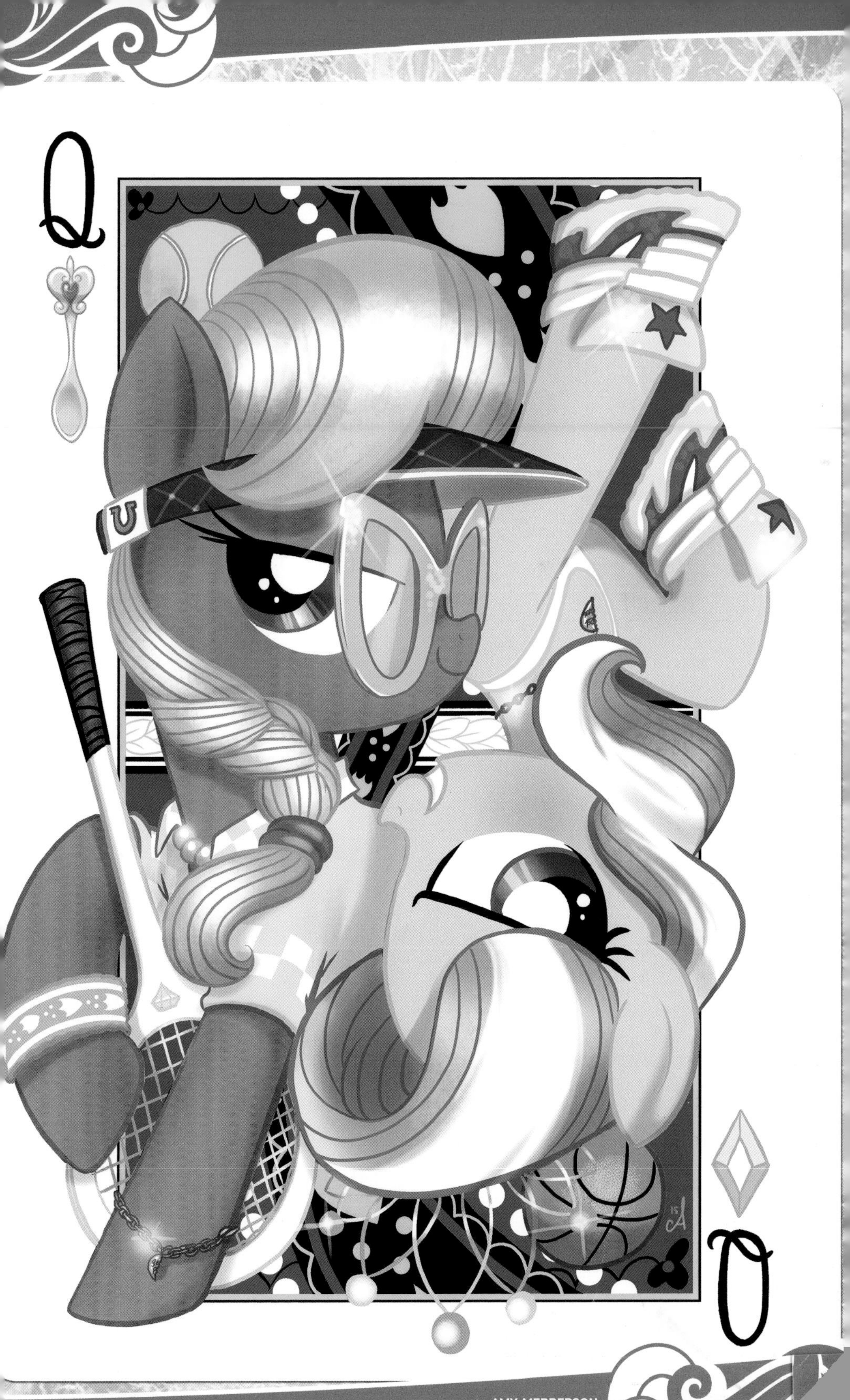
Q
Q

art by AMY MEBBERSON

Twilight Sparkle & Big Mac

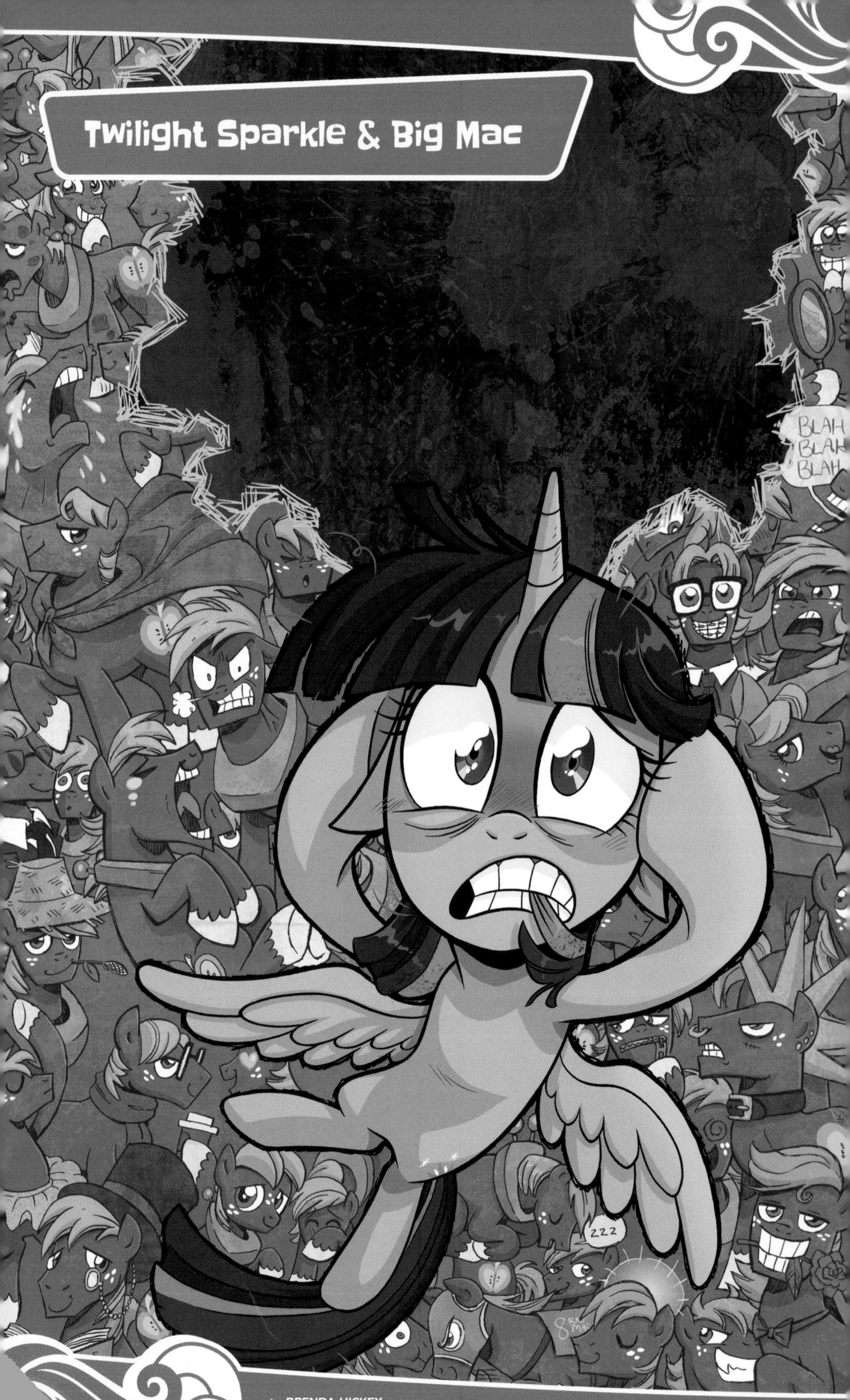
BLAH BLAH BLAH
ZZZ

art by BRENDA HICKEY

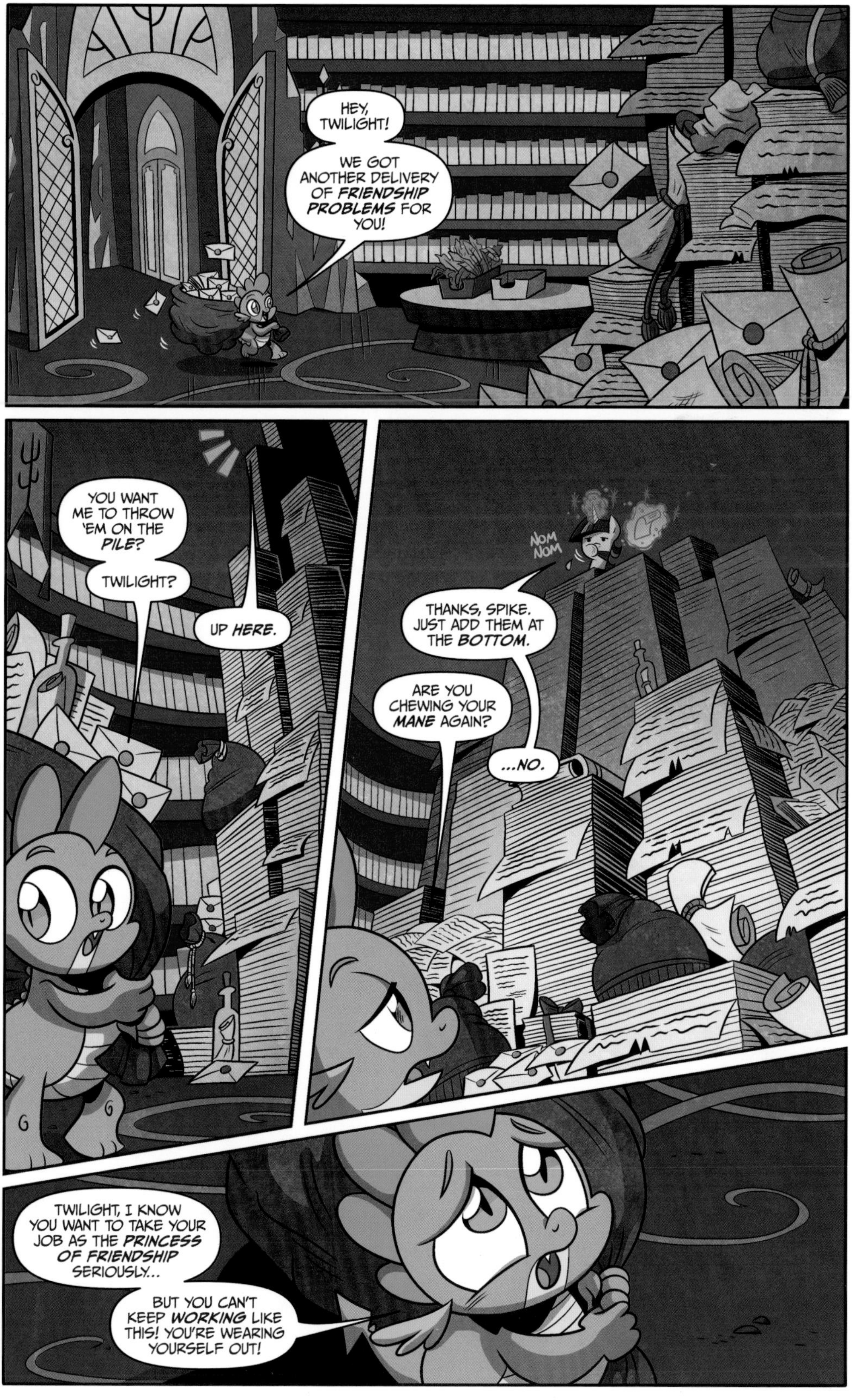
HEY, TWILIGHT!
WE GOT ANOTHER DELIVERY OF FRIENDSHIP PROBLEMS FOR YOU!
YOU WANT ME TO THROW 'EM ON THE PILE?
TWILIGHT?
UP HERE.
NOM NOM
THANKS, SPIKE. JUST ADD THEM AT THE BOTTOM.
ARE YOU CHEWING YOUR MANE AGAIN?
...NO.
TWILIGHT, I KNOW YOU WANT TO TAKE YOUR JOB AS THE PRINCESS OF FRIENDSHIP SERIOUSLY...
BUT YOU CAN'T KEEP WORKING LIKE THIS! YOU'RE WEARING YOURSELF OUT!

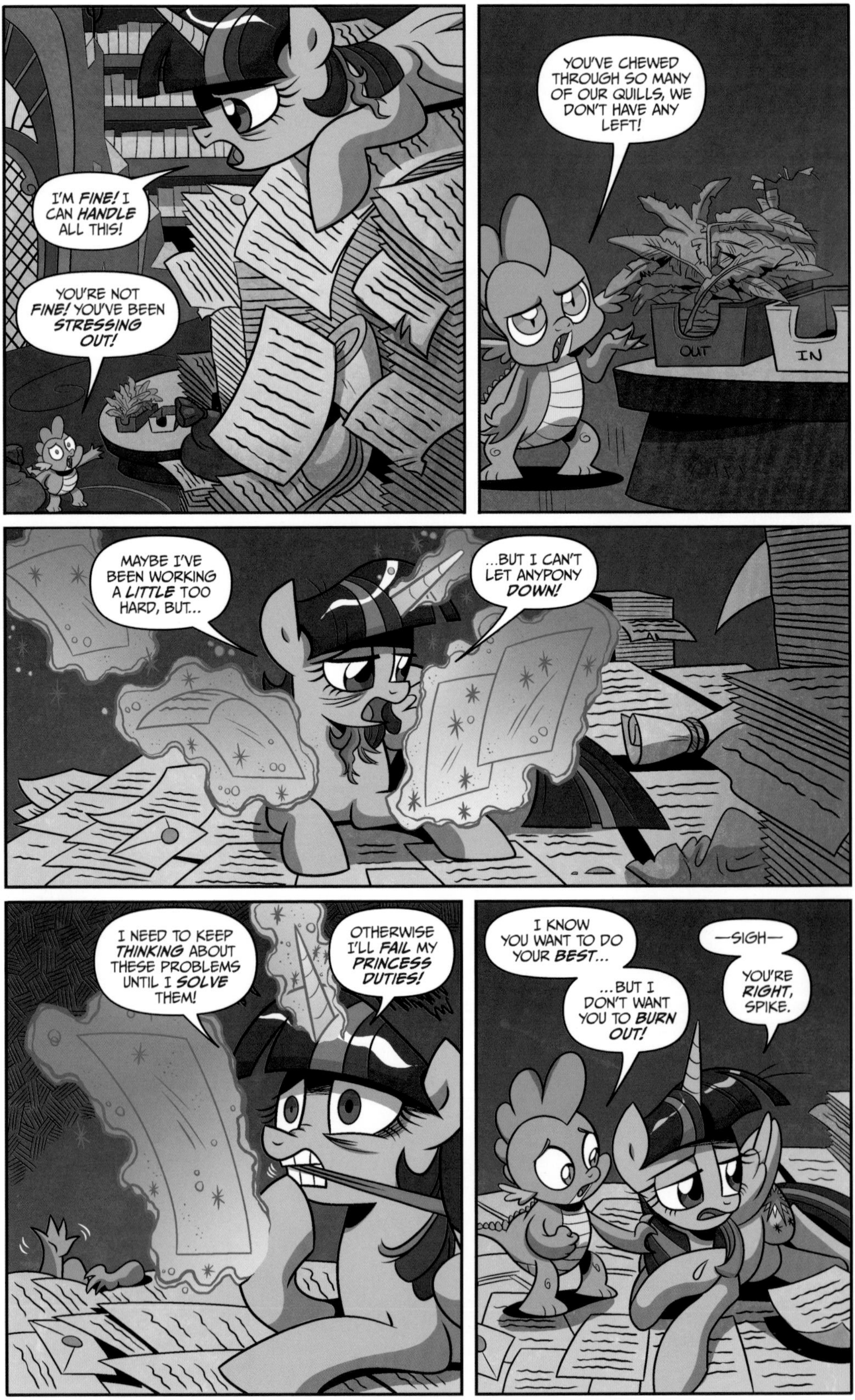
I'M FINE! I CAN HANDLE ALL THIS!
YOU'RE NOT FINE! YOU'VE BEEN STRESSING OUT!
YOU'VE CHEWED THROUGH SO MANY OF OUR QUILLS, WE DON'T HAVE ANY LEFT!
OUT
IN
MAYBE I'VE BEEN WORKING A LITTLE TOO HARD, BUT...
...BUT I CAN'T LET ANYPONY DOWN!
I NEED TO KEEP THINKING ABOUT THESE PROBLEMS UNTIL I SOLVE THEM!
OTHERWISE I'LL FAIL MY PRINCESS DUTIES!
I KNOW YOU WANT TO DO YOUR BEST...
...BUT I DON'T WANT YOU TO BURN OUT!
—SIGH—
YOU'RE RIGHT, SPIKE.

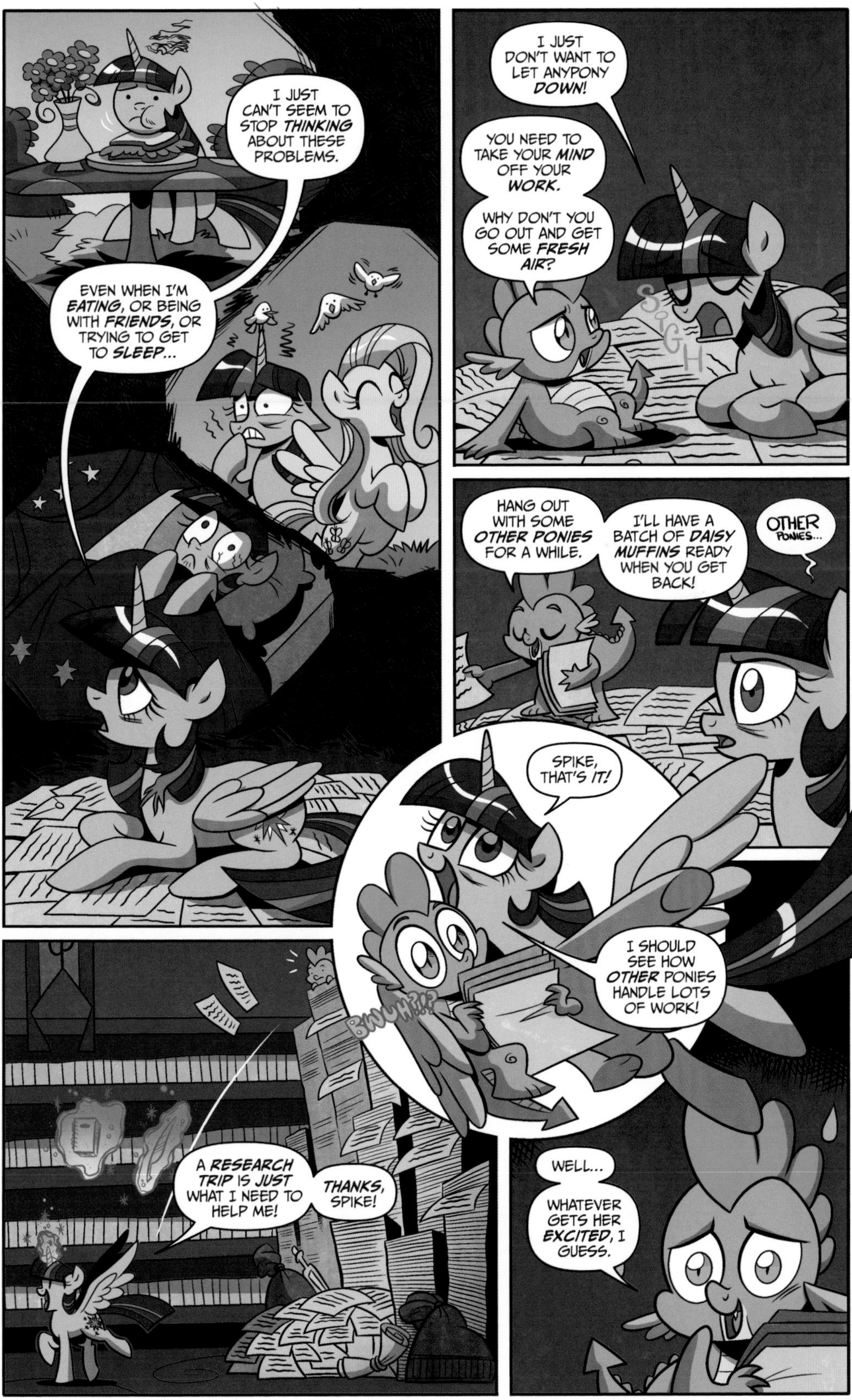
I JUST CAN'T SEEM TO STOP THINKING ABOUT THESE PROBLEMS.
EVEN WHEN I'M EATING, OR BEING WITH FRIENDS, OR TRYING TO GET TO SLEEP...
I JUST DON'T WANT TO LET ANYPONY DOWN!
YOU NEED TO TAKE YOUR MIND OFF YOUR WORK.
WHY DON'T YOU GO OUT AND GET SOME FRESH AIR?
SIGH
HANG OUT WITH SOME OTHER PONIES FOR A WHILE.
I'LL HAVE A BATCH OF DAISY MUFFINS READY WHEN YOU GET BACK!
OTHER PONIES...
SPIKE, THAT'S IT!
I SHOULD SEE HOW OTHER PONIES HANDLE LOTS OF WORK!
BWUH!?!?
A RESEARCH TRIP IS JUST WHAT I NEED TO HELP ME!
THANKS, SPIKE!
WELL...
WHATEVER GETS HER EXCITED, I GUESS.

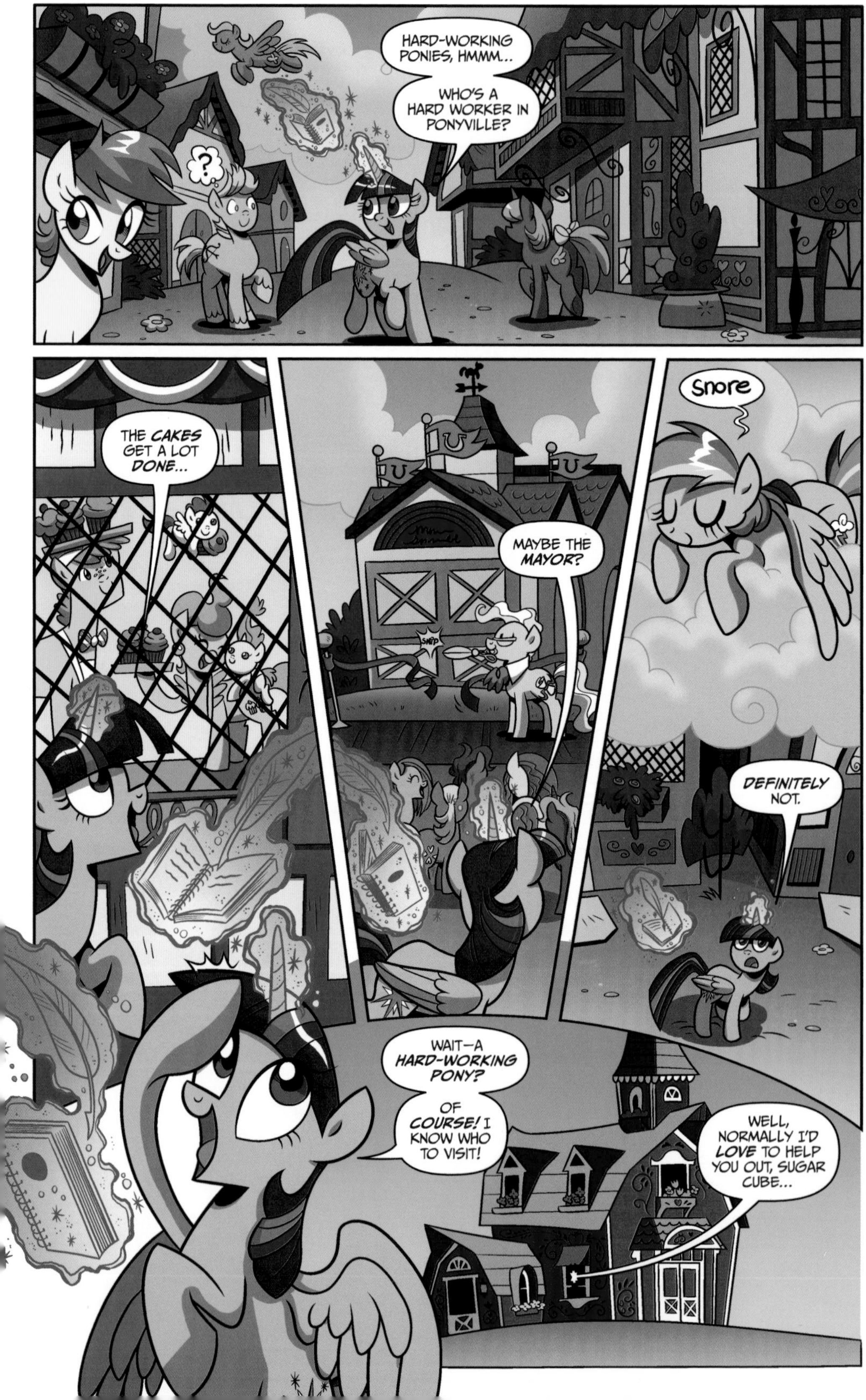
HARD-WORKING PONIES, HMMM...
WHO'S A HARD WORKER IN PONYVILLE?
?
THE CAKES GET A LOT DONE...
MAYBE THE MAYOR?
SNIP
Snore
DEFINITELY NOT.
WAIT—A HARD-WORKING PONY?
OF COURSE! I KNOW WHO TO VISIT!
WELL, NORMALLY I'D LOVE TO HELP YOU OUT, SUGAR CUBE...

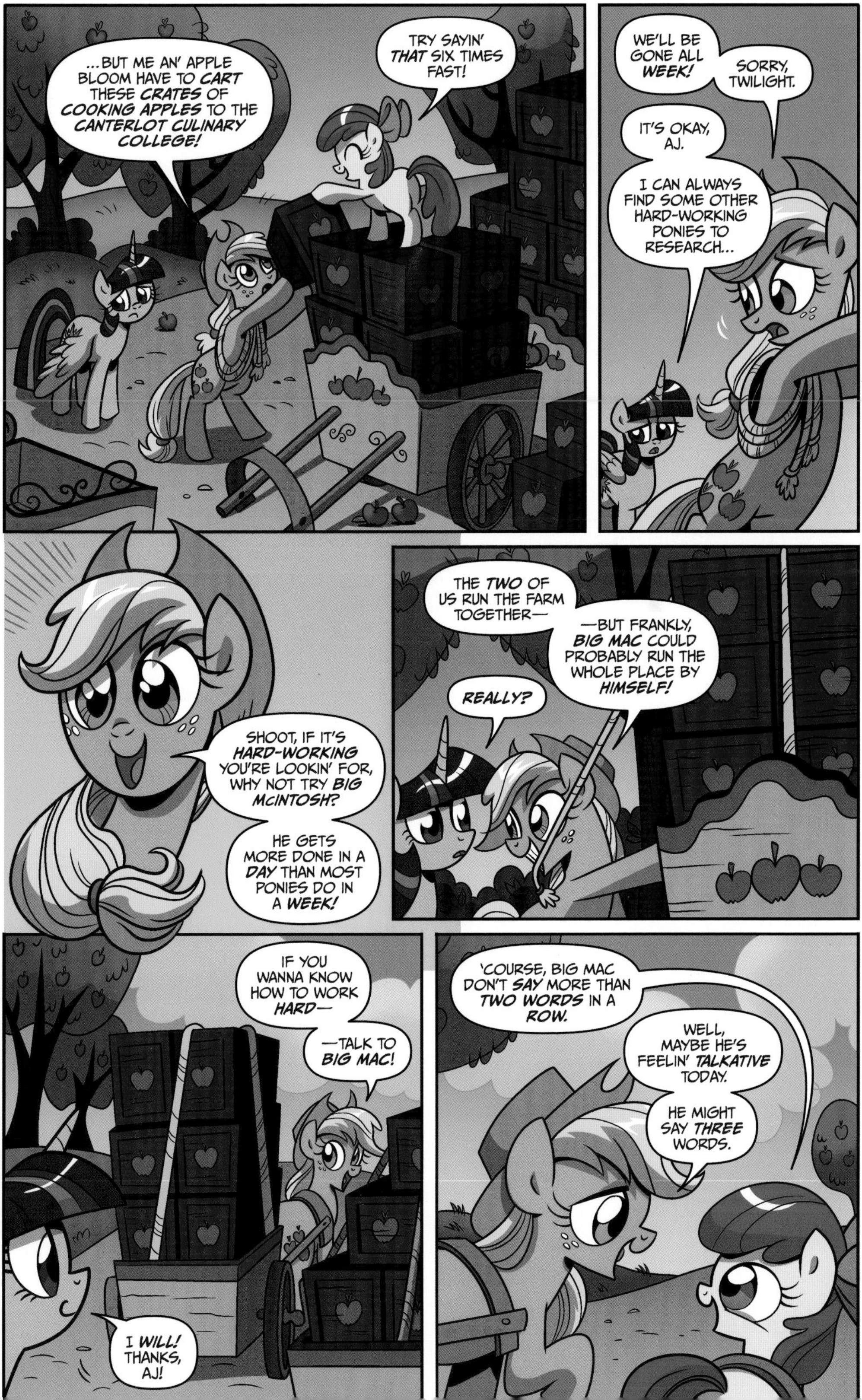
...BUT ME AN' APPLE BLOOM HAVE TO CART THESE CRATES OF COOKING APPLES TO THE CANTERLOT CULINARY COLLEGE!
TRY SAYIN' THAT SIX TIMES FAST!
WE'LL BE GONE ALL WEEK!
SORRY, TWILIGHT.
IT'S OKAY, AJ.
I CAN ALWAYS FIND SOME OTHER HARD-WORKING PONIES TO RESEARCH...
SHOOT, IF IT'S HARD-WORKING YOU'RE LOOKIN' FOR, WHY NOT TRY BIG McINTOSH?
HE GETS MORE DONE IN A DAY THAN MOST PONIES DO IN A WEEK!
THE TWO OF US RUN THE FARM TOGETHER—
—BUT FRANKLY, BIG MAC COULD PROBABLY RUN THE WHOLE PLACE BY HIMSELF!
REALLY?
IF YOU WANNA KNOW HOW TO WORK HARD—
—TALK TO BIG MAC!
I WILL! THANKS, AJ!
'COURSE, BIG MAC DON'T SAY MORE THAN TWO WORDS IN A ROW.
WELL, MAYBE HE'S FEELIN' TALKATIVE TODAY.
HE MIGHT SAY THREE WORDS.

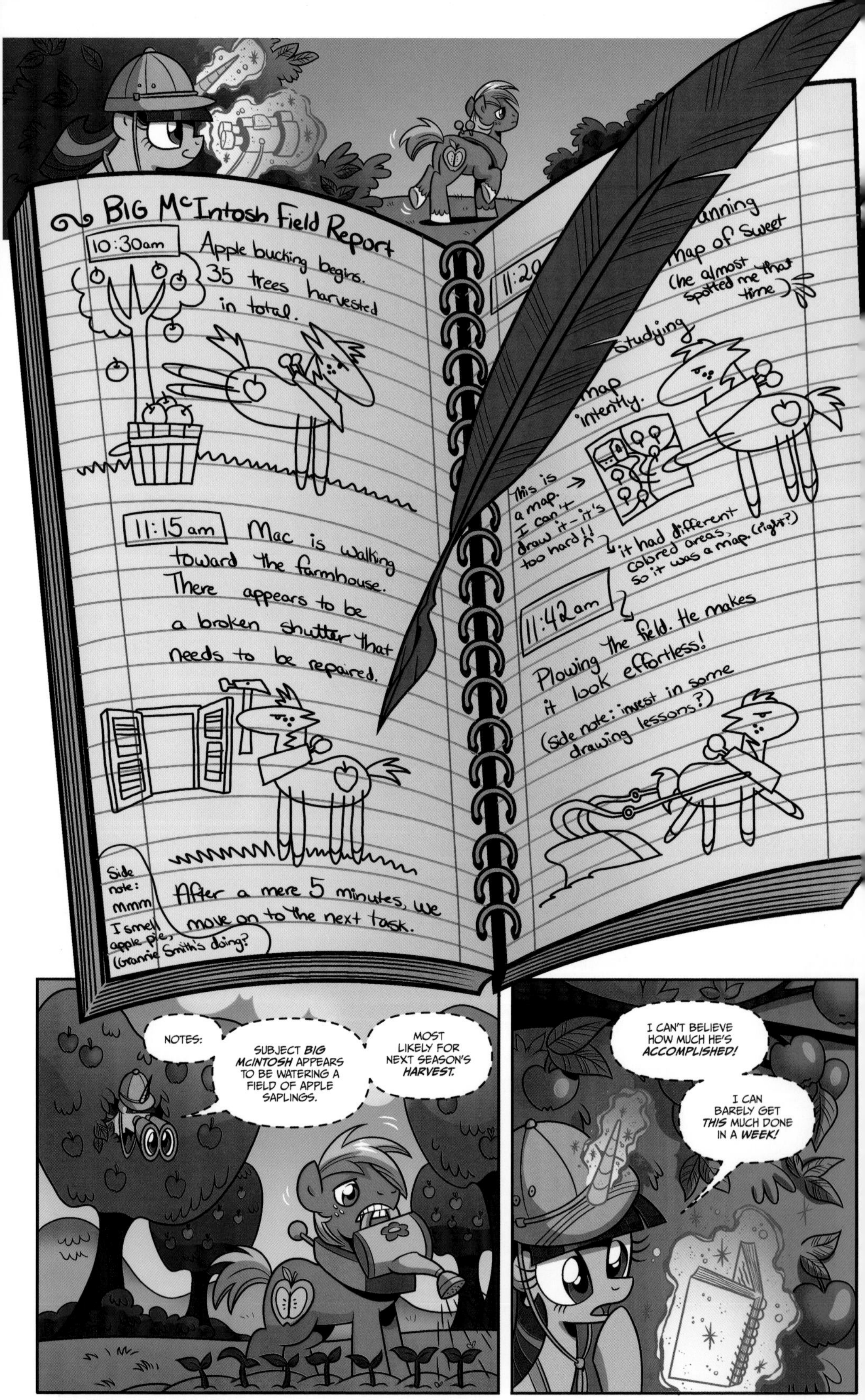
BIG McIntosh Field Report
10:30am
Apple bucking begins. 35 trees harvested in total.
11:15 am
Mac is walking toward the farmhouse. There appears to be a broken shutter that needs to be repaired.
Side note: mmm I smell apple pie, (Granny Smith's doing?
After a mere 5 minutes, we move on to the next task.
11:20
anning
map of Sweet
(he almost spotted me that time)
studying
map intently.
this is a map. I can't draw it - it's too hard!!
it had different colored areas, so it was a map. (right?)
11:42am
Plowing the field. He makes it look effortless!
(Side note: invest in some drawing lessons?)
NOTES:
SUBJECT BIG McINTOSH APPEARS TO BE WATERING A FIELD OF APPLE SAPLINGS.
MOST LIKELY FOR NEXT SEASON'S HARVEST.
I CAN'T BELIEVE HOW MUCH HE'S ACCOMPLISHED!
I CAN BARELY GET THIS MUCH DONE IN A WEEK!

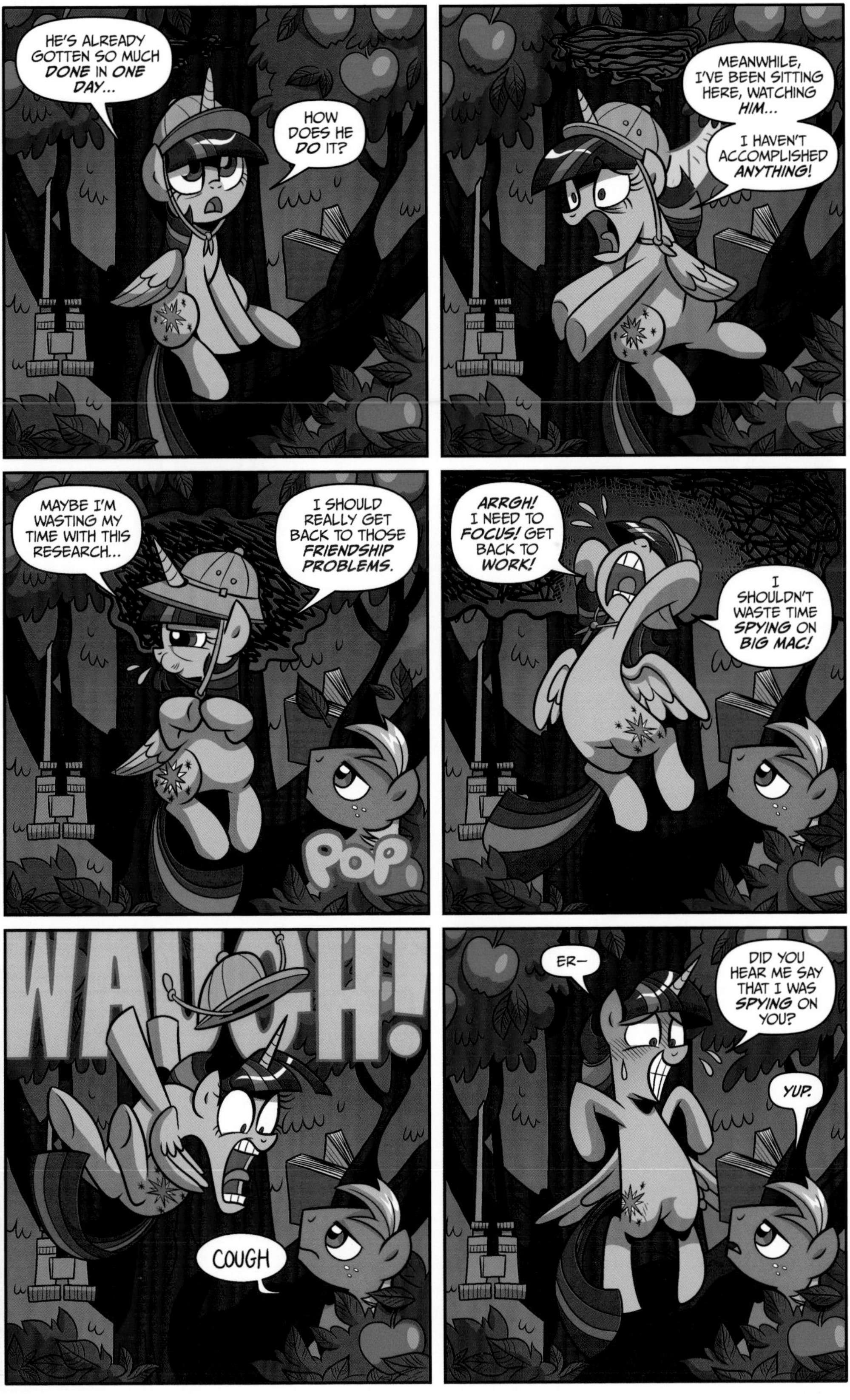
HE'S ALREADY GOTTEN SO MUCH DONE IN ONE DAY...
HOW DOES HE DO IT?
MEANWHILE, I'VE BEEN SITTING HERE, WATCHING HIM...
I HAVEN'T ACCOMPLISHED ANYTHING!
MAYBE I'M WASTING MY TIME WITH THIS RESEARCH...
I SHOULD REALLY GET BACK TO THOSE FRIENDSHIP PROBLEMS.
POP
ARRGH! I NEED TO FOCUS! GET BACK TO WORK!
I SHOULDN'T WASTE TIME SPYING ON BIG MAC!
COUGH
ER—
DID YOU HEAR ME SAY THAT I WAS SPYING ON YOU?
YUP.

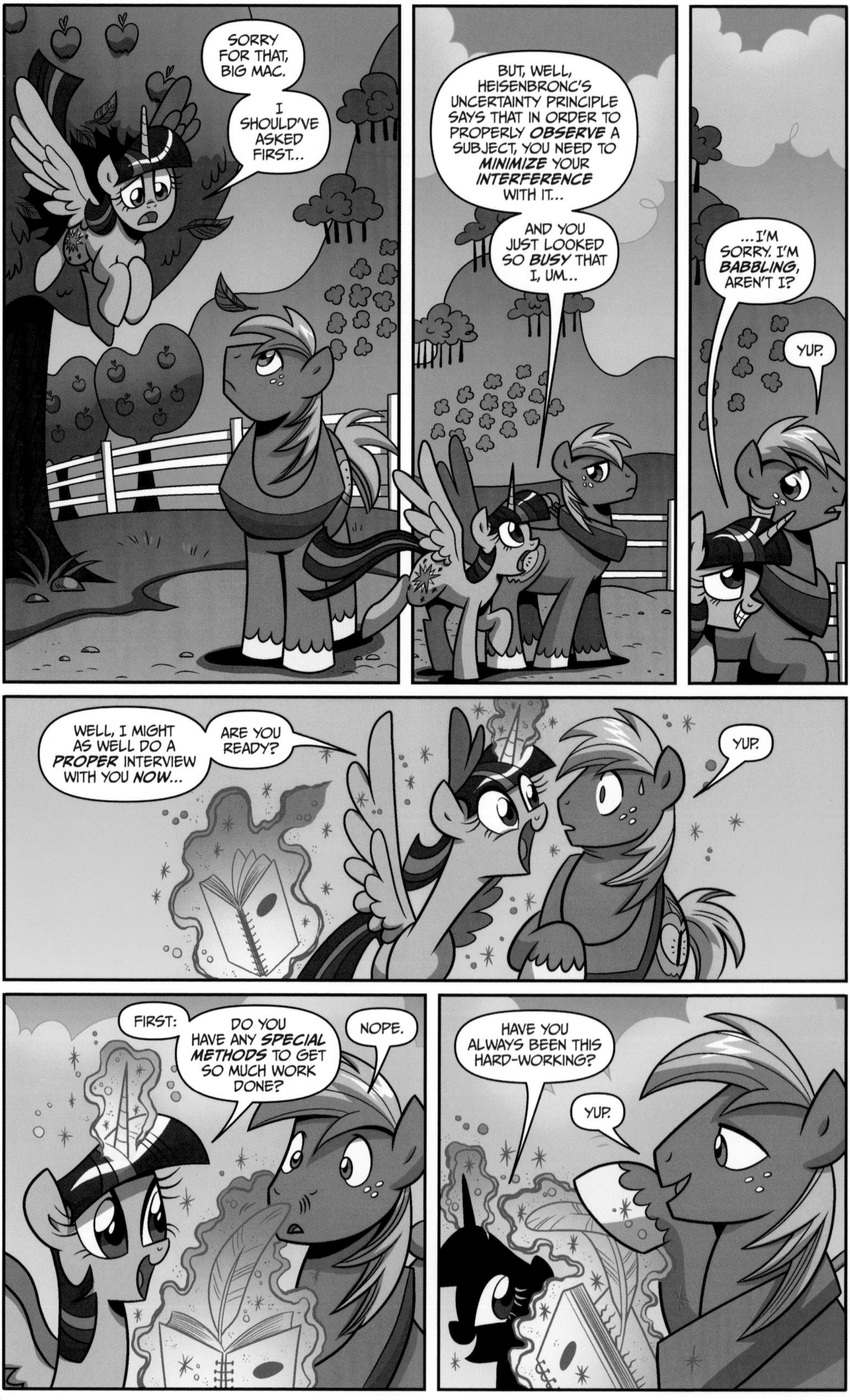
SORRY FOR THAT, BIG MAC.
I SHOULD'VE ASKED FIRST...
BUT, WELL, HEISENBRONC'S UNCERTAINTY PRINCIPLE SAYS THAT IN ORDER TO PROPERLY *OBSERVE* A SUBJECT, YOU NEED TO *MINIMIZE* YOUR *INTERFERENCE* WITH IT...
AND YOU JUST LOOKED SO *BUSY* THAT I, UM...
...I'M SORRY. I'M *BABBLING*, AREN'T I?
YUP.
WELL, I MIGHT AS WELL DO A *PROPER* INTERVIEW WITH YOU *NOW*...
ARE YOU READY?
YUP.
FIRST:
DO YOU HAVE ANY *SPECIAL METHODS* TO GET SO MUCH WORK DONE?
NOPE.
HAVE YOU ALWAYS BEEN THIS HARD-WORKING?
YUP.

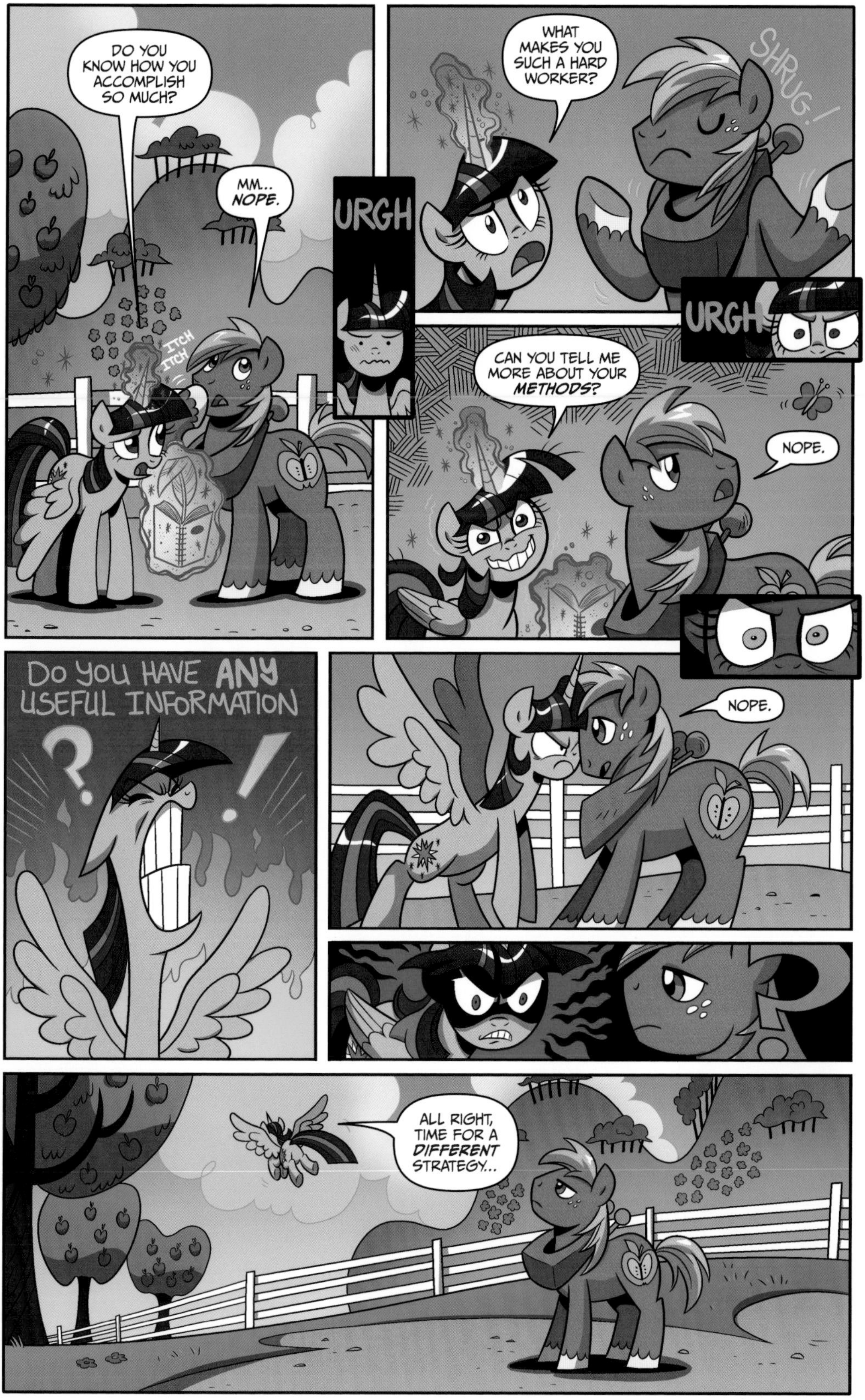
DO YOU KNOW HOW YOU ACCOMPLISH SO MUCH?
MM... NOPE.
ITCH ITCH
URGH
WHAT MAKES YOU SUCH A HARD WORKER?
SHRUG!
URGH
CAN YOU TELL ME MORE ABOUT YOUR METHODS?
NOPE.
DO YOU HAVE ANY USEFUL INFORMATION
?!
NOPE.
ALL RIGHT, TIME FOR A DIFFERENT STRATEGY...

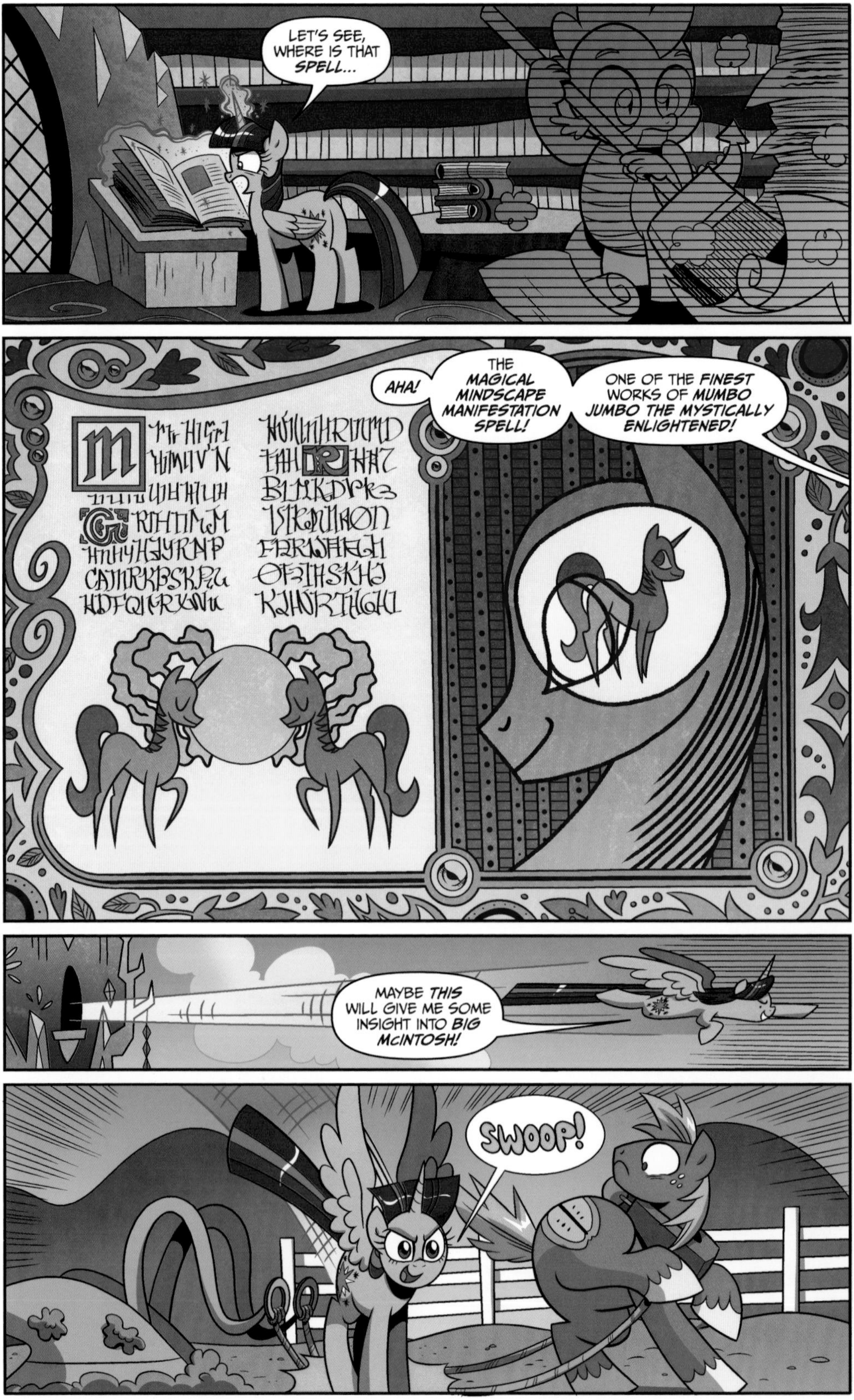
LET'S SEE, WHERE IS THAT SPELL...
AHA!
THE MAGICAL MINDSCAPE MANIFESTATION SPELL!
ONE OF THE FINEST WORKS OF MUMBO JUMBO THE MYSTICALLY ENLIGHTENED!
MAYBE THIS WILL GIVE ME SOME INSIGHT INTO BIG McINTOSH!
SWOOP!

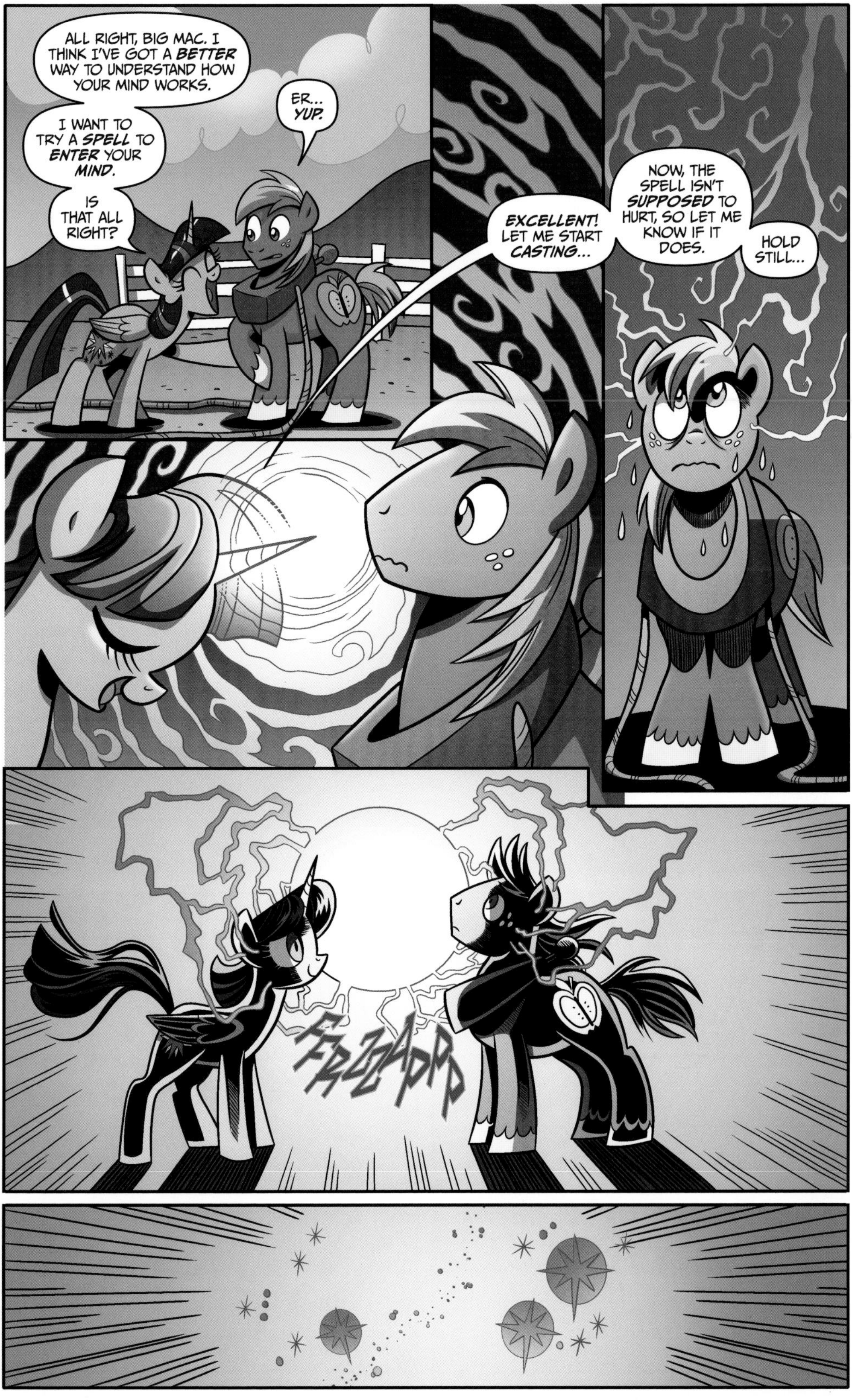
ALL RIGHT, BIG MAC. I THINK I'VE GOT A BETTER WAY TO UNDERSTAND HOW YOUR MIND WORKS.
I WANT TO TRY A SPELL TO ENTER YOUR MIND.
IS THAT ALL RIGHT?
ER... YUP.
EXCELLENT! LET ME START CASTING...
NOW, THE SPELL ISN'T SUPPOSED TO HURT, SO LET ME KNOW IF IT DOES.
HOLD STILL...
FRZZAPP

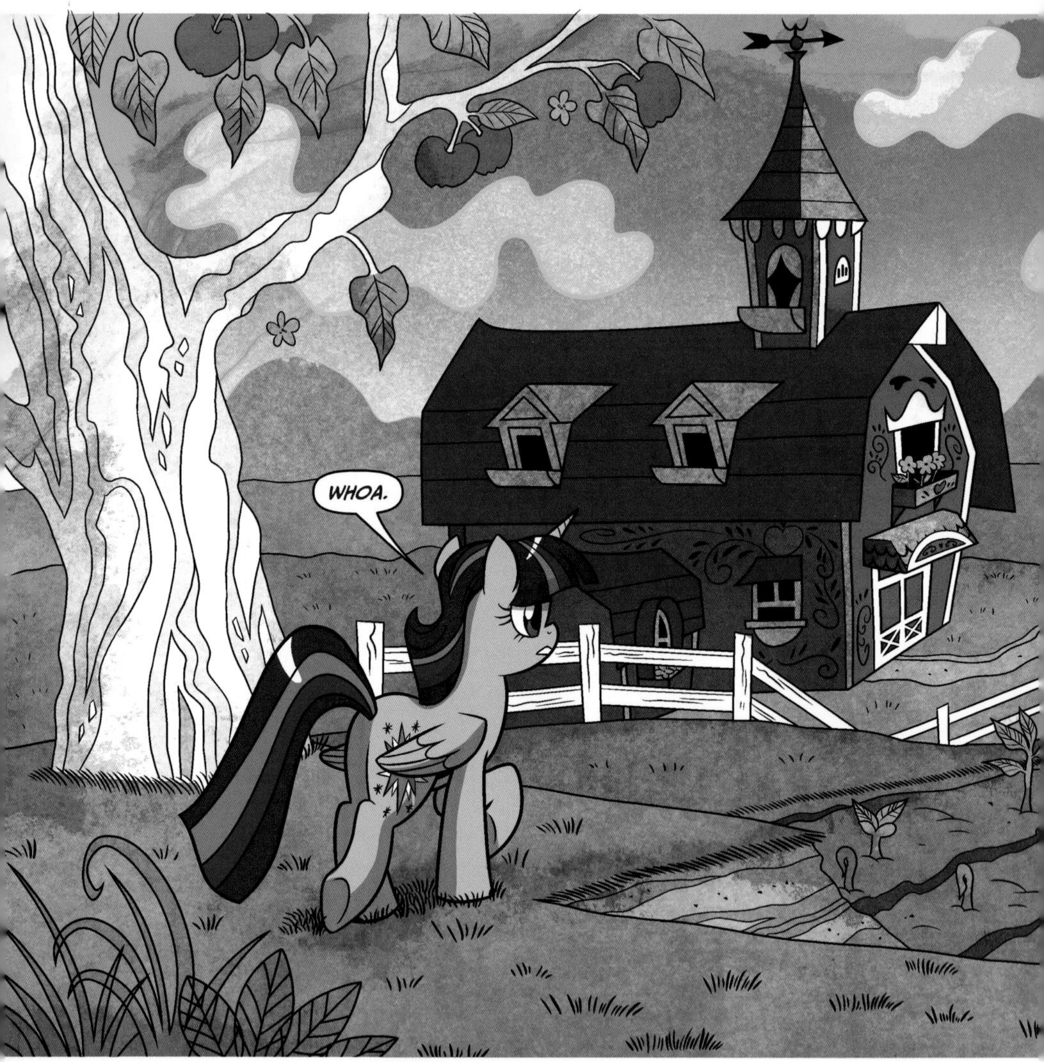
WHOA.

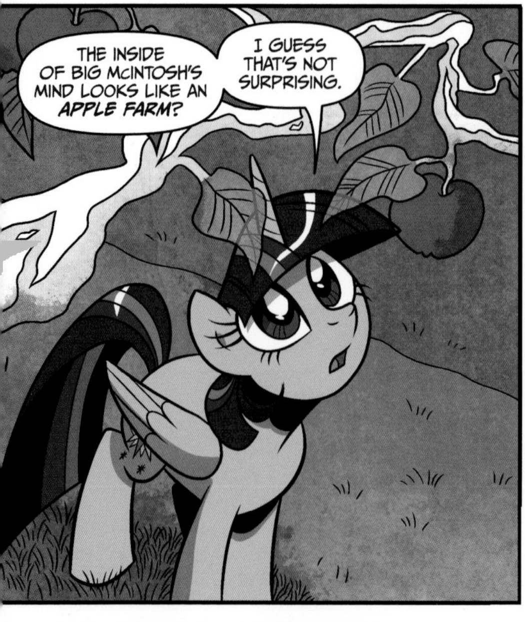
THE INSIDE OF BIG McINTOSH'S MIND LOOKS LIKE AN *APPLE FARM*?
I GUESS THAT'S NOT SURPRISING.

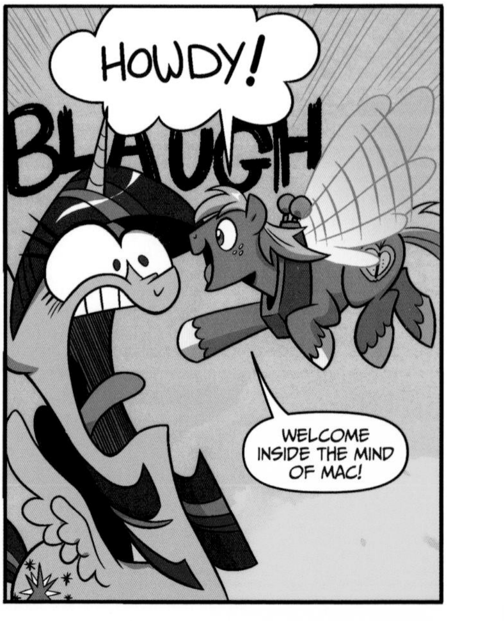
HOWDY!
BLAUGH
WELCOME INSIDE THE MIND OF MAC!

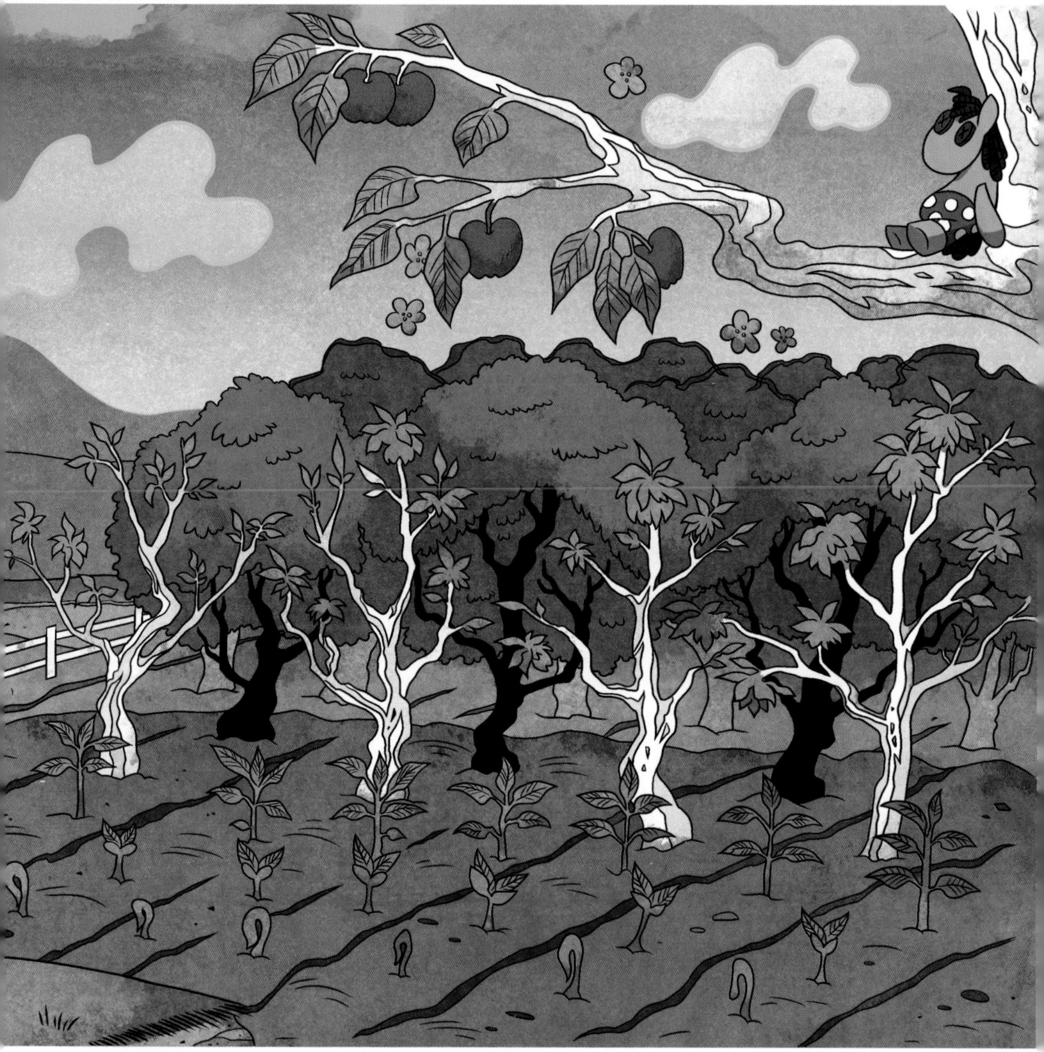

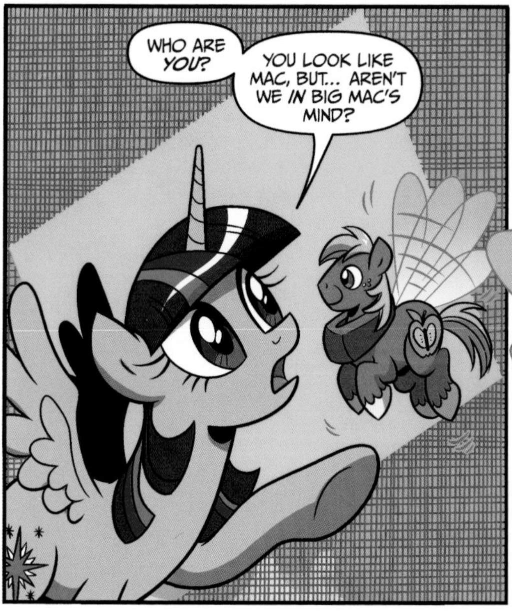
WHO ARE *YOU*?
YOU LOOK LIKE MAC, BUT... AREN'T WE *IN* BIG MAC'S MIND?

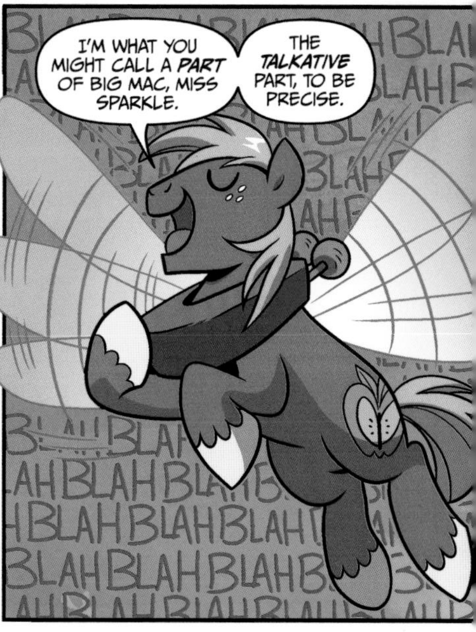
I'M WHAT YOU MIGHT CALL A *PART* OF BIG MAC, MISS SPARKLE.
THE *TALKATIVE* PART, TO BE PRECISE.

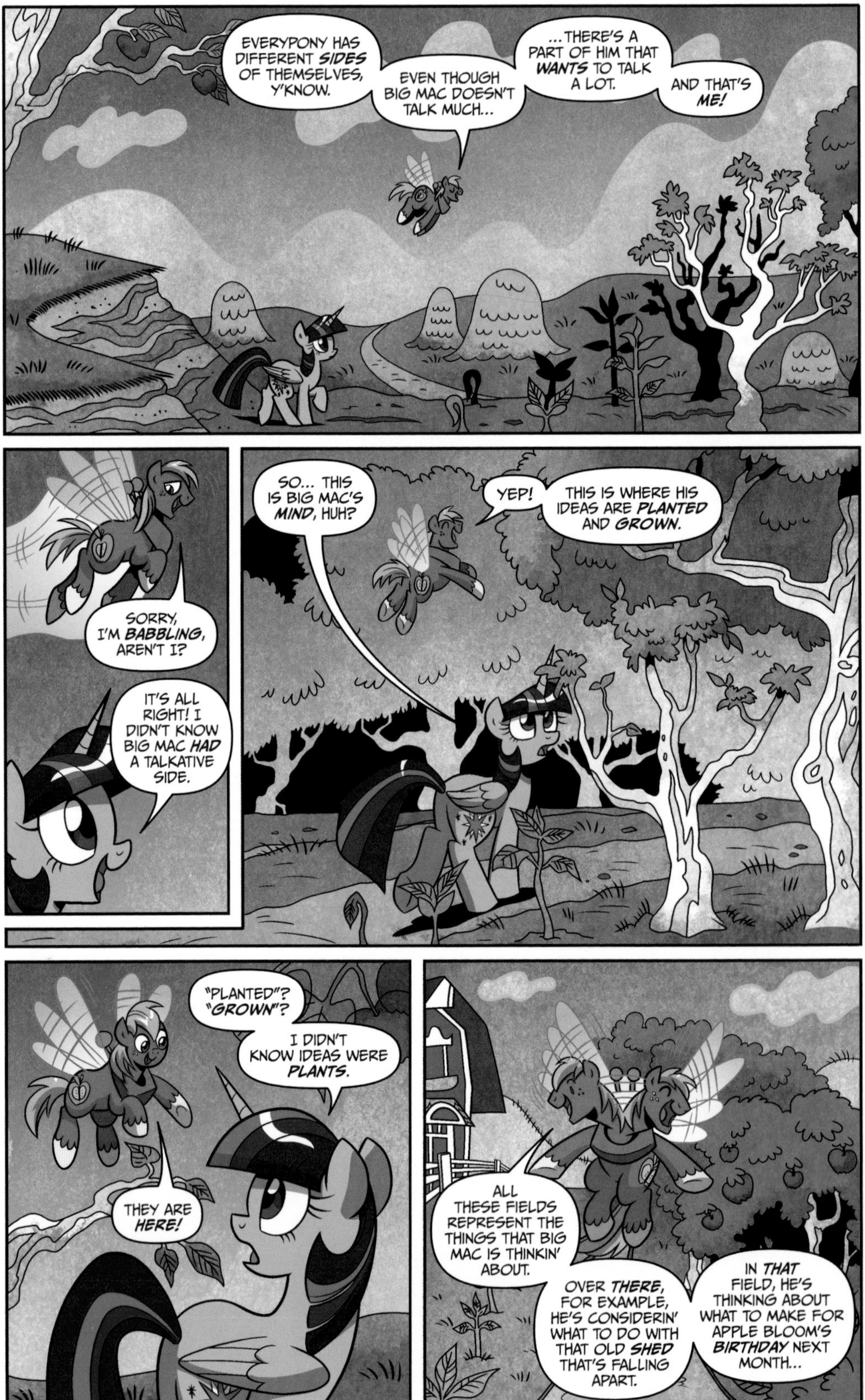
EVERYPONY HAS DIFFERENT SIDES OF THEMSELVES, Y'KNOW.
EVEN THOUGH BIG MAC DOESN'T TALK MUCH...
...THERE'S A PART OF HIM THAT WANTS TO TALK A LOT.
AND THAT'S ME!
SORRY, I'M BABBLING, AREN'T I?
IT'S ALL RIGHT! I DIDN'T KNOW BIG MAC HAD A TALKATIVE SIDE.
SO... THIS IS BIG MAC'S MIND, HUH?
YEP!
THIS IS WHERE HIS IDEAS ARE PLANTED AND GROWN.
"PLANTED"? "GROWN"?
I DIDN'T KNOW IDEAS WERE PLANTS.
THEY ARE HERE!
ALL THESE FIELDS REPRESENT THE THINGS THAT BIG MAC IS THINKIN' ABOUT.
OVER THERE, FOR EXAMPLE, HE'S CONSIDERIN' WHAT TO DO WITH THAT OLD SHED THAT'S FALLING APART.
IN THAT FIELD, HE'S THINKING ABOUT WHAT TO MAKE FOR APPLE BLOOM'S BIRTHDAY NEXT MONTH...

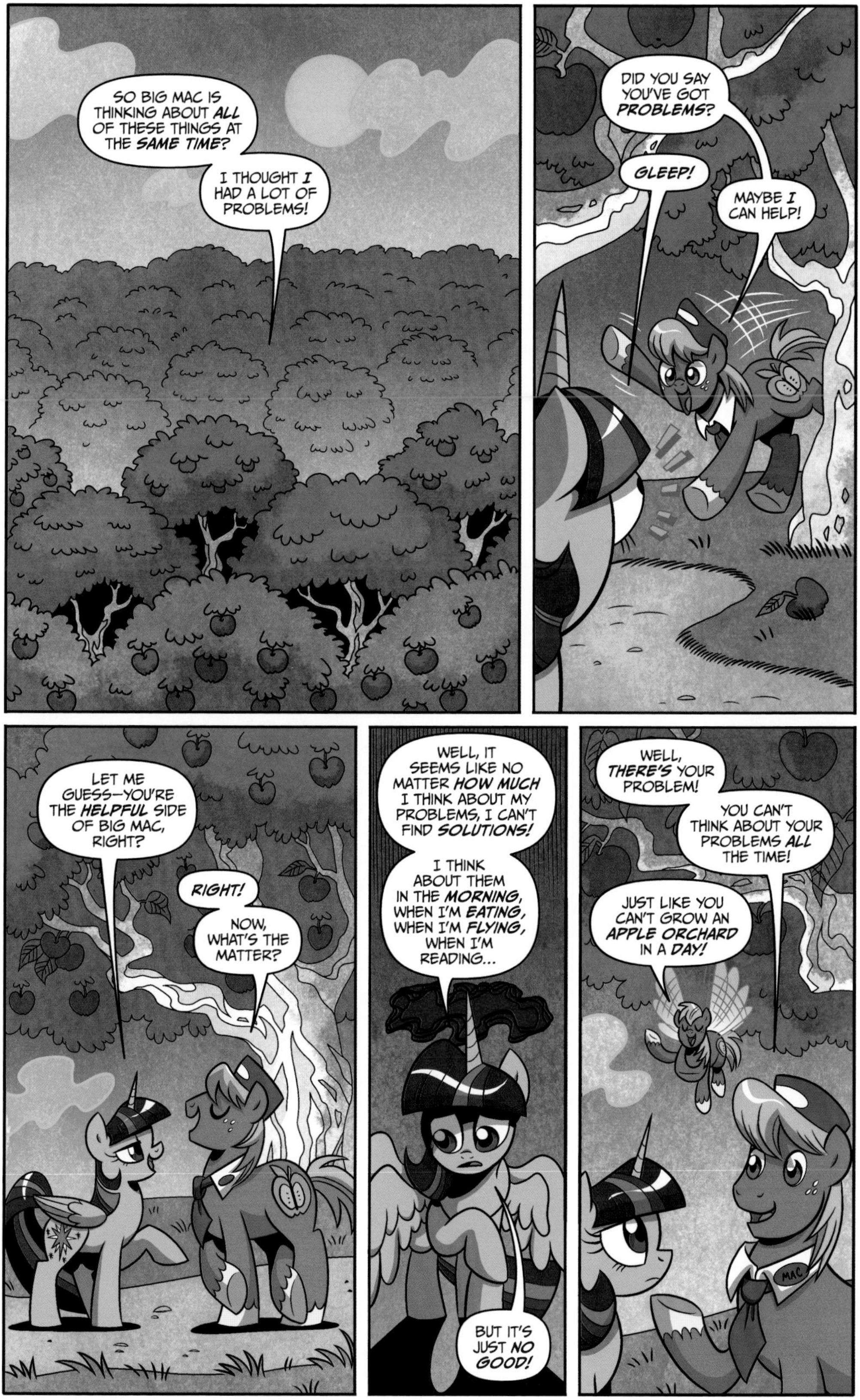
SO BIG MAC IS THINKING ABOUT ALL OF THESE THINGS AT THE SAME TIME?
I THOUGHT I HAD A LOT OF PROBLEMS!
DID YOU SAY YOU'VE GOT PROBLEMS?
GLEEP!
MAYBE I CAN HELP!
LET ME GUESS—YOU'RE THE HELPFUL SIDE OF BIG MAC, RIGHT?
RIGHT!
NOW, WHAT'S THE MATTER?
WELL, IT SEEMS LIKE NO MATTER HOW MUCH I THINK ABOUT MY PROBLEMS, I CAN'T FIND SOLUTIONS!
I THINK ABOUT THEM IN THE MORNING, WHEN I'M EATING, WHEN I'M FLYING, WHEN I'M READING...
BUT IT'S JUST NO GOOD!
WELL, THERE'S YOUR PROBLEM!
YOU CAN'T THINK ABOUT YOUR PROBLEMS ALL THE TIME!
JUST LIKE YOU CAN'T GROW AN APPLE ORCHARD IN A DAY!
MAC

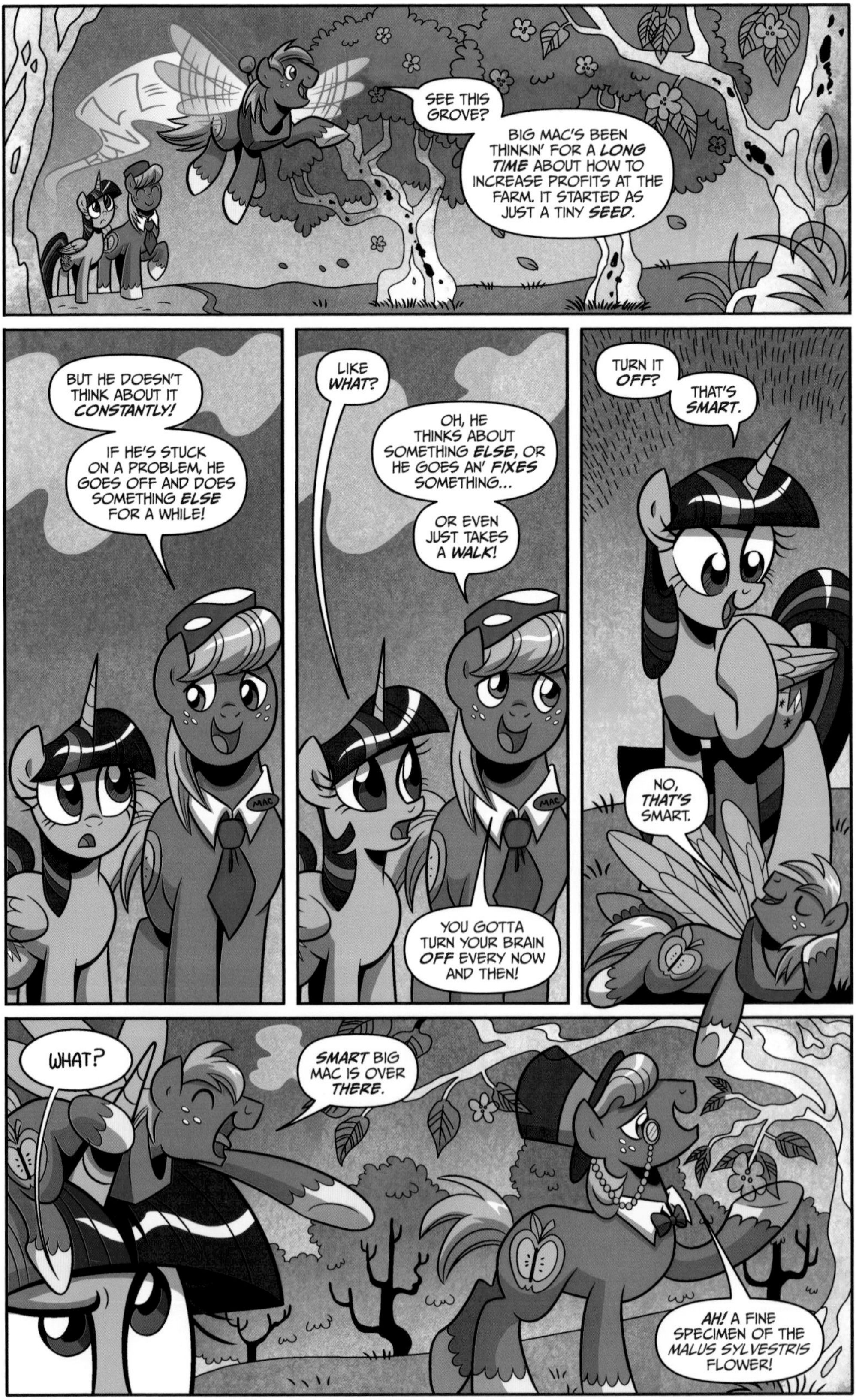
SEE THIS GROVE?
BIG MAC'S BEEN THINKIN' FOR A LONG TIME ABOUT HOW TO INCREASE PROFITS AT THE FARM. IT STARTED AS JUST A TINY SEED.
BUT HE DOESN'T THINK ABOUT IT CONSTANTLY!
IF HE'S STUCK ON A PROBLEM, HE GOES OFF AND DOES SOMETHING ELSE FOR A WHILE!
LIKE WHAT?
OH, HE THINKS ABOUT SOMETHING ELSE, OR HE GOES AN' FIXES SOMETHING...
OR EVEN JUST TAKES A WALK!
YOU GOTTA TURN YOUR BRAIN OFF EVERY NOW AND THEN!
TURN IT OFF?
THAT'S SMART.
NO, THAT'S SMART.
WHAT?
SMART BIG MAC IS OVER THERE.
AH! A FINE SPECIMEN OF THE MALUS SYLVESTRIS FLOWER!
MAC
MAC

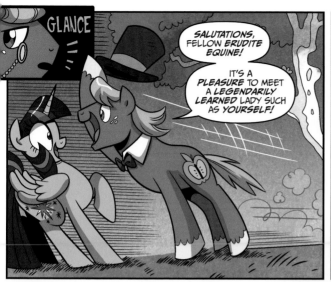

GLANCE

SALUTATIONS, FELLOW *ERUDITE* EQUINE!

IT'S A *PLEASURE* TO MEET A *LEGENDARILY LEARNED* LADY SUCH AS *YOURSELF!*

YOUR *BULBOUS BRAINPAN* IS MOST *BEWITCHING!*

WELL, LET'S SEE...

SO THIS IS BIG MAC'S *SMART* SIDE?

JUST HOW MANY SIDES OF BIG MAC *ARE* THERE?

THERE'S *SULLEN* BIG MAC...

OVERPROTECTIVE BIG MAC...

DON'T WANNA TALK ABOUT IT.

YOU LOOKIN' AT MY *SISTER*, MISTER?

UUURP!

RUDE BIG MAC...

CURIOUS BIG MAC...

OOH! SOMEONE *NEW* IS HERE!

IS *YOUR* HEAD THIS CROWDED, TOO?

UM—I DON'T KNOW?

I'VE NEVER BEEN *INSIDE* MY OWN HEAD.

WELL, LET'S TAKE A *LOOK!*

. . . .

wiggle wiggle

POUNCE

WHA— *HEY!*

NO GOING INSIDE MY HEAD UNLESS YOU'RE *INVITED!*

FZORP!
WHOA!
WHEE!
A-ARE WE *INSIDE* MY *OWN MIND?!*
LOOKS THAT WAY!
OOH... IT'S LIKE A GIANT *LIBRARY!*
WHY, IT *IS* A LIBRARY!
IT'S *WONDERFUL!*
YES... KINDA *CLUTTERED*, THOUGH, ISN'T IT?
YOU'VE GOT ALL THESE *FACTS* AND *IDEAS* HERE, BUT...
EH?
HOW DO YOU *FIND* ANYTHING?
HOW CAN YOU KEEP TRACK OF WHAT NEEDS *DOING?*

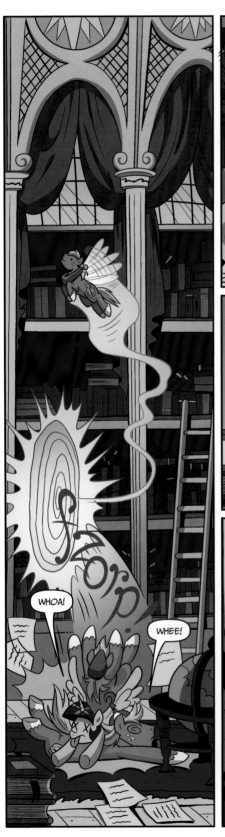

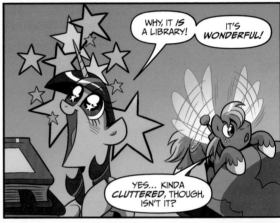

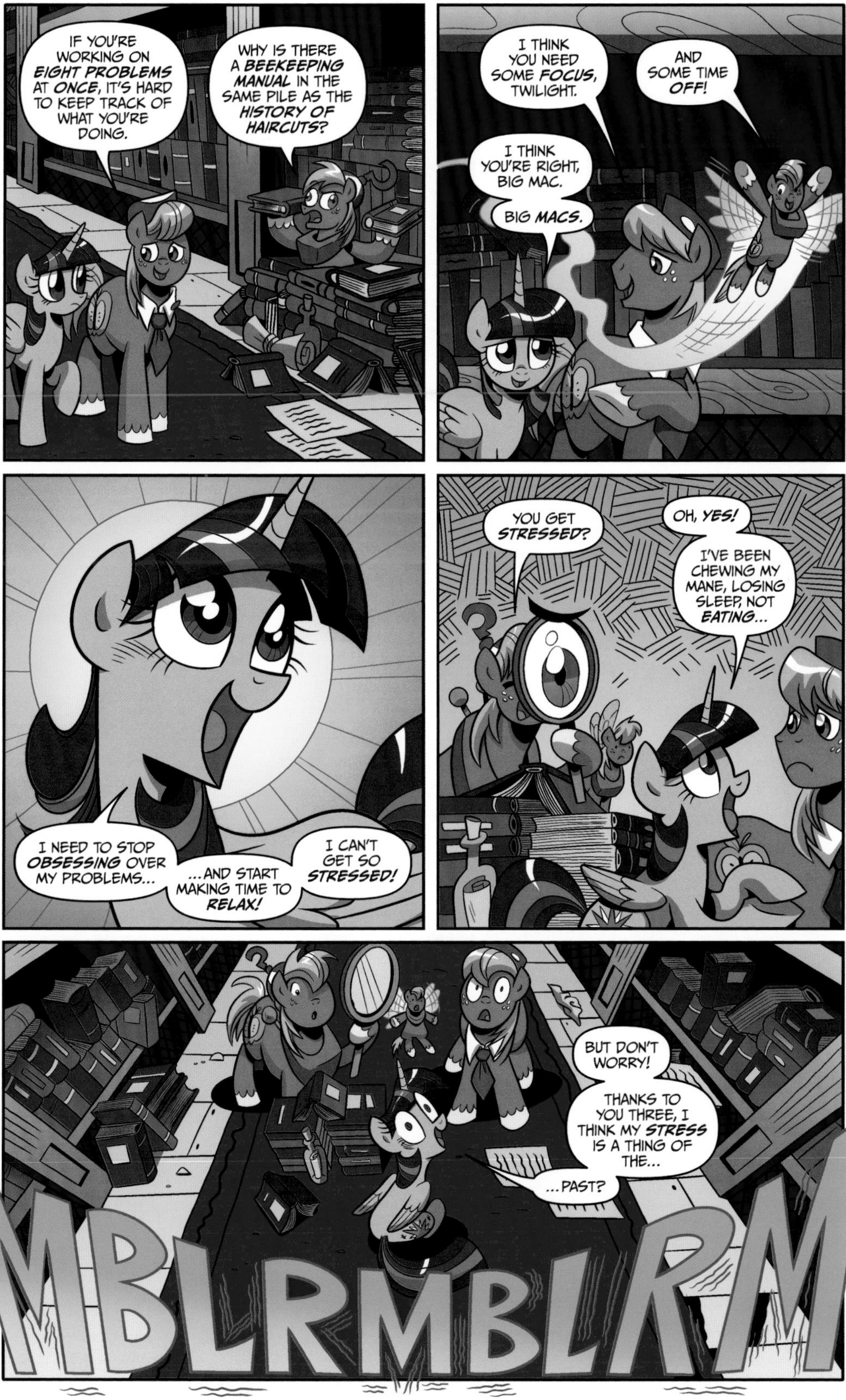
IF YOU'RE WORKING ON EIGHT PROBLEMS AT ONCE, IT'S HARD TO KEEP TRACK OF WHAT YOU'RE DOING.
WHY IS THERE A BEEKEEPING MANUAL IN THE SAME PILE AS THE HISTORY OF HAIRCUTS?
I THINK YOU NEED SOME FOCUS, TWILIGHT.
AND SOME TIME OFF!
I THINK YOU'RE RIGHT, BIG MAC.
BIG MACS.
I NEED TO STOP OBSESSING OVER MY PROBLEMS...
...AND START MAKING TIME TO RELAX!
I CAN'T GET SO STRESSED!
YOU GET STRESSED?
OH, YES!
I'VE BEEN CHEWING MY MANE, LOSING SLEEP, NOT EATING...
BUT DON'T WORRY!
THANKS TO YOU THREE, I THINK MY STRESS IS A THING OF THE...
...PAST?
MBLRMBLRM

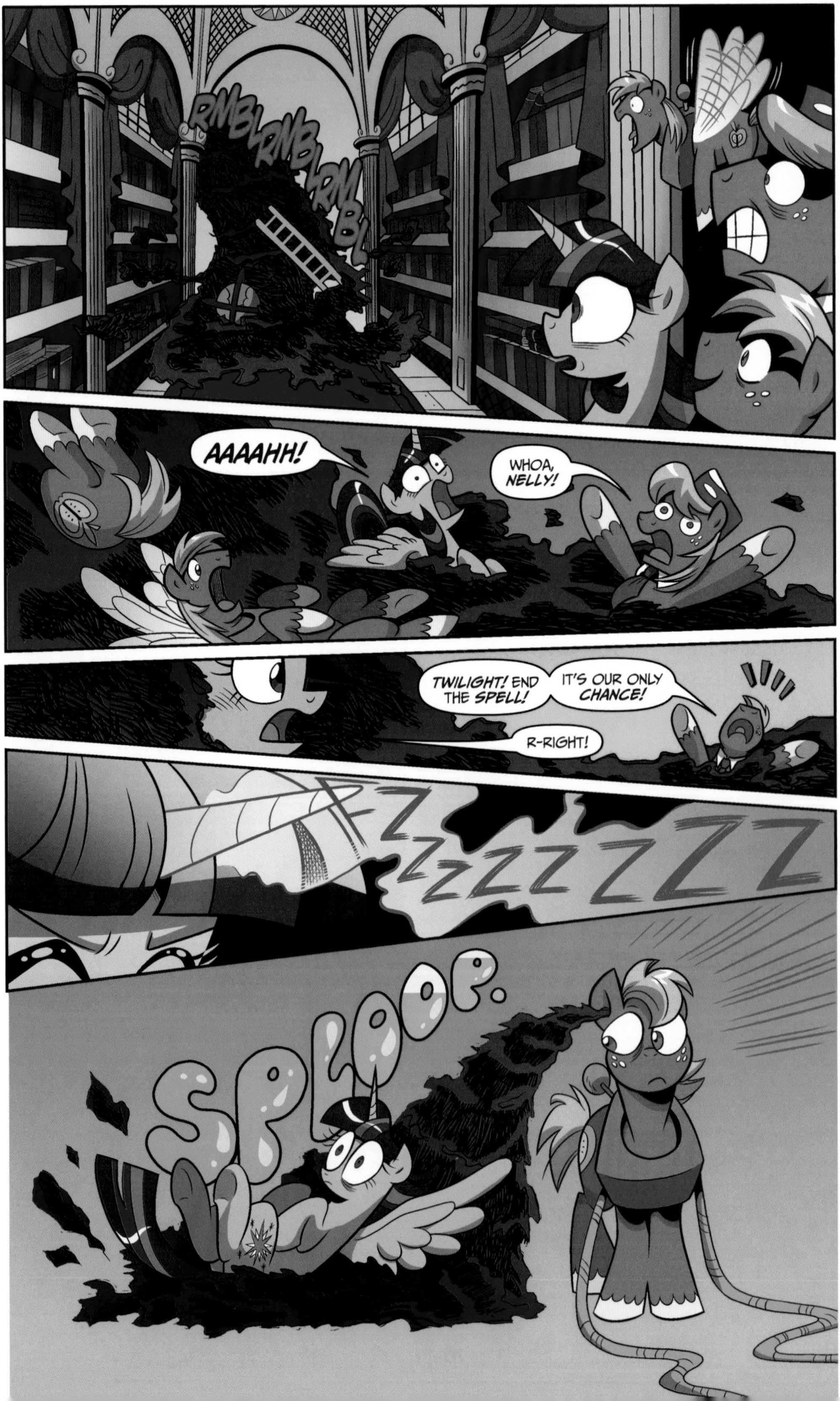
RMBLRMBLRMBL
AAAAHH!
WHOA, NELLY!
TWILIGHT! END THE SPELL!
IT'S OUR ONLY CHANCE!
R-RIGHT!
ZZZZZZZZZ
SPLOOP.

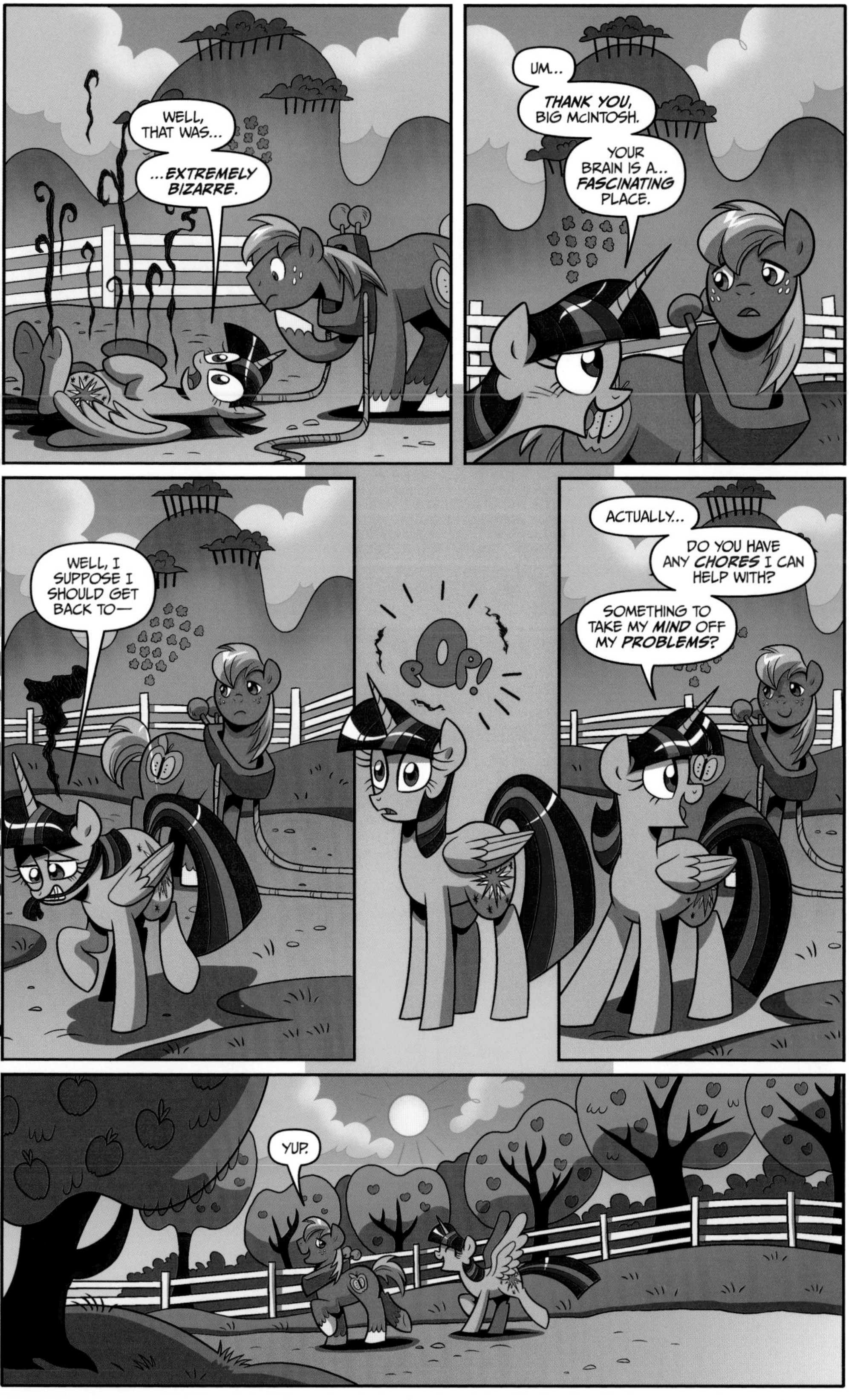
WELL, THAT WAS...
...EXTREMELY BIZARRE.
UM...
THANK YOU, BIG McINTOSH.
YOUR BRAIN IS A... FASCINATING PLACE.
WELL, I SUPPOSE I SHOULD GET BACK TO—
POP!
ACTUALLY...
DO YOU HAVE ANY CHORES I CAN HELP WITH?
SOMETHING TO TAKE MY MIND OFF MY PROBLEMS?
YUP.

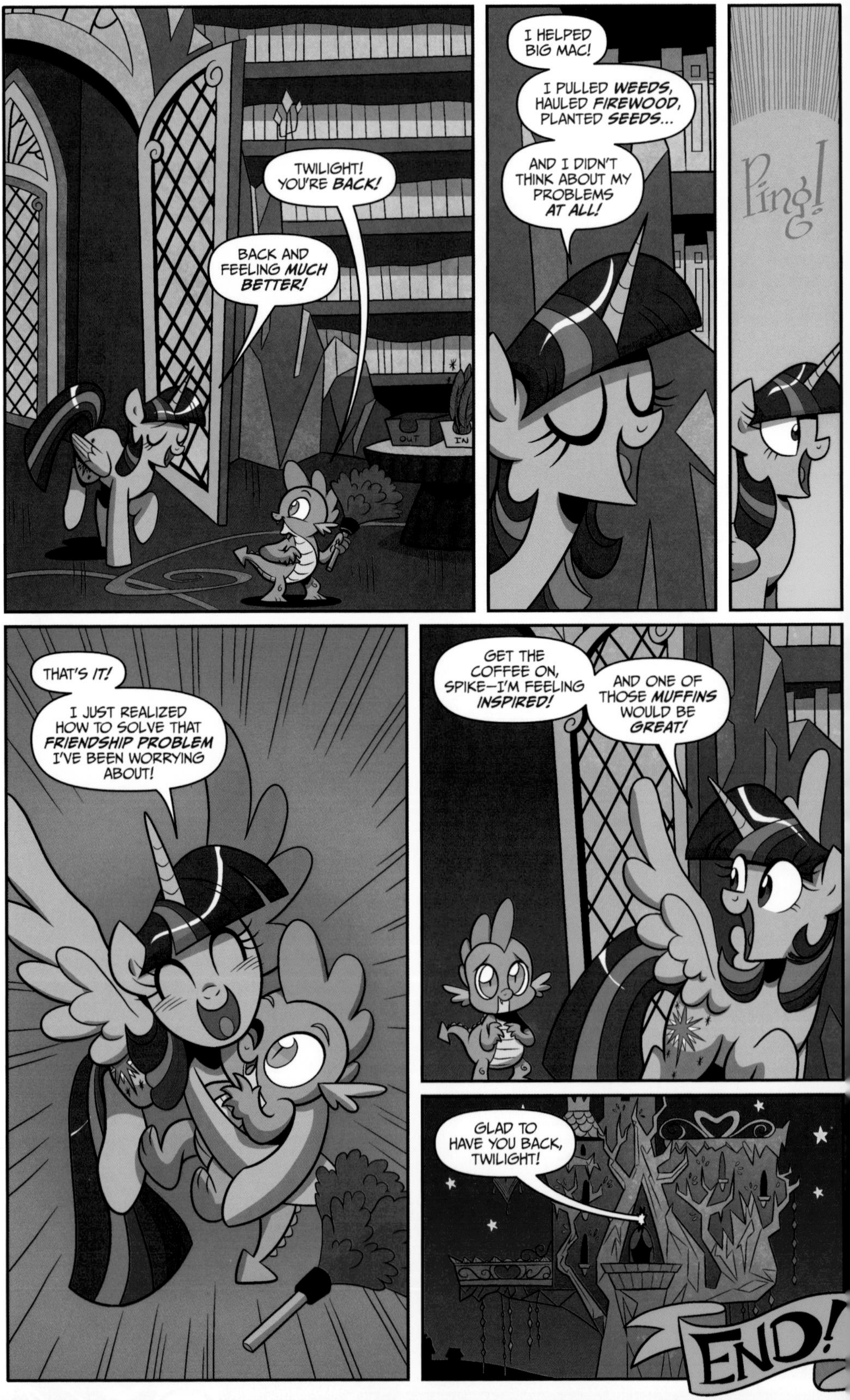
TWILIGHT! YOU'RE BACK!
BACK AND FEELING MUCH BETTER!
I HELPED BIG MAC!
I PULLED WEEDS, HAULED FIREWOOD, PLANTED SEEDS...
AND I DIDN'T THINK ABOUT MY PROBLEMS AT ALL!
OUT
IN
Ping!
THAT'S IT!
I JUST REALIZED HOW TO SOLVE THAT FRIENDSHIP PROBLEM I'VE BEEN WORRYING ABOUT!
GET THE COFFEE ON, SPIKE—I'M FEELING INSPIRED!
AND ONE OF THOSE MUFFINS WOULD BE GREAT!
GLAD TO HAVE YOU BACK, TWILIGHT!
END!

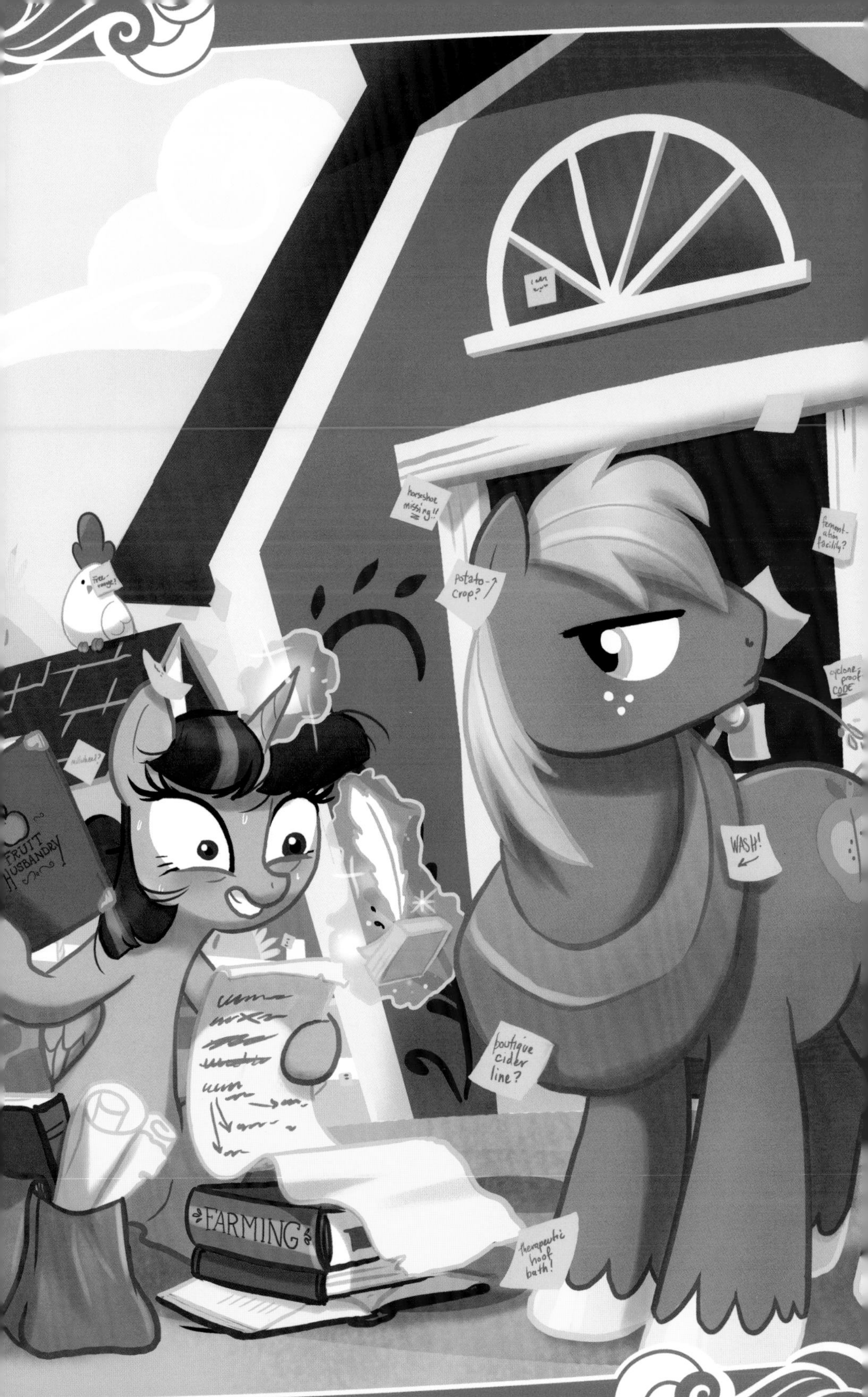
horseshoe missing!!
ferment-ation facility?
potato-crop?
cyclone proof CODE
FRUIT HUSBANDRY
WASH!
boutique cider line?
FARMING
therapeutic hoof bath!

art by AMY MEBBERSON

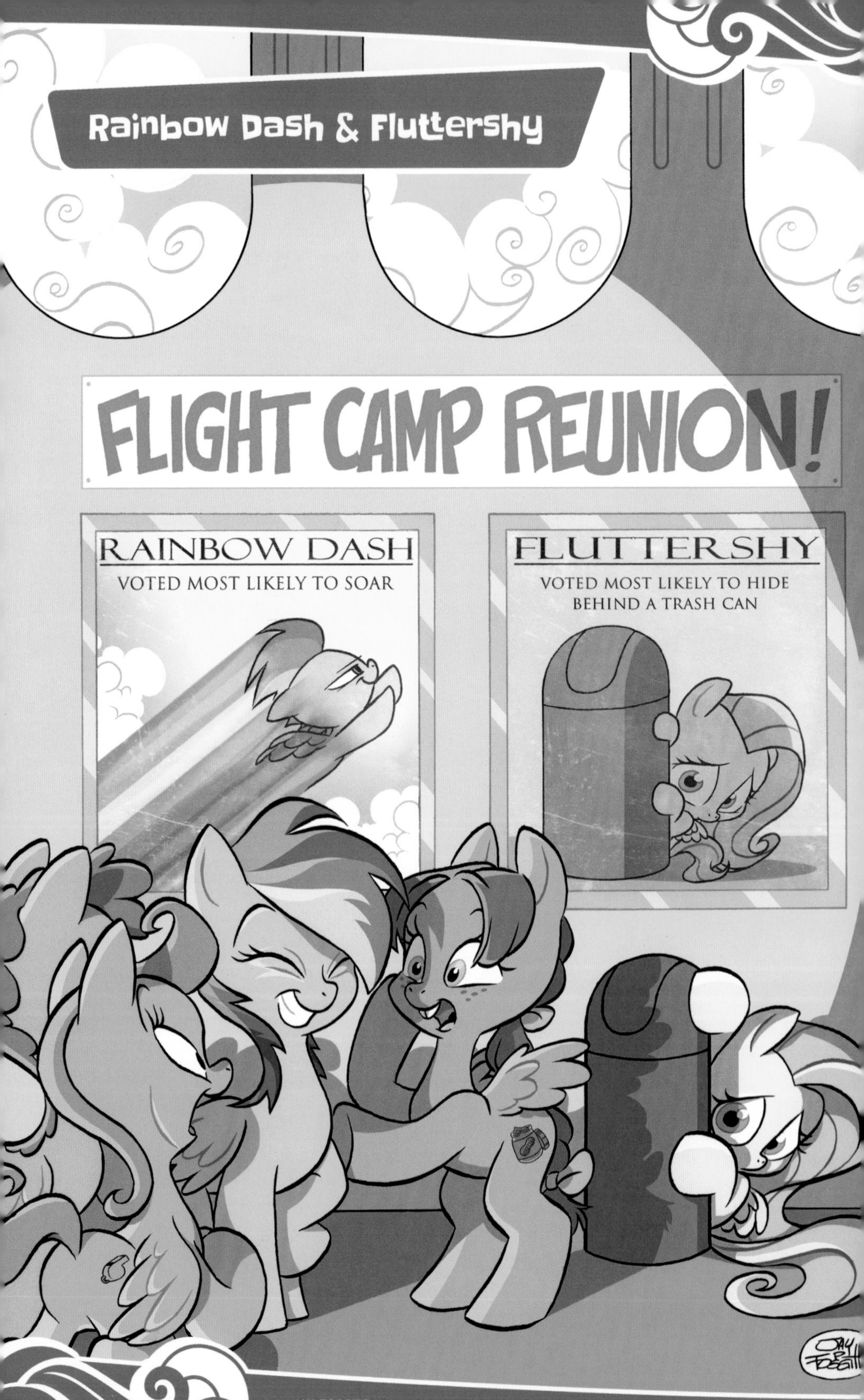
Rainbow Dash & Fluttershy
FLIGHT CAMP REUNION!
RAINBOW DASH
VOTED MOST LIKELY TO SOAR
FLUTTERSHY
VOTED MOST LIKELY TO HIDE BEHIND A TRASH CAN

art by JAY FOSGITT

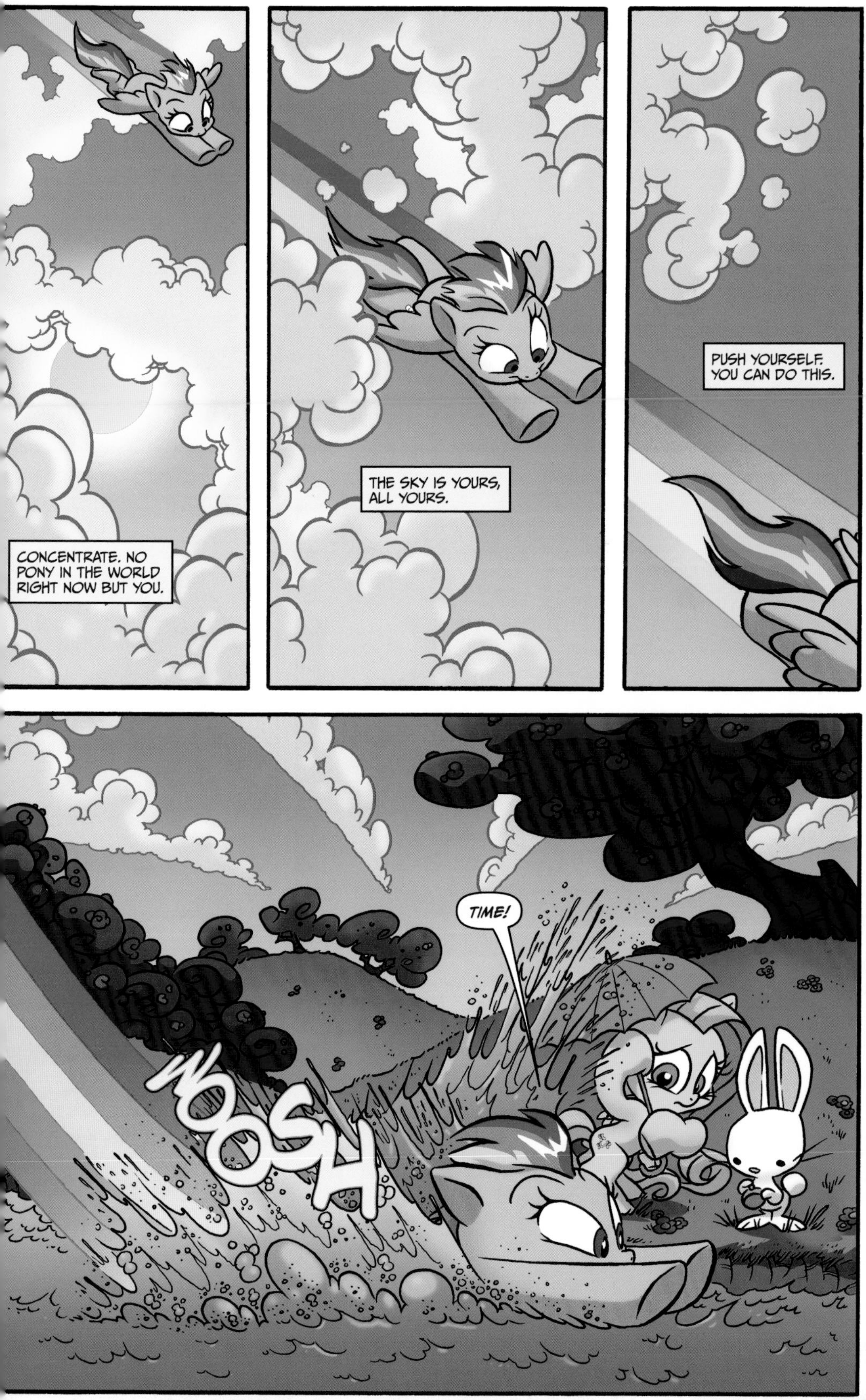
CONCENTRATE. NO PONY IN THE WORLD RIGHT NOW BUT YOU.
THE SKY IS YOURS, ALL YOURS.
PUSH YOURSELF. YOU CAN DO THIS.
WOOSH
TIME!

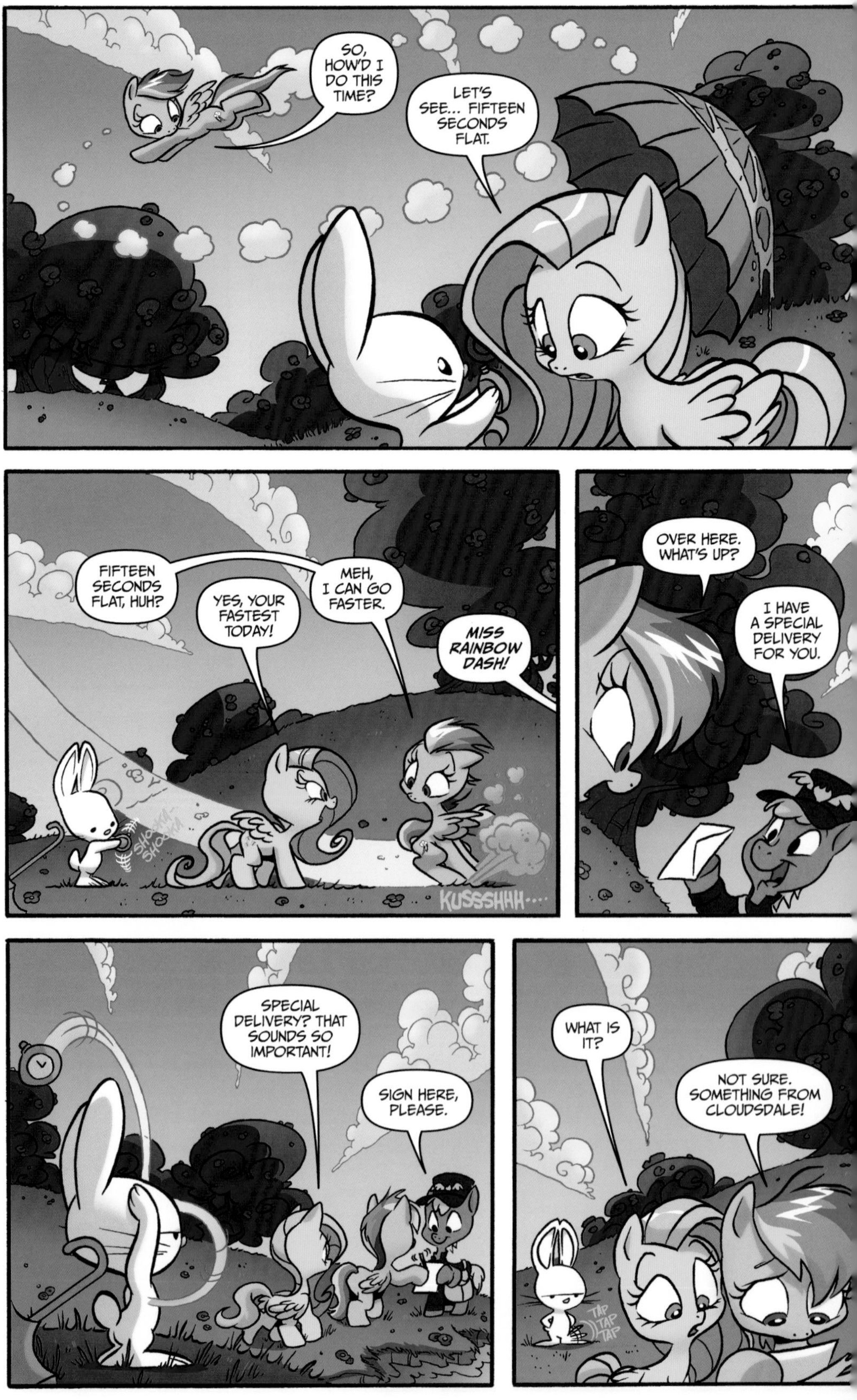
SO, HOW'D I DO THIS TIME?
LET'S SEE... FIFTEEN SECONDS FLAT.
FIFTEEN SECONDS FLAT, HUH?
YES, YOUR FASTEST TODAY!
MEH, I CAN GO FASTER.
MISS RAINBOW DASH!
SHOOKA- SHOOKA
KUSSSHHH....
OVER HERE. WHAT'S UP?
I HAVE A SPECIAL DELIVERY FOR YOU.
SPECIAL DELIVERY? THAT SOUNDS SO IMPORTANT!
SIGN HERE, PLEASE.
WHAT IS IT?
NOT SURE. SOMETHING FROM CLOUDSDALE!
TAP TAP TAP

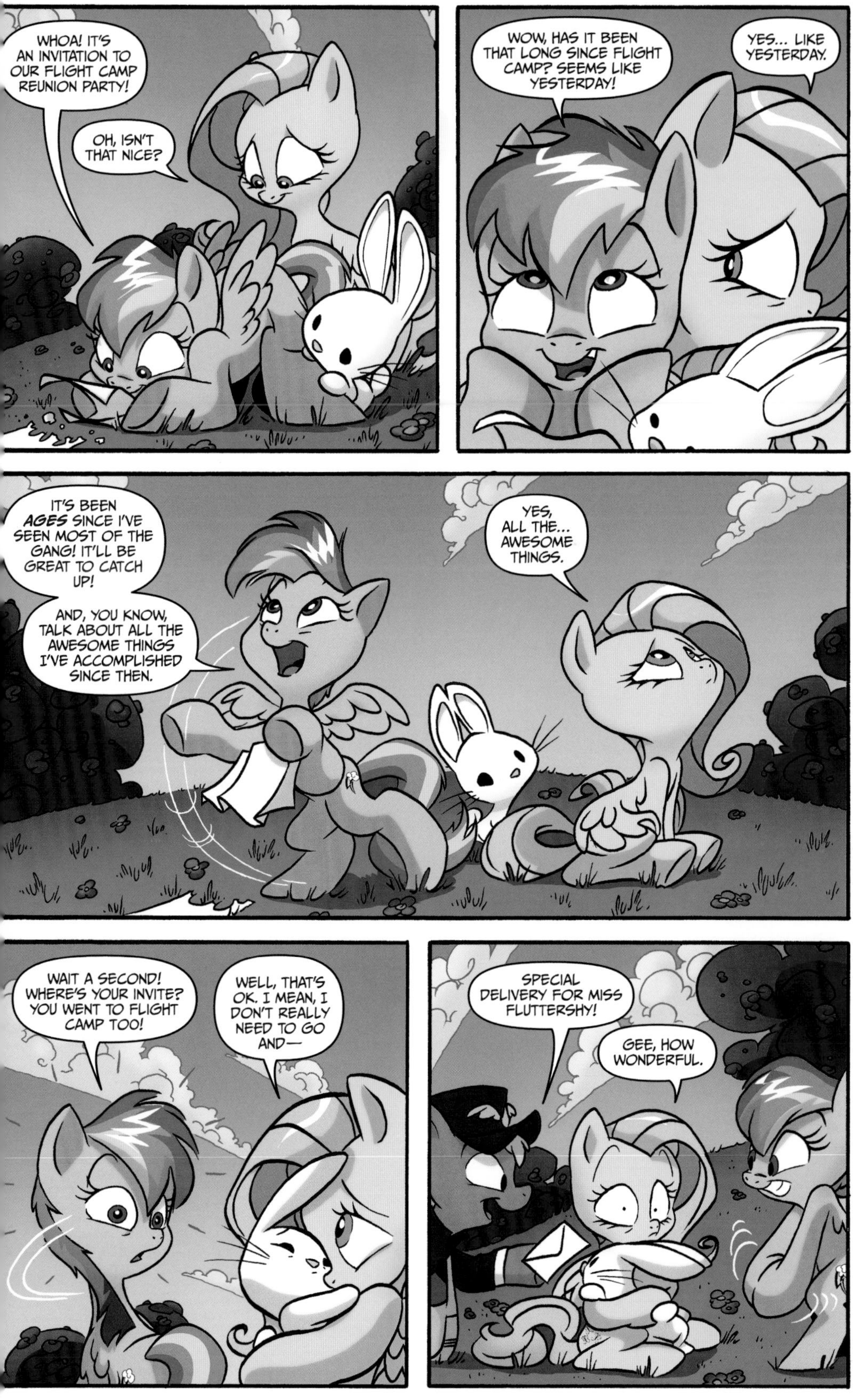

WHOA! IT'S AN INVITATION TO OUR FLIGHT CAMP REUNION PARTY!
OH, ISN'T THAT NICE?
WOW, HAS IT BEEN THAT LONG SINCE FLIGHT CAMP? SEEMS LIKE YESTERDAY!
YES... LIKE YESTERDAY.
IT'S BEEN AGES SINCE I'VE SEEN MOST OF THE GANG! IT'LL BE GREAT TO CATCH UP!
AND, YOU KNOW, TALK ABOUT ALL THE AWESOME THINGS I'VE ACCOMPLISHED SINCE THEN.
YES, ALL THE... AWESOME THINGS.
WAIT A SECOND! WHERE'S YOUR INVITE? YOU WENT TO FLIGHT CAMP TOO!
WELL, THAT'S OK. I MEAN, I DON'T REALLY NEED TO GO AND—
SPECIAL DELIVERY FOR MISS FLUTTERSHY!
GEE, HOW WONDERFUL.

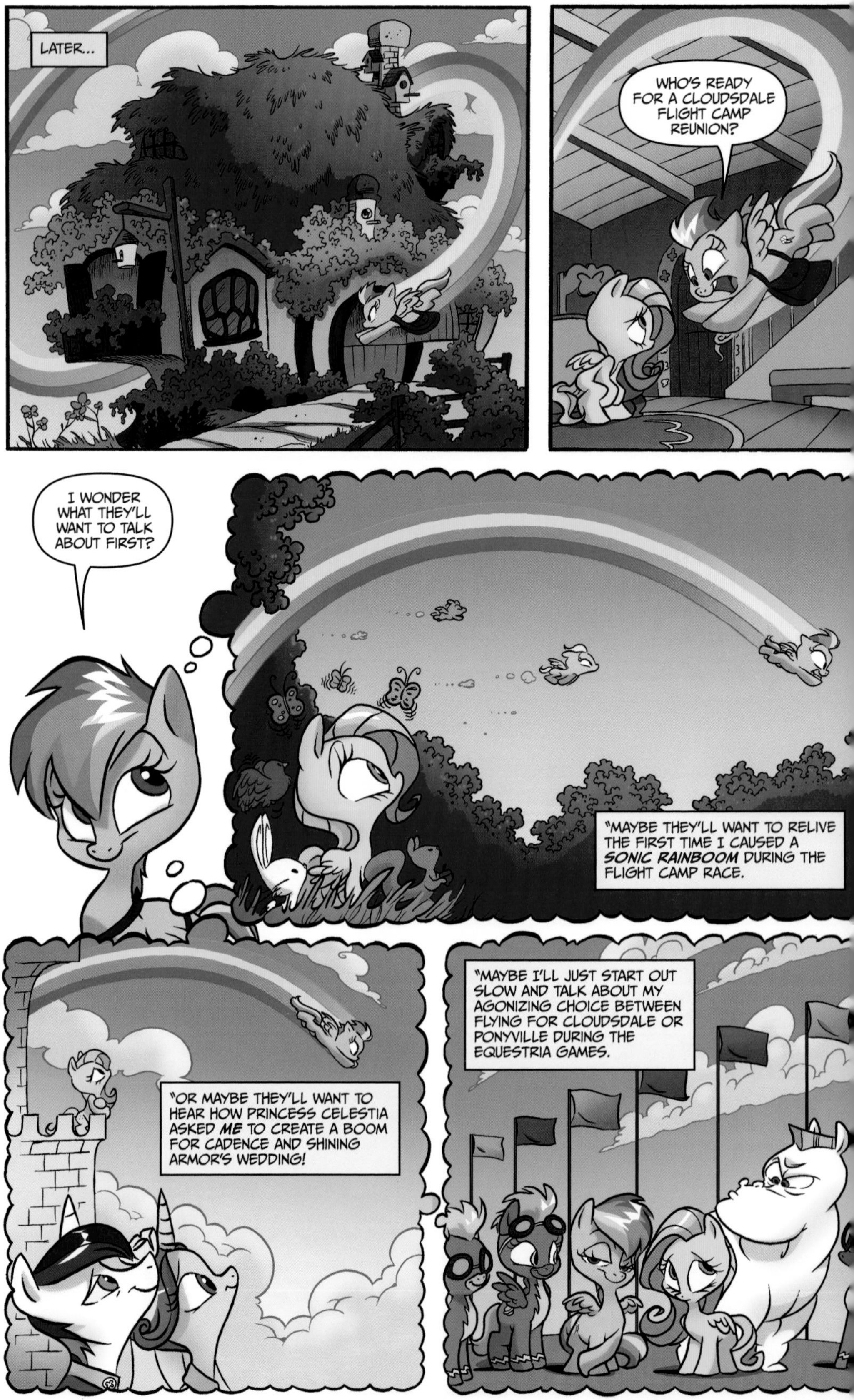
LATER...
WHO'S READY FOR A CLOUDSDALE FLIGHT CAMP REUNION?
I WONDER WHAT THEY'LL WANT TO TALK ABOUT FIRST?
"MAYBE THEY'LL WANT TO RELIVE THE FIRST TIME I CAUSED A SONIC RAINBOOM DURING THE FLIGHT CAMP RACE.
"OR MAYBE THEY'LL WANT TO HEAR HOW PRINCESS CELESTIA ASKED ME TO CREATE A BOOM FOR CADENCE AND SHINING ARMOR'S WEDDING!
"MAYBE I'LL JUST START OUT SLOW AND TALK ABOUT MY AGONIZING CHOICE BETWEEN FLYING FOR CLOUDSDALE OR PONYVILLE DURING THE EQUESTRIA GAMES.

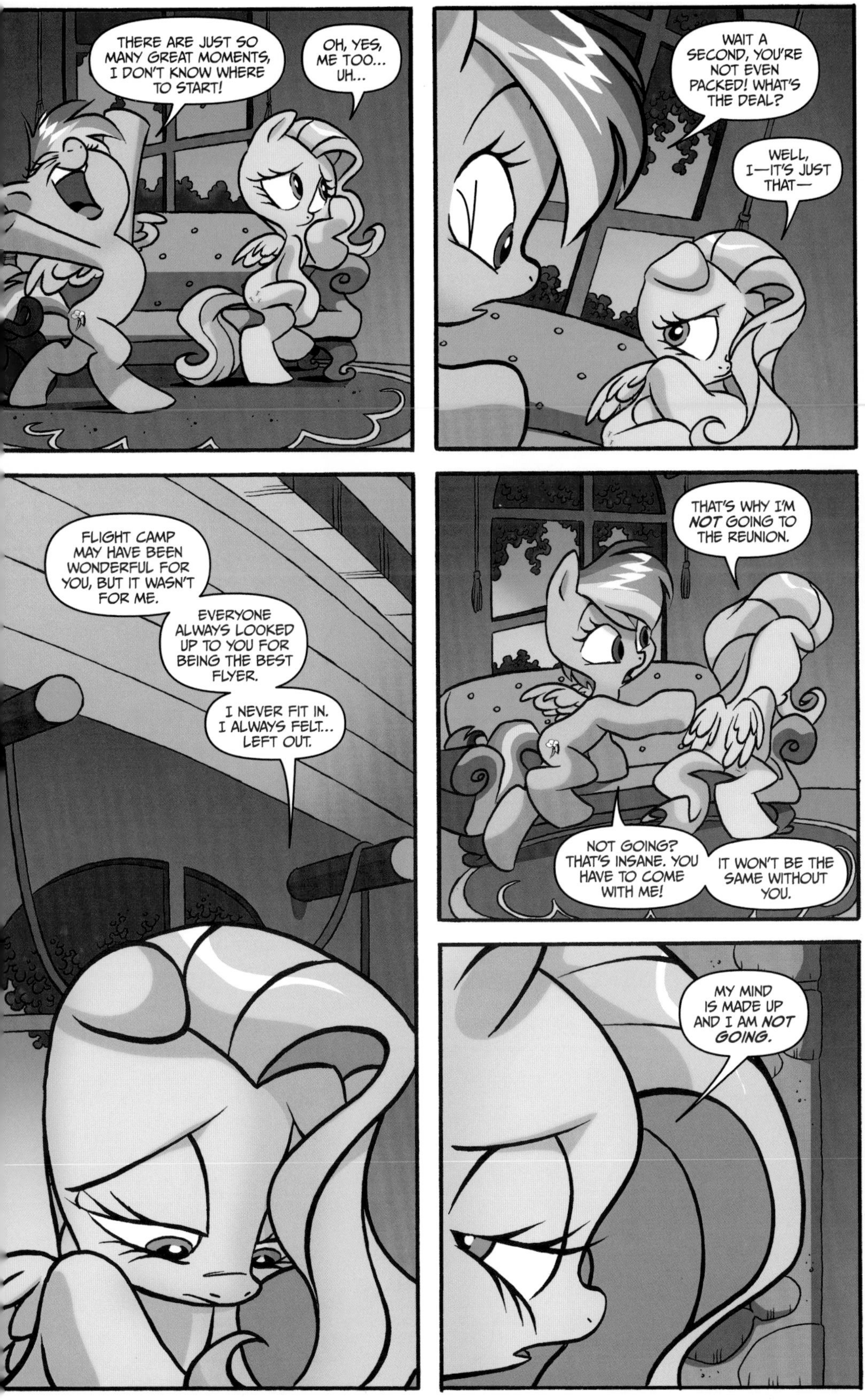
THERE ARE JUST SO MANY GREAT MOMENTS, I DON'T KNOW WHERE TO START!
OH, YES, ME TOO... UH...
WAIT A SECOND, YOU'RE NOT EVEN PACKED! WHAT'S THE DEAL?
WELL, I—IT'S JUST THAT—
FLIGHT CAMP MAY HAVE BEEN WONDERFUL FOR YOU, BUT IT WASN'T FOR ME.
EVERYONE ALWAYS LOOKED UP TO YOU FOR BEING THE BEST FLYER.
I NEVER FIT IN. I ALWAYS FELT... LEFT OUT.
THAT'S WHY I'M *NOT* GOING TO THE REUNION.
NOT GOING? THAT'S INSANE. YOU HAVE TO COME WITH ME!
IT WON'T BE THE SAME WITHOUT YOU.
MY MIND IS MADE UP AND I AM *NOT GOING.*

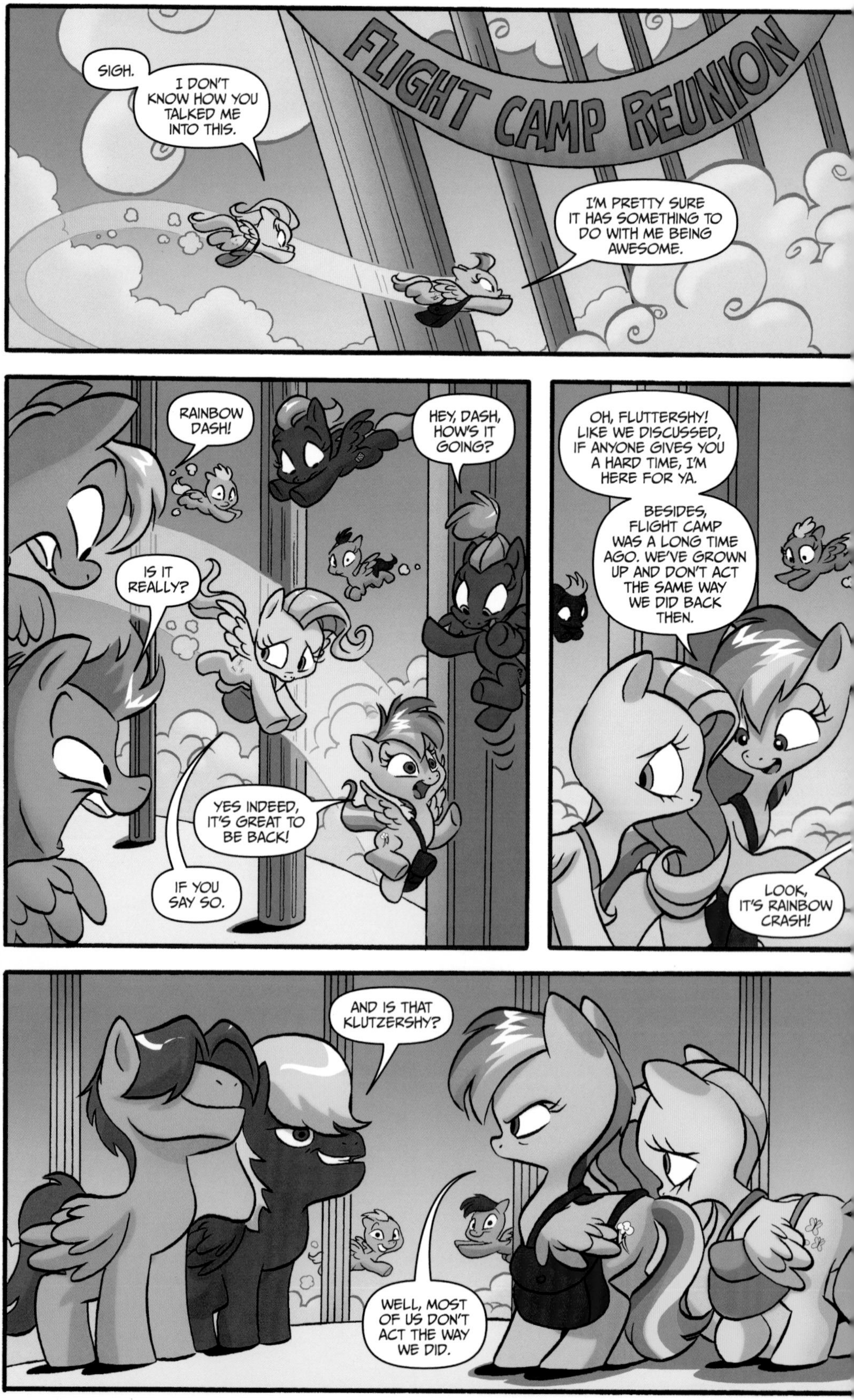
FLIGHT CAMP REUNION
SIGH.
I DON'T KNOW HOW YOU TALKED ME INTO THIS.
I'M PRETTY SURE IT HAS SOMETHING TO DO WITH ME BEING AWESOME.
RAINBOW DASH!
HEY, DASH, HOW'S IT GOING?
IS IT REALLY?
YES INDEED, IT'S GREAT TO BE BACK!
IF YOU SAY SO.
OH, FLUTTERSHY! LIKE WE DISCUSSED, IF ANYONE GIVES YOU A HARD TIME, I'M HERE FOR YA.
BESIDES, FLIGHT CAMP WAS A LONG TIME AGO. WE'VE GROWN UP AND DON'T ACT THE SAME WAY WE DID BACK THEN.
LOOK, IT'S RAINBOW CRASH!
AND IS THAT KLUTZERSHY?
WELL, MOST OF US DON'T ACT THE WAY WE DID.

WHAT DO YOU SAY, CRASH? UP FOR A LITTLE RACE?

SERIOUSLY? DON'T YOU TWO EVER LEARN?

WE'VE BEEN PRACTICING.

AND WAITING FOR THIS MOMENT FOR A LONG TIME.

OH PLEASE, YOU TWO DON'T STAND A CHANCE!

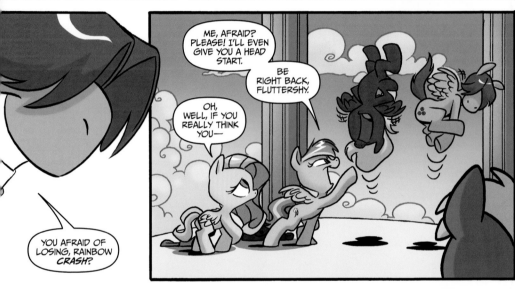

ME, AFRAID? PLEASE! I'LL EVEN GIVE YOU A HEAD START.

BE RIGHT BACK, FLUTTERSHY.

OH, WELL, IF YOU REALLY THINK YOU—

YOU AFRAID OF LOSING, RAINBOW CRASH?

...

—HAVE TO.

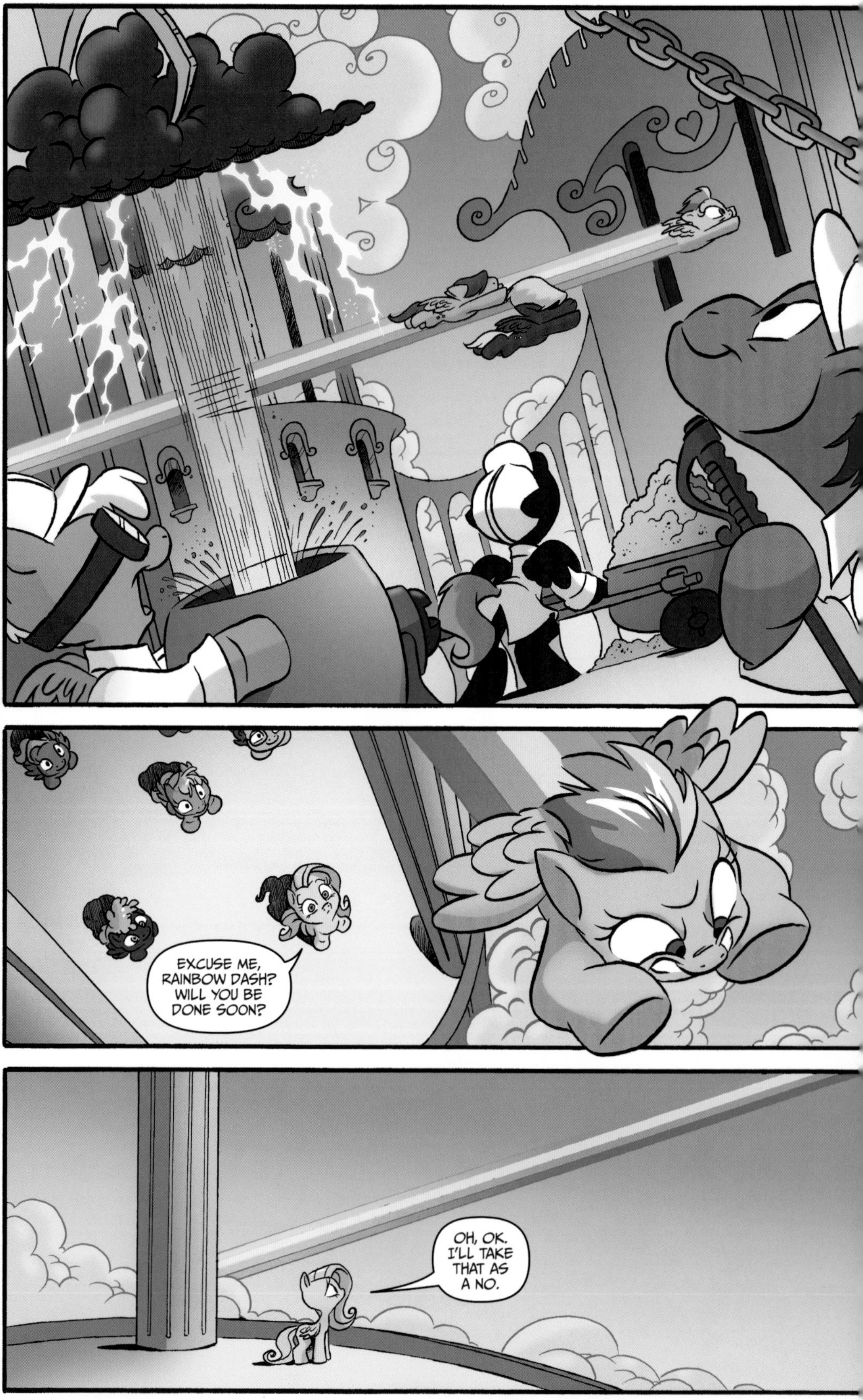
EXCUSE ME, RAINBOW DASH? WILL YOU BE DONE SOON?
OH, OK. I'LL TAKE THAT AS A NO.

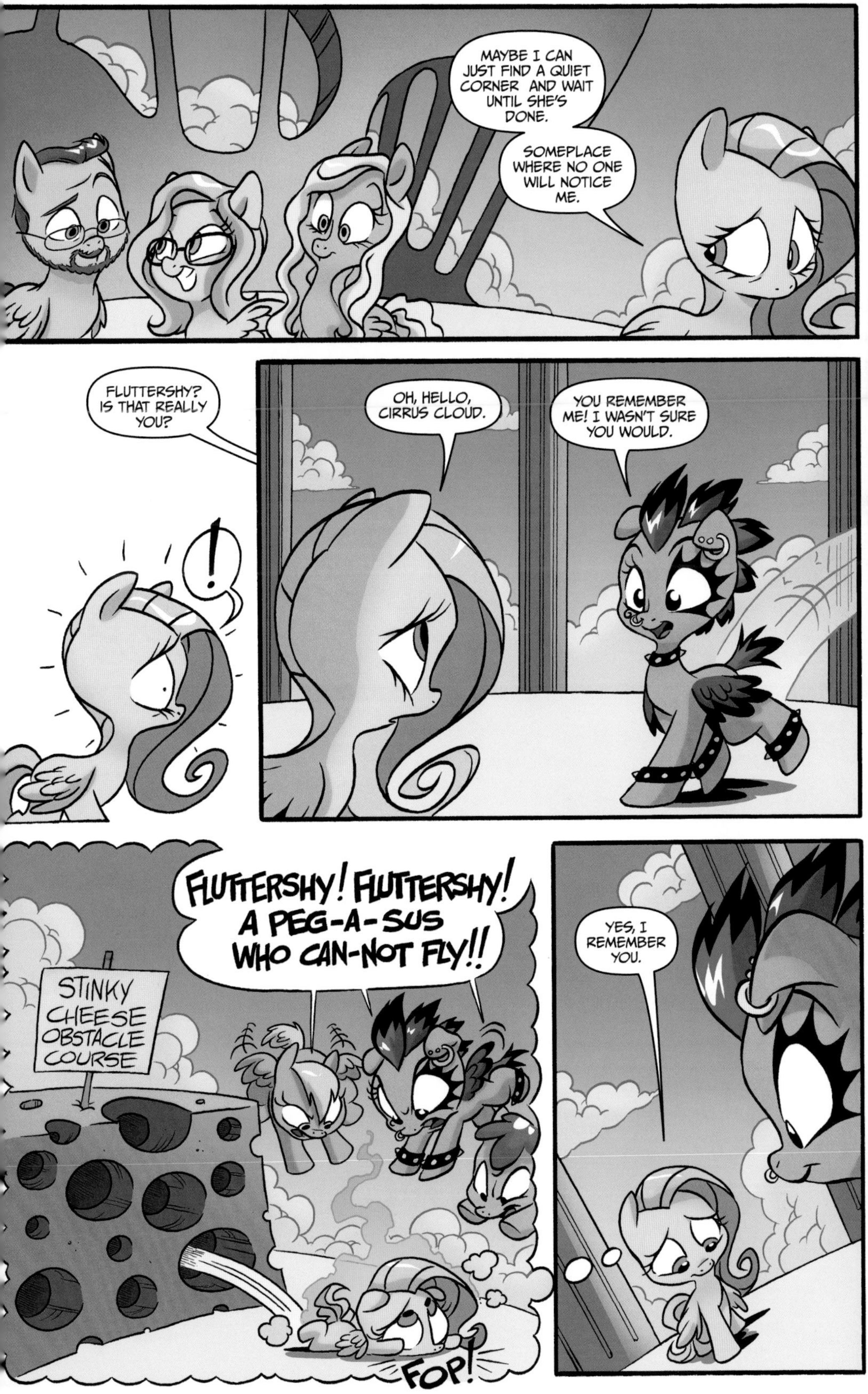
MAYBE I CAN JUST FIND A QUIET CORNER AND WAIT UNTIL SHE'S DONE.
SOMEPLACE WHERE NO ONE WILL NOTICE ME.
FLUTTERSHY? IS THAT REALLY YOU?
!
OH, HELLO, CIRRUS CLOUD.
YOU REMEMBER ME! I WASN'T SURE YOU WOULD.
FLUTTERSHY! FLUTTERSHY! A PEG-A-SUS WHO CAN-NOT FLY!!
STINKY CHEESE OBSTACLE COURSE
FOP!
YES, I REMEMBER YOU.

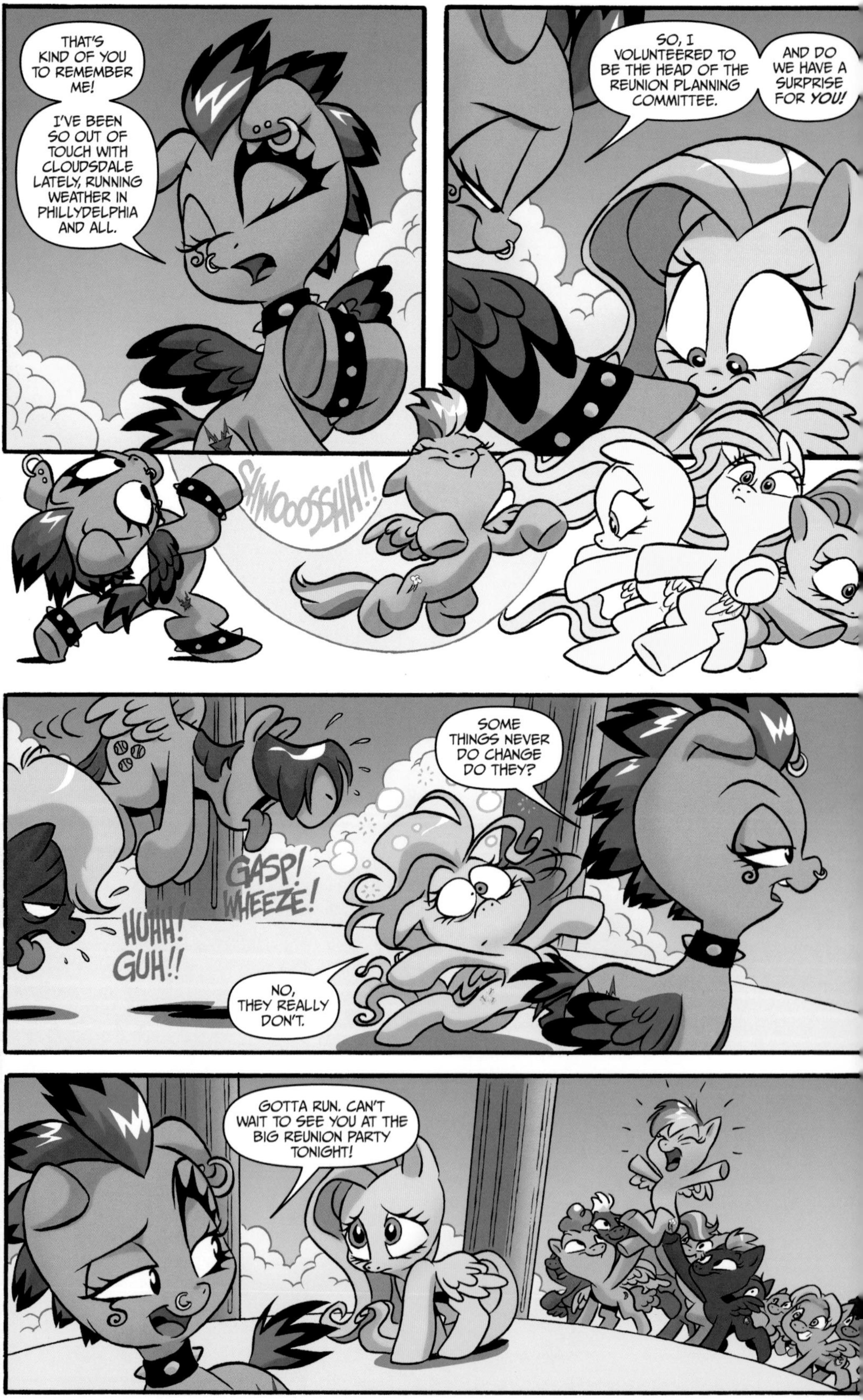
THAT'S KIND OF YOU TO REMEMBER ME!
I'VE BEEN SO OUT OF TOUCH WITH CLOUDSDALE LATELY, RUNNING WEATHER IN PHILLYDELPHIA AND ALL.
SO, I VOLUNTEERED TO BE THE HEAD OF THE REUNION PLANNING COMMITTEE.
AND DO WE HAVE A SURPRISE FOR *YOU!*
SHWOOOSSHH!!
SOME THINGS NEVER DO CHANGE DO THEY?
GASP! WHEEZE!
HUHH! GUH!!
NO, THEY REALLY DON'T.
GOTTA RUN. CAN'T WAIT TO SEE YOU AT THE BIG REUNION PARTY TONIGHT!

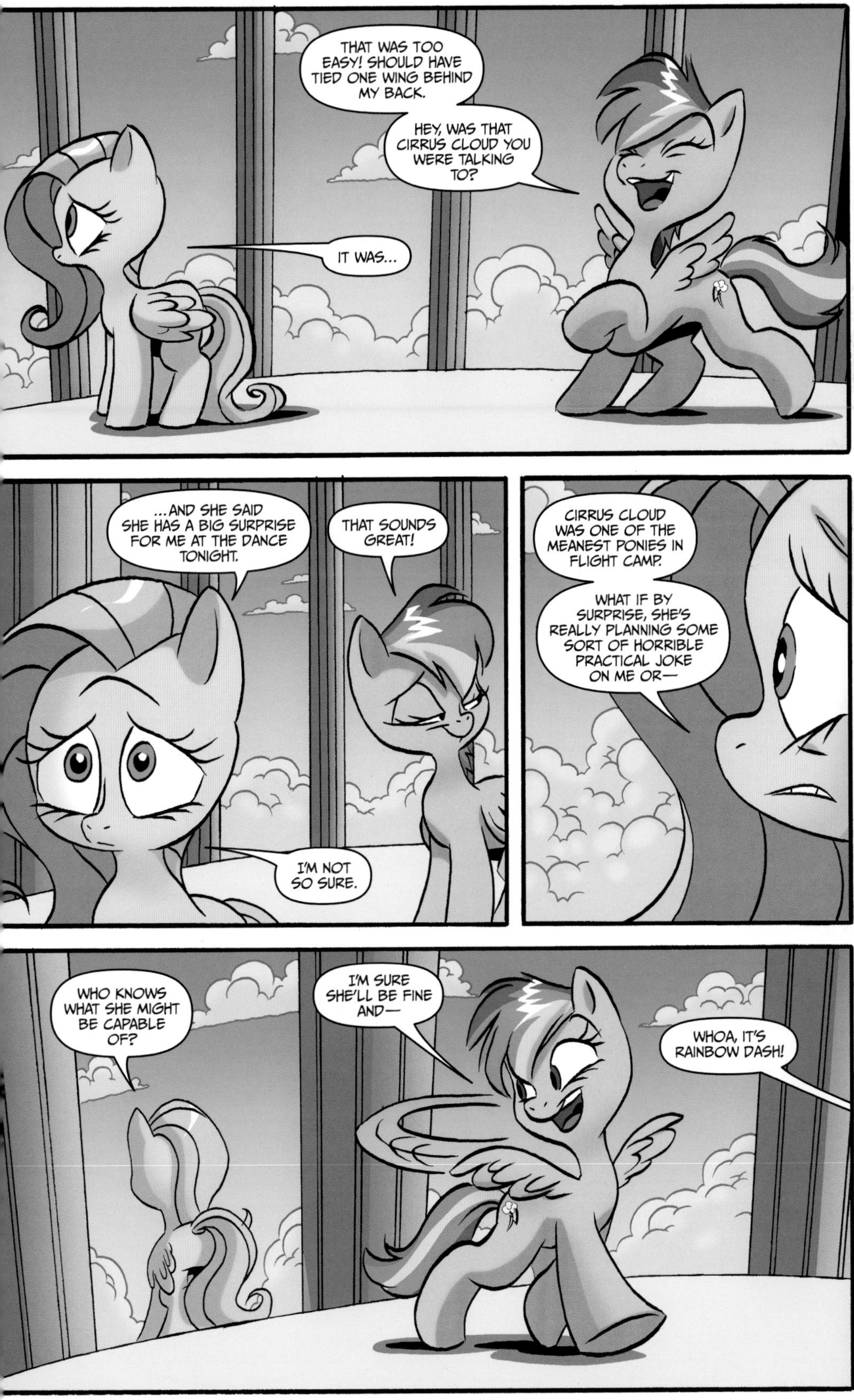
THAT WAS TOO EASY! SHOULD HAVE TIED ONE WING BEHIND MY BACK.
HEY, WAS THAT CIRRUS CLOUD YOU WERE TALKING TO?
IT WAS...
...AND SHE SAID SHE HAS A BIG SURPRISE FOR ME AT THE DANCE TONIGHT.
THAT SOUNDS GREAT!
I'M NOT SO SURE.
CIRRUS CLOUD WAS ONE OF THE MEANEST PONIES IN FLIGHT CAMP.
WHAT IF BY SURPRISE, SHE'S REALLY PLANNING SOME SORT OF HORRIBLE PRACTICAL JOKE ON ME OR—
WHO KNOWS WHAT SHE MIGHT BE CAPABLE OF?
I'M SURE SHE'LL BE FINE AND—
WHOA, IT'S RAINBOW DASH!

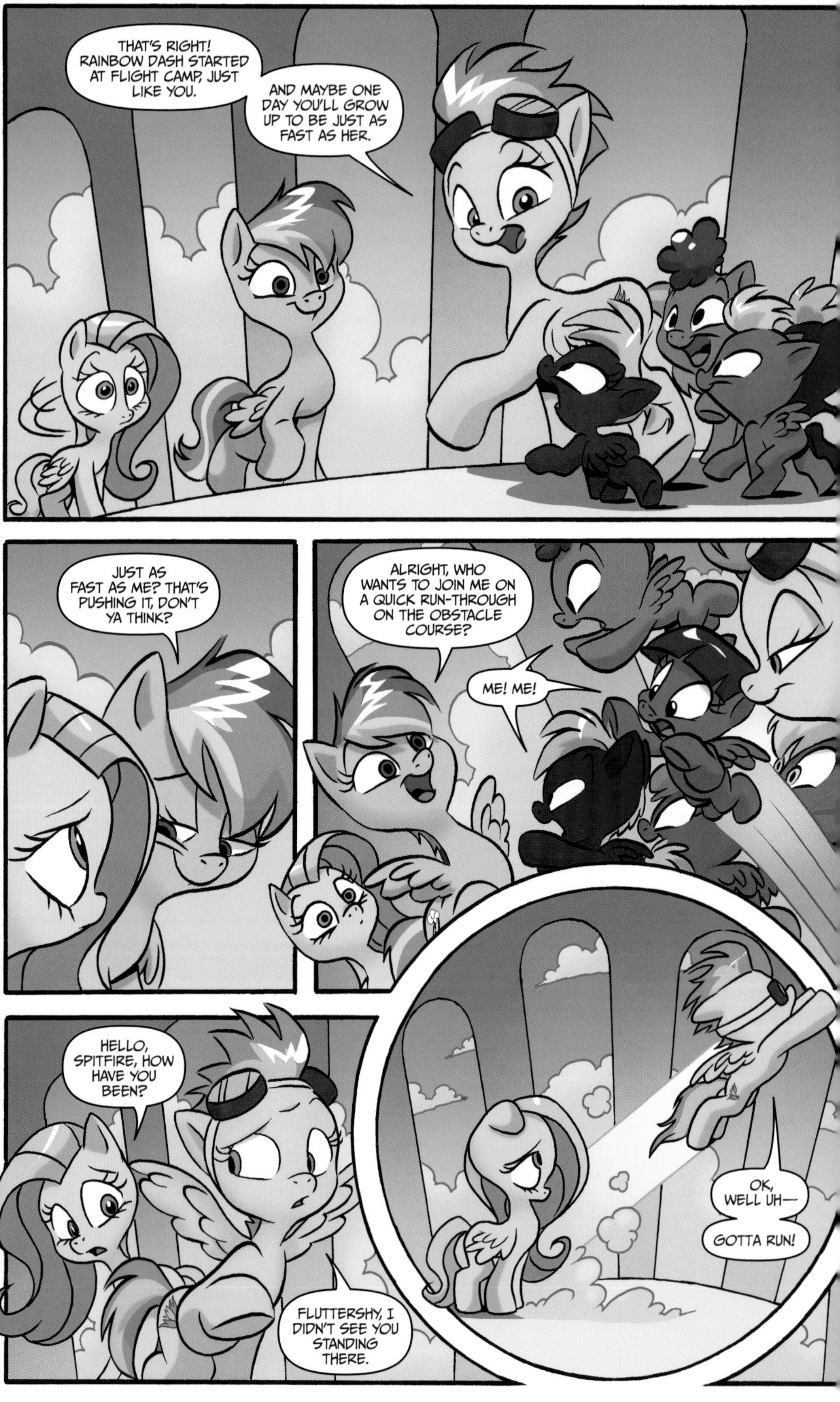
THAT'S RIGHT! RAINBOW DASH STARTED AT FLIGHT CAMP, JUST LIKE YOU.
AND MAYBE ONE DAY YOU'LL GROW UP TO BE JUST AS FAST AS HER.
JUST AS FAST AS ME? THAT'S PUSHING IT, DON'T YA THINK?
ALRIGHT, WHO WANTS TO JOIN ME ON A QUICK RUN-THROUGH ON THE OBSTACLE COURSE?
ME! ME!
HELLO, SPITFIRE, HOW HAVE YOU BEEN?
FLUTTERSHY, I DIDN'T SEE YOU STANDING THERE.
OK, WELL UH—
GOTTA RUN!

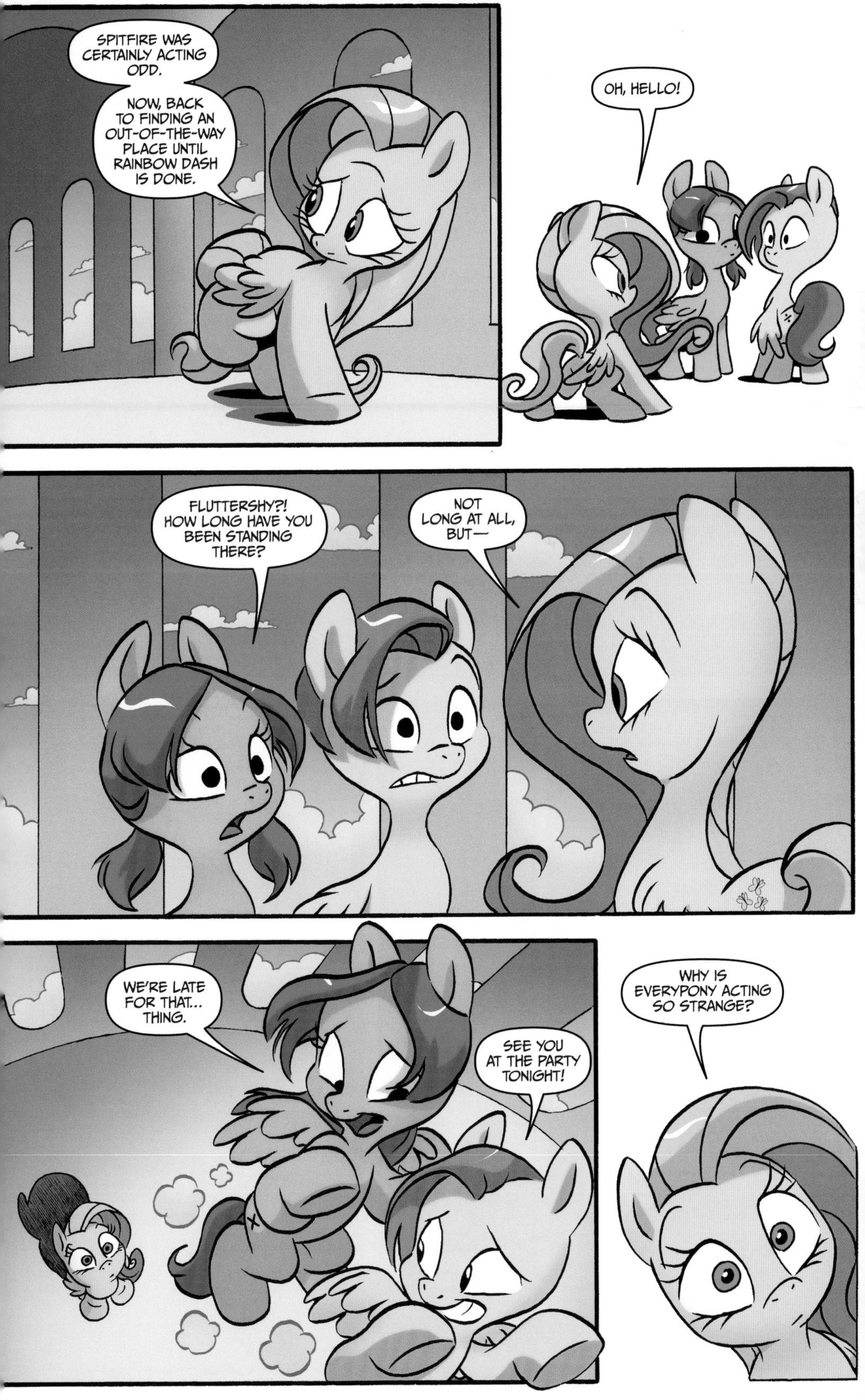
SPITFIRE WAS CERTAINLY ACTING ODD.
NOW, BACK TO FINDING AN OUT-OF-THE-WAY PLACE UNTIL RAINBOW DASH IS DONE.
OH, HELLO!
FLUTTERSHY?! HOW LONG HAVE YOU BEEN STANDING THERE?
NOT LONG AT ALL, BUT—
WE'RE LATE FOR THAT... THING.
SEE YOU AT THE PARTY TONIGHT!
WHY IS EVERYPONY ACTING SO STRANGE?

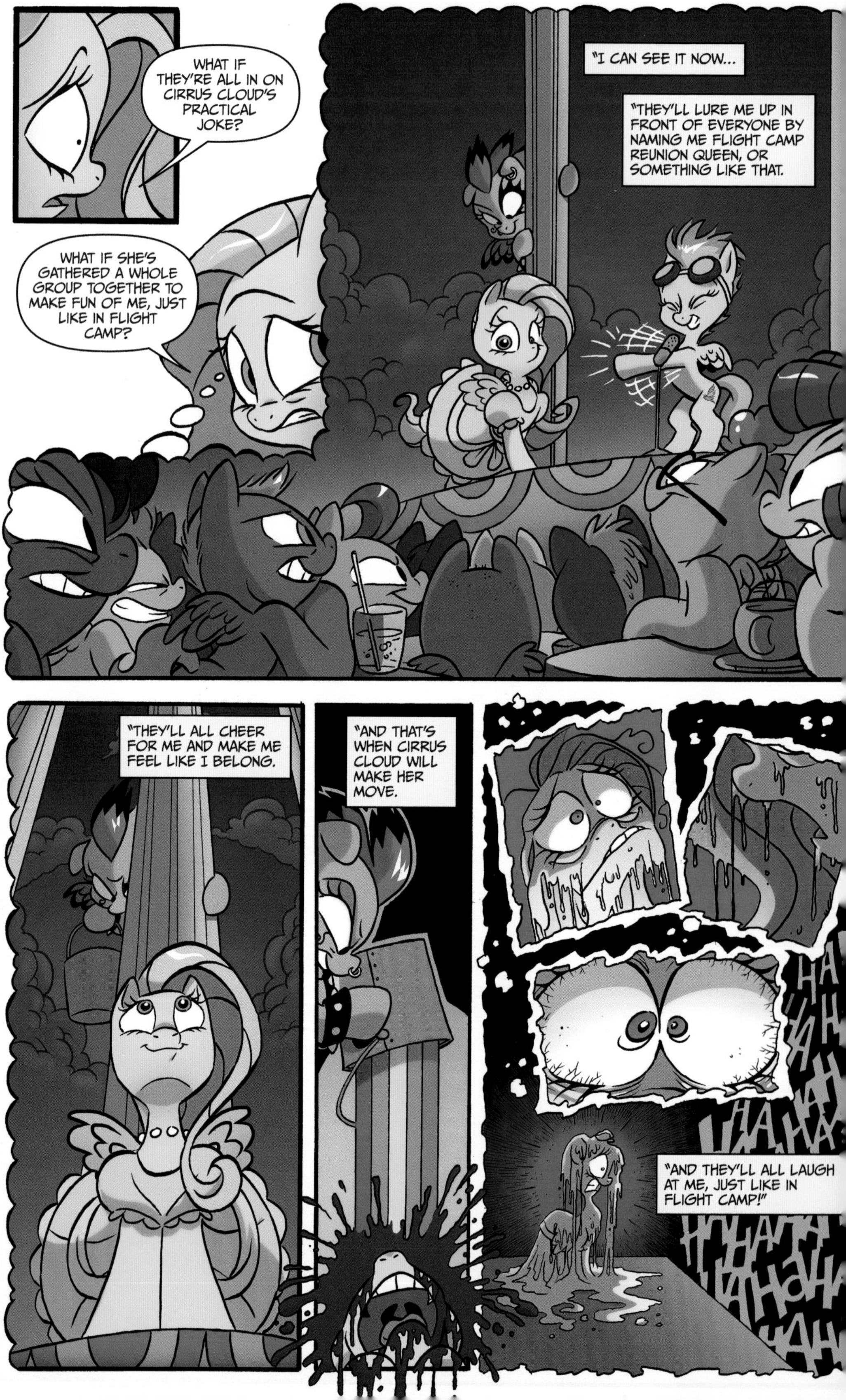
WHAT IF THEY'RE ALL IN ON CIRRUS CLOUD'S PRACTICAL JOKE?
WHAT IF SHE'S GATHERED A WHOLE GROUP TOGETHER TO MAKE FUN OF ME, JUST LIKE IN FLIGHT CAMP?
"I CAN SEE IT NOW...
"THEY'LL LURE ME UP IN FRONT OF EVERYONE BY NAMING ME FLIGHT CAMP REUNION QUEEN, OR SOMETHING LIKE THAT.
"THEY'LL ALL CHEER FOR ME AND MAKE ME FEEL LIKE I BELONG.
"AND THAT'S WHEN CIRRUS CLOUD WILL MAKE HER MOVE.
"AND THEY'LL ALL LAUGH AT ME, JUST LIKE IN FLIGHT CAMP!"

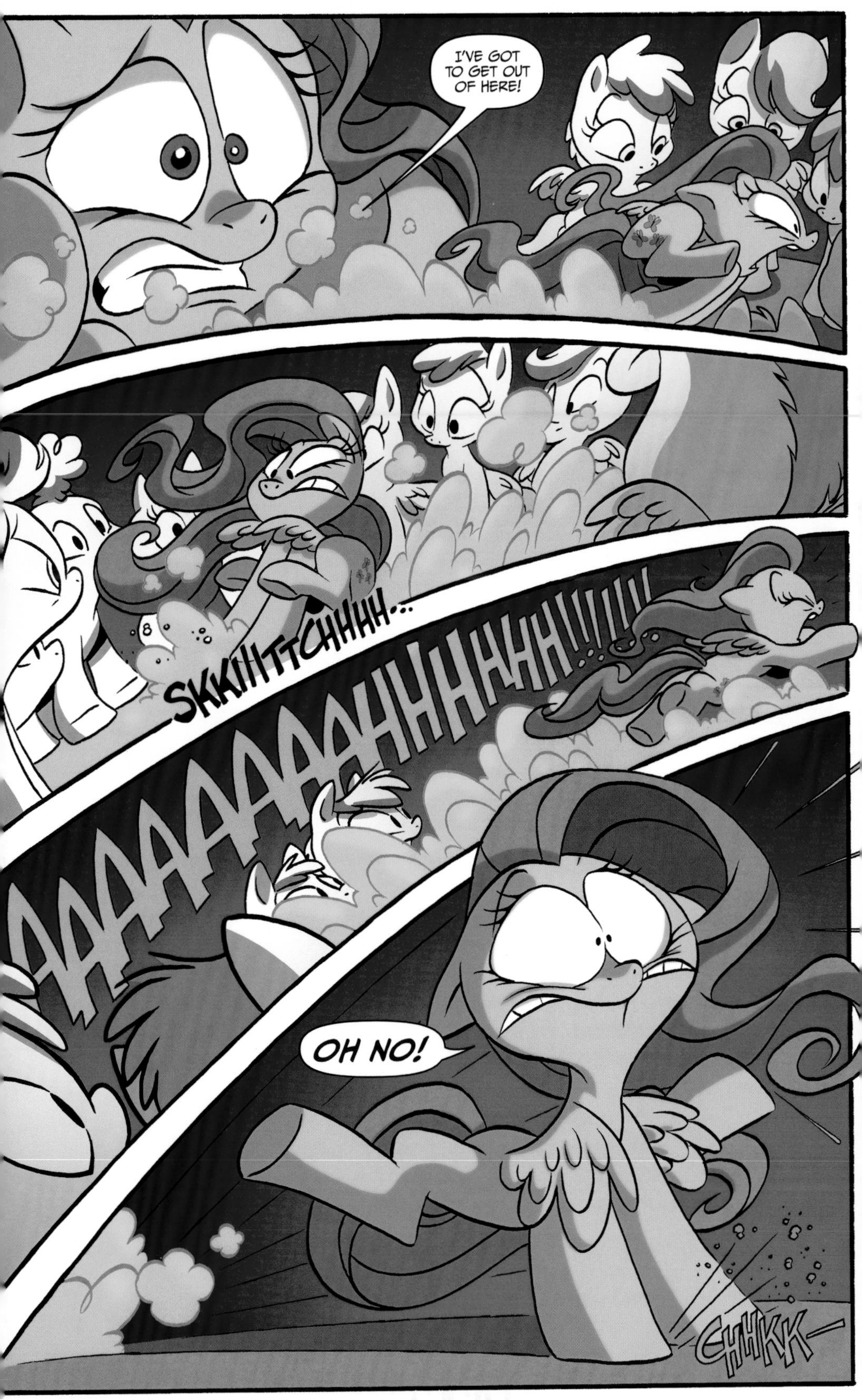
I'VE GOT TO GET OUT OF HERE!
SKKIIIITTCHHHH..
AAAAAAAAAAHHHHHHHHH!!!!!!!
OH NO!
CHHKK—

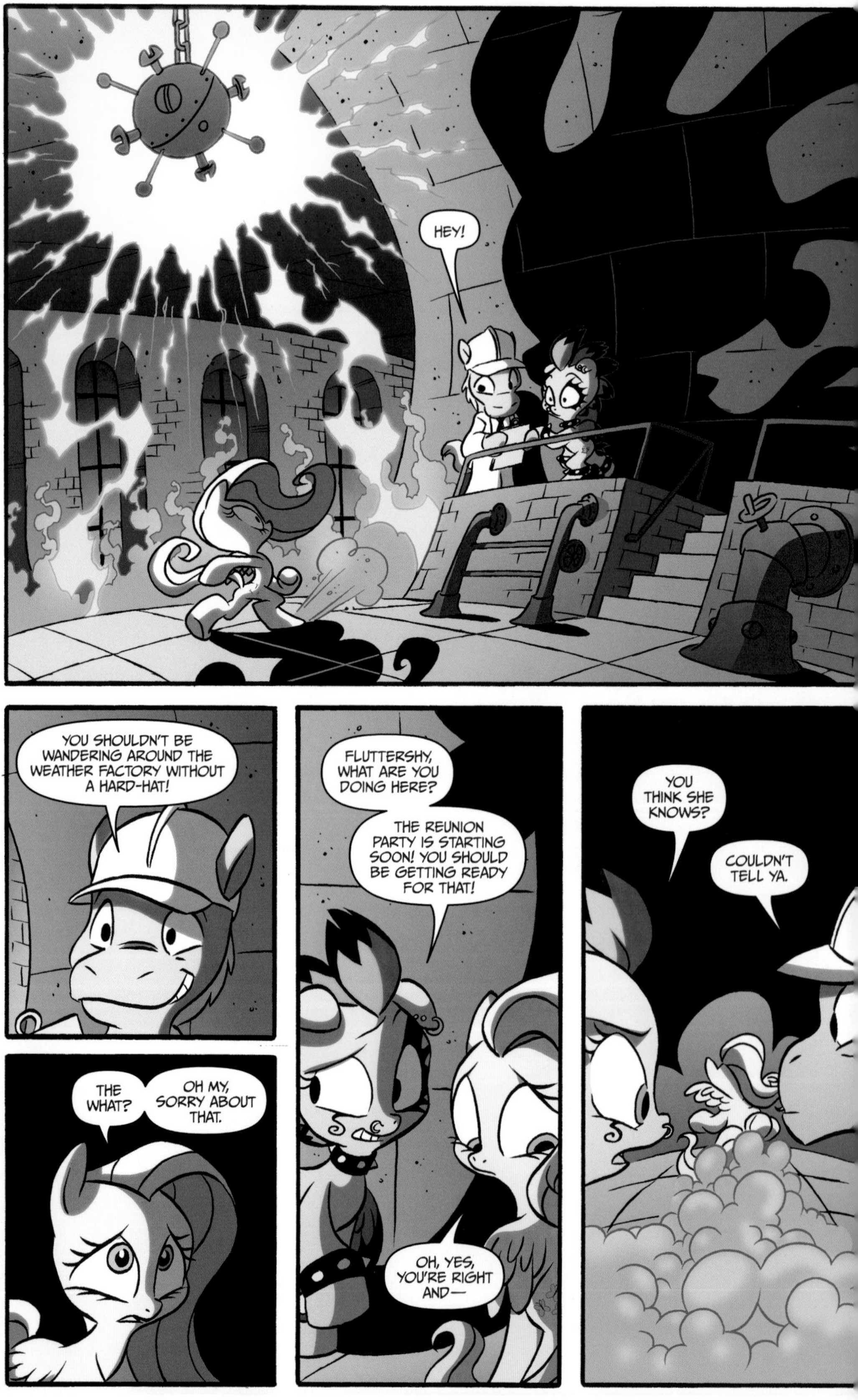
HEY!
YOU SHOULDN'T BE WANDERING AROUND THE WEATHER FACTORY WITHOUT A HARD-HAT!
THE WHAT?
OH MY, SORRY ABOUT THAT.
FLUTTERSHY, WHAT ARE YOU DOING HERE?
THE REUNION PARTY IS STARTING SOON! YOU SHOULD BE GETTING READY FOR THAT!
OH, YES, YOU'RE RIGHT AND—
YOU THINK SHE KNOWS?
COULDN'T TELL YA.

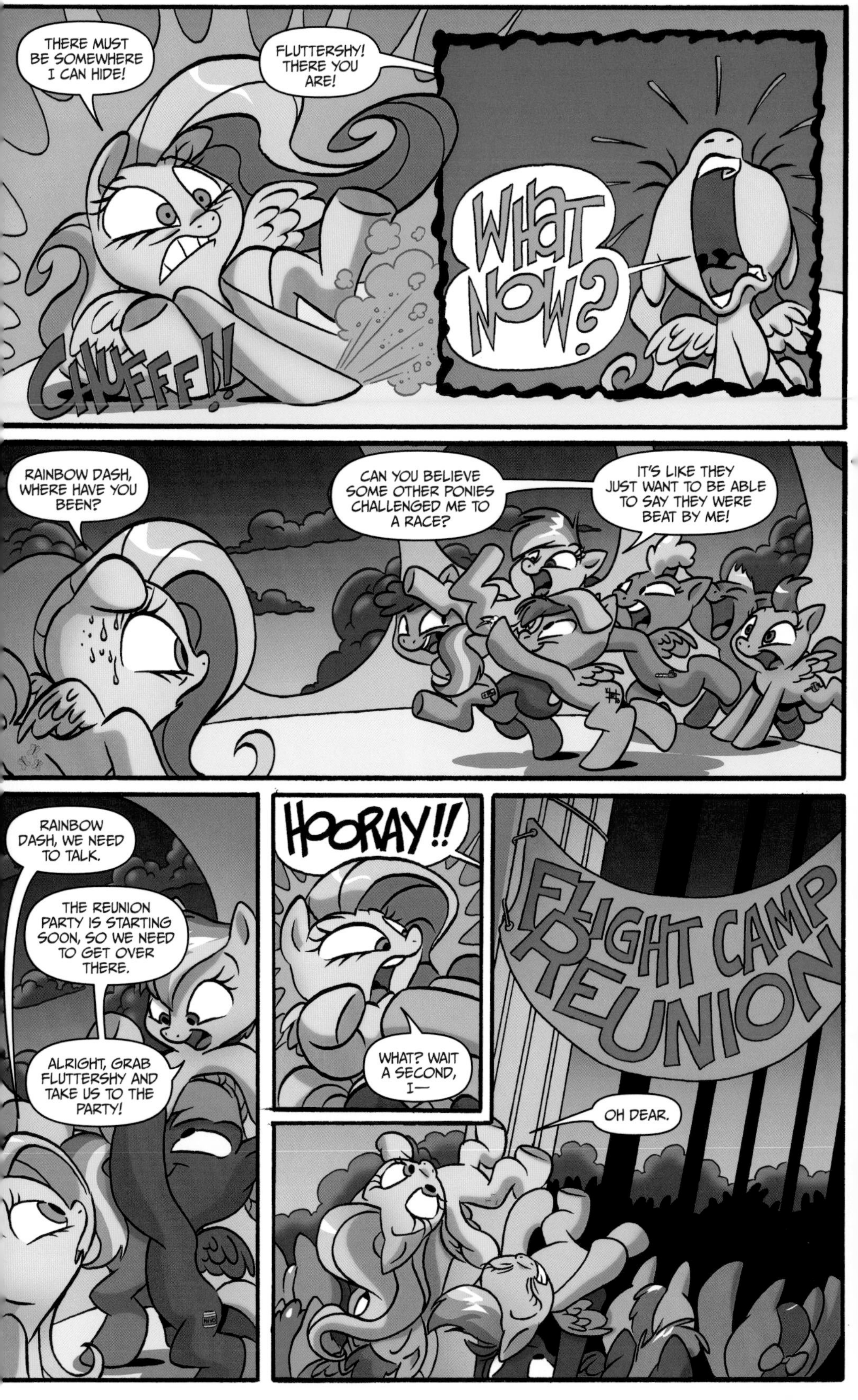
THERE MUST BE SOMEWHERE I CAN HIDE!
GHUFFFF!!
FLUTTERSHY! THERE YOU ARE!
WHAT NOW?
RAINBOW DASH, WHERE HAVE YOU BEEN?
CAN YOU BELIEVE SOME OTHER PONIES CHALLENGED ME TO A RACE?
IT'S LIKE THEY JUST WANT TO BE ABLE TO SAY THEY WERE BEAT BY ME!
RAINBOW DASH, WE NEED TO TALK.
THE REUNION PARTY IS STARTING SOON, SO WE NEED TO GET OVER THERE.
ALRIGHT, GRAB FLUTTERSHY AND TAKE US TO THE PARTY!
HOORAY!!
WHAT? WAIT A SECOND, I—
FLIGHT CAMP REUNION
OH DEAR.

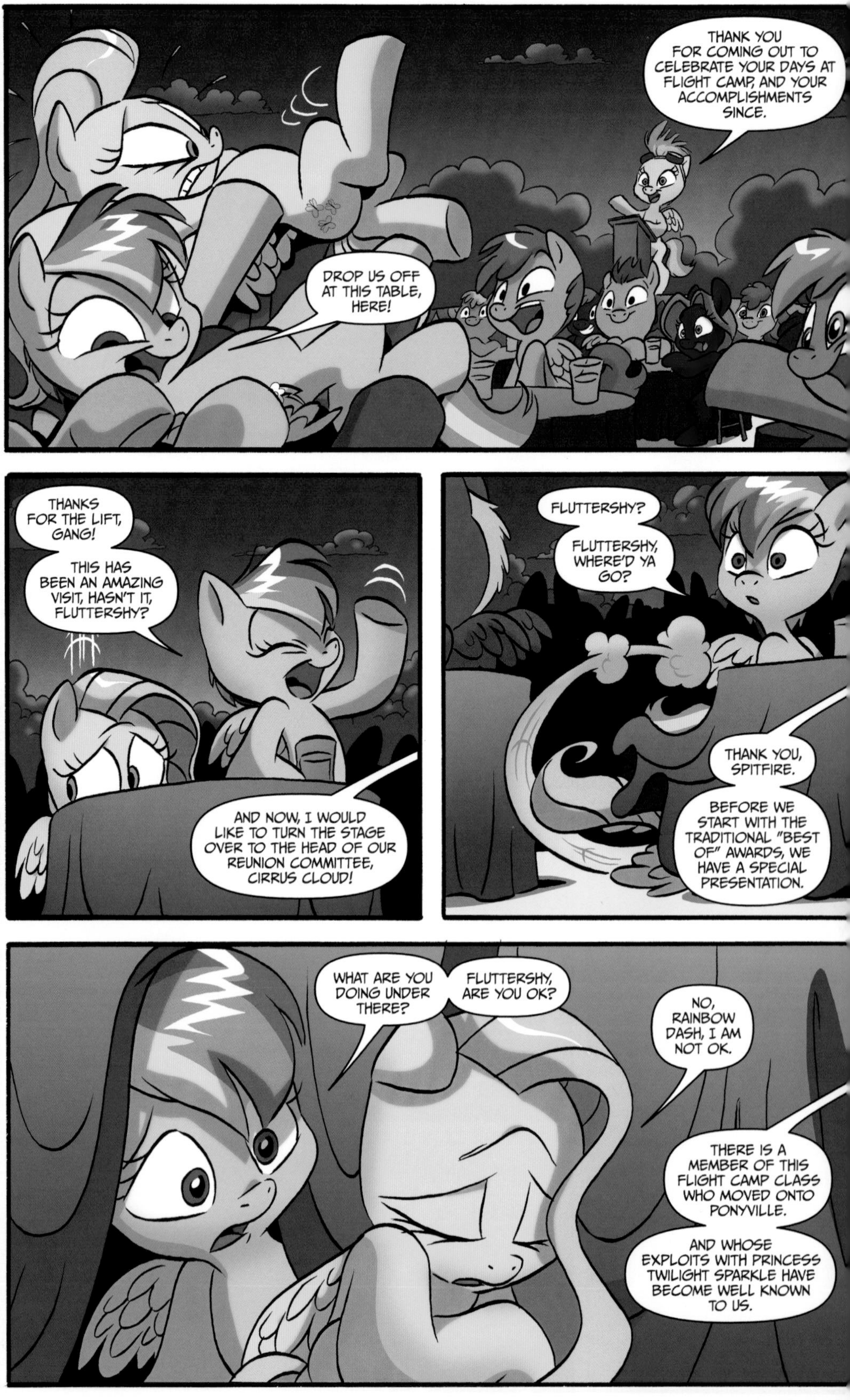
THANK YOU FOR COMING OUT TO CELEBRATE YOUR DAYS AT FLIGHT CAMP, AND YOUR ACCOMPLISHMENTS SINCE.
DROP US OFF AT THIS TABLE, HERE!
THANKS FOR THE LIFT, GANG!
THIS HAS BEEN AN AMAZING VISIT, HASN'T IT, FLUTTERSHY?
AND NOW, I WOULD LIKE TO TURN THE STAGE OVER TO THE HEAD OF OUR REUNION COMMITTEE, CIRRUS CLOUD!
FLUTTERSHY?
FLUTTERSHY, WHERE'D YA GO?
THANK YOU, SPITFIRE.
BEFORE WE START WITH THE TRADITIONAL "BEST OF" AWARDS, WE HAVE A SPECIAL PRESENTATION.
WHAT ARE YOU DOING UNDER THERE?
FLUTTERSHY, ARE YOU OK?
NO, RAINBOW DASH, I AM NOT OK.
THERE IS A MEMBER OF THIS FLIGHT CAMP CLASS WHO MOVED ONTO PONYVILLE.
AND WHOSE EXPLOITS WITH PRINCESS TWILIGHT SPARKLE HAVE BECOME WELL KNOWN TO US.

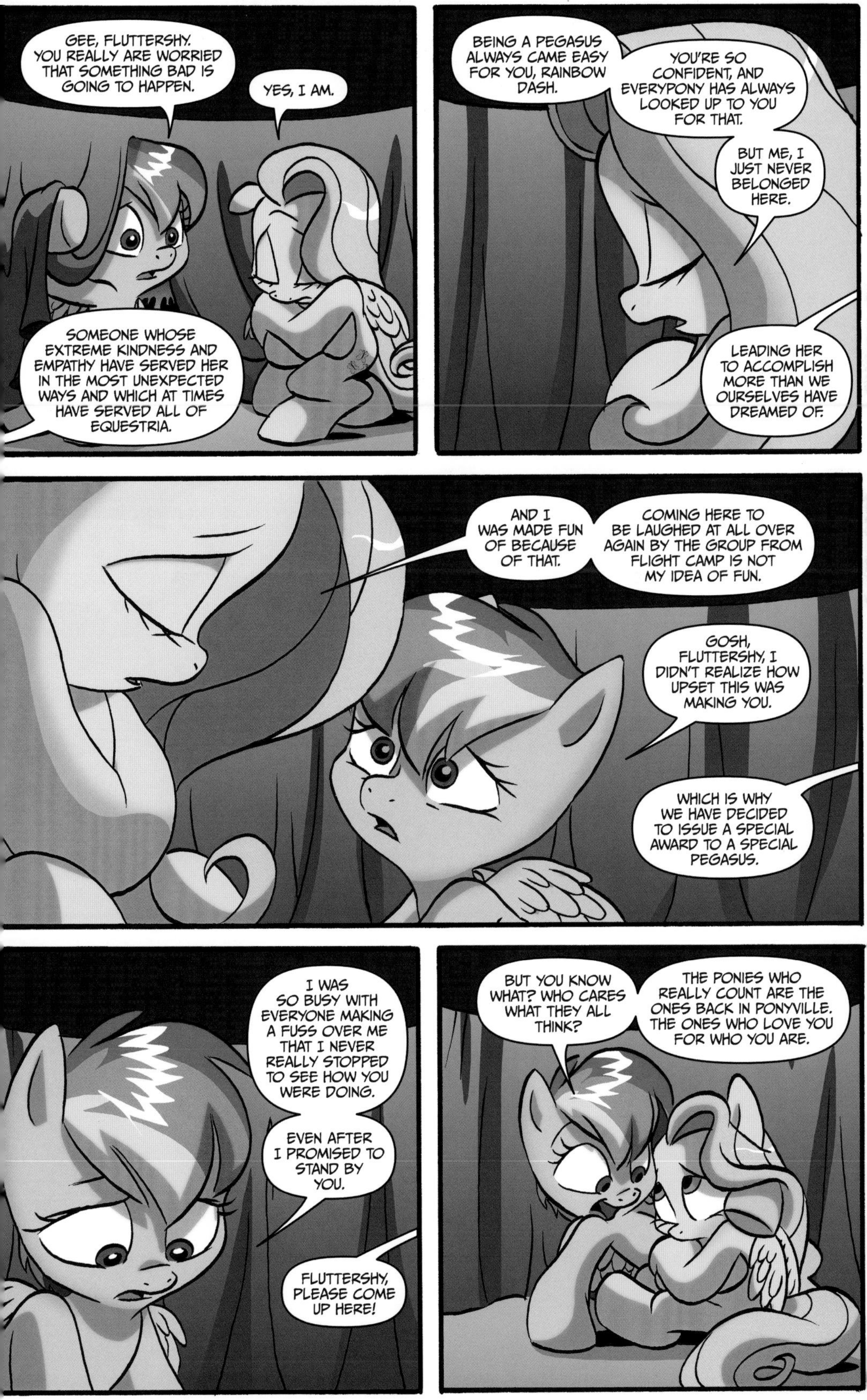
GEE, FLUTTERSHY. YOU REALLY ARE WORRIED THAT SOMETHING BAD IS GOING TO HAPPEN.
YES, I AM.
SOMEONE WHOSE EXTREME KINDNESS AND EMPATHY HAVE SERVED HER IN THE MOST UNEXPECTED WAYS AND WHICH AT TIMES HAVE SERVED ALL OF EQUESTRIA.
BEING A PEGASUS ALWAYS CAME EASY FOR YOU, RAINBOW DASH.
YOU'RE SO CONFIDENT, AND EVERYPONY HAS ALWAYS LOOKED UP TO YOU FOR THAT.
BUT ME, I JUST NEVER BELONGED HERE.
LEADING HER TO ACCOMPLISH MORE THAN WE OURSELVES HAVE DREAMED OF.
AND I WAS MADE FUN OF BECAUSE OF THAT.
COMING HERE TO BE LAUGHED AT ALL OVER AGAIN BY THE GROUP FROM FLIGHT CAMP IS NOT MY IDEA OF FUN.
GOSH, FLUTTERSHY, I DIDN'T REALIZE HOW UPSET THIS WAS MAKING YOU.
WHICH IS WHY WE HAVE DECIDED TO ISSUE A SPECIAL AWARD TO A SPECIAL PEGASUS.
I WAS SO BUSY WITH EVERYONE MAKING A FUSS OVER ME THAT I NEVER REALLY STOPPED TO SEE HOW YOU WERE DOING.
EVEN AFTER I PROMISED TO STAND BY YOU.
FLUTTERSHY, PLEASE COME UP HERE!
BUT YOU KNOW WHAT? WHO CARES WHAT THEY ALL THINK?
THE PONIES WHO REALLY COUNT ARE THE ONES BACK IN PONYVILLE. THE ONES WHO LOVE YOU FOR WHO YOU ARE.

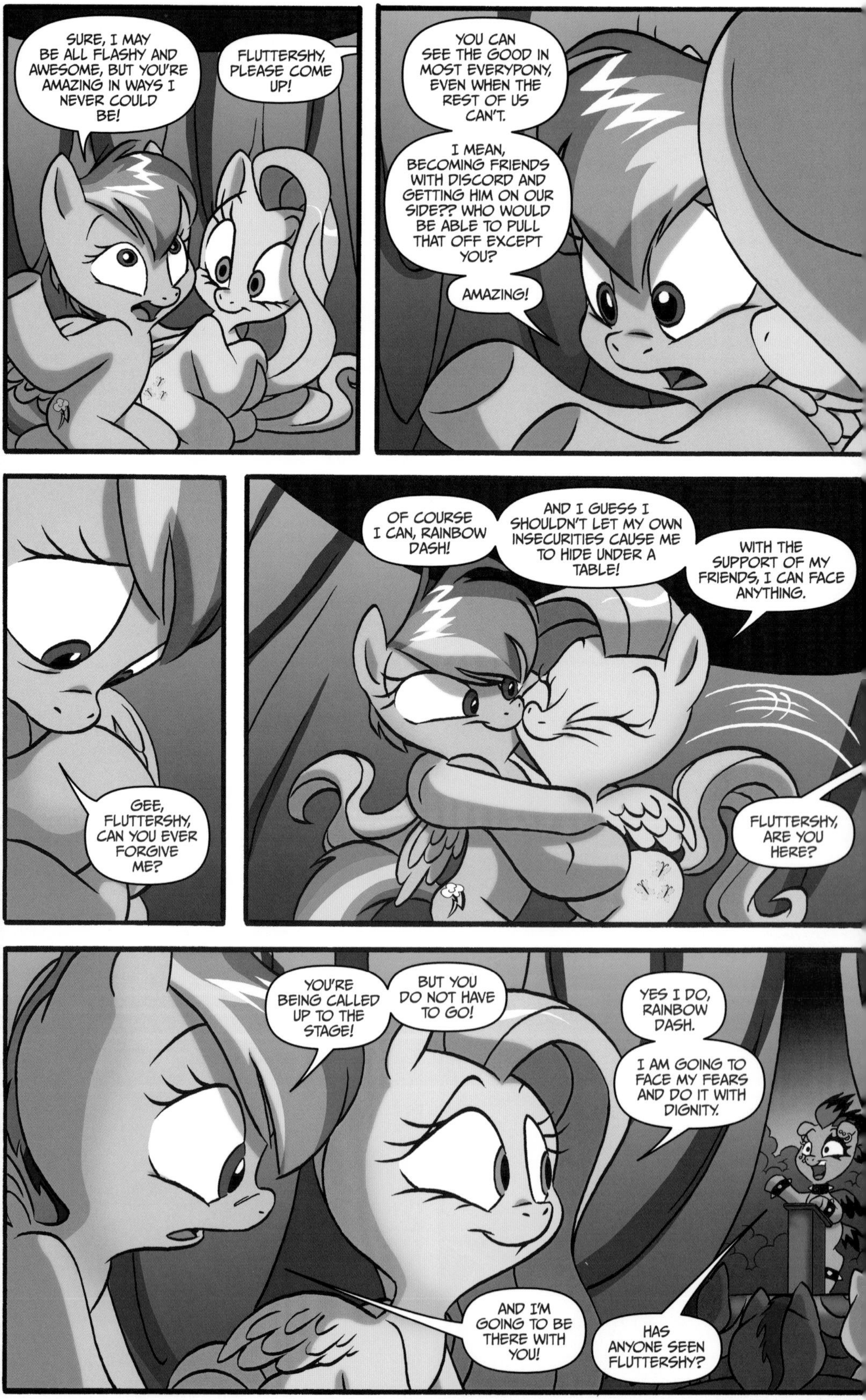
SURE, I MAY BE ALL FLASHY AND AWESOME, BUT YOU'RE AMAZING IN WAYS I NEVER COULD BE!
FLUTTERSHY, PLEASE COME UP!
YOU CAN SEE THE GOOD IN MOST EVERYPONY, EVEN WHEN THE REST OF US CAN'T.
I MEAN, BECOMING FRIENDS WITH DISCORD AND GETTING HIM ON OUR SIDE?? WHO WOULD BE ABLE TO PULL THAT OFF EXCEPT YOU?
AMAZING!
GEE, FLUTTERSHY, CAN YOU EVER FORGIVE ME?
OF COURSE I CAN, RAINBOW DASH!
AND I GUESS I SHOULDN'T LET MY OWN INSECURITIES CAUSE ME TO HIDE UNDER A TABLE!
WITH THE SUPPORT OF MY FRIENDS, I CAN FACE ANYTHING.
FLUTTERSHY, ARE YOU HERE?
YOU'RE BEING CALLED UP TO THE STAGE!
BUT YOU DO NOT HAVE TO GO!
YES I DO, RAINBOW DASH.
I AM GOING TO FACE MY FEARS AND DO IT WITH DIGNITY.
AND I'M GOING TO BE THERE WITH YOU!
HAS ANYONE SEEN FLUTTERSHY?

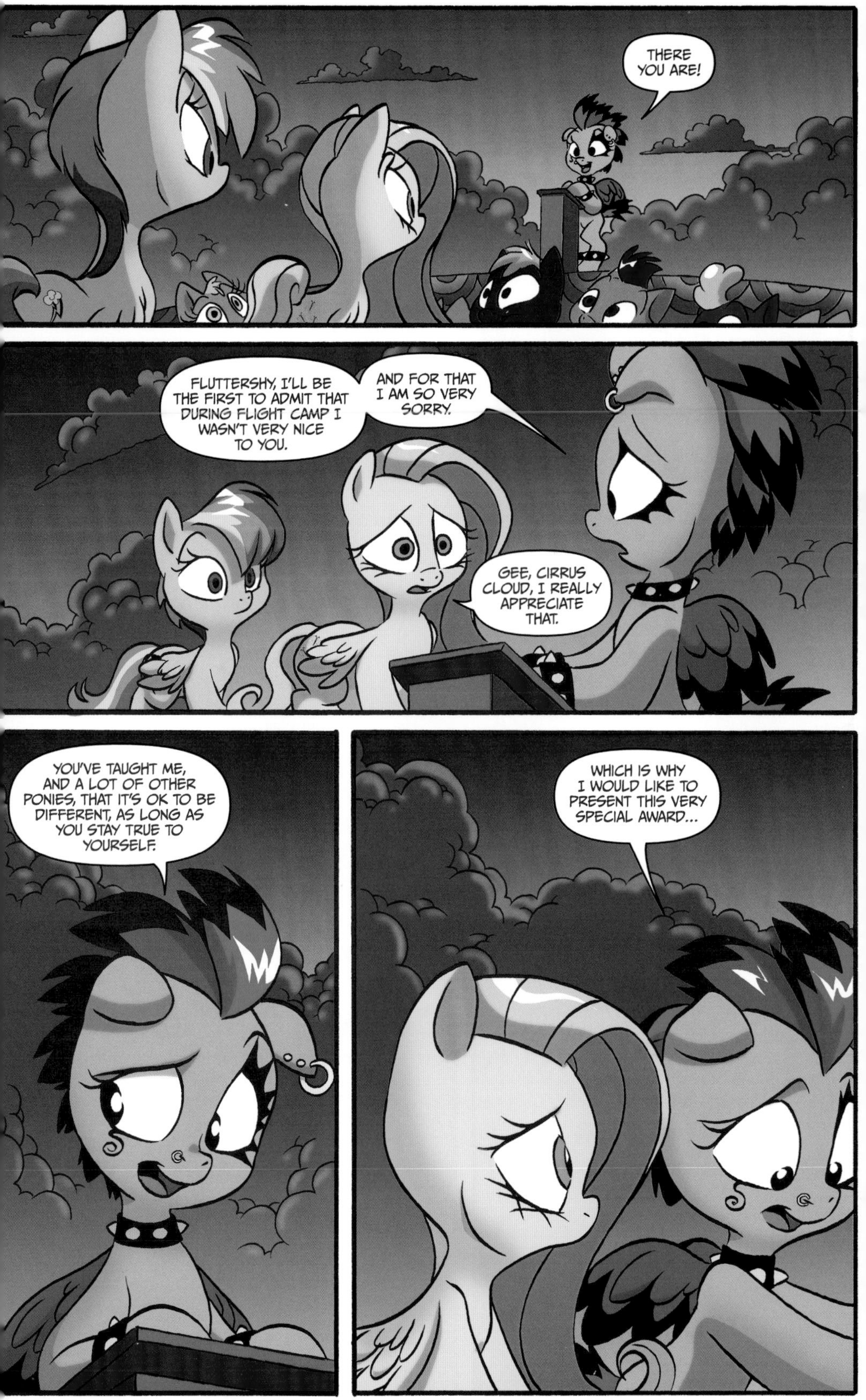

THERE YOU ARE!
FLUTTERSHY, I'LL BE THE FIRST TO ADMIT THAT DURING FLIGHT CAMP I WASN'T VERY NICE TO YOU.
AND FOR THAT I AM SO VERY SORRY.
GEE, CIRRUS CLOUD, I REALLY APPRECIATE THAT.
YOU'VE TAUGHT ME, AND A LOT OF OTHER PONIES, THAT IT'S OK TO BE DIFFERENT, AS LONG AS YOU STAY TRUE TO YOURSELF.
WHICH IS WHY I WOULD LIKE TO PRESENT THIS VERY SPECIAL AWARD...

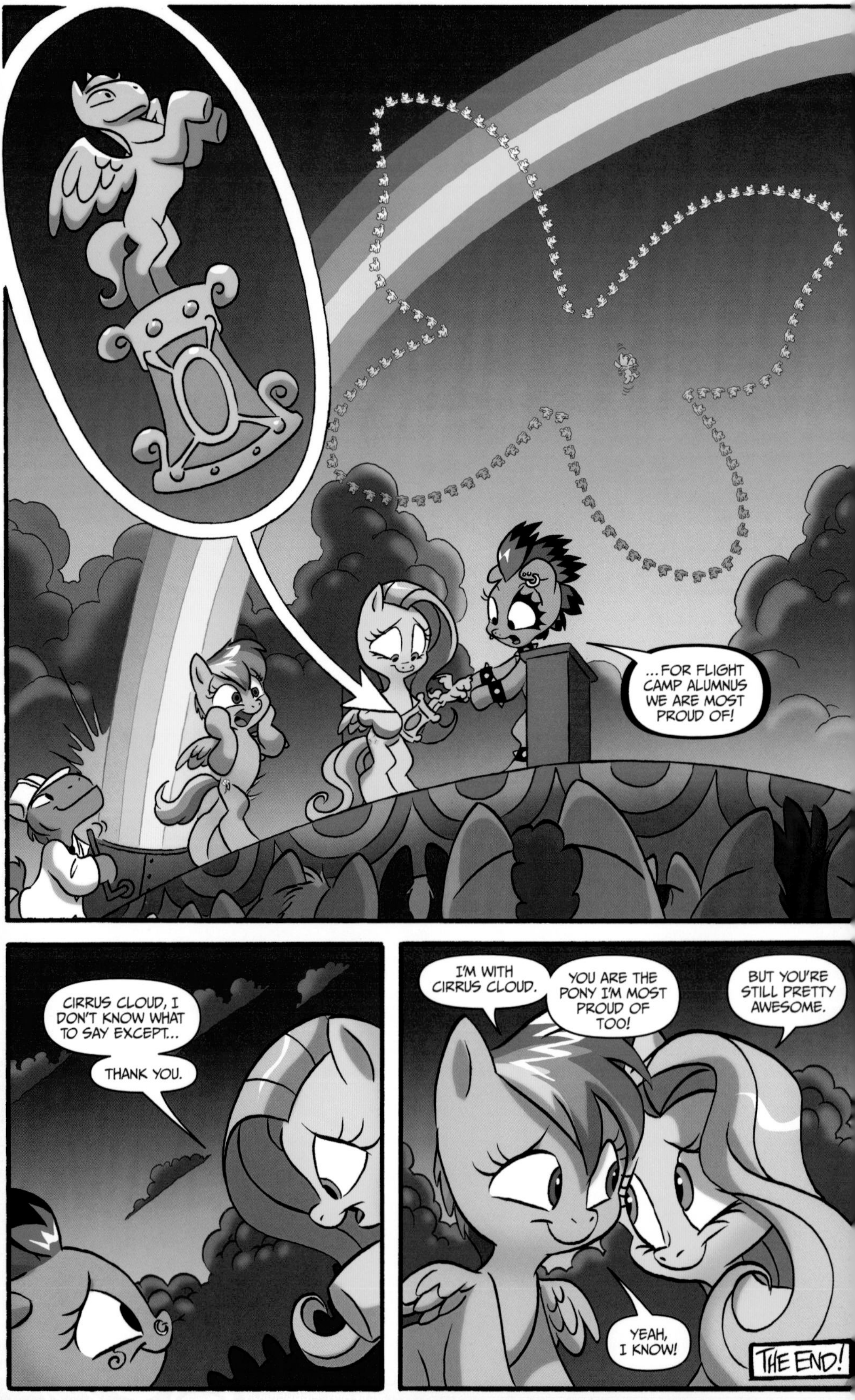
...FOR FLIGHT CAMP ALUMNUS WE ARE MOST PROUD OF!
CIRRUS CLOUD, I DON'T KNOW WHAT TO SAY EXCEPT...
THANK YOU.
I'M WITH CIRRUS CLOUD.
YOU ARE THE PONY I'M MOST PROUD OF TOO!
BUT YOU'RE STILL PRETTY AWESOME.
YEAH, I KNOW!
THE END!

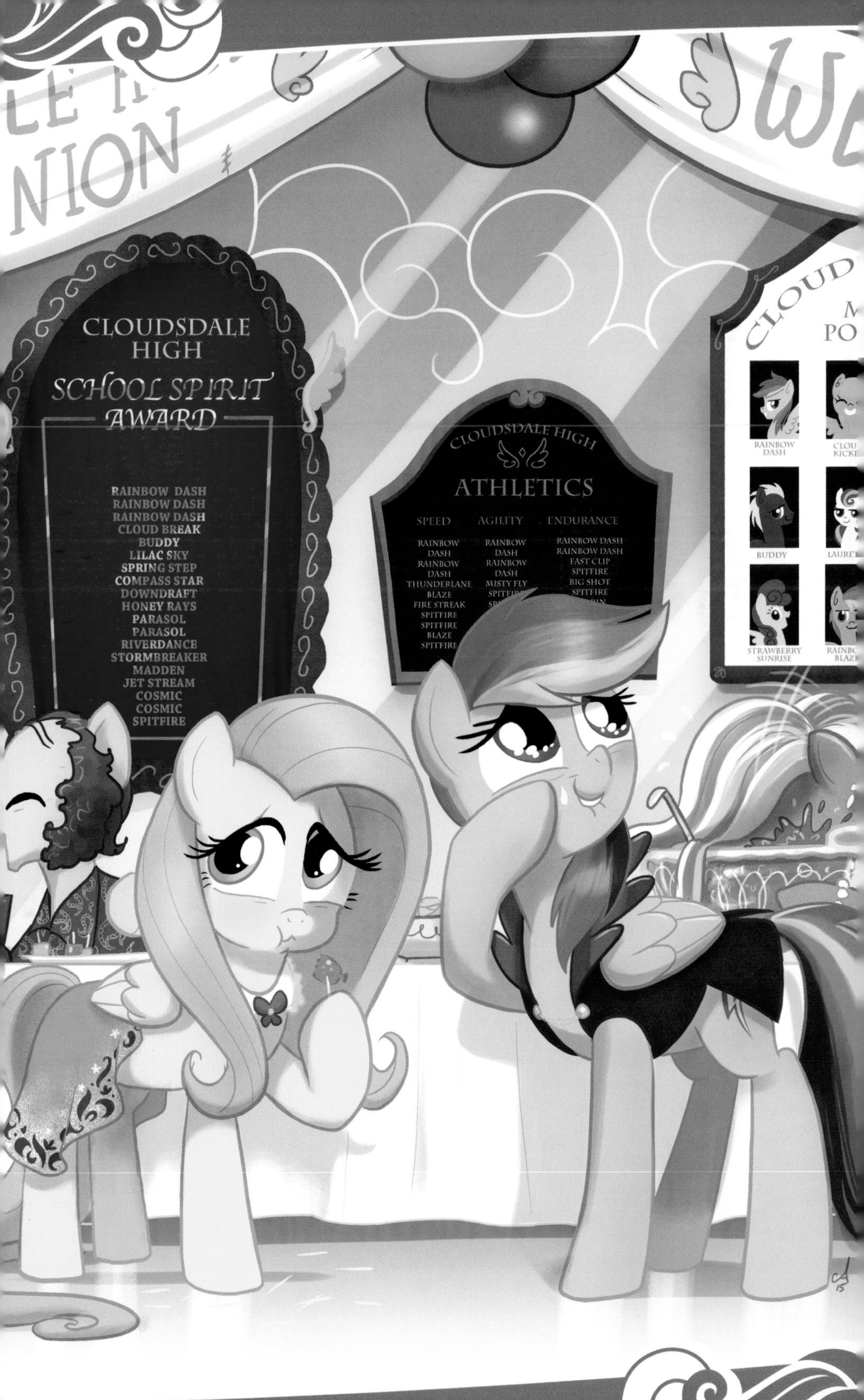
CLOUDSDALE HIGH
SCHOOL SPIRIT AWARD
RAINBOW DASH
RAINBOW DASH
RAINBOW DASH
CLOUD BREAK
BUDDY
LILAC SKY
SPRING STEP
COMPASS STAR
DOWNDRAFT
HONEY RAYS
PARASOL
PARASOL
RIVERDANCE
STORMBREAKER
MADDEN
JET STREAM
COSMIC
COSMIC
SPITFIRE
CLOUDSDALE HIGH
ATHLETICS
SPEED
RAINBOW DASH
RAINBOW DASH
THUNDERLANE
BLAZE
FIRE STREAK
SPITFIRE
SPITFIRE
BLAZE
SPITFIRE
AGILITY
RAINBOW DASH
RAINBOW DASH
MISTY FLY
ENDURANCE
RAINBOW DASH
RAINBOW DASH
FAST CLIP
SPITFIRE
BIG SHOT
SPITFIRE
RAINBOW DASH
BUDDY
STRAWBERRY SUNRISE

art by AMY MEBBERSON

Rarity & The Cakes

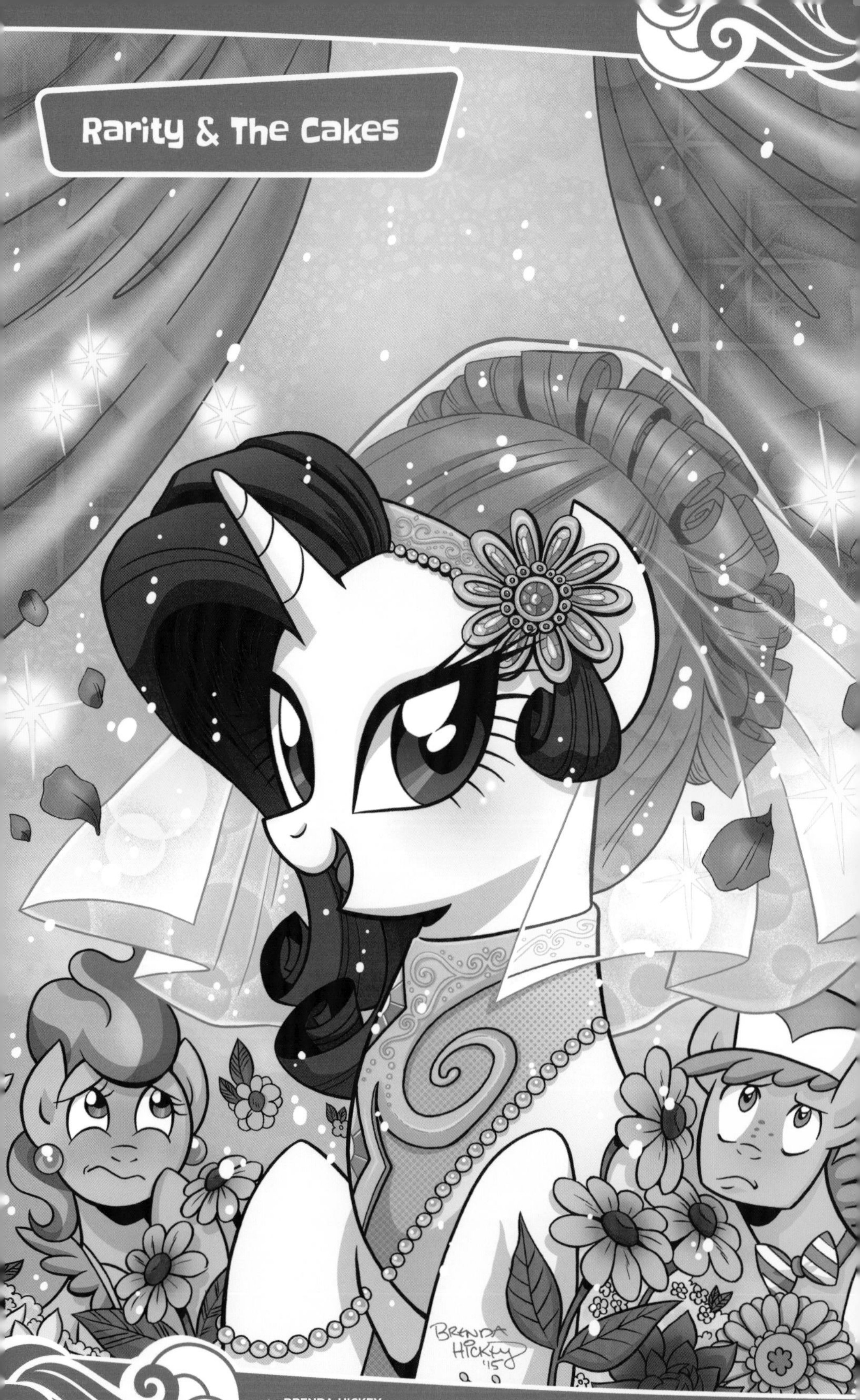
BRENDA HICKEY '15

art by BRENDA HICKEY

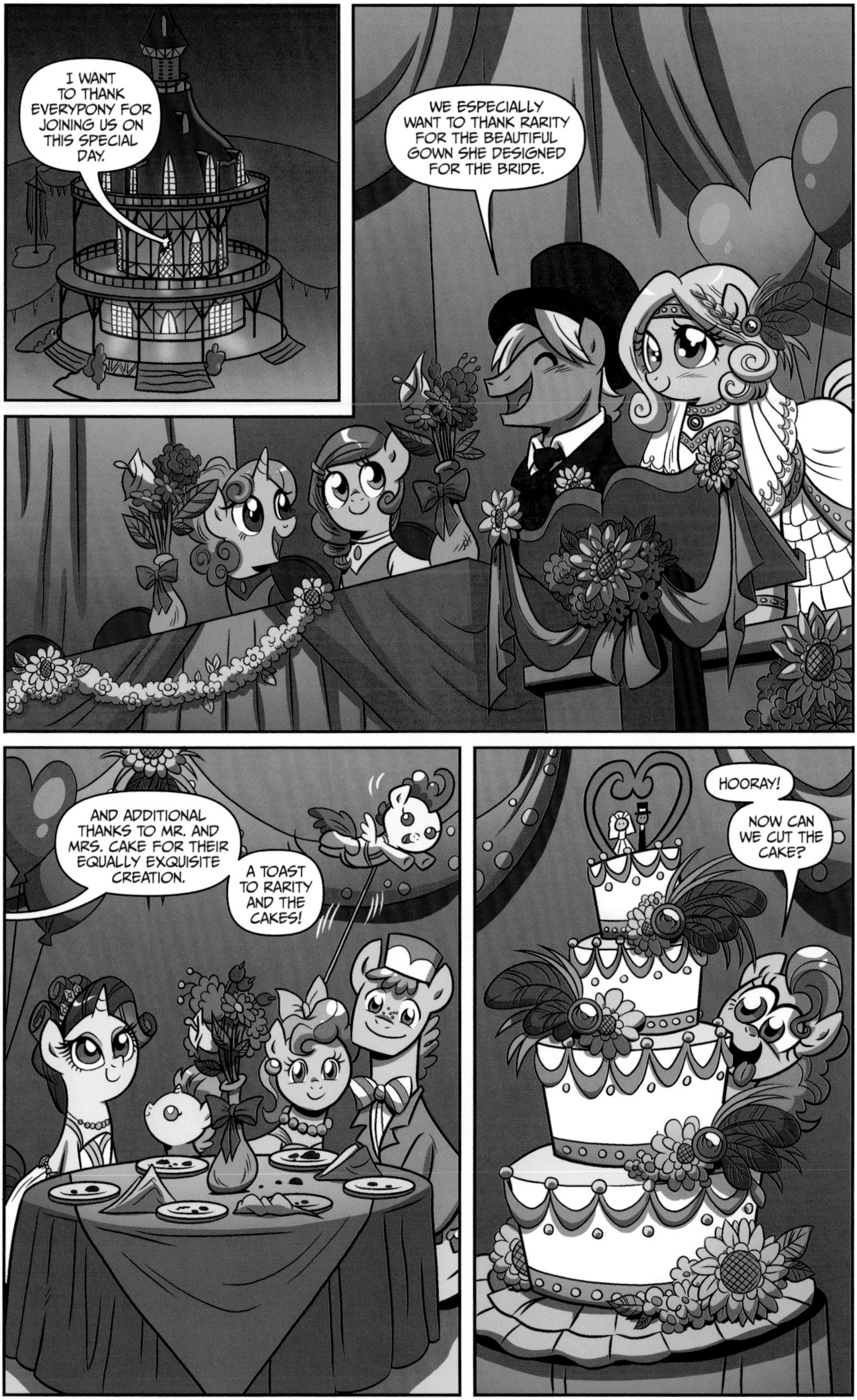
I WANT TO THANK EVERYPONY FOR JOINING US ON THIS SPECIAL DAY.
WE ESPECIALLY WANT TO THANK RARITY FOR THE BEAUTIFUL GOWN SHE DESIGNED FOR THE BRIDE.
AND ADDITIONAL THANKS TO MR. AND MRS. CAKE FOR THEIR EQUALLY EXQUISITE CREATION.
A TOAST TO RARITY AND THE CAKES!
HOORAY!
NOW CAN WE CUT THE CAKE?

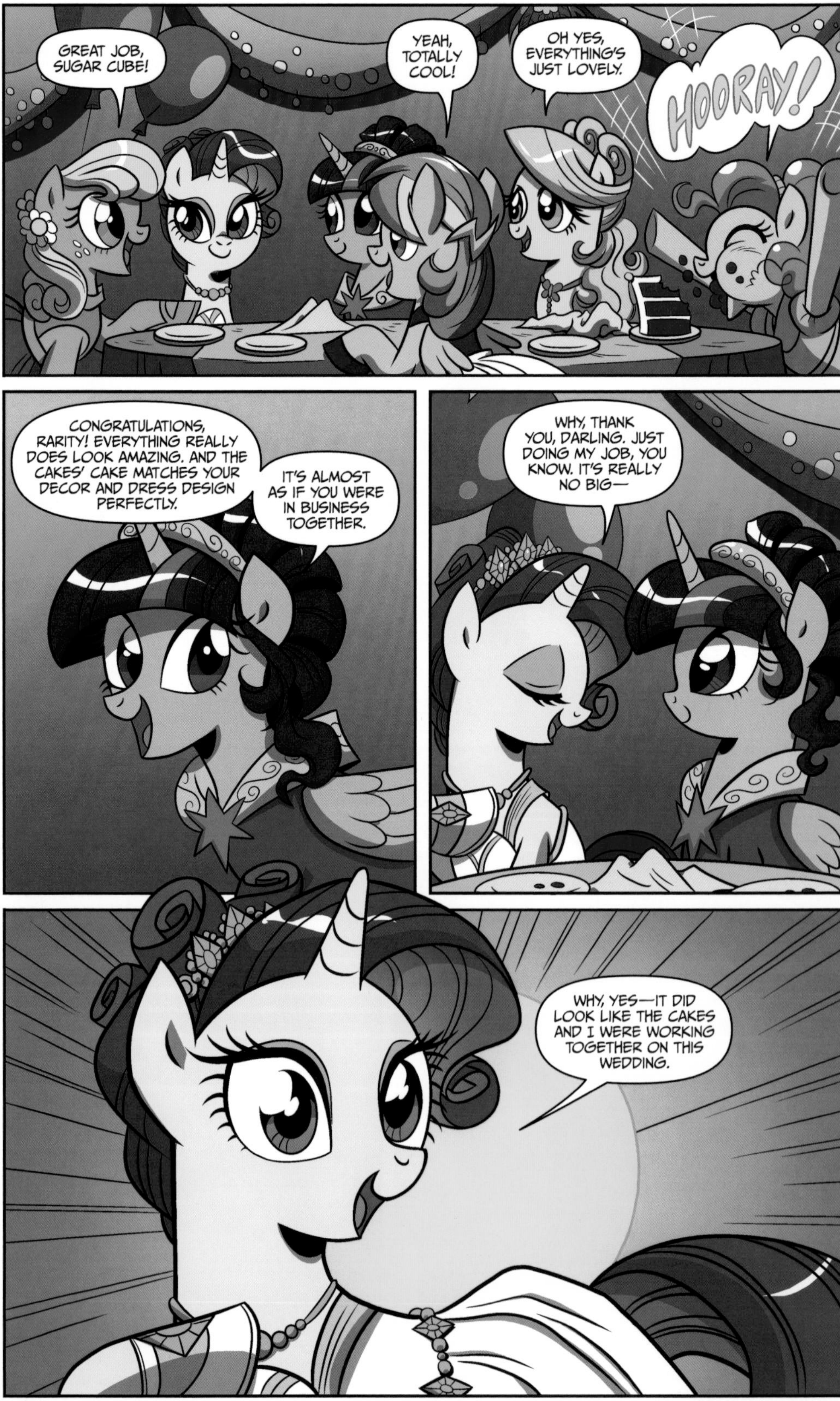
GREAT JOB, SUGAR CUBE!
YEAH, TOTALLY COOL!
OH YES, EVERYTHING'S JUST LOVELY.
HOORAY!
CONGRATULATIONS, RARITY! EVERYTHING REALLY DOES LOOK AMAZING. AND THE CAKES' CAKE MATCHES YOUR DECOR AND DRESS DESIGN PERFECTLY.
IT'S ALMOST AS IF YOU WERE IN BUSINESS TOGETHER.
WHY, THANK YOU, DARLING. JUST DOING MY JOB, YOU KNOW. IT'S REALLY NO BIG—
WHY, YES—IT DID LOOK LIKE THE CAKES AND I WERE WORKING TOGETHER ON THIS WEDDING.

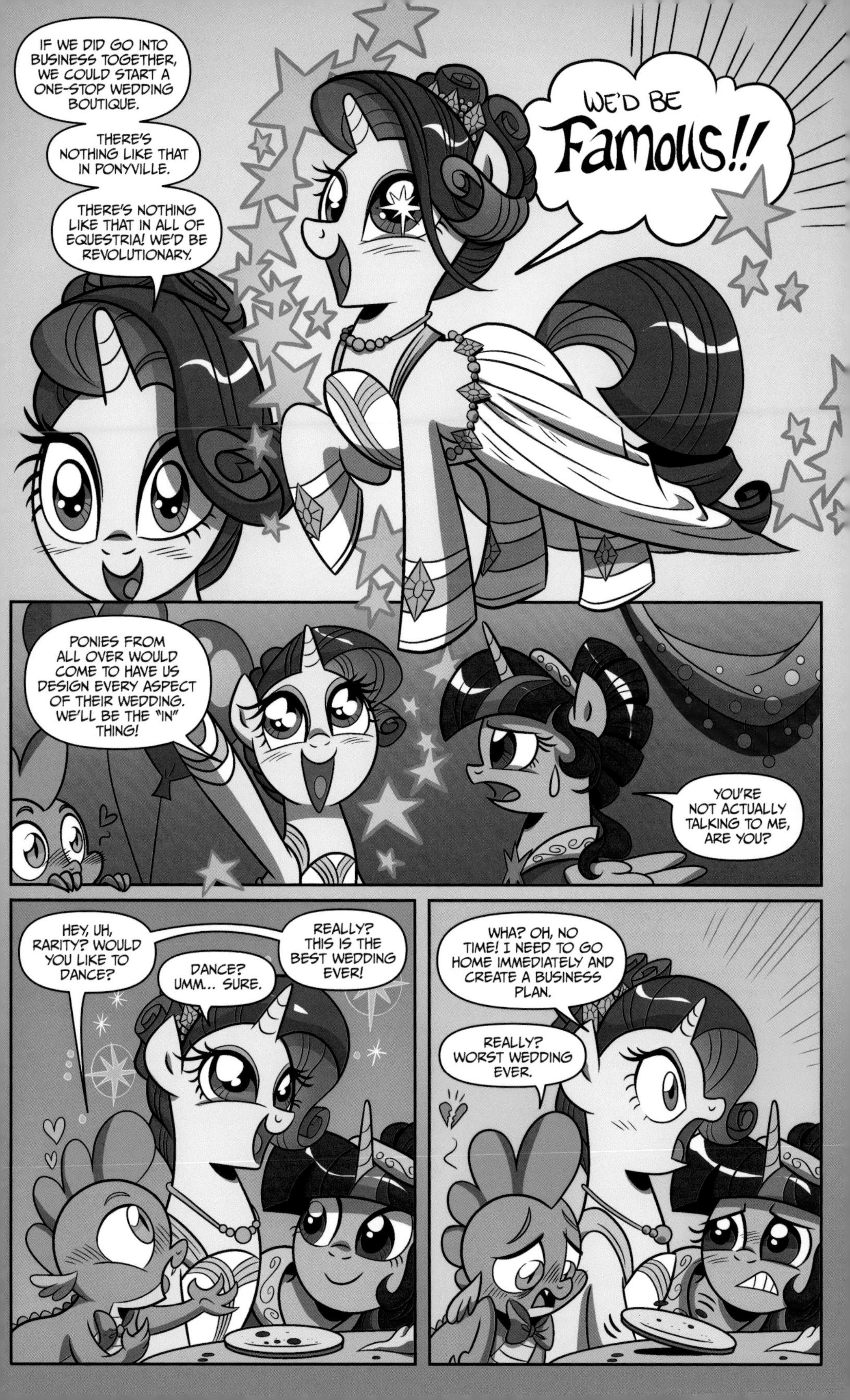
IF WE DID GO INTO BUSINESS TOGETHER, WE COULD START A ONE-STOP WEDDING BOUTIQUE.
THERE'S NOTHING LIKE THAT IN PONYVILLE.
THERE'S NOTHING LIKE THAT IN ALL OF EQUESTRIA! WE'D BE REVOLUTIONARY.
WE'D BE Famous!!
PONIES FROM ALL OVER WOULD COME TO HAVE US DESIGN EVERY ASPECT OF THEIR WEDDING. WE'LL BE THE "IN" THING!
YOU'RE NOT ACTUALLY TALKING TO ME, ARE YOU?
HEY, UH, RARITY? WOULD YOU LIKE TO DANCE?
DANCE? UMM... SURE.
REALLY? THIS IS THE BEST WEDDING EVER!
WHA? OH, NO TIME! I NEED TO GO HOME IMMEDIATELY AND CREATE A BUSINESS PLAN.
REALLY? WORST WEDDING EVER.

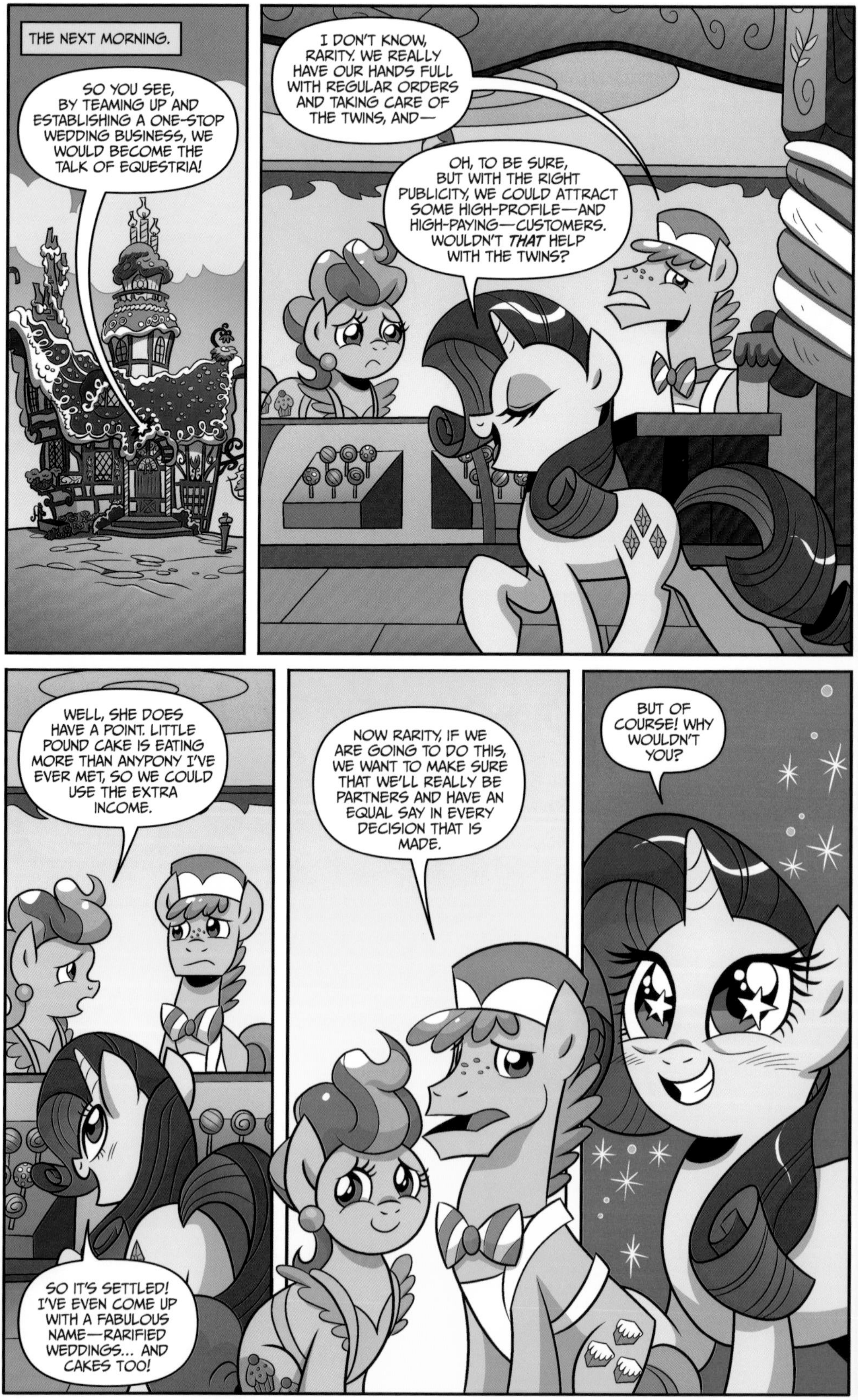
THE NEXT MORNING.
SO YOU SEE, BY TEAMING UP AND ESTABLISHING A ONE-STOP WEDDING BUSINESS, WE WOULD BECOME THE TALK OF EQUESTRIA!
I DON'T KNOW, RARITY. WE REALLY HAVE OUR HANDS FULL WITH REGULAR ORDERS AND TAKING CARE OF THE TWINS, AND—
OH, TO BE SURE, BUT WITH THE RIGHT PUBLICITY, WE COULD ATTRACT SOME HIGH-PROFILE—AND HIGH-PAYING—CUSTOMERS. WOULDN'T *THAT* HELP WITH THE TWINS?
WELL, SHE DOES HAVE A POINT. LITTLE POUND CAKE IS EATING MORE THAN ANYPONY I'VE EVER MET, SO WE COULD USE THE EXTRA INCOME.
SO IT'S SETTLED! I'VE EVEN COME UP WITH A FABULOUS NAME—RARIFIED WEDDINGS... AND CAKES TOO!
NOW RARITY, IF WE ARE GOING TO DO THIS, WE WANT TO MAKE SURE THAT WE'LL REALLY BE PARTNERS AND HAVE AN EQUAL SAY IN EVERY DECISION THAT IS MADE.
BUT OF COURSE! WHY WOULDN'T YOU?

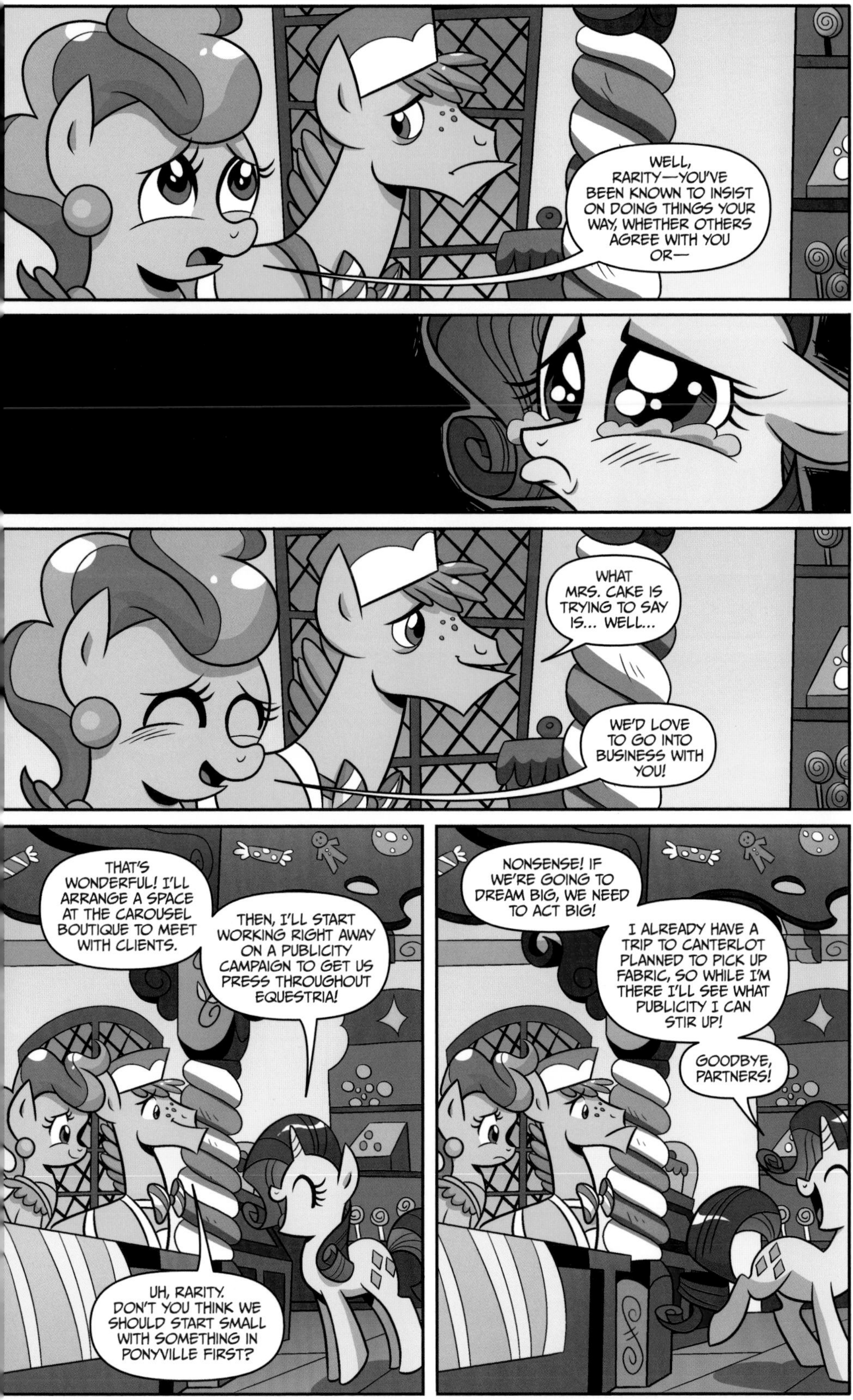
WELL, RARITY—YOU'VE BEEN KNOWN TO INSIST ON DOING THINGS YOUR WAY, WHETHER OTHERS AGREE WITH YOU OR—
WHAT MRS. CAKE IS TRYING TO SAY IS... WELL...
WE'D LOVE TO GO INTO BUSINESS WITH YOU!
THAT'S WONDERFUL! I'LL ARRANGE A SPACE AT THE CAROUSEL BOUTIQUE TO MEET WITH CLIENTS.
THEN, I'LL START WORKING RIGHT AWAY ON A PUBLICITY CAMPAIGN TO GET US PRESS THROUGHOUT EQUESTRIA!
UH, RARITY. DON'T YOU THINK WE SHOULD START SMALL WITH SOMETHING IN PONYVILLE FIRST?
NONSENSE! IF WE'RE GOING TO DREAM BIG, WE NEED TO ACT BIG!
I ALREADY HAVE A TRIP TO CANTERLOT PLANNED TO PICK UP FABRIC, SO WHILE I'M THERE I'LL SEE WHAT PUBLICITY I CAN STIR UP!
GOODBYE, PARTNERS!

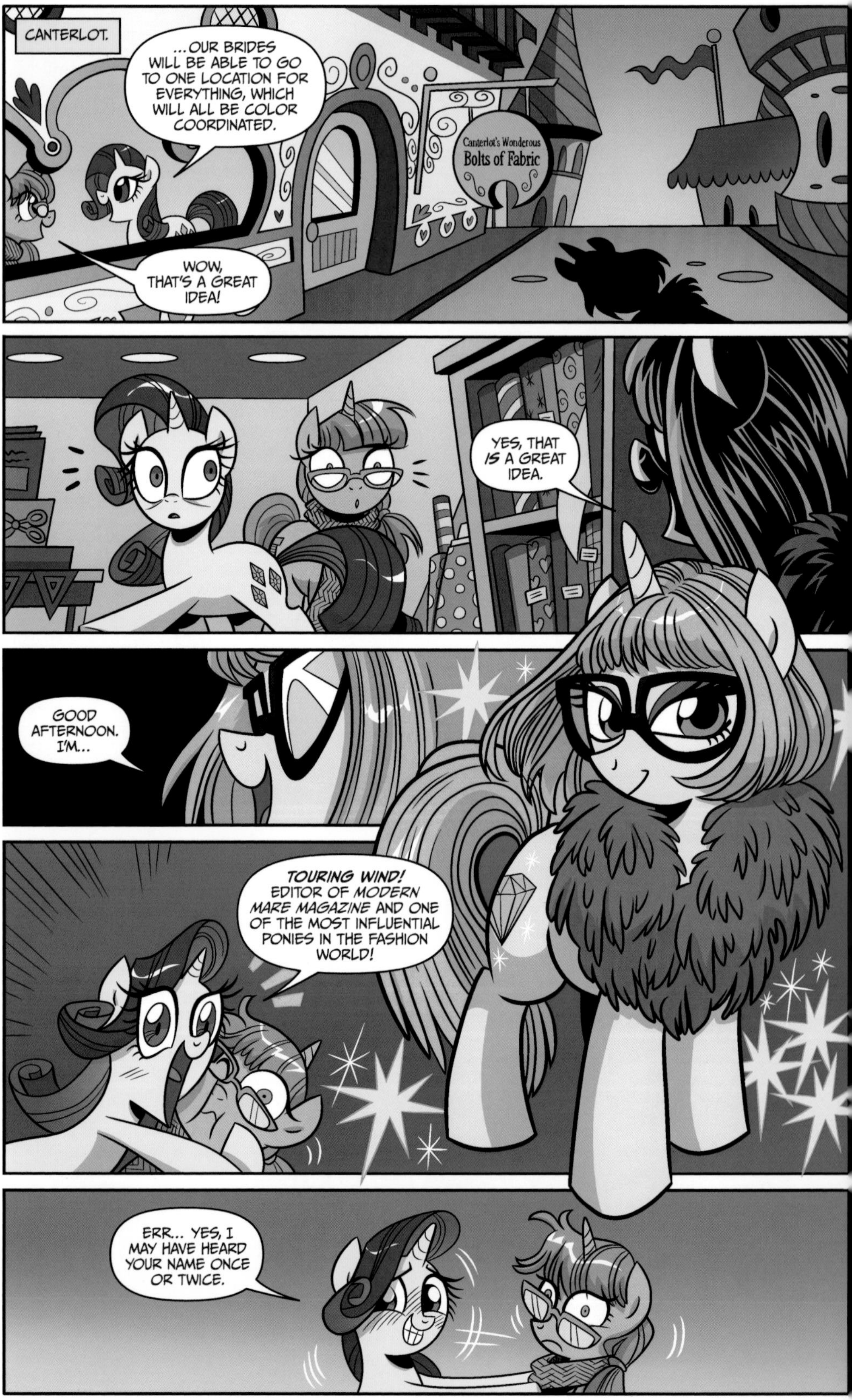
CANTERLOT.
...OUR BRIDES WILL BE ABLE TO GO TO ONE LOCATION FOR EVERYTHING, WHICH WILL ALL BE COLOR COORDINATED.
Canterlot's Wonderous Bolts of Fabric
WOW, THAT'S A GREAT IDEA!
YES, THAT IS A GREAT IDEA.
GOOD AFTERNOON. I'M...
TOURING WIND! EDITOR OF MODERN MARE MAGAZINE AND ONE OF THE MOST INFLUENTIAL PONIES IN THE FASHION WORLD!
ERR... YES, I MAY HAVE HEARD YOUR NAME ONCE OR TWICE.

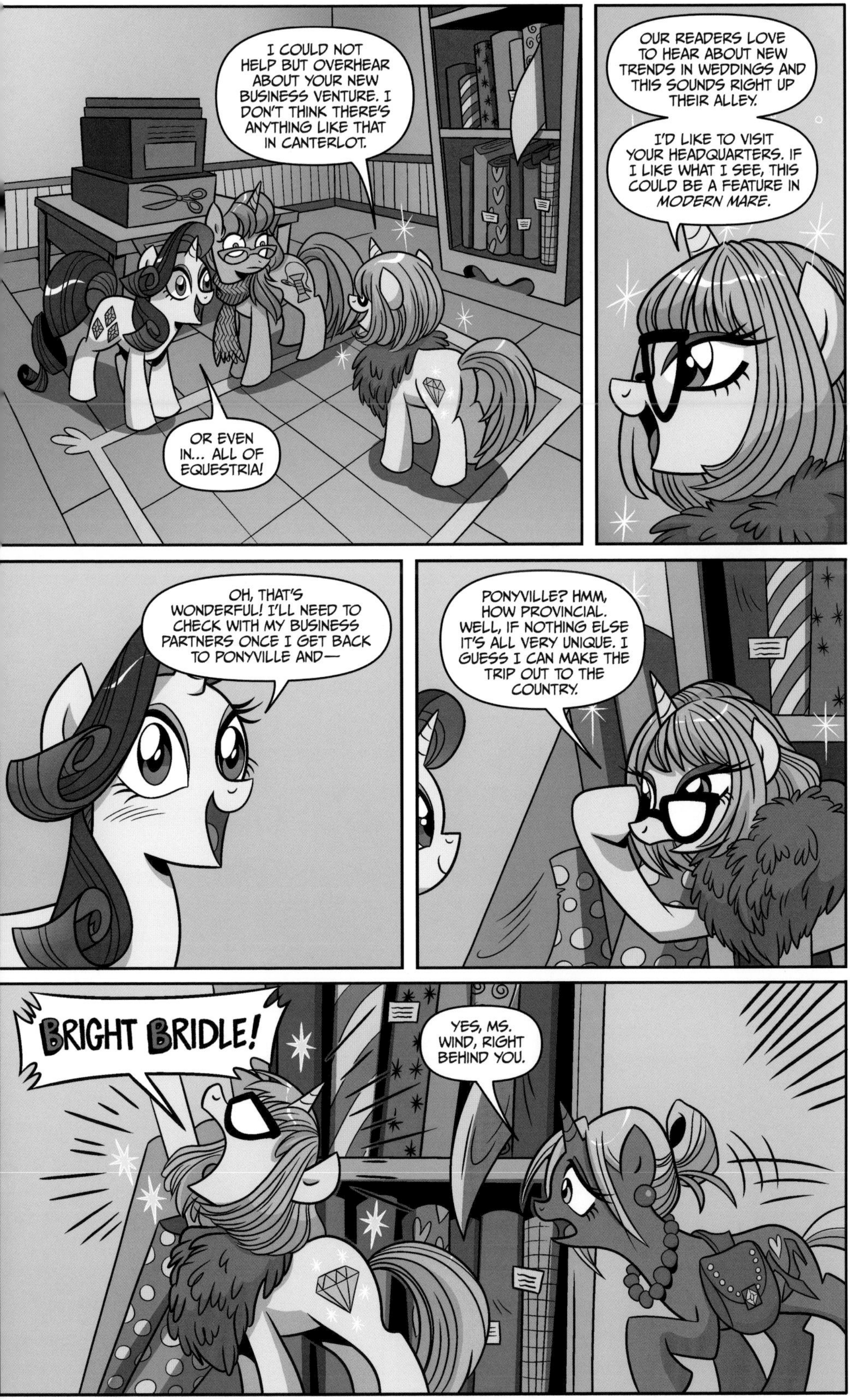
I COULD NOT HELP BUT OVERHEAR ABOUT YOUR NEW BUSINESS VENTURE. I DON'T THINK THERE'S ANYTHING LIKE THAT IN CANTERLOT.
OR EVEN IN... ALL OF EQUESTRIA!
OUR READERS LOVE TO HEAR ABOUT NEW TRENDS IN WEDDINGS AND THIS SOUNDS RIGHT UP THEIR ALLEY.
I'D LIKE TO VISIT YOUR HEADQUARTERS. IF I LIKE WHAT I SEE, THIS COULD BE A FEATURE IN *MODERN MARE*.
OH, THAT'S WONDERFUL! I'LL NEED TO CHECK WITH MY BUSINESS PARTNERS ONCE I GET BACK TO PONYVILLE AND—
PONYVILLE? HMM, HOW PROVINCIAL. WELL, IF NOTHING ELSE IT'S ALL VERY UNIQUE. I GUESS I CAN MAKE THE TRIP OUT TO THE COUNTRY.
BRIGHT BRIDLE!
YES, MS. WIND, RIGHT BEHIND YOU.

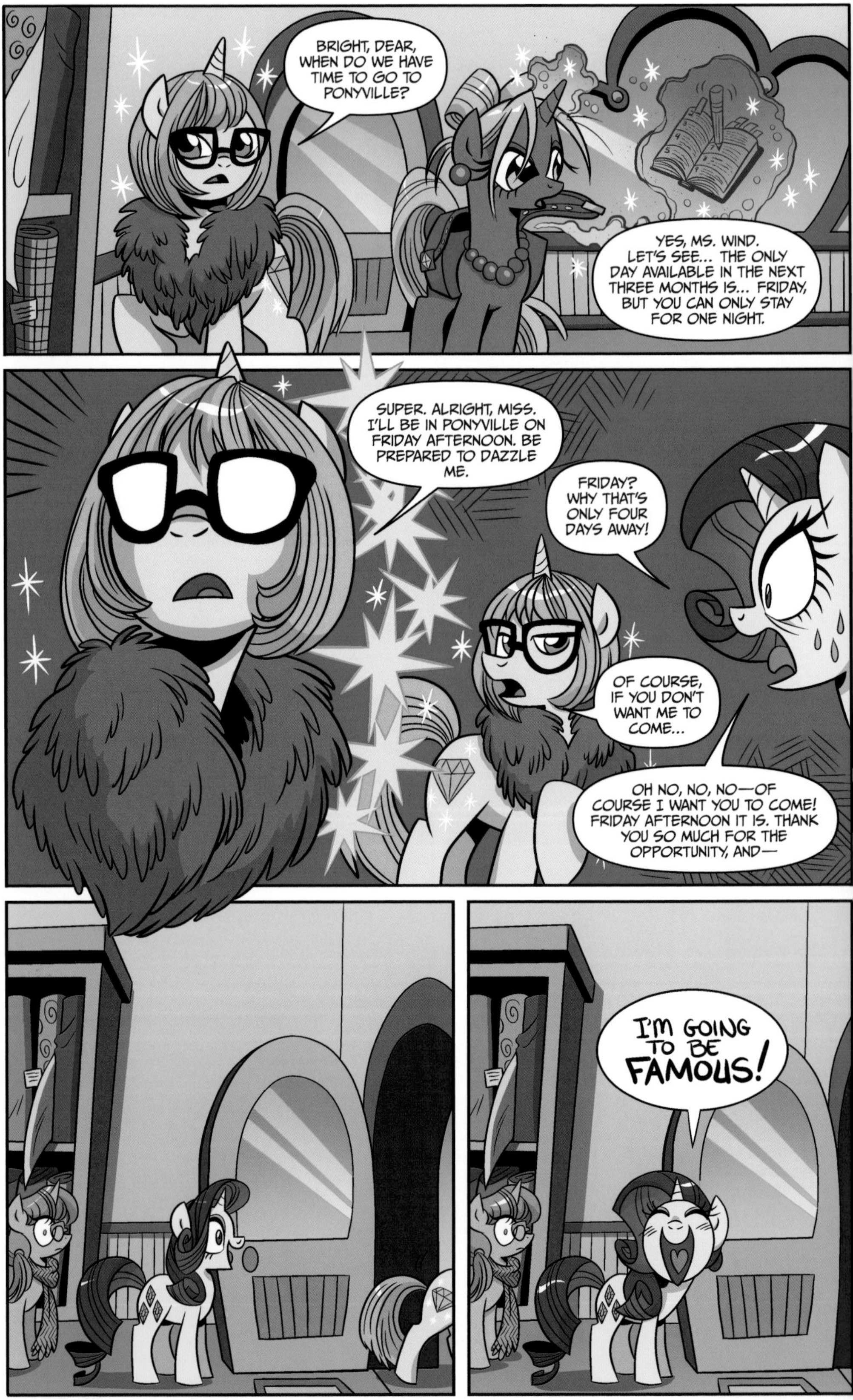
BRIGHT, DEAR, WHEN DO WE HAVE TIME TO GO TO PONYVILLE?
YES, MS. WIND. LET'S SEE... THE ONLY DAY AVAILABLE IN THE NEXT THREE MONTHS IS... FRIDAY, BUT YOU CAN ONLY STAY FOR ONE NIGHT.
SUPER. ALRIGHT, MISS. I'LL BE IN PONYVILLE ON FRIDAY AFTERNOON. BE PREPARED TO DAZZLE ME.
FRIDAY? WHY THAT'S ONLY FOUR DAYS AWAY!
OF COURSE, IF YOU DON'T WANT ME TO COME...
OH NO, NO, NO—OF COURSE I WANT YOU TO COME! FRIDAY AFTERNOON IT IS. THANK YOU SO MUCH FOR THE OPPORTUNITY, AND—
I'M GOING TO BE FAMOUS!

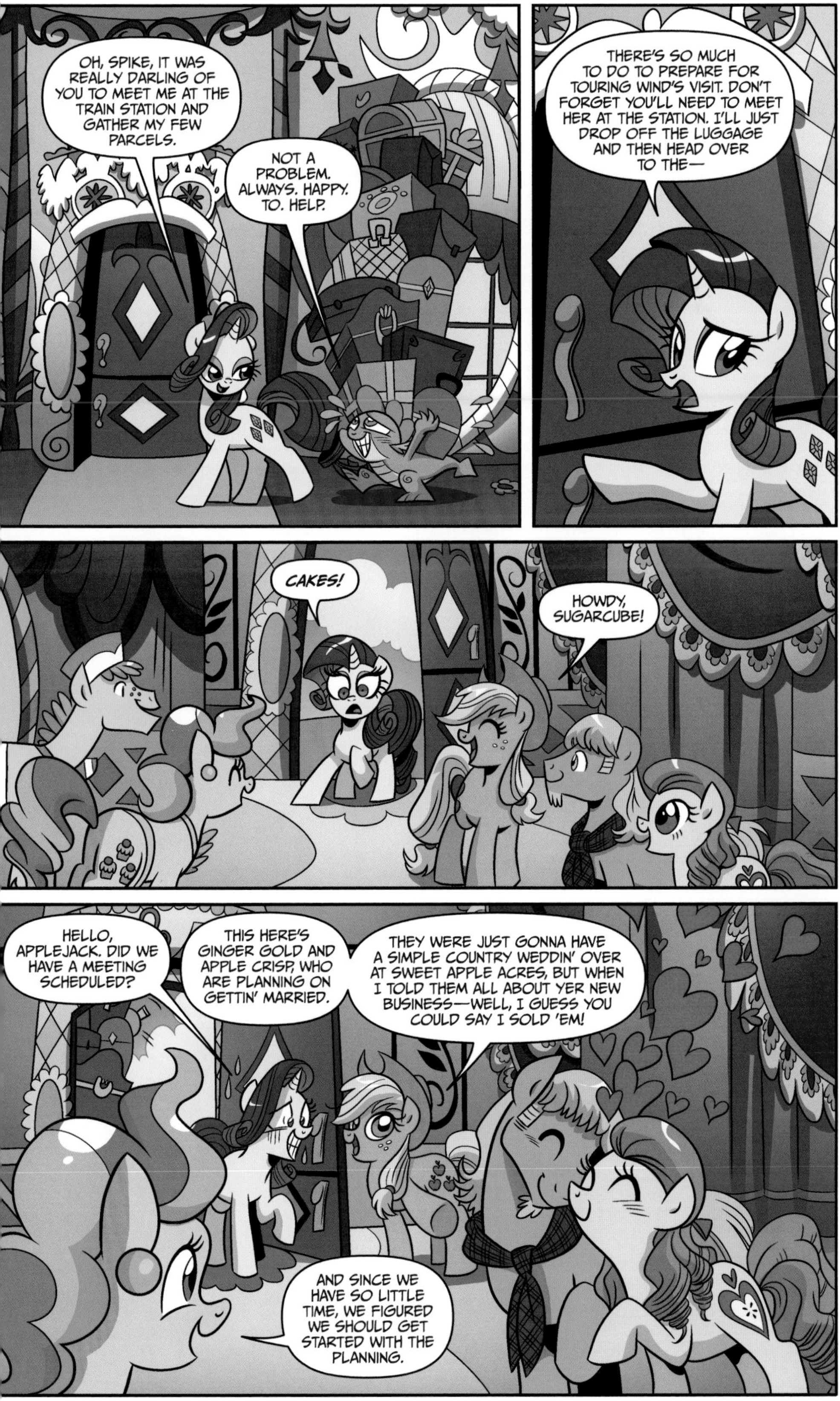
OH, SPIKE, IT WAS REALLY DARLING OF YOU TO MEET ME AT THE TRAIN STATION AND GATHER MY FEW PARCELS.
NOT A PROBLEM. ALWAYS. HAPPY. TO. HELP.
THERE'S SO MUCH TO DO TO PREPARE FOR TOURING WIND'S VISIT. DON'T FORGET YOU'LL NEED TO MEET HER AT THE STATION. I'LL JUST DROP OFF THE LUGGAGE AND THEN HEAD OVER TO THE—
CAKES!
HOWDY, SUGARCUBE!
HELLO, APPLEJACK. DID WE HAVE A MEETING SCHEDULED?
THIS HERE'S GINGER GOLD AND APPLE CRISP, WHO ARE PLANNING ON GETTIN' MARRIED.
THEY WERE JUST GONNA HAVE A SIMPLE COUNTRY WEDDIN' OVER AT SWEET APPLE ACRES, BUT WHEN I TOLD THEM ALL ABOUT YER NEW BUSINESS—WELL, I GUESS YOU COULD SAY I SOLD 'EM!
AND SINCE WE HAVE SO LITTLE TIME, WE FIGURED WE SHOULD GET STARTED WITH THE PLANNING.

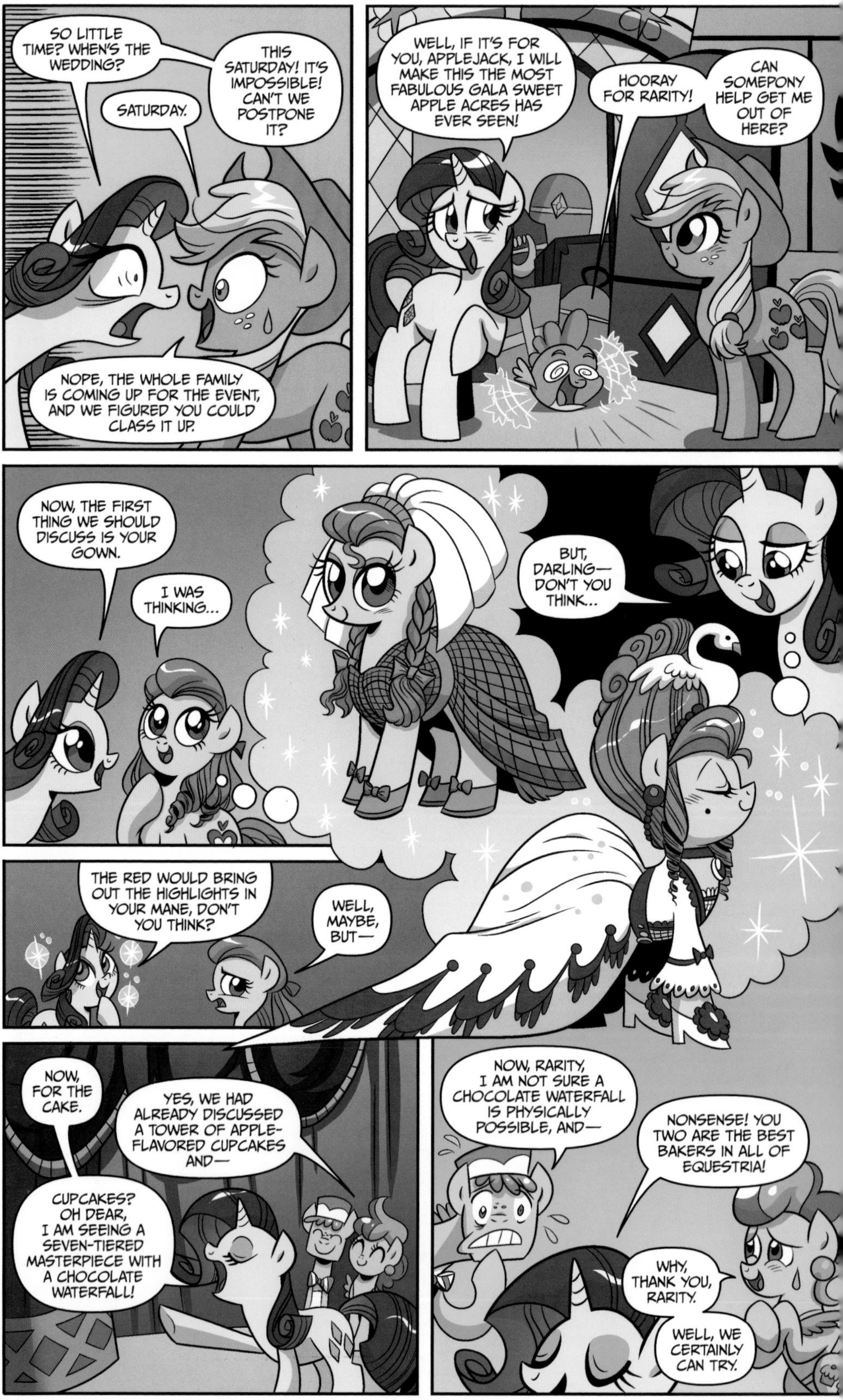
SO LITTLE TIME? WHEN'S THE WEDDING?
SATURDAY.
THIS SATURDAY! IT'S IMPOSSIBLE! CAN'T WE POSTPONE IT?
NOPE, THE WHOLE FAMILY IS COMING UP FOR THE EVENT, AND WE FIGURED YOU COULD CLASS IT UP.
WELL, IF IT'S FOR YOU, APPLEJACK, I WILL MAKE THIS THE MOST FABULOUS GALA SWEET APPLE ACRES HAS EVER SEEN!
HOORAY FOR RARITY!
CAN SOMEPONY HELP GET ME OUT OF HERE?
NOW, THE FIRST THING WE SHOULD DISCUSS IS YOUR GOWN.
I WAS THINKING...
BUT, DARLING— DON'T YOU THINK...
THE RED WOULD BRING OUT THE HIGHLIGHTS IN YOUR MANE, DON'T YOU THINK?
WELL, MAYBE, BUT—
NOW, FOR THE CAKE.
YES, WE HAD ALREADY DISCUSSED A TOWER OF APPLE-FLAVORED CUPCAKES AND—
CUPCAKES? OH DEAR, I AM SEEING A SEVEN-TIERED MASTERPIECE WITH A CHOCOLATE WATERFALL!
NOW, RARITY, I AM NOT SURE A CHOCOLATE WATERFALL IS PHYSICALLY POSSIBLE, AND—
NONSENSE! YOU TWO ARE THE BEST BAKERS IN ALL OF EQUESTRIA!
WHY, THANK YOU, RARITY.
WELL, WE CERTAINLY CAN TRY.

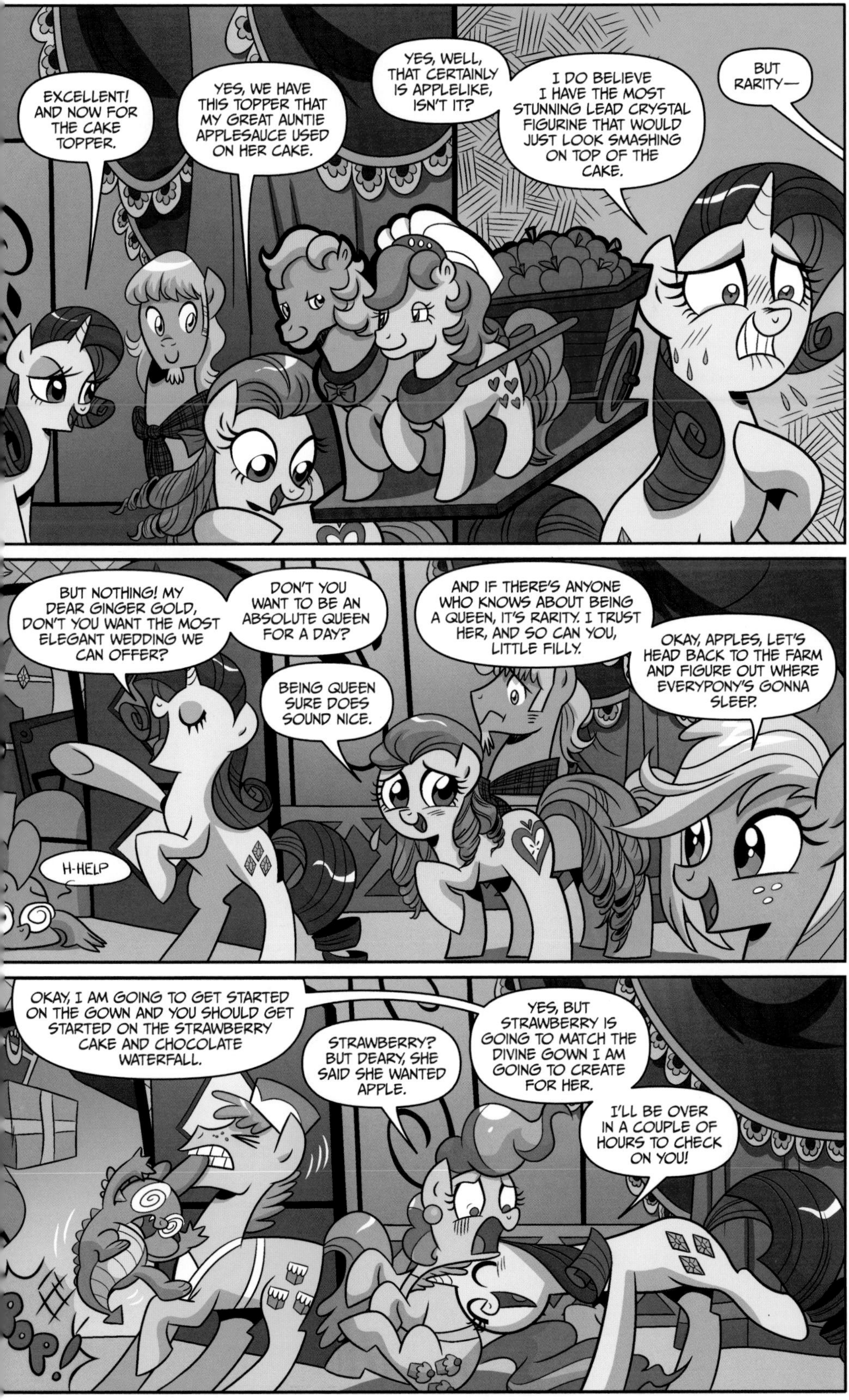
EXCELLENT! AND NOW FOR THE CAKE TOPPER.
YES, WE HAVE THIS TOPPER THAT MY GREAT AUNTIE APPLESAUCE USED ON HER CAKE.
YES, WELL, THAT CERTAINLY IS APPLELIKE, ISN'T IT?
I DO BELIEVE I HAVE THE MOST STUNNING LEAD CRYSTAL FIGURINE THAT WOULD JUST LOOK SMASHING ON TOP OF THE CAKE.
BUT RARITY—
BUT NOTHING! MY DEAR GINGER GOLD, DON'T YOU WANT THE MOST ELEGANT WEDDING WE CAN OFFER?
DON'T YOU WANT TO BE AN ABSOLUTE QUEEN FOR A DAY?
BEING QUEEN SURE DOES SOUND NICE.
AND IF THERE'S ANYONE WHO KNOWS ABOUT BEING A QUEEN, IT'S RARITY. I TRUST HER, AND SO CAN YOU, LITTLE FILLY.
OKAY, APPLES, LET'S HEAD BACK TO THE FARM AND FIGURE OUT WHERE EVERYPONY'S GONNA SLEEP.
H-HELP
OKAY, I AM GOING TO GET STARTED ON THE GOWN AND YOU SHOULD GET STARTED ON THE STRAWBERRY CAKE AND CHOCOLATE WATERFALL.
STRAWBERRY? BUT DEARY, SHE SAID SHE WANTED APPLE.
YES, BUT STRAWBERRY IS GOING TO MATCH THE DIVINE GOWN I AM GOING TO CREATE FOR HER.
I'LL BE OVER IN A COUPLE OF HOURS TO CHECK ON YOU!
BOP!

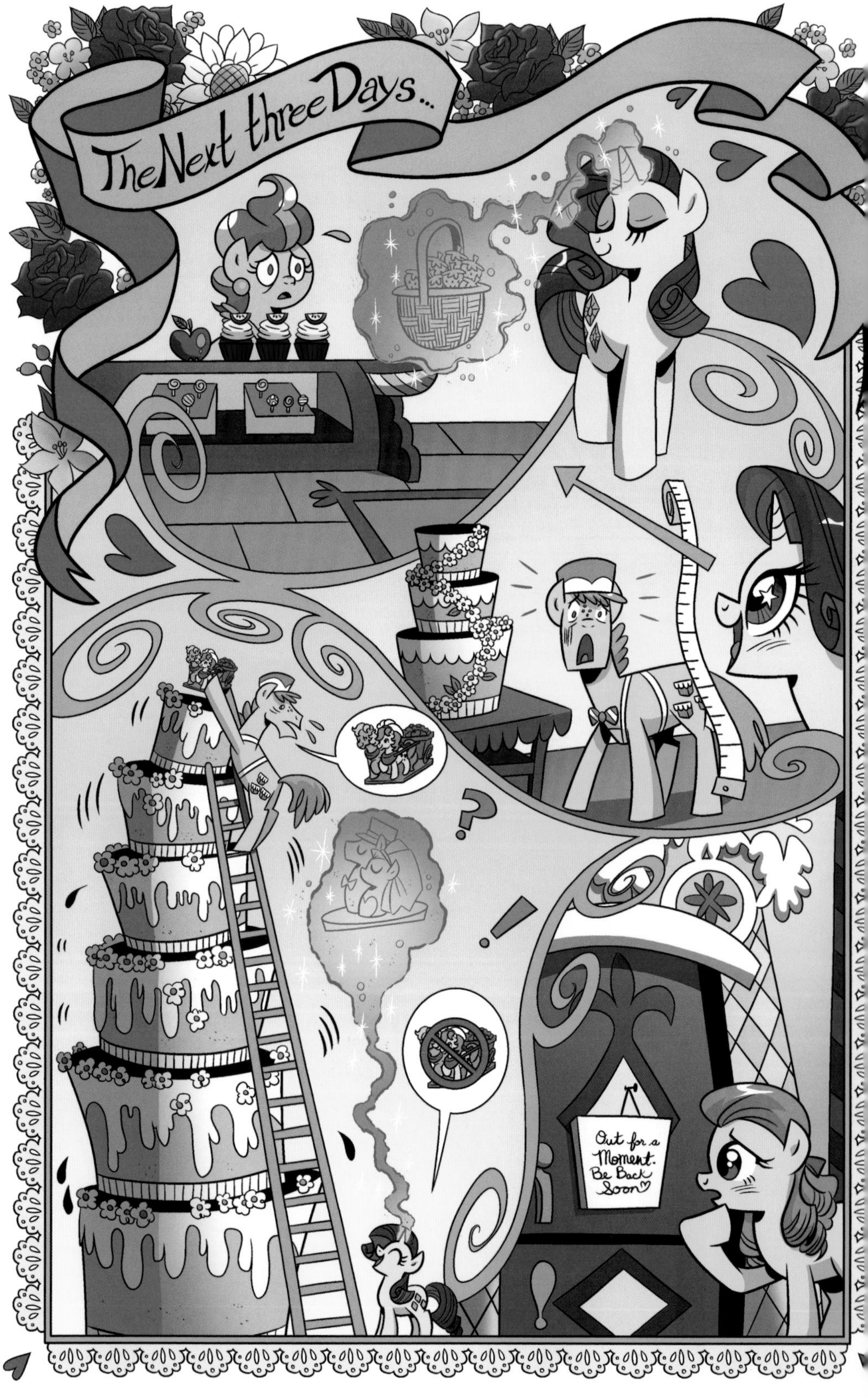
The Next three Days...
?
!
Out for a Moment. Be Back Soon♡

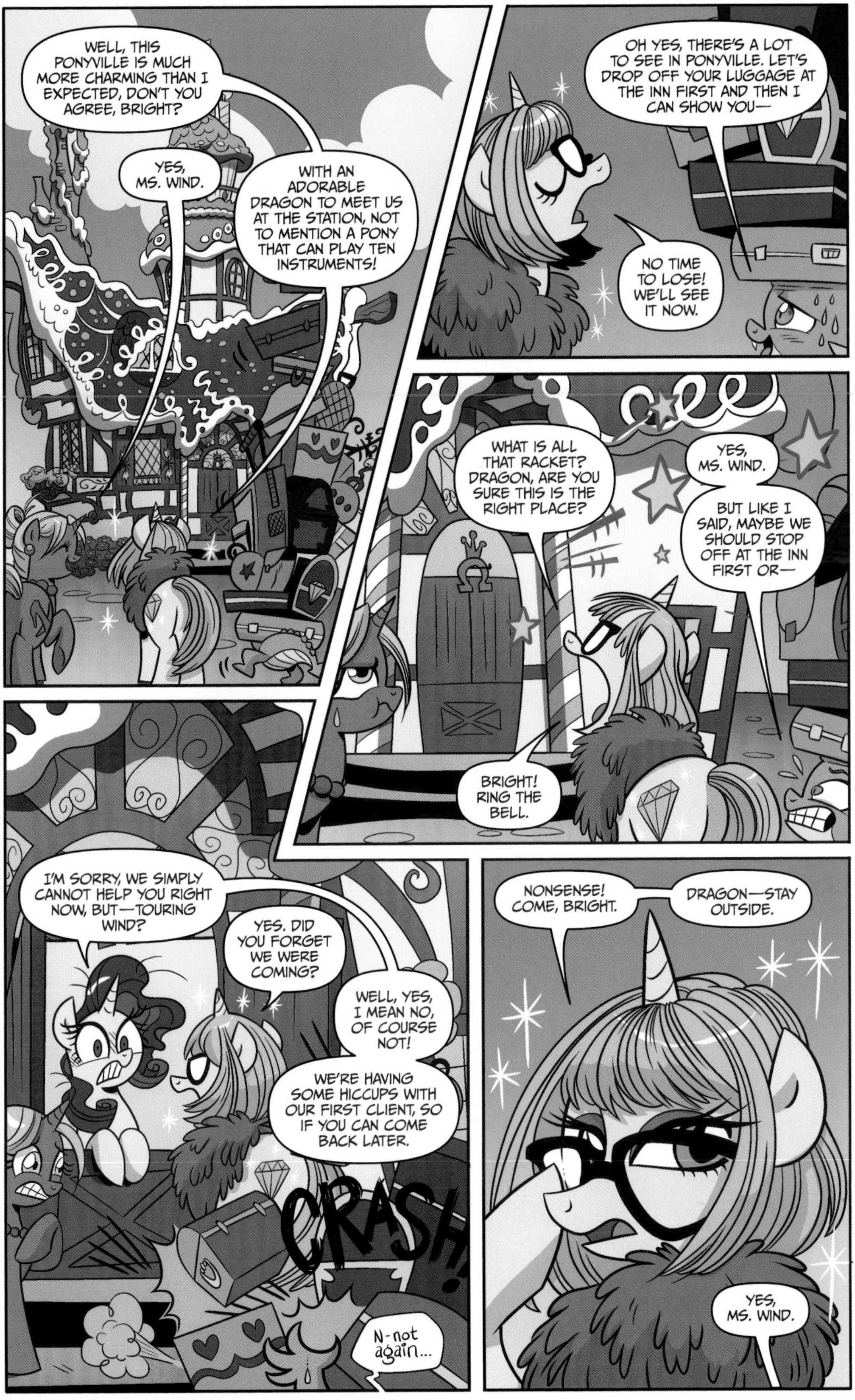
WELL, THIS PONYVILLE IS MUCH MORE CHARMING THAN I EXPECTED, DON'T YOU AGREE, BRIGHT?
YES, MS. WIND.
WITH AN ADORABLE DRAGON TO MEET US AT THE STATION, NOT TO MENTION A PONY THAT CAN PLAY TEN INSTRUMENTS!
OH YES, THERE'S A LOT TO SEE IN PONYVILLE. LET'S DROP OFF YOUR LUGGAGE AT THE INN FIRST AND THEN I CAN SHOW YOU—
NO TIME TO LOSE! WE'LL SEE IT NOW.
WHAT IS ALL THAT RACKET? DRAGON, ARE YOU SURE THIS IS THE RIGHT PLACE?
YES, MS. WIND.
BUT LIKE I SAID, MAYBE WE SHOULD STOP OFF AT THE INN FIRST OR—
BRIGHT! RING THE BELL.
I'M SORRY, WE SIMPLY CANNOT HELP YOU RIGHT NOW, BUT—TOURING WIND?
YES. DID YOU FORGET WE WERE COMING?
WELL, YES, I MEAN NO, OF COURSE NOT!
WE'RE HAVING SOME HICCUPS WITH OUR FIRST CLIENT, SO IF YOU CAN COME BACK LATER.
CRASH!
N-not again...
NONSENSE! COME, BRIGHT.
DRAGON—STAY OUTSIDE.
YES, MS. WIND.

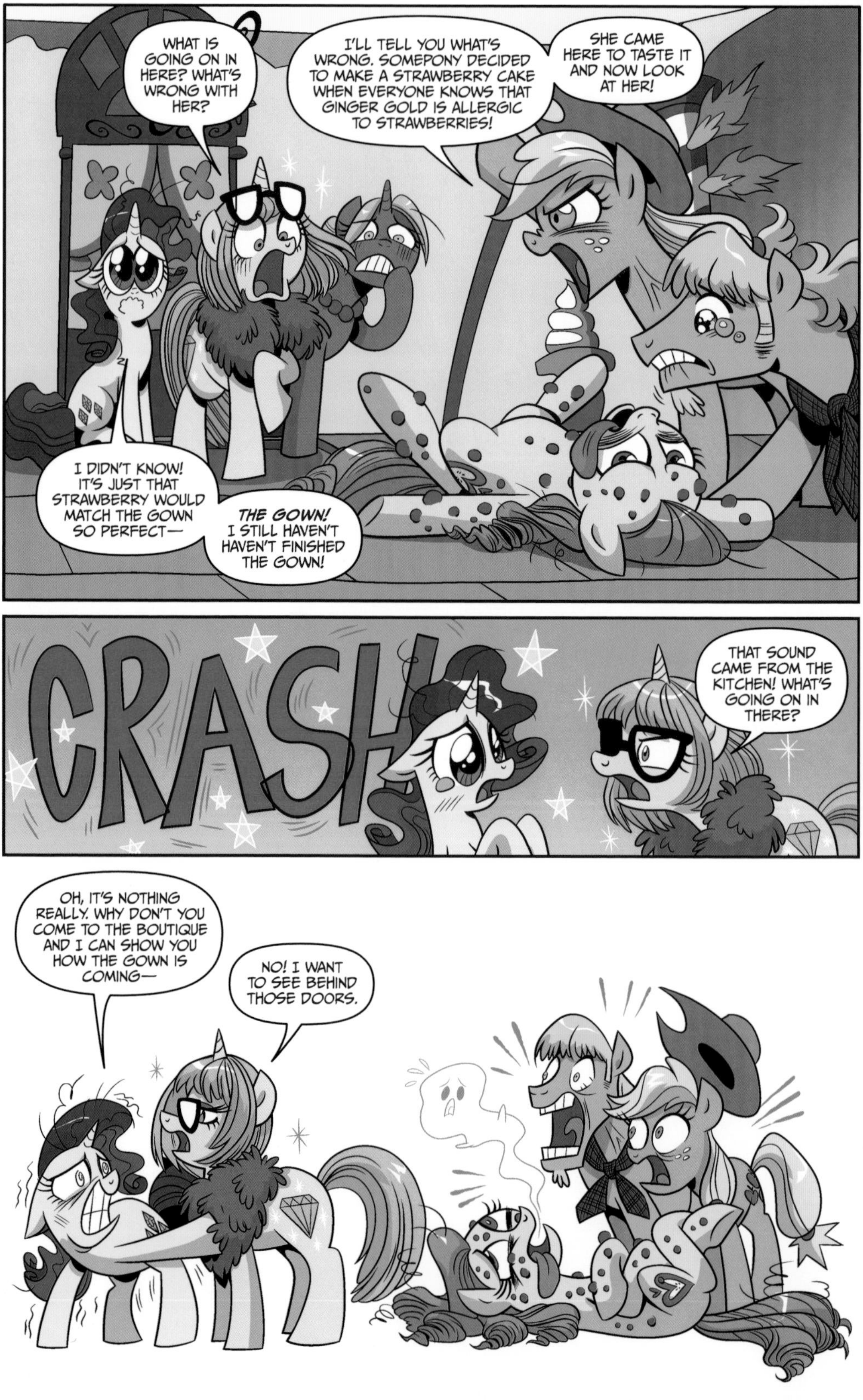
WHAT IS GOING ON IN HERE? WHAT'S WRONG WITH HER?
I'LL TELL YOU WHAT'S WRONG. SOMEPONY DECIDED TO MAKE A STRAWBERRY CAKE WHEN EVERYONE KNOWS THAT GINGER GOLD IS ALLERGIC TO STRAWBERRIES!
SHE CAME HERE TO TASTE IT AND NOW LOOK AT HER!
I DIDN'T KNOW! IT'S JUST THAT STRAWBERRY WOULD MATCH THE GOWN SO PERFECT—
THE GOWN! I STILL HAVEN'T HAVEN'T FINISHED THE GOWN!
CRASH!
THAT SOUND CAME FROM THE KITCHEN! WHAT'S GOING ON IN THERE?
OH, IT'S NOTHING REALLY. WHY DON'T YOU COME TO THE BOUTIQUE AND I CAN SHOW YOU HOW THE GOWN IS COMING—
NO! I WANT TO SEE BEHIND THOSE DOORS.

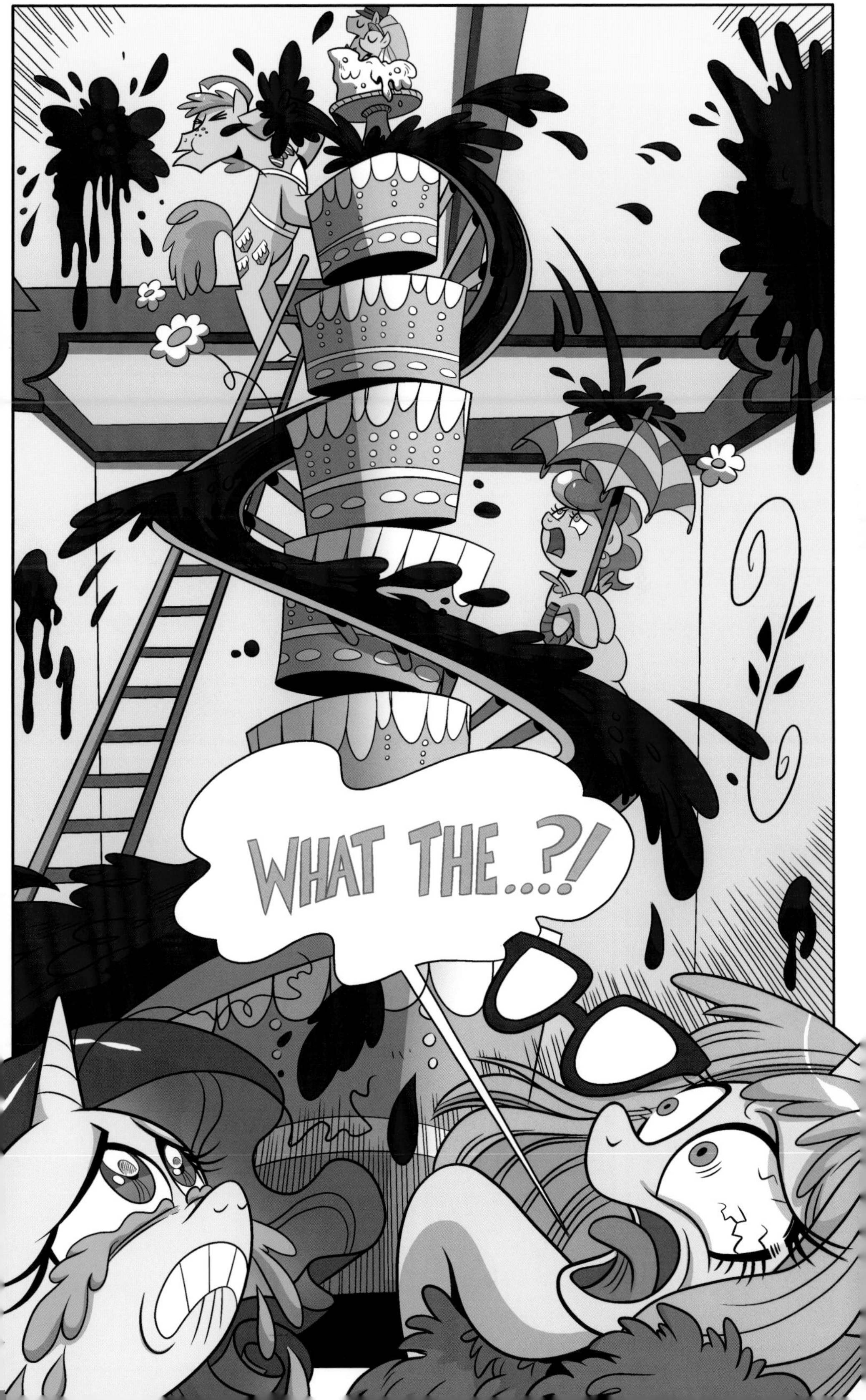
WHAT THE...?!

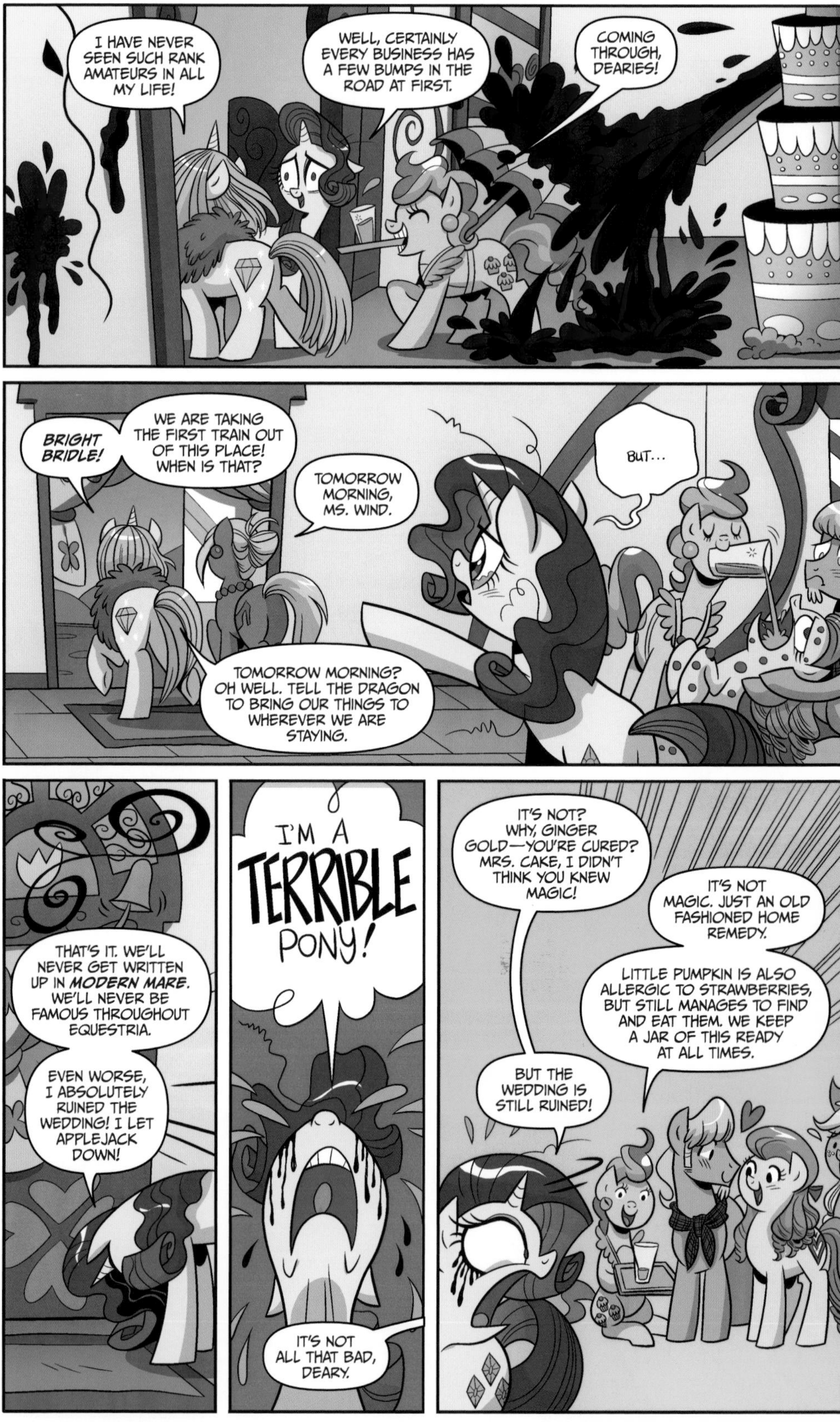
I HAVE NEVER SEEN SUCH RANK AMATEURS IN ALL MY LIFE!
WELL, CERTAINLY EVERY BUSINESS HAS A FEW BUMPS IN THE ROAD AT FIRST.
COMING THROUGH, DEARIES!
BRIGHT BRIDLE!
WE ARE TAKING THE FIRST TRAIN OUT OF THIS PLACE! WHEN IS THAT?
TOMORROW MORNING, MS. WIND.
TOMORROW MORNING? OH WELL. TELL THE DRAGON TO BRING OUR THINGS TO WHEREVER WE ARE STAYING.
BUT...
THAT'S IT. WE'LL NEVER GET WRITTEN UP IN MODERN MARE. WE'LL NEVER BE FAMOUS THROUGHOUT EQUESTRIA.
EVEN WORSE, I ABSOLUTELY RUINED THE WEDDING! I LET APPLEJACK DOWN!
I'M A TERRIBLE PONY!
IT'S NOT ALL THAT BAD, DEARY.
IT'S NOT? WHY, GINGER GOLD—YOU'RE CURED? MRS. CAKE, I DIDN'T THINK YOU KNEW MAGIC!
IT'S NOT MAGIC. JUST AN OLD FASHIONED HOME REMEDY.
LITTLE PUMPKIN IS ALSO ALLERGIC TO STRAWBERRIES, BUT STILL MANAGES TO FIND AND EAT THEM. WE KEEP A JAR OF THIS READY AT ALL TIMES.
BUT THE WEDDING IS STILL RUINED!

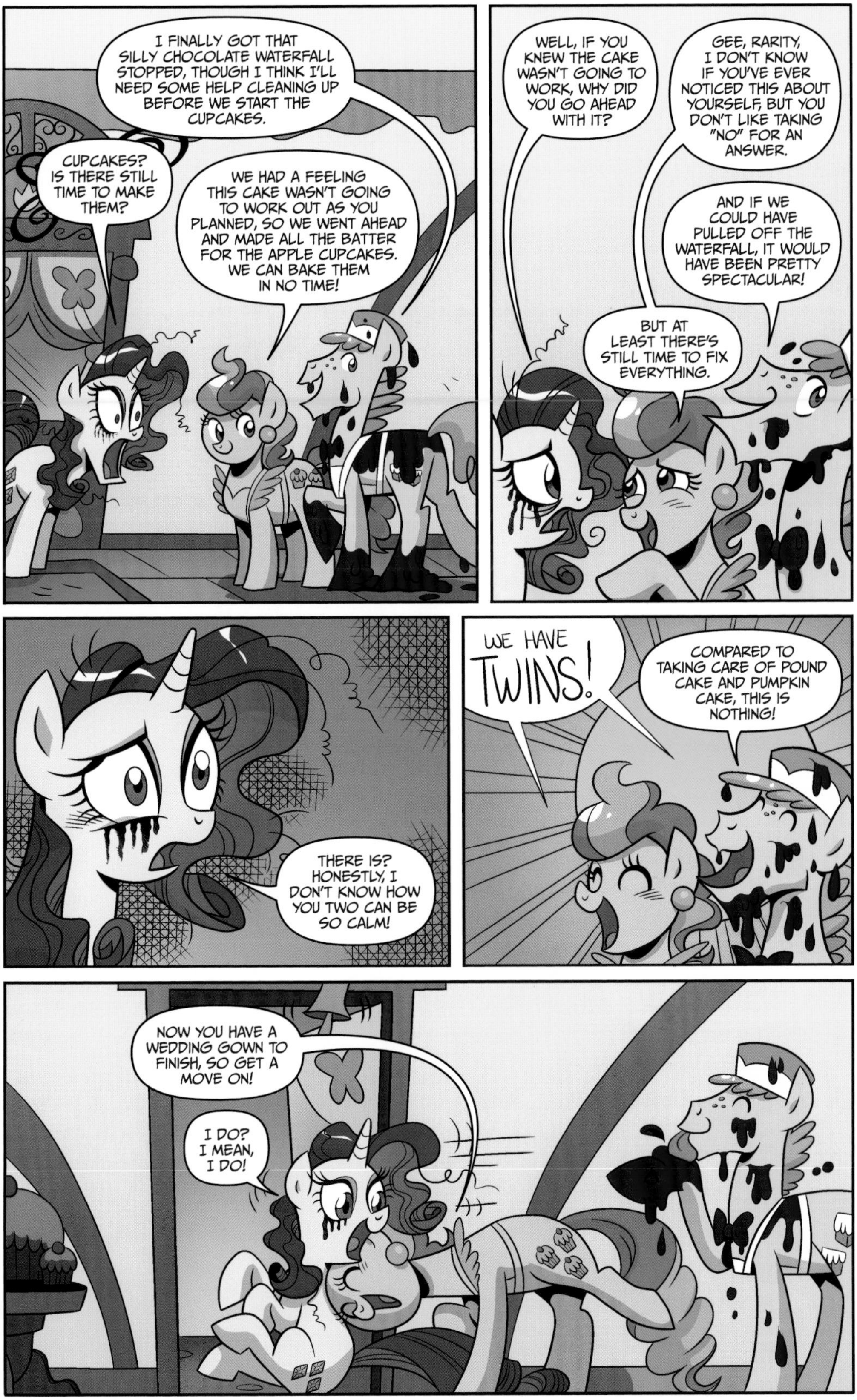
I FINALLY GOT THAT SILLY CHOCOLATE WATERFALL STOPPED, THOUGH I THINK I'LL NEED SOME HELP CLEANING UP BEFORE WE START THE CUPCAKES.
CUPCAKES? IS THERE STILL TIME TO MAKE THEM?
WE HAD A FEELING THIS CAKE WASN'T GOING TO WORK OUT AS YOU PLANNED, SO WE WENT AHEAD AND MADE ALL THE BATTER FOR THE APPLE CUPCAKES. WE CAN BAKE THEM IN NO TIME!
WELL, IF YOU KNEW THE CAKE WASN'T GOING TO WORK, WHY DID YOU GO AHEAD WITH IT?
GEE, RARITY, I DON'T KNOW IF YOU'VE EVER NOTICED THIS ABOUT YOURSELF, BUT YOU DON'T LIKE TAKING "NO" FOR AN ANSWER.
AND IF WE COULD HAVE PULLED OFF THE WATERFALL, IT WOULD HAVE BEEN PRETTY SPECTACULAR!
BUT AT LEAST THERE'S STILL TIME TO FIX EVERYTHING.
THERE IS? HONESTLY, I DON'T KNOW HOW YOU TWO CAN BE SO CALM!
WE HAVE TWINS!
COMPARED TO TAKING CARE OF POUND CAKE AND PUMPKIN CAKE, THIS IS NOTHING!
NOW YOU HAVE A WEDDING GOWN TO FINISH, SO GET A MOVE ON!
I DO? I MEAN, I DO!

NEXT MORNING.

WELL, AT LEAST IT WASN'T A TOTAL LOSS. THAT CRITTER CONCERT IN THE PARK LAST NIGHT CONDUCTED BY FLUTTERSHY WAS SIMPLY ENCHANTING. DON'T YOU THINK?

YES, MS. WIND.

MS. WIND?

WE DO WISH YOU WOULD RECONSIDER REVIEWING OUR BUSINESS.

OUR DEAR RARITY MAY HAVE BEEN A BIT OVER-AMBITIOUS FOR OUR FIRST WEDDING, BUT WE'VE GOT IT ALL STRAIGHTENED OUT.

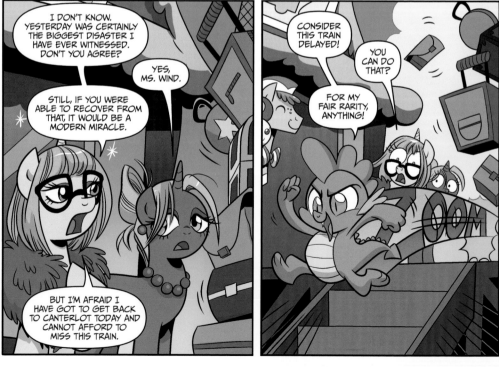

I DON'T KNOW. YESTERDAY WAS CERTAINLY THE BIGGEST DISASTER I HAVE EVER WITNESSED. DON'T YOU AGREE?

YES, MS. WIND.

STILL, IF YOU WERE ABLE TO RECOVER FROM THAT, IT WOULD BE A MODERN MIRACLE.

BUT I'M AFRAID I HAVE GOT TO GET BACK TO CANTERLOT TODAY AND CANNOT AFFORD TO MISS THIS TRAIN.

CONSIDER THIS TRAIN DELAYED!

YOU CAN DO THAT?

FOR MY FAIR RARITY, ANYTHING!

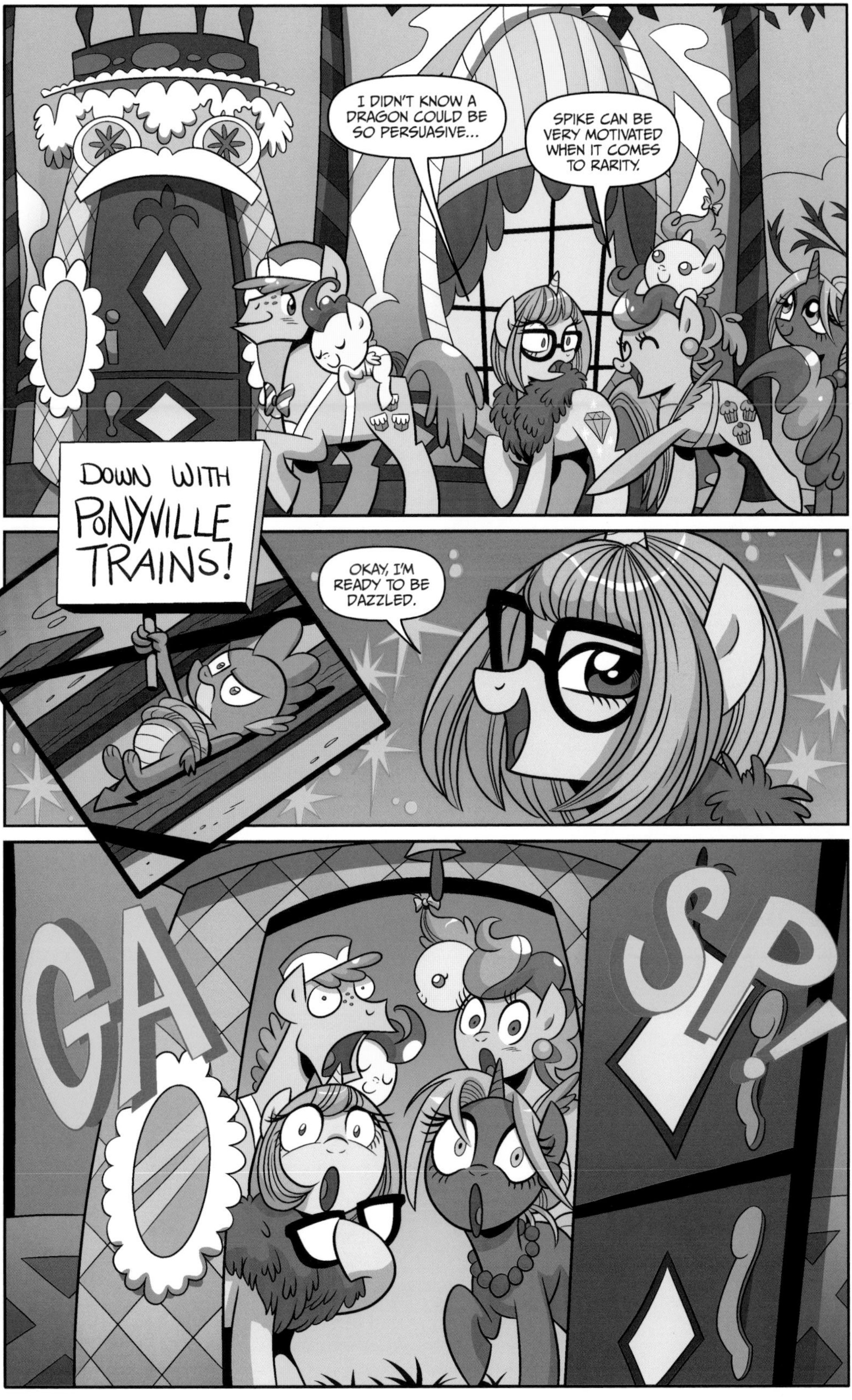
I DIDN'T KNOW A DRAGON COULD BE SO PERSUASIVE...
SPIKE CAN BE VERY MOTIVATED WHEN IT COMES TO RARITY.
DOWN WITH PONYVILLE TRAINS!
OKAY, I'M READY TO BE DAZZLED.
GASP!

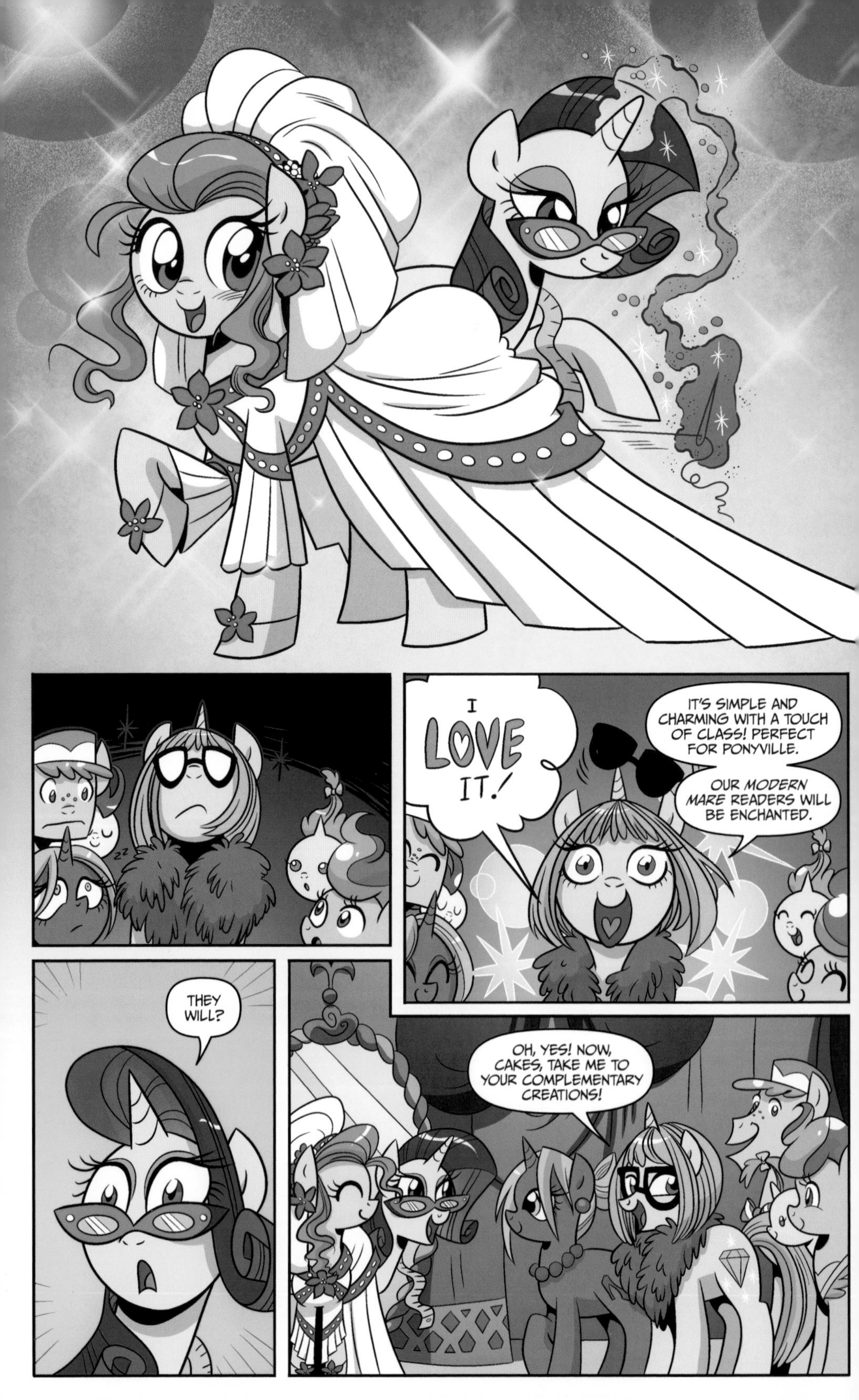
I LOVE IT!
IT'S SIMPLE AND CHARMING WITH A TOUCH OF CLASS! PERFECT FOR PONYVILLE.
OUR MODERN MARE READERS WILL BE ENCHANTED.
THEY WILL?
OH, YES! NOW, CAKES, TAKE ME TO YOUR COMPLEMENTARY CREATIONS!

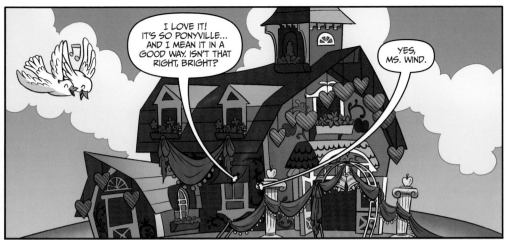

I LOVE IT! IT'S SO PONYVILLE... AND I MEAN IT IN A GOOD WAY. ISN'T THAT RIGHT, BRIGHT?

YES, MS. WIND.

EVEN THE CUPCAKE TOWER IS CHARMING. I WOULD CALL THIS A COMPLETE SUCCESS!

IF IT IS A COMPLETE SUCCESS, IT'S ONLY BECAUSE OF YOU TWO.

I REALLY MUST APOLOGIZE. WE'RE SUPPOSED TO BE IN BUSINESS *TOGETHER* AND I TRIED TO DICTATE EVERYTHING! CAN YOU EVER FORGIVE ME?

OH, RARITY, THERE'S NOTHING TO FORGIVE. YOUR SELF-CONFIDENCE IS ONE OF THE REASONS WHY WE LOVE YOU.

BUT SOMETIMES, YOU NEED TO TRUST OUR JUDGMENT TOO!

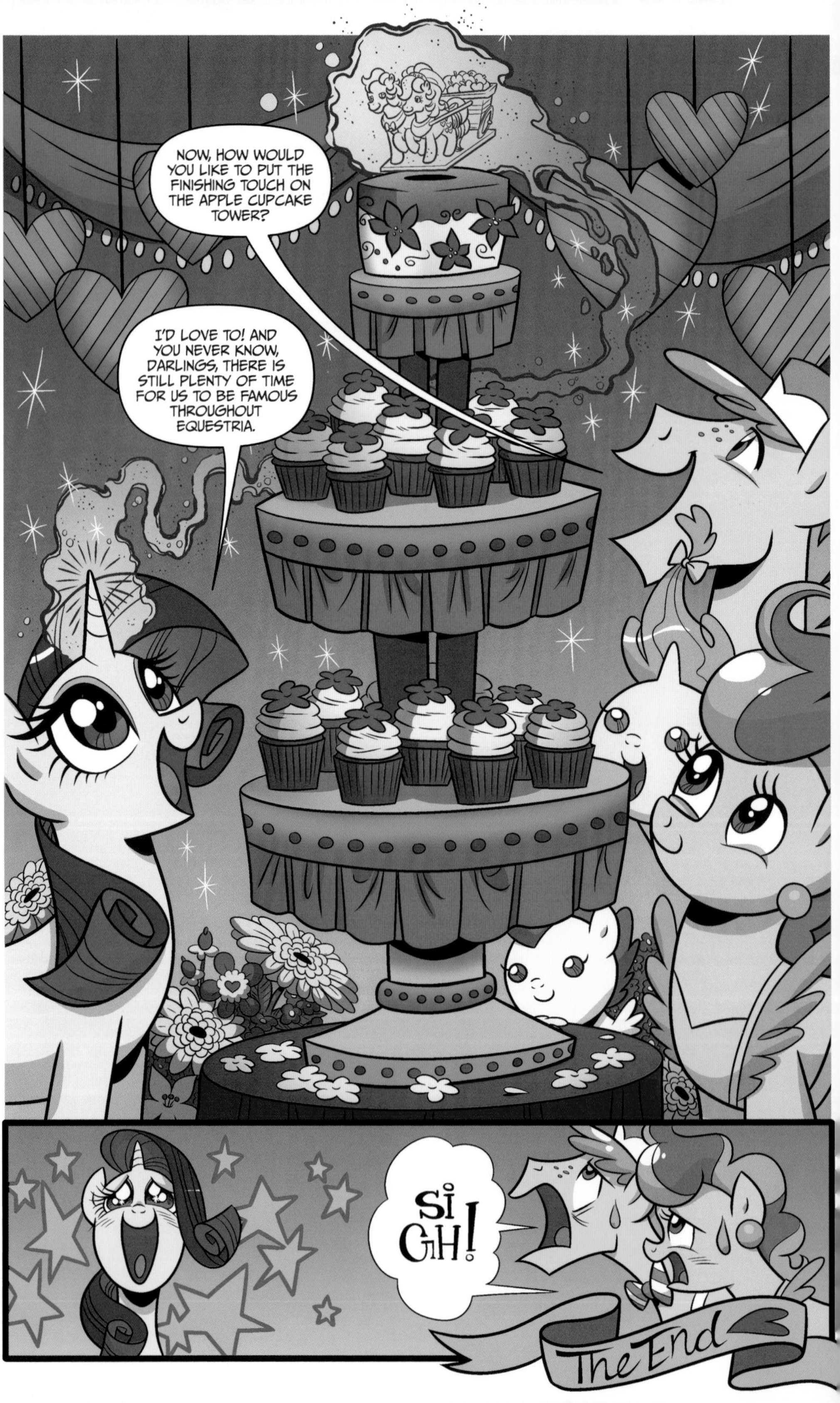
NOW, HOW WOULD YOU LIKE TO PUT THE FINISHING TOUCH ON THE APPLE CUPCAKE TOWER?
I'D LOVE TO! AND YOU NEVER KNOW, DARLINGS, THERE IS STILL PLENTY OF TIME FOR US TO BE FAMOUS THROUGHOUT EQUESTRIA.
SIGH!
The End

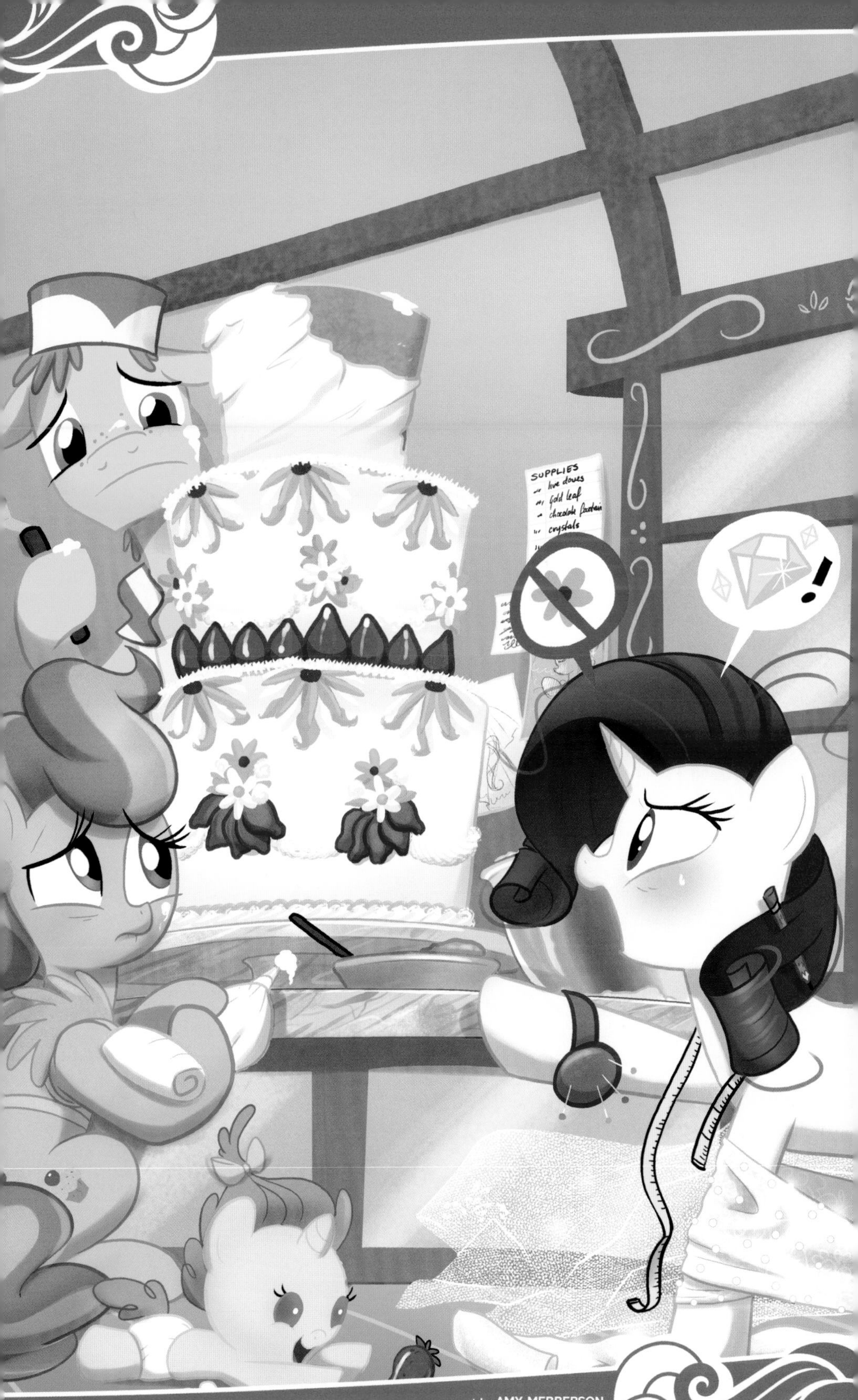
SUPPLIES
live doves
gold leaf
chocolate fountain
crystals
!
art by AMY MEBBERSON

Princess Luna & Discord

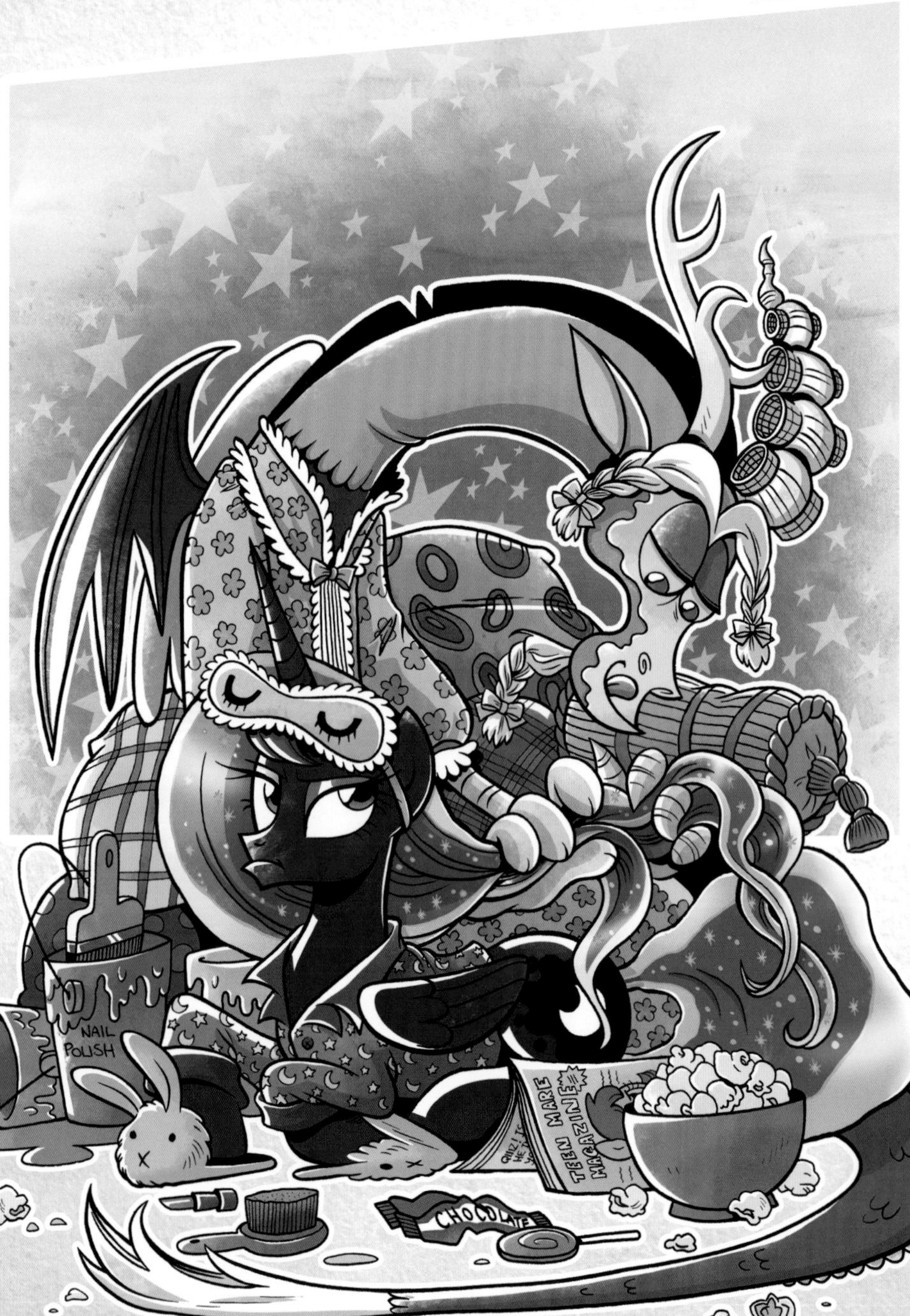
NAIL
POLISH
TEEN MARE
MAGAZINE
CHOCOLATE
BRENDA HICKEY

art by BRENDA HICKEY

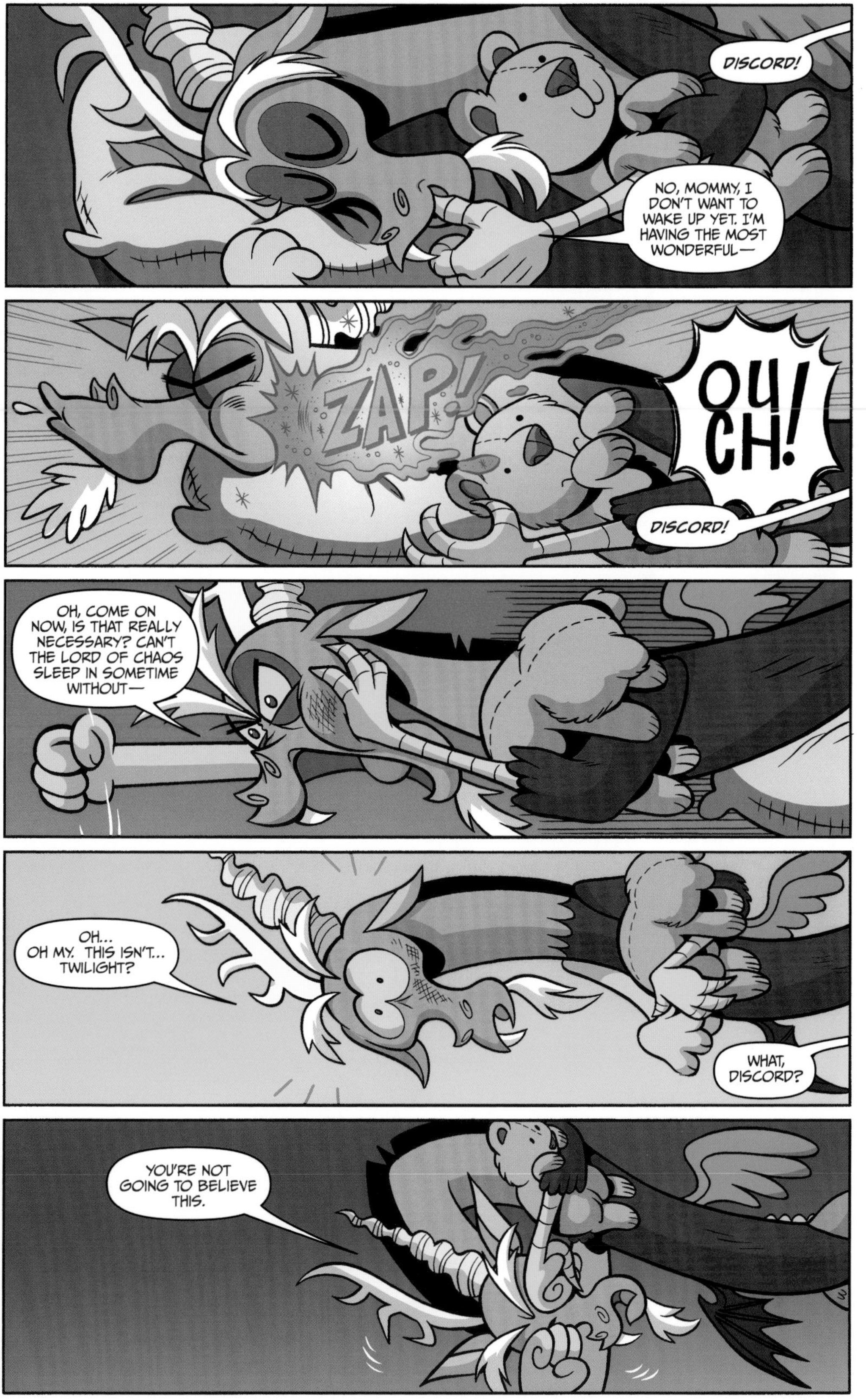
DISCORD!
NO, MOMMY, I DON'T WANT TO WAKE UP YET. I'M HAVING THE MOST WONDERFUL—
ZAP!
OUCH!
DISCORD!
OH, COME ON NOW, IS THAT REALLY NECESSARY? CAN'T THE LORD OF CHAOS SLEEP IN SOMETIME WITHOUT—
OH... OH MY. THIS ISN'T... TWILIGHT?
WHAT, DISCORD?
YOU'RE NOT GOING TO BELIEVE THIS.

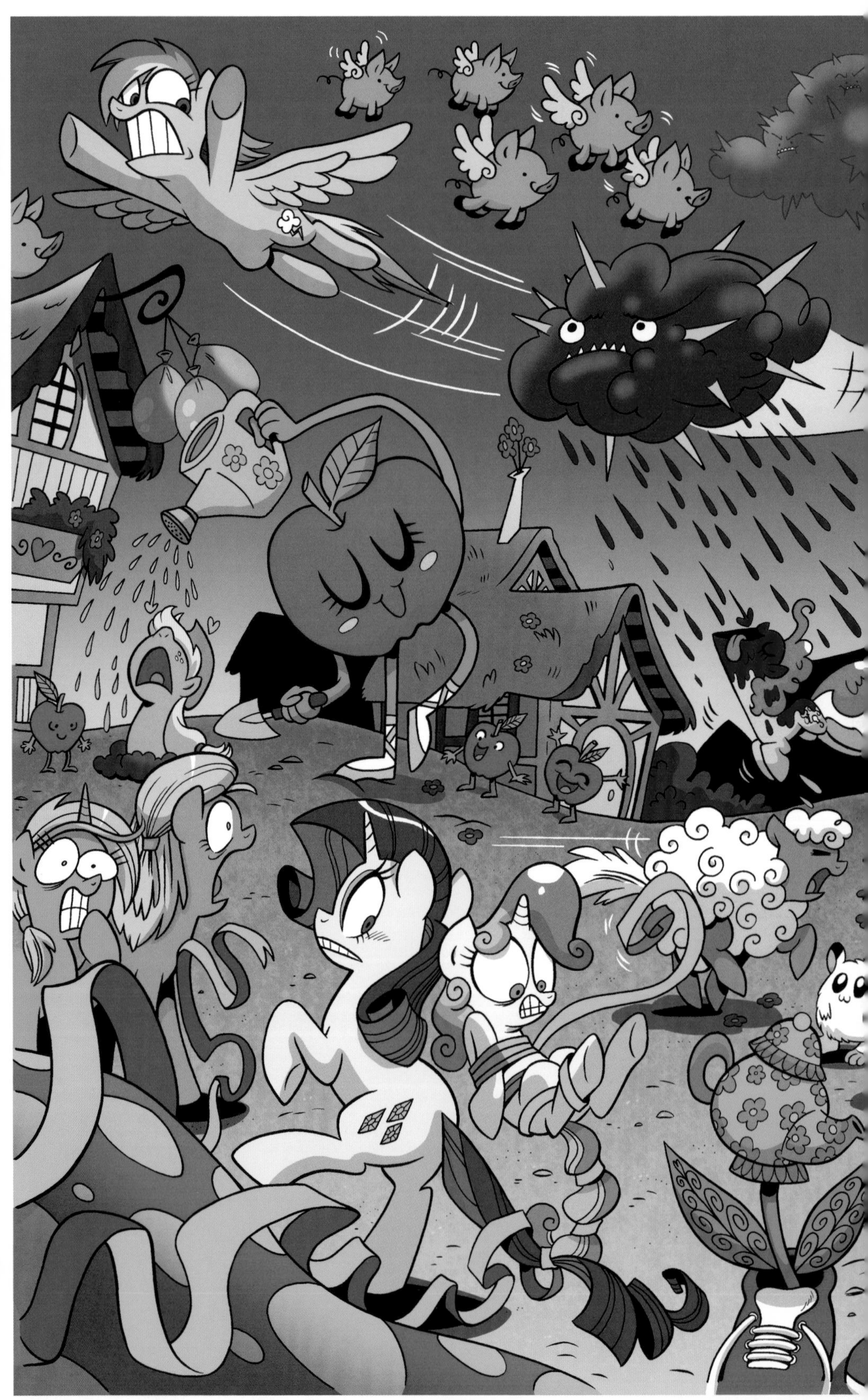

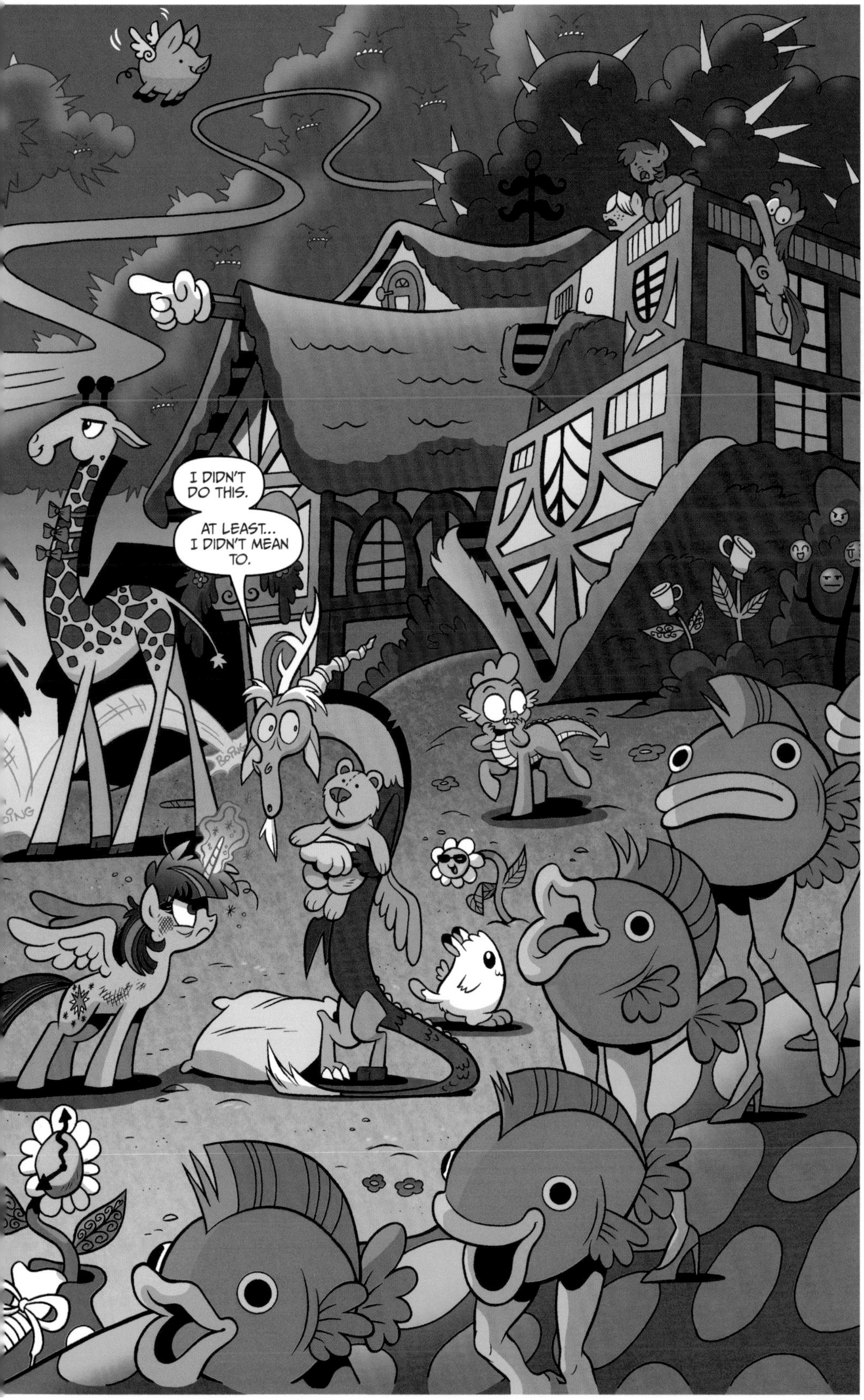
I DIDN'T DO THIS.
AT LEAST... I DIDN'T MEAN TO.

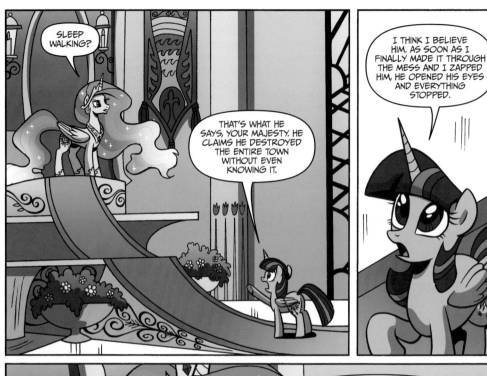

SLEEP WALKING?

THAT'S WHAT HE SAYS, YOUR MAJESTY. HE CLAIMS HE DESTROYED THE ENTIRE TOWN WITHOUT EVEN KNOWING IT.

I THINK I BELIEVE HIM. AS SOON AS I FINALLY MADE IT THROUGH THE MESS AND I ZAPPED HIM, HE OPENED HIS EYES AND EVERYTHING STOPPED.

BUT... SLEEPWALKING IS USUALLY A SIGN OF NIGHTMARES. SOMETHING UNDERLYING THAT'S BOTHERING A PONY. SOMETHING A PONY IS AFRAID OF. WHAT IS DISCORD AFRAID OF?

"WHERE IS DISCORD NOW?"

"HE'S WITH FLUTTERSHY AT HER COTTAGE. PRINCESS, WHAT ARE WE GOING TO DO? PONYVILLE CAN'T GO THROUGH THAT AGAIN."

"INDEED IT CAN'T. WE HAVE TO PUT A STOP TO THIS FOR GOOD."

KNOCK KNOCK KNOCK

"FOR GOOD? WHAT DO YOU MEAN?"

"TWILIGHT, I'M SENDING IN A SPECIALIST."

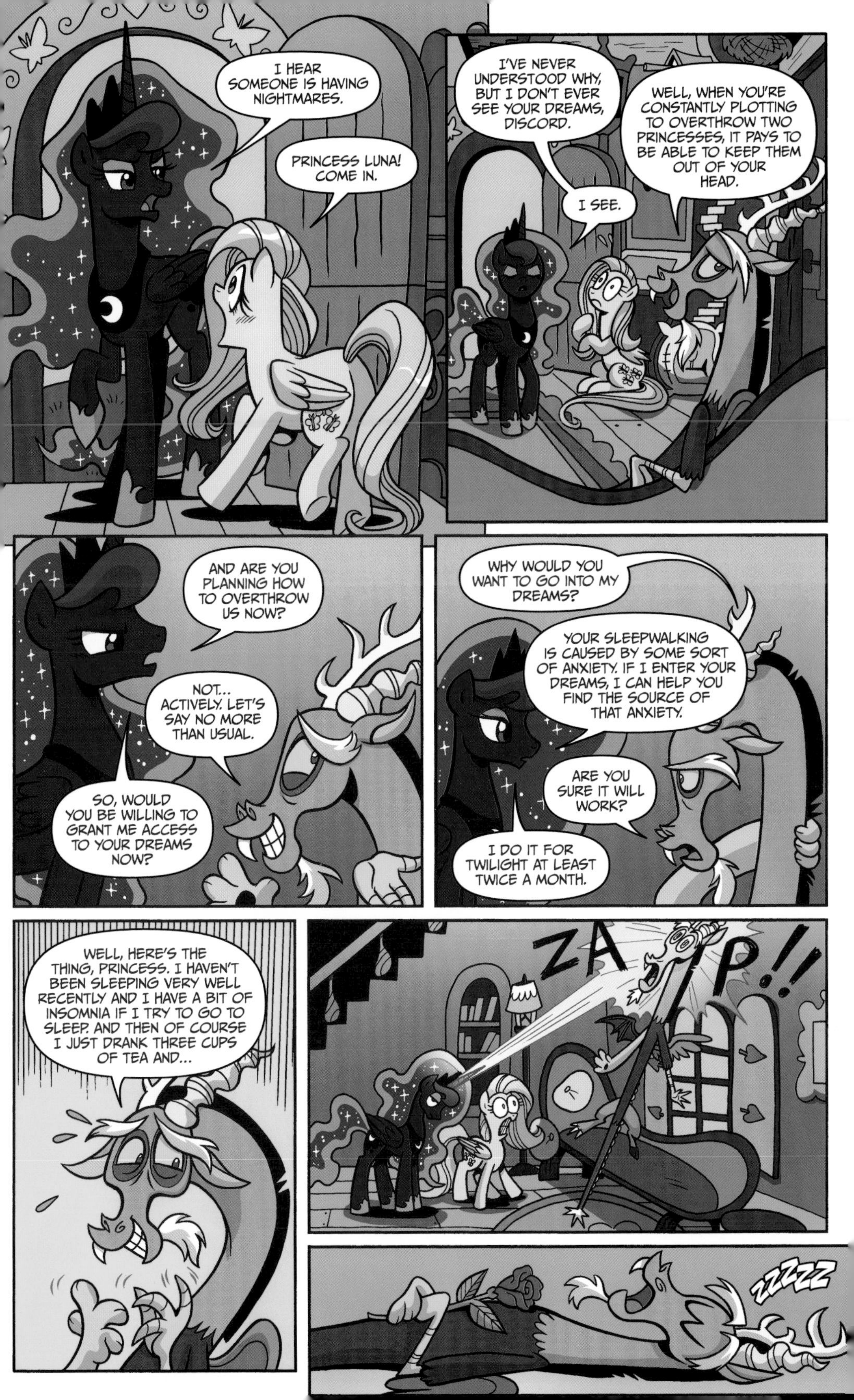
I HEAR SOMEONE IS HAVING NIGHTMARES.
PRINCESS LUNA! COME IN.
I'VE NEVER UNDERSTOOD WHY, BUT I DON'T EVER SEE YOUR DREAMS, DISCORD.
WELL, WHEN YOU'RE CONSTANTLY PLOTTING TO OVERTHROW TWO PRINCESSES, IT PAYS TO BE ABLE TO KEEP THEM OUT OF YOUR HEAD.
I SEE.
AND ARE YOU PLANNING HOW TO OVERTHROW US NOW?
NOT... ACTIVELY. LET'S SAY NO MORE THAN USUAL.
SO, WOULD YOU BE WILLING TO GRANT ME ACCESS TO YOUR DREAMS NOW?
WHY WOULD YOU WANT TO GO INTO MY DREAMS?
YOUR SLEEPWALKING IS CAUSED BY SOME SORT OF ANXIETY. IF I ENTER YOUR DREAMS, I CAN HELP YOU FIND THE SOURCE OF THAT ANXIETY.
ARE YOU SURE IT WILL WORK?
I DO IT FOR TWILIGHT AT LEAST TWICE A MONTH.
WELL, HERE'S THE THING, PRINCESS. I HAVEN'T BEEN SLEEPING VERY WELL RECENTLY AND I HAVE A BIT OF INSOMNIA IF I TRY TO GO TO SLEEP. AND THEN OF COURSE I JUST DRANK THREE CUPS OF TEA AND...
ZAP!!
ZZZZZ

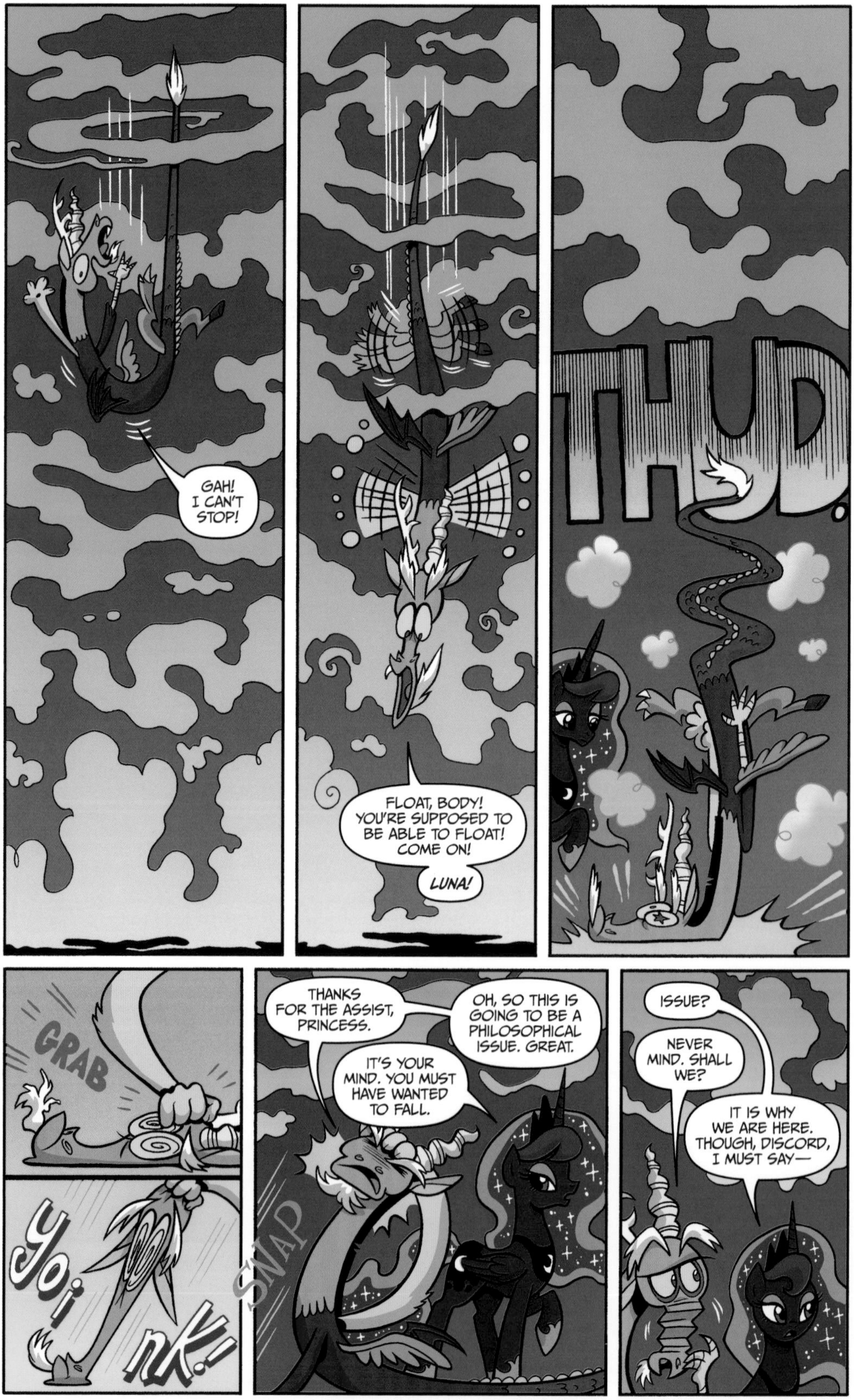
GAH! I CAN'T STOP!
FLOAT, BODY! YOU'RE SUPPOSED TO BE ABLE TO FLOAT! COME ON!
LUNA!
THUD.
GRAB
Yoink!
THANKS FOR THE ASSIST, PRINCESS.
IT'S YOUR MIND. YOU MUST HAVE WANTED TO FALL.
SNAP
OH, SO THIS IS GOING TO BE A PHILOSOPHICAL ISSUE. GREAT.
ISSUE?
NEVER MIND. SHALL WE?
IT IS WHY WE ARE HERE. THOUGH, DISCORD, I MUST SAY—

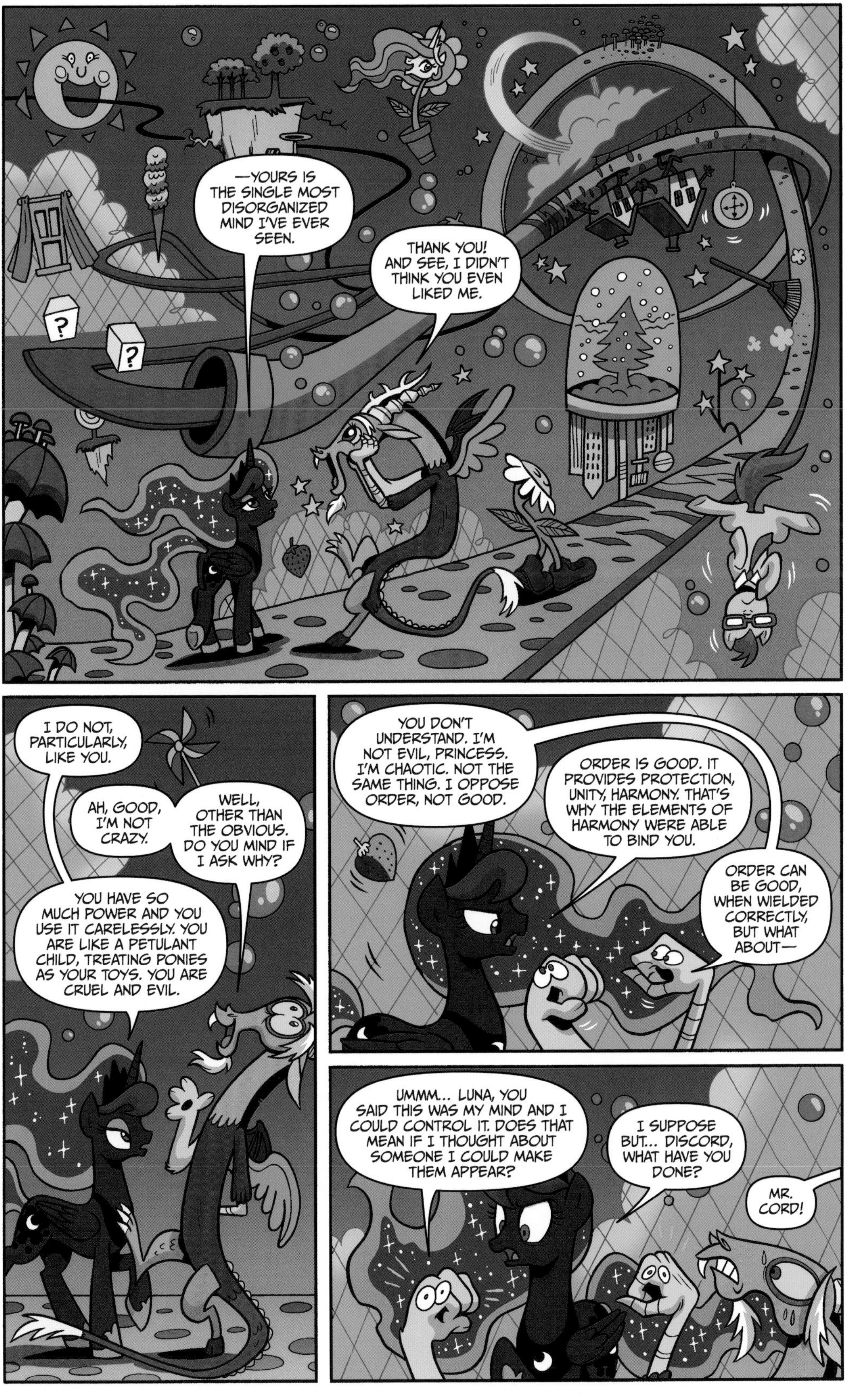
—YOURS IS THE SINGLE MOST DISORGANIZED MIND I'VE EVER SEEN.
THANK YOU! AND SEE, I DIDN'T THINK YOU EVEN LIKED ME.
I DO NOT, PARTICULARLY, LIKE YOU.
AH, GOOD, I'M NOT CRAZY.
WELL, OTHER THAN THE OBVIOUS. DO YOU MIND IF I ASK WHY?
YOU HAVE SO MUCH POWER AND YOU USE IT CARELESSLY. YOU ARE LIKE A PETULANT CHILD, TREATING PONIES AS YOUR TOYS. YOU ARE CRUEL AND EVIL.
YOU DON'T UNDERSTAND. I'M NOT EVIL, PRINCESS. I'M CHAOTIC. NOT THE SAME THING. I OPPOSE ORDER, NOT GOOD.
ORDER IS GOOD. IT PROVIDES PROTECTION, UNITY, HARMONY. THAT'S WHY THE ELEMENTS OF HARMONY WERE ABLE TO BIND YOU.
ORDER CAN BE GOOD, WHEN WIELDED CORRECTLY, BUT WHAT ABOUT—
UMMM... LUNA, YOU SAID THIS WAS MY MIND AND I COULD CONTROL IT. DOES THAT MEAN IF I THOUGHT ABOUT SOMEONE I COULD MAKE THEM APPEAR?
I SUPPOSE BUT... DISCORD, WHAT HAVE YOU DONE?
MR. CORD!

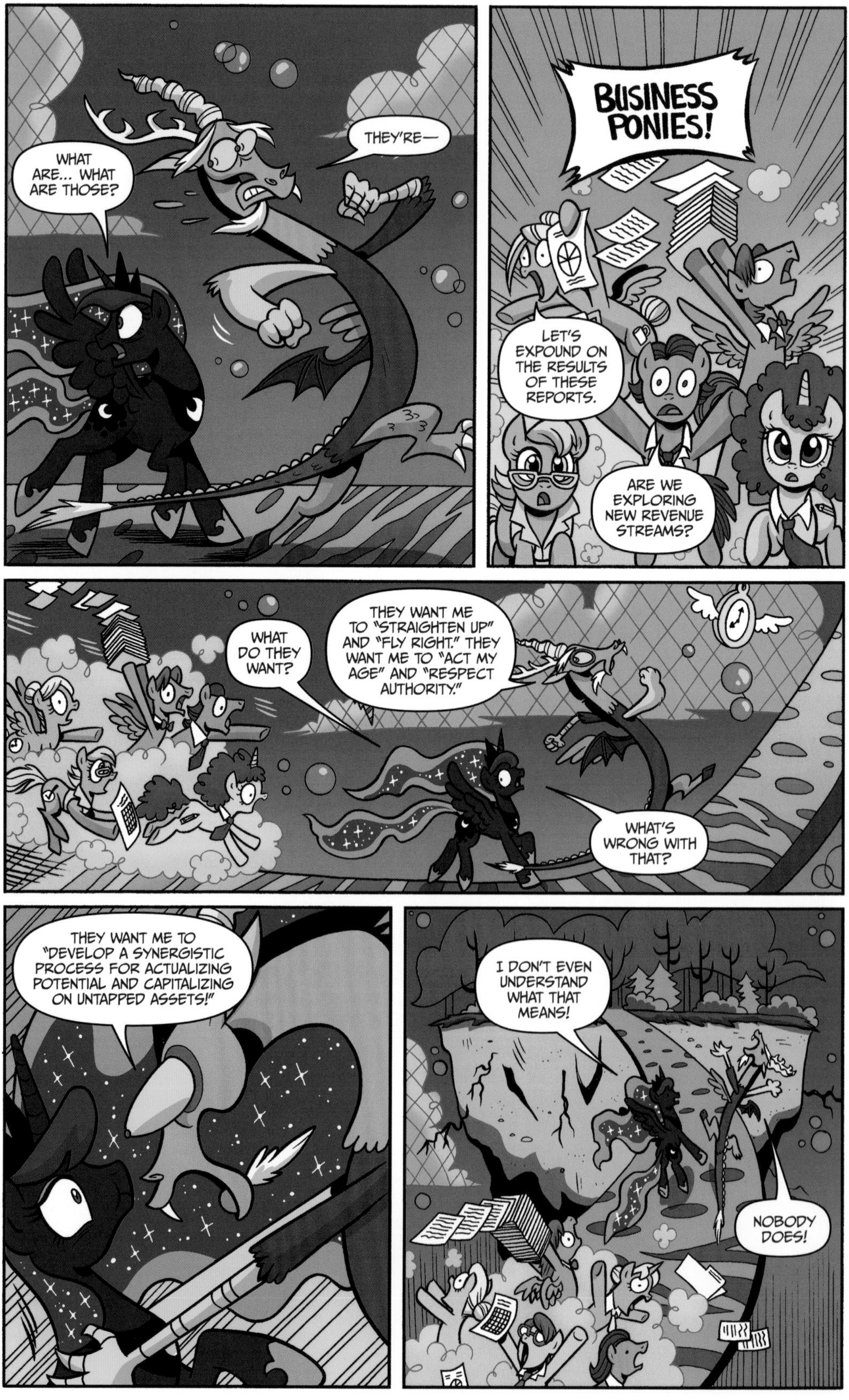
WHAT ARE... WHAT ARE THOSE?
THEY'RE—
BUSINESS PONIES!
LET'S EXPOUND ON THE RESULTS OF THESE REPORTS.
ARE WE EXPLORING NEW REVENUE STREAMS?
WHAT DO THEY WANT?
THEY WANT ME TO "STRAIGHTEN UP" AND "FLY RIGHT." THEY WANT ME TO "ACT MY AGE" AND "RESPECT AUTHORITY."
WHAT'S WRONG WITH THAT?
THEY WANT ME TO "DEVELOP A SYNERGISTIC PROCESS FOR ACTUALIZING POTENTIAL AND CAPITALIZING ON UNTAPPED ASSETS!"
I DON'T EVEN UNDERSTAND WHAT THAT MEANS!
NOBODY DOES!

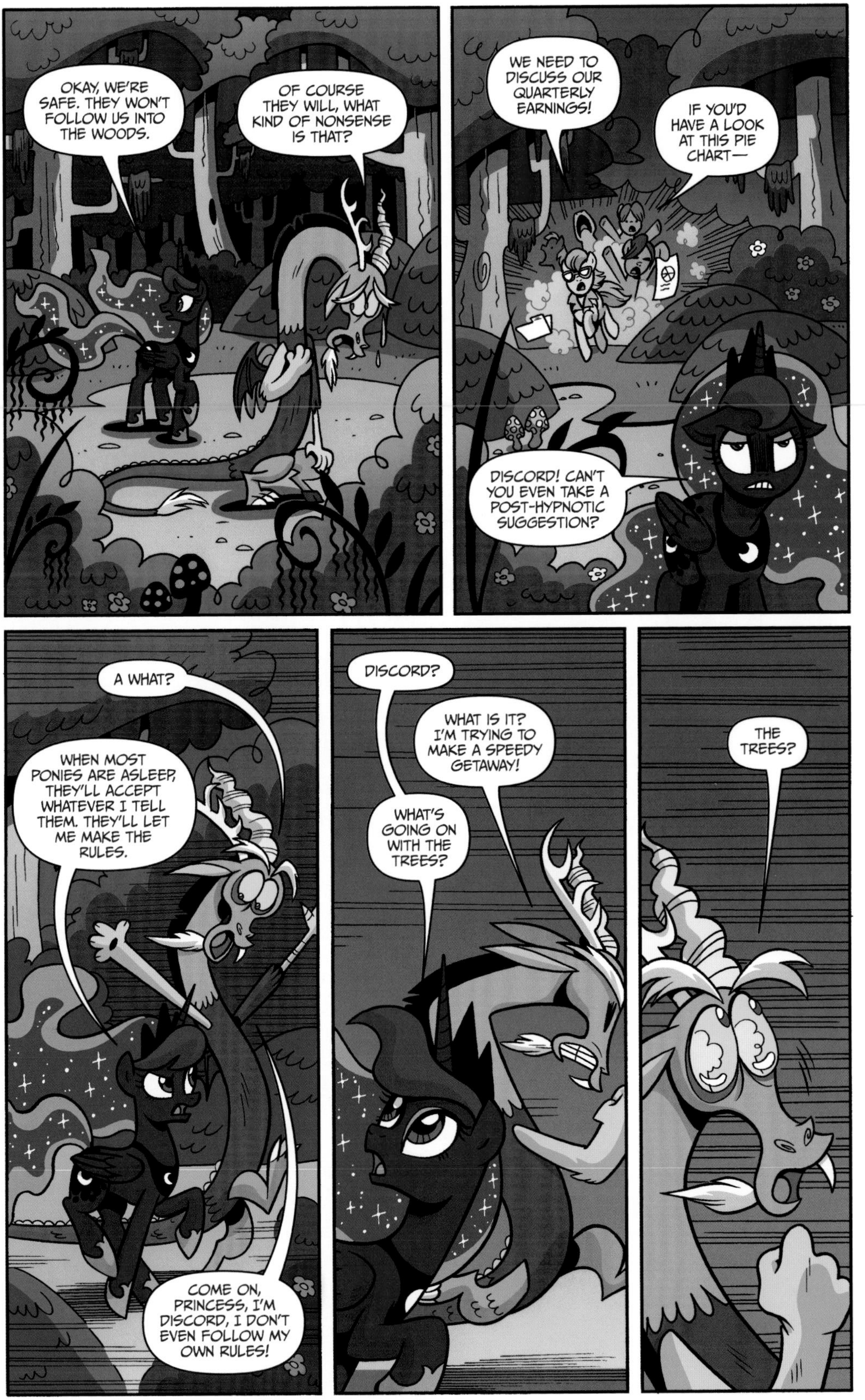
OKAY, WE'RE SAFE. THEY WON'T FOLLOW US INTO THE WOODS.
OF COURSE THEY WILL, WHAT KIND OF NONSENSE IS THAT?
WE NEED TO DISCUSS OUR QUARTERLY EARNINGS!
IF YOU'D HAVE A LOOK AT THIS PIE CHART—
DISCORD! CAN'T YOU EVEN TAKE A POST-HYPNOTIC SUGGESTION?
A WHAT?
WHEN MOST PONIES ARE ASLEEP, THEY'LL ACCEPT WHATEVER I TELL THEM. THEY'LL LET ME MAKE THE RULES.
COME ON, PRINCESS, I'M DISCORD, I DON'T EVEN FOLLOW MY OWN RULES!
DISCORD?
WHAT IS IT? I'M TRYING TO MAKE A SPEEDY GETAWAY!
WHAT'S GOING ON WITH THE TREES?
THE TREES?

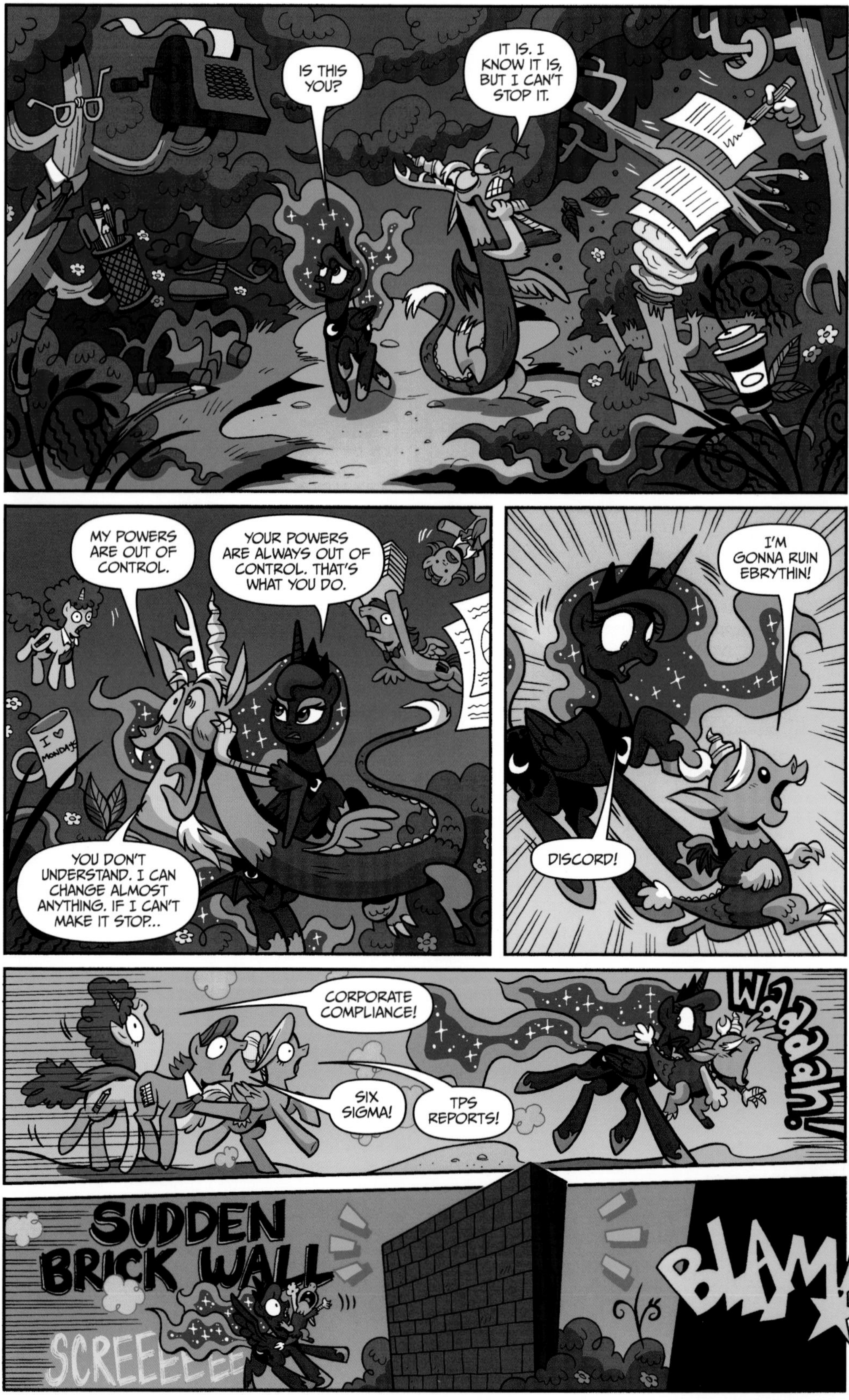
IS THIS YOU?
IT IS. I KNOW IT IS, BUT I CAN'T STOP IT.
MY POWERS ARE OUT OF CONTROL.
YOUR POWERS ARE ALWAYS OUT OF CONTROL. THAT'S WHAT YOU DO.
I ♥ MONDAYS
YOU DON'T UNDERSTAND. I CAN CHANGE ALMOST ANYTHING. IF I CAN'T MAKE IT STOP...
I'M GONNA RUIN EBRYTHIN!
DISCORD!
CORPORATE COMPLIANCE!
SIX SIGMA!
TPS REPORTS!
WAAAAAH!
SUDDEN BRICK WALL
SCREEEEEEE
BLAM!

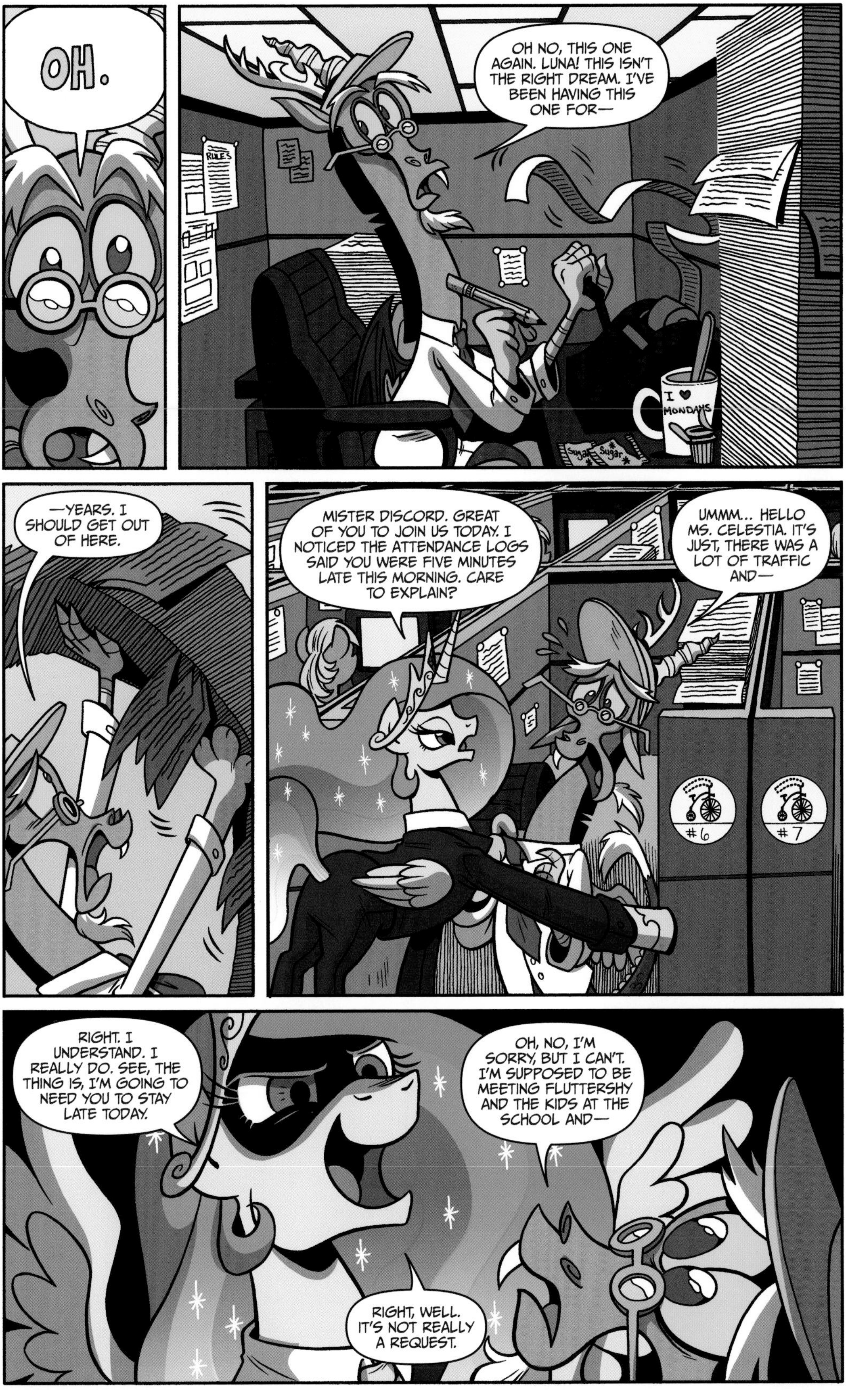
OH.
OH NO, THIS ONE AGAIN. LUNA! THIS ISN'T THE RIGHT DREAM. I'VE BEEN HAVING THIS ONE FOR—
RULES
I ♥ MONDAYS
Sugar
Sugar
—YEARS. I SHOULD GET OUT OF HERE.
MISTER DISCORD. GREAT OF YOU TO JOIN US TODAY. I NOTICED THE ATTENDANCE LOGS SAID YOU WERE FIVE MINUTES LATE THIS MORNING. CARE TO EXPLAIN?
UMMM... HELLO MS. CELESTIA. IT'S JUST, THERE WAS A LOT OF TRAFFIC AND—
#6
#7
RIGHT. I UNDERSTAND. I REALLY DO. SEE, THE THING IS, I'M GOING TO NEED YOU TO STAY LATE TODAY.
OH, NO, I'M SORRY, BUT I CAN'T. I'M SUPPOSED TO BE MEETING FLUTTERSHY AND THE KIDS AT THE SCHOOL AND—
RIGHT, WELL. IT'S NOT REALLY A REQUEST.

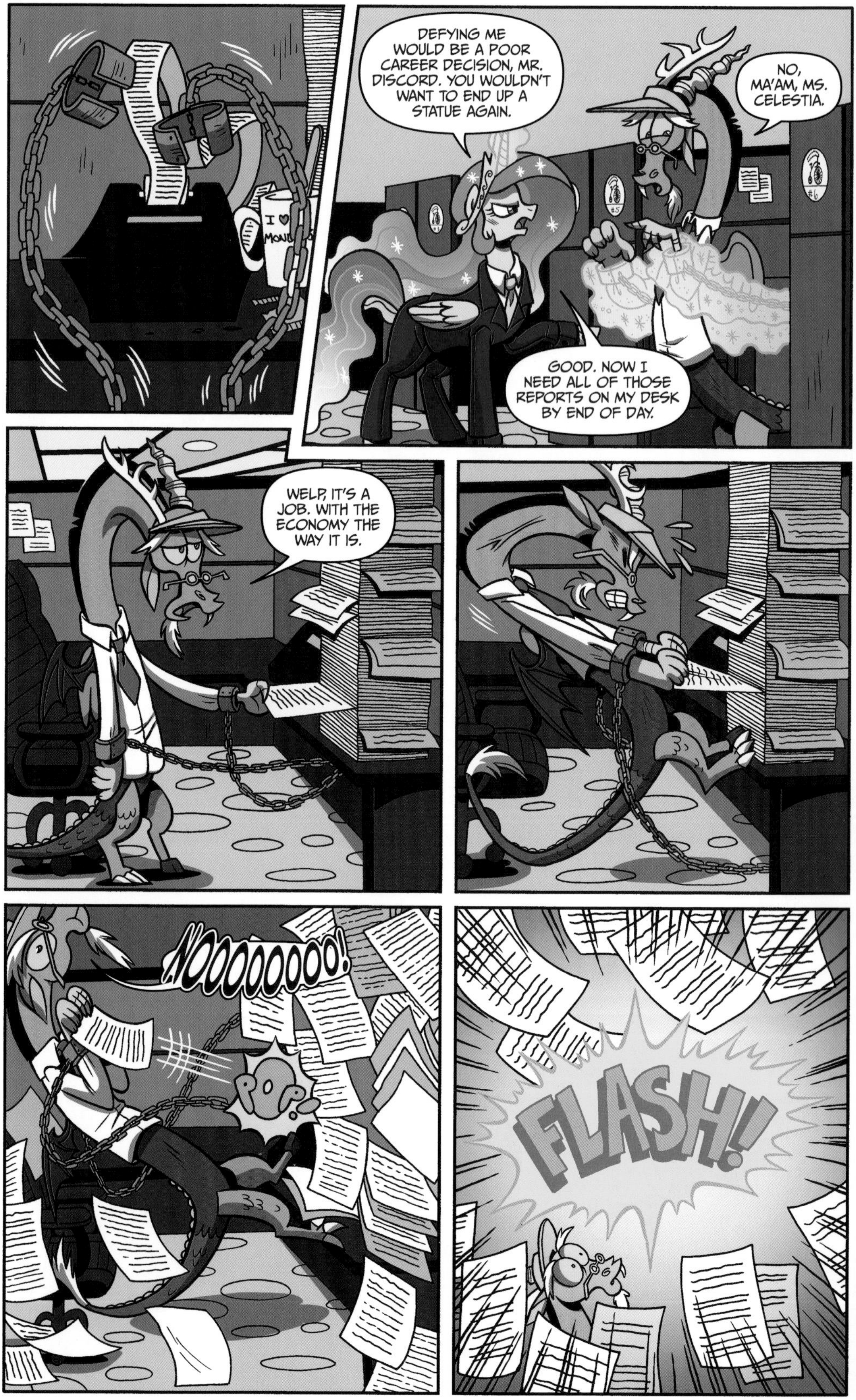

DEFYING ME WOULD BE A POOR CAREER DECISION, MR. DISCORD. YOU WOULDN'T WANT TO END UP A STATUE AGAIN.
NO, MA'AM, MS. CELESTIA.
GOOD. NOW I NEED ALL OF THOSE REPORTS ON MY DESK BY END OF DAY.
WELP, IT'S A JOB. WITH THE ECONOMY THE WAY IT IS.
NOOOOOOOO!
POP!
FLASH!

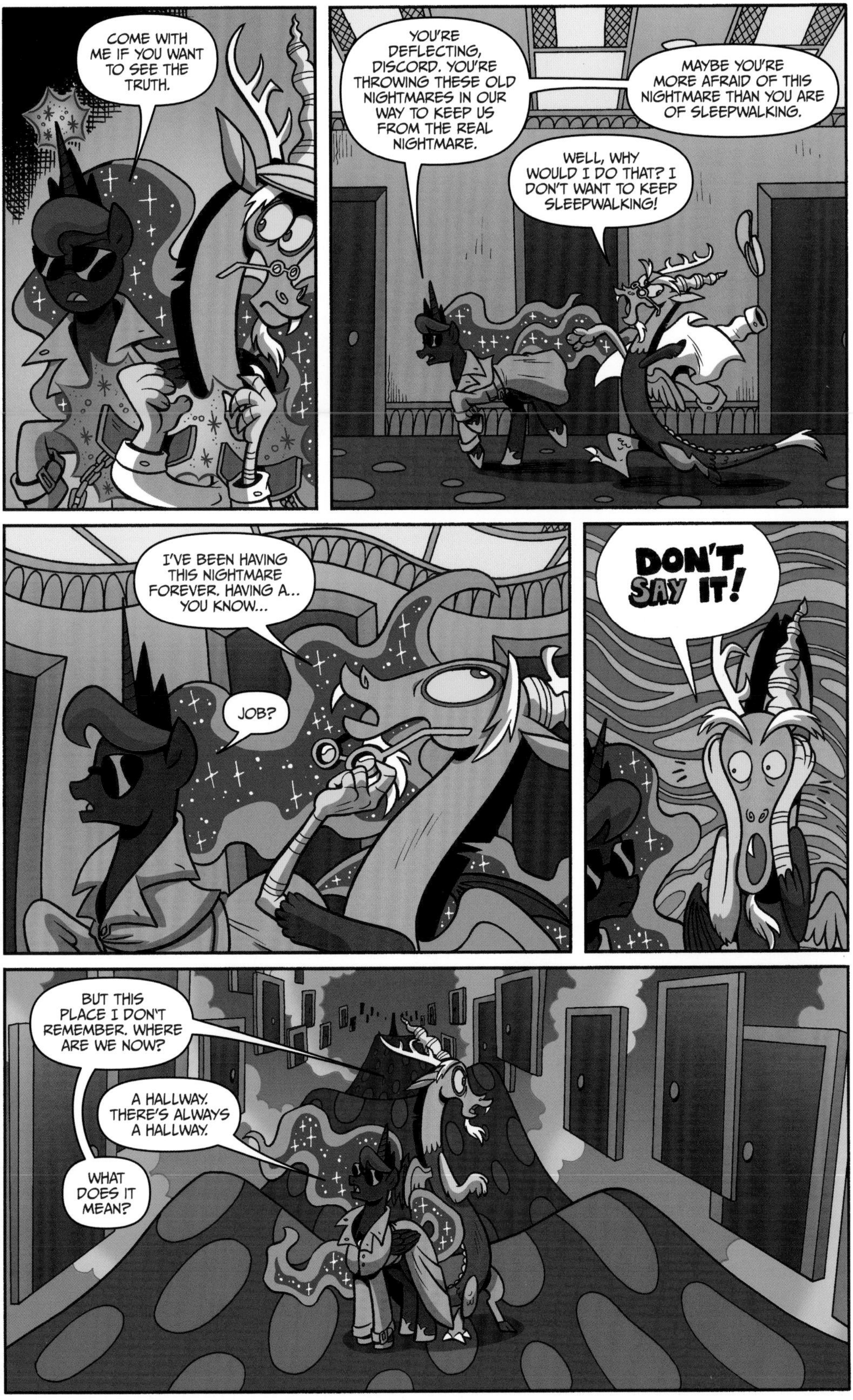
COME WITH ME IF YOU WANT TO SEE THE TRUTH.
YOU'RE DEFLECTING, DISCORD. YOU'RE THROWING THESE OLD NIGHTMARES IN OUR WAY TO KEEP US FROM THE REAL NIGHTMARE.
MAYBE YOU'RE MORE AFRAID OF THIS NIGHTMARE THAN YOU ARE OF SLEEPWALKING.
WELL, WHY WOULD I DO THAT? I DON'T WANT TO KEEP SLEEPWALKING!
I'VE BEEN HAVING THIS NIGHTMARE FOREVER. HAVING A... YOU KNOW...
JOB?
DON'T SAY IT!
BUT THIS PLACE I DON'T REMEMBER. WHERE ARE WE NOW?
A HALLWAY. THERE'S ALWAYS A HALLWAY.
WHAT DOES IT MEAN?

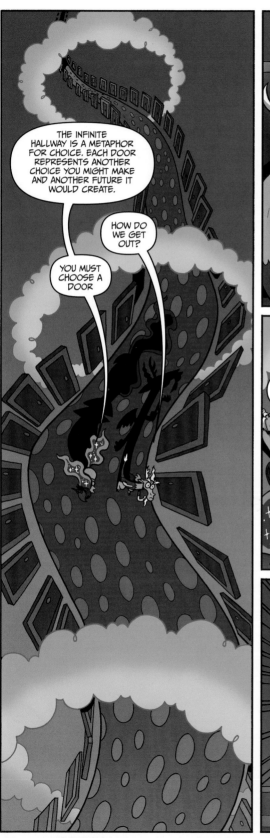

THE INFINITE HALLWAY IS A METAPHOR FOR CHOICE. EACH DOOR REPRESENTS ANOTHER CHOICE YOU MIGHT MAKE AND ANOTHER FUTURE IT WOULD CREATE.

HOW DO WE GET OUT?

YOU MUST CHOOSE A DOOR

THIS ONE HAS DIAMONDS. THAT MUST BE A GOOD SIGN, RIGHT?

THAT HARDLY SEEMS LIKE THE BEST BASIS TO CHOOSE.

WHAT ABOUT THIS ONE? IT LOOKS IMPORTANT.

NONSENSE, THIS IS CLEARLY THE BEST CHOICE.

CAUTION CAUTION CAUTION

STOP

CAUTION CAUTION CAUTION CAUTION

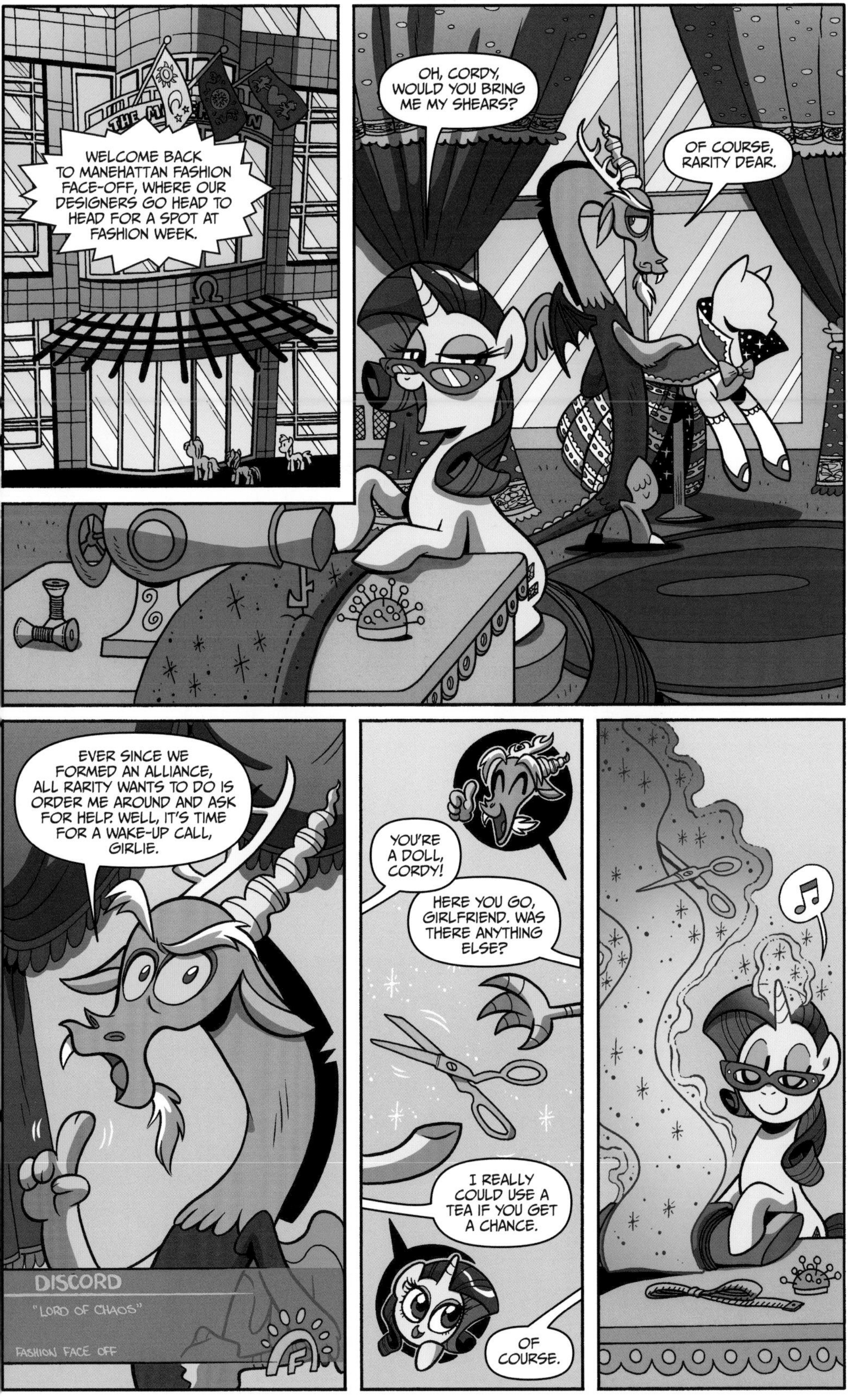
THE M[...]
WELCOME BACK TO MANEHATTAN FASHION FACE-OFF, WHERE OUR DESIGNERS GO HEAD TO HEAD FOR A SPOT AT FASHION WEEK.
OH, CORDY, WOULD YOU BRING ME MY SHEARS?
OF COURSE, RARITY DEAR.
EVER SINCE WE FORMED AN ALLIANCE, ALL RARITY WANTS TO DO IS ORDER ME AROUND AND ASK FOR HELP. WELL, IT'S TIME FOR A WAKE-UP CALL, GIRLIE.
DISCORD
"LORD OF CHAOS"
FASHION FACE OFF
YOU'RE A DOLL, CORDY!
HERE YOU GO, GIRLFRIEND. WAS THERE ANYTHING ELSE?
I REALLY COULD USE A TEA IF YOU GET A CHANCE.
OF COURSE.

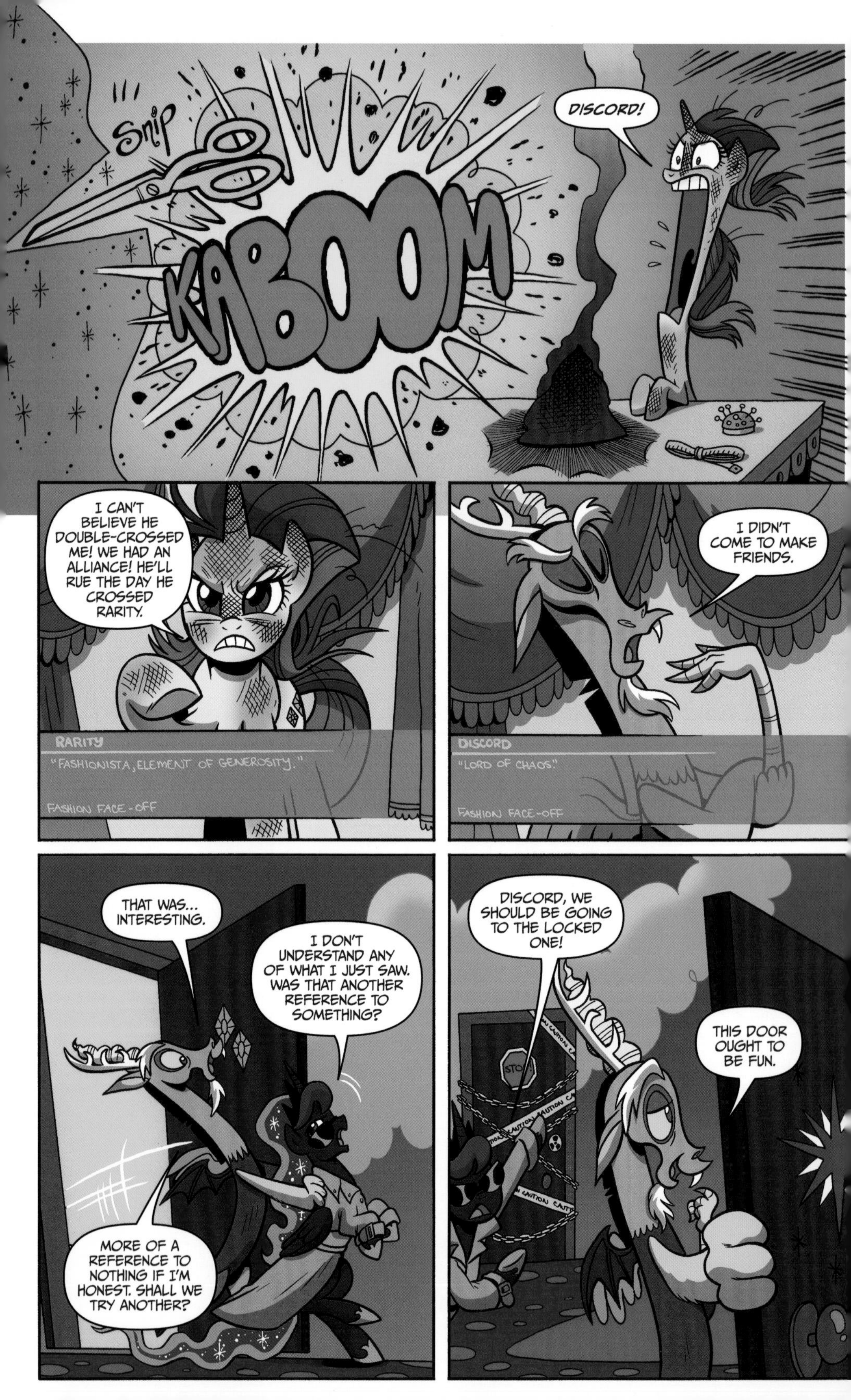
SNIP
KABOOM
DISCORD!
I CAN'T BELIEVE HE DOUBLE-CROSSED ME! WE HAD AN ALLIANCE! HE'LL RUE THE DAY HE CROSSED RARITY.
RARITY
"FASHIONISTA, ELEMENT OF GENEROSITY."
FASHION FACE-OFF
I DIDN'T COME TO MAKE FRIENDS.
DISCORD
"LORD OF CHAOS."
FASHION FACE-OFF
THAT WAS... INTERESTING.
I DON'T UNDERSTAND ANY OF WHAT I JUST SAW. WAS THAT ANOTHER REFERENCE TO SOMETHING?
MORE OF A REFERENCE TO NOTHING IF I'M HONEST. SHALL WE TRY ANOTHER?
DISCORD, WE SHOULD BE GOING TO THE LOCKED ONE!
THIS DOOR OUGHT TO BE FUN.

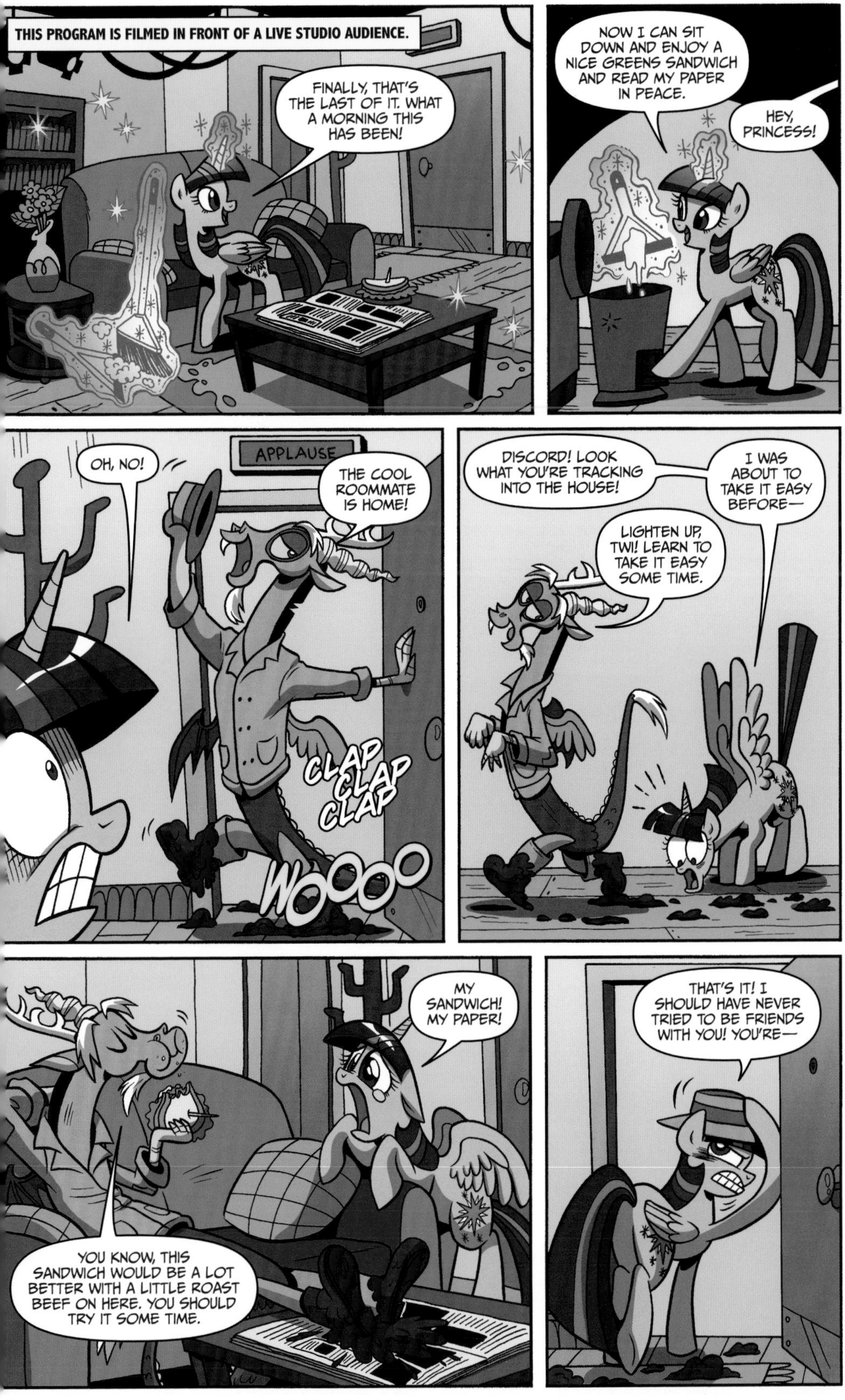
THIS PROGRAM IS FILMED IN FRONT OF A LIVE STUDIO AUDIENCE.
FINALLY, THAT'S THE LAST OF IT. WHAT A MORNING THIS HAS BEEN!
NOW I CAN SIT DOWN AND ENJOY A NICE GREENS SANDWICH AND READ MY PAPER IN PEACE.
HEY, PRINCESS!
OH, NO!
APPLAUSE
THE COOL ROOMMATE IS HOME!
CLAP CLAP CLAP
WOOOO
DISCORD! LOOK WHAT YOU'RE TRACKING INTO THE HOUSE!
I WAS ABOUT TO TAKE IT EASY BEFORE—
LIGHTEN UP, TWI! LEARN TO TAKE IT EASY SOME TIME.
MY SANDWICH! MY PAPER!
YOU KNOW, THIS SANDWICH WOULD BE A LOT BETTER WITH A LITTLE ROAST BEEF ON HERE. YOU SHOULD TRY IT SOME TIME.
THAT'S IT! I SHOULD HAVE NEVER TRIED TO BE FRIENDS WITH YOU! YOU'RE—

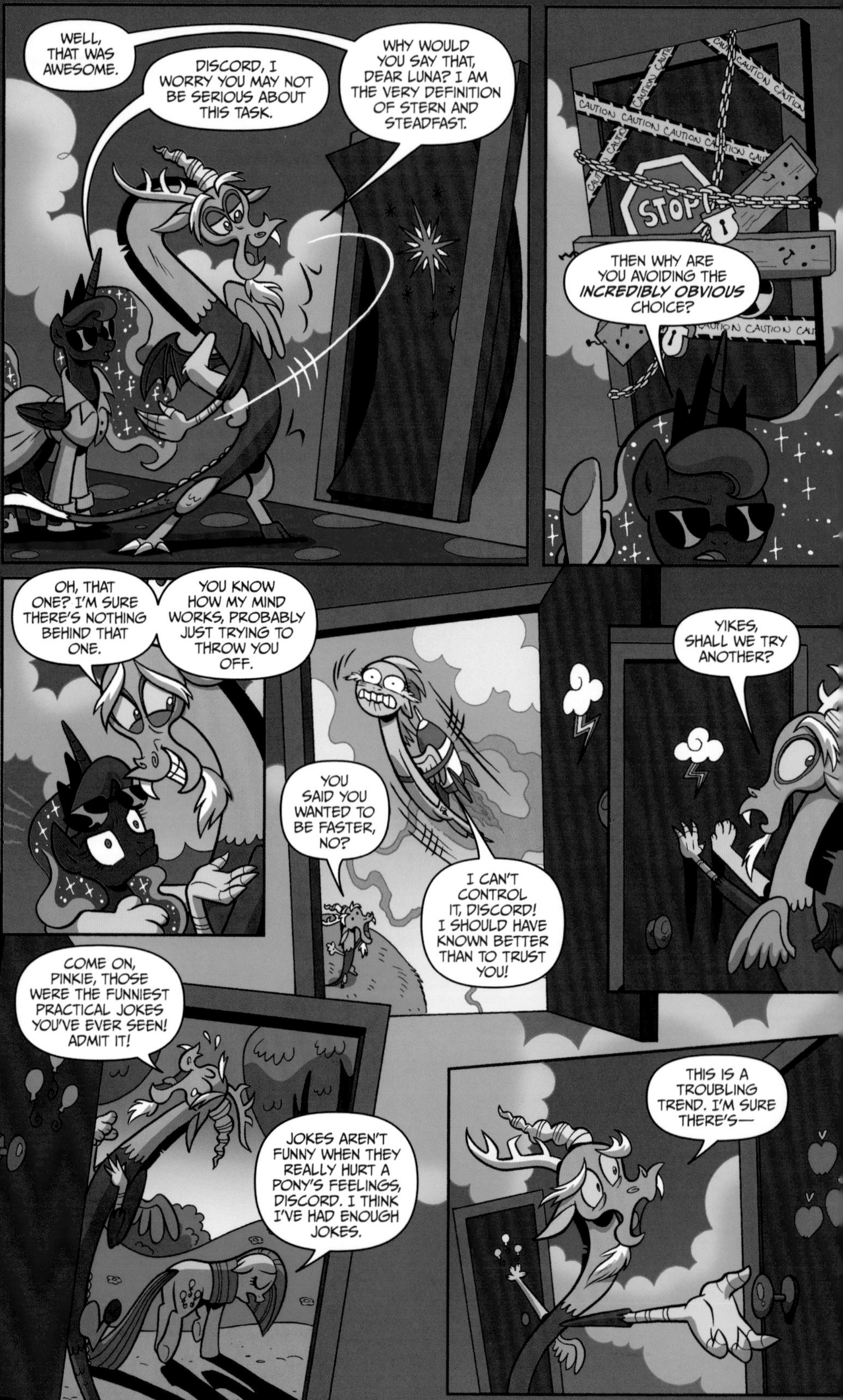
WELL, THAT WAS AWESOME.
DISCORD, I WORRY YOU MAY NOT BE SERIOUS ABOUT THIS TASK.
WHY WOULD YOU SAY THAT, DEAR LUNA? I AM THE VERY DEFINITION OF STERN AND STEADFAST.
CAUTION CAUTION CAUTION
STOP
THEN WHY ARE YOU AVOIDING THE *INCREDIBLY OBVIOUS* CHOICE?
OH, THAT ONE? I'M SURE THERE'S NOTHING BEHIND THAT ONE.
YOU KNOW HOW MY MIND WORKS, PROBABLY JUST TRYING TO THROW YOU OFF.
YOU SAID YOU WANTED TO BE FASTER, NO?
I CAN'T CONTROL IT, DISCORD! I SHOULD HAVE KNOWN BETTER THAN TO TRUST YOU!
YIKES, SHALL WE TRY ANOTHER?
COME ON, PINKIE, THOSE WERE THE FUNNIEST PRACTICAL JOKES YOU'VE EVER SEEN! ADMIT IT!
JOKES AREN'T FUNNY WHEN THEY REALLY HURT A PONY'S FEELINGS, DISCORD. I THINK I'VE HAD ENOUGH JOKES.
THIS IS A TROUBLING TREND. I'M SURE THERE'S—

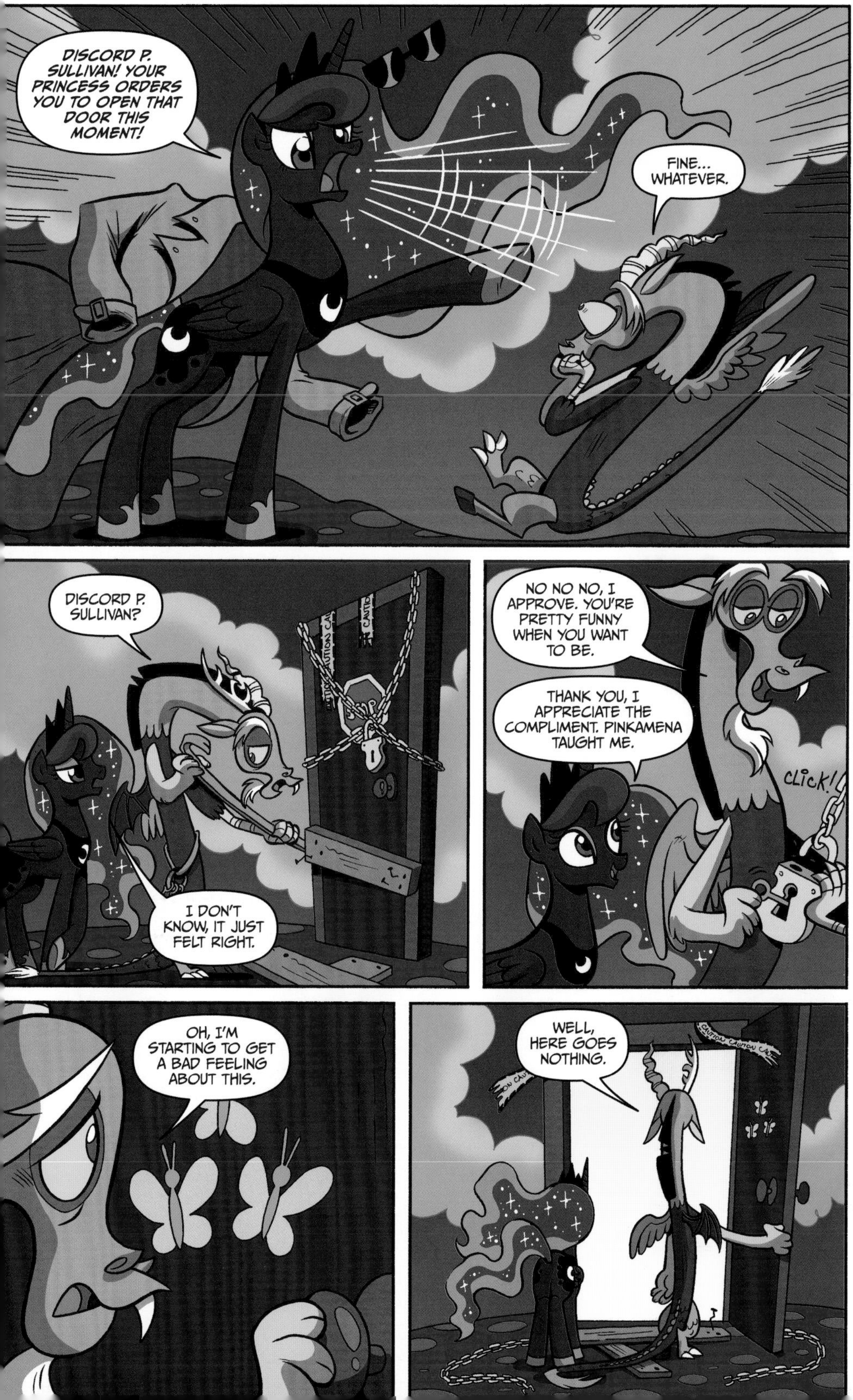
DISCORD P. SULLIVAN! YOUR PRINCESS ORDERS YOU TO OPEN THAT DOOR THIS MOMENT!
FINE... WHATEVER.
DISCORD P. SULLIVAN?
I DON'T KNOW, IT JUST FELT RIGHT.
NO NO NO, I APPROVE. YOU'RE PRETTY FUNNY WHEN YOU WANT TO BE.
THANK YOU, I APPRECIATE THE COMPLIMENT. PINKAMENA TAUGHT ME.
CLICK!
OH, I'M STARTING TO GET A BAD FEELING ABOUT THIS.
WELL, HERE GOES NOTHING.

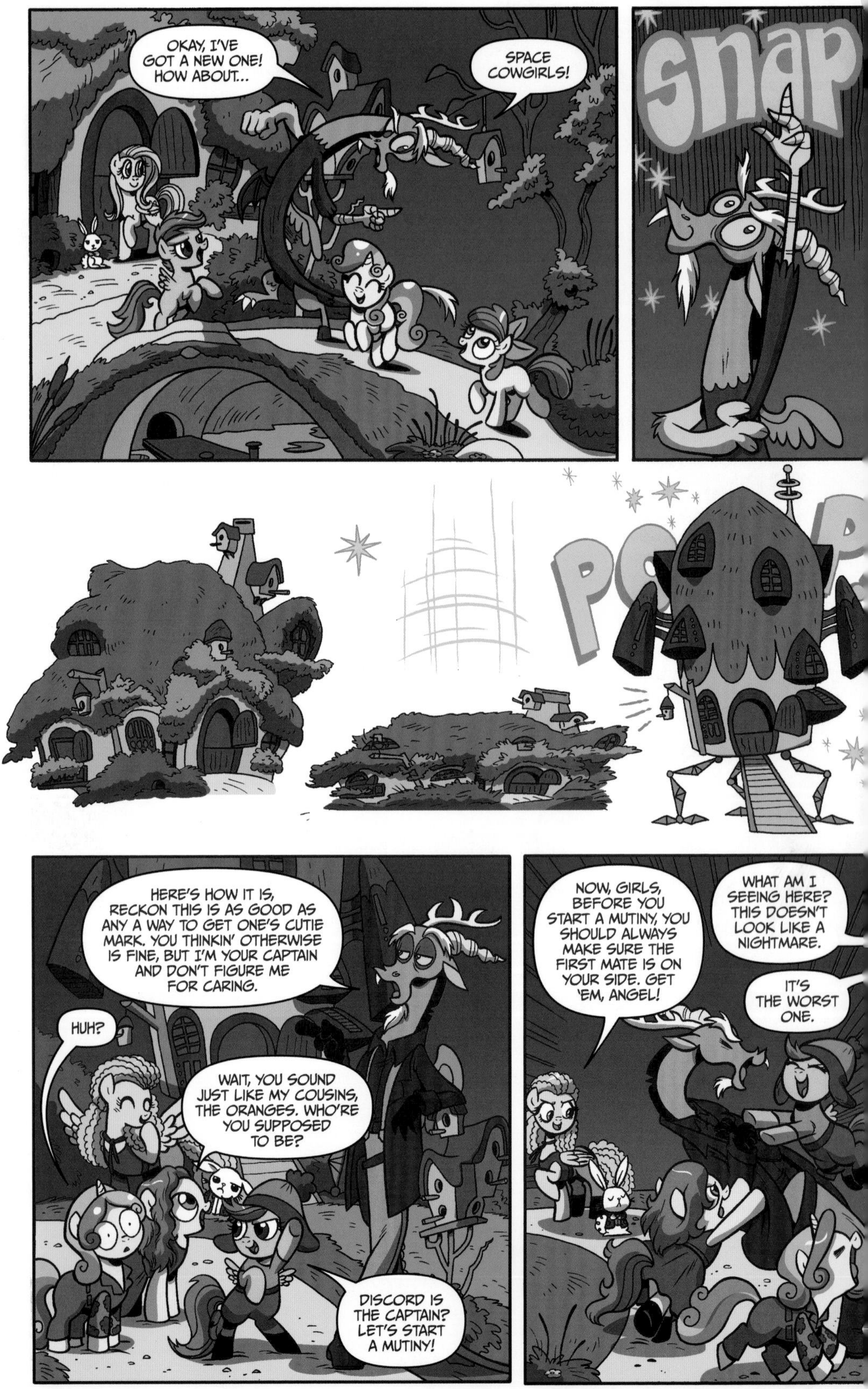
OKAY, I'VE GOT A NEW ONE! HOW ABOUT...
SPACE COWGIRLS!
SNAP
PO
HERE'S HOW IT IS, RECKON THIS IS AS GOOD AS ANY A WAY TO GET ONE'S CUTIE MARK. YOU THINKIN' OTHERWISE IS FINE, BUT I'M YOUR CAPTAIN AND DON'T FIGURE ME FOR CARING.
HUH?
WAIT, YOU SOUND JUST LIKE MY COUSINS, THE ORANGES. WHO'RE YOU SUPPOSED TO BE?
DISCORD IS THE CAPTAIN? LET'S START A MUTINY!
NOW, GIRLS, BEFORE YOU START A MUTINY, YOU SHOULD ALWAYS MAKE SURE THE FIRST MATE IS ON YOUR SIDE. GET 'EM, ANGEL!
WHAT AM I SEEING HERE? THIS DOESN'T LOOK LIKE A NIGHTMARE.
IT'S THE WORST ONE.

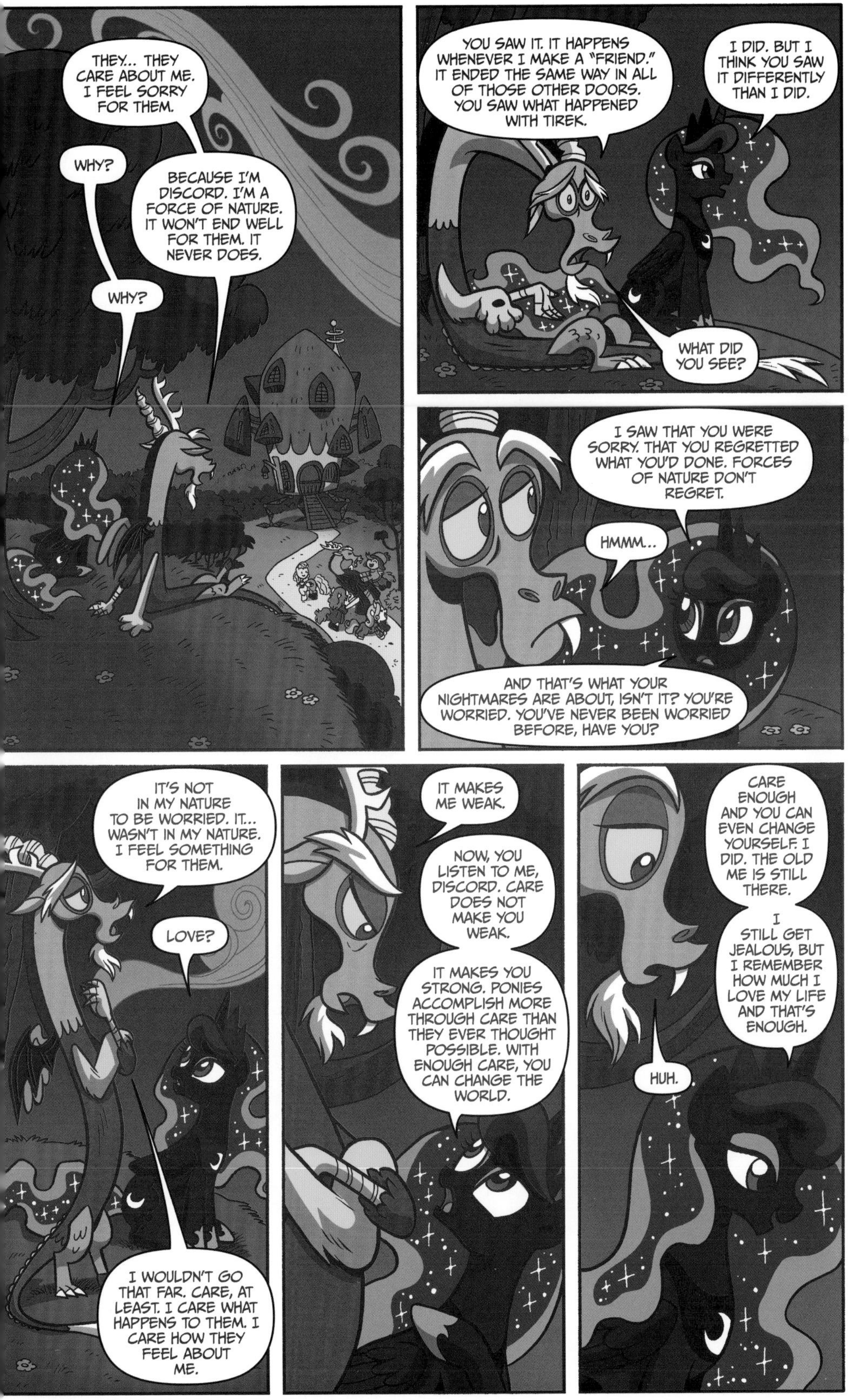
THEY... THEY CARE ABOUT ME. I FEEL SORRY FOR THEM.
WHY?
BECAUSE I'M DISCORD. I'M A FORCE OF NATURE. IT WON'T END WELL FOR THEM. IT NEVER DOES.
WHY?
YOU SAW IT. IT HAPPENS WHENEVER I MAKE A "FRIEND." IT ENDED THE SAME WAY IN ALL OF THOSE OTHER DOORS. YOU SAW WHAT HAPPENED WITH TIREK.
I DID. BUT I THINK YOU SAW IT DIFFERENTLY THAN I DID.
WHAT DID YOU SEE?
I SAW THAT YOU WERE SORRY. THAT YOU REGRETTED WHAT YOU'D DONE. FORCES OF NATURE DON'T REGRET.
HMMM...
AND THAT'S WHAT YOUR NIGHTMARES ARE ABOUT, ISN'T IT? YOU'RE WORRIED. YOU'VE NEVER BEEN WORRIED BEFORE, HAVE YOU?
IT'S NOT IN MY NATURE TO BE WORRIED. IT... WASN'T IN MY NATURE. I FEEL SOMETHING FOR THEM.
LOVE?
I WOULDN'T GO THAT FAR. CARE, AT LEAST. I CARE WHAT HAPPENS TO THEM. I CARE HOW THEY FEEL ABOUT ME.
IT MAKES ME WEAK.
NOW, YOU LISTEN TO ME, DISCORD. CARE DOES NOT MAKE YOU WEAK.
IT MAKES YOU STRONG. PONIES ACCOMPLISH MORE THROUGH CARE THAN THEY EVER THOUGHT POSSIBLE. WITH ENOUGH CARE, YOU CAN CHANGE THE WORLD.
CARE ENOUGH AND YOU CAN EVEN CHANGE YOURSELF. I DID. THE OLD ME IS STILL THERE.
I STILL GET JEALOUS, BUT I REMEMBER HOW MUCH I LOVE MY LIFE AND THAT'S ENOUGH.
HUH.

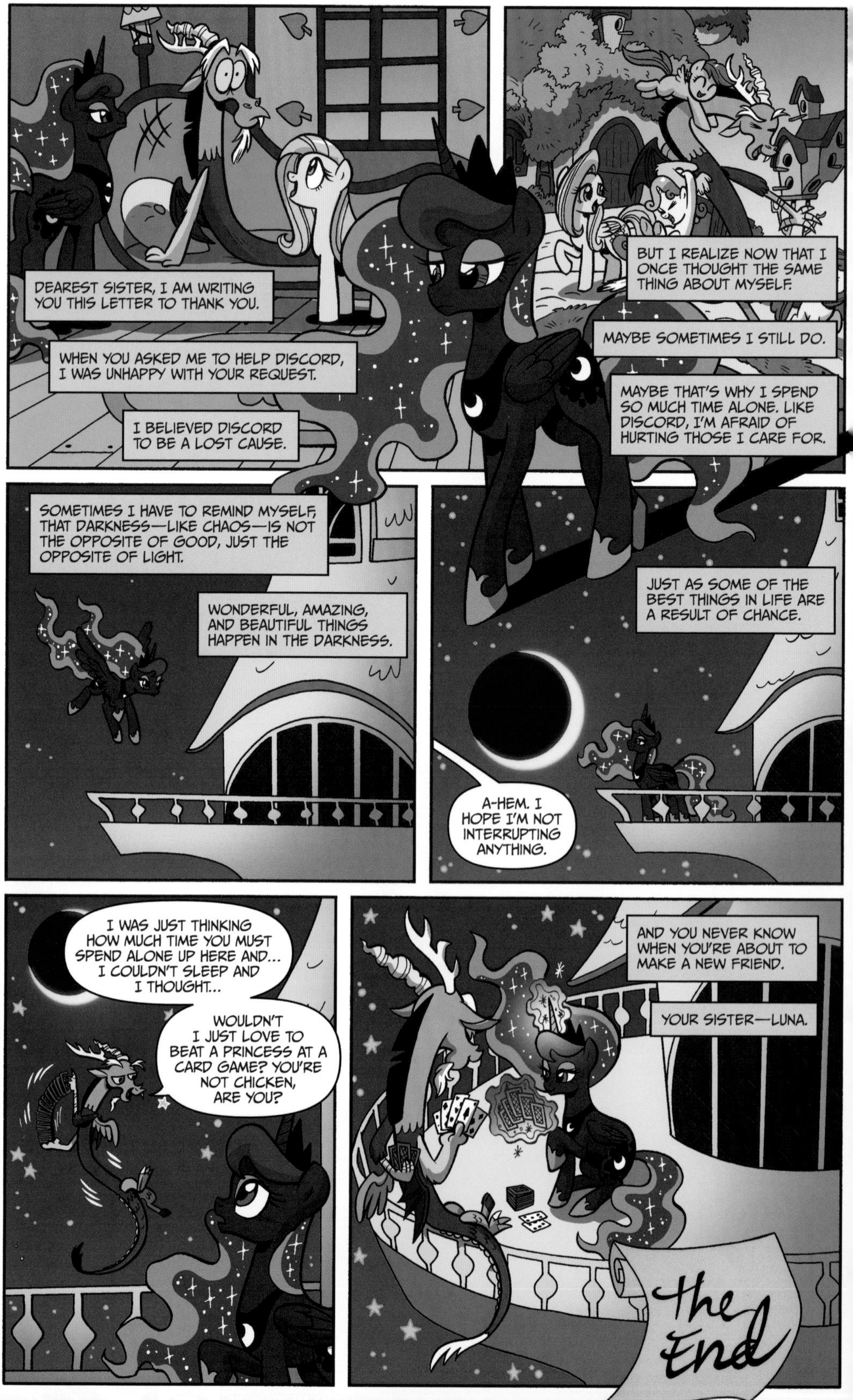
DEAREST SISTER, I AM WRITING YOU THIS LETTER TO THANK YOU.
WHEN YOU ASKED ME TO HELP DISCORD, I WAS UNHAPPY WITH YOUR REQUEST.
I BELIEVED DISCORD TO BE A LOST CAUSE.
BUT I REALIZE NOW THAT I ONCE THOUGHT THE SAME THING ABOUT MYSELF.
MAYBE SOMETIMES I STILL DO.
MAYBE THAT'S WHY I SPEND SO MUCH TIME ALONE. LIKE DISCORD, I'M AFRAID OF HURTING THOSE I CARE FOR.
SOMETIMES I HAVE TO REMIND MYSELF, THAT DARKNESS—LIKE CHAOS—IS NOT THE OPPOSITE OF GOOD, JUST THE OPPOSITE OF LIGHT.
WONDERFUL, AMAZING, AND BEAUTIFUL THINGS HAPPEN IN THE DARKNESS.
JUST AS SOME OF THE BEST THINGS IN LIFE ARE A RESULT OF CHANCE.
A-HEM. I HOPE I'M NOT INTERRUPTING ANYTHING.
I WAS JUST THINKING HOW MUCH TIME YOU MUST SPEND ALONE UP HERE AND... I COULDN'T SLEEP AND I THOUGHT...
WOULDN'T I JUST LOVE TO BEAT A PRINCESS AT A CARD GAME? YOU'RE NOT CHICKEN, ARE YOU?
AND YOU NEVER KNOW WHEN YOU'RE ABOUT TO MAKE A NEW FRIEND.
YOUR SISTER—LUNA.
the End

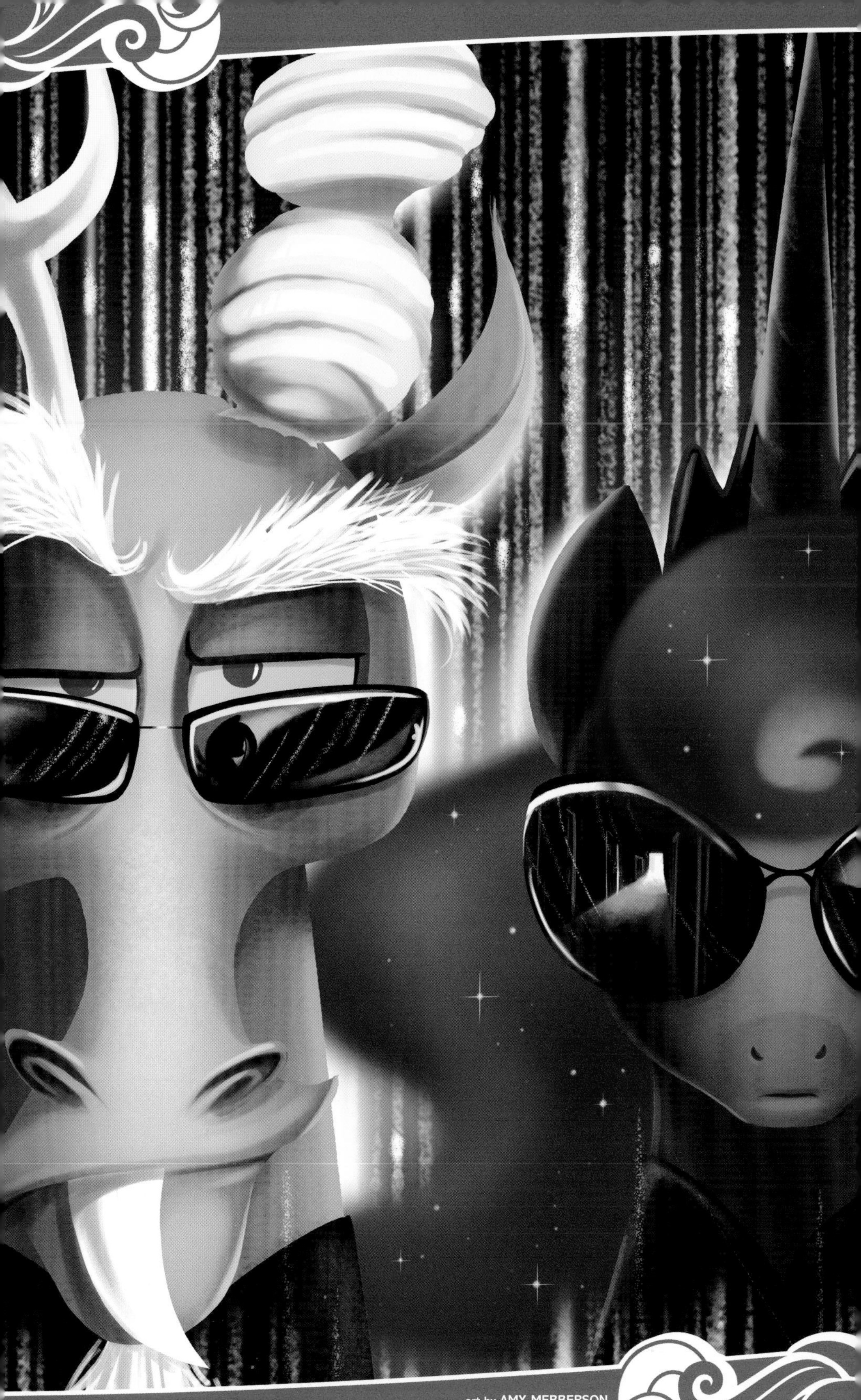

art by AMY MEBBERSON

Zecora & Spike

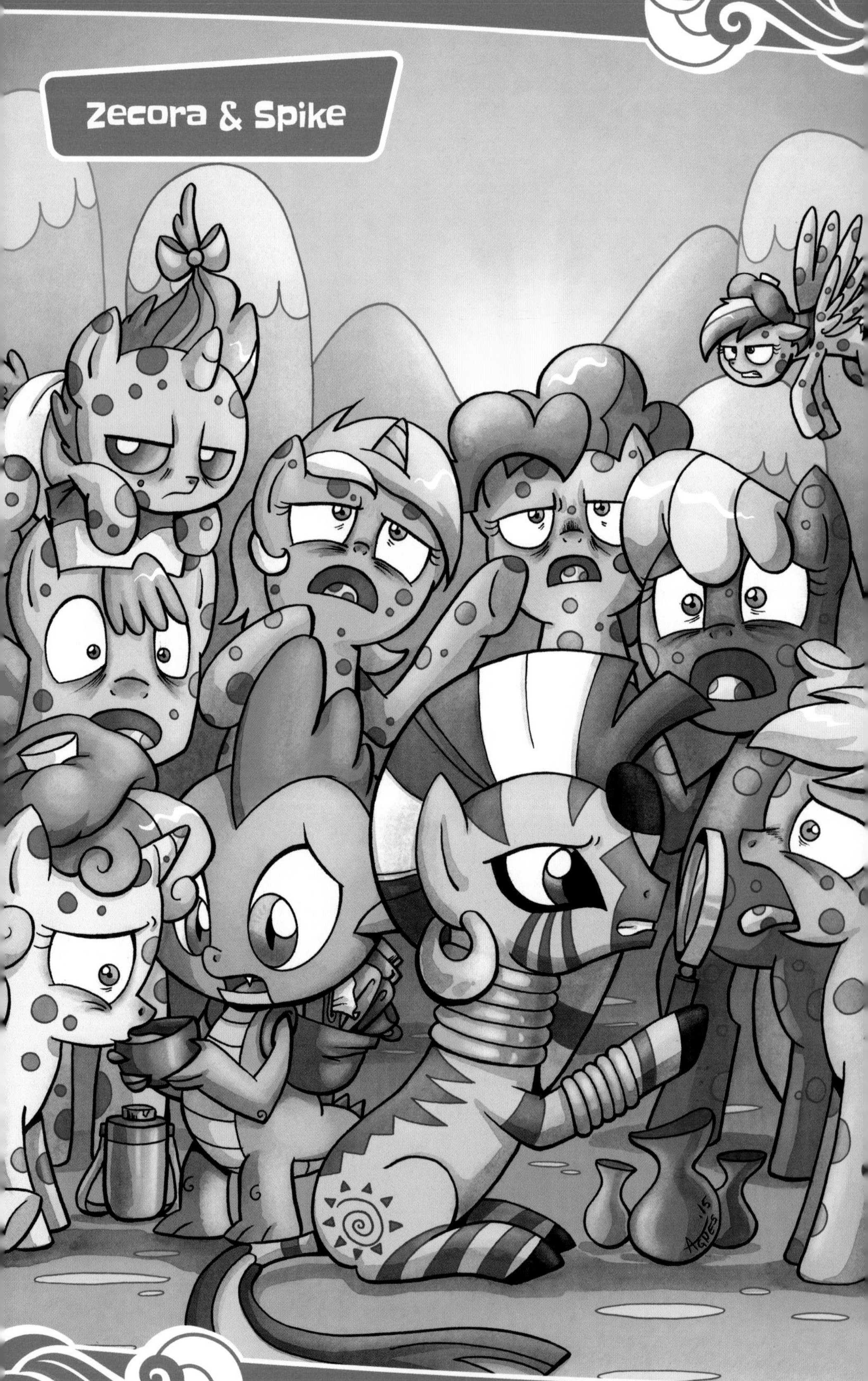

art by AGNES GARBOWSKA

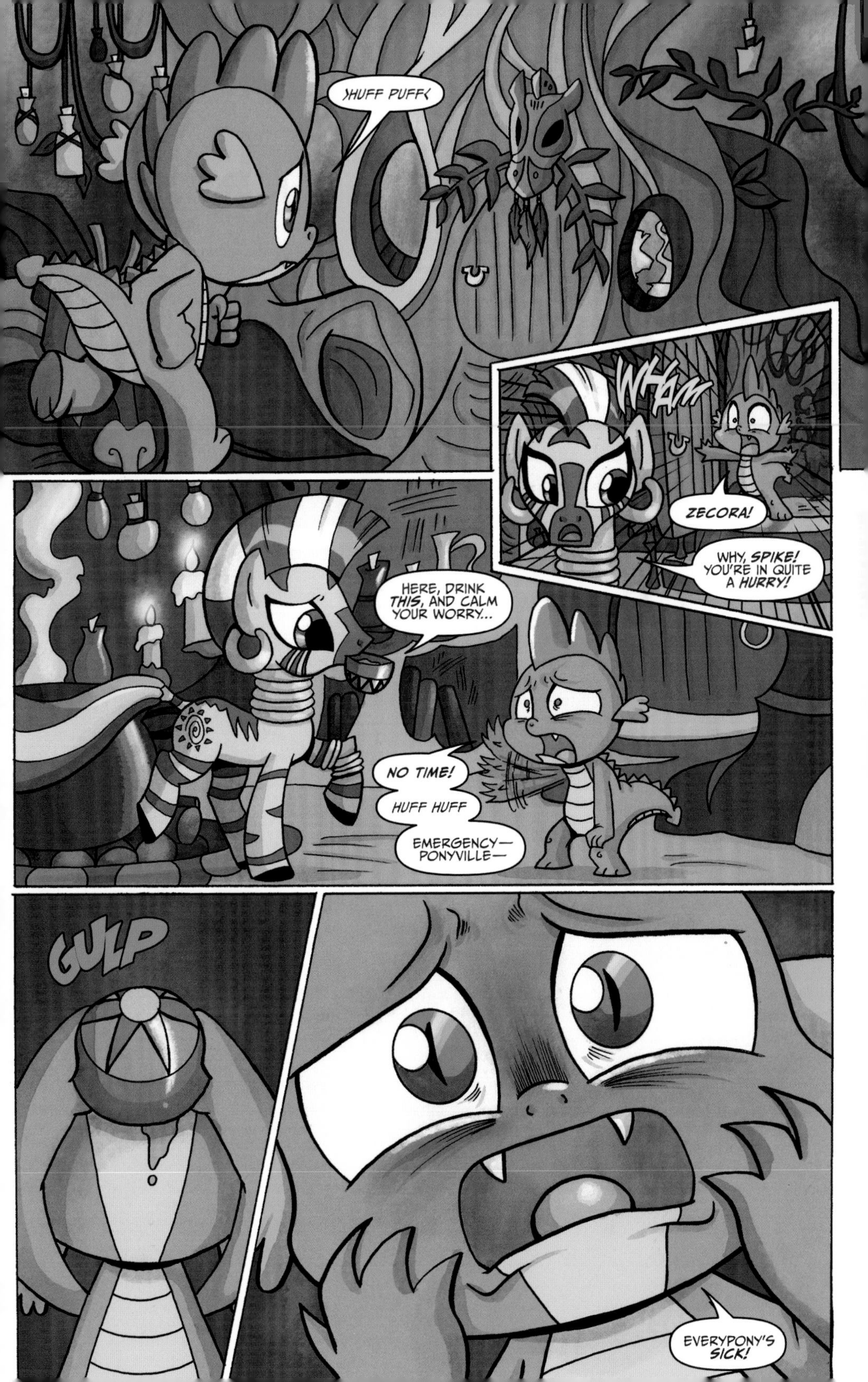

›HUFF PUFF‹
WHAM
ZECORA!
WHY, SPIKE! YOU'RE IN QUITE A HURRY!
HERE, DRINK THIS, AND CALM YOUR WORRY...
NO TIME!
HUFF HUFF
EMERGENCY— PONYVILLE—
GULP
EVERYPONY'S SICK!

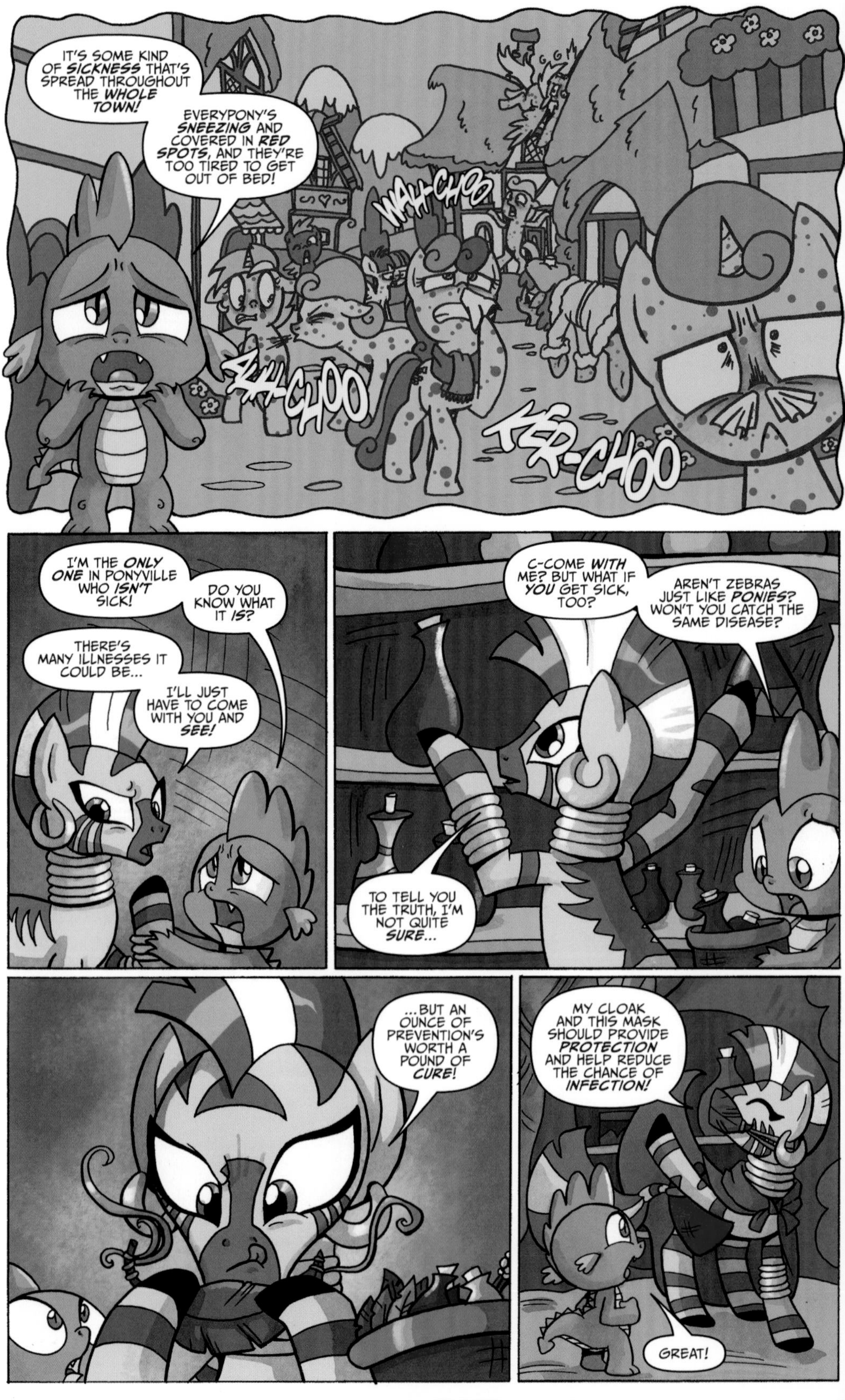
IT'S SOME KIND OF SICKNESS THAT'S SPREAD THROUGHOUT THE WHOLE TOWN!
EVERYPONY'S SNEEZING AND COVERED IN RED SPOTS, AND THEY'RE TOO TIRED TO GET OUT OF BED!
WAH-CHOO
AHH-CHOO
KER-CHOO
I'M THE ONLY ONE IN PONYVILLE WHO ISN'T SICK!
DO YOU KNOW WHAT IT IS?
THERE'S MANY ILLNESSES IT COULD BE...
I'LL JUST HAVE TO COME WITH YOU AND SEE!
C-COME WITH ME? BUT WHAT IF YOU GET SICK, TOO?
AREN'T ZEBRAS JUST LIKE PONIES? WON'T YOU CATCH THE SAME DISEASE?
TO TELL YOU THE TRUTH, I'M NOT QUITE SURE...
...BUT AN OUNCE OF PREVENTION'S WORTH A POUND OF CURE!
MY CLOAK AND THIS MASK SHOULD PROVIDE PROTECTION AND HELP REDUCE THE CHANCE OF INFECTION!
GREAT!

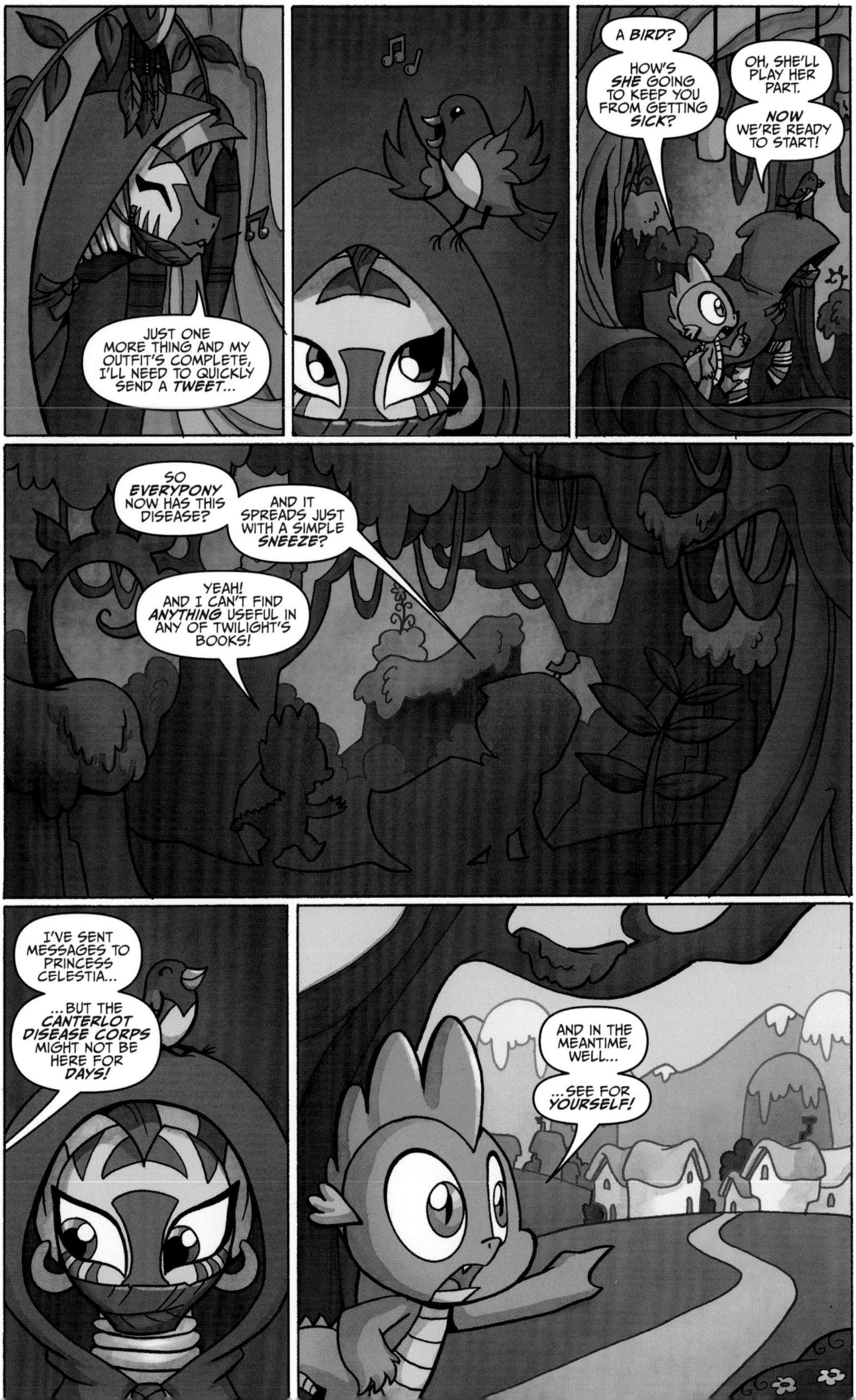

JUST ONE MORE THING AND MY OUTFIT'S COMPLETE, I'LL NEED TO QUICKLY SEND A TWEET...
A BIRD?
HOW'S SHE GOING TO KEEP YOU FROM GETTING SICK?
OH, SHE'LL PLAY HER PART.
NOW WE'RE READY TO START!
SO EVERYPONY NOW HAS THIS DISEASE?
AND IT SPREADS JUST WITH A SIMPLE SNEEZE?
YEAH! AND I CAN'T FIND ANYTHING USEFUL IN ANY OF TWILIGHT'S BOOKS!
I'VE SENT MESSAGES TO PRINCESS CELESTIA...
...BUT THE CANTERLOT DISEASE CORPS MIGHT NOT BE HERE FOR DAYS!
AND IN THE MEANTIME, WELL...
...SEE FOR YOURSELF!

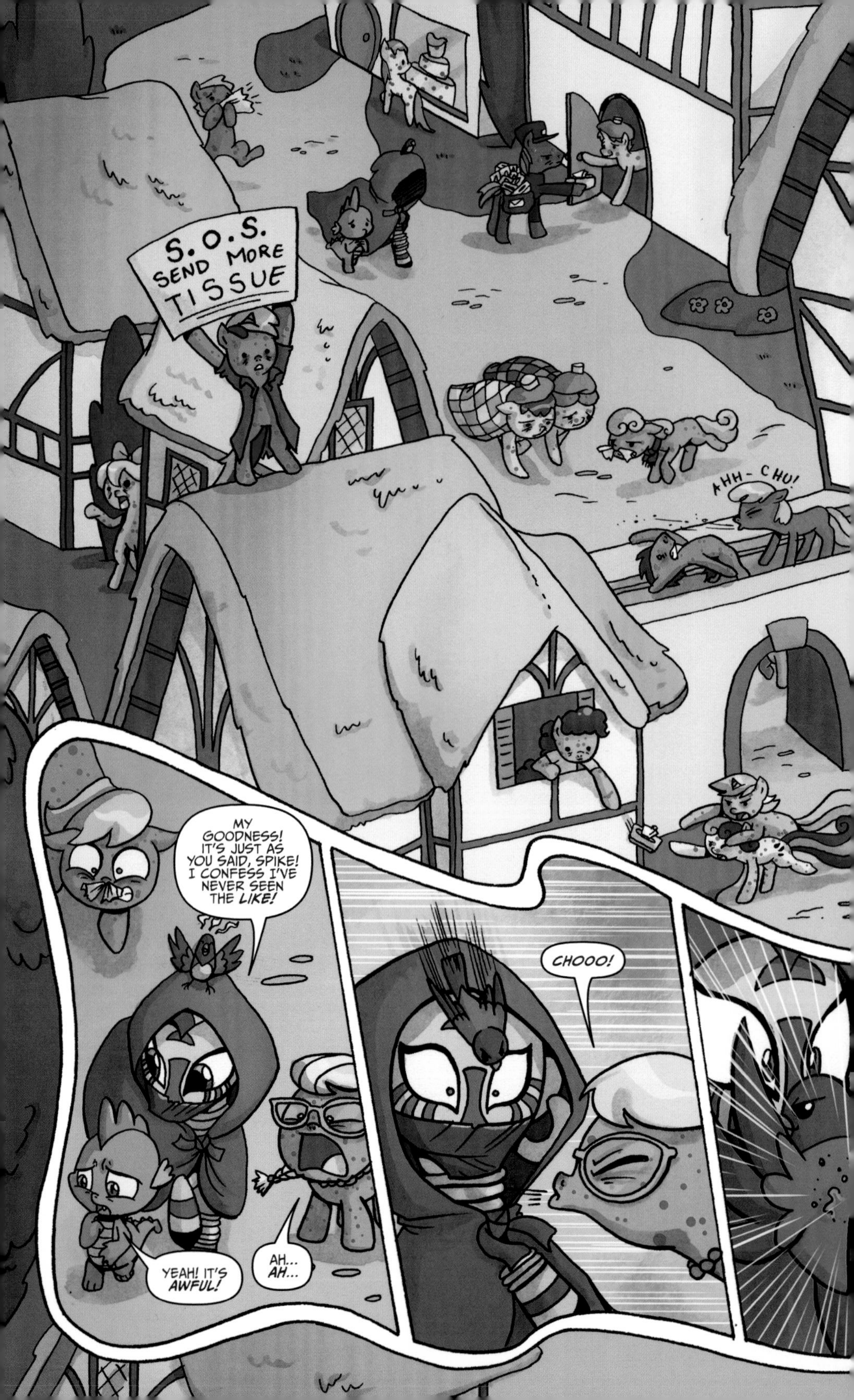
S.O.S. SEND MORE TISSUE
AHH-CHU!
MY GOODNESS! IT'S JUST AS YOU SAID, SPIKE! I CONFESS I'VE NEVER SEEN THE *LIKE*!
YEAH! IT'S *AWFUL*!
AH... *AH*...
CHOOO!

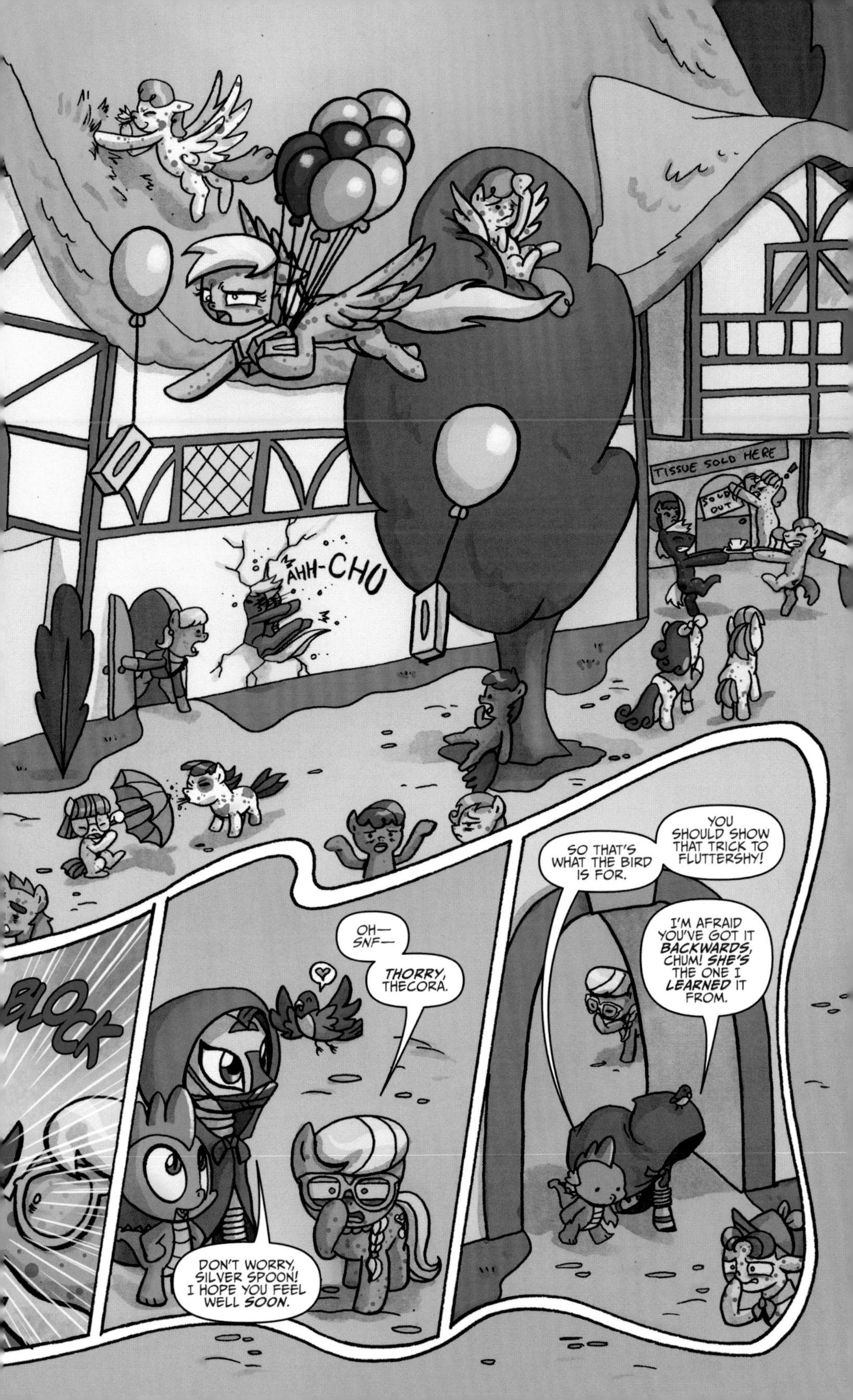
TISSUE SOLD HERE
SOLD OUT
AHH-CHU
BLOCK
OH— SNF—
THORRY, THECORA.
DON'T WORRY, SILVER SPOON! I HOPE YOU FEEL WELL SOON.
SO THAT'S WHAT THE BIRD IS FOR.
YOU SHOULD SHOW THAT TRICK TO FLUTTERSHY!
I'M AFRAID YOU'VE GOT IT BACKWARDS, CHUM! SHE'S THE ONE I LEARNED IT FROM.

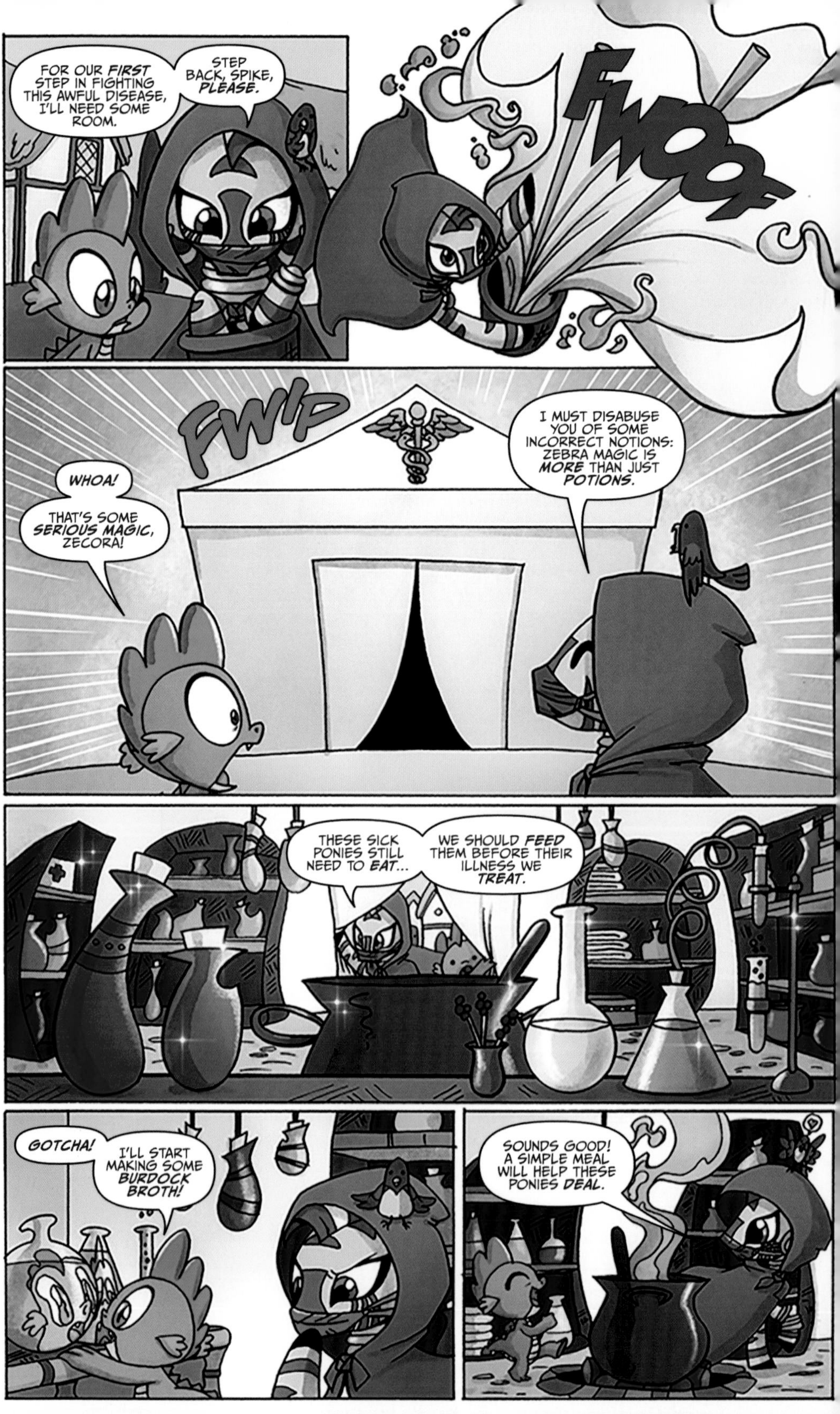

FOR OUR FIRST STEP IN FIGHTING THIS AWFUL DISEASE, I'LL NEED SOME ROOM.
STEP BACK, SPIKE, PLEASE.
FWOOF
FWIP
WHOA!
THAT'S SOME SERIOUS MAGIC, ZECORA!
I MUST DISABUSE YOU OF SOME INCORRECT NOTIONS: ZEBRA MAGIC IS MORE THAN JUST POTIONS.
THESE SICK PONIES STILL NEED TO EAT...
WE SHOULD FEED THEM BEFORE THEIR ILLNESS WE TREAT.
GOTCHA!
I'LL START MAKING SOME BURDOCK BROTH!
SOUNDS GOOD! A SIMPLE MEAL WILL HELP THESE PONIES DEAL.

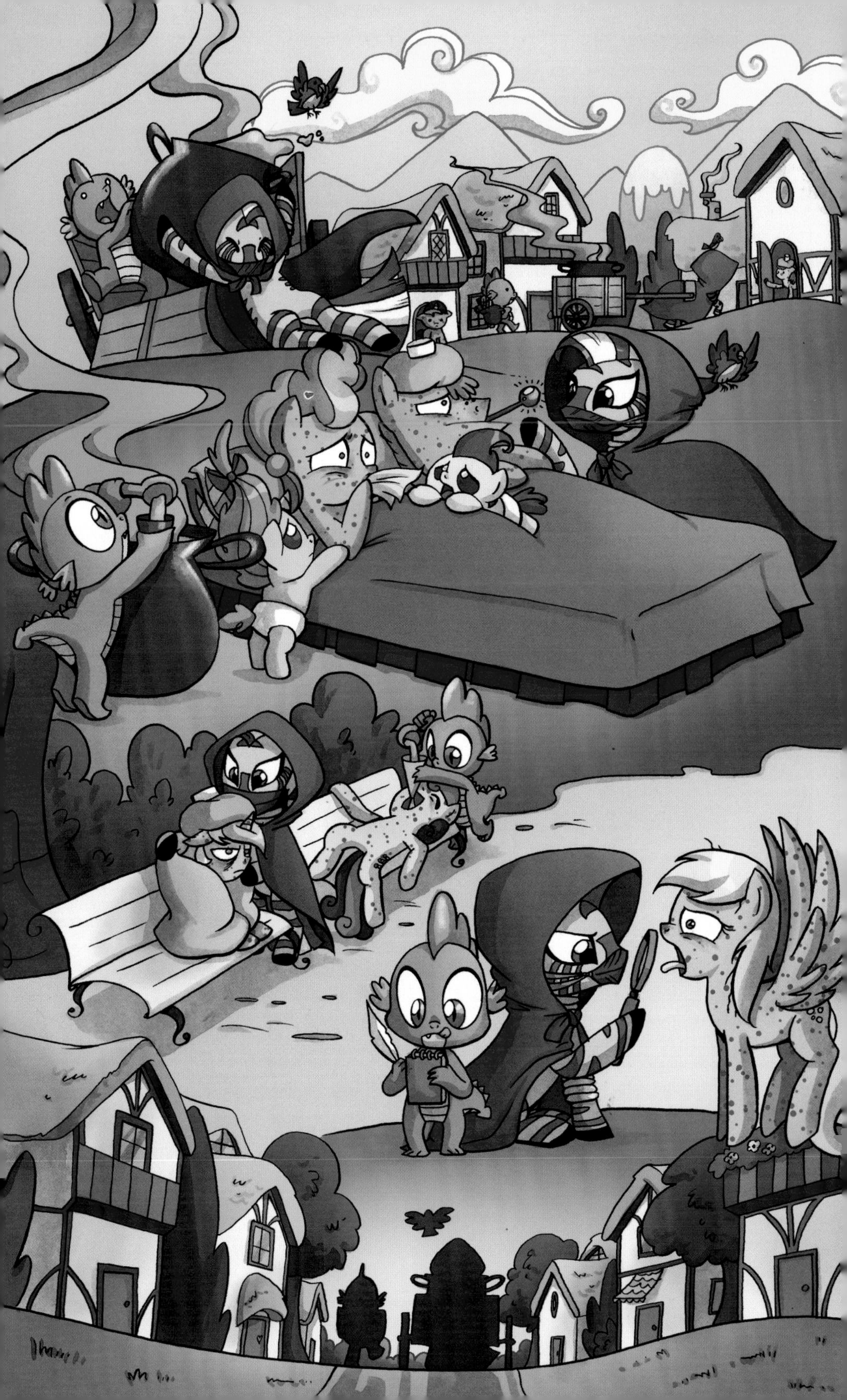

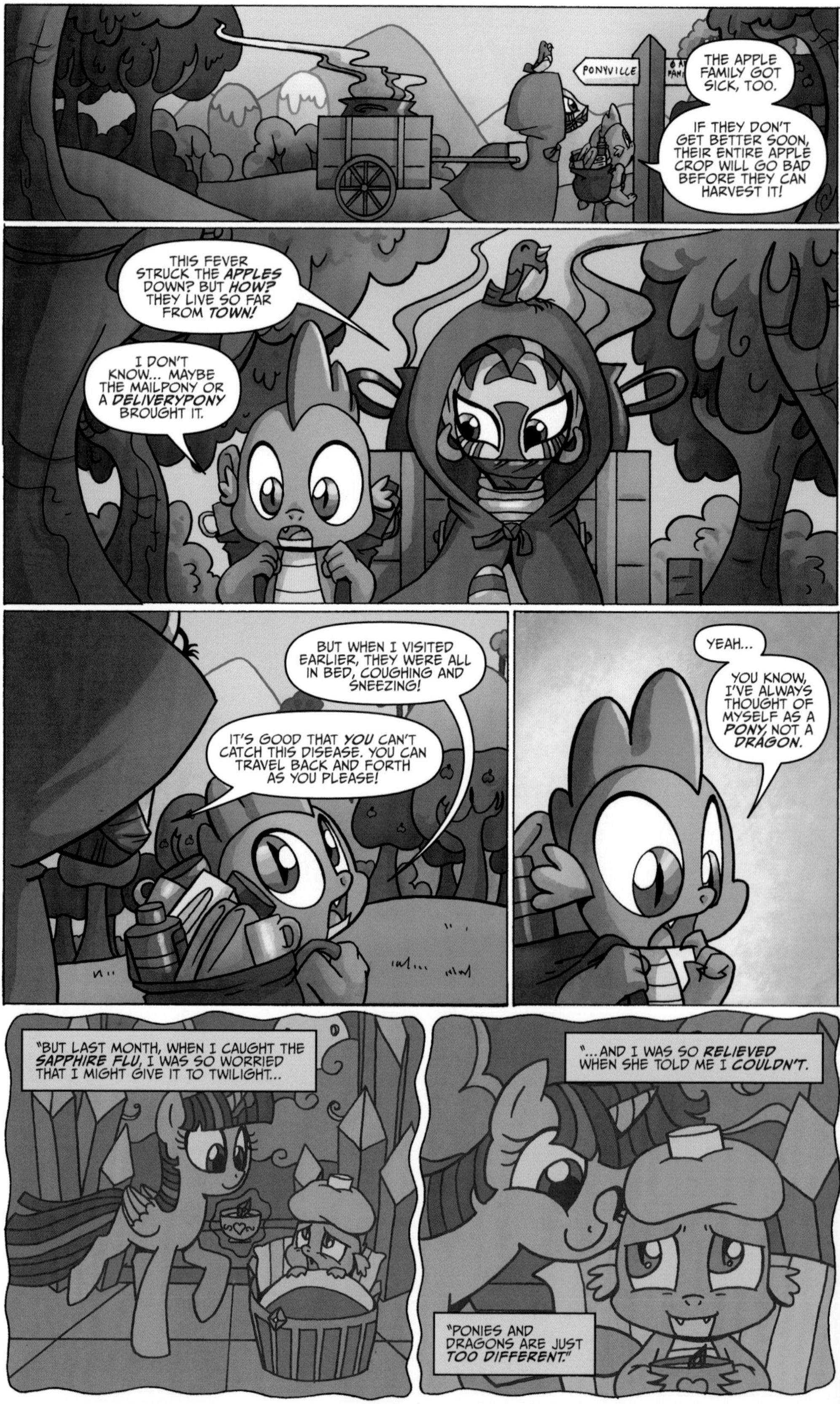
PONYVILLE
THE APPLE FAMILY GOT SICK, TOO.
IF THEY DON'T GET BETTER SOON, THEIR ENTIRE APPLE CROP WILL GO BAD BEFORE THEY CAN HARVEST IT!
THIS FEVER STRUCK THE *APPLES* DOWN? BUT *HOW?* THEY LIVE SO FAR FROM *TOWN!*
I DON'T KNOW... MAYBE THE MAILPONY OR A *DELIVERYPONY* BROUGHT IT.
BUT WHEN I VISITED EARLIER, THEY WERE ALL IN BED, COUGHING AND SNEEZING!
IT'S GOOD THAT *YOU* CAN'T CATCH THIS DISEASE. YOU CAN TRAVEL BACK AND FORTH AS YOU PLEASE!
YEAH...
YOU KNOW, I'VE ALWAYS THOUGHT OF MYSELF AS A *PONY*, NOT A *DRAGON*.
"BUT LAST MONTH, WHEN I CAUGHT THE *SAPPHIRE FLU*, I WAS SO WORRIED THAT I MIGHT GIVE IT TO TWILIGHT...
"...AND I WAS SO *RELIEVED* WHEN SHE TOLD ME I *COULDN'T*.
"PONIES AND DRAGONS ARE JUST *TOO DIFFERENT*."

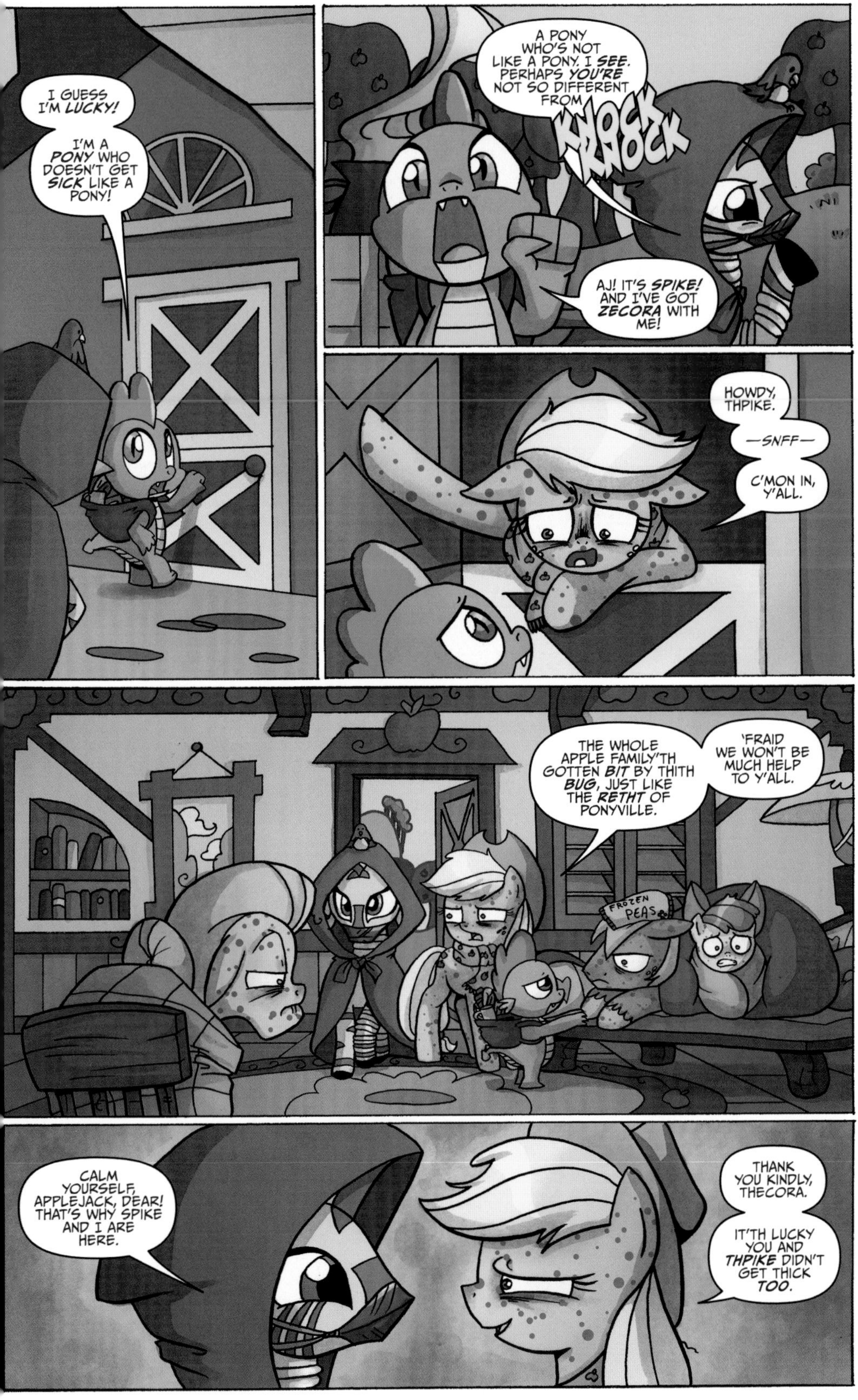

I GUESS I'M *LUCKY!*
I'M A *PONY* WHO DOESN'T GET *SICK* LIKE A PONY!
A PONY WHO'S NOT LIKE A PONY. I *SEE.* PERHAPS *YOU'RE* NOT SO DIFFERENT FROM
KNOCK KNOCK
AJ! IT'S *SPIKE!* AND I'VE GOT *ZECORA* WITH ME!
HOWDY, THPIKE.
—SNFF—
C'MON IN, Y'ALL.
THE WHOLE APPLE FAMILY'TH GOTTEN *BIT* BY THITH *BUG*, JUST LIKE THE *RETHT* OF PONYVILLE.
'FRAID WE WON'T BE MUCH HELP TO Y'ALL.
FROZEN PEAS
CALM YOURSELF, APPLEJACK, DEAR! THAT'S WHY SPIKE AND I ARE HERE.
THANK YOU KINDLY, THECORA.
IT'TH LUCKY YOU AND *THPIKE* DIDN'T GET THICK *TOO.*

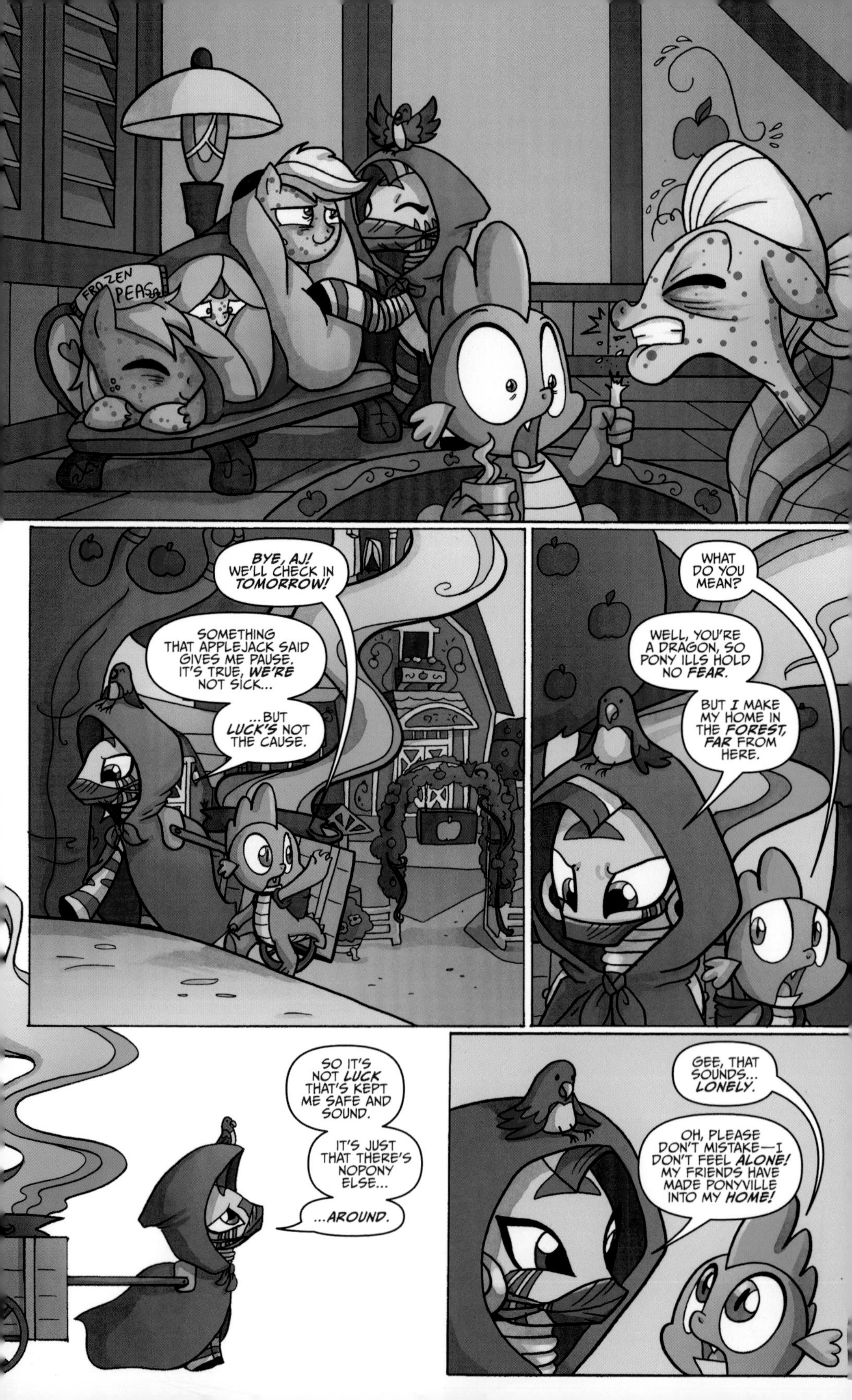
FROZEN PEAS
BYE, AJ! WE'LL CHECK IN TOMORROW!
SOMETHING THAT APPLEJACK SAID GIVES ME PAUSE. IT'S TRUE, WE'RE NOT SICK...
...BUT LUCK'S NOT THE CAUSE.
WHAT DO YOU MEAN?
WELL, YOU'RE A DRAGON, SO PONY ILLS HOLD NO FEAR.
BUT I MAKE MY HOME IN THE FOREST, FAR FROM HERE.
SO IT'S NOT LUCK THAT'S KEPT ME SAFE AND SOUND.
IT'S JUST THAT THERE'S NOPONY ELSE...
...AROUND.
GEE, THAT SOUNDS... LONELY.
OH, PLEASE DON'T MISTAKE—I DON'T FEEL ALONE! MY FRIENDS HAVE MADE PONYVILLE INTO MY HOME!

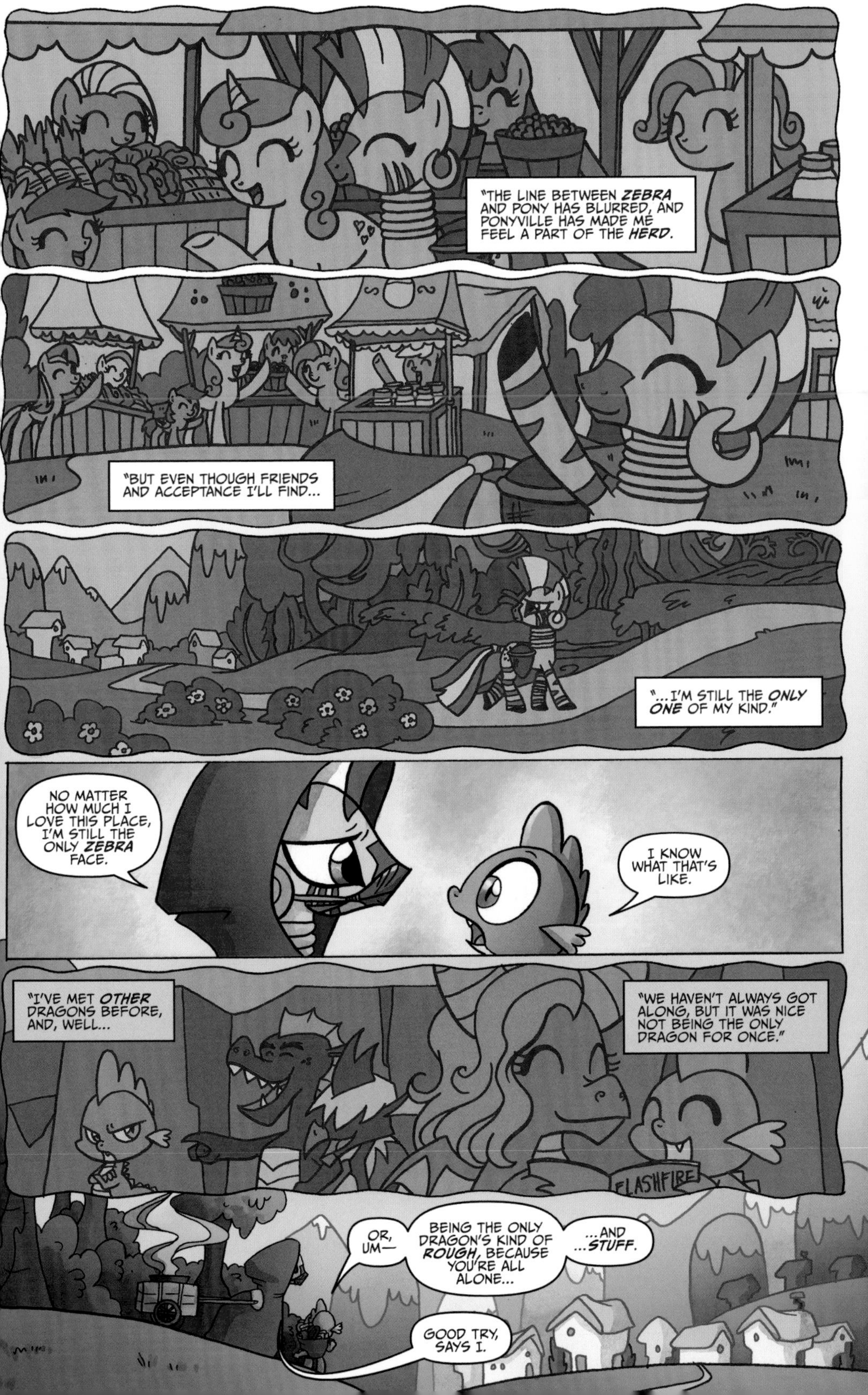
"THE LINE BETWEEN ZEBRA AND PONY HAS BLURRED, AND PONYVILLE HAS MADE ME FEEL A PART OF THE HERD.
"BUT EVEN THOUGH FRIENDS AND ACCEPTANCE I'LL FIND...
"...I'M STILL THE ONLY ONE OF MY KIND."
NO MATTER HOW MUCH I LOVE THIS PLACE, I'M STILL THE ONLY ZEBRA FACE.
I KNOW WHAT THAT'S LIKE.
"I'VE MET OTHER DRAGONS BEFORE, AND, WELL...
"WE HAVEN'T ALWAYS GOT ALONG, BUT IT WAS NICE NOT BEING THE ONLY DRAGON FOR ONCE."
FLASHFIRE
OR, UM—
BEING THE ONLY DRAGON'S KIND OF ROUGH, BECAUSE YOU'RE ALL ALONE...
...AND ...STUFF.
GOOD TRY, SAYS I.

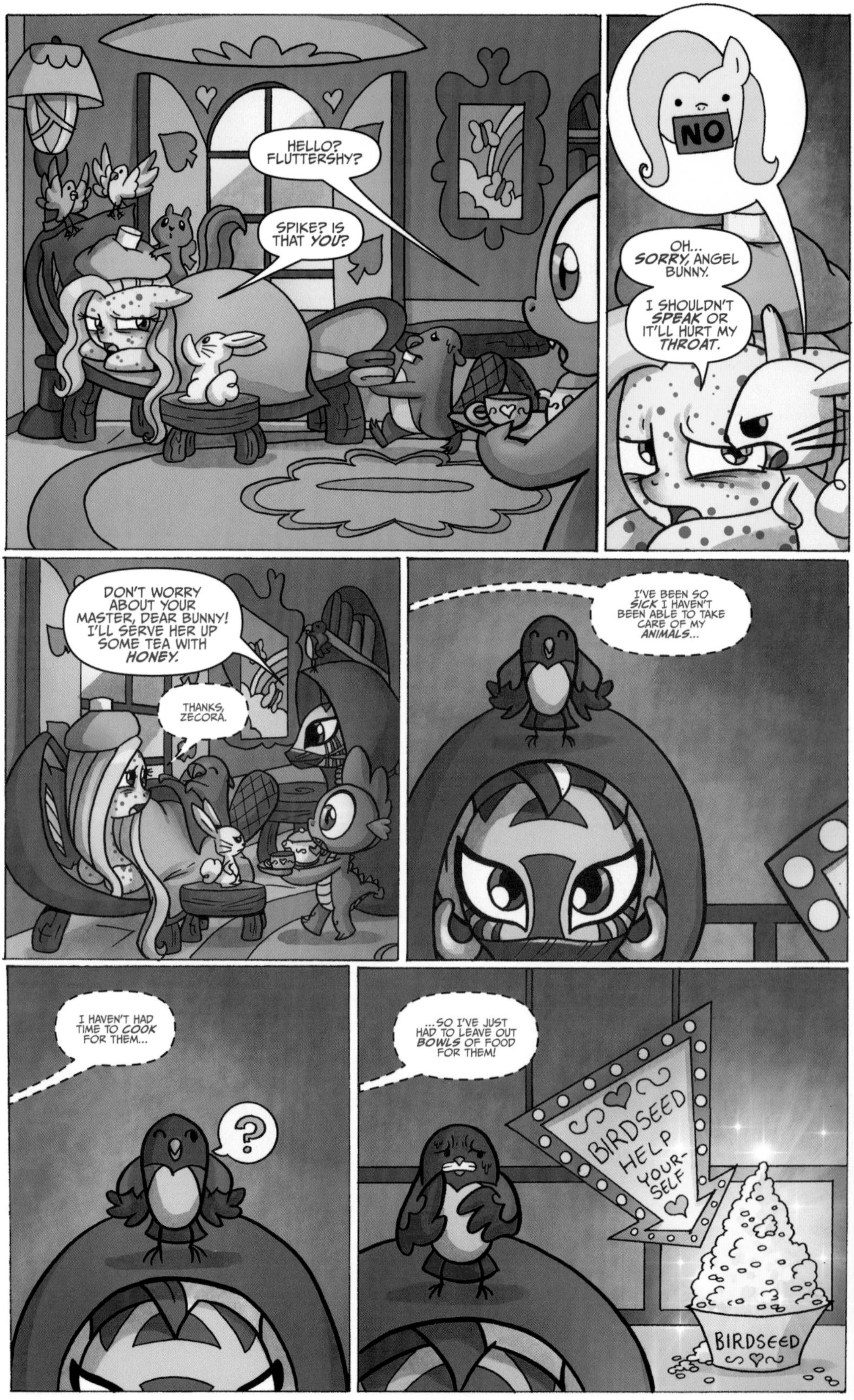
HELLO? FLUTTERSHY?
SPIKE? IS THAT YOU?
NO
OH... SORRY, ANGEL BUNNY.
I SHOULDN'T SPEAK OR IT'LL HURT MY THROAT.
DON'T WORRY ABOUT YOUR MASTER, DEAR BUNNY! I'LL SERVE HER UP SOME TEA WITH HONEY.
THANKS, ZECORA.
I'VE BEEN SO SICK I HAVEN'T BEEN ABLE TO TAKE CARE OF MY ANIMALS...
I HAVEN'T HAD TIME TO COOK FOR THEM...
?
...SO I'VE JUST HAD TO LEAVE OUT BOWLS OF FOOD FOR THEM!
BIRDSEED HELP YOUR-SELF
BIRDSEED

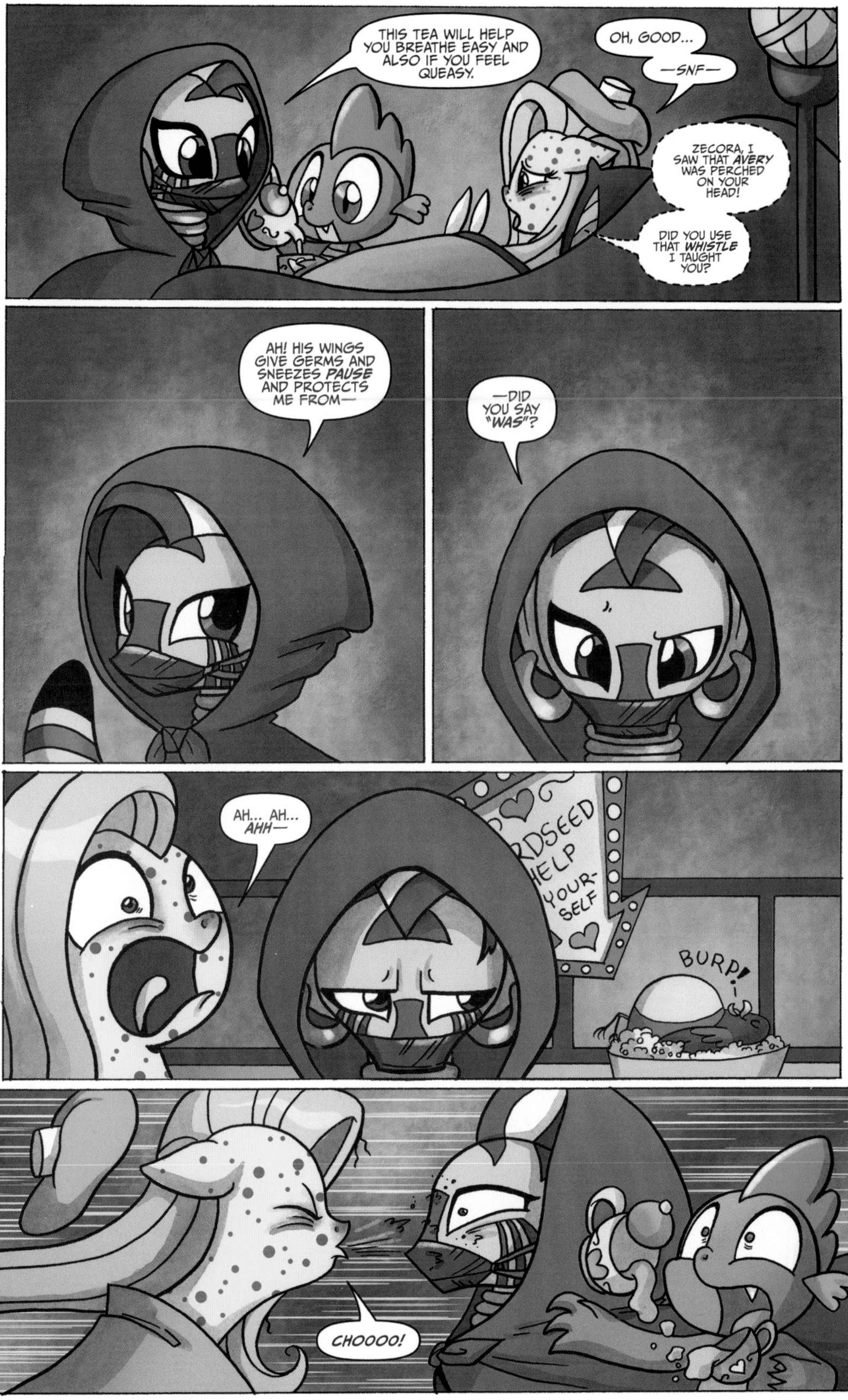
THIS TEA WILL HELP YOU BREATHE EASY AND ALSO IF YOU FEEL QUEASY.
OH, GOOD...
—SNF—
ZECORA, I SAW THAT AVERY WAS PERCHED ON YOUR HEAD!
DID YOU USE THAT WHISTLE I TAUGHT YOU?
AH! HIS WINGS GIVE GERMS AND SNEEZES PAUSE AND PROTECTS ME FROM—
—DID YOU SAY "WAS"?
AH... AH... AHH—
RDSEED
HELP
YOUR-SELF
BURP!
CHOOOO!

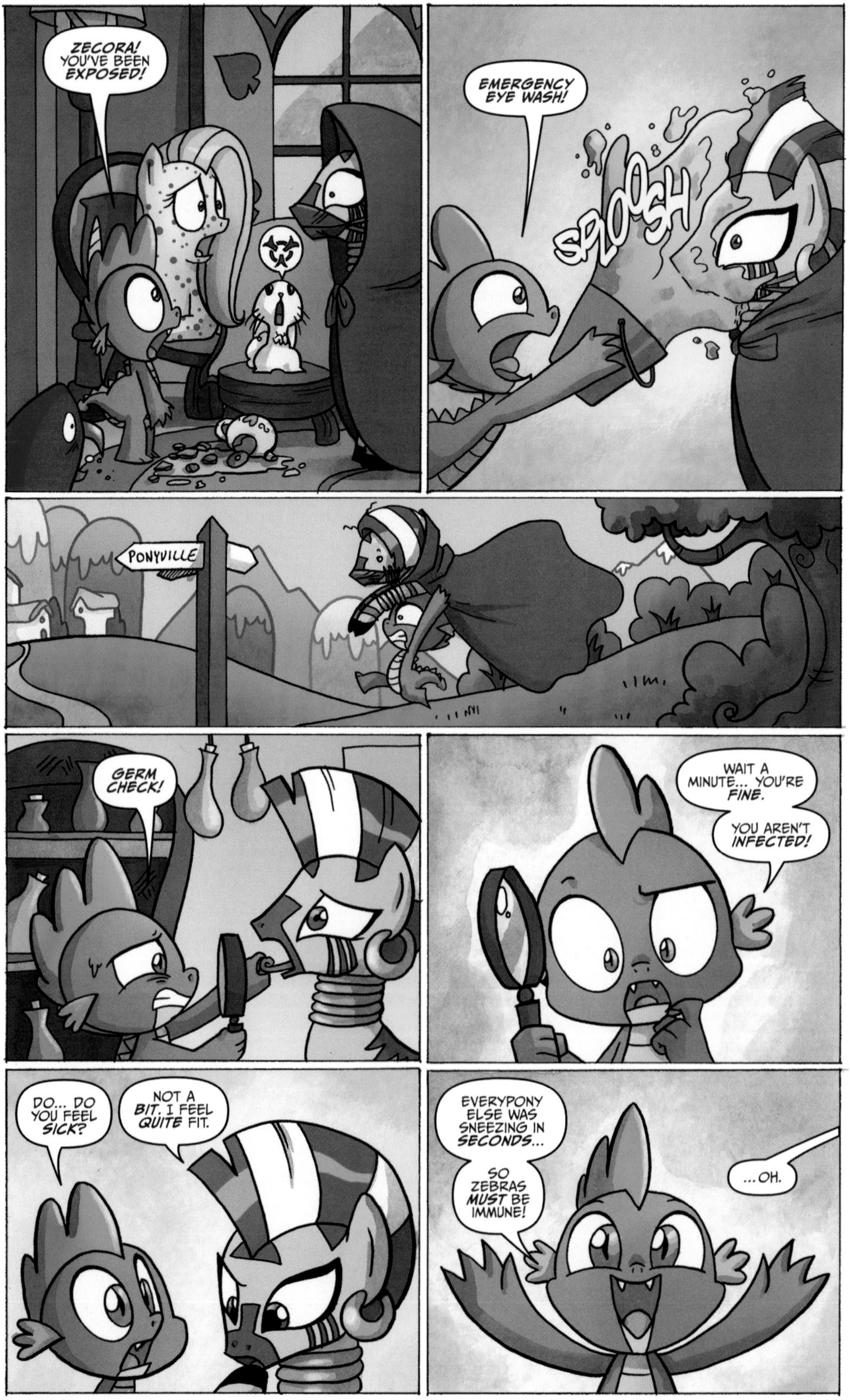
ZECORA! YOU'VE BEEN EXPOSED!
EMERGENCY EYE WASH!
SPLOOSH
PONYVILLE
GERM CHECK!
WAIT A MINUTE... YOU'RE FINE.
YOU AREN'T INFECTED!
DO... DO YOU FEEL SICK?
NOT A BIT. I FEEL QUITE FIT.
EVERYPONY ELSE WAS SNEEZING IN SECONDS...
SO ZEBRAS MUST BE IMMUNE!
...OH.

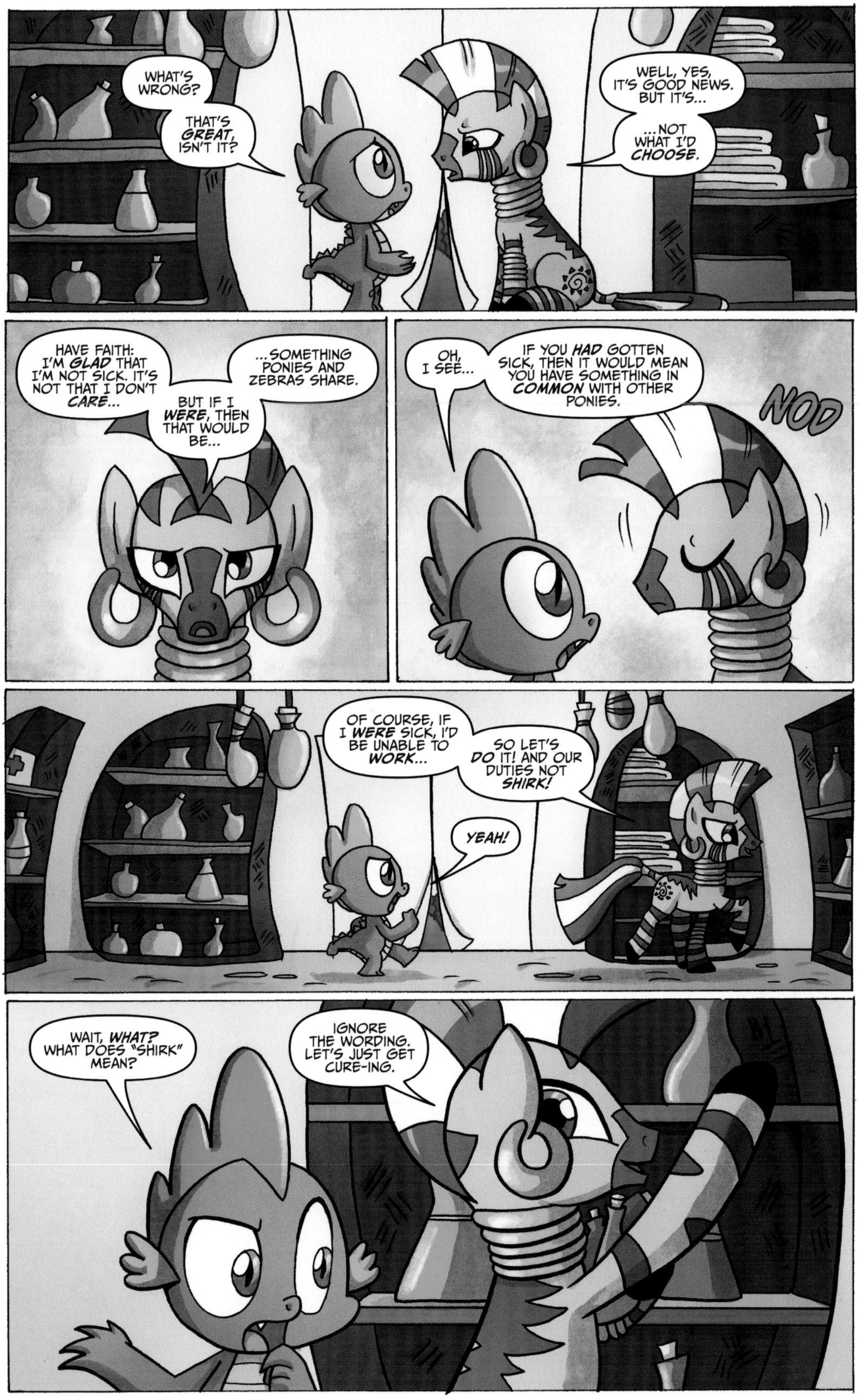
WHAT'S WRONG?
THAT'S *GREAT*, ISN'T IT?
WELL, YES, IT'S GOOD NEWS. BUT IT'S...
...NOT WHAT I'D *CHOOSE*.
HAVE FAITH: I'M *GLAD* THAT I'M NOT SICK. IT'S NOT THAT I DON'T *CARE*...
BUT IF I *WERE*, THEN THAT WOULD BE...
...SOMETHING PONIES AND ZEBRAS SHARE.
OH, I SEE...
IF YOU *HAD* GOTTEN SICK, THEN IT WOULD MEAN YOU HAVE SOMETHING IN *COMMON* WITH OTHER PONIES.
NOD
OF COURSE, IF I *WERE* SICK, I'D BE UNABLE TO *WORK*...
SO LET'S *DO* IT! AND OUR DUTIES NOT *SHIRK*!
YEAH!
WAIT, *WHAT?* WHAT DOES "SHIRK" MEAN?
IGNORE THE WORDING. LET'S JUST GET CURE-ING.

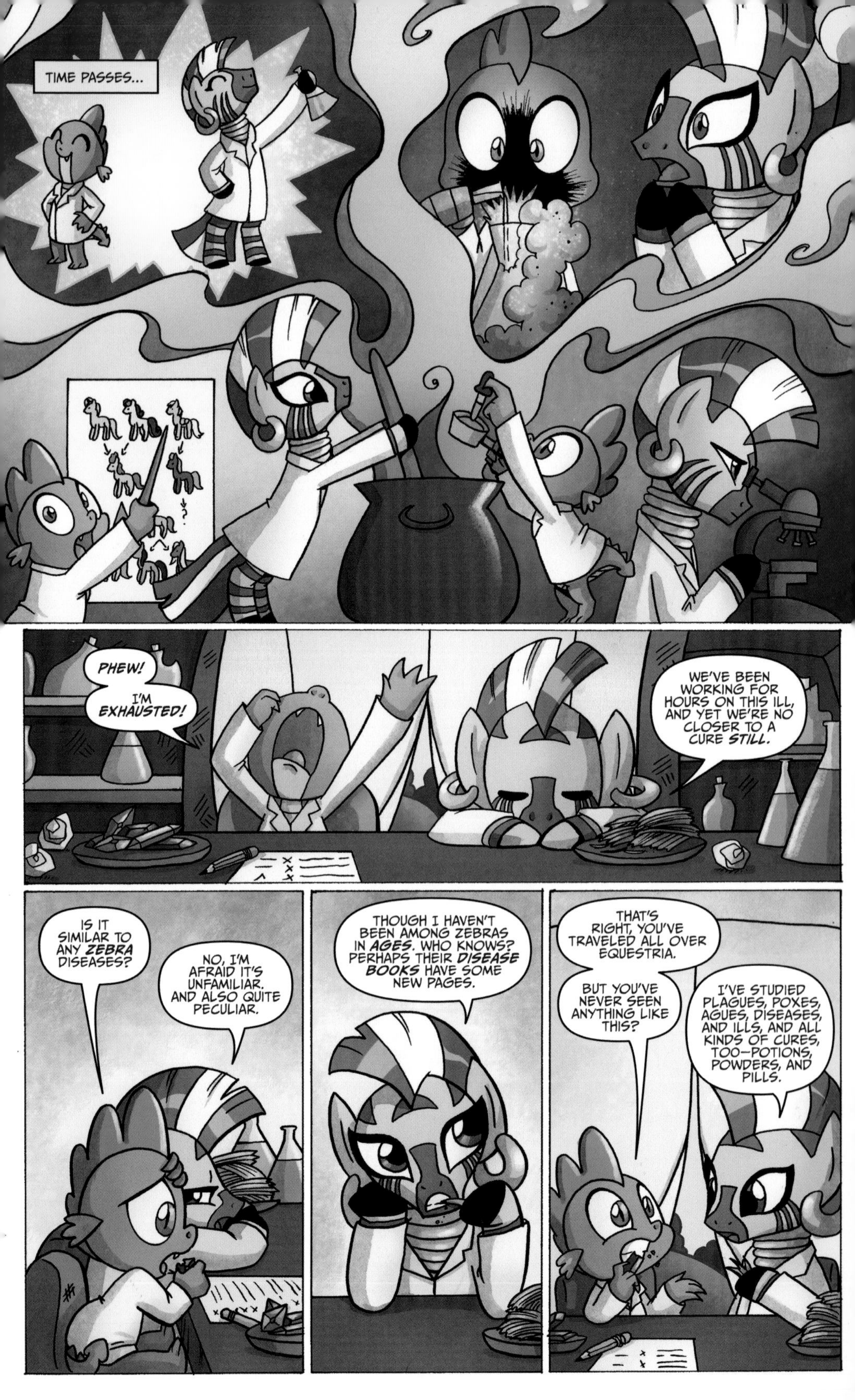
TIME PASSES...
PHEW! I'M EXHAUSTED!
WE'VE BEEN WORKING FOR HOURS ON THIS ILL, AND YET WE'RE NO CLOSER TO A CURE STILL.
IS IT SIMILAR TO ANY ZEBRA DISEASES?
NO, I'M AFRAID IT'S UNFAMILIAR. AND ALSO QUITE PECULIAR.
THOUGH I HAVEN'T BEEN AMONG ZEBRAS IN AGES. WHO KNOWS? PERHAPS THEIR DISEASE BOOKS HAVE SOME NEW PAGES.
THAT'S RIGHT, YOU'VE TRAVELED ALL OVER EQUESTRIA.
BUT YOU'VE NEVER SEEN ANYTHING LIKE THIS?
I'VE STUDIED PLAGUES, POXES, AGUES, DISEASES, AND ILLS, AND ALL KINDS OF CURES, TOO—POTIONS, POWDERS, AND PILLS.

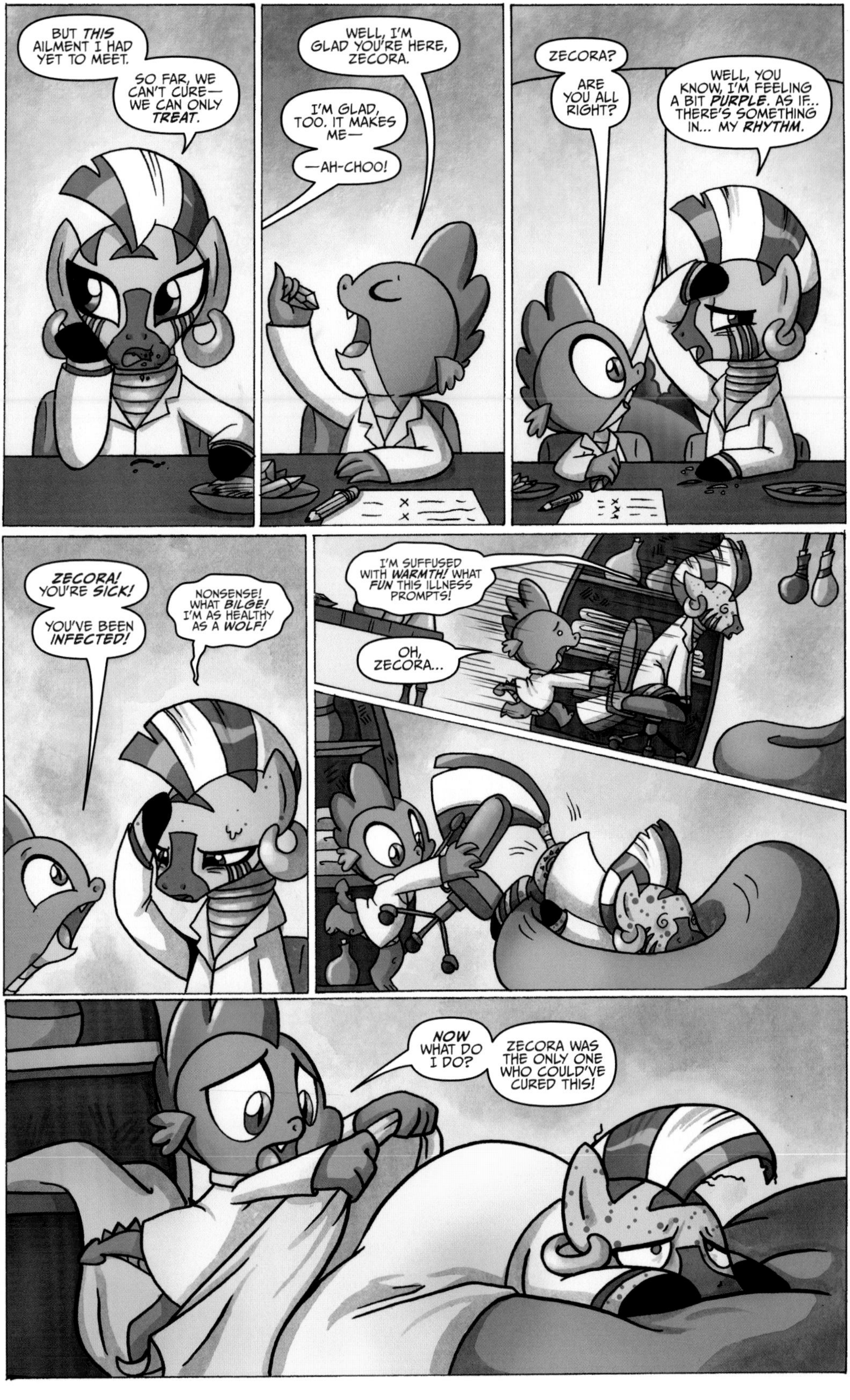

BUT THIS AILMENT I HAD YET TO MEET.
SO FAR, WE CAN'T CURE— WE CAN ONLY TREAT.
WELL, I'M GLAD YOU'RE HERE, ZECORA.
I'M GLAD, TOO. IT MAKES ME—
—AH-CHOO!
ZECORA?
ARE YOU ALL RIGHT?
WELL, YOU KNOW, I'M FEELING A BIT PURPLE. AS IF... THERE'S SOMETHING IN... MY RHYTHM.
ZECORA! YOU'RE SICK!
YOU'VE BEEN INFECTED!
NONSENSE! WHAT BILGE! I'M AS HEALTHY AS A WOLF!
I'M SUFFUSED WITH WARMTH! WHAT FUN THIS ILLNESS PROMPTS!
OH, ZECORA...
NOW WHAT DO I DO?
ZECORA WAS THE ONLY ONE WHO COULD'VE CURED THIS!

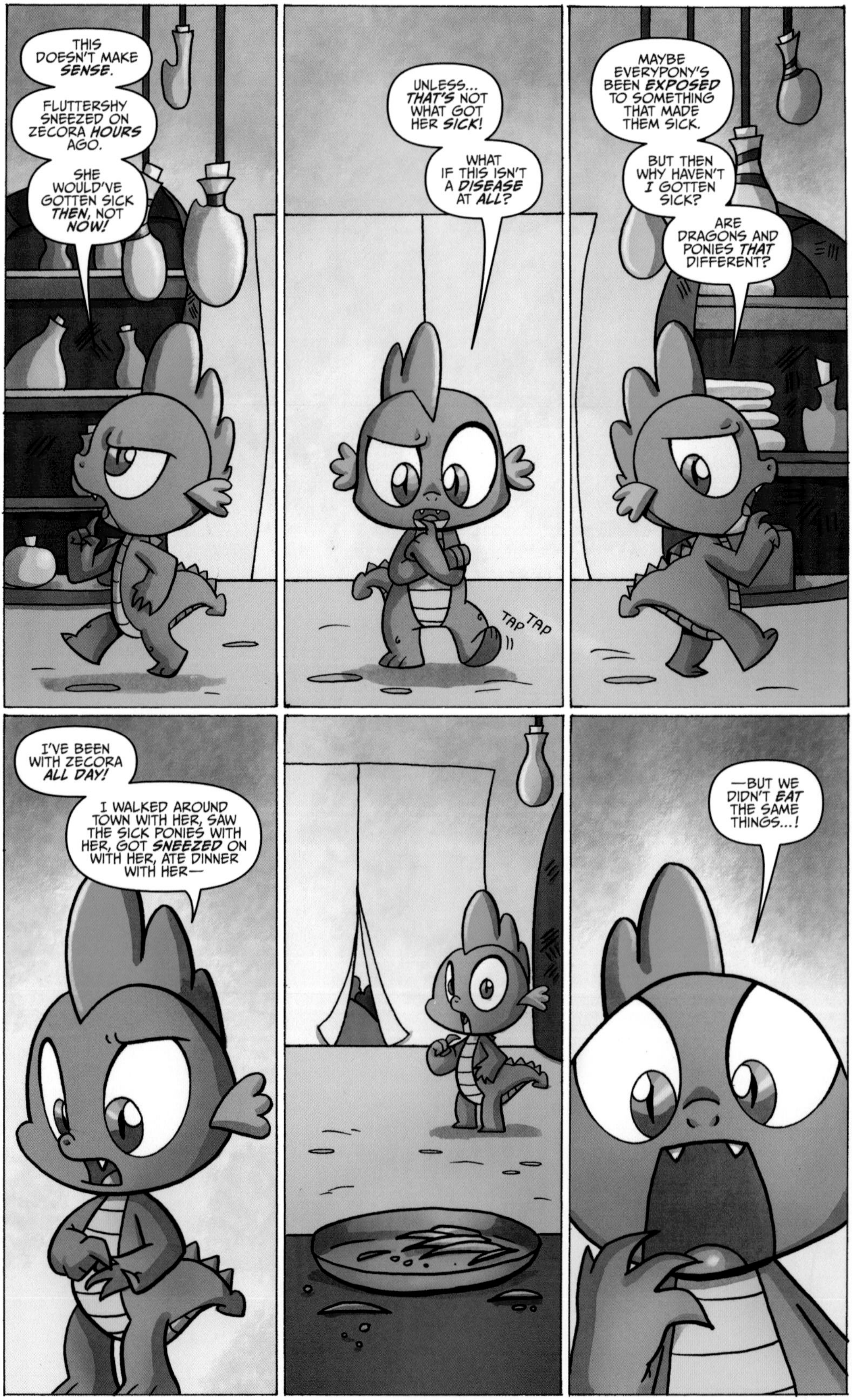
THIS DOESN'T MAKE SENSE.
FLUTTERSHY SNEEZED ON ZECORA HOURS AGO.
SHE WOULD'VE GOTTEN SICK THEN, NOT NOW!
UNLESS... THAT'S NOT WHAT GOT HER SICK!
WHAT IF THIS ISN'T A DISEASE AT ALL?
TAP TAP
MAYBE EVERYPONY'S BEEN EXPOSED TO SOMETHING THAT MADE THEM SICK.
BUT THEN WHY HAVEN'T I GOTTEN SICK?
ARE DRAGONS AND PONIES THAT DIFFERENT?
I'VE BEEN WITH ZECORA ALL DAY!
I WALKED AROUND TOWN WITH HER, SAW THE SICK PONIES WITH HER, GOT SNEEZED ON WITH HER, ATE DINNER WITH HER—
—BUT WE DIDN'T EAT THE SAME THINGS...!

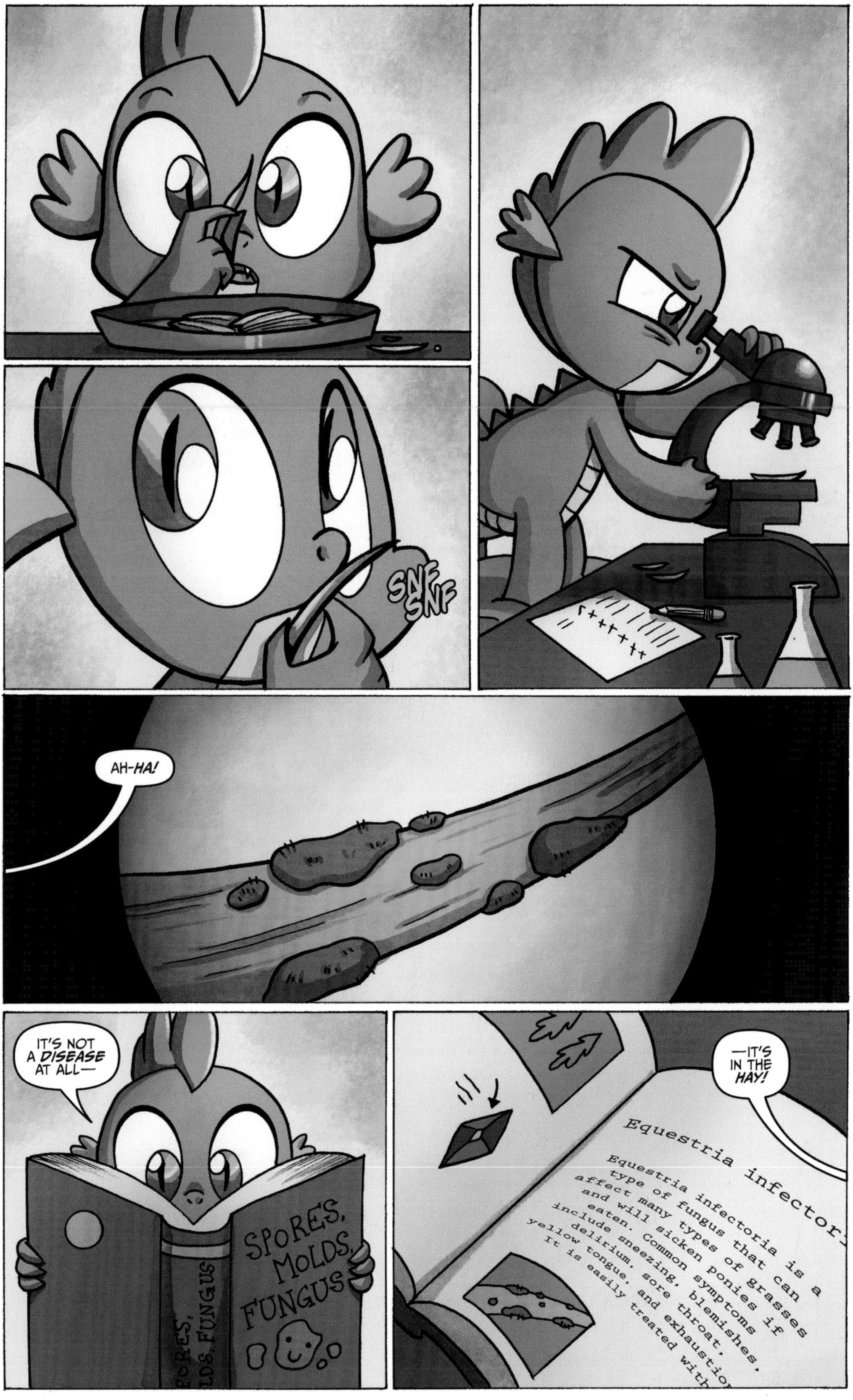
SNF SNF
AH-HA!
IT'S NOT A DISEASE AT ALL—
SPORES, MOLDS, FUNGUS
SPORES, MOLDS, FUNGUS
—IT'S IN THE HAY!
Equestria infectori
Equestria infectoria is a
type of fungus that can
affect many types of grasses
and will sicken ponies if
eaten. Common symptoms
include sneezing, blemishes,
delirium, sore throat,
yellow tongue, and exhaustio
It is easily treated with

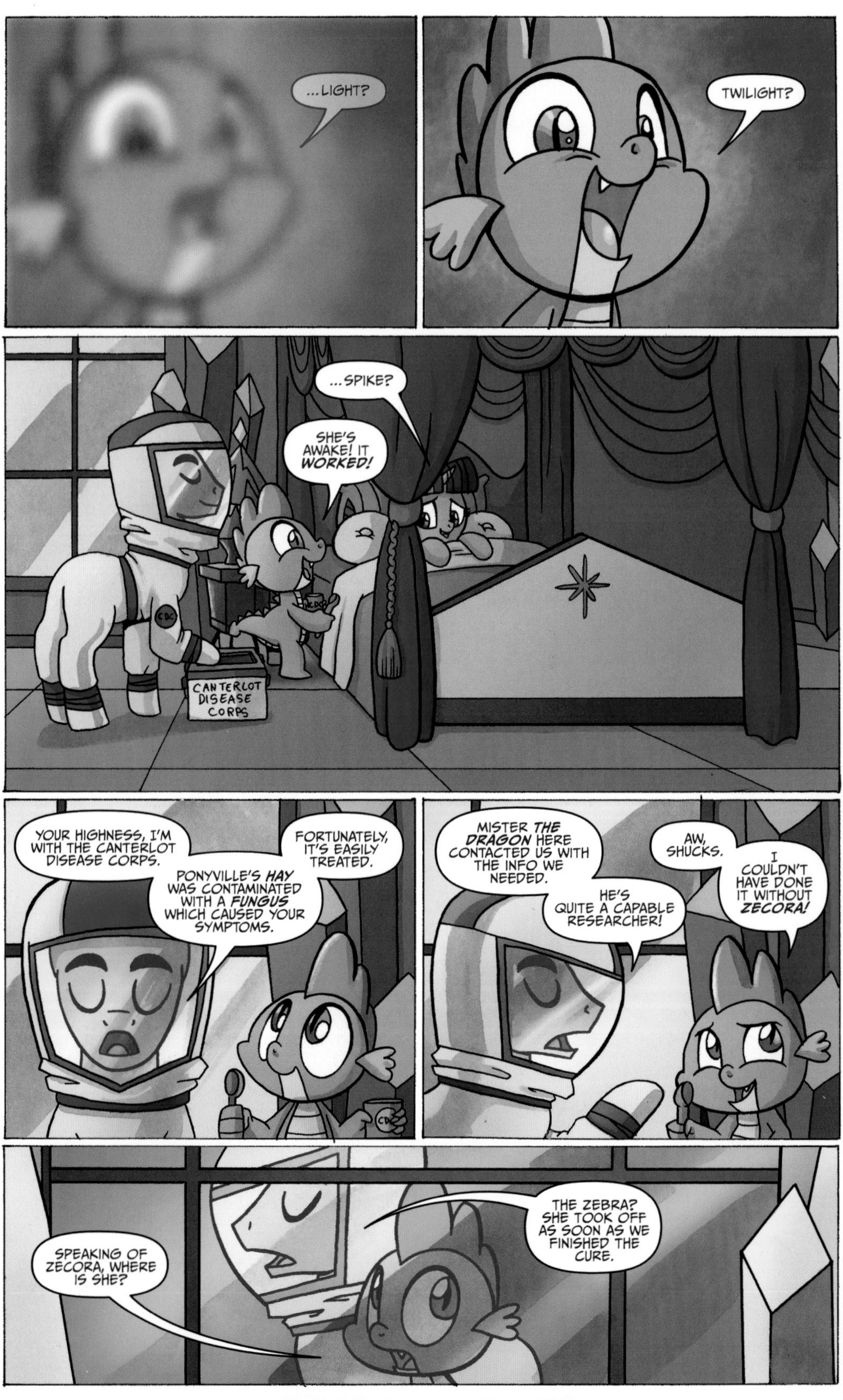
...LIGHT?
TWILIGHT?
...SPIKE?
SHE'S AWAKE! IT WORKED!
CANTERLOT DISEASE CORPS
YOUR HIGHNESS, I'M WITH THE CANTERLOT DISEASE CORPS.
PONYVILLE'S HAY WAS CONTAMINATED WITH A FUNGUS WHICH CAUSED YOUR SYMPTOMS.
FORTUNATELY, IT'S EASILY TREATED.
MISTER THE DRAGON HERE CONTACTED US WITH THE INFO WE NEEDED.
HE'S QUITE A CAPABLE RESEARCHER!
AW, SHUCKS.
I COULDN'T HAVE DONE IT WITHOUT ZECORA!
SPEAKING OF ZECORA, WHERE IS SHE?
THE ZEBRA? SHE TOOK OFF AS SOON AS WE FINISHED THE CURE.

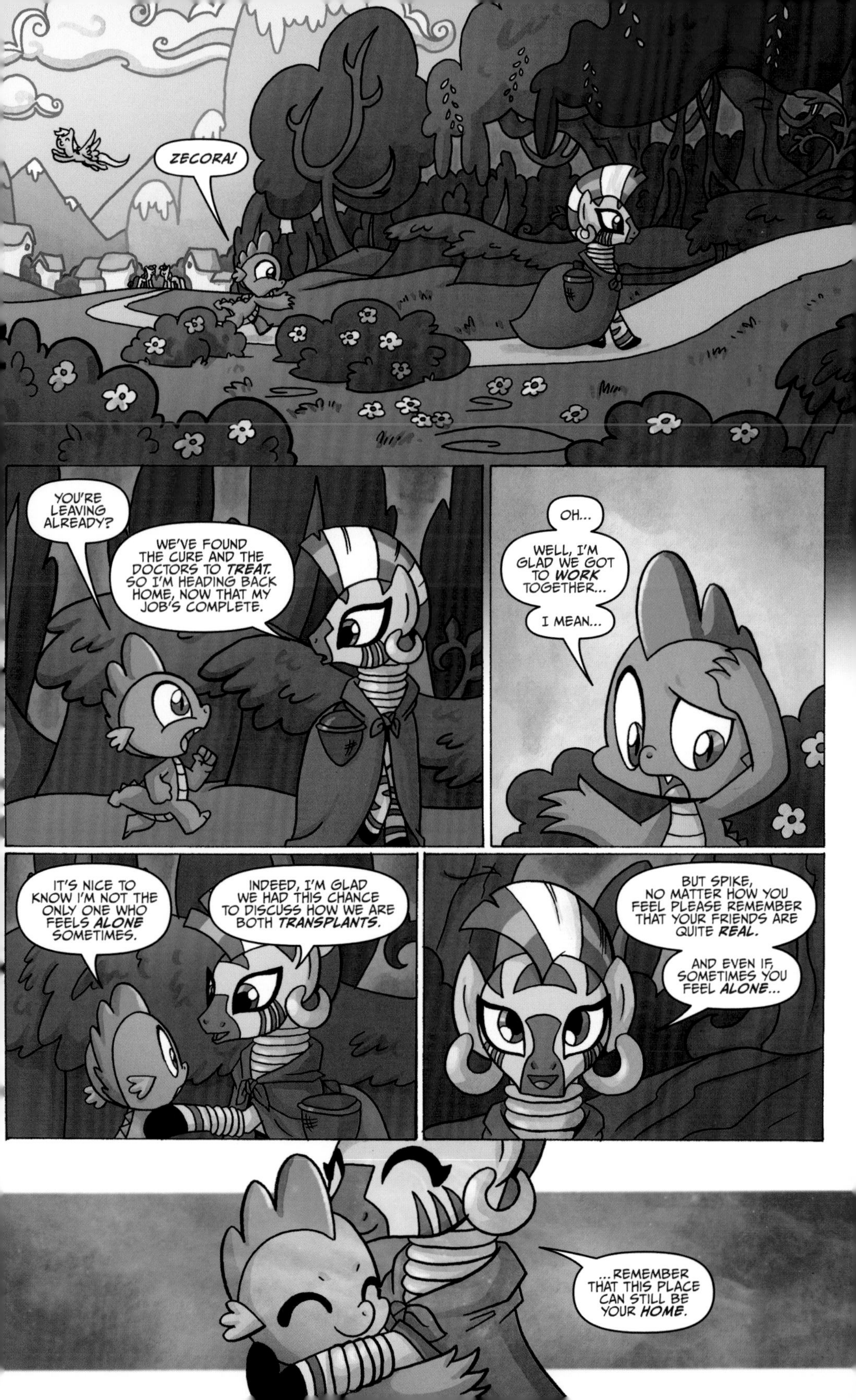
ZECORA!
YOU'RE LEAVING ALREADY?
WE'VE FOUND THE CURE AND THE DOCTORS TO *TREAT.* SO I'M HEADING BACK HOME, NOW THAT MY JOB'S COMPLETE.
OH...
WELL, I'M GLAD WE GOT TO *WORK* TOGETHER...
I MEAN...
IT'S NICE TO KNOW I'M NOT THE ONLY ONE WHO FEELS *ALONE* SOMETIMES.
INDEED, I'M GLAD WE HAD THIS CHANCE TO DISCUSS HOW WE ARE BOTH *TRANSPLANTS.*
BUT SPIKE, NO MATTER HOW YOU FEEL PLEASE REMEMBER THAT YOUR FRIENDS ARE QUITE *REAL.*
AND EVEN IF, SOMETIMES YOU FEEL *ALONE*...
...REMEMBER THAT THIS PLACE CAN STILL BE YOUR *HOME.*

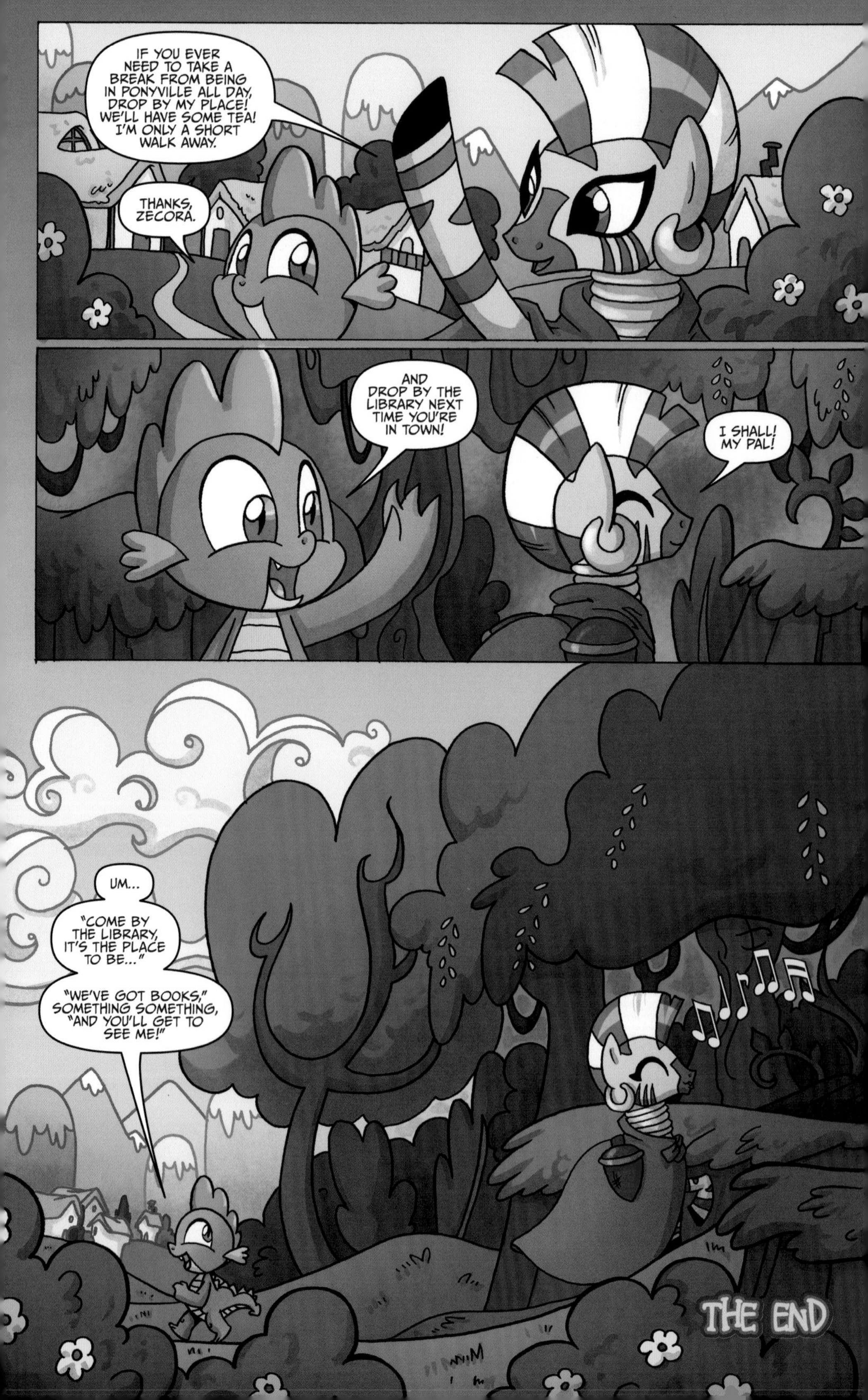
IF YOU EVER NEED TO TAKE A BREAK FROM BEING IN PONYVILLE ALL DAY, DROP BY MY PLACE! WE'LL HAVE SOME TEA! I'M ONLY A SHORT WALK AWAY.
THANKS, ZECORA.
AND DROP BY THE LIBRARY NEXT TIME YOU'RE IN TOWN!
I SHALL! MY PAL!
UM...
"COME BY THE LIBRARY, IT'S THE PLACE TO BE..."
"WE'VE GOT BOOKS," SOMETHING SOMETHING, "AND YOU'LL GET TO SEE ME!"
THE END

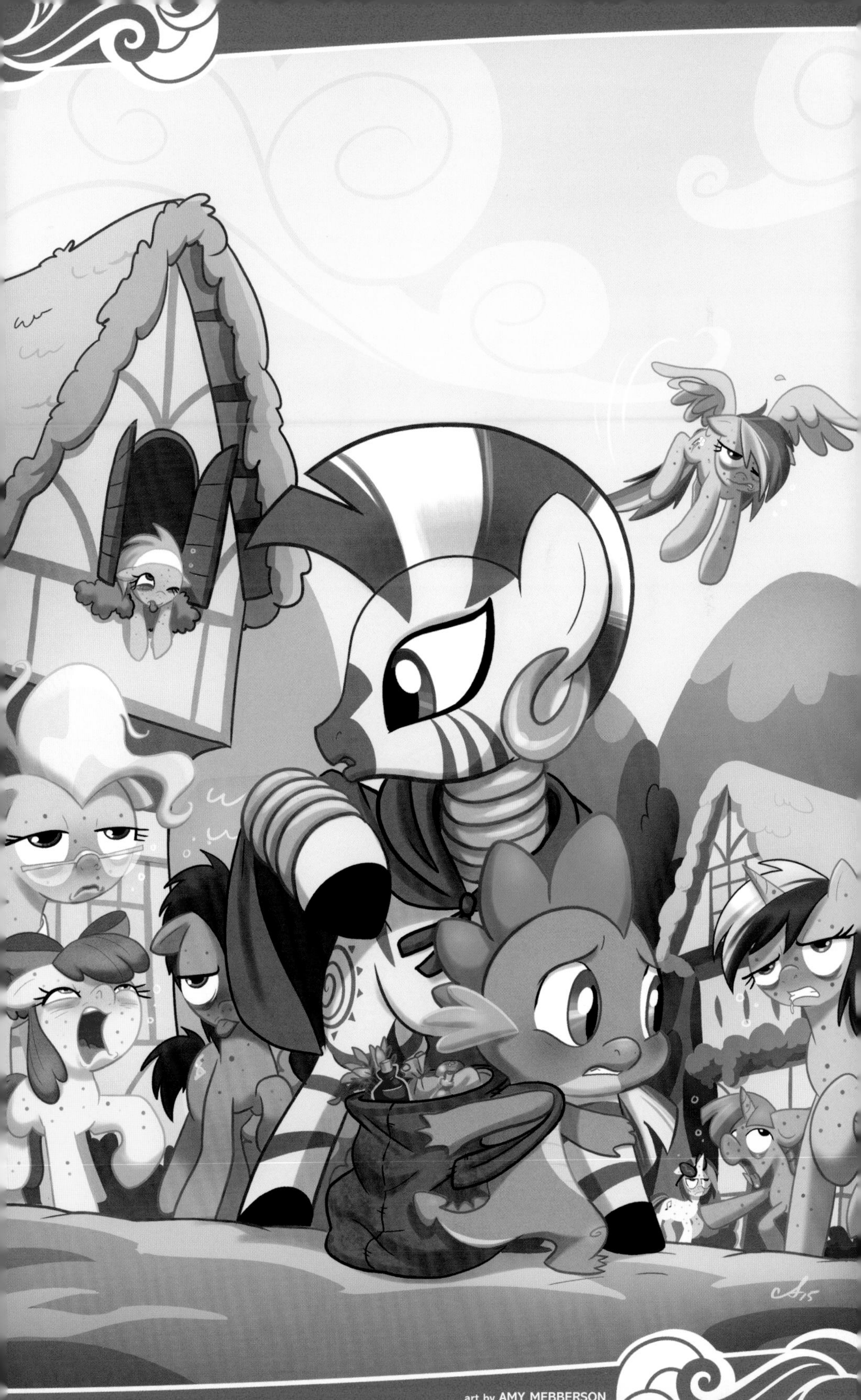

art by AMY MEBBERSON

Princess Celestia & Pinkie Pie

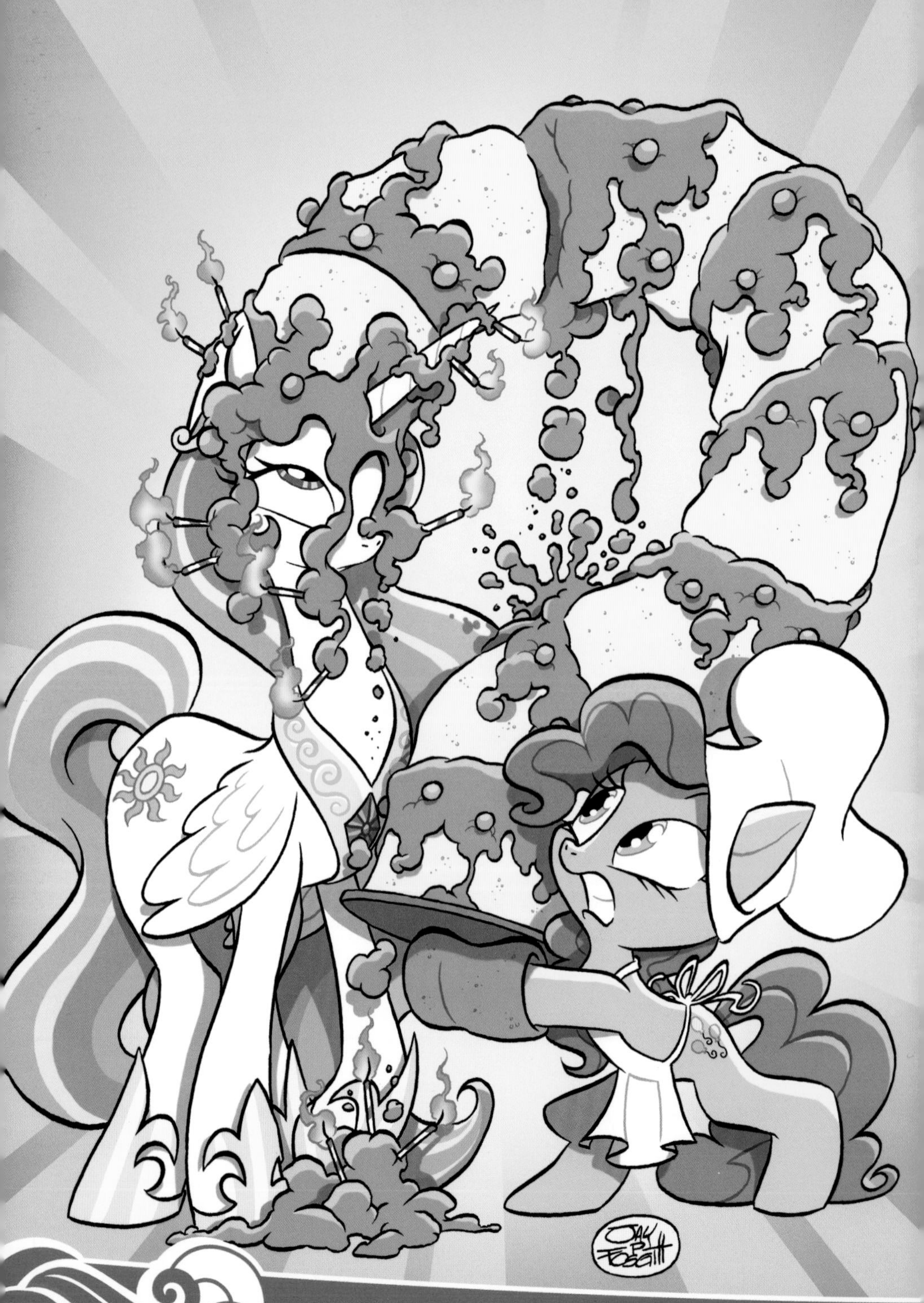

art by JAY FOSGITT

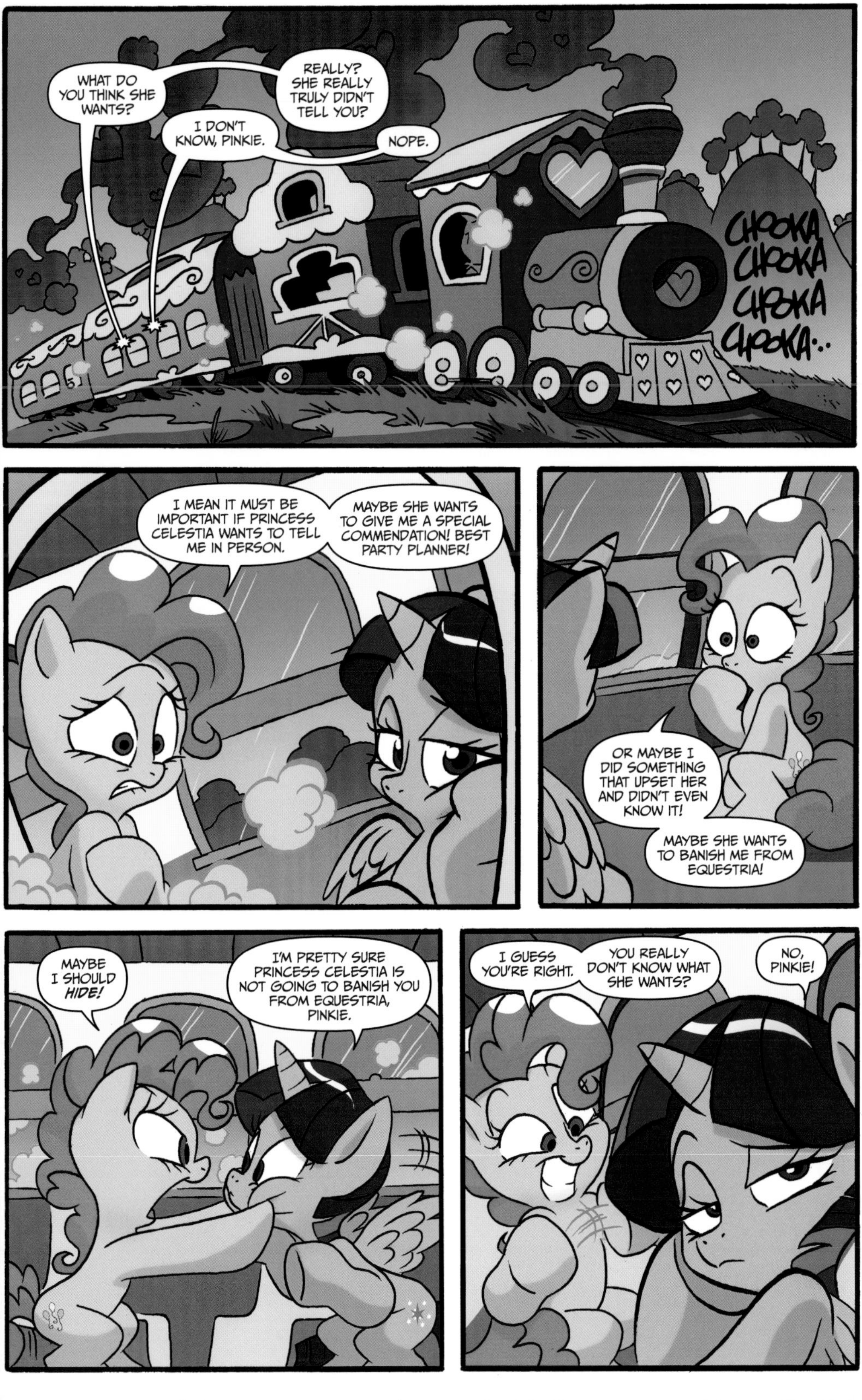
WHAT DO YOU THINK SHE WANTS?
REALLY? SHE REALLY TRULY DIDN'T TELL YOU?
I DON'T KNOW, PINKIE.
NOPE.
CHOOKA CHOOKA CHOOKA CHOOKA...
I MEAN IT MUST BE IMPORTANT IF PRINCESS CELESTIA WANTS TO TELL ME IN PERSON.
MAYBE SHE WANTS TO GIVE ME A SPECIAL COMMENDATION! BEST PARTY PLANNER!
OR MAYBE I DID SOMETHING THAT UPSET HER AND DIDN'T EVEN KNOW IT!
MAYBE SHE WANTS TO BANISH ME FROM EQUESTRIA!
MAYBE I SHOULD *HIDE!*
I'M PRETTY SURE PRINCESS CELESTIA IS NOT GOING TO BANISH YOU FROM EQUESTRIA, PINKIE.
I GUESS YOU'RE RIGHT.
YOU REALLY DON'T KNOW WHAT SHE WANTS?
NO, PINKIE!

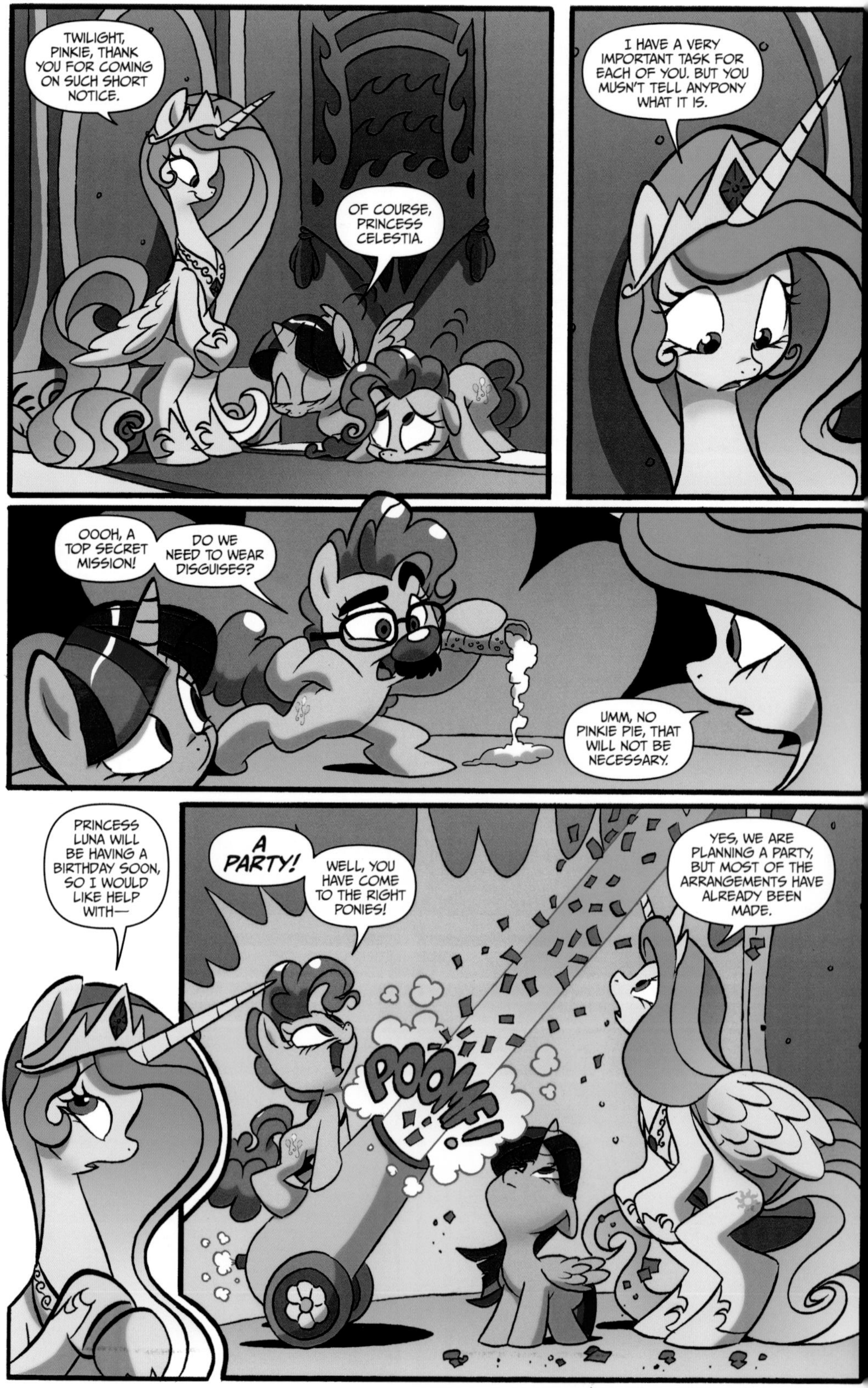
TWILIGHT, PINKIE, THANK YOU FOR COMING ON SUCH SHORT NOTICE.
OF COURSE, PRINCESS CELESTIA.
I HAVE A VERY IMPORTANT TASK FOR EACH OF YOU. BUT YOU MUSN'T TELL ANYPONY WHAT IT IS.
OOOH, A TOP SECRET MISSION!
DO WE NEED TO WEAR DISGUISES?
UMM, NO PINKIE PIE, THAT WILL NOT BE NECESSARY.
PRINCESS LUNA WILL BE HAVING A BIRTHDAY SOON, SO I WOULD LIKE HELP WITH—
A PARTY!
WELL, YOU HAVE COME TO THE RIGHT PONIES!
POOMF!
YES, WE ARE PLANNING A PARTY, BUT MOST OF THE ARRANGEMENTS HAVE ALREADY BEEN MADE.

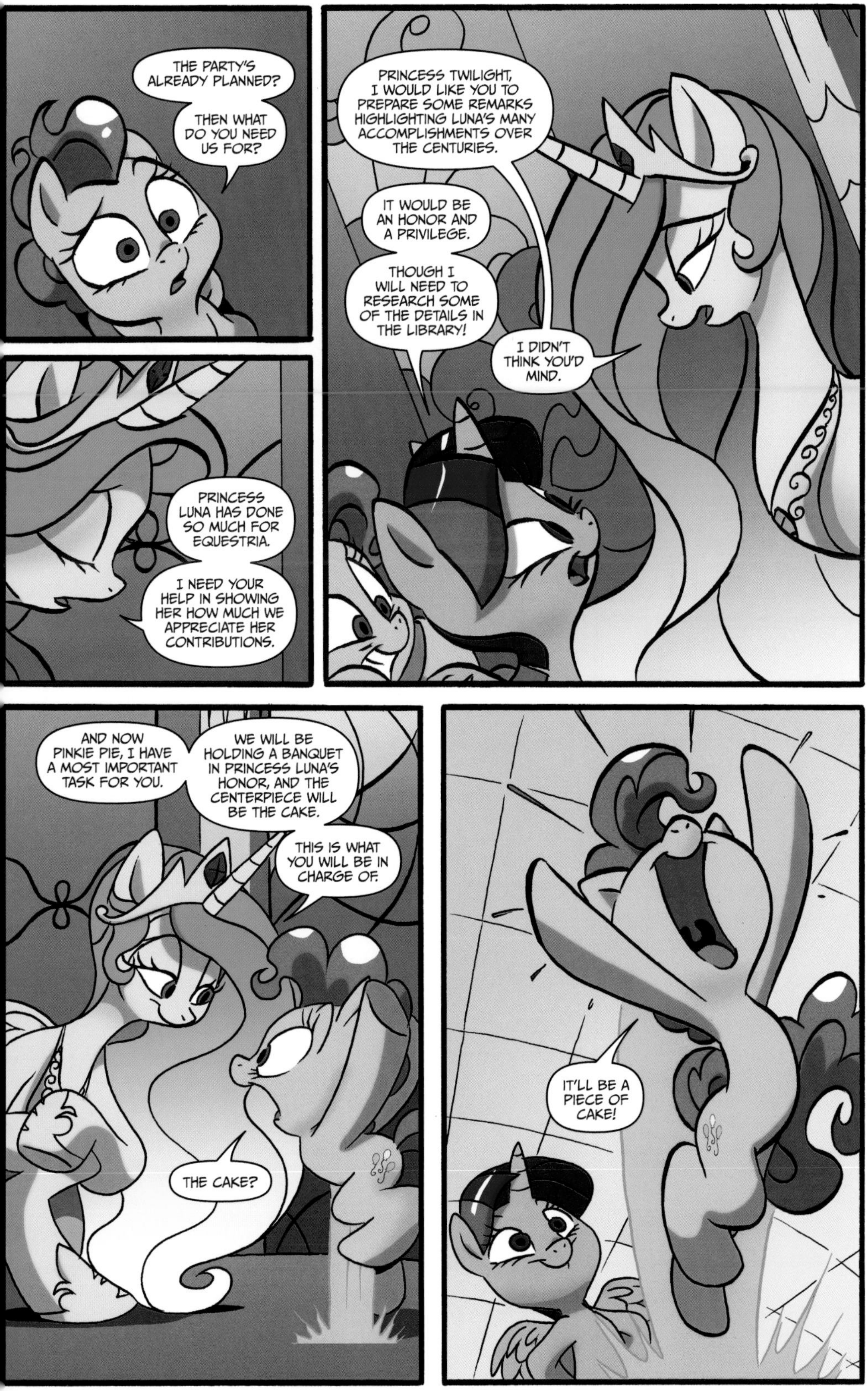
THE PARTY'S ALREADY PLANNED?
THEN WHAT DO YOU NEED US FOR?
PRINCESS TWILIGHT, I WOULD LIKE YOU TO PREPARE SOME REMARKS HIGHLIGHTING LUNA'S MANY ACCOMPLISHMENTS OVER THE CENTURIES.
IT WOULD BE AN HONOR AND A PRIVILEGE.
THOUGH I WILL NEED TO RESEARCH SOME OF THE DETAILS IN THE LIBRARY!
I DIDN'T THINK YOU'D MIND.
PRINCESS LUNA HAS DONE SO MUCH FOR EQUESTRIA.
I NEED YOUR HELP IN SHOWING HER HOW MUCH WE APPRECIATE HER CONTRIBUTIONS.
AND NOW PINKIE PIE, I HAVE A MOST IMPORTANT TASK FOR YOU.
WE WILL BE HOLDING A BANQUET IN PRINCESS LUNA'S HONOR, AND THE CENTERPIECE WILL BE THE CAKE.
THIS IS WHAT YOU WILL BE IN CHARGE OF.
THE CAKE?
IT'LL BE A PIECE OF CAKE!

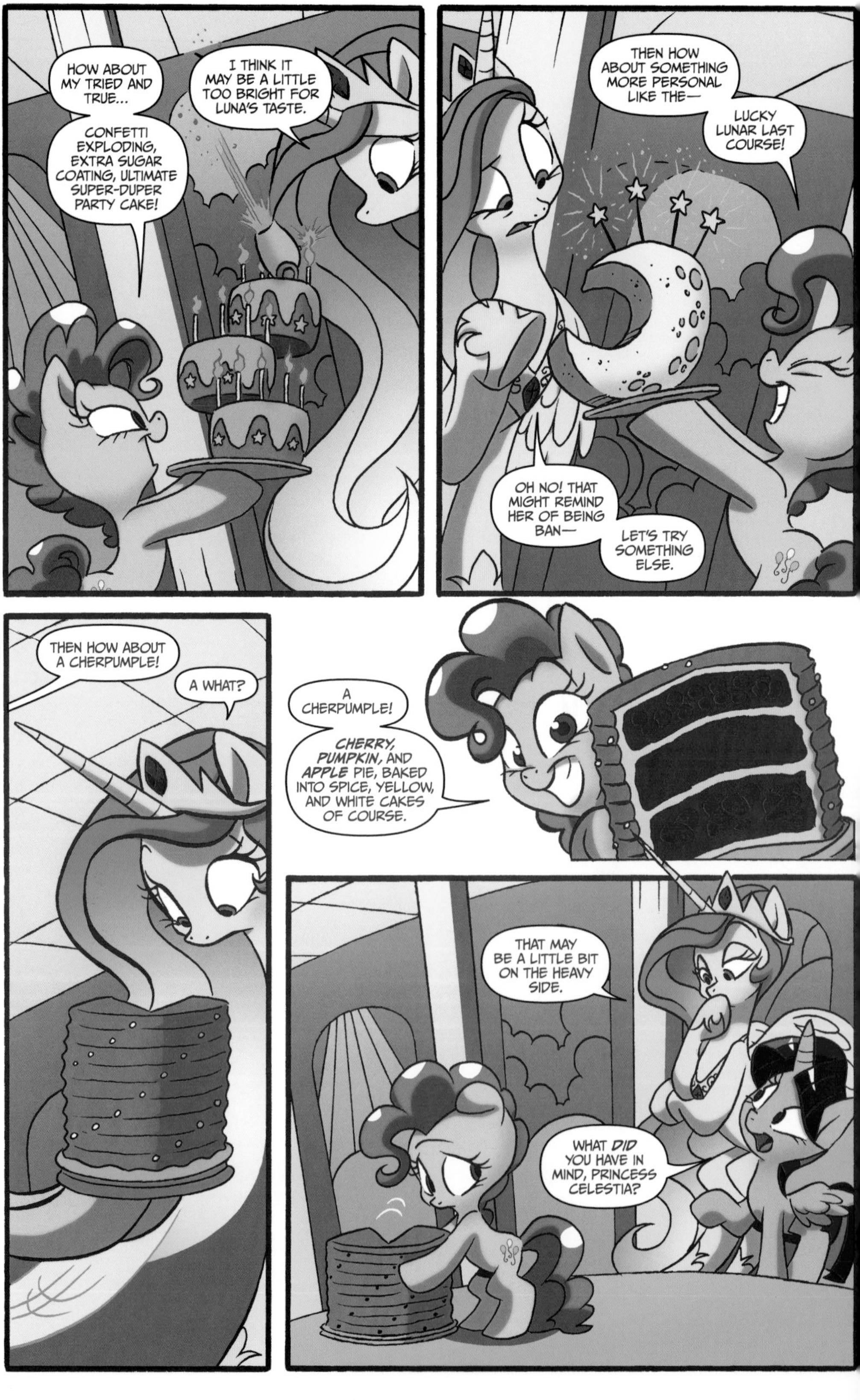
HOW ABOUT MY TRIED AND TRUE...
CONFETTI EXPLODING, EXTRA SUGAR COATING, ULTIMATE SUPER-DUPER PARTY CAKE!
I THINK IT MAY BE A LITTLE TOO BRIGHT FOR LUNA'S TASTE.
THEN HOW ABOUT SOMETHING MORE PERSONAL LIKE THE—
LUCKY LUNAR LAST COURSE!
OH NO! THAT MIGHT REMIND HER OF BEING BAN—
LET'S TRY SOMETHING ELSE.
THEN HOW ABOUT A CHERPUMPLE!
A WHAT?
A CHERPUMPLE!
CHERRY, PUMPKIN, AND *APPLE* PIE, BAKED INTO SPICE, YELLOW, AND WHITE CAKES OF COURSE.
THAT MAY BE A LITTLE BIT ON THE HEAVY SIDE.
WHAT *DID* YOU HAVE IN MIND, PRINCESS CELESTIA?

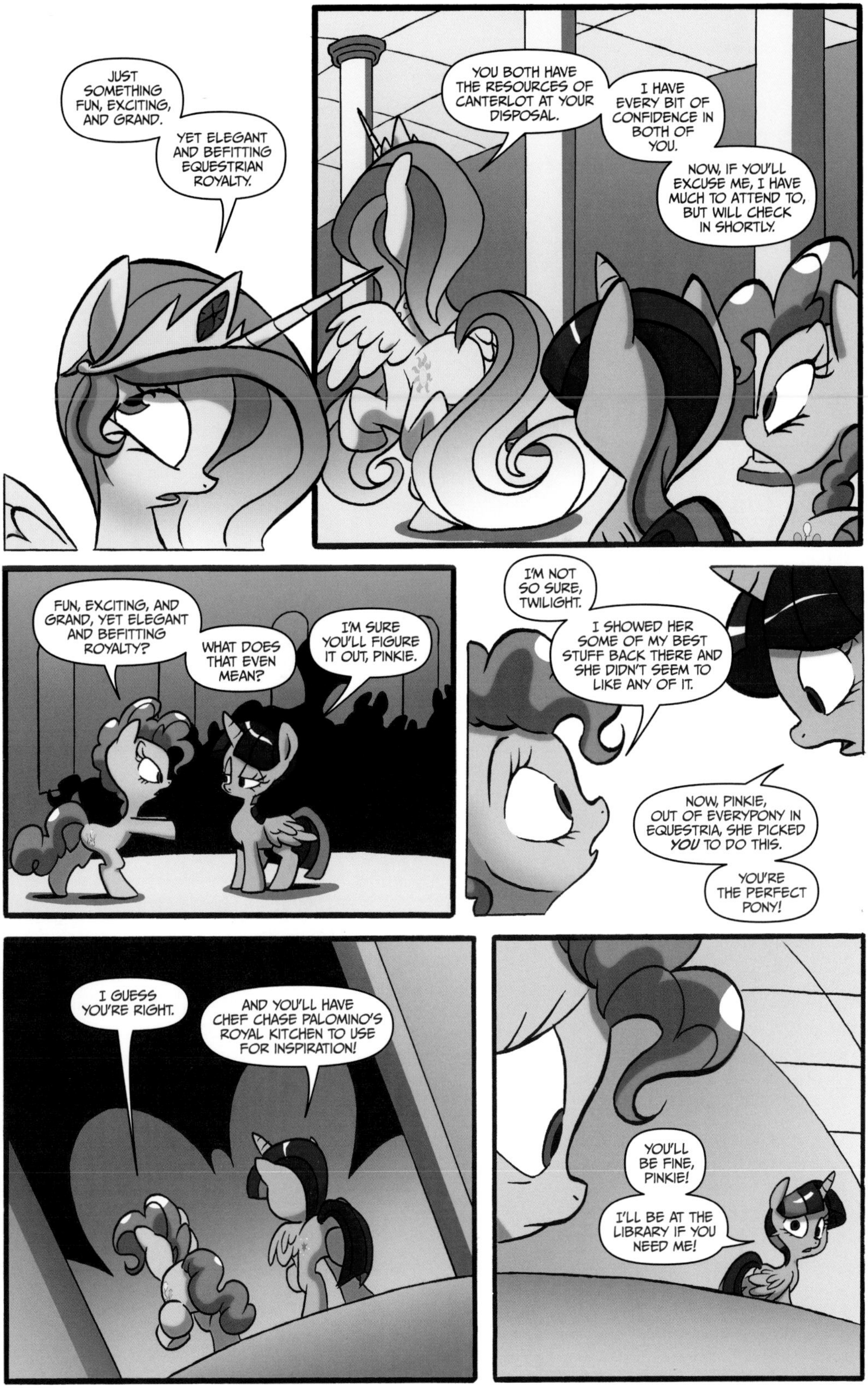
JUST SOMETHING FUN, EXCITING, AND GRAND.
YET ELEGANT AND BEFITTING EQUESTRIAN ROYALTY.
YOU BOTH HAVE THE RESOURCES OF CANTERLOT AT YOUR DISPOSAL.
I HAVE EVERY BIT OF CONFIDENCE IN BOTH OF YOU.
NOW, IF YOU'LL EXCUSE ME, I HAVE MUCH TO ATTEND TO, BUT WILL CHECK IN SHORTLY.
FUN, EXCITING, AND GRAND, YET ELEGANT AND BEFITTING ROYALTY?
WHAT DOES THAT EVEN MEAN?
I'M SURE YOU'LL FIGURE IT OUT, PINKIE.
I'M NOT SO SURE, TWILIGHT.
I SHOWED HER SOME OF MY BEST STUFF BACK THERE AND SHE DIDN'T SEEM TO LIKE ANY OF IT.
NOW, PINKIE, OUT OF EVERYPONY IN EQUESTRIA, SHE PICKED *YOU* TO DO THIS.
YOU'RE THE PERFECT PONY!
I GUESS YOU'RE RIGHT.
AND YOU'LL HAVE CHEF CHASE PALOMINO'S ROYAL KITCHEN TO USE FOR INSPIRATION!
YOU'LL BE FINE, PINKIE!
I'LL BE AT THE LIBRARY IF YOU NEED ME!

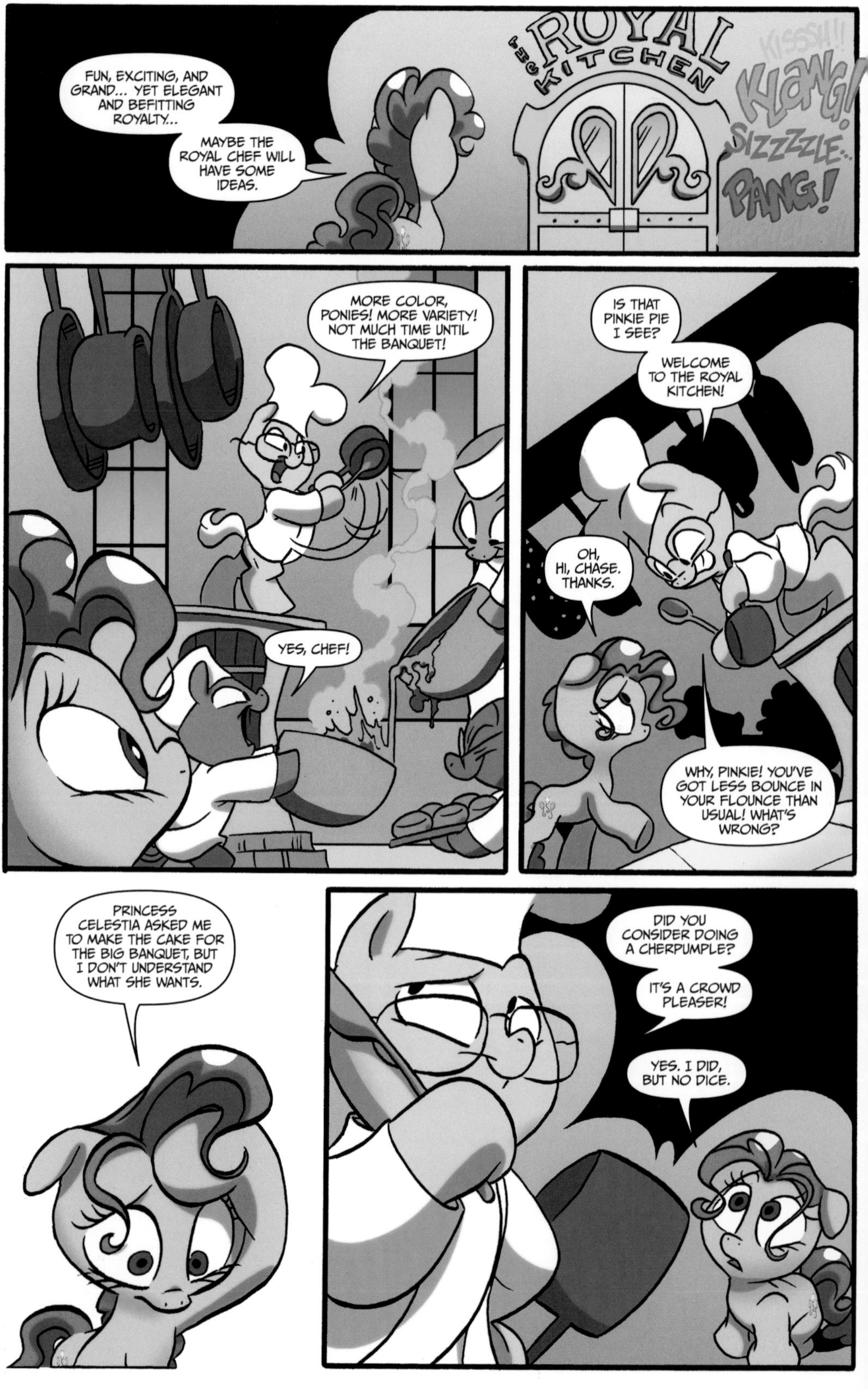
FUN, EXCITING, AND GRAND... YET ELEGANT AND BEFITTING ROYALTY...
MAYBE THE ROYAL CHEF WILL HAVE SOME IDEAS.
ROYAL KITCHEN
KISSSH!!
KLANG!
SIZZZZLE...
PANG!
MORE COLOR, PONIES! MORE VARIETY! NOT MUCH TIME UNTIL THE BANQUET!
YES, CHEF!
IS THAT PINKIE PIE I SEE?
WELCOME TO THE ROYAL KITCHEN!
OH, HI, CHASE. THANKS.
WHY, PINKIE! YOU'VE GOT LESS BOUNCE IN YOUR FLOUNCE THAN USUAL! WHAT'S WRONG?
PRINCESS CELESTIA ASKED ME TO MAKE THE CAKE FOR THE BIG BANQUET, BUT I DON'T UNDERSTAND WHAT SHE WANTS.
DID YOU CONSIDER DOING A CHERPUMPLE?
IT'S A CROWD PLEASER!
YES. I DID, BUT NO DICE.

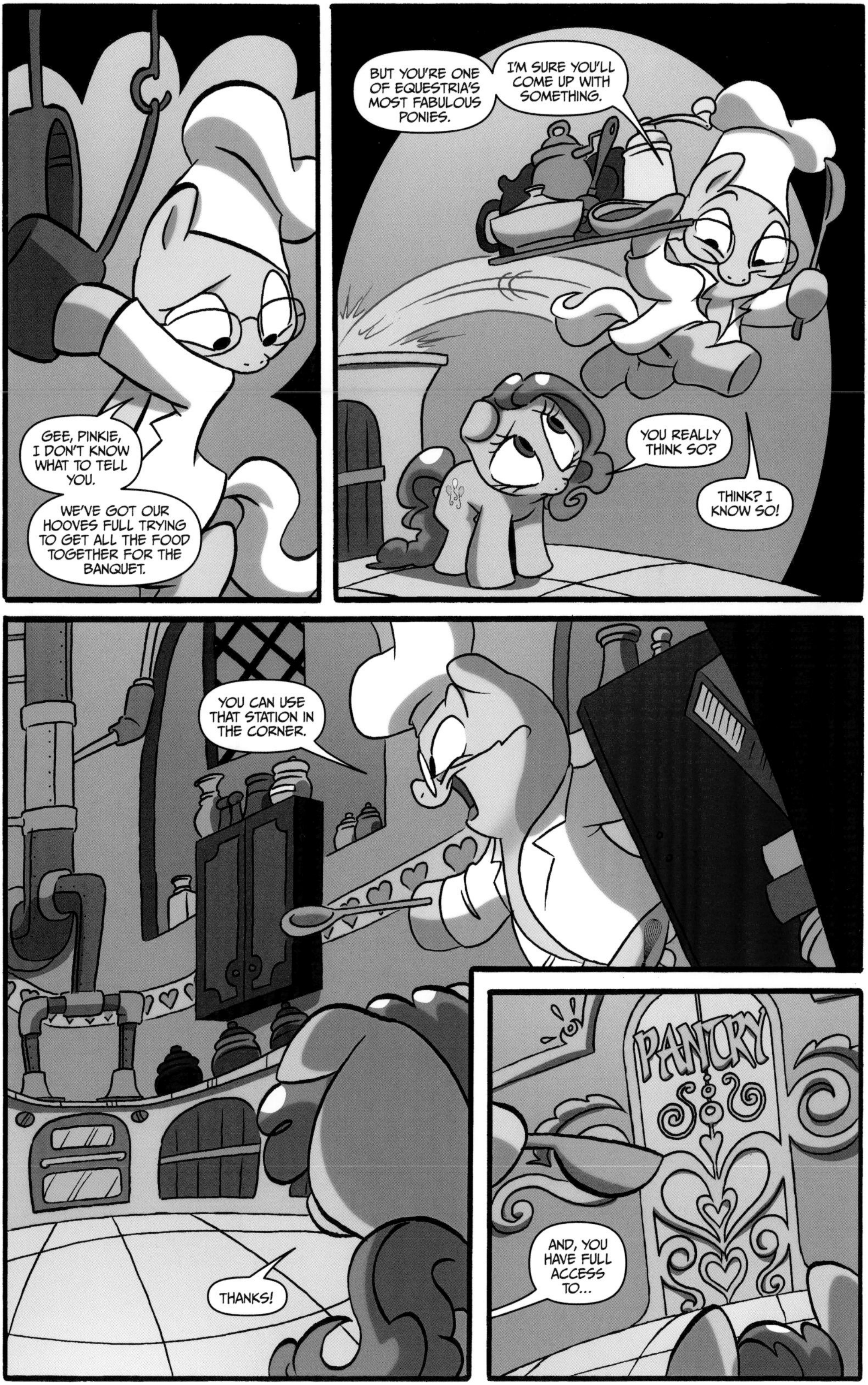
GEE, PINKIE, I DON'T KNOW WHAT TO TELL YOU.
WE'VE GOT OUR HOOVES FULL TRYING TO GET ALL THE FOOD TOGETHER FOR THE BANQUET.
BUT YOU'RE ONE OF EQUESTRIA'S MOST FABULOUS PONIES.
I'M SURE YOU'LL COME UP WITH SOMETHING.
YOU REALLY THINK SO?
THINK? I KNOW SO!
YOU CAN USE THAT STATION IN THE CORNER.
THANKS!
PANTRY
AND, YOU HAVE FULL ACCESS TO...

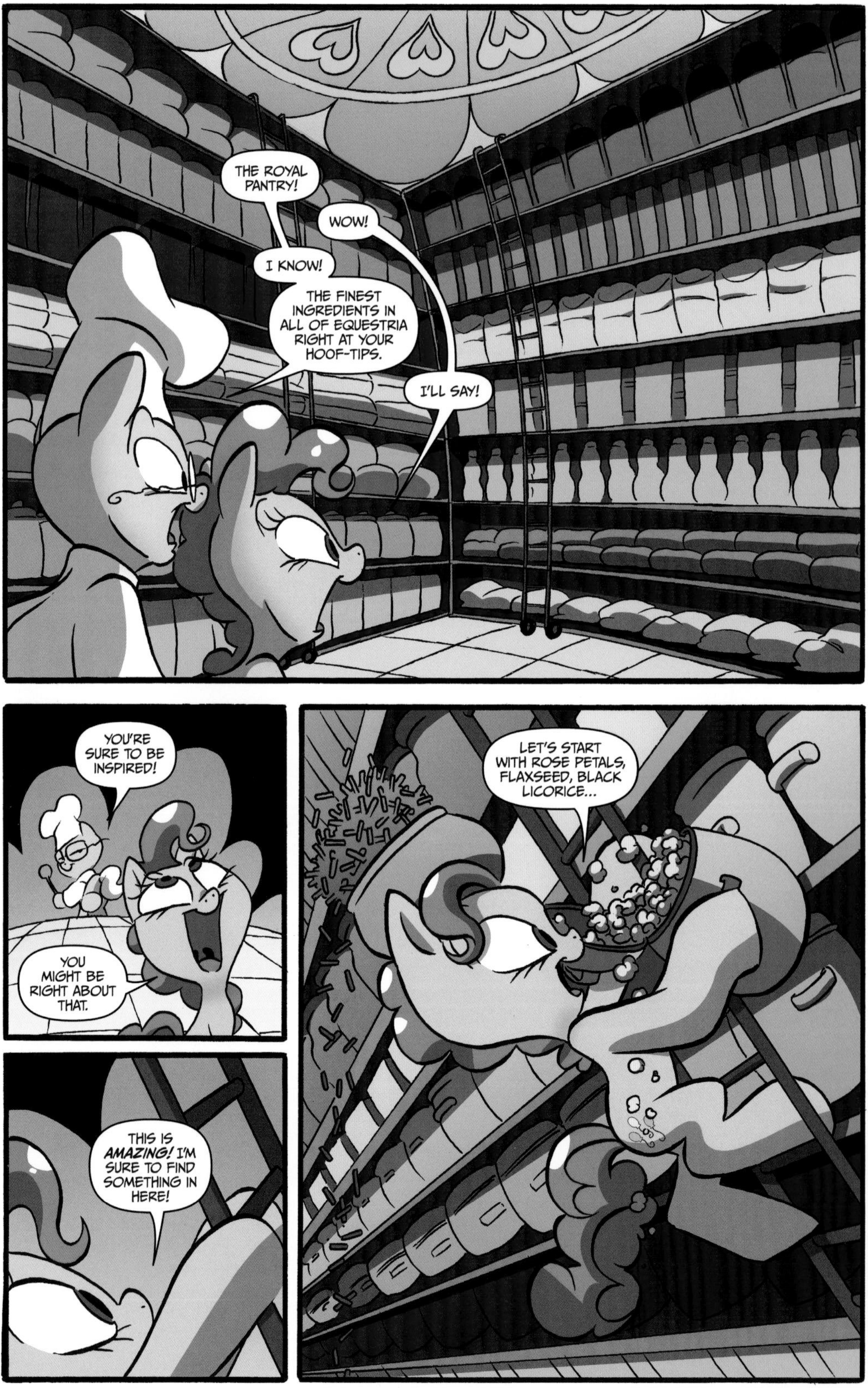
THE ROYAL PANTRY!
WOW!
I KNOW!
THE FINEST INGREDIENTS IN ALL OF EQUESTRIA RIGHT AT YOUR HOOF-TIPS.
I'LL SAY!
YOU'RE SURE TO BE INSPIRED!
YOU MIGHT BE RIGHT ABOUT THAT.
THIS IS AMAZING! I'M SURE TO FIND SOMETHING IN HERE!
LET'S START WITH ROSE PETALS, FLAXSEED, BLACK LICORICE...

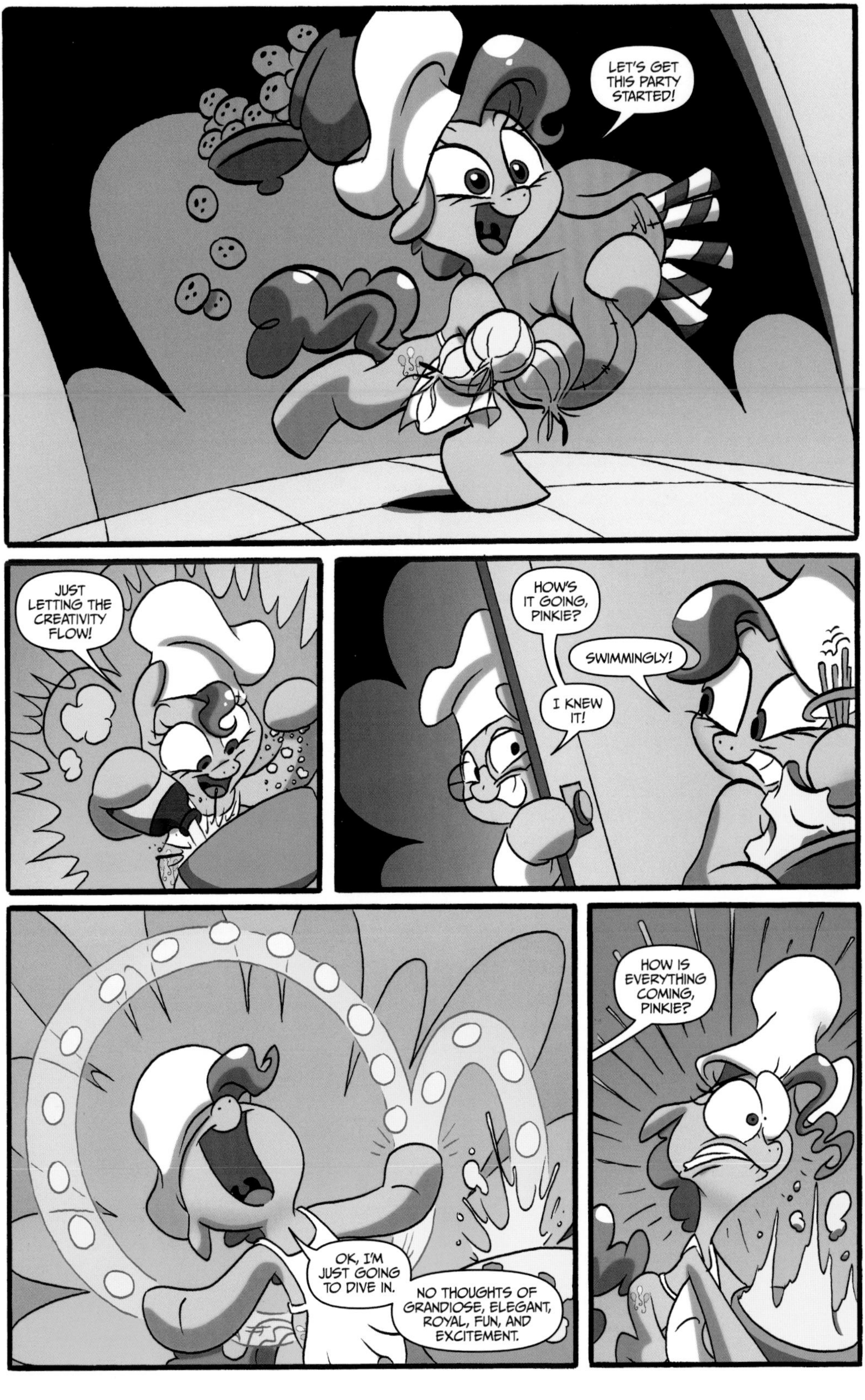
LET'S GET THIS PARTY STARTED!
JUST LETTING THE CREATIVITY FLOW!
HOW'S IT GOING, PINKIE?
SWIMMINGLY!
I KNEW IT!
OK, I'M JUST GOING TO DIVE IN.
NO THOUGHTS OF GRANDIOSE, ELEGANT, ROYAL, FUN, AND EXCITEMENT.
HOW IS EVERYTHING COMING, PINKIE?

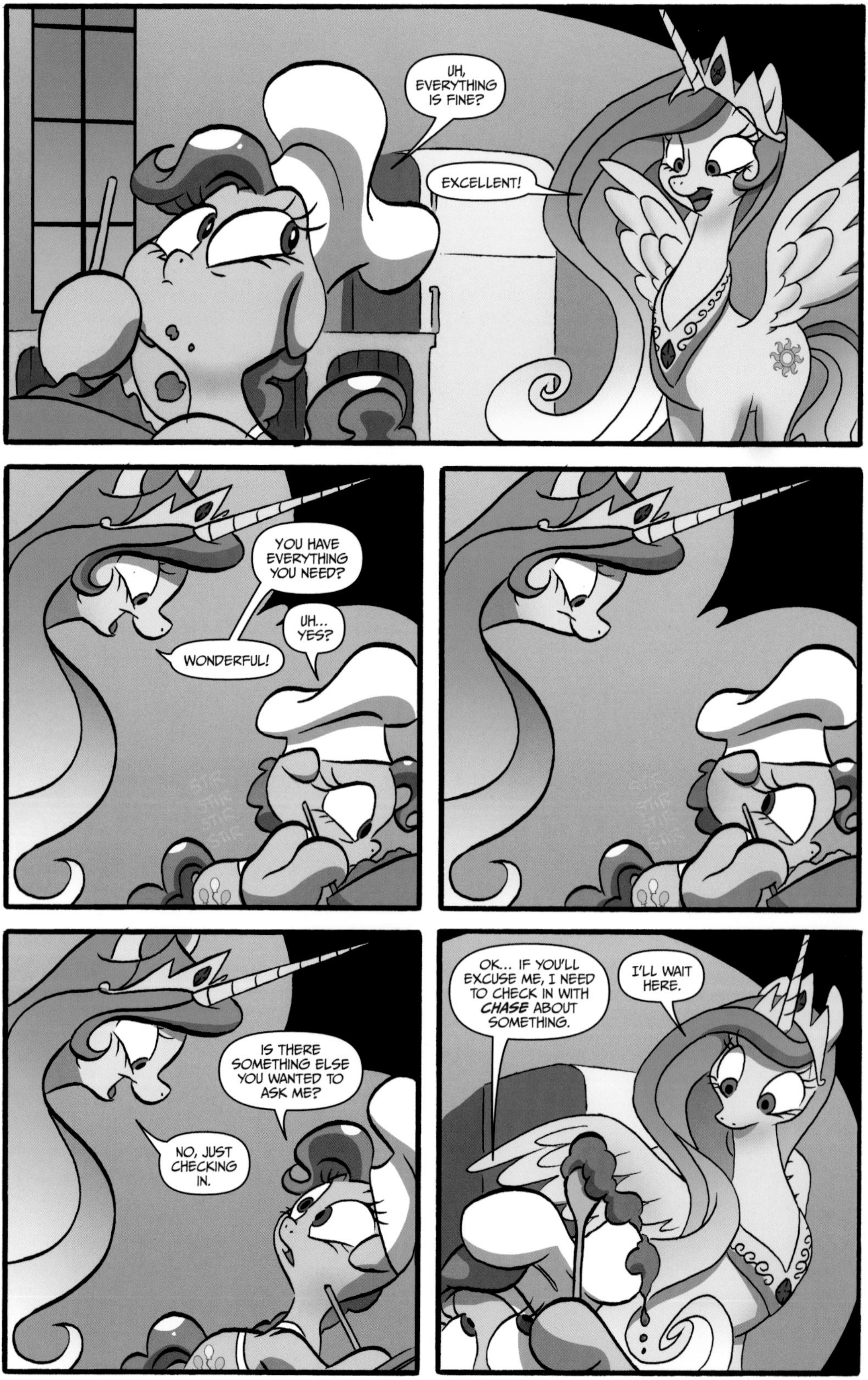
UH, EVERYTHING IS FINE?
EXCELLENT!
YOU HAVE EVERYTHING YOU NEED?
UH... YES?
WONDERFUL!
STIR STIR STIR STIR
STIR STIR STIR STIR
IS THERE SOMETHING ELSE YOU WANTED TO ASK ME?
NO, JUST CHECKING IN.
OK... IF YOU'LL EXCUSE ME, I NEED TO CHECK IN WITH *CHASE* ABOUT SOMETHING.
I'LL WAIT HERE.

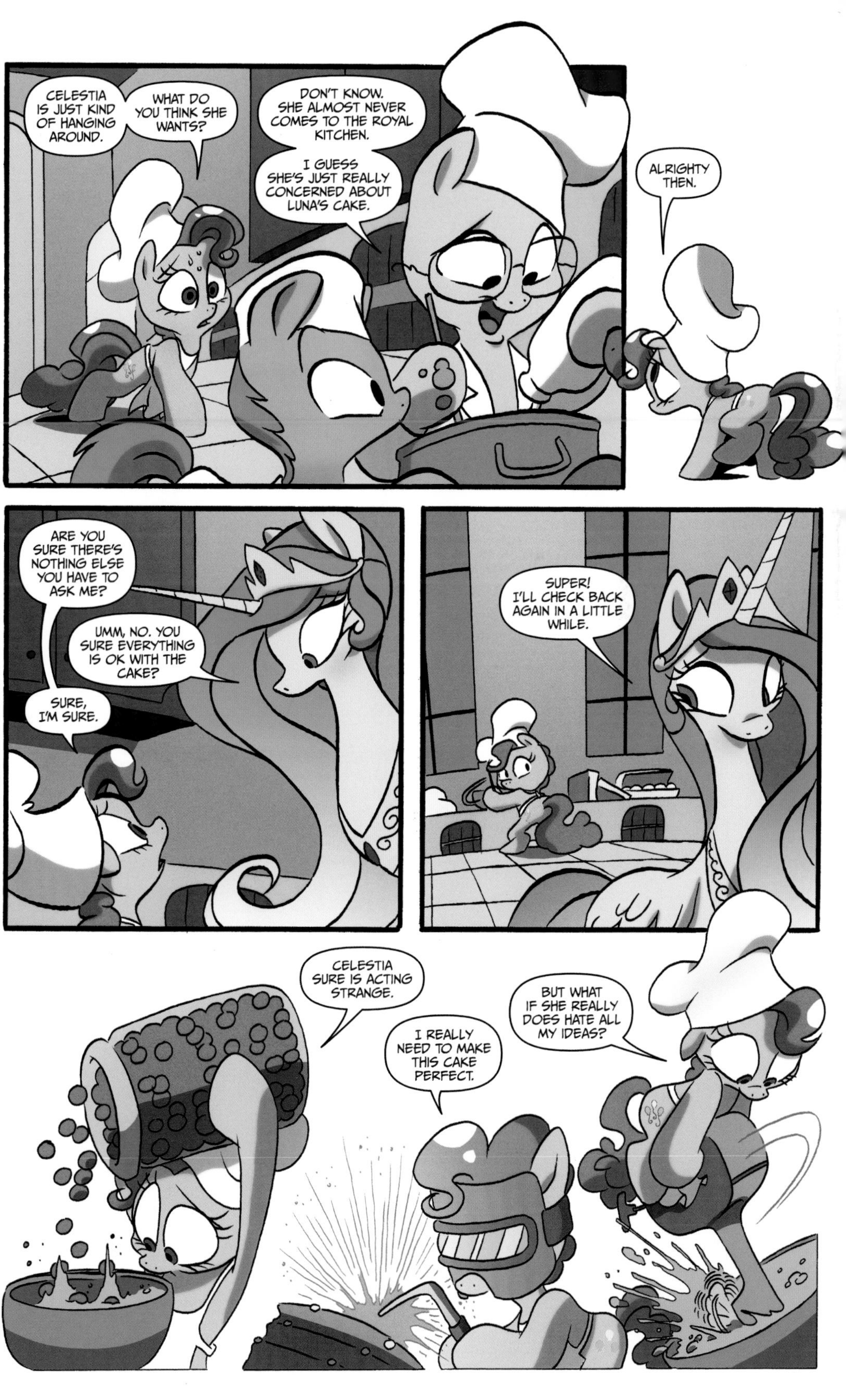
CELESTIA IS JUST KIND OF HANGING AROUND.
WHAT DO YOU THINK SHE WANTS?
DON'T KNOW. SHE ALMOST NEVER COMES TO THE ROYAL KITCHEN.
I GUESS SHE'S JUST REALLY CONCERNED ABOUT LUNA'S CAKE.
ALRIGHTY THEN.
ARE YOU SURE THERE'S NOTHING ELSE YOU HAVE TO ASK ME?
UMM, NO. YOU SURE EVERYTHING IS OK WITH THE CAKE?
SURE, I'M SURE.
SUPER! I'LL CHECK BACK AGAIN IN A LITTLE WHILE.
CELESTIA SURE IS ACTING STRANGE.
I REALLY NEED TO MAKE THIS CAKE PERFECT.
BUT WHAT IF SHE REALLY DOES HATE ALL MY IDEAS?

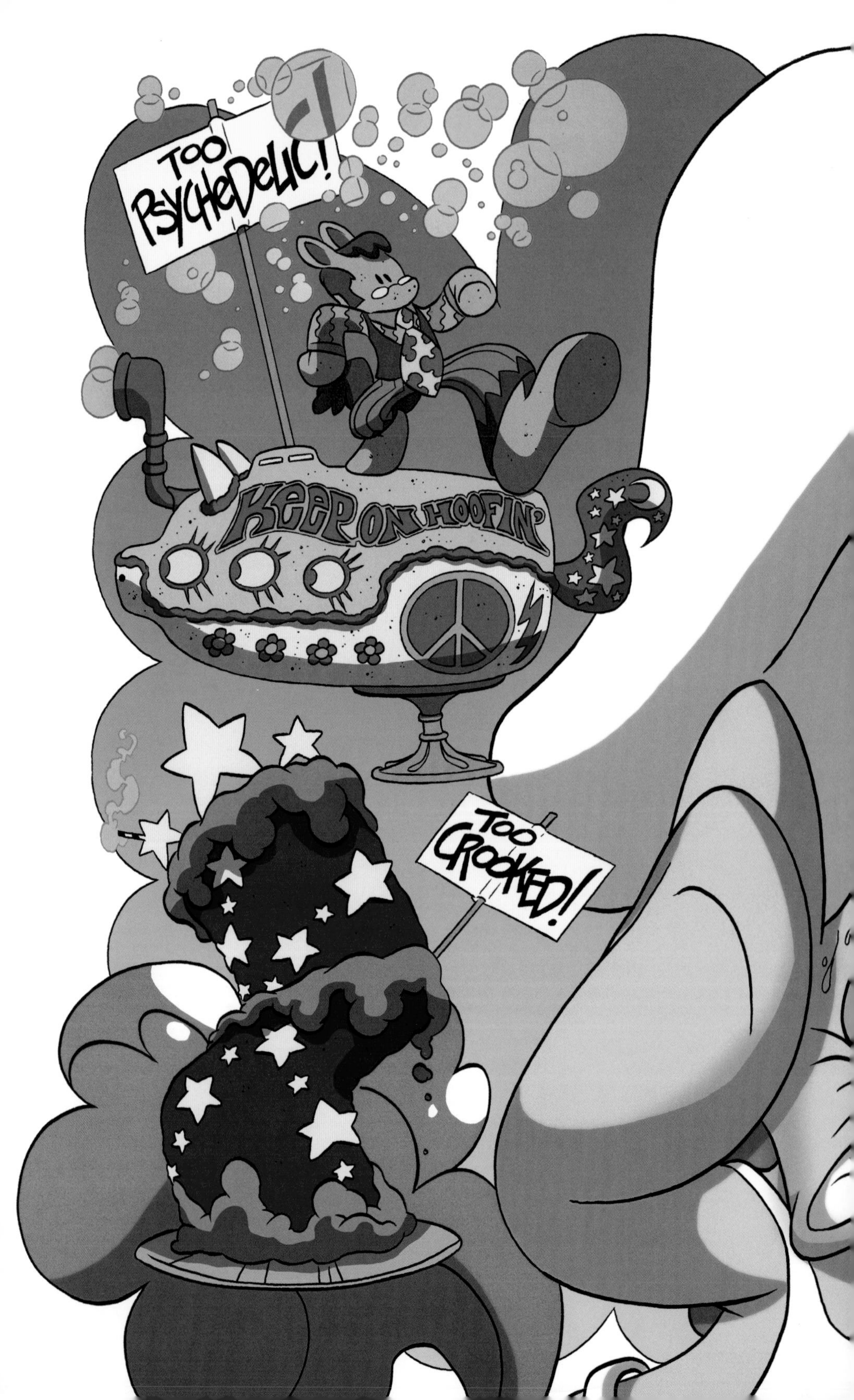
TOO PSYCHEDELIC!
KEEP ON HOOFIN'
TOO CROOKED!

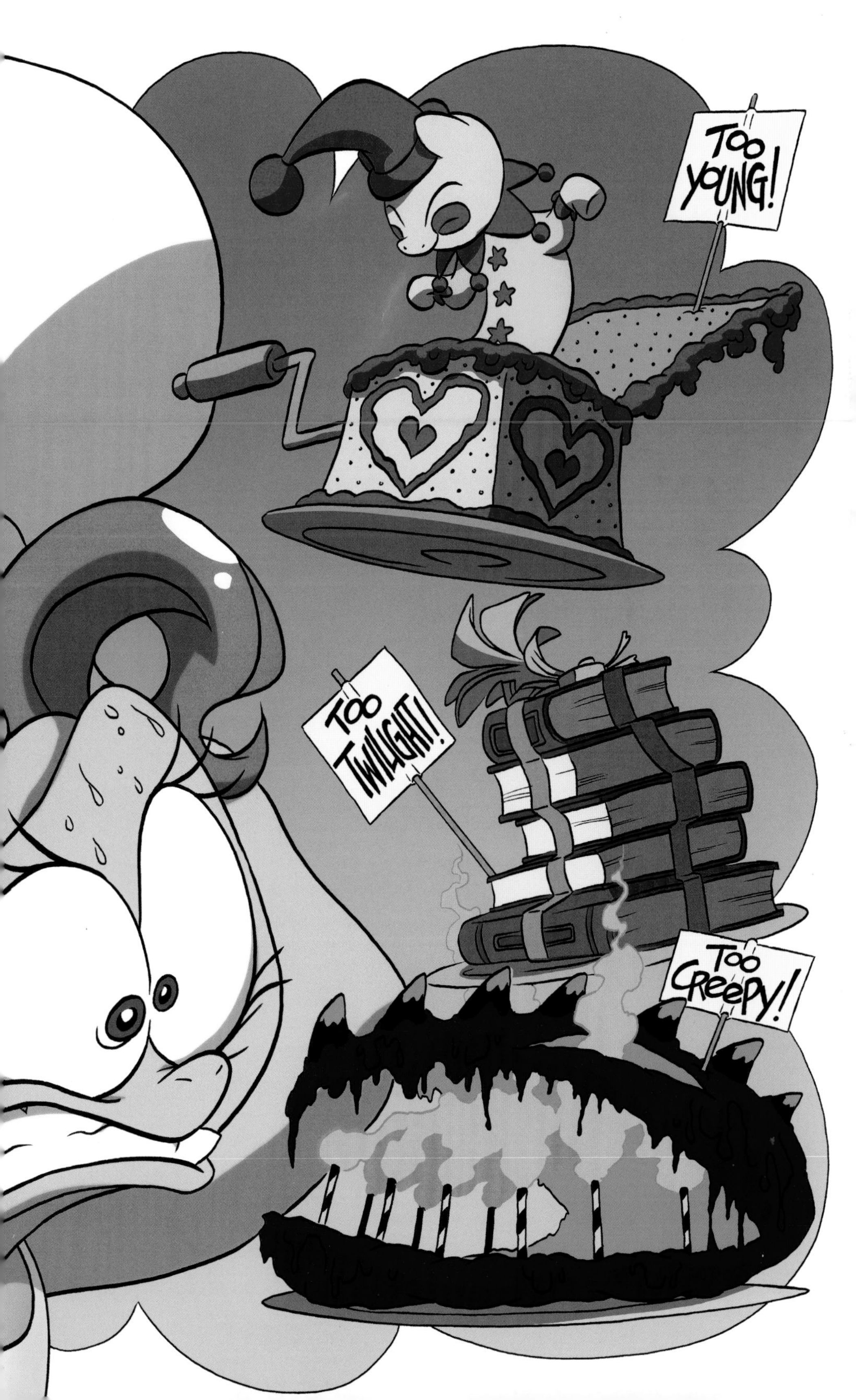
TOO YOUNG!
TOO TWILIGHT!
TOO CREEPY!

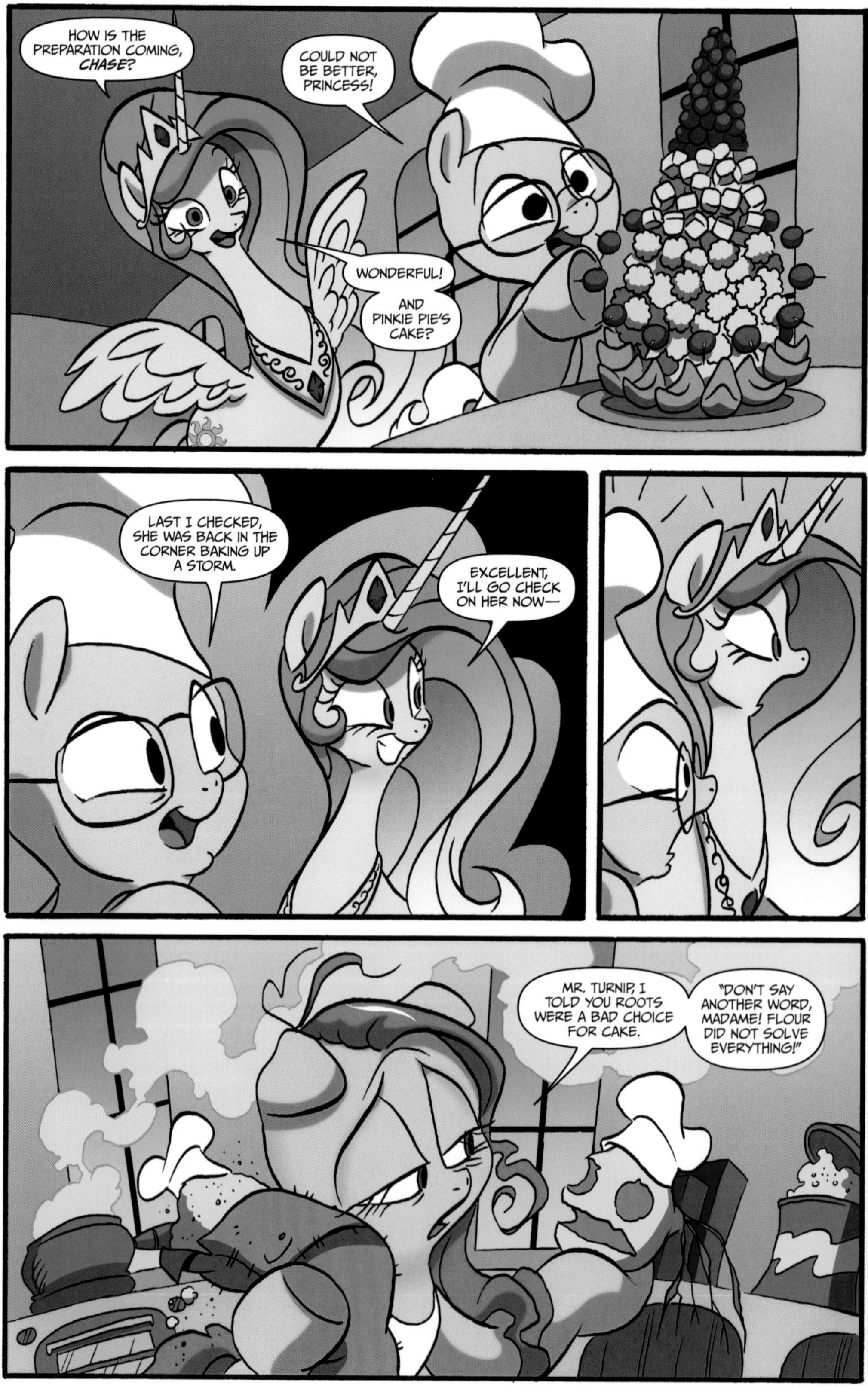
HOW IS THE PREPARATION COMING, CHASE?
COULD NOT BE BETTER, PRINCESS!
WONDERFUL!
AND PINKIE PIE'S CAKE?
LAST I CHECKED, SHE WAS BACK IN THE CORNER BAKING UP A STORM.
EXCELLENT, I'LL GO CHECK ON HER NOW—
MR. TURNIP, I TOLD YOU ROOTS WERE A BAD CHOICE FOR CAKE.
"DON'T SAY ANOTHER WORD, MADAME! FLOUR DID NOT SOLVE EVERYTHING!"

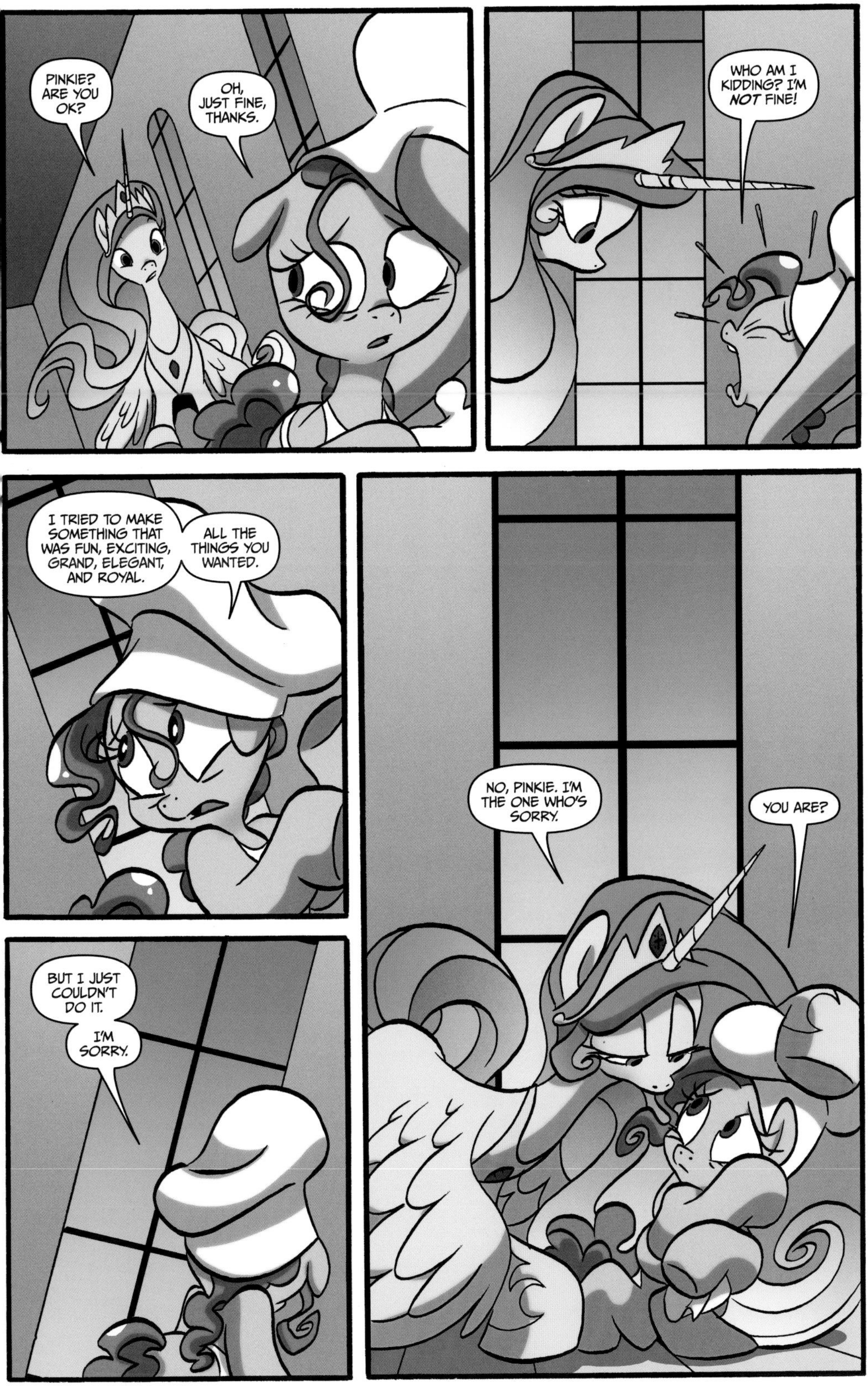
PINKIE? ARE YOU OK?
OH, JUST FINE, THANKS.
WHO AM I KIDDING? I'M *NOT* FINE!
I TRIED TO MAKE SOMETHING THAT WAS FUN, EXCITING, GRAND, ELEGANT, AND ROYAL.
ALL THE THINGS YOU WANTED.
BUT I JUST COULDN'T DO IT.
I'M SORRY.
NO, PINKIE. I'M THE ONE WHO'S SORRY.
YOU ARE?

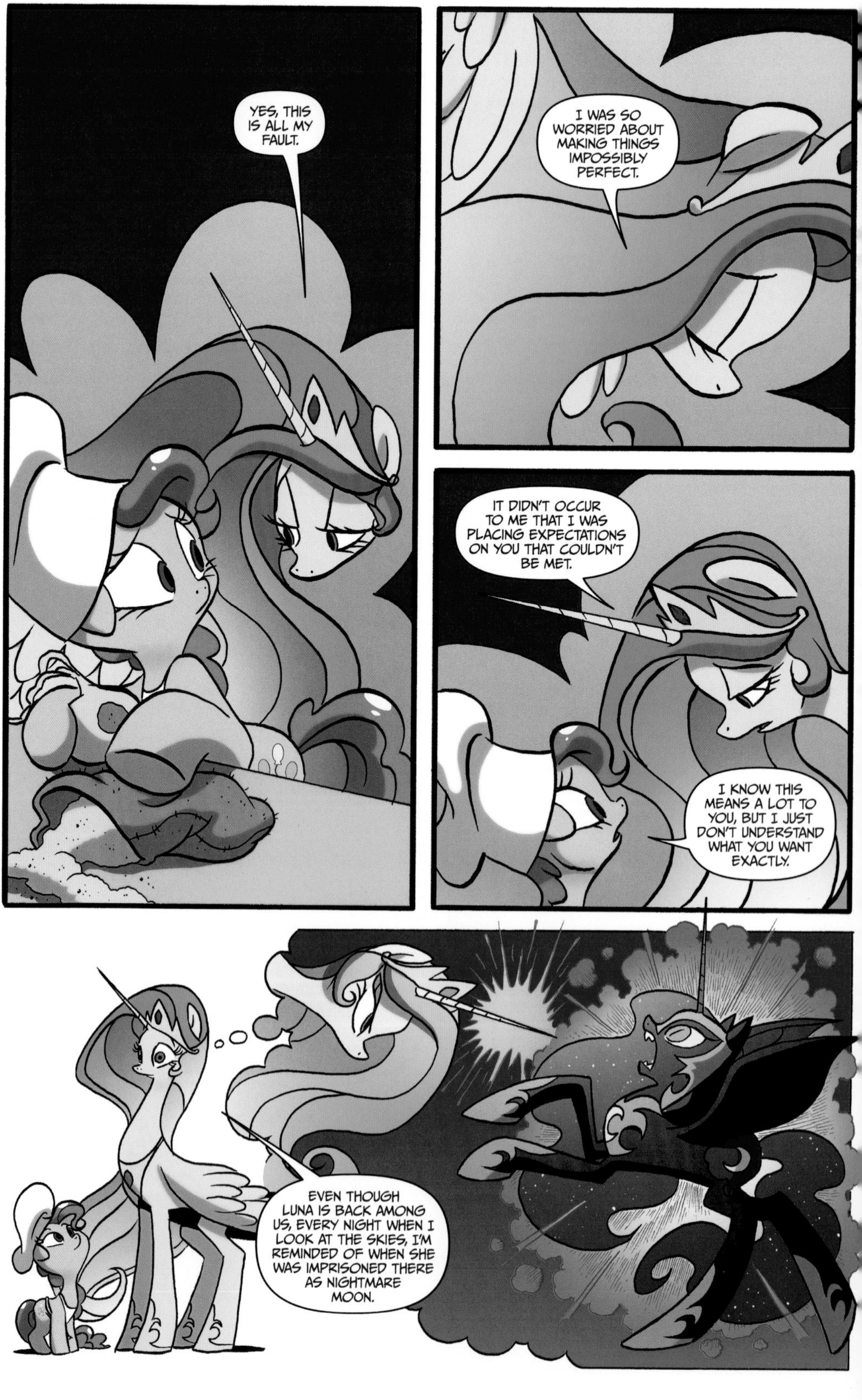

YES, THIS IS ALL MY FAULT.
I WAS SO WORRIED ABOUT MAKING THINGS IMPOSSIBLY PERFECT.
IT DIDN'T OCCUR TO ME THAT I WAS PLACING EXPECTATIONS ON YOU THAT COULDN'T BE MET.
I KNOW THIS MEANS A LOT TO YOU, BUT I JUST DON'T UNDERSTAND WHAT YOU WANT EXACTLY.
EVEN THOUGH LUNA IS BACK AMONG US, EVERY NIGHT WHEN I LOOK AT THE SKIES, I'M REMINDED OF WHEN SHE WAS IMPRISONED THERE AS NIGHTMARE MOON.

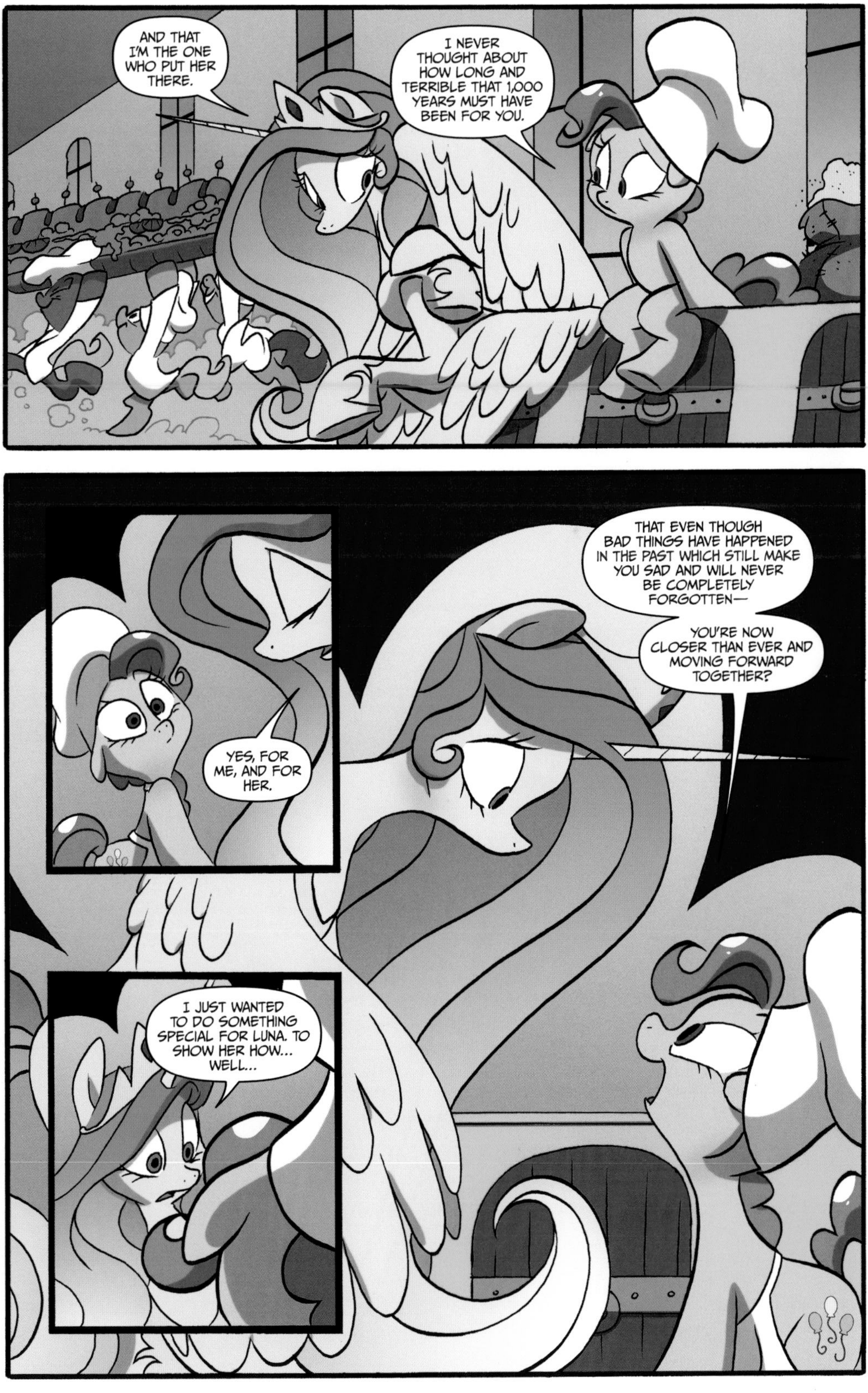
AND THAT I'M THE ONE WHO PUT HER THERE.
I NEVER THOUGHT ABOUT HOW LONG AND TERRIBLE THAT 1,000 YEARS MUST HAVE BEEN FOR YOU.
I JUST WANTED TO DO SOMETHING SPECIAL FOR LUNA. TO SHOW HER HOW... WELL...
THAT EVEN THOUGH BAD THINGS HAVE HAPPENED IN THE PAST WHICH STILL MAKE YOU SAD AND WILL NEVER BE COMPLETELY FORGOTTEN—
YOU'RE NOW CLOSER THAN EVER AND MOVING FORWARD TOGETHER?
YES, FOR ME, AND FOR HER.

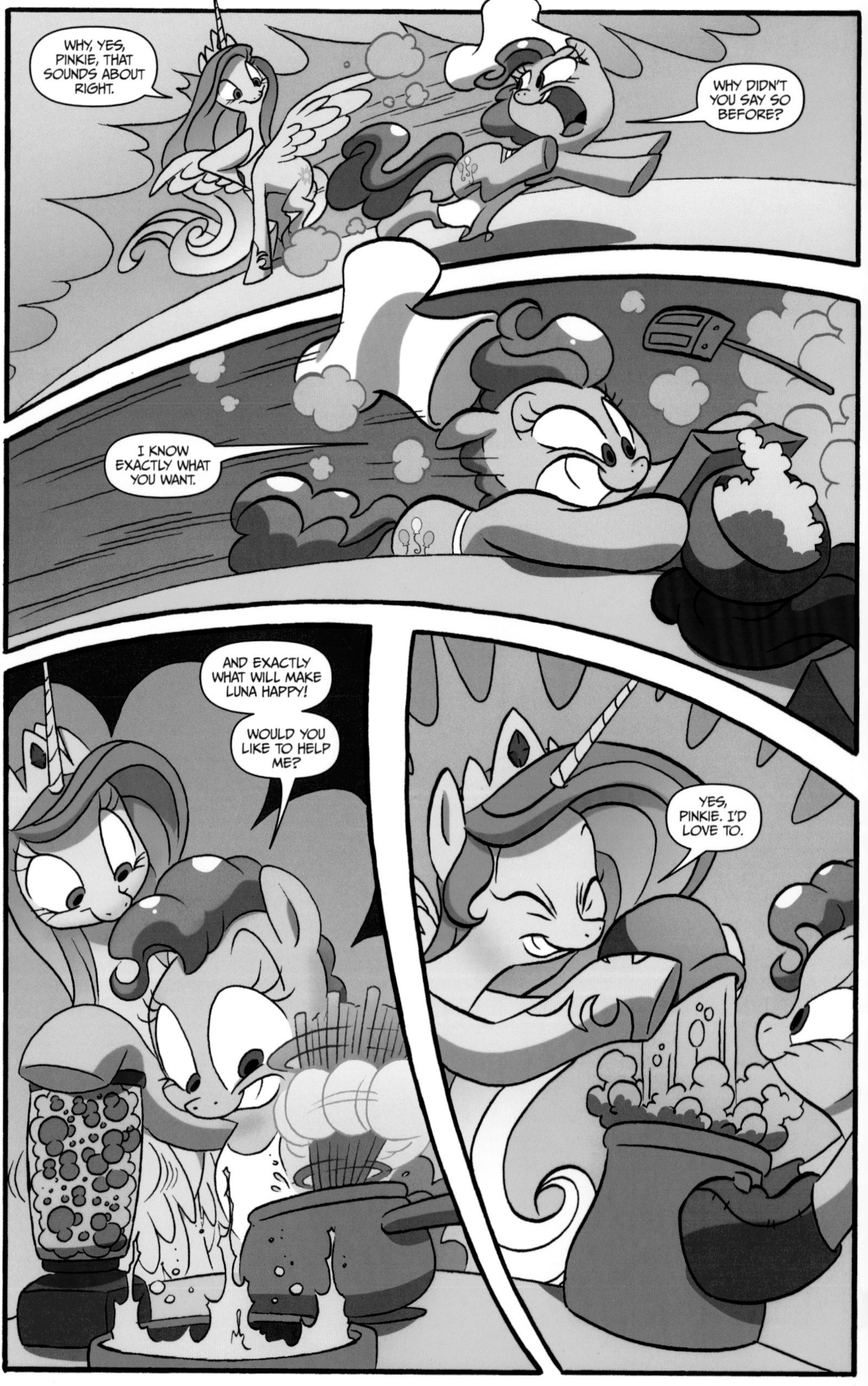
WHY, YES, PINKIE, THAT SOUNDS ABOUT RIGHT.
WHY DIDN'T YOU SAY SO BEFORE?
I KNOW EXACTLY WHAT YOU WANT.
AND EXACTLY WHAT WILL MAKE LUNA HAPPY!
WOULD YOU LIKE TO HELP ME?
YES, PINKIE. I'D LOVE TO.

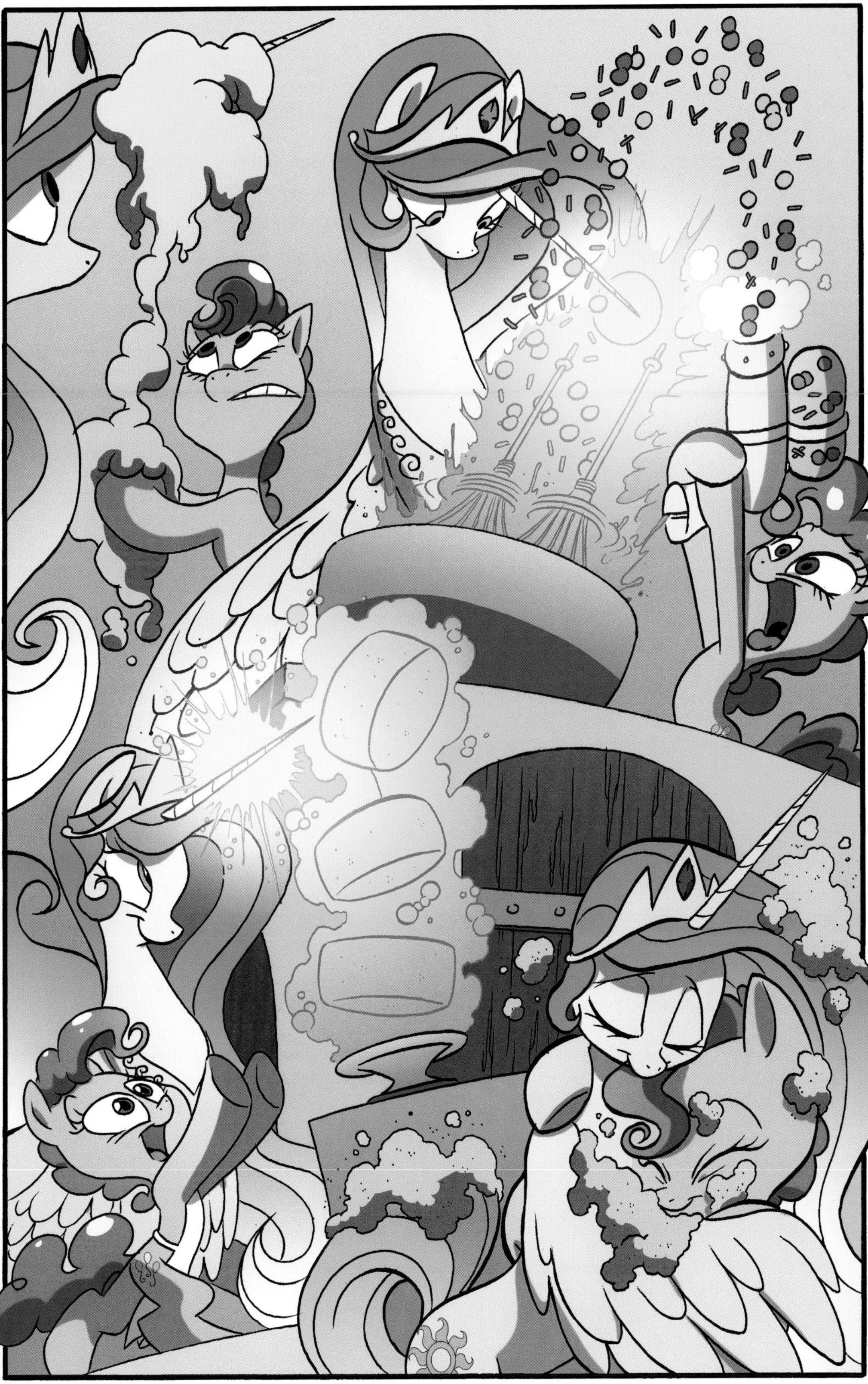

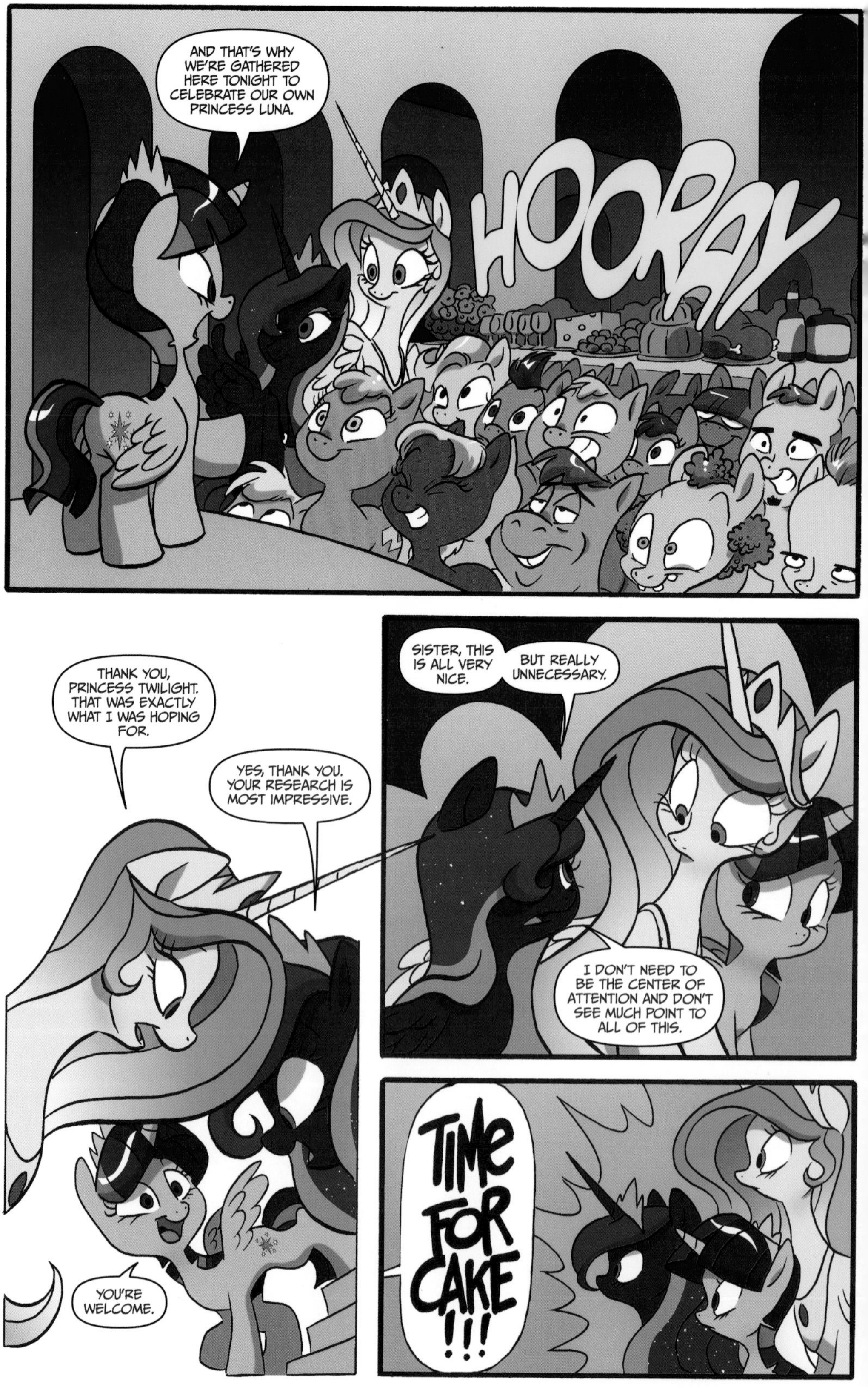
AND THAT'S WHY WE'RE GATHERED HERE TONIGHT TO CELEBRATE OUR OWN PRINCESS LUNA.
HOORAY
THANK YOU, PRINCESS TWILIGHT. THAT WAS EXACTLY WHAT I WAS HOPING FOR.
YES, THANK YOU. YOUR RESEARCH IS MOST IMPRESSIVE.
YOU'RE WELCOME.
SISTER, THIS IS ALL VERY NICE.
BUT REALLY UNNECESSARY.
I DON'T NEED TO BE THE CENTER OF ATTENTION AND DON'T SEE MUCH POINT TO ALL OF THIS.
TIME FOR CAKE!!!

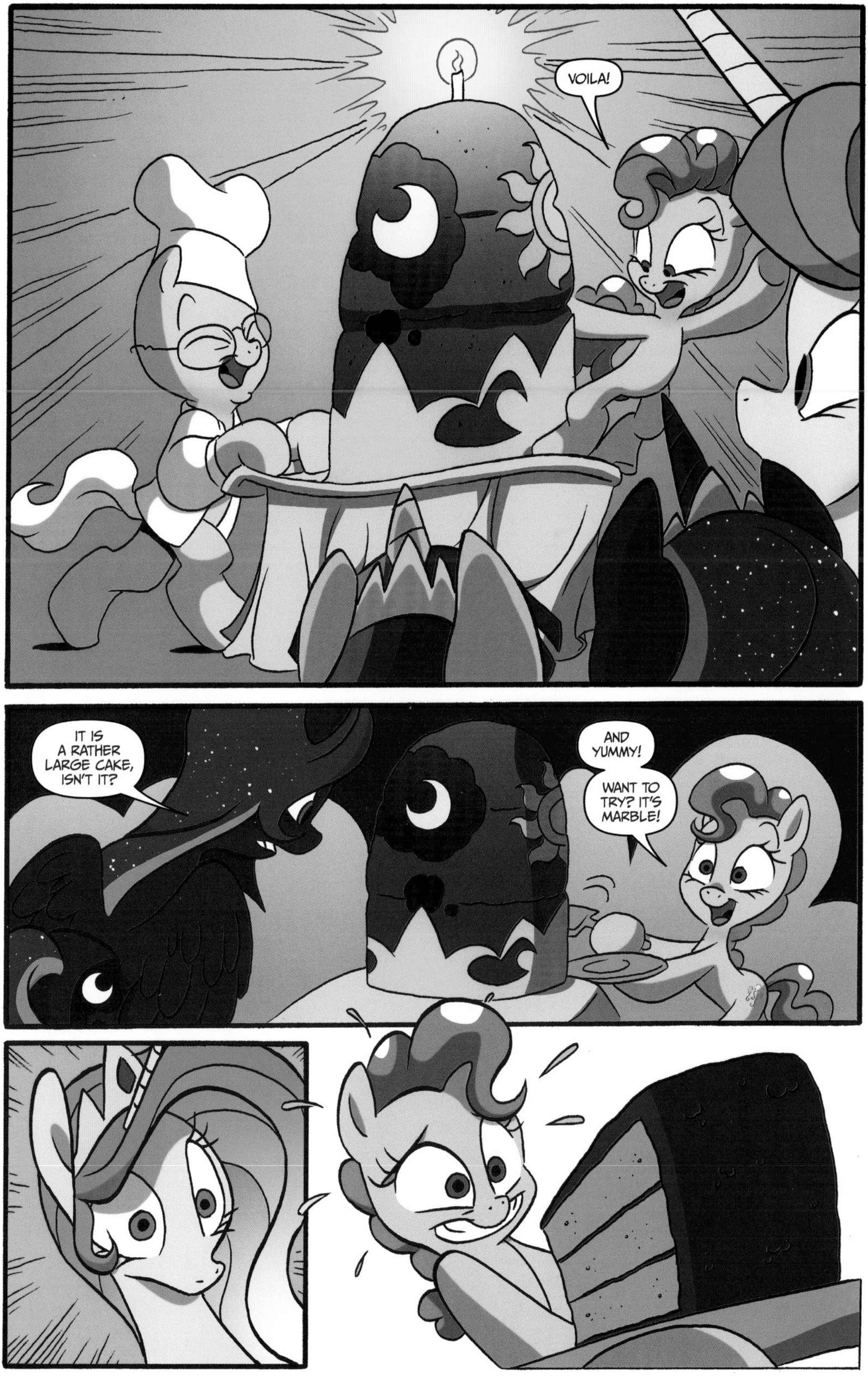
VOILA!
IT IS A RATHER LARGE CAKE, ISN'T IT?
AND YUMMY!
WANT TO TRY? IT'S MARBLE!

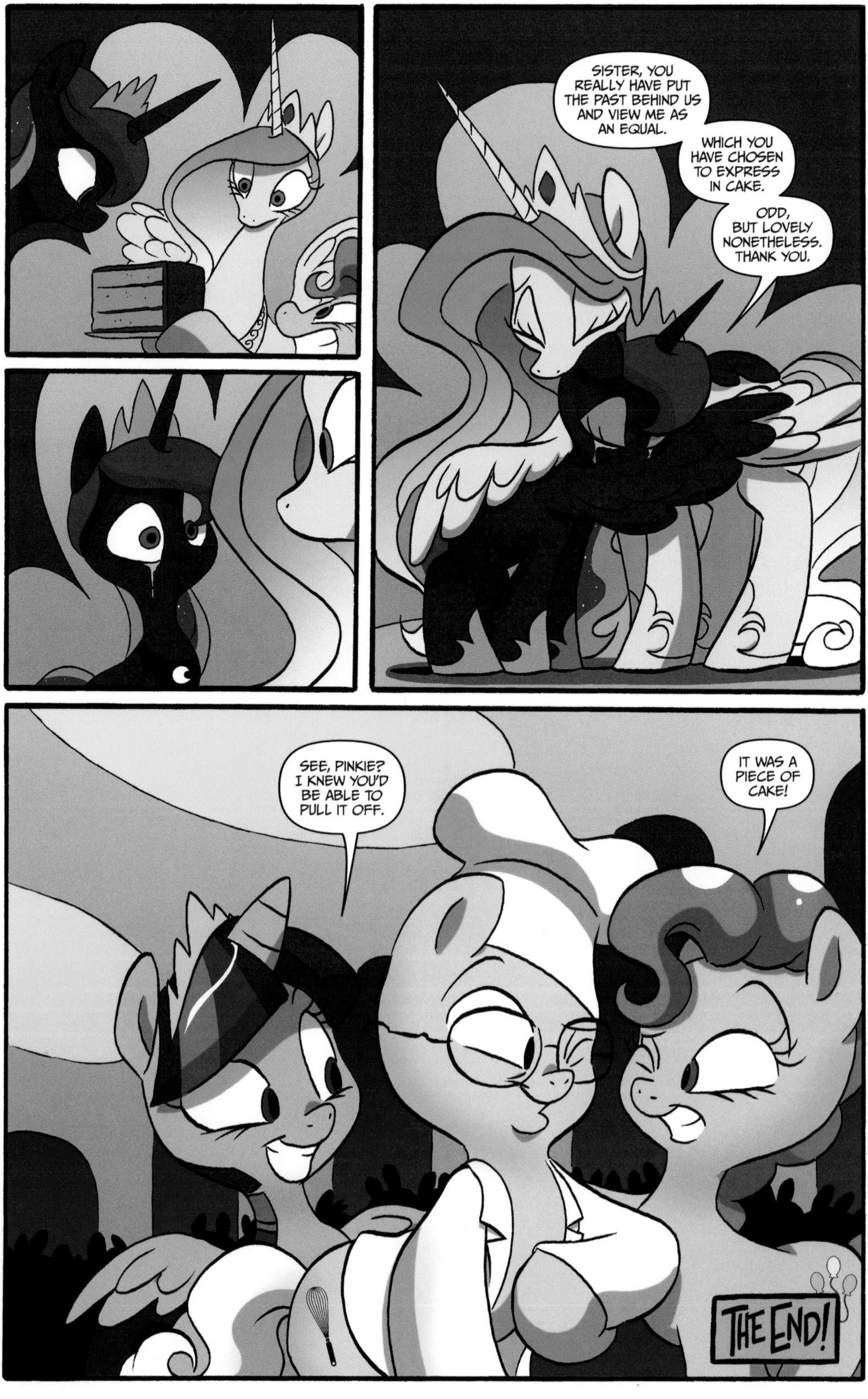
SISTER, YOU REALLY HAVE PUT THE PAST BEHIND US AND VIEW ME AS AN EQUAL.
WHICH YOU HAVE CHOSEN TO EXPRESS IN CAKE.
ODD, BUT LOVELY NONETHELESS. THANK YOU.
SEE, PINKIE? I KNEW YOU'D BE ABLE TO PULL IT OFF.
IT WAS A PIECE OF CAKE!
THE END!

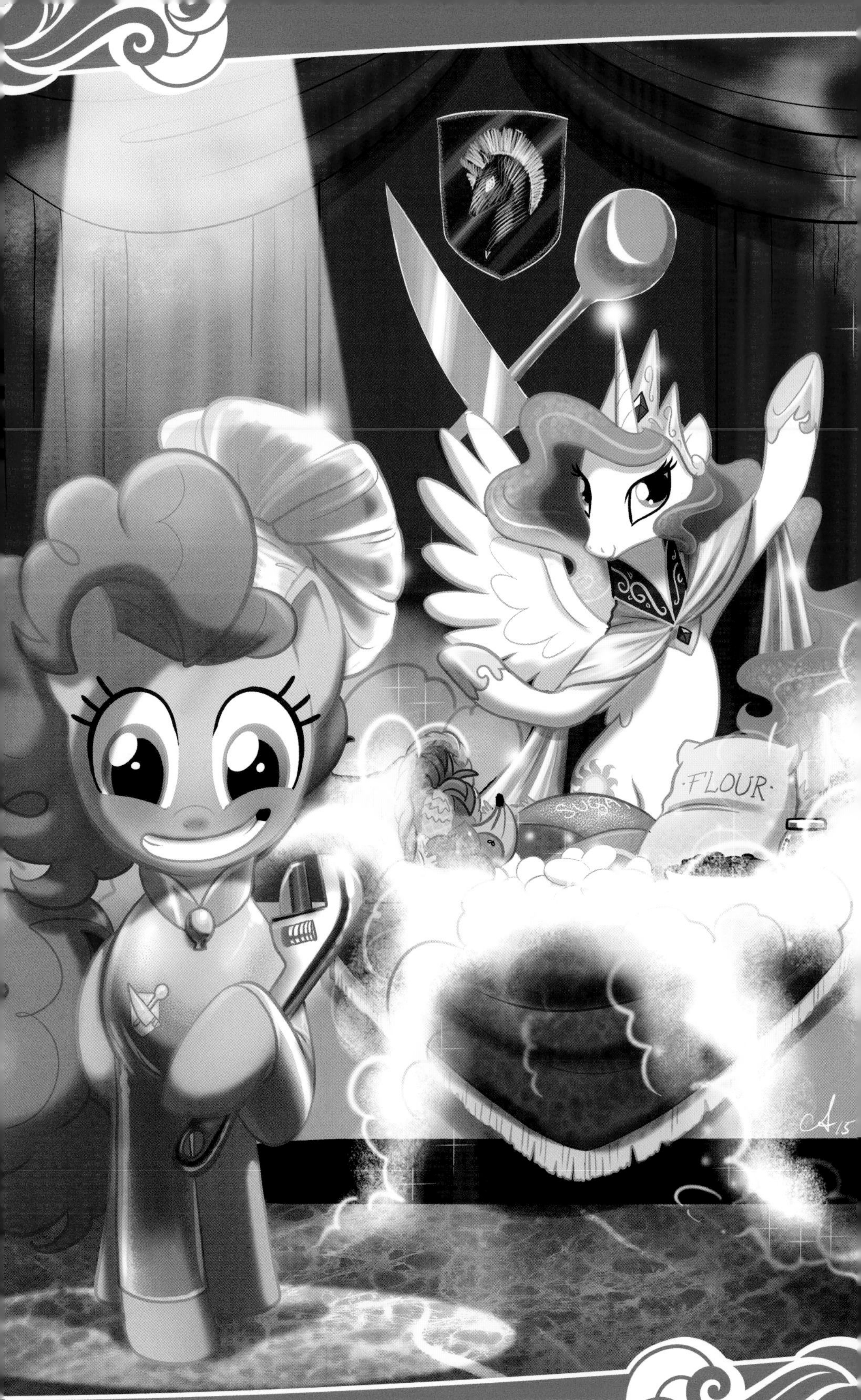

FLOUR

art by AMY MEBBERSON

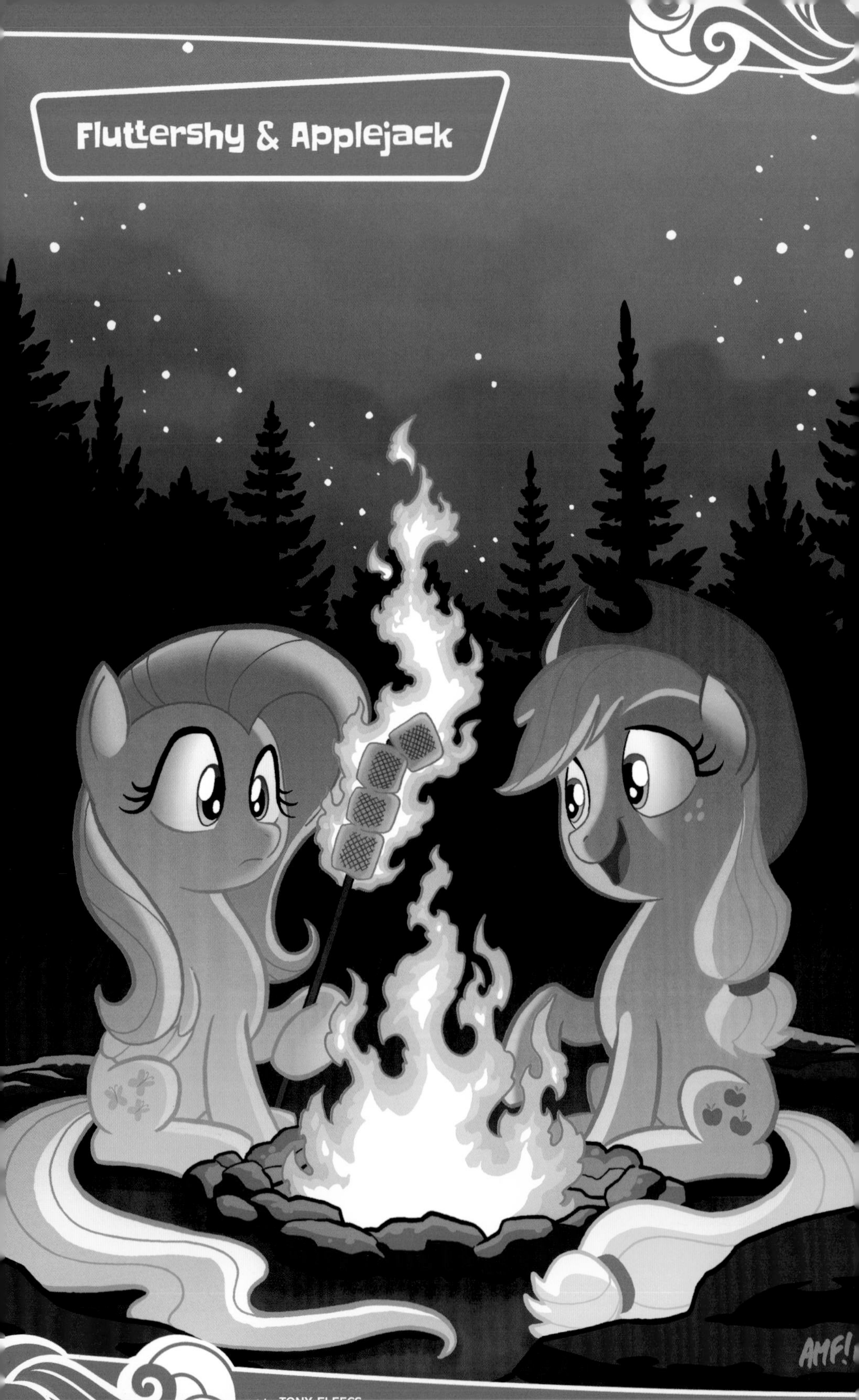
Fluttershy & Applejack
AMF!

art by TONY FLEECS

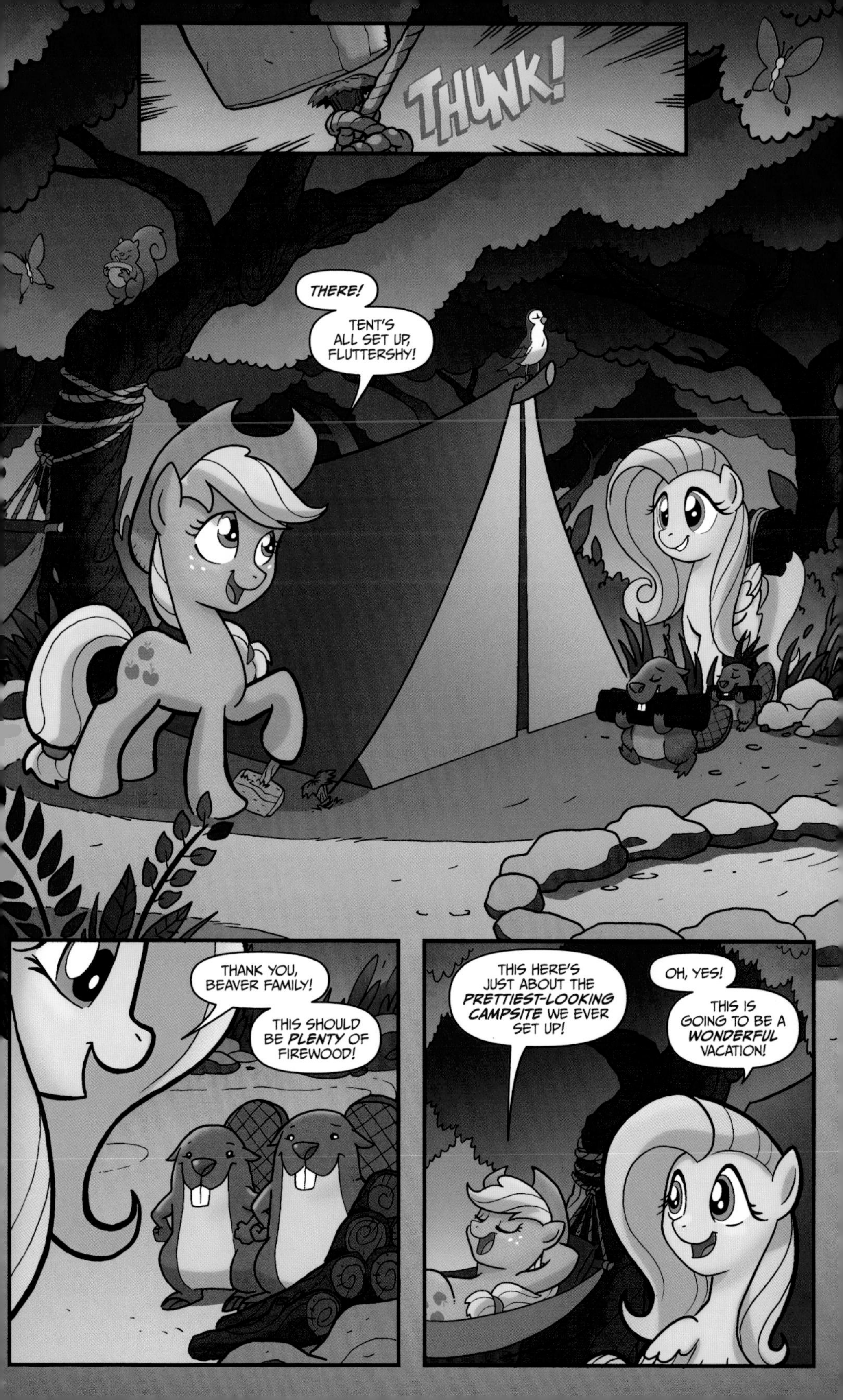
THUNK!
THERE!
TENT'S ALL SET UP, FLUTTERSHY!
THANK YOU, BEAVER FAMILY!
THIS SHOULD BE PLENTY OF FIREWOOD!
THIS HERE'S JUST ABOUT THE PRETTIEST-LOOKING CAMPSITE WE EVER SET UP!
OH, YES!
THIS IS GOING TO BE A WONDERFUL VACATION!

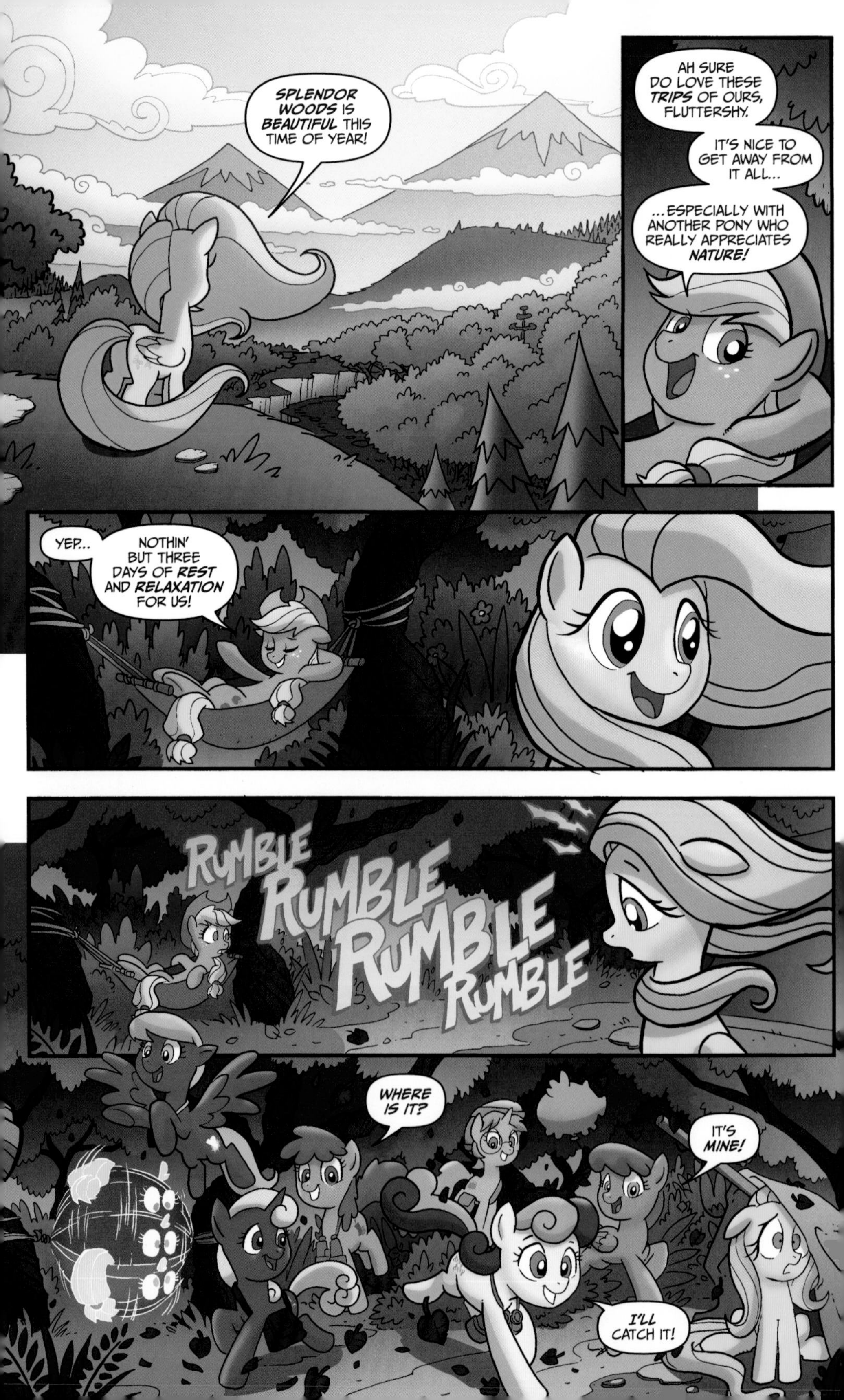
SPLENDOR WOODS IS BEAUTIFUL THIS TIME OF YEAR!
AH SURE DO LOVE THESE TRIPS OF OURS, FLUTTERSHY.
IT'S NICE TO GET AWAY FROM IT ALL...
...ESPECIALLY WITH ANOTHER PONY WHO REALLY APPRECIATES NATURE!
YEP...
NOTHIN' BUT THREE DAYS OF REST AND RELAXATION FOR US!
RUMBLE
RUMBLE
RUMBLE
RUMBLE
WHERE IS IT?
IT'S MINE!
I'LL CATCH IT!

WHAT TH' *HAY* WAS THAT?

A *STAMPEDE?*

NOT QUITE!

WE'RE ON THE HUNT FOR THE MOST *FANTASTIC LEGENDARY CREATURE* IN *ALL* OF *EQUESTRIA!*

"*LEGENDARY CREATURE*"?

AN' JUST *WHO* ARE *YOU?*

THE NAME'S *NOSEY NEWS,* REPORTER FOR *CANTERLOT DAILY,* AND I'M HERE INVESTIGATING A RECENT *SIGHTING* OF—

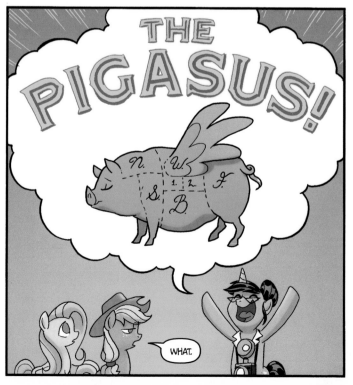

THE **PIGASUS!**

WHAT.

A *NOBLE BEAST* WITH THE BODY OF A *PIG* AND THE WINGS OF A *BIRD!*

I TOOK THIS PICTURE JUST *LAST WEEK,* HERE IN *SPLENDOR WOODS!*

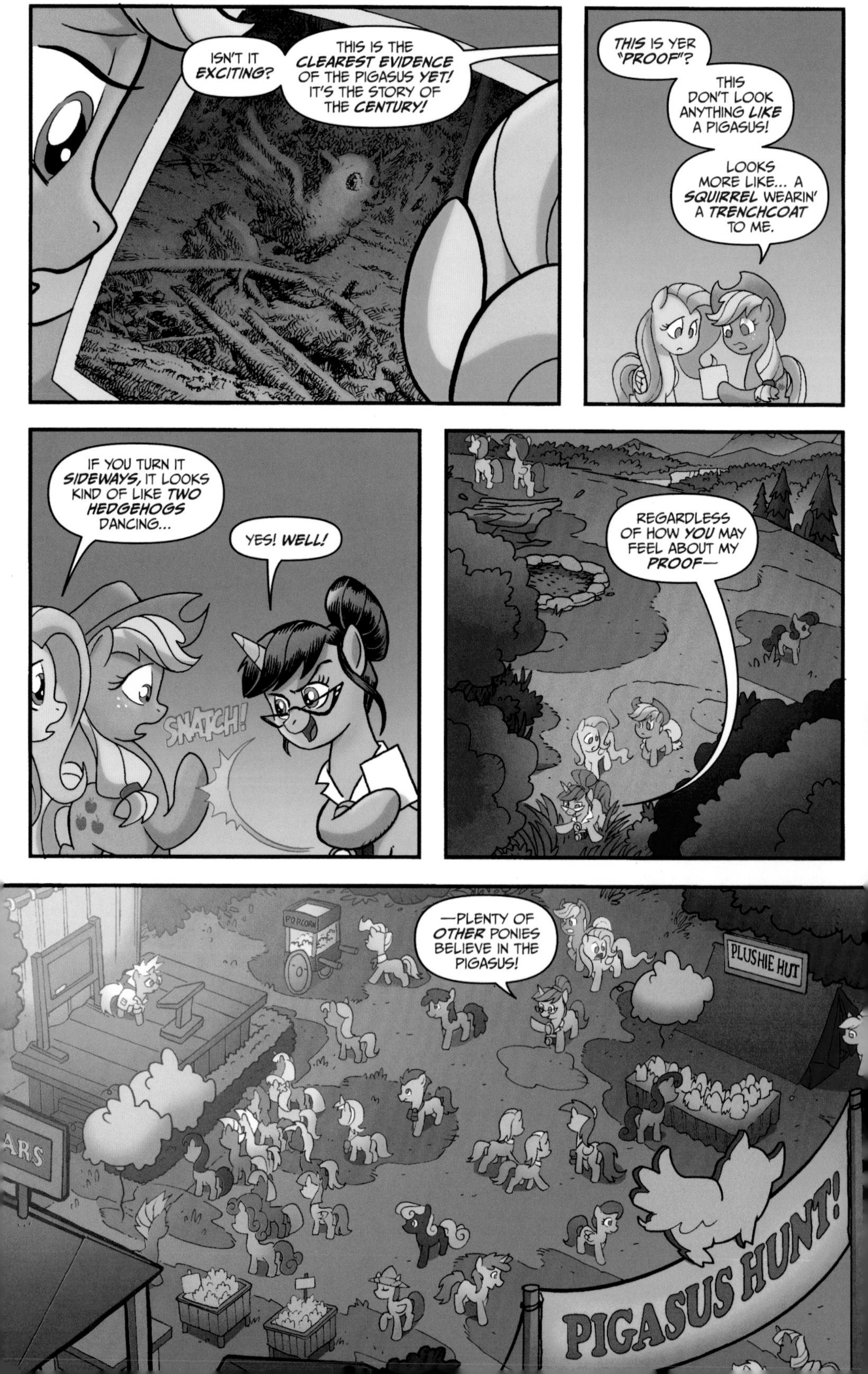

ISN'T IT EXCITING?
THIS IS THE CLEAREST EVIDENCE OF THE PIGASUS YET! IT'S THE STORY OF THE CENTURY!
THIS IS YER "PROOF"?
THIS DON'T LOOK ANYTHING LIKE A PIGASUS!
LOOKS MORE LIKE... A SQUIRREL WEARIN' A TRENCHCOAT TO ME.
IF YOU TURN IT SIDEWAYS, IT LOOKS KIND OF LIKE TWO HEDGEHOGS DANCING...
YES! WELL!
SNATCH!
REGARDLESS OF HOW YOU MAY FEEL ABOUT MY PROOF—
—PLENTY OF OTHER PONIES BELIEVE IN THE PIGASUS!
POPCORN
PLUSHIE HUT
ARS
PIGASUS HUNT!

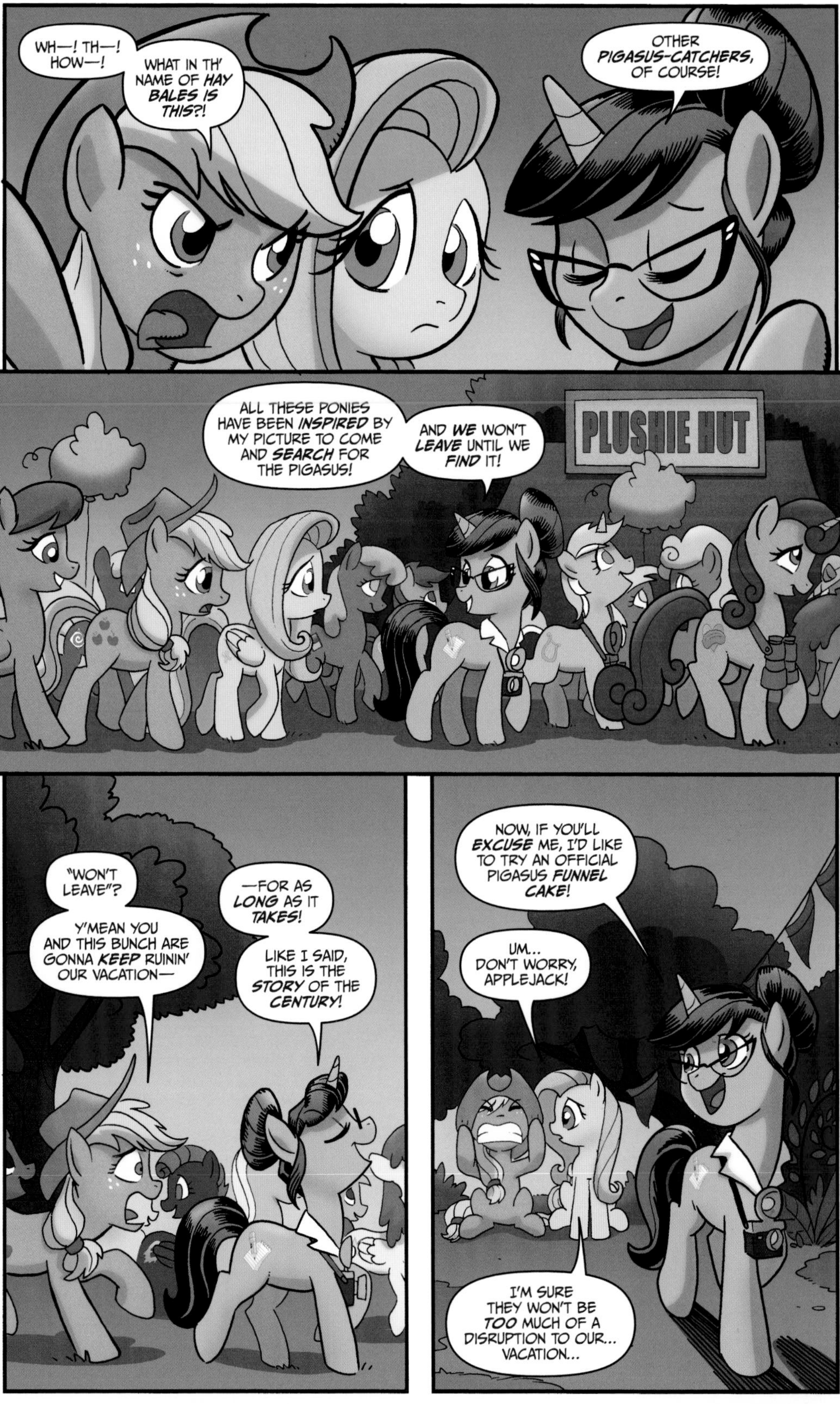
WH—! TH—! HOW—!
WHAT IN TH' NAME OF HAY BALES IS THIS?!
OTHER PIGASUS-CATCHERS, OF COURSE!
ALL THESE PONIES HAVE BEEN INSPIRED BY MY PICTURE TO COME AND SEARCH FOR THE PIGASUS!
AND WE WON'T LEAVE UNTIL WE FIND IT!
PLUSHIE HUT
"WON'T LEAVE"?
Y'MEAN YOU AND THIS BUNCH ARE GONNA KEEP RUININ' OUR VACATION—
—FOR AS LONG AS IT TAKES!
LIKE I SAID, THIS IS THE STORY OF THE CENTURY!
NOW, IF YOU'LL EXCUSE ME, I'D LIKE TO TRY AN OFFICIAL PIGASUS FUNNEL CAKE!
UM... DON'T WORRY, APPLEJACK!
I'M SURE THEY WON'T BE TOO MUCH OF A DISRUPTION TO OUR... VACATION...

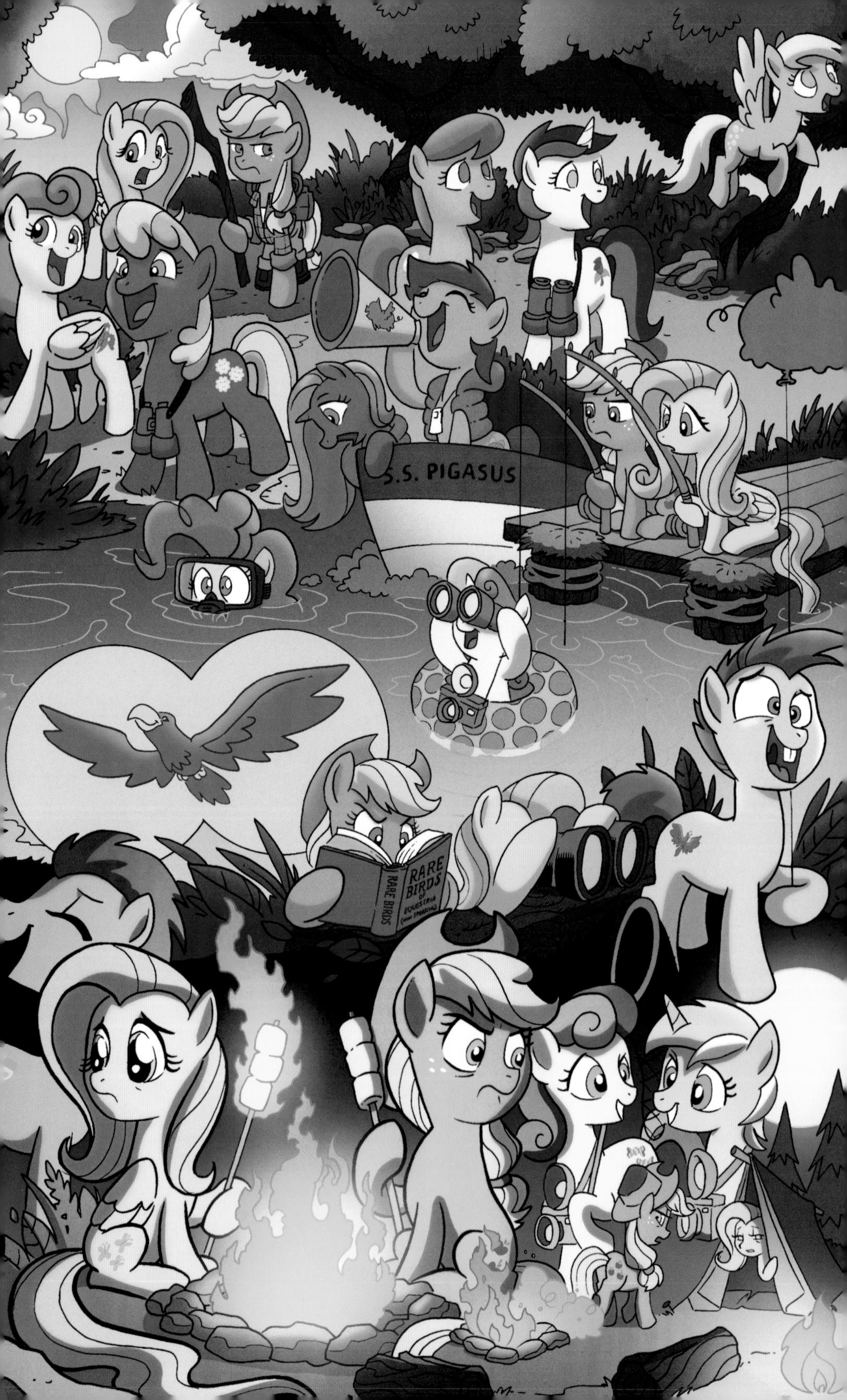
S.S. PIGASUS
RARE BIRDS OF EQUESTRIA
RARE BIRDS

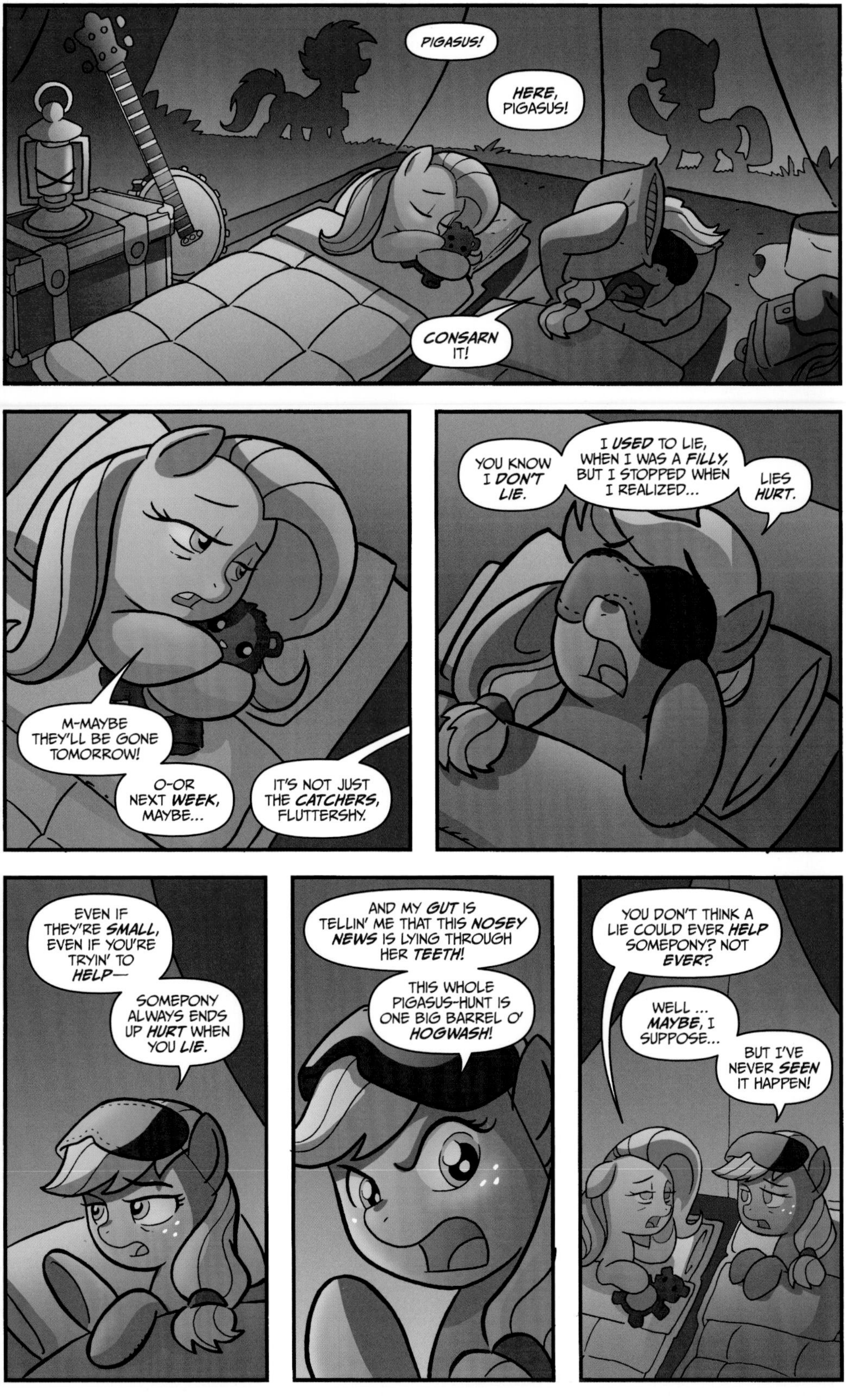
PIGASUS!
HERE, PIGASUS!
CONSARN IT!
M-MAYBE THEY'LL BE GONE TOMORROW!
O-OR NEXT WEEK, MAYBE...
IT'S NOT JUST THE CATCHERS, FLUTTERSHY.
YOU KNOW I DON'T LIE.
I USED TO LIE, WHEN I WAS A FILLY, BUT I STOPPED WHEN I REALIZED...
LIES HURT.
EVEN IF THEY'RE SMALL, EVEN IF YOU'RE TRYIN' TO HELP—
SOMEPONY ALWAYS ENDS UP HURT WHEN YOU LIE.
AND MY GUT IS TELLIN' ME THAT THIS NOSEY NEWS IS LYING THROUGH HER TEETH!
THIS WHOLE PIGASUS-HUNT IS ONE BIG BARREL O' HOGWASH!
YOU DON'T THINK A LIE COULD EVER HELP SOMEPONY? NOT EVER?
WELL ... MAYBE, I SUPPOSE...
BUT I'VE NEVER SEEN IT HAPPEN!

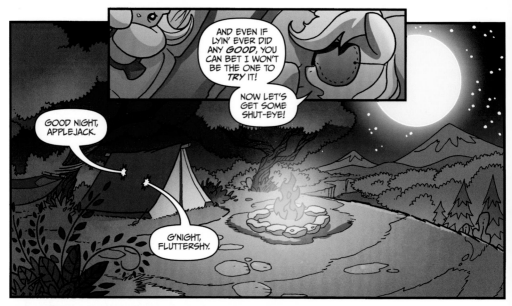

AND EVEN IF LYIN' EVER DID ANY *GOOD*, YOU CAN BET I WON'T BE THE ONE TO *TRY* IT!

NOW LET'S GET SOME SHUT-EYE!

GOOD NIGHT, APPLEJACK.

G'NIGHT, FLUTTERSHY.

YAAAWWWWNN...

smack smack

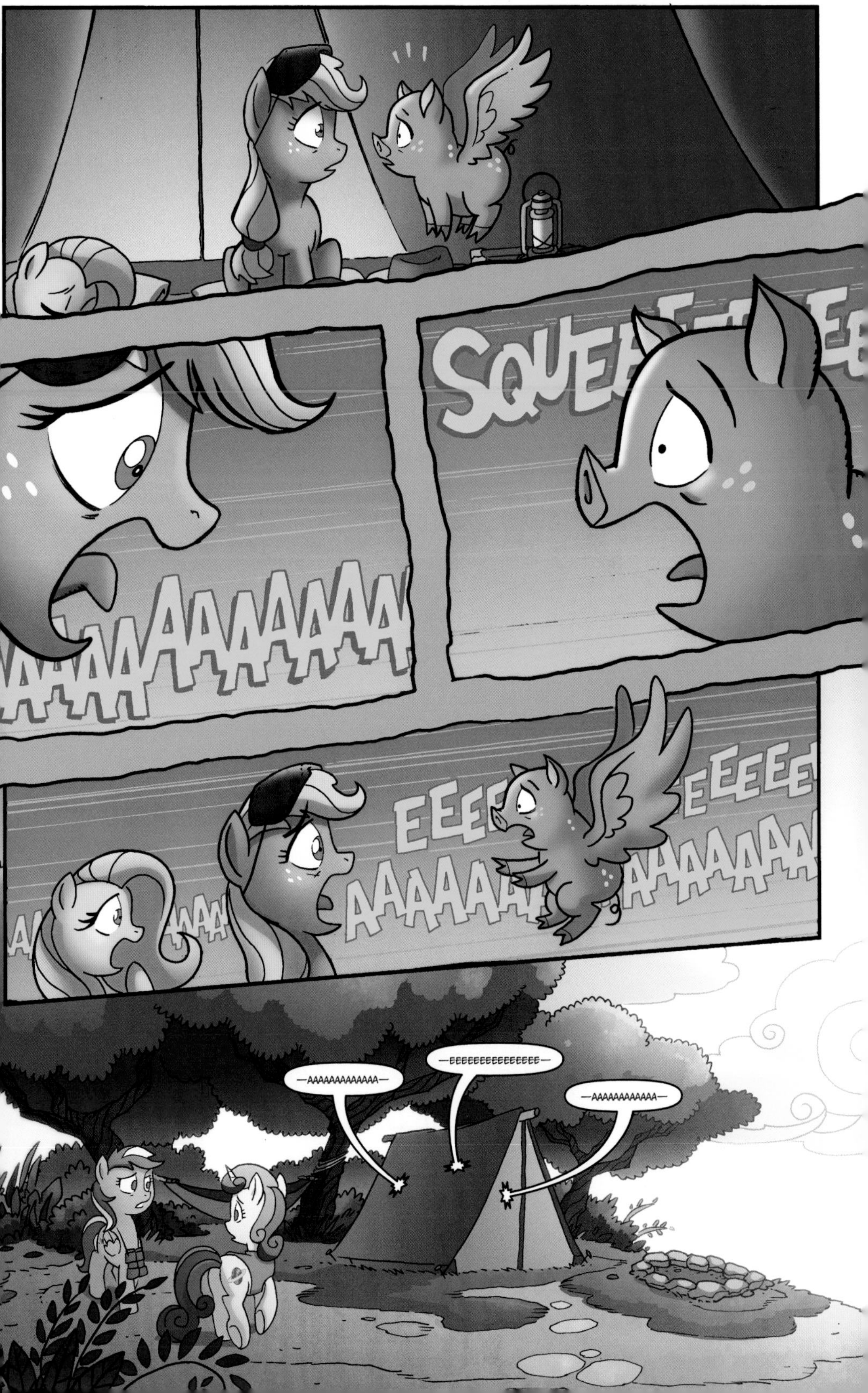
—AAAAAAAAAAAAAA—
—EEEEEEEEEEEEEEEEE—
—AAAAAAAAAAAAA—

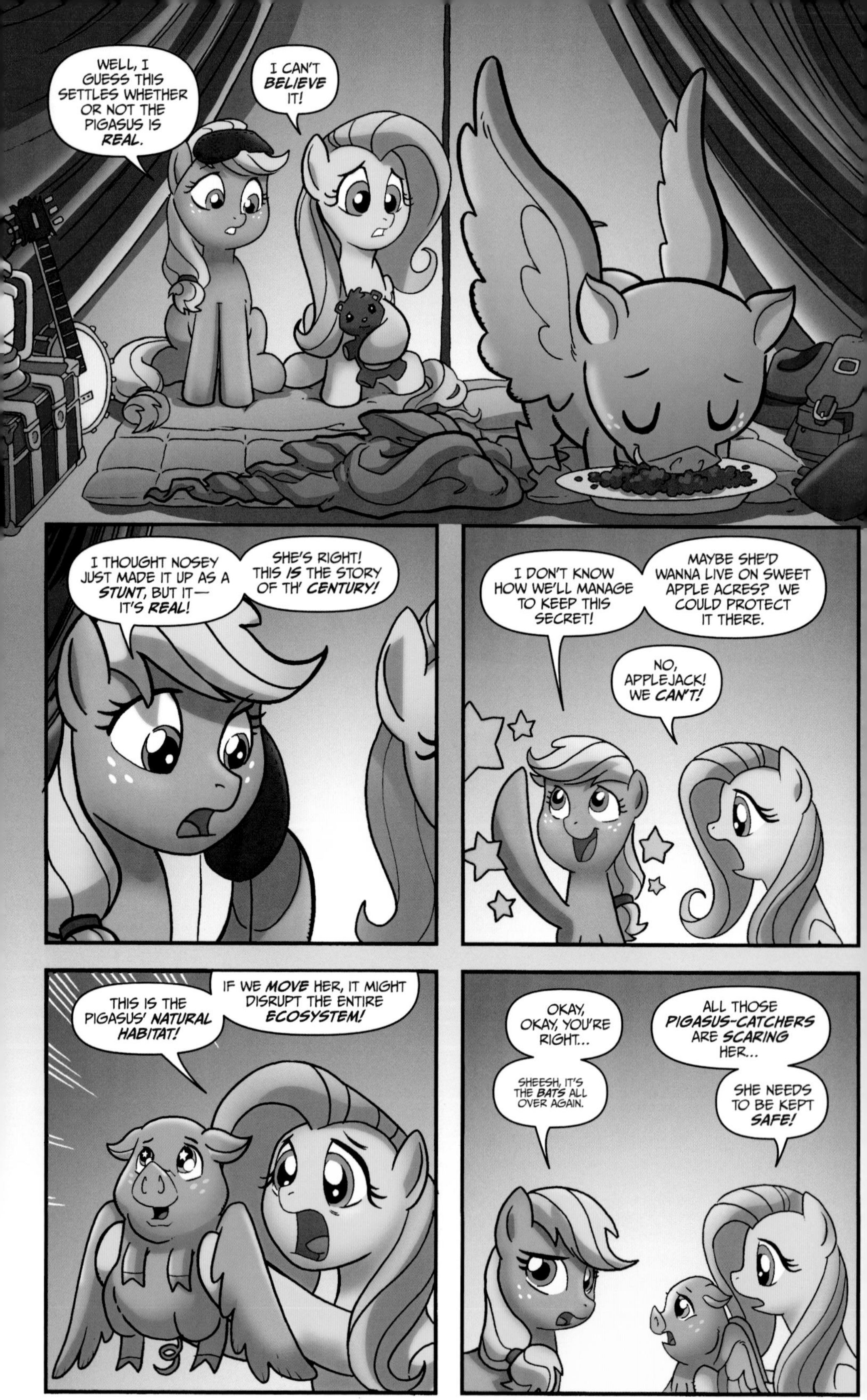
WELL, I GUESS THIS SETTLES WHETHER OR NOT THE PIGASUS IS REAL.
I CAN'T BELIEVE IT!
I THOUGHT NOSEY JUST MADE IT UP AS A STUNT, BUT IT— IT'S REAL!
SHE'S RIGHT! THIS IS THE STORY OF TH' CENTURY!
I DON'T KNOW HOW WE'LL MANAGE TO KEEP THIS SECRET!
MAYBE SHE'D WANNA LIVE ON SWEET APPLE ACRES? WE COULD PROTECT IT THERE.
NO, APPLEJACK! WE CAN'T!
THIS IS THE PIGASUS' NATURAL HABITAT!
IF WE MOVE HER, IT MIGHT DISRUPT THE ENTIRE ECOSYSTEM!
OKAY, OKAY, YOU'RE RIGHT...
SHEESH, IT'S THE BATS ALL OVER AGAIN.
ALL THOSE PIGASUS-CATCHERS ARE SCARING HER...
SHE NEEDS TO BE KEPT SAFE!

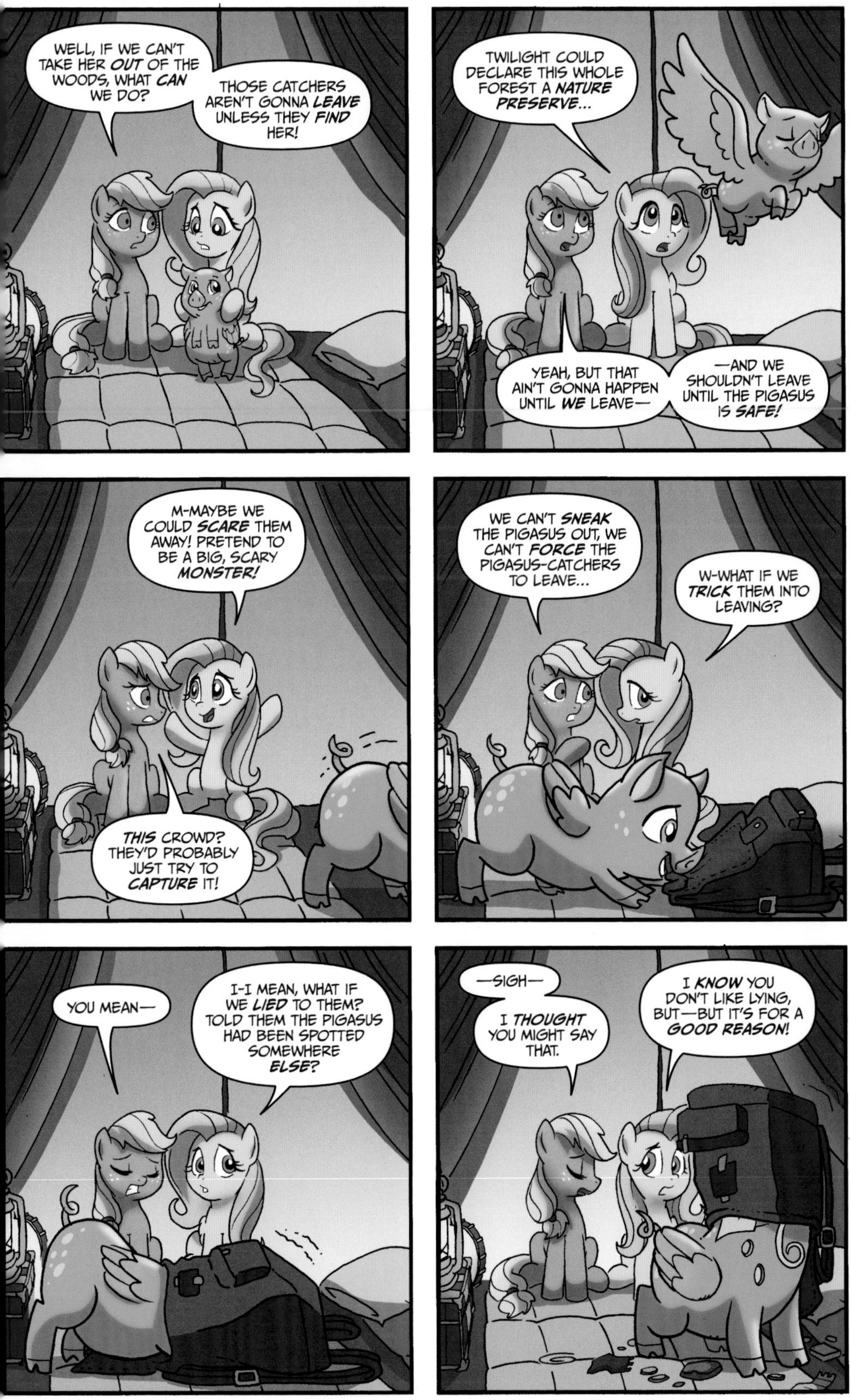
WELL, IF WE CAN'T TAKE HER *OUT* OF THE WOODS, WHAT *CAN* WE DO?
THOSE CATCHERS AREN'T GONNA *LEAVE* UNLESS THEY *FIND* HER!
TWILIGHT COULD DECLARE THIS WHOLE FOREST A *NATURE PRESERVE*...
YEAH, BUT THAT AIN'T GONNA HAPPEN UNTIL *WE* LEAVE—
—AND WE SHOULDN'T LEAVE UNTIL THE PIGASUS IS *SAFE!*
M-MAYBE WE COULD *SCARE* THEM AWAY! PRETEND TO BE A BIG, SCARY *MONSTER!*
THIS CROWD? THEY'D PROBABLY JUST TRY TO *CAPTURE* IT!
WE CAN'T *SNEAK* THE PIGASUS OUT, WE CAN'T *FORCE* THE PIGASUS-CATCHERS TO LEAVE...
W-WHAT IF WE *TRICK* THEM INTO LEAVING?
YOU MEAN—
I-I MEAN, WHAT IF WE *LIED* TO THEM? TOLD THEM THE PIGASUS HAD BEEN SPOTTED SOMEWHERE *ELSE?*
—SIGH—
I *THOUGHT* YOU MIGHT SAY THAT.
I *KNOW* YOU DON'T LIKE LYING, BUT—BUT IT'S FOR A *GOOD REASON!*

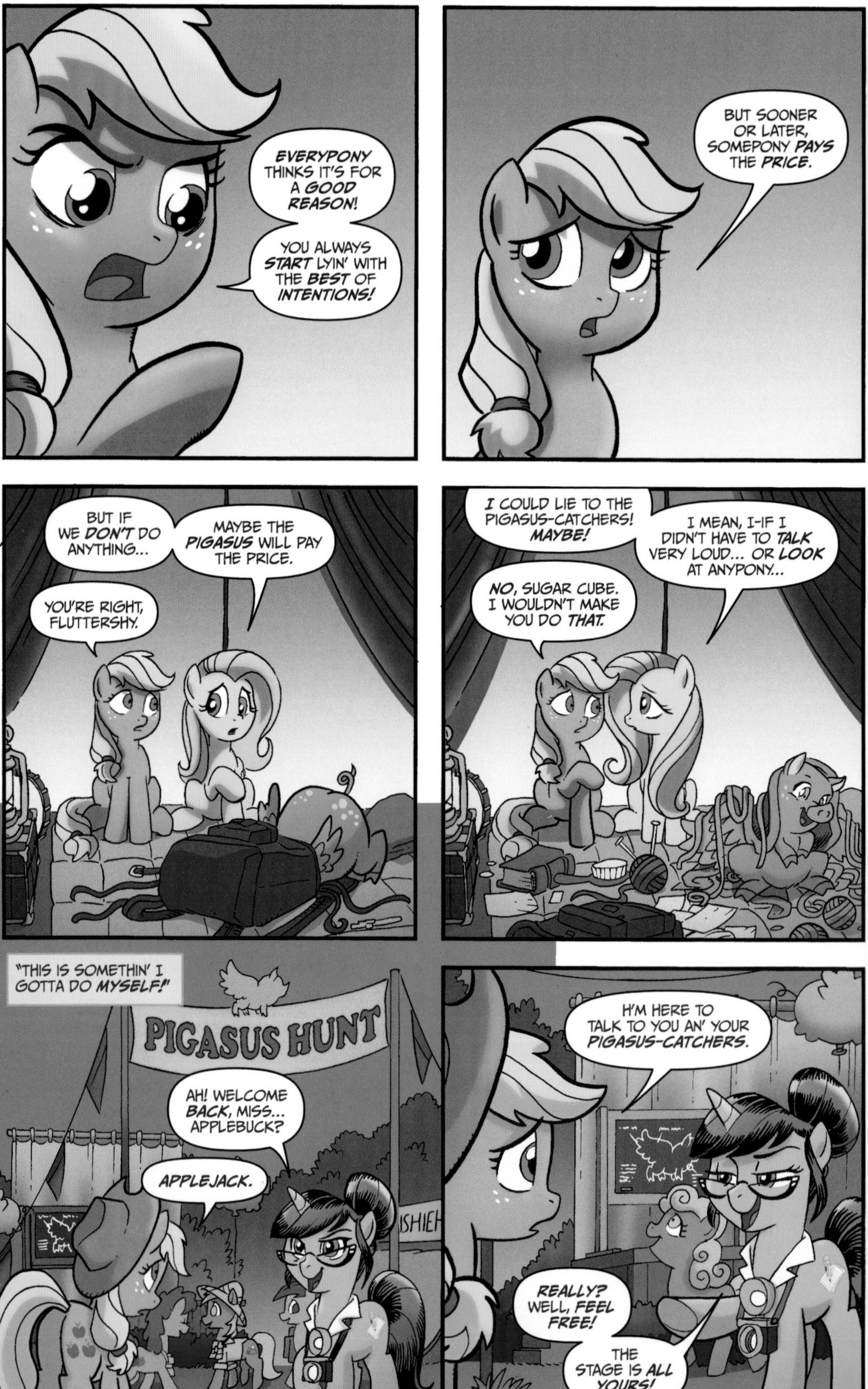
EVERYPONY THINKS IT'S FOR A GOOD REASON!
YOU ALWAYS START LYIN' WITH THE BEST OF INTENTIONS!
BUT SOONER OR LATER, SOMEPONY PAYS THE PRICE.
BUT IF WE DON'T DO ANYTHING...
MAYBE THE PIGASUS WILL PAY THE PRICE.
YOU'RE RIGHT, FLUTTERSHY.
I COULD LIE TO THE PIGASUS-CATCHERS! MAYBE!
I MEAN, I-IF I DIDN'T HAVE TO TALK VERY LOUD... OR LOOK AT ANYPONY...
NO, SUGAR CUBE. I WOULDN'T MAKE YOU DO THAT.
"THIS IS SOMETHIN' I GOTTA DO MYSELF!"
PIGASUS HUNT
AH! WELCOME BACK, MISS... APPLEBUCK?
APPLEJACK.
H'M HERE TO TALK TO YOU AN' YOUR PIGASUS-CATCHERS.
REALLY? WELL, FEEL FREE!
THE STAGE IS ALL YOURS!

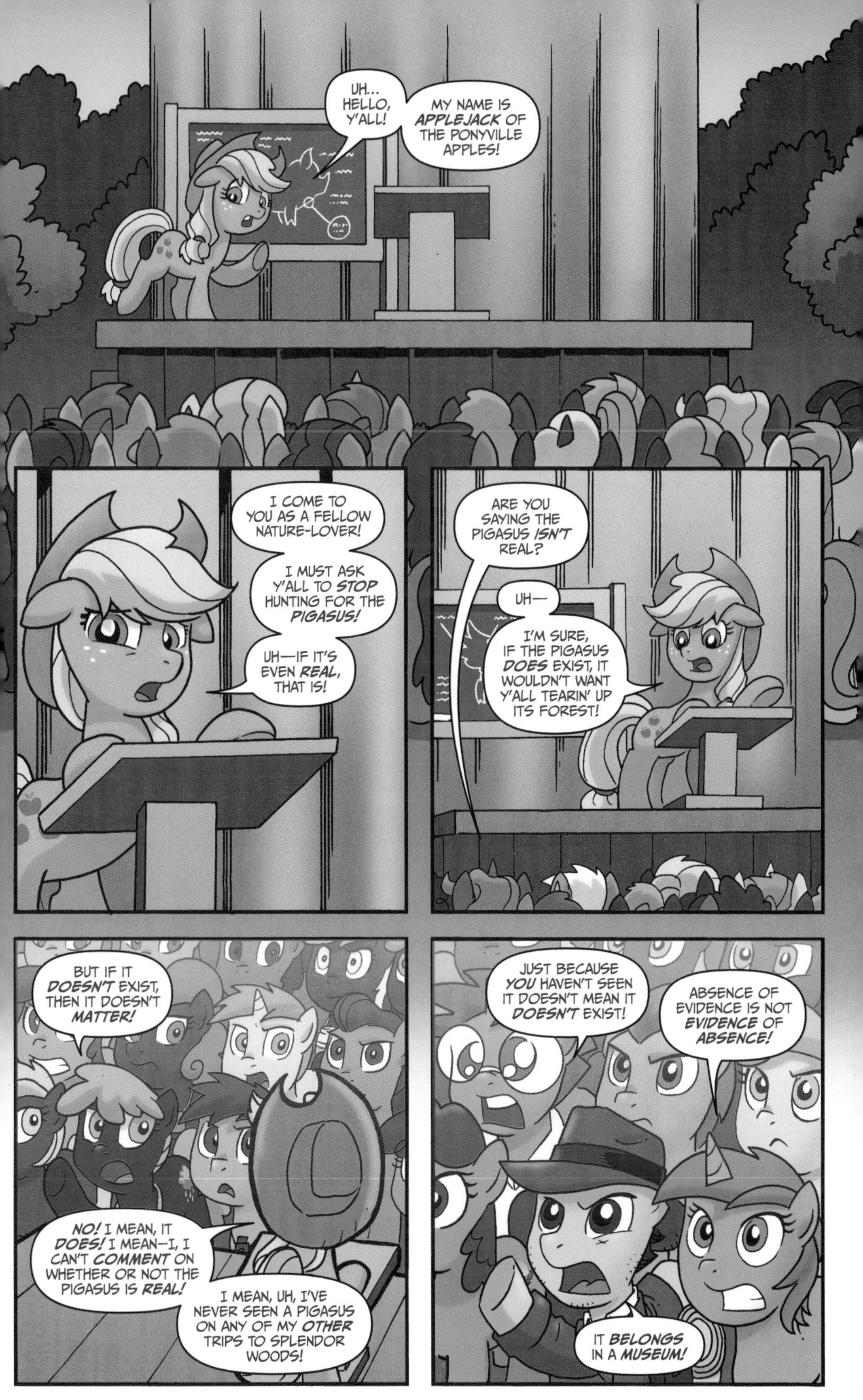
UH... HELLO, Y'ALL!
MY NAME IS APPLEJACK OF THE PONYVILLE APPLES!
I COME TO YOU AS A FELLOW NATURE-LOVER!
I MUST ASK Y'ALL TO STOP HUNTING FOR THE PIGASUS!
UH—IF IT'S EVEN REAL, THAT IS!
ARE YOU SAYING THE PIGASUS ISN'T REAL?
UH—
I'M SURE, IF THE PIGASUS DOES EXIST, IT WOULDN'T WANT Y'ALL TEARIN' UP ITS FOREST!
BUT IF IT DOESN'T EXIST, THEN IT DOESN'T MATTER!
NO! I MEAN, IT DOES! I MEAN—I, I CAN'T COMMENT ON WHETHER OR NOT THE PIGASUS IS REAL!
I MEAN, UH, I'VE NEVER SEEN A PIGASUS ON ANY OF MY OTHER TRIPS TO SPLENDOR WOODS!
JUST BECAUSE YOU HAVEN'T SEEN IT DOESN'T MEAN IT DOESN'T EXIST!
ABSENCE OF EVIDENCE IS NOT EVIDENCE OF ABSENCE!
IT BELONGS IN A MUSEUM!

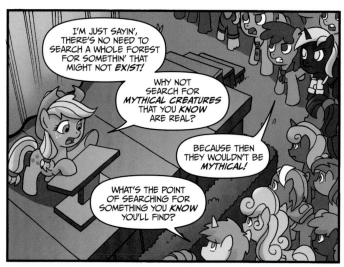

I'M JUST SAYIN', THERE'S NO NEED TO SEARCH A WHOLE FOREST FOR SOMETHIN' THAT MIGHT NOT *EXIST*!

WHY NOT SEARCH FOR *MYTHICAL CREATURES* THAT YOU *KNOW* ARE REAL?

BECAUSE THEN THEY WOULDN'T BE *MYTHICAL*!

WHAT'S THE POINT OF SEARCHING FOR SOMETHING YOU *KNOW* YOU'LL FIND?

BUT—ER—THAT IS TO SAY, UH—

I SURE DON'T *SEE* ANY PIGASUS AROUND HERE RIGHT *NOW*!

SO, UH...

OH, NO...

...THIS ISN'T WORKING WELL AT *ALL*.

I *KNEW* THIS WOULD BE HARD FOR HER!

APPLEJACK TRYING TO *LIE* IS LIKE A *PIG* TRYING TO *FLY*!

OH, UM—

ANY *OTHER* PIG, I MEAN.

SNERK?

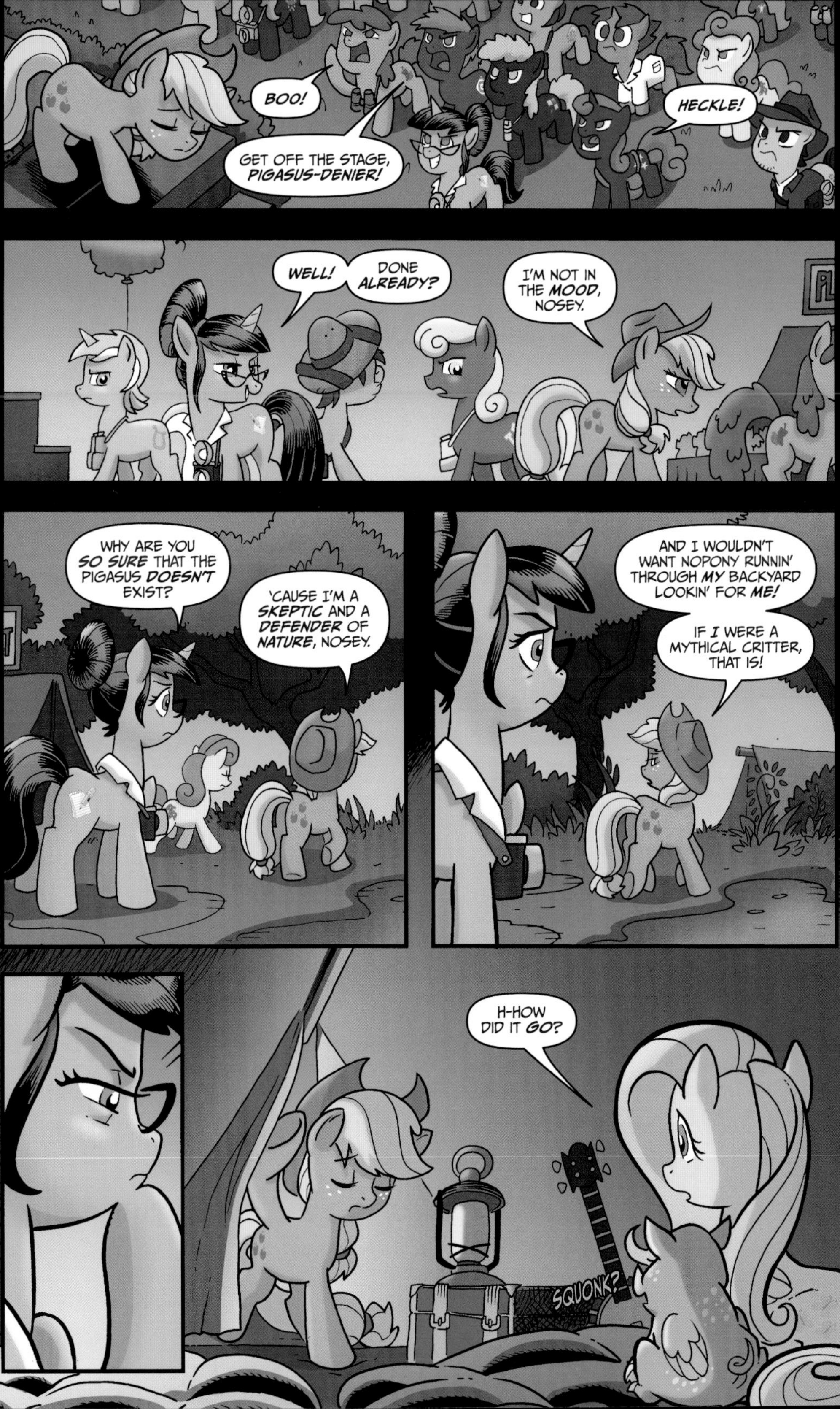
BOO!
GET OFF THE STAGE, PIGASUS-DENIER!
HECKLE!
WELL!
DONE ALREADY?
I'M NOT IN THE MOOD, NOSEY.
WHY ARE YOU SO SURE THAT THE PIGASUS DOESN'T EXIST?
'CAUSE I'M A SKEPTIC AND A DEFENDER OF NATURE, NOSEY.
AND I WOULDN'T WANT NOPONY RUNNIN' THROUGH MY BACKYARD LOOKIN' FOR ME!
IF I WERE A MYTHICAL CRITTER, THAT IS!
H-HOW DID IT GO?
SQUONK?

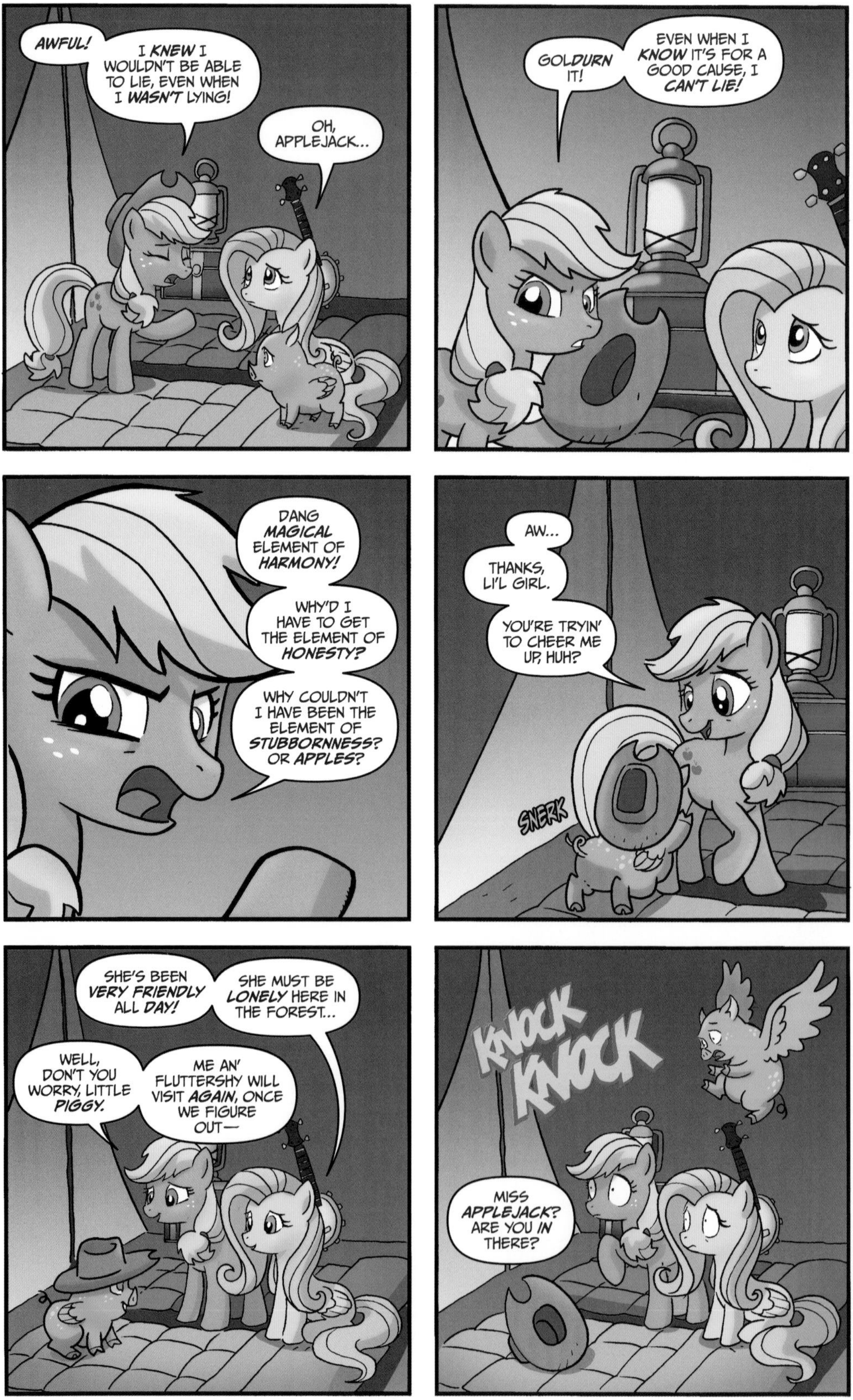

AWFUL!
I KNEW I WOULDN'T BE ABLE TO LIE, EVEN WHEN I WASN'T LYING!
OH, APPLEJACK...
GOLDURN IT!
EVEN WHEN I KNOW IT'S FOR A GOOD CAUSE, I CAN'T LIE!
DANG MAGICAL ELEMENT OF HARMONY!
WHY'D I HAVE TO GET THE ELEMENT OF HONESTY?
WHY COULDN'T I HAVE BEEN THE ELEMENT OF STUBBORNNESS? OR APPLES?
AW...
THANKS, LI'L GIRL.
YOU'RE TRYIN' TO CHEER ME UP, HUH?
SNERK
SHE'S BEEN VERY FRIENDLY ALL DAY!
SHE MUST BE LONELY HERE IN THE FOREST...
WELL, DON'T YOU WORRY, LITTLE PIGGY.
ME AN' FLUTTERSHY WILL VISIT AGAIN, ONCE WE FIGURE OUT—
KNOCK KNOCK
MISS APPLEJACK? ARE YOU IN THERE?

IT'S *NOSEY!*

DID SHE *HEAR US?*

I DON'T KNOW!

HOW DID SHE *KNOCK* ON THE *TENT?*

I DON'T KNOW!

YOU RAN OFF SO *SUDDENLY* AFTER YOUR, UH, *SPEECH...*

WOULD YOU CARE TO *CLARIFY* YOUR *REMARKS?*

QUICK! HERE!

KEEP HER *QUIET!*

UH, *HELLO!* CASUAL HELLO, Y'ALL!

WHAT CAN I *HELP* YOU WITH?

WELL, SOME OF US WERE *CURIOUS* AS TO YOUR *QUALIFICATIONS.*

HOW DO YOU KNOW SO MUCH ABOUT *LEGENDARY CREATURES?*

UH...

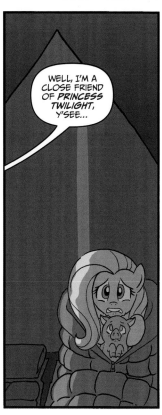

WELL, I'M A *CLOSE FRIEND* OF *PRINCESS TWILIGHT,* Y'SEE...

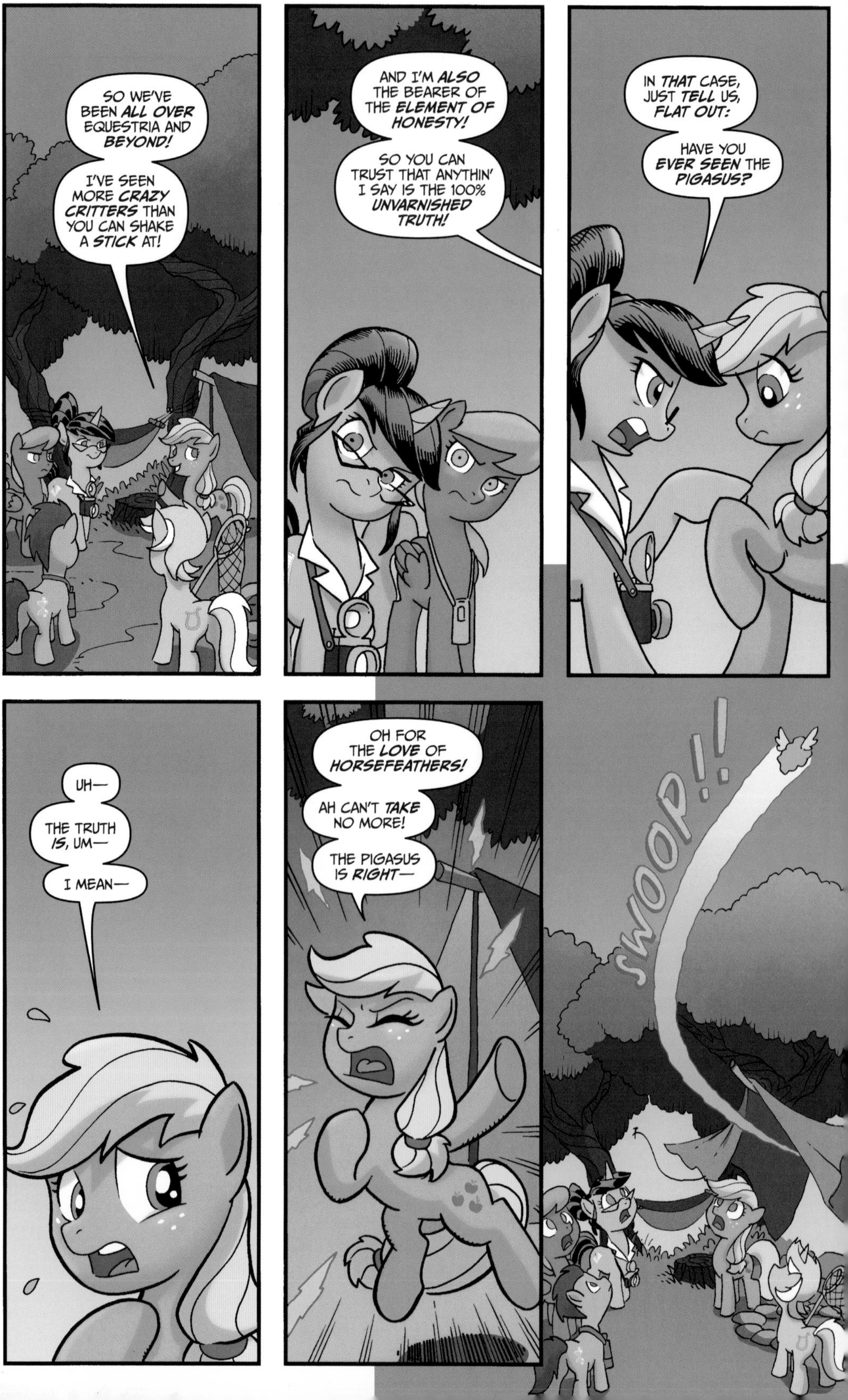

SO WE'VE BEEN ALL OVER EQUESTRIA AND BEYOND!
I'VE SEEN MORE CRAZY CRITTERS THAN YOU CAN SHAKE A STICK AT!
AND I'M ALSO THE BEARER OF THE ELEMENT OF HONESTY!
SO YOU CAN TRUST THAT ANYTHIN' I SAY IS THE 100% UNVARNISHED TRUTH!
IN THAT CASE, JUST TELL US, FLAT OUT:
HAVE YOU EVER SEEN THE PIGASUS?
UH—
THE TRUTH IS, UM—
I MEAN—
OH FOR THE LOVE OF HORSEFEATHERS!
AH CAN'T TAKE NO MORE!
THE PIGASUS IS RIGHT—
SWOOP!!

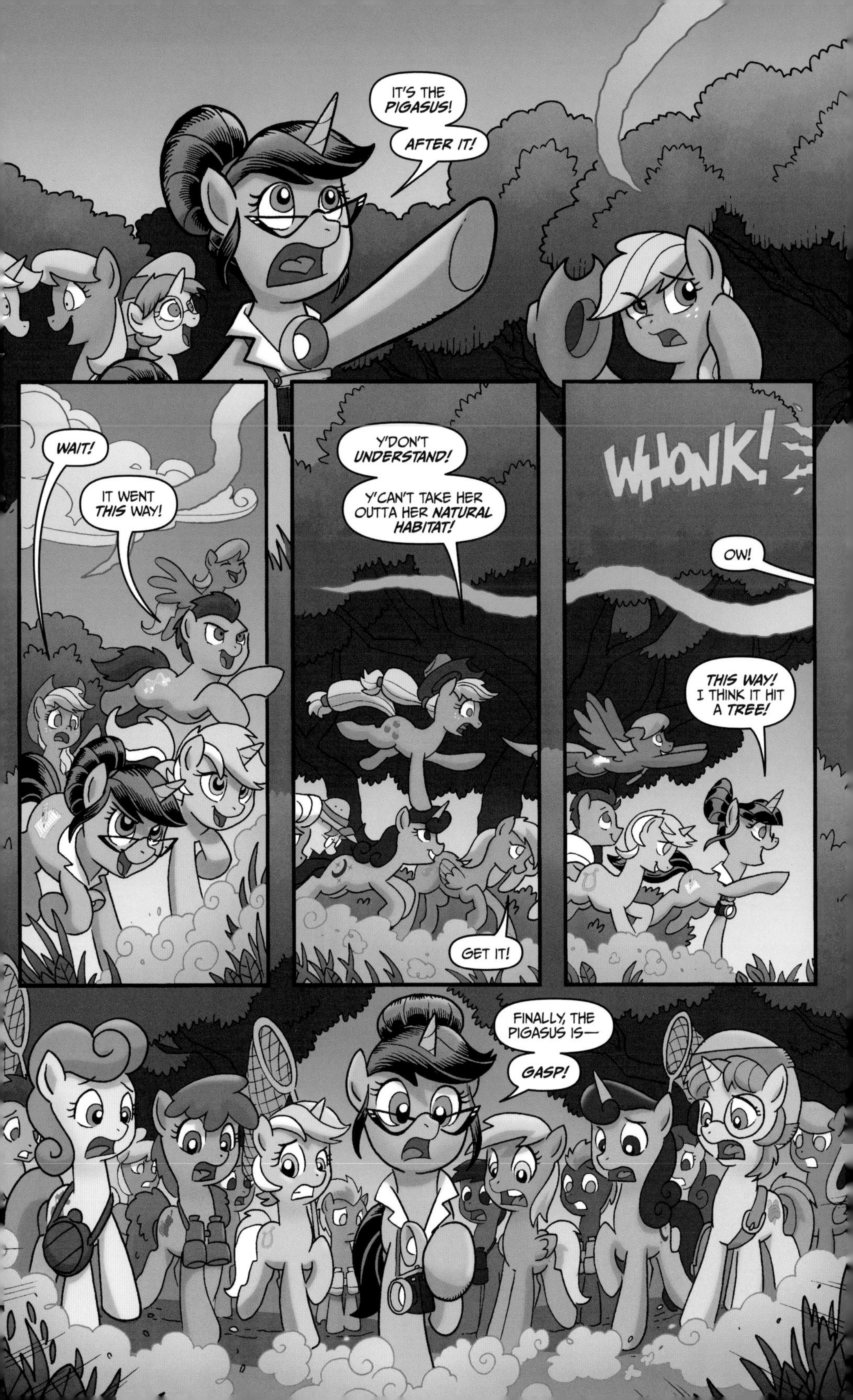
IT'S THE PIGASUS!
AFTER IT!
WAIT!
IT WENT THIS WAY!
Y'DON'T UNDERSTAND!
Y'CAN'T TAKE HER OUTTA HER NATURAL HABITAT!
GET IT!
WHONK!
OW!
THIS WAY! I THINK IT HIT A TREE!
FINALLY, THE PIGASUS IS—
GASP!

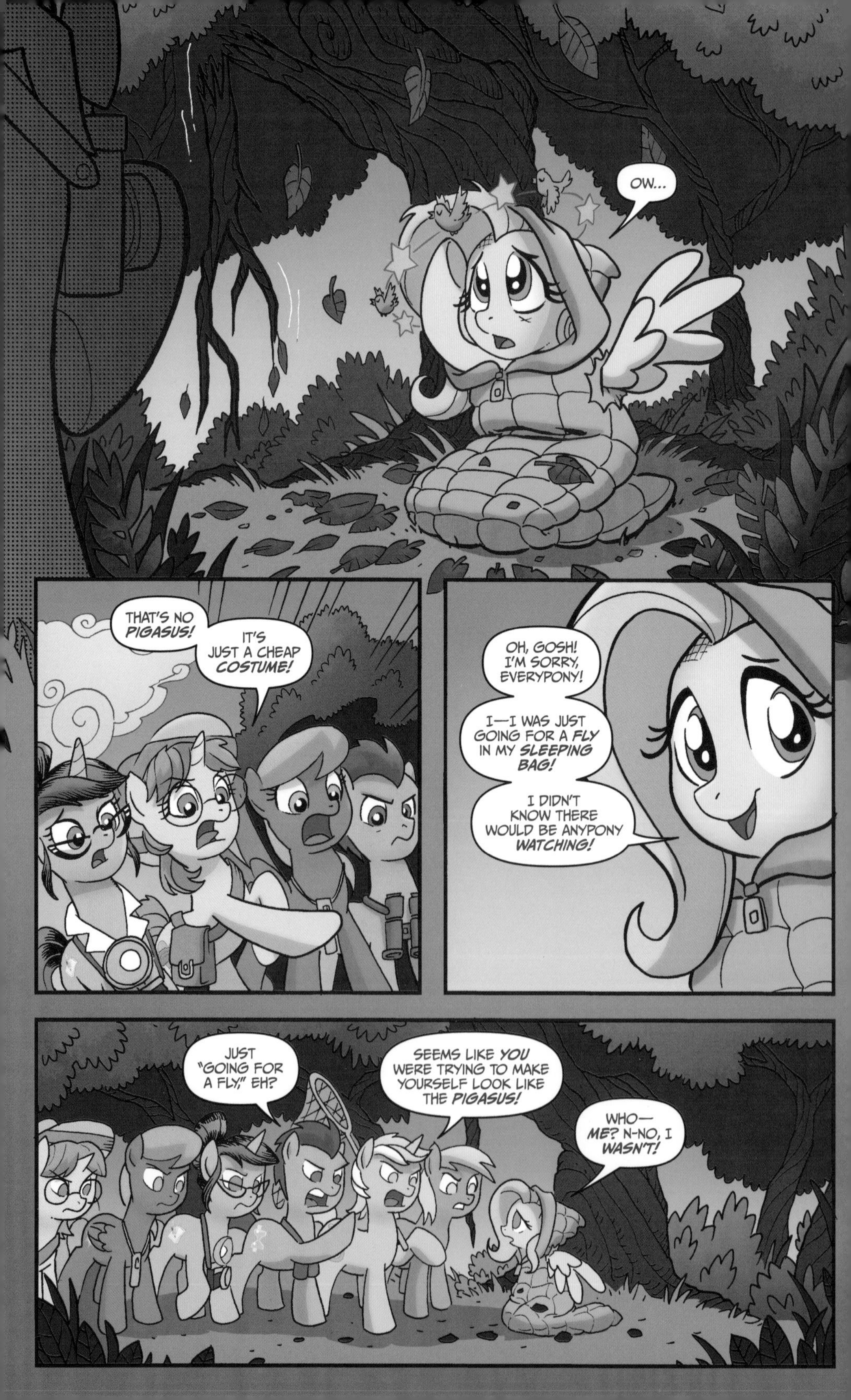
OW...
THAT'S NO PIGASUS!
IT'S JUST A CHEAP COSTUME!
OH, GOSH! I'M SORRY, EVERYPONY!
I—I WAS JUST GOING FOR A FLY IN MY SLEEPING BAG!
I DIDN'T KNOW THERE WOULD BE ANYPONY WATCHING!
JUST "GOING FOR A FLY," EH?
SEEMS LIKE YOU WERE TRYING TO MAKE YOURSELF LOOK LIKE THE PIGASUS!
WHO— ME? N-NO, I WASN'T!

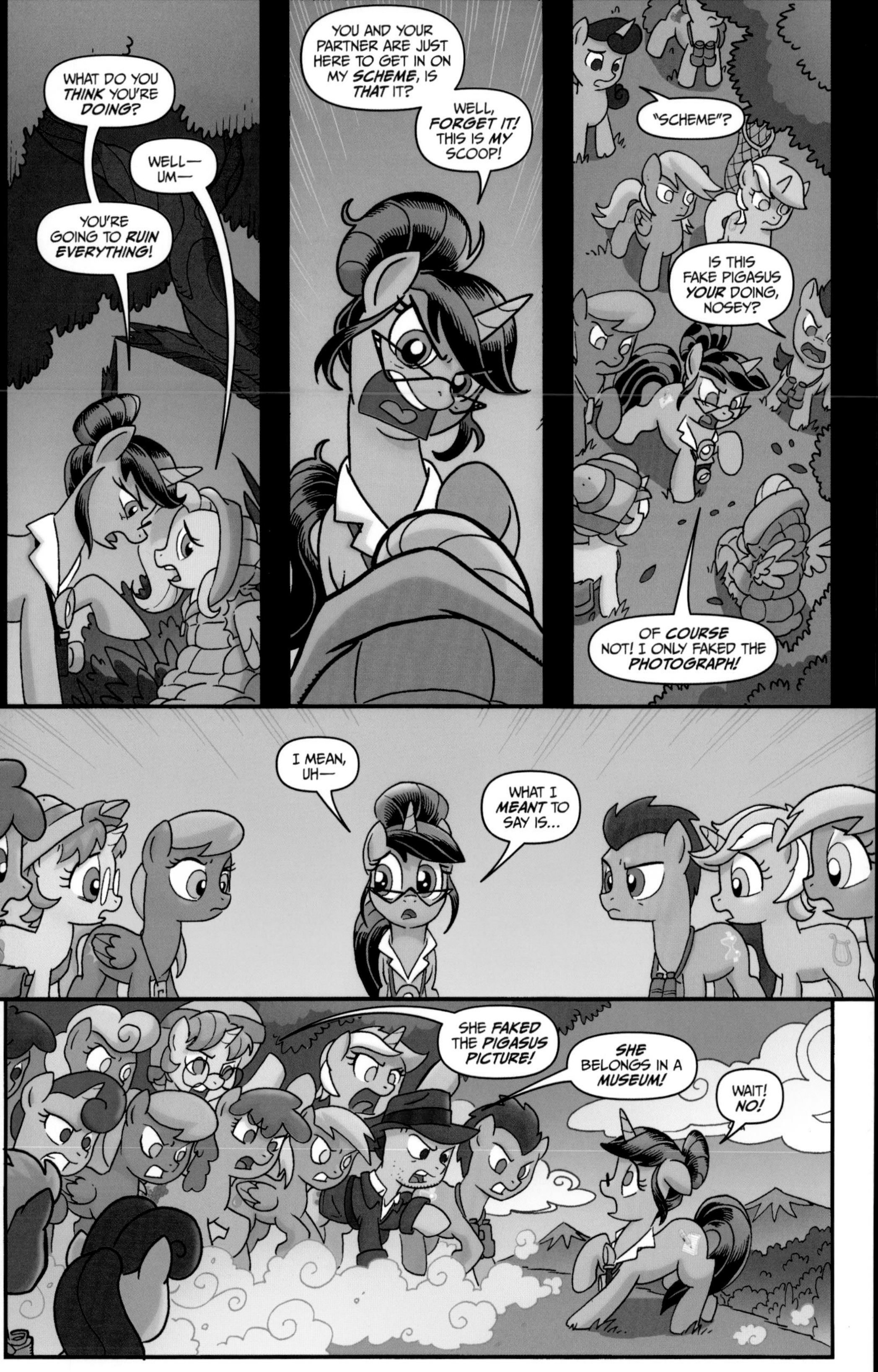

WHAT DO YOU THINK YOU'RE DOING?
WELL— UM—
YOU'RE GOING TO RUIN EVERYTHING!
YOU AND YOUR PARTNER ARE JUST HERE TO GET IN ON MY SCHEME, IS THAT IT?
WELL, FORGET IT! THIS IS MY SCOOP!
"SCHEME"?
IS THIS FAKE PIGASUS YOUR DOING, NOSEY?
OF COURSE NOT! I ONLY FAKED THE PHOTOGRAPH!
I MEAN, UH—
WHAT I MEANT TO SAY IS...
SHE FAKED THE PIGASUS PICTURE!
SHE BELONGS IN A MUSEUM!
WAIT! NO!

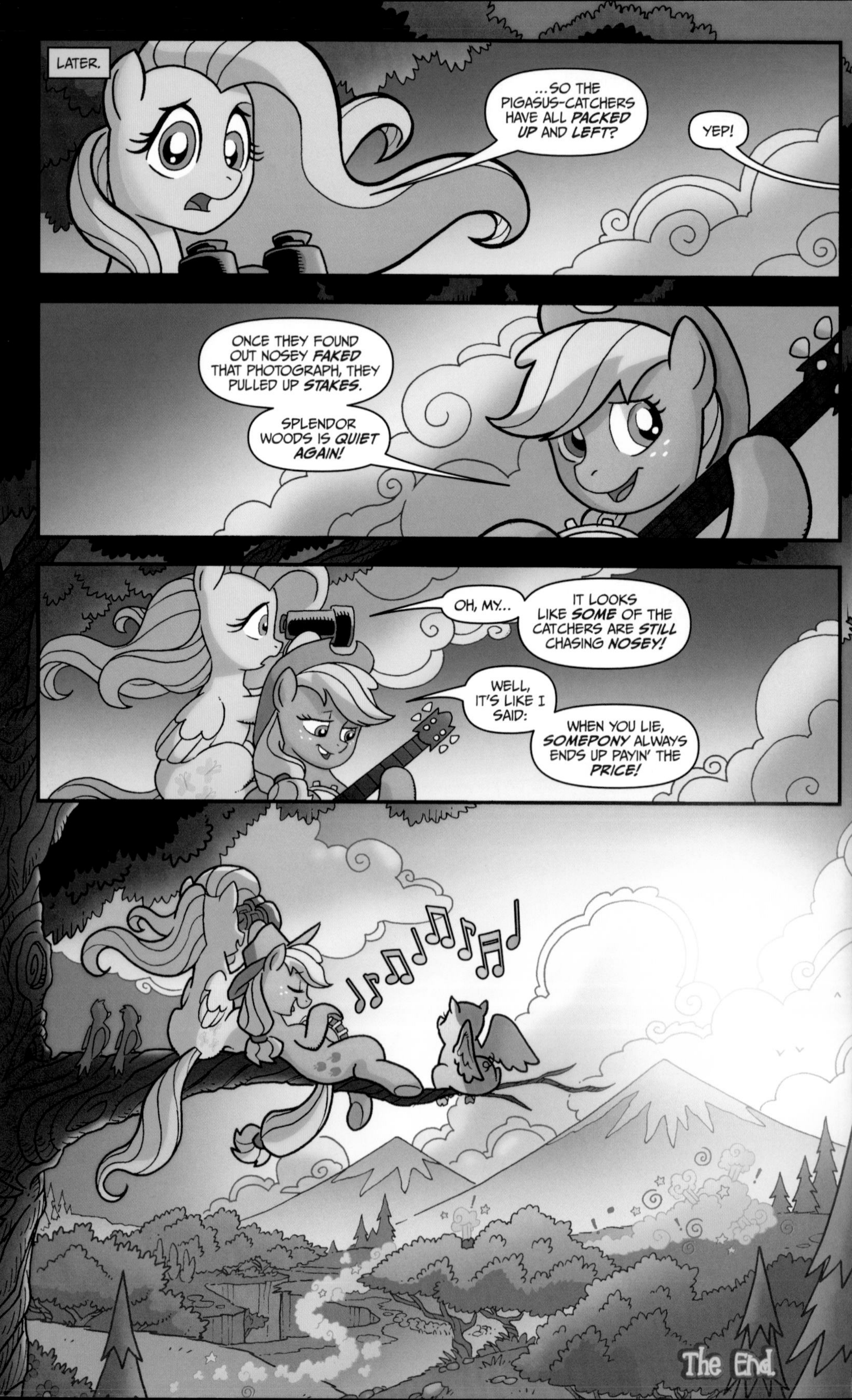
LATER.
...SO THE PIGASUS-CATCHERS HAVE ALL PACKED UP AND LEFT?
YEP!
ONCE THEY FOUND OUT NOSEY FAKED THAT PHOTOGRAPH, THEY PULLED UP STAKES.
SPLENDOR WOODS IS QUIET AGAIN!
OH, MY...
IT LOOKS LIKE SOME OF THE CATCHERS ARE STILL CHASING NOSEY!
WELL, IT'S LIKE I SAID:
WHEN YOU LIE, SOMEPONY ALWAYS ENDS UP PAYIN' THE PRICE!
The End.

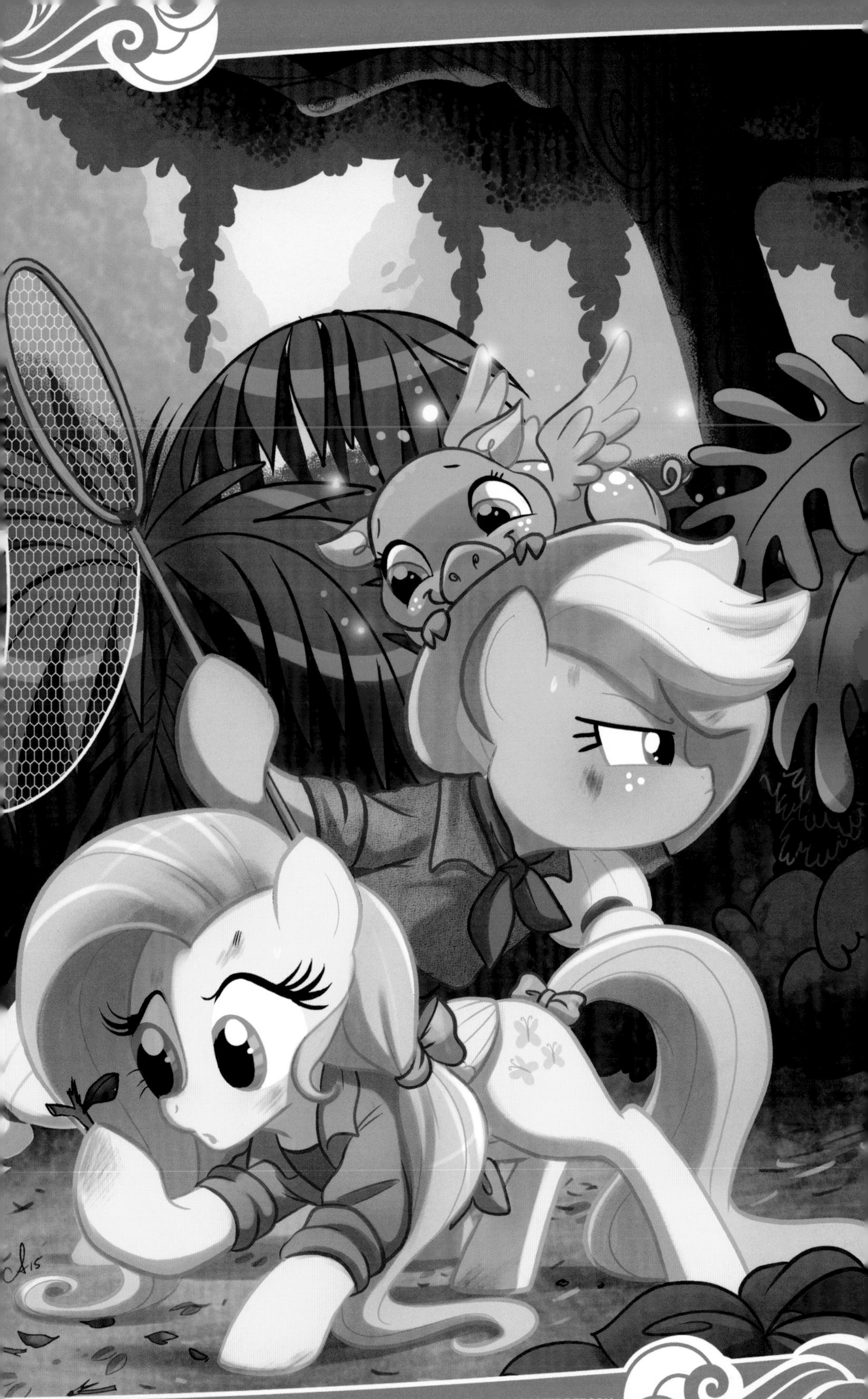

art by AMY MEBBERSON

Rarity & Gilda

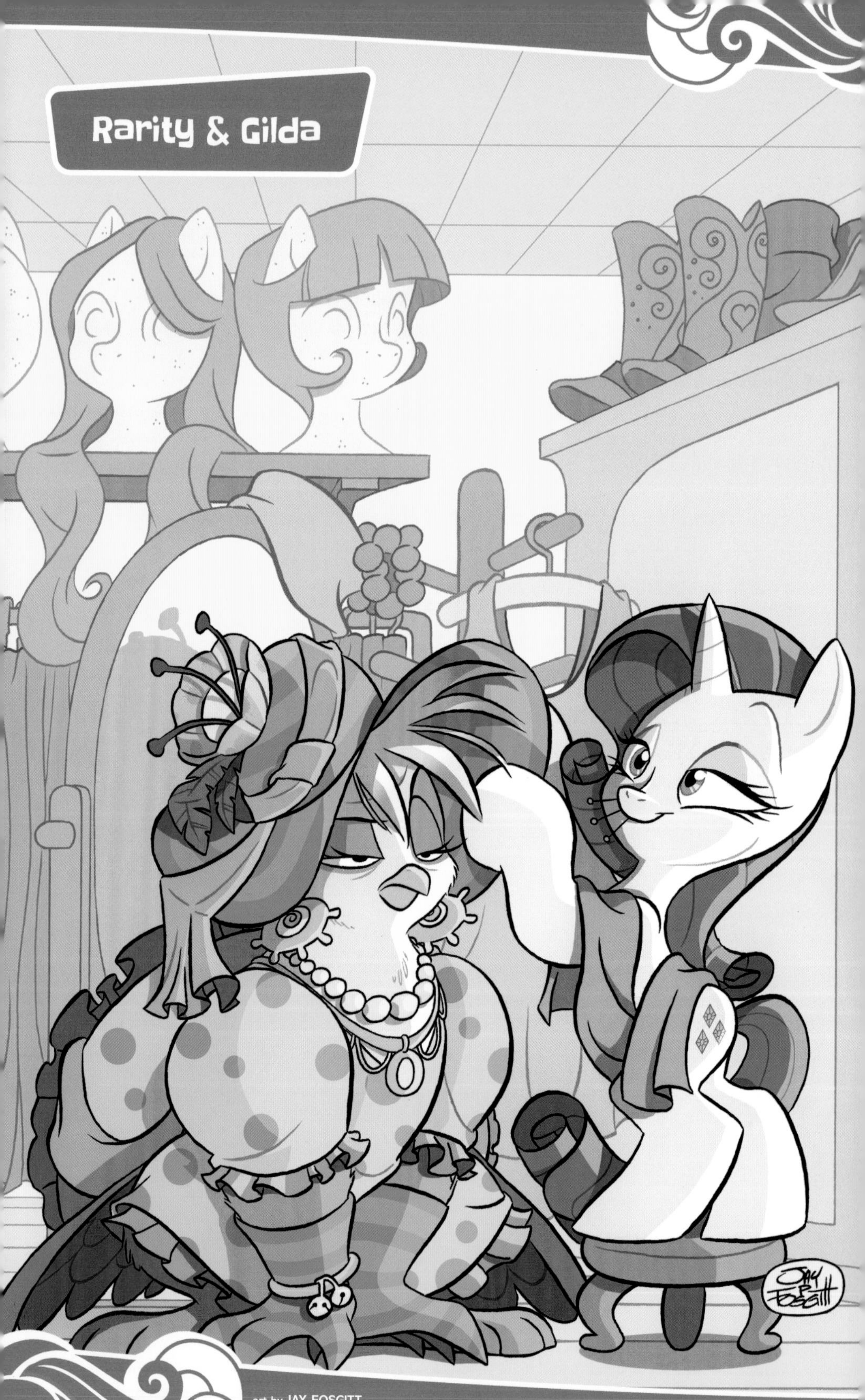

art by JAY FOSGITT

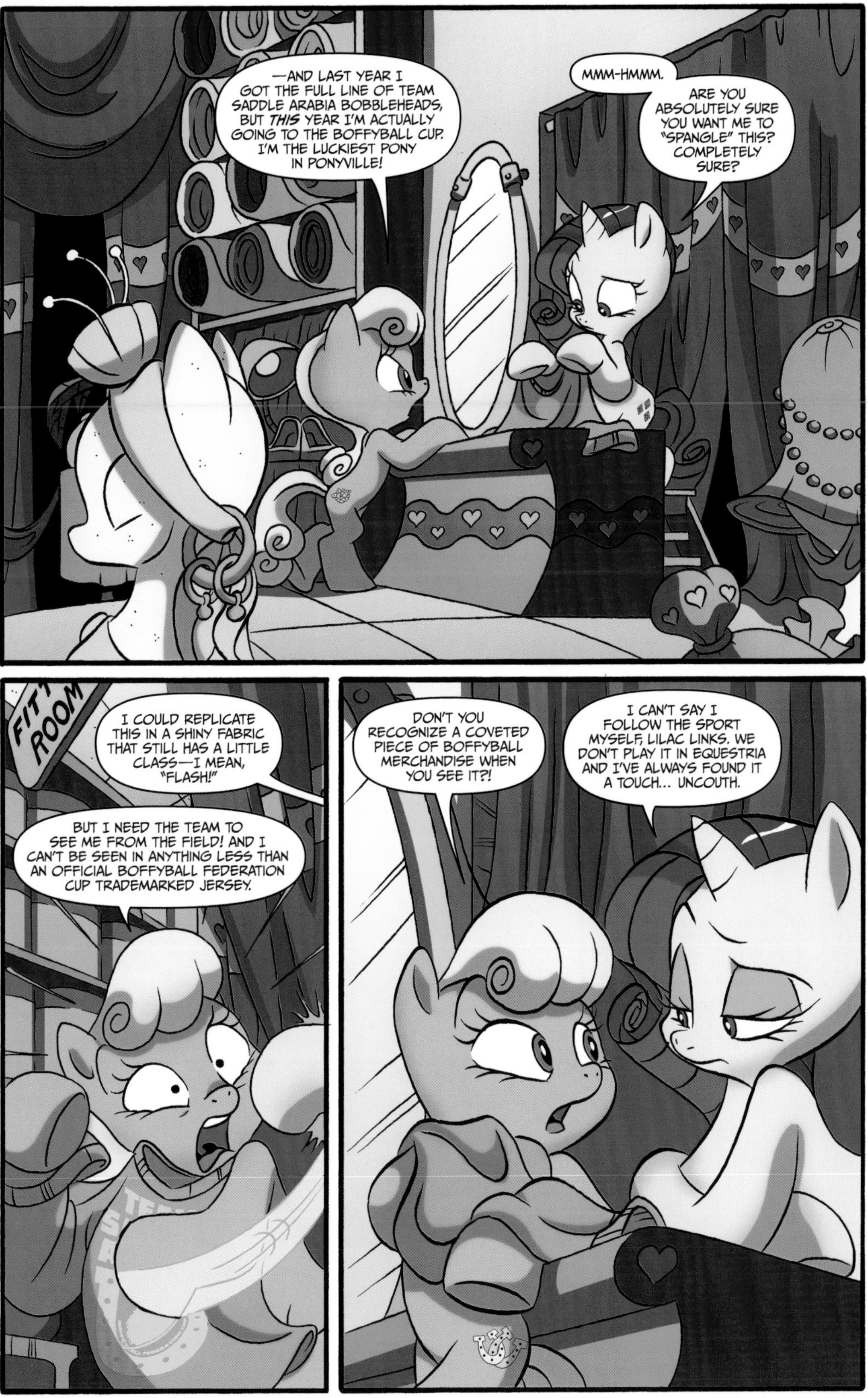
—AND LAST YEAR I GOT THE FULL LINE OF TEAM SADDLE ARABIA BOBBLEHEADS, BUT *THIS* YEAR I'M ACTUALLY GOING TO THE BOFFYBALL CUP. I'M THE LUCKIEST PONY IN PONYVILLE!
MMM-HMMM.
ARE YOU ABSOLUTELY SURE YOU WANT ME TO "SPANGLE" THIS? COMPLETELY SURE?
I COULD REPLICATE THIS IN A SHINY FABRIC THAT STILL HAS A LITTLE CLASS—I MEAN, "FLASH!"
BUT I NEED THE TEAM TO SEE ME FROM THE FIELD! AND I CAN'T BE SEEN IN ANYTHING LESS THAN AN OFFICIAL BOFFYBALL FEDERATION CUP TRADEMARKED JERSEY.
DON'T YOU RECOGNIZE A COVETED PIECE OF BOFFYBALL MERCHANDISE WHEN YOU SEE IT?!
I CAN'T SAY I FOLLOW THE SPORT MYSELF, LILAC LINKS. WE DON'T PLAY IT IN EQUESTRIA AND I'VE ALWAYS FOUND IT A TOUCH... UNCOUTH.

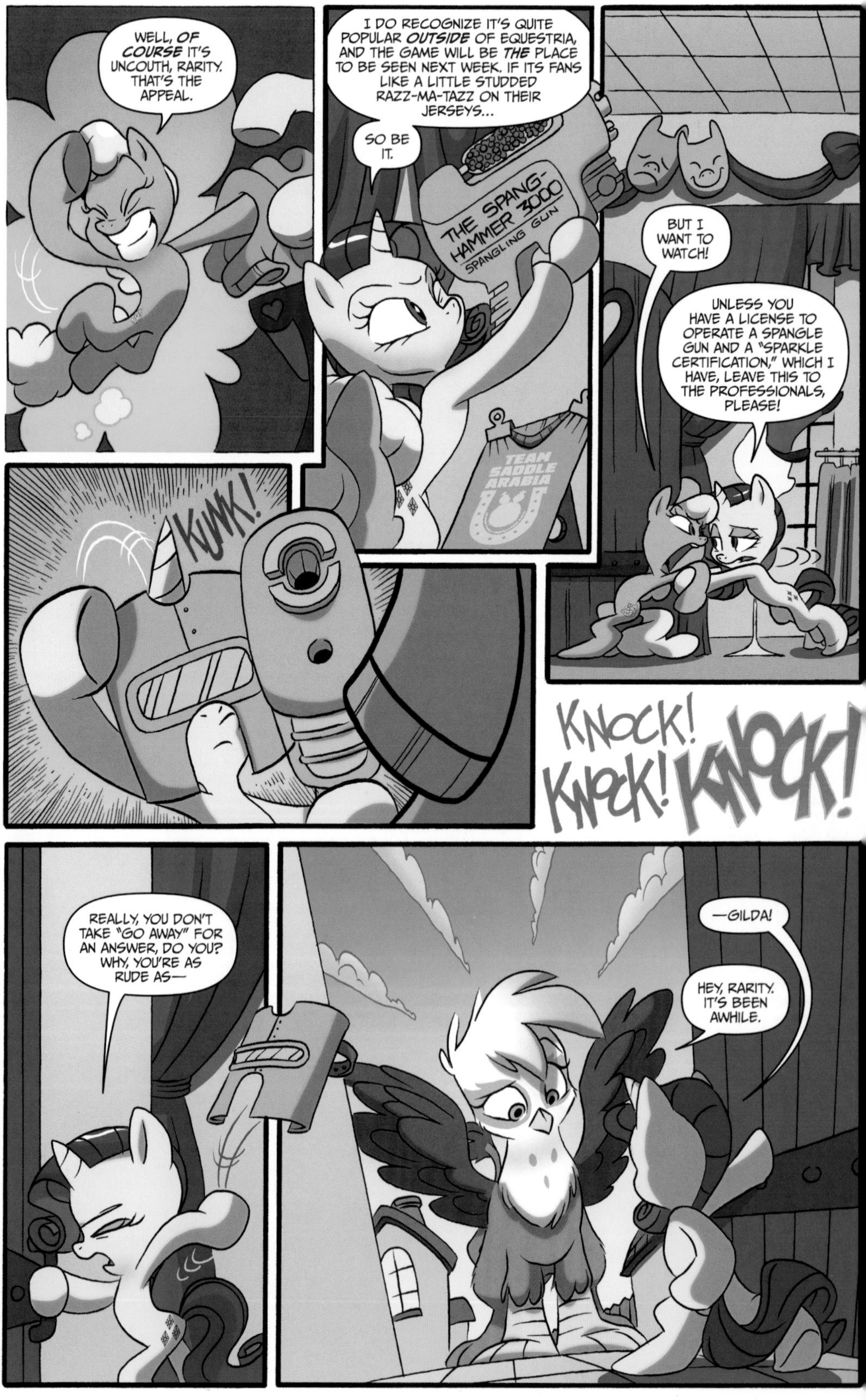
WELL, OF COURSE IT'S UNCOUTH, RARITY. THAT'S THE APPEAL.
I DO RECOGNIZE IT'S QUITE POPULAR OUTSIDE OF EQUESTRIA, AND THE GAME WILL BE THE PLACE TO BE SEEN NEXT WEEK. IF ITS FANS LIKE A LITTLE STUDDED RAZZ-MA-TAZZ ON THEIR JERSEYS...
SO BE IT.
THE SPANG-HAMMER 3000
SPANGLING GUN
TEAM SADDLE ARABIA
BUT I WANT TO WATCH!
UNLESS YOU HAVE A LICENSE TO OPERATE A SPANGLE GUN AND A "SPARKLE CERTIFICATION," WHICH I HAVE, LEAVE THIS TO THE PROFESSIONALS, PLEASE!
KUNK!
KNOCK! KNOCK! KNOCK!
REALLY, YOU DON'T TAKE "GO AWAY" FOR AN ANSWER, DO YOU? WHY, YOU'RE AS RUDE AS—
—GILDA!
HEY, RARITY. IT'S BEEN AWHILE.

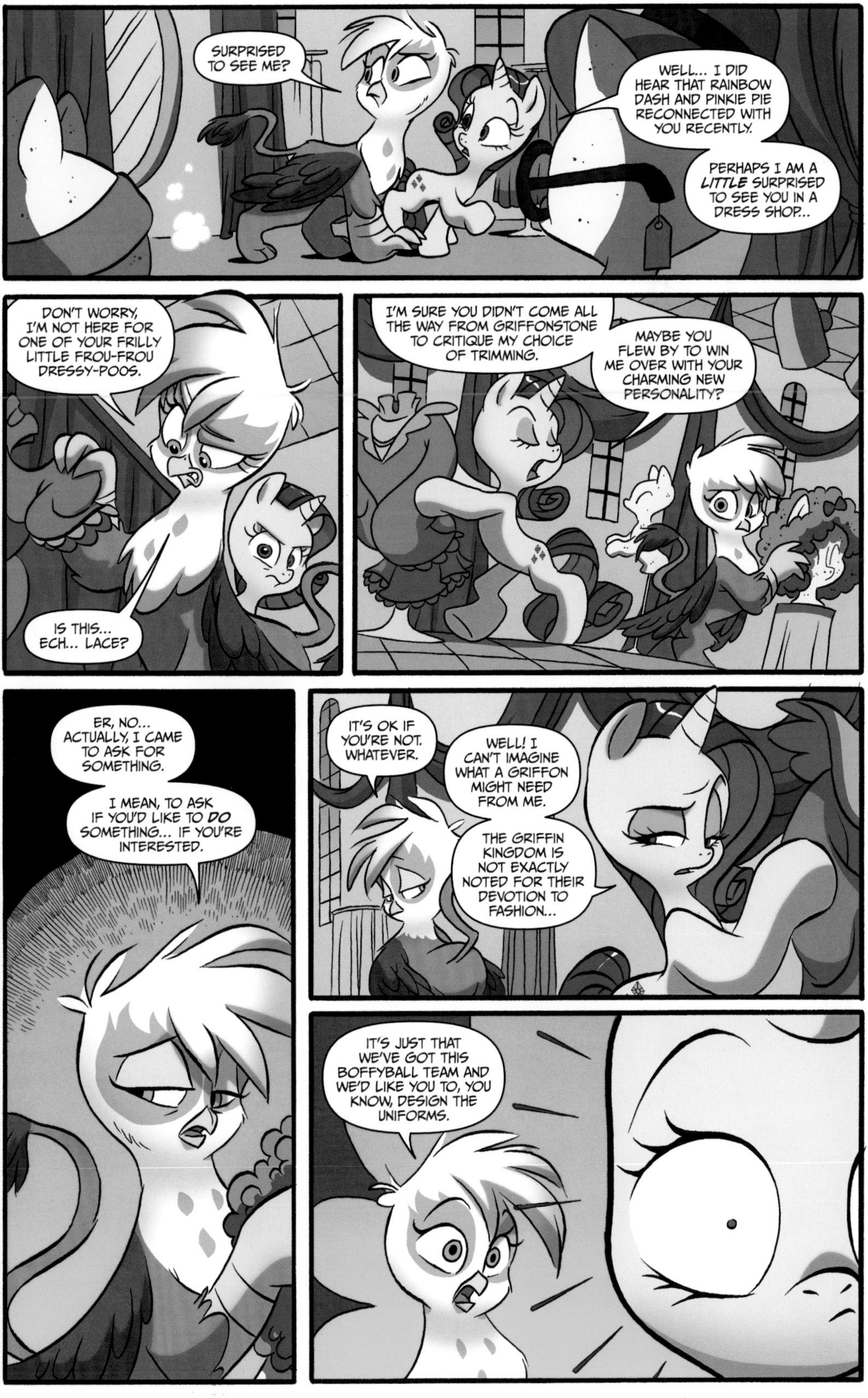

SURPRISED TO SEE ME?
WELL... I DID HEAR THAT RAINBOW DASH AND PINKIE PIE RECONNECTED WITH YOU RECENTLY.
PERHAPS I AM A *LITTLE* SURPRISED TO SEE YOU IN A DRESS SHOP...
DON'T WORRY, I'M NOT HERE FOR ONE OF YOUR FRILLY LITTLE FROU-FROU DRESSY-POOS.
IS THIS... ECH... LACE?
I'M SURE YOU DIDN'T COME ALL THE WAY FROM GRIFFONSTONE TO CRITIQUE MY CHOICE OF TRIMMING.
MAYBE YOU FLEW BY TO WIN ME OVER WITH YOUR CHARMING NEW PERSONALITY?
ER, NO... ACTUALLY, I CAME TO ASK FOR SOMETHING.
I MEAN, TO ASK IF YOU'D LIKE TO *DO* SOMETHING... IF YOU'RE INTERESTED.
IT'S OK IF YOU'RE NOT. WHATEVER.
WELL! I CAN'T IMAGINE WHAT A GRIFFON MIGHT NEED FROM ME.
THE GRIFFIN KINGDOM IS NOT EXACTLY NOTED FOR THEIR DEVOTION TO FASHION...
IT'S JUST THAT WE'VE GOT THIS BOFFYBALL TEAM AND WE'D LIKE YOU TO, YOU KNOW, DESIGN THE UNIFORMS.

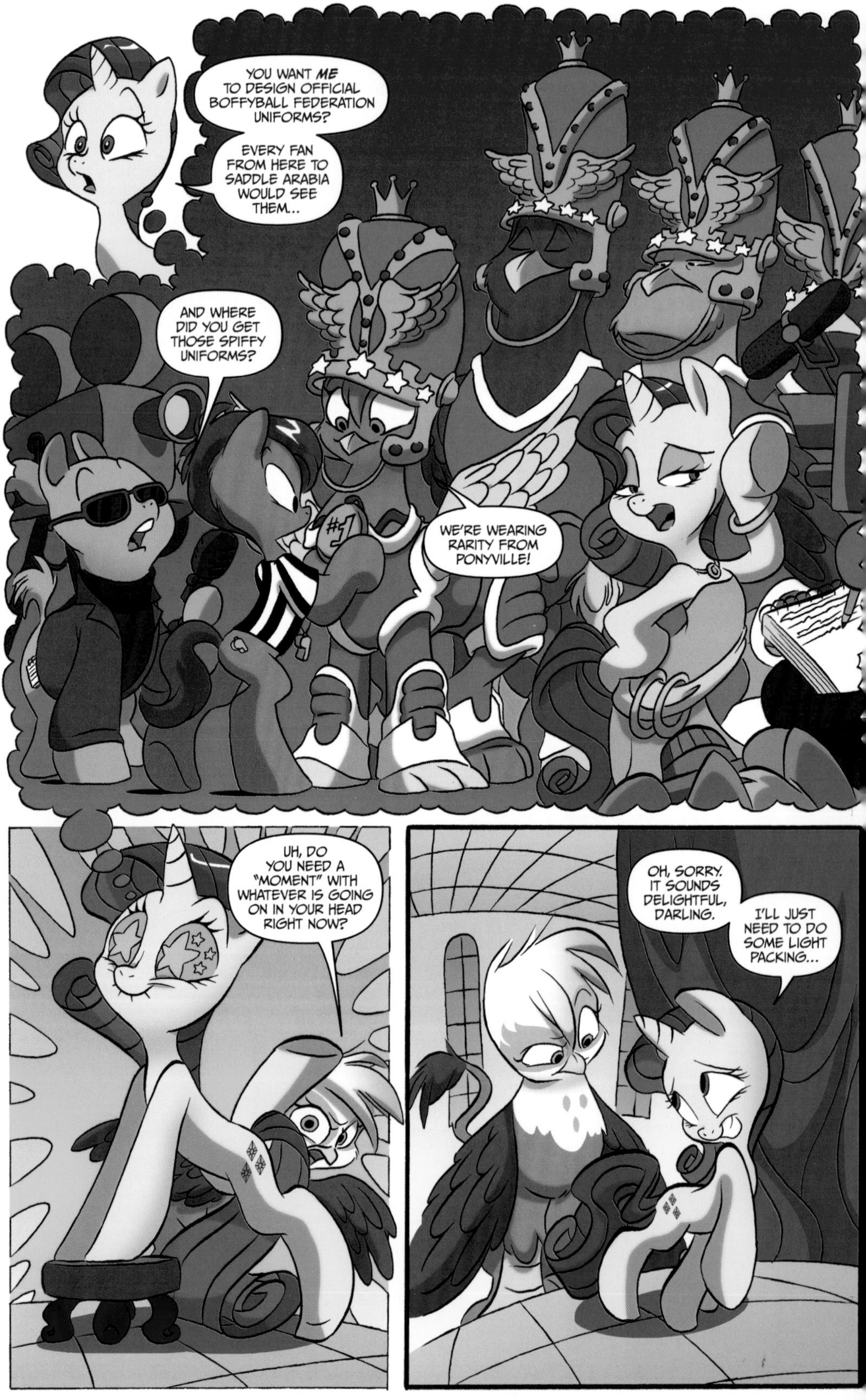
YOU WANT *ME* TO DESIGN OFFICIAL BOFFYBALL FEDERATION UNIFORMS?
EVERY FAN FROM HERE TO SADDLE ARABIA WOULD SEE THEM...
AND WHERE DID YOU GET THOSE SPIFFY UNIFORMS?
WE'RE WEARING RARITY FROM PONYVILLE!
UH, DO YOU NEED A "MOMENT" WITH WHATEVER IS GOING ON IN YOUR HEAD RIGHT NOW?
OH, SORRY. IT SOUNDS DELIGHTFUL, DARLING.
I'LL JUST NEED TO DO SOME LIGHT PACKING...

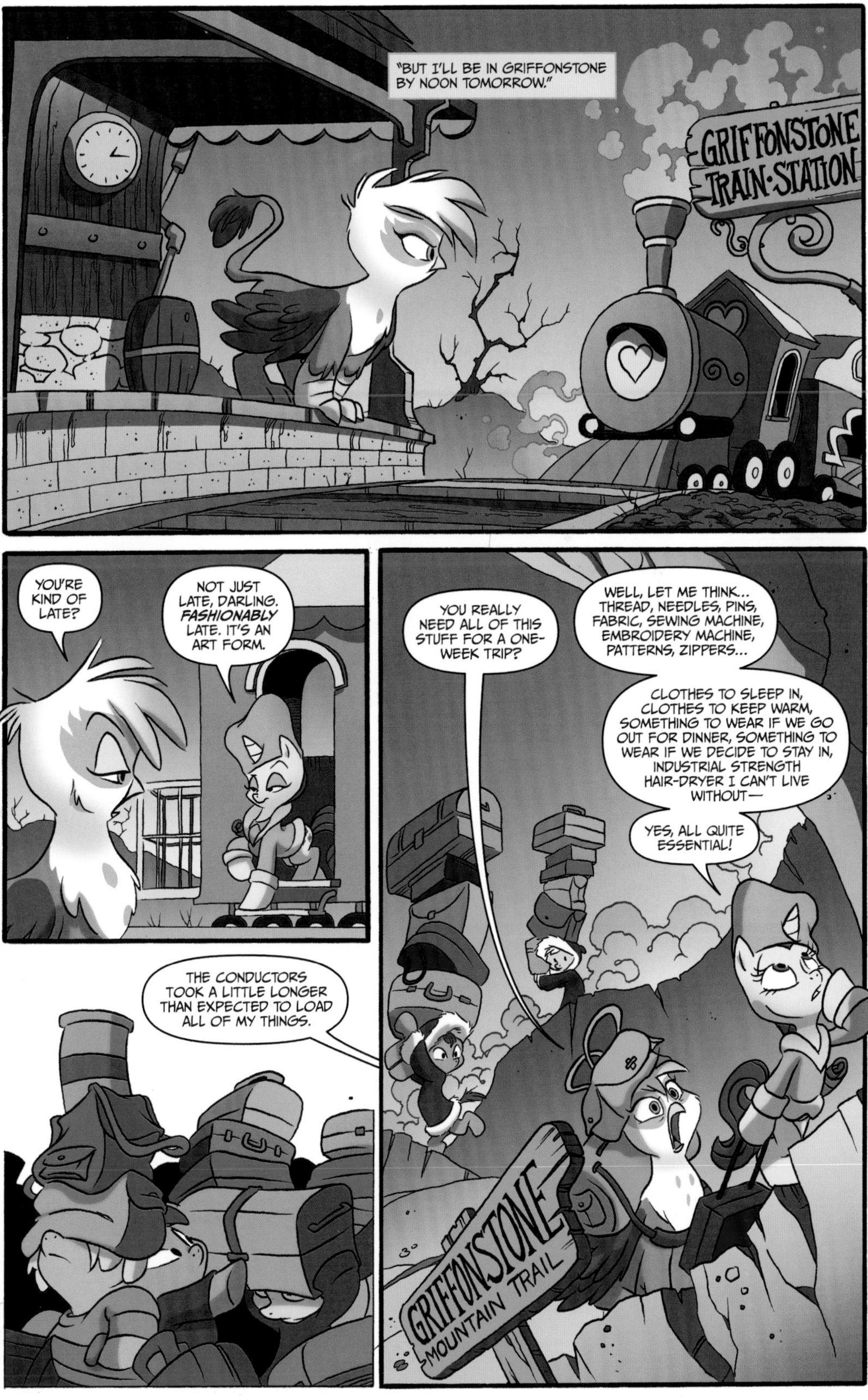
"BUT I'LL BE IN GRIFFONSTONE BY NOON TOMORROW."
GRIFFONSTONE TRAIN·STATION
YOU'RE KIND OF LATE?
NOT JUST LATE, DARLING. *FASHIONABLY* LATE. IT'S AN ART FORM.
THE CONDUCTORS TOOK A LITTLE LONGER THAN EXPECTED TO LOAD ALL OF MY THINGS.
YOU REALLY NEED ALL OF THIS STUFF FOR A ONE-WEEK TRIP?
WELL, LET ME THINK... THREAD, NEEDLES, PINS, FABRIC, SEWING MACHINE, EMBROIDERY MACHINE, PATTERNS, ZIPPERS...
CLOTHES TO SLEEP IN, CLOTHES TO KEEP WARM, SOMETHING TO WEAR IF WE GO OUT FOR DINNER, SOMETHING TO WEAR IF WE DECIDE TO STAY IN, INDUSTRIAL STRENGTH HAIR-DRYER I CAN'T LIVE WITHOUT—
YES, ALL QUITE ESSENTIAL!
GRIFFONSTONE MOUNTAIN TRAIL

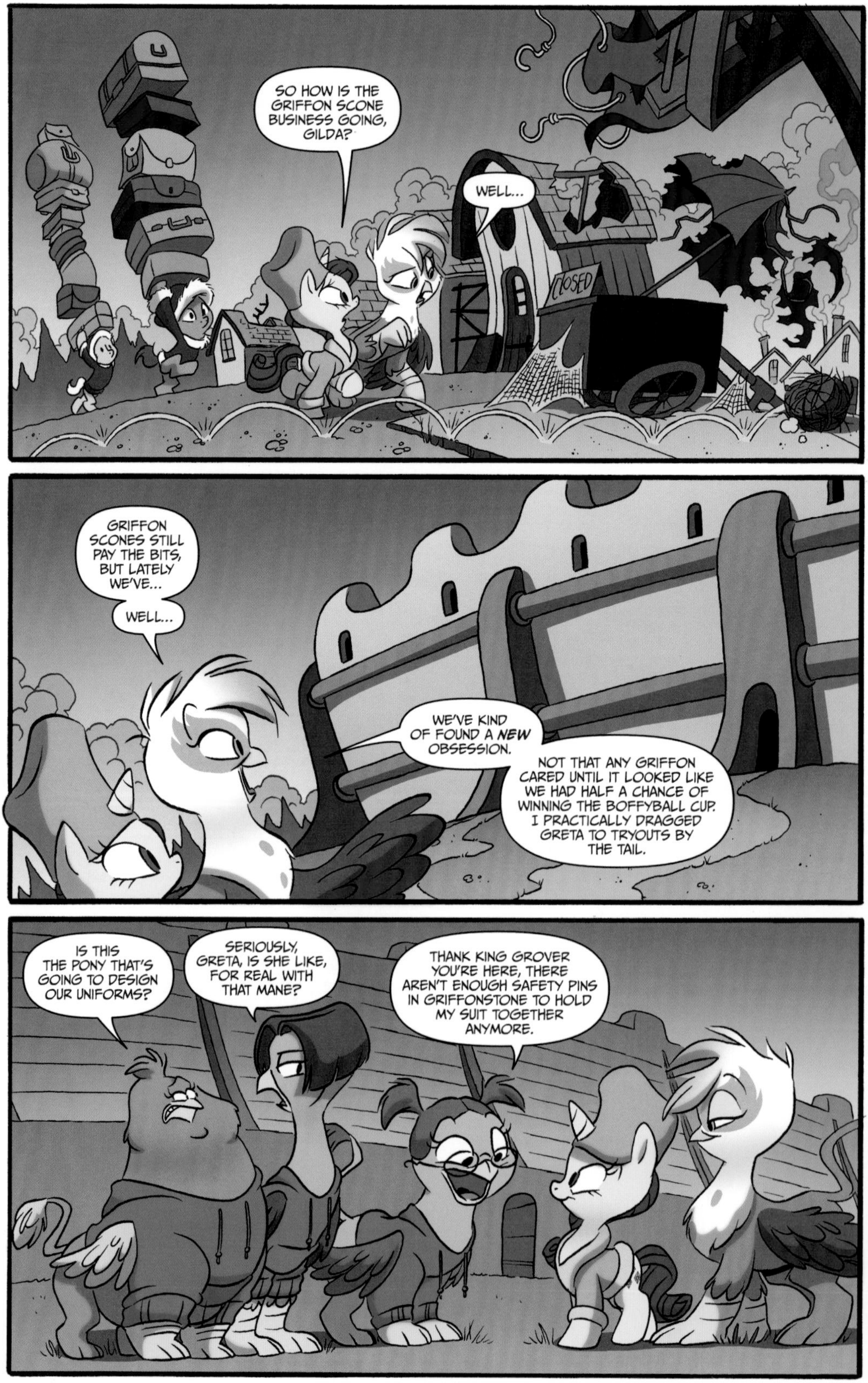
SO HOW IS THE GRIFFON SCONE BUSINESS GOING, GILDA?
WELL...
CLOSED
GRIFFON SCONES STILL PAY THE BITS, BUT LATELY WE'VE...
WELL...
WE'VE KIND OF FOUND A *NEW* OBSESSION.
NOT THAT ANY GRIFFON CARED UNTIL IT LOOKED LIKE WE HAD HALF A CHANCE OF WINNING THE BOFFYBALL CUP. I PRACTICALLY DRAGGED GRETA TO TRYOUTS BY THE TAIL.
IS THIS THE PONY THAT'S GOING TO DESIGN OUR UNIFORMS?
SERIOUSLY, GRETA, IS SHE LIKE, FOR REAL WITH THAT MANE?
THANK KING GROVER YOU'RE HERE, THERE AREN'T ENOUGH SAFETY PINS IN GRIFFONSTONE TO HOLD MY SUIT TOGETHER ANYMORE.

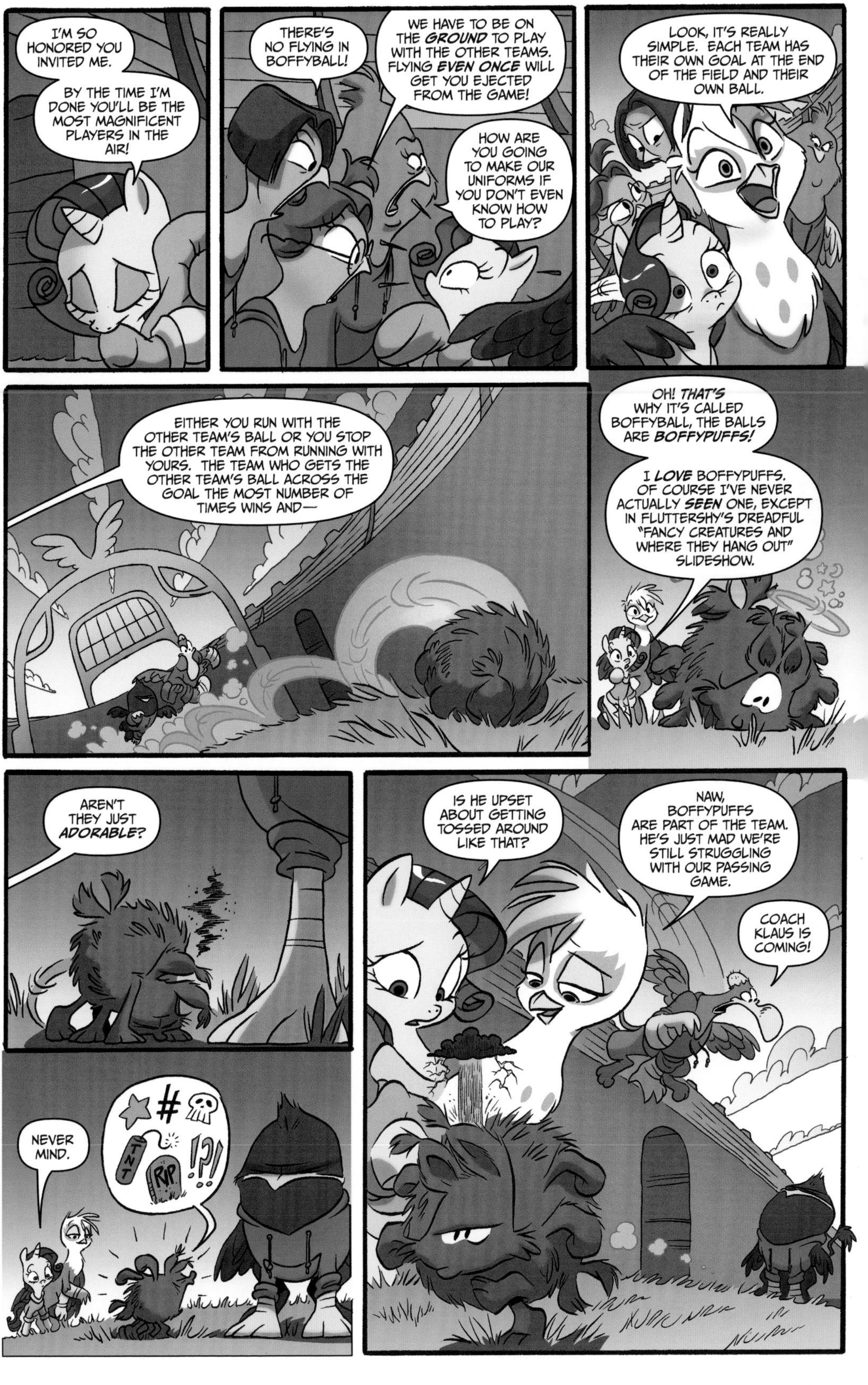

I'M SO HONORED YOU INVITED ME.
BY THE TIME I'M DONE YOU'LL BE THE MOST MAGNIFICENT PLAYERS IN THE AIR!
THERE'S NO FLYING IN BOFFYBALL!
WE HAVE TO BE ON THE GROUND TO PLAY WITH THE OTHER TEAMS. FLYING EVEN ONCE WILL GET YOU EJECTED FROM THE GAME!
HOW ARE YOU GOING TO MAKE OUR UNIFORMS IF YOU DON'T EVEN KNOW HOW TO PLAY?
LOOK, IT'S REALLY SIMPLE. EACH TEAM HAS THEIR OWN GOAL AT THE END OF THE FIELD AND THEIR OWN BALL.
EITHER YOU RUN WITH THE OTHER TEAM'S BALL OR YOU STOP THE OTHER TEAM FROM RUNNING WITH YOURS. THE TEAM WHO GETS THE OTHER TEAM'S BALL ACROSS THE GOAL THE MOST NUMBER OF TIMES WINS AND—
OH! THAT'S WHY IT'S CALLED BOFFYBALL, THE BALLS ARE BOFFYPUFFS!
I LOVE BOFFYPUFFS. OF COURSE I'VE NEVER ACTUALLY SEEN ONE, EXCEPT IN FLUTTERSHY'S DREADFUL "FANCY CREATURES AND WHERE THEY HANG OUT" SLIDESHOW.
AREN'T THEY JUST ADORABLE?
NEVER MIND.
TNT RIP !?!
IS HE UPSET ABOUT GETTING TOSSED AROUND LIKE THAT?
NAW, BOFFYPUFFS ARE PART OF THE TEAM. HE'S JUST MAD WE'RE STILL STRUGGLING WITH OUR PASSING GAME.
COACH KLAUS IS COMING!

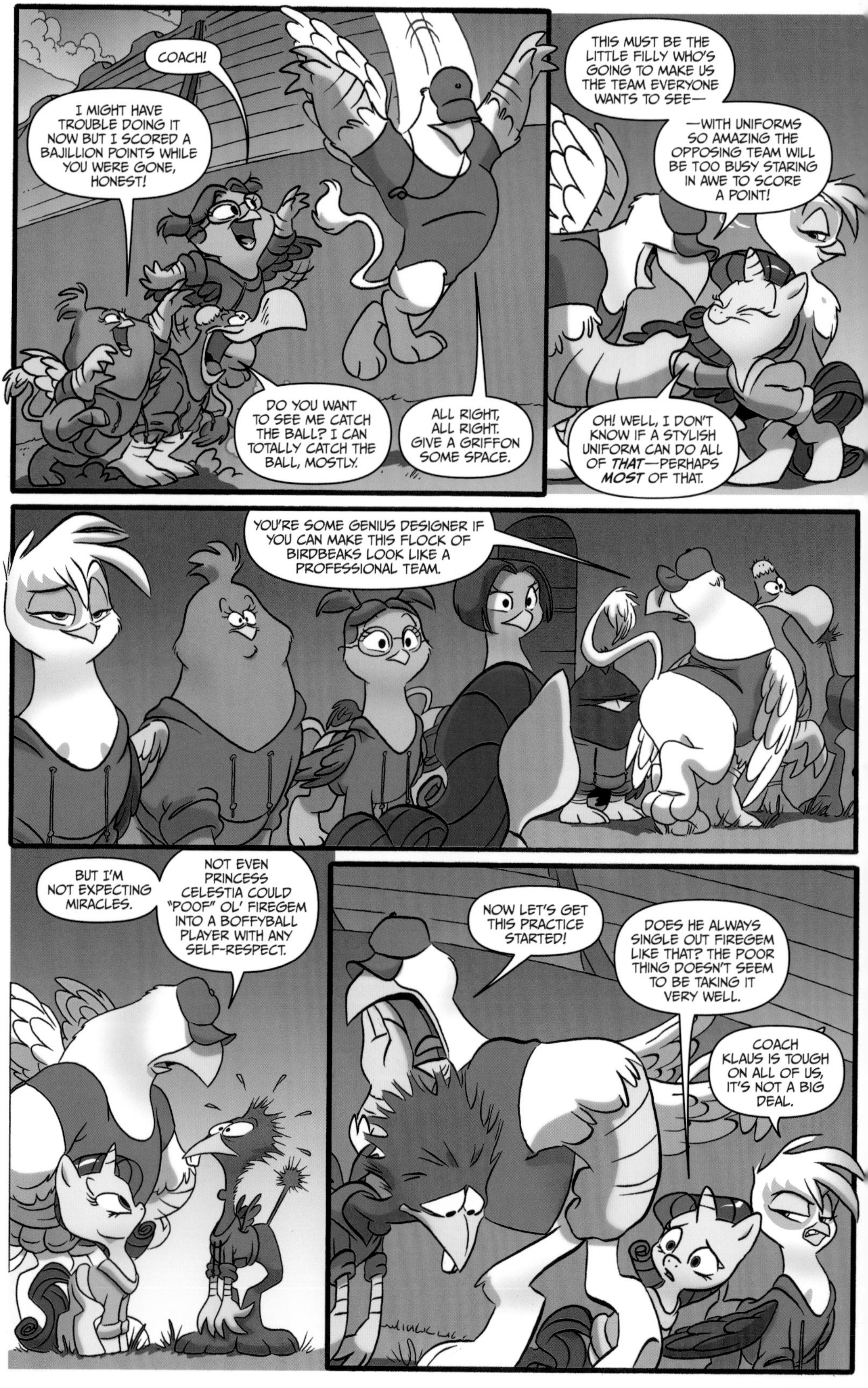
COACH!
I MIGHT HAVE TROUBLE DOING IT NOW BUT I SCORED A BAJILLION POINTS WHILE YOU WERE GONE, HONEST!
DO YOU WANT TO SEE ME CATCH THE BALL? I CAN TOTALLY CATCH THE BALL, MOSTLY.
ALL RIGHT, ALL RIGHT. GIVE A GRIFFON SOME SPACE.
THIS MUST BE THE LITTLE FILLY WHO'S GOING TO MAKE US THE TEAM EVERYONE WANTS TO SEE—
—WITH UNIFORMS SO AMAZING THE OPPOSING TEAM WILL BE TOO BUSY STARING IN AWE TO SCORE A POINT!
OH! WELL, I DON'T KNOW IF A STYLISH UNIFORM CAN DO ALL OF *THAT*—PERHAPS ***MOST*** OF THAT.
YOU'RE SOME GENIUS DESIGNER IF YOU CAN MAKE THIS FLOCK OF BIRDBEAKS LOOK LIKE A PROFESSIONAL TEAM.
BUT I'M NOT EXPECTING MIRACLES.
NOT EVEN PRINCESS CELESTIA COULD "POOF" OL' FIREGEM INTO A BOFFYBALL PLAYER WITH ANY SELF-RESPECT.
NOW LET'S GET THIS PRACTICE STARTED!
DOES HE ALWAYS SINGLE OUT FIREGEM LIKE THAT? THE POOR THING DOESN'T SEEM TO BE TAKING IT VERY WELL.
COACH KLAUS IS TOUGH ON ALL OF US, IT'S NOT A BIG DEAL.

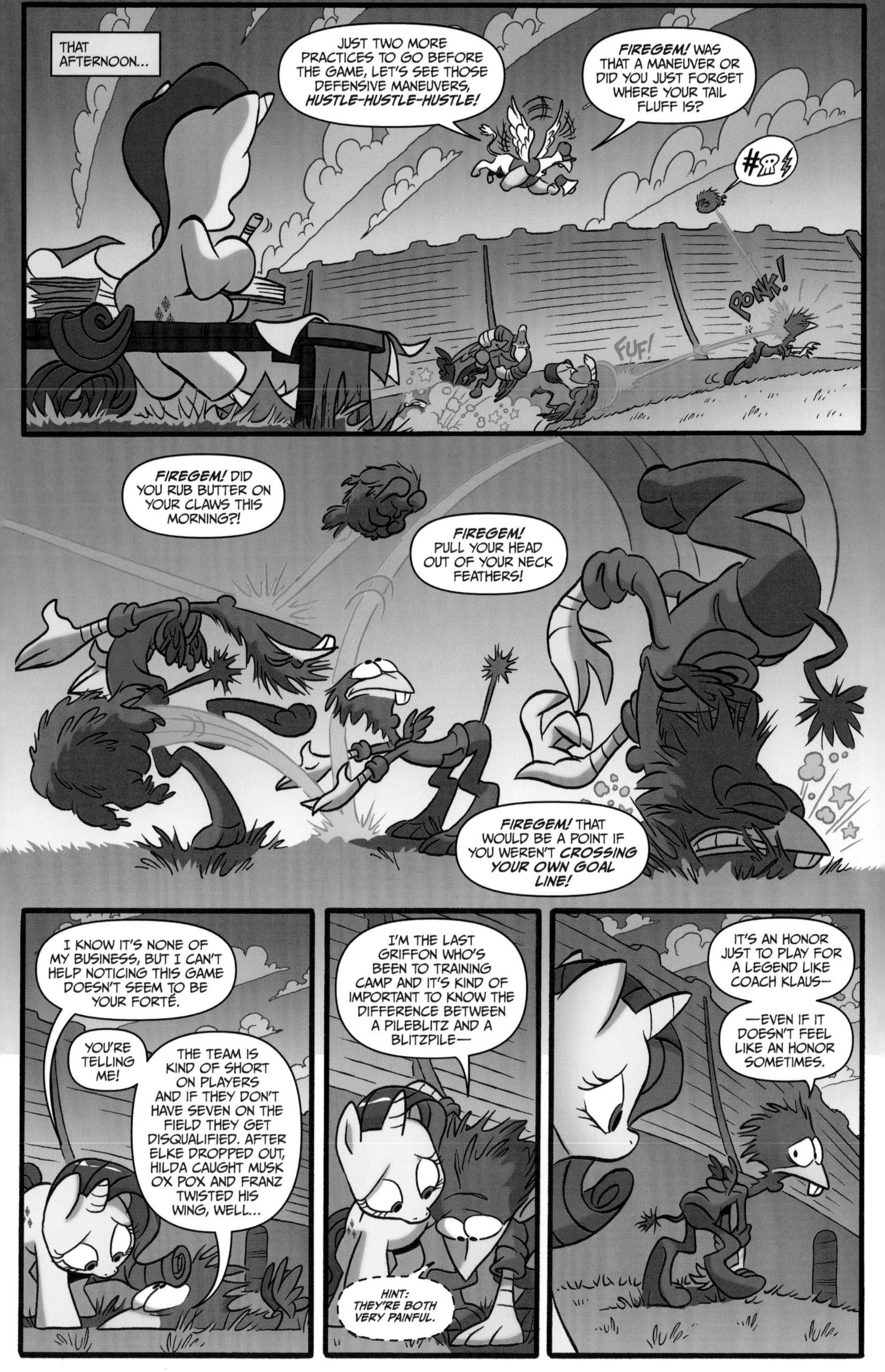
THAT AFTERNOON...
JUST TWO MORE PRACTICES TO GO BEFORE THE GAME, LET'S SEE THOSE DEFENSIVE MANEUVERS, HUSTLE-HUSTLE-HUSTLE!
FIREGEM! WAS THAT A MANEUVER OR DID YOU JUST FORGET WHERE YOUR TAIL FLUFF IS?
FUF!
PONK!
FIREGEM! DID YOU RUB BUTTER ON YOUR CLAWS THIS MORNING?!
FIREGEM! PULL YOUR HEAD OUT OF YOUR NECK FEATHERS!
FIREGEM! THAT WOULD BE A POINT IF YOU WEREN'T CROSSING YOUR OWN GOAL LINE!
I KNOW IT'S NONE OF MY BUSINESS, BUT I CAN'T HELP NOTICING THIS GAME DOESN'T SEEM TO BE YOUR FORTÉ.
YOU'RE TELLING ME!
THE TEAM IS KIND OF SHORT ON PLAYERS AND IF THEY DON'T HAVE SEVEN ON THE FIELD THEY GET DISQUALIFIED. AFTER ELKE DROPPED OUT, HILDA CAUGHT MUSK OX POX AND FRANZ TWISTED HIS WING, WELL...
I'M THE LAST GRIFFON WHO'S BEEN TO TRAINING CAMP AND IT'S KIND OF IMPORTANT TO KNOW THE DIFFERENCE BETWEEN A PILEBLITZ AND A BLITZPILE—
HINT: THEY'RE BOTH VERY PAINFUL.
IT'S AN HONOR JUST TO PLAY FOR A LEGEND LIKE COACH KLAUS—
—EVEN IF IT DOESN'T FEEL LIKE AN HONOR SOMETIMES.

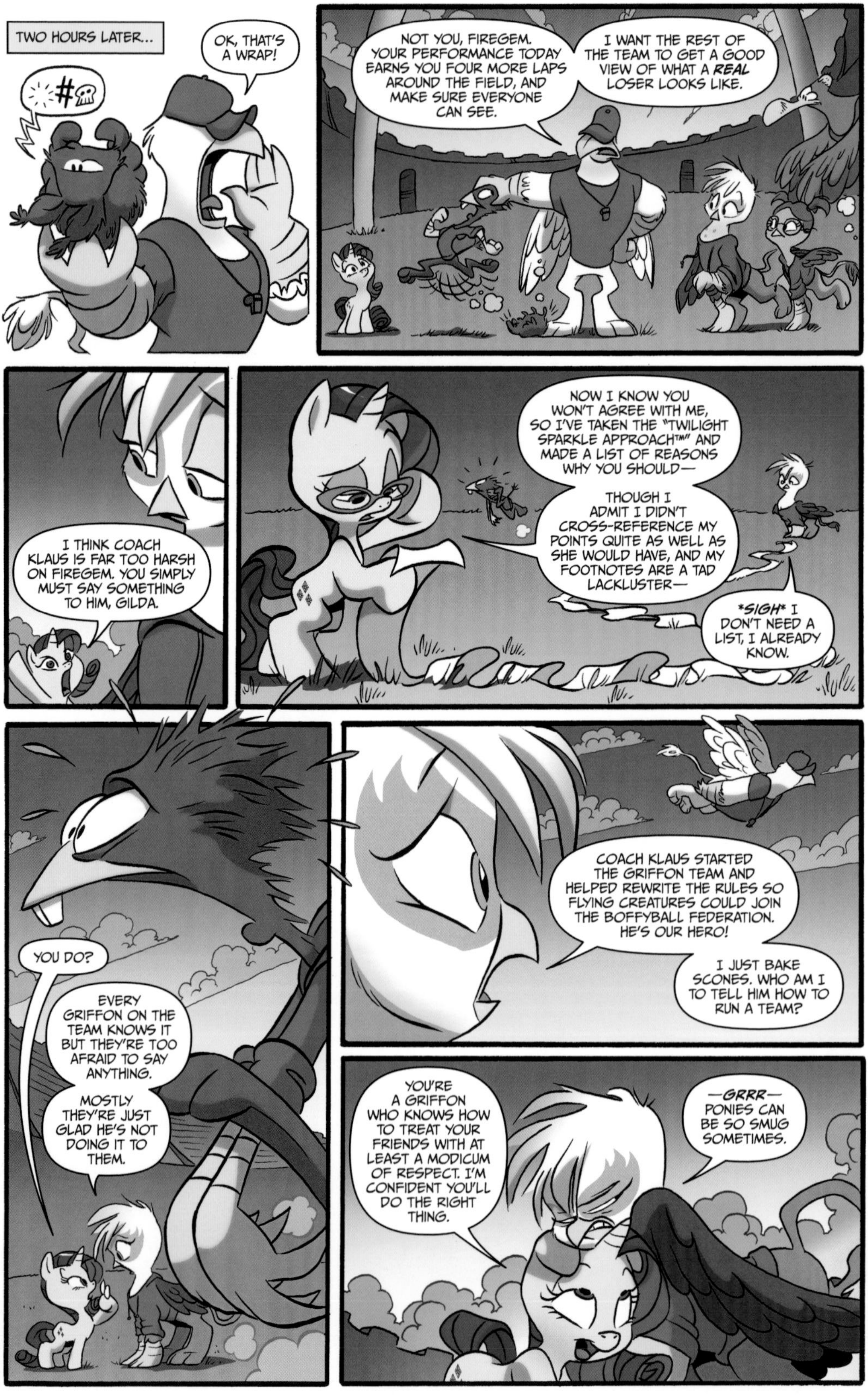
TWO HOURS LATER...
OK, THAT'S A WRAP!
#
NOT YOU, FIREGEM. YOUR PERFORMANCE TODAY EARNS YOU FOUR MORE LAPS AROUND THE FIELD, AND MAKE SURE EVERYONE CAN SEE.
I WANT THE REST OF THE TEAM TO GET A GOOD VIEW OF WHAT A *REAL* LOSER LOOKS LIKE.
I THINK COACH KLAUS IS FAR TOO HARSH ON FIREGEM. YOU SIMPLY MUST SAY SOMETHING TO HIM, GILDA.
NOW I KNOW YOU WON'T AGREE WITH ME, SO I'VE TAKEN THE "TWILIGHT SPARKLE APPROACH™" AND MADE A LIST OF REASONS WHY YOU SHOULD—
THOUGH I ADMIT I DIDN'T CROSS-REFERENCE MY POINTS QUITE AS WELL AS SHE WOULD HAVE, AND MY FOOTNOTES ARE A TAD LACKLUSTER—
SIGH I DON'T NEED A LIST, I ALREADY KNOW.
YOU DO?
EVERY GRIFFON ON THE TEAM KNOWS IT BUT THEY'RE TOO AFRAID TO SAY ANYTHING.
MOSTLY THEY'RE JUST GLAD HE'S NOT DOING IT TO THEM.
COACH KLAUS STARTED THE GRIFFON TEAM AND HELPED REWRITE THE RULES SO FLYING CREATURES COULD JOIN THE BOFFYBALL FEDERATION. HE'S OUR HERO!
I JUST BAKE SCONES. WHO AM I TO TELL HIM HOW TO RUN A TEAM?
YOU'RE A GRIFFON WHO KNOWS HOW TO TREAT YOUR FRIENDS WITH AT LEAST A MODICUM OF RESPECT. I'M CONFIDENT YOU'LL DO THE RIGHT THING.
—*GRRR*— PONIES CAN BE SO SMUG SOMETIMES.

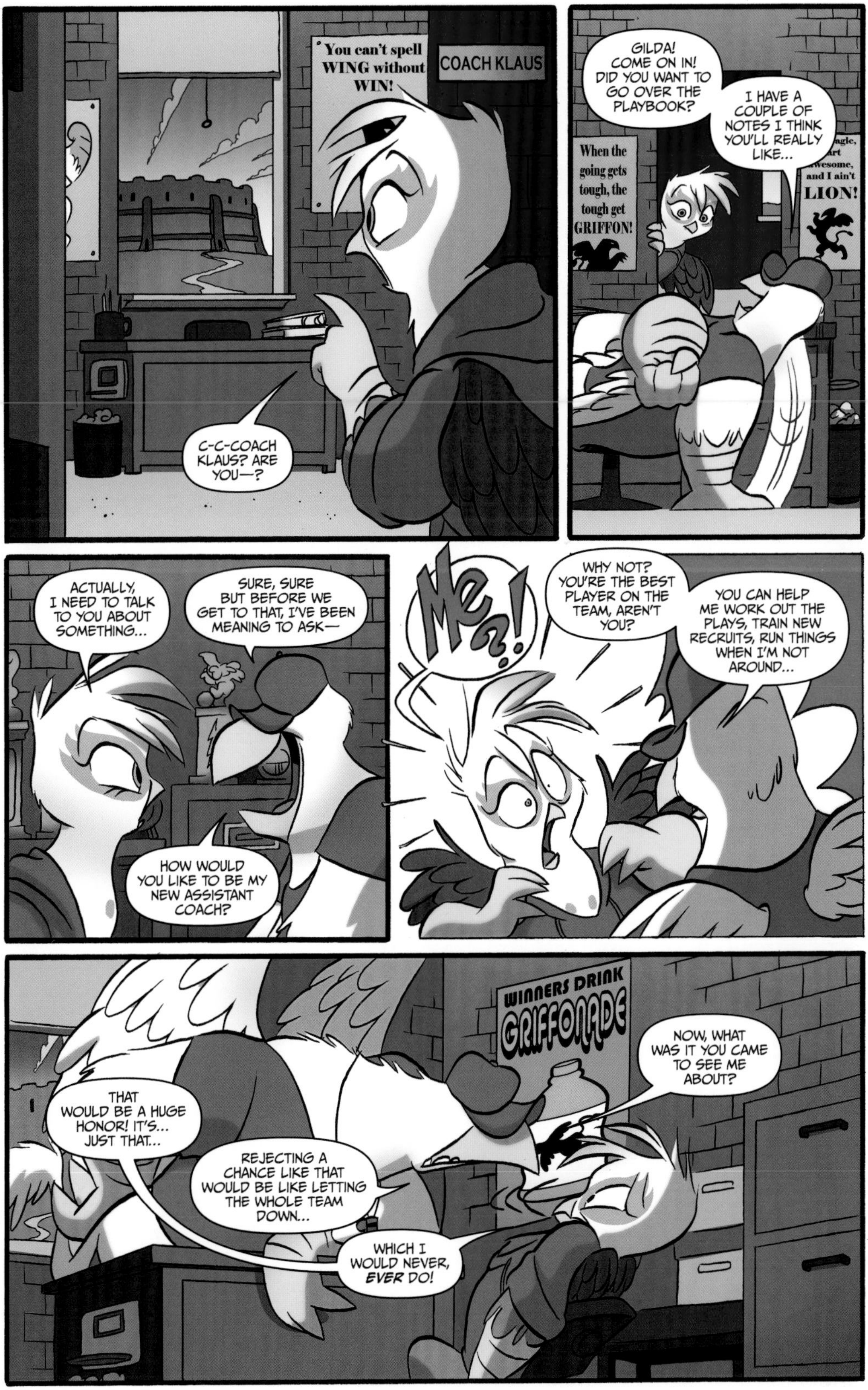
You can't spell WING without WIN!
COACH KLAUS
C-C-COACH KLAUS? ARE YOU—?
GILDA! COME ON IN! DID YOU WANT TO GO OVER THE PLAYBOOK?
I HAVE A COUPLE OF NOTES I THINK YOU'LL REALLY LIKE...
When the going gets tough, the tough get GRIFFON!
and I ain't LION!
ACTUALLY, I NEED TO TALK TO YOU ABOUT SOMETHING...
SURE, SURE BUT BEFORE WE GET TO THAT, I'VE BEEN MEANING TO ASK—
HOW WOULD YOU LIKE TO BE MY NEW ASSISTANT COACH?
ME?!
WHY NOT? YOU'RE THE BEST PLAYER ON THE TEAM, AREN'T YOU?
YOU CAN HELP ME WORK OUT THE PLAYS, TRAIN NEW RECRUITS, RUN THINGS WHEN I'M NOT AROUND...
WINNERS DRINK GRIFFONADE
THAT WOULD BE A HUGE HONOR! IT'S... JUST THAT...
NOW, WHAT WAS IT YOU CAME TO SEE ME ABOUT?
REJECTING A CHANCE LIKE THAT WOULD BE LIKE LETTING THE WHOLE TEAM DOWN...
WHICH I WOULD NEVER, *EVER* DO!

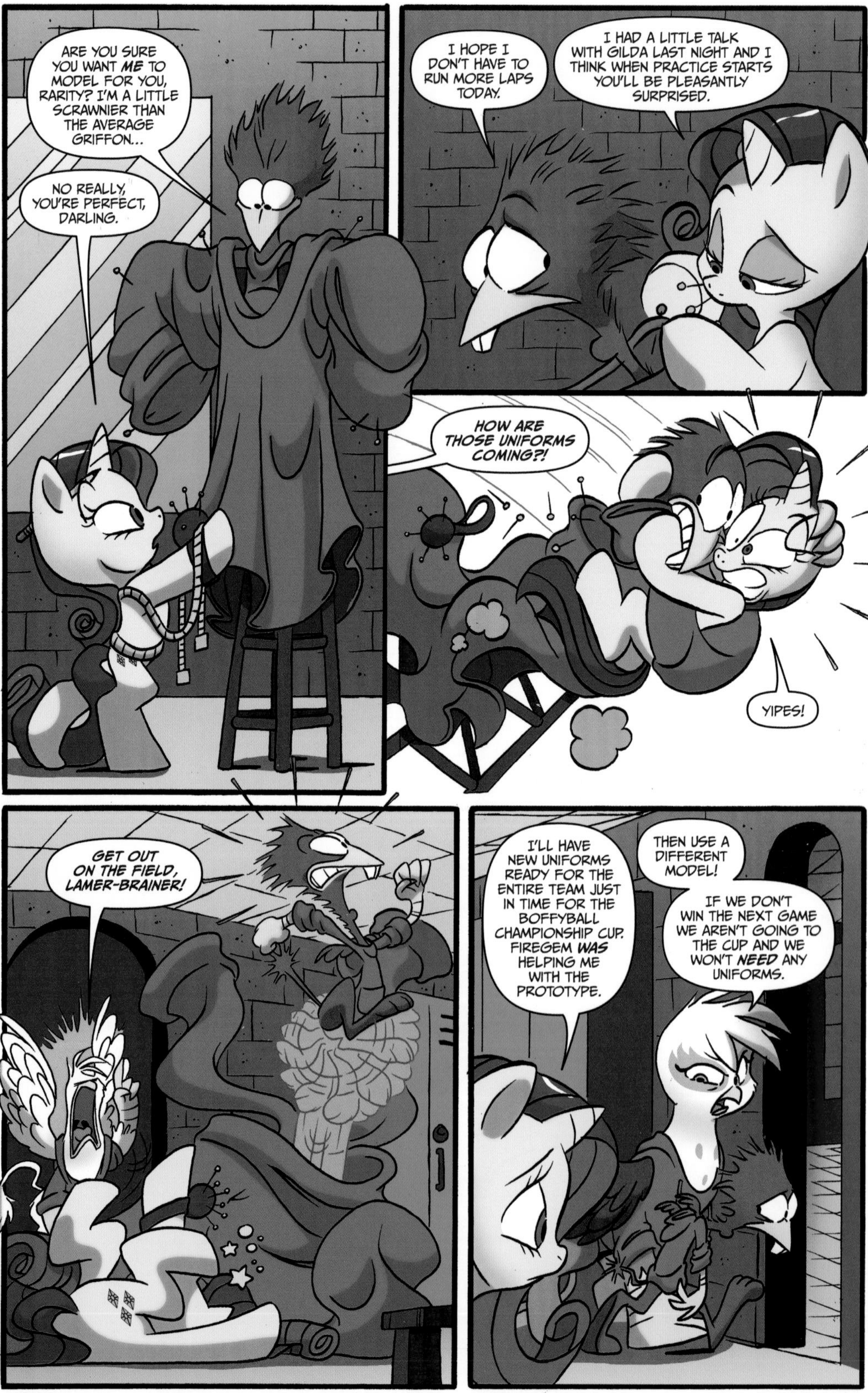
ARE YOU SURE YOU WANT ME TO MODEL FOR YOU, RARITY? I'M A LITTLE SCRAWNIER THAN THE AVERAGE GRIFFON...
NO REALLY, YOU'RE PERFECT, DARLING.
I HOPE I DON'T HAVE TO RUN MORE LAPS TODAY.
I HAD A LITTLE TALK WITH GILDA LAST NIGHT AND I THINK WHEN PRACTICE STARTS YOU'LL BE PLEASANTLY SURPRISED.
HOW ARE THOSE UNIFORMS COMING?!
YIPES!
GET OUT ON THE FIELD, LAMER-BRAINER!
I'LL HAVE NEW UNIFORMS READY FOR THE ENTIRE TEAM JUST IN TIME FOR THE BOFFYBALL CHAMPIONSHIP CUP. FIREGEM WAS HELPING ME WITH THE PROTOTYPE.
THEN USE A DIFFERENT MODEL!
IF WE DON'T WIN THE NEXT GAME WE AREN'T GOING TO THE CUP AND WE WON'T NEED ANY UNIFORMS.

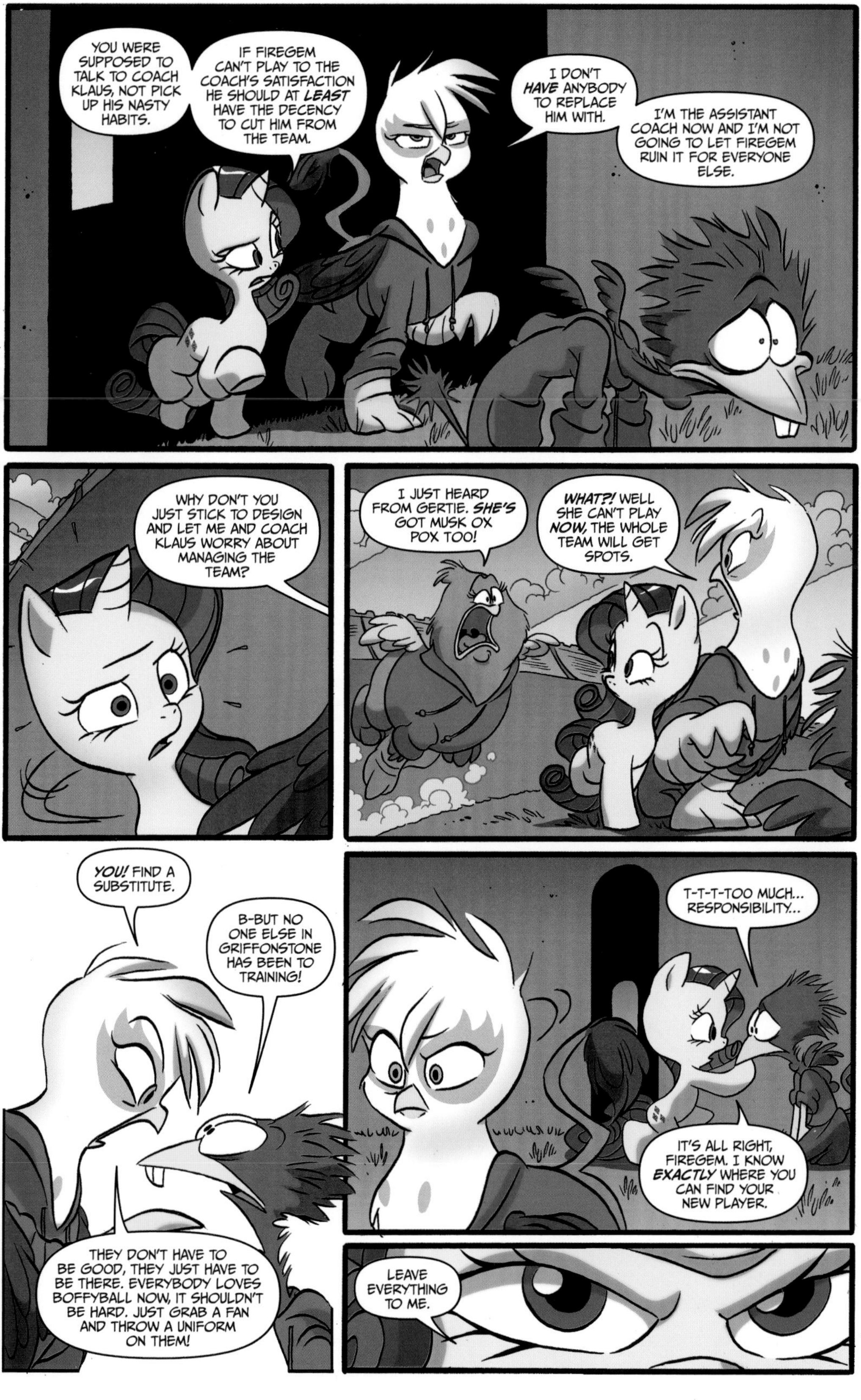

YOU WERE SUPPOSED TO TALK TO COACH KLAUS, NOT PICK UP HIS NASTY HABITS.
IF FIREGEM CAN'T PLAY TO THE COACH'S SATISFACTION HE SHOULD AT LEAST HAVE THE DECENCY TO CUT HIM FROM THE TEAM.
I DON'T HAVE ANYBODY TO REPLACE HIM WITH.
I'M THE ASSISTANT COACH NOW AND I'M NOT GOING TO LET FIREGEM RUIN IT FOR EVERYONE ELSE.
WHY DON'T YOU JUST STICK TO DESIGN AND LET ME AND COACH KLAUS WORRY ABOUT MANAGING THE TEAM?
I JUST HEARD FROM GERTIE. SHE'S GOT MUSK OX POX TOO!
WHAT?! WELL SHE CAN'T PLAY NOW, THE WHOLE TEAM WILL GET SPOTS.
YOU! FIND A SUBSTITUTE.
B-BUT NO ONE ELSE IN GRIFFONSTONE HAS BEEN TO TRAINING!
THEY DON'T HAVE TO BE GOOD, THEY JUST HAVE TO BE THERE. EVERYBODY LOVES BOFFYBALL NOW, IT SHOULDN'T BE HARD. JUST GRAB A FAN AND THROW A UNIFORM ON THEM!
T-T-T-TOO MUCH... RESPONSIBILITY...
IT'S ALL RIGHT, FIREGEM. I KNOW EXACTLY WHERE YOU CAN FIND YOUR NEW PLAYER.
LEAVE EVERYTHING TO ME.

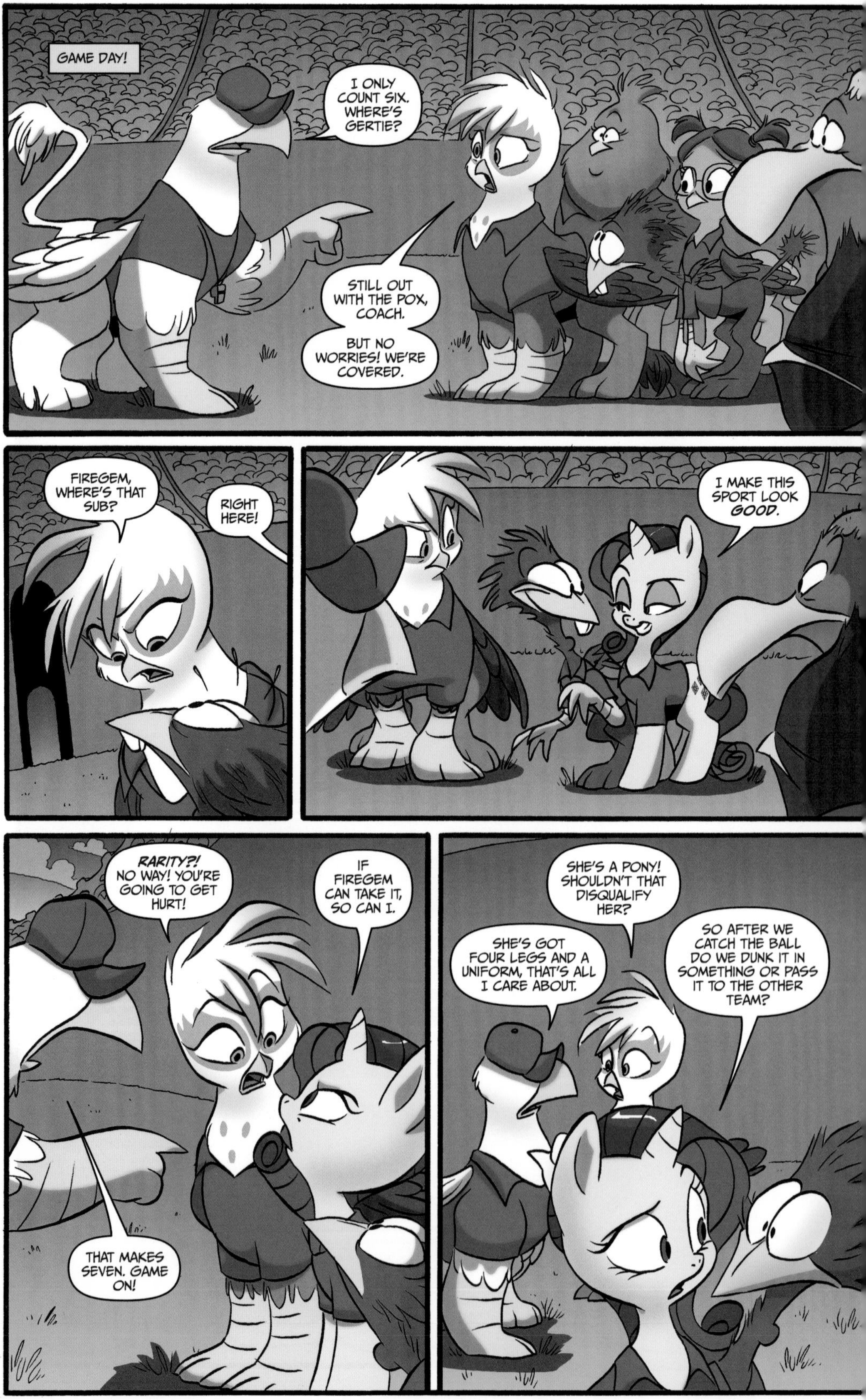
GAME DAY!
I ONLY COUNT SIX. WHERE'S GERTIE?
STILL OUT WITH THE POX, COACH.
BUT NO WORRIES! WE'RE COVERED.
FIREGEM, WHERE'S THAT SUB?
RIGHT HERE!
I MAKE THIS SPORT LOOK *GOOD*.
RARITY?! NO WAY! YOU'RE GOING TO GET HURT!
IF FIREGEM CAN TAKE IT, SO CAN I.
THAT MAKES SEVEN. GAME ON!
SHE'S A PONY! SHOULDN'T THAT DISQUALIFY HER?
SHE'S GOT FOUR LEGS AND A UNIFORM, THAT'S ALL I CARE ABOUT.
SO AFTER WE CATCH THE BALL DO WE DUNK IT IN SOMETHING OR PASS IT TO THE OTHER TEAM?

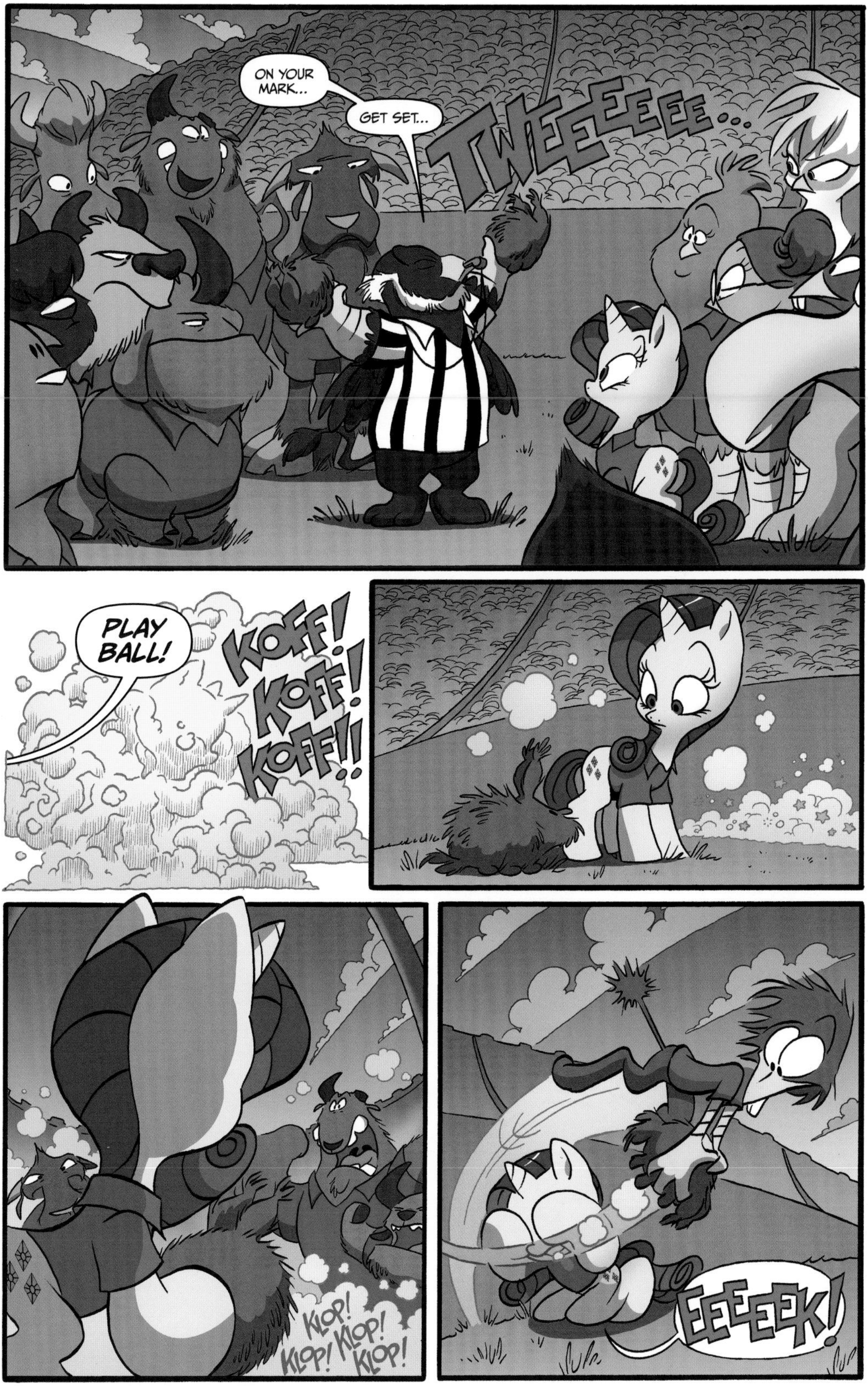
ON YOUR MARK...
GET SET...
TWEEEEEEE...
PLAY BALL!
KOFF! KOFF! KOFF!!
KLOP! KLOP! KLOP! KLOP!
EEEEEK!

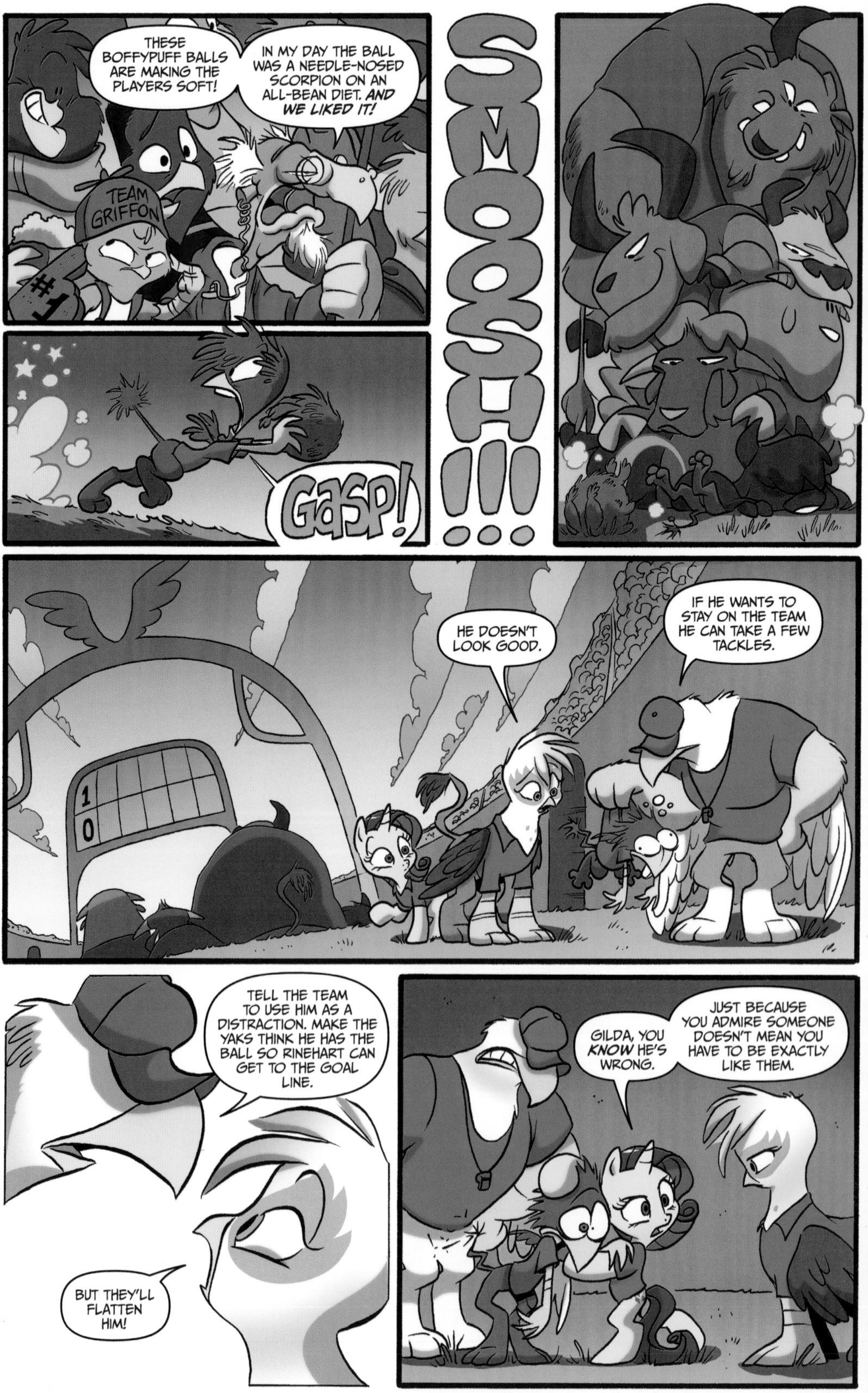
THESE BOFFYPUFF BALLS ARE MAKING THE PLAYERS SOFT!
IN MY DAY THE BALL WAS A NEEDLE-NOSED SCORPION ON AN ALL-BEAN DIET. AND WE LIKED IT!
TEAM GRIFFON
#1
GASP!
SMOOSH!!!...
HE DOESN'T LOOK GOOD.
IF HE WANTS TO STAY ON THE TEAM HE CAN TAKE A FEW TACKLES.
1
0
TELL THE TEAM TO USE HIM AS A DISTRACTION. MAKE THE YAKS THINK HE HAS THE BALL SO RINEHART CAN GET TO THE GOAL LINE.
BUT THEY'LL FLATTEN HIM!
GILDA, YOU KNOW HE'S WRONG.
JUST BECAUSE YOU ADMIRE SOMEONE DOESN'T MEAN YOU HAVE TO BE EXACTLY LIKE THEM.

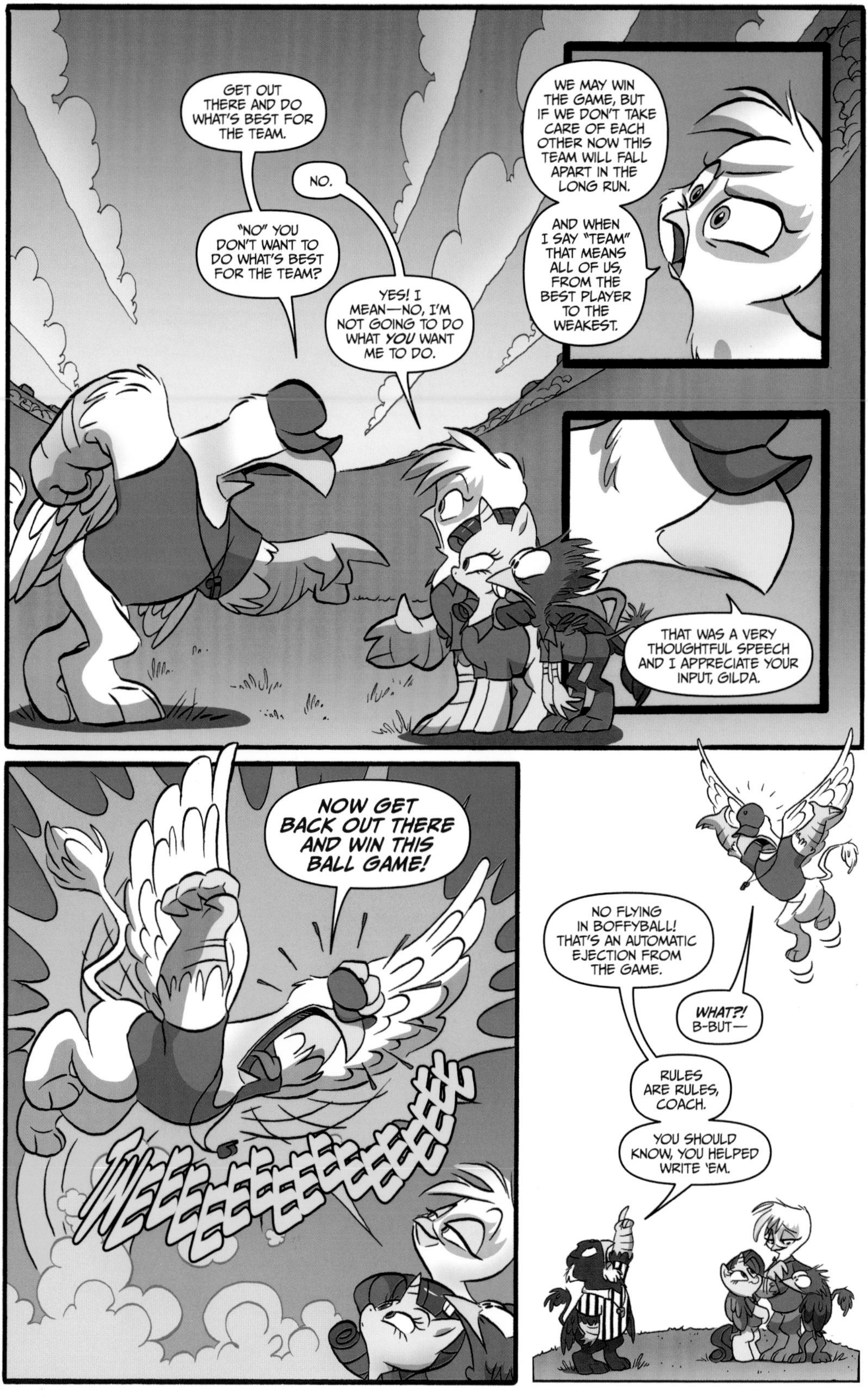
GET OUT THERE AND DO WHAT'S BEST FOR THE TEAM.
NO.
"NO" YOU DON'T WANT TO DO WHAT'S BEST FOR THE TEAM?
YES! I MEAN—NO, I'M NOT GOING TO DO WHAT *YOU* WANT ME TO DO.
WE MAY WIN THE GAME, BUT IF WE DON'T TAKE CARE OF EACH OTHER NOW THIS TEAM WILL FALL APART IN THE LONG RUN.
AND WHEN I SAY "TEAM" THAT MEANS ALL OF US, FROM THE BEST PLAYER TO THE WEAKEST.
THAT WAS A VERY THOUGHTFUL SPEECH AND I APPRECIATE YOUR INPUT, GILDA.
NOW GET BACK OUT THERE AND WIN THIS BALL GAME!
TWEEEEEEEEEEEEEEEEEEEEET
NO FLYING IN BOFFYBALL! THAT'S AN AUTOMATIC EJECTION FROM THE GAME.
WHAT?! B-BUT—
RULES ARE RULES, COACH.
YOU SHOULD KNOW, YOU HELPED WRITE 'EM.

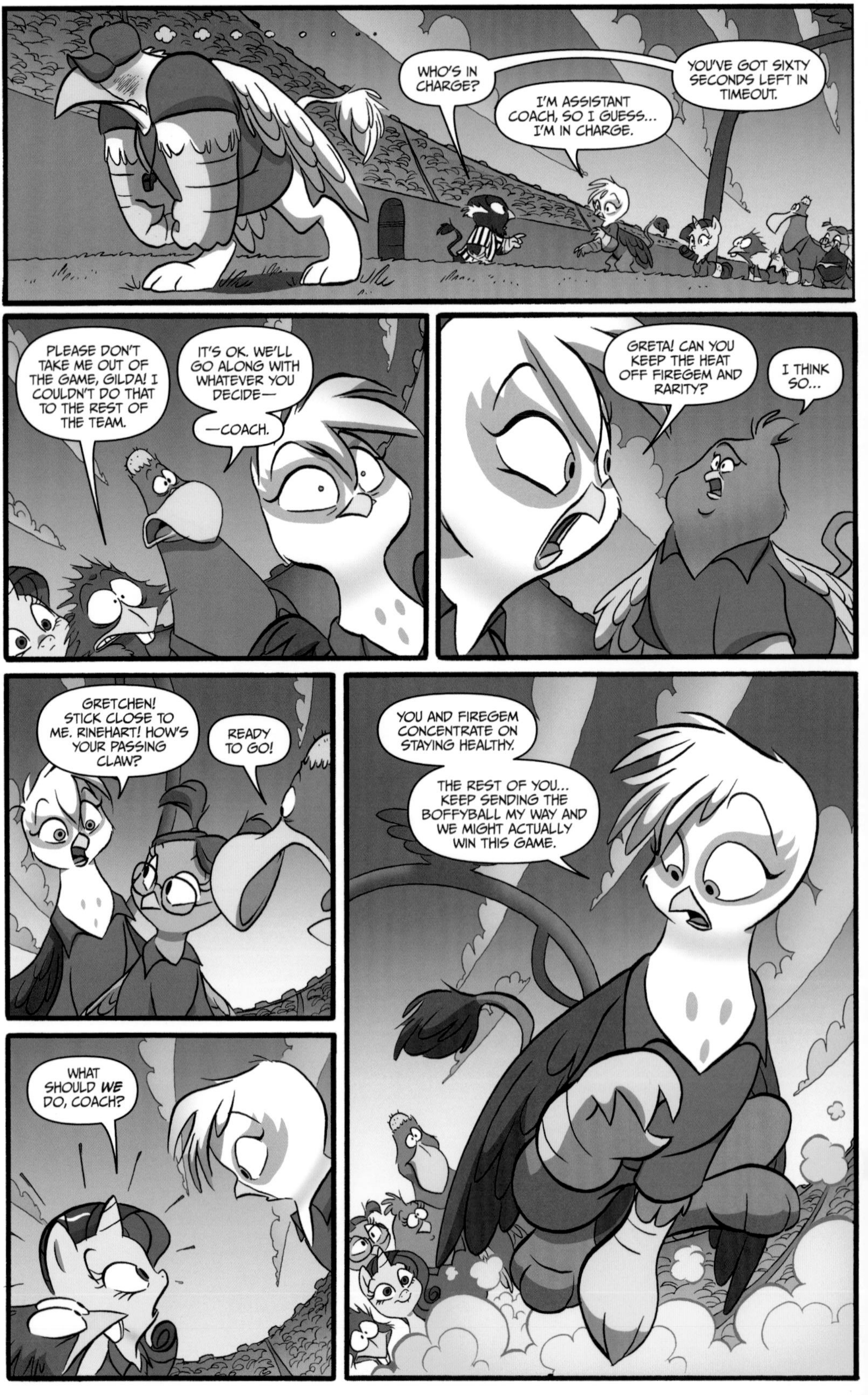
WHO'S IN CHARGE?
YOU'VE GOT SIXTY SECONDS LEFT IN TIMEOUT.
I'M ASSISTANT COACH, SO I GUESS... I'M IN CHARGE.
PLEASE DON'T TAKE ME OUT OF THE GAME, GILDA! I COULDN'T DO THAT TO THE REST OF THE TEAM.
IT'S OK. WE'LL GO ALONG WITH WHATEVER YOU DECIDE—
—COACH.
GRETA! CAN YOU KEEP THE HEAT OFF FIREGEM AND RARITY?
I THINK SO...
GRETCHEN! STICK CLOSE TO ME. RINEHART! HOW'S YOUR PASSING CLAW?
READY TO GO!
WHAT SHOULD *WE* DO, COACH?
YOU AND FIREGEM CONCENTRATE ON STAYING HEALTHY.
THE REST OF YOU... KEEP SENDING THE BOFFYBALL MY WAY AND WE MIGHT ACTUALLY WIN THIS GAME.

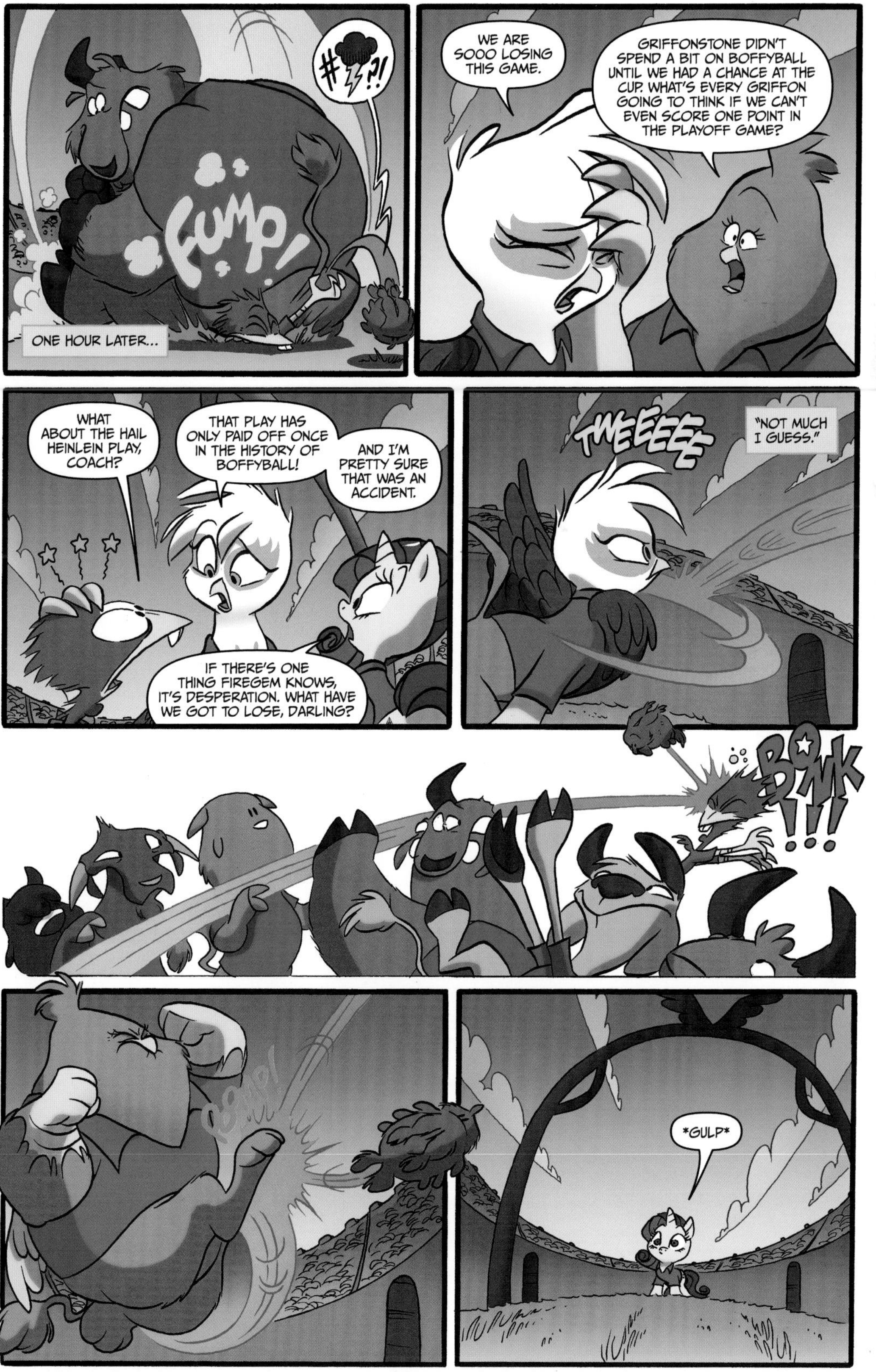

#?!
FUMP!
ONE HOUR LATER...
WE ARE SOOO LOSING THIS GAME.
GRIFFONSTONE DIDN'T SPEND A BIT ON BOFFYBALL UNTIL WE HAD A CHANCE AT THE CUP. WHAT'S EVERY GRIFFON GOING TO THINK IF WE CAN'T EVEN SCORE ONE POINT IN THE PLAYOFF GAME?
WHAT ABOUT THE HAIL HEINLEIN PLAY, COACH?
THAT PLAY HAS ONLY PAID OFF ONCE IN THE HISTORY OF BOFFYBALL!
AND I'M PRETTY SURE THAT WAS AN ACCIDENT.
IF THERE'S ONE THING FIREGEM KNOWS, IT'S DESPERATION. WHAT HAVE WE GOT TO LOSE, DARLING?
TWEEEEE
"NOT MUCH I GUESS."
BONK!!!
GULP

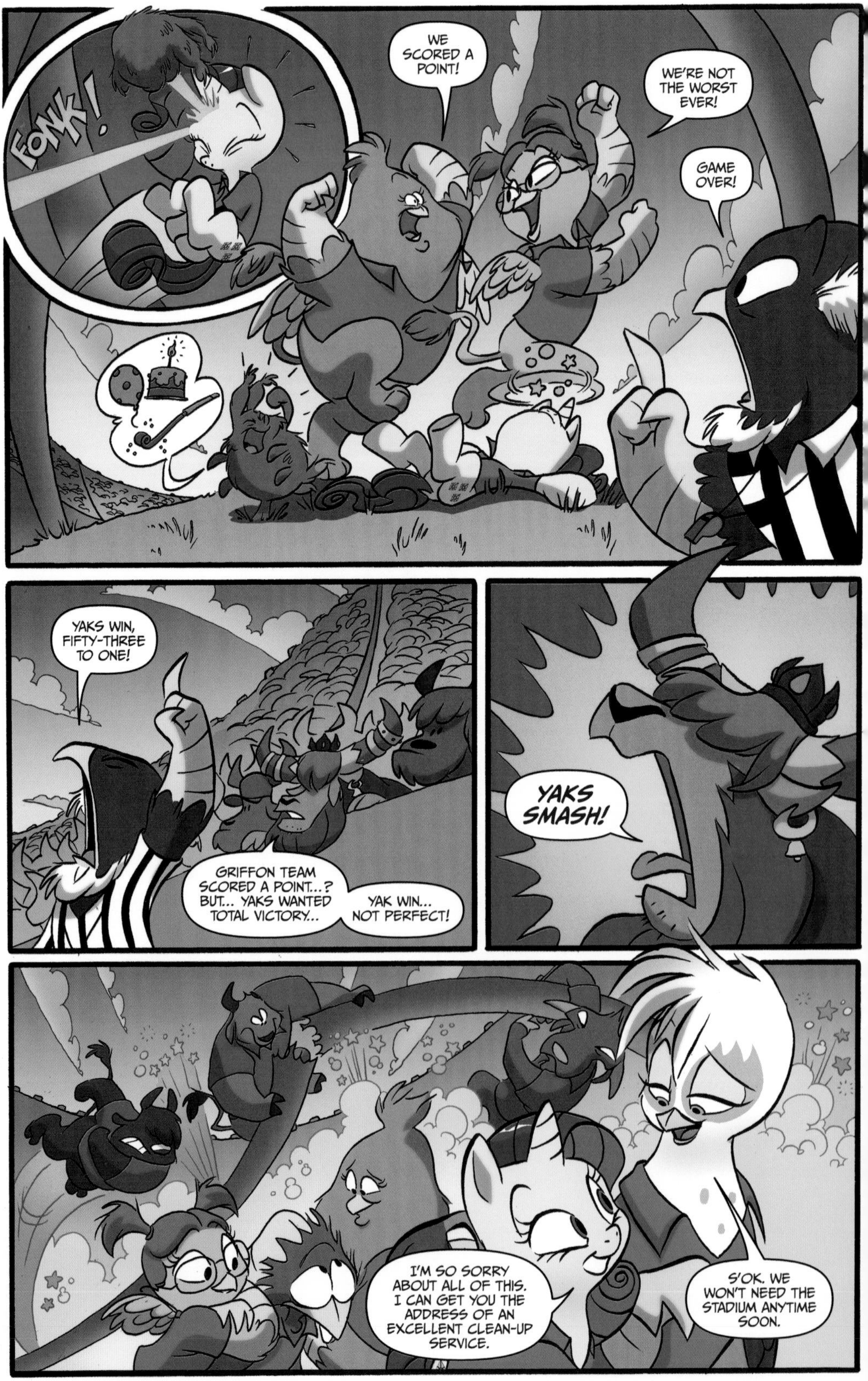
FONK!
WE SCORED A POINT!
WE'RE NOT THE WORST EVER!
GAME OVER!
YAKS WIN, FIFTY-THREE TO ONE!
GRIFFON TEAM SCORED A POINT...? BUT... YAKS WANTED TOTAL VICTORY...
YAK WIN... NOT PERFECT!
YAKS SMASH!
I'M SO SORRY ABOUT ALL OF THIS. I CAN GET YOU THE ADDRESS OF AN EXCELLENT CLEAN-UP SERVICE.
S'OK. WE WON'T NEED THE STADIUM ANYTIME SOON.

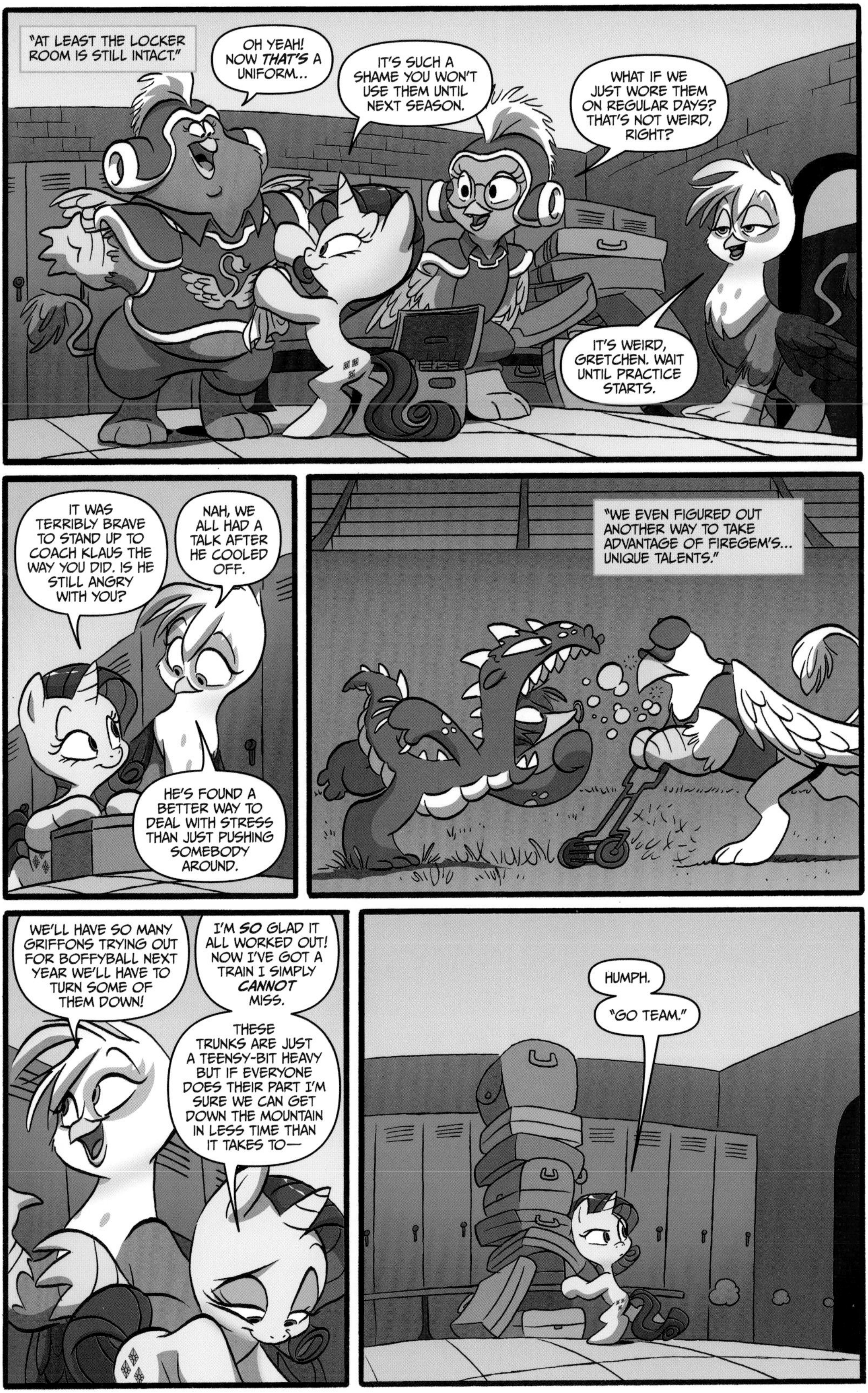
"AT LEAST THE LOCKER ROOM IS STILL INTACT."
OH YEAH! NOW *THAT'S* A UNIFORM...
IT'S SUCH A SHAME YOU WON'T USE THEM UNTIL NEXT SEASON.
WHAT IF WE JUST WORE THEM ON REGULAR DAYS? THAT'S NOT WEIRD, RIGHT?
IT'S WEIRD, GRETCHEN. WAIT UNTIL PRACTICE STARTS.
IT WAS TERRIBLY BRAVE TO STAND UP TO COACH KLAUS THE WAY YOU DID. IS HE STILL ANGRY WITH YOU?
NAH, WE ALL HAD A TALK AFTER HE COOLED OFF.
HE'S FOUND A BETTER WAY TO DEAL WITH STRESS THAN JUST PUSHING SOMEBODY AROUND.
"WE EVEN FIGURED OUT ANOTHER WAY TO TAKE ADVANTAGE OF FIREGEM'S... UNIQUE TALENTS."
WE'LL HAVE SO MANY GRIFFONS TRYING OUT FOR BOFFYBALL NEXT YEAR WE'LL HAVE TO TURN SOME OF THEM DOWN!
I'M *SO* GLAD IT ALL WORKED OUT! NOW I'VE GOT A TRAIN I SIMPLY *CANNOT* MISS.
THESE TRUNKS ARE JUST A TEENSY-BIT HEAVY BUT IF EVERYONE DOES THEIR PART I'M SURE WE CAN GET DOWN THE MOUNTAIN IN LESS TIME THAN IT TAKES TO—
HUMPH.
"GO TEAM."

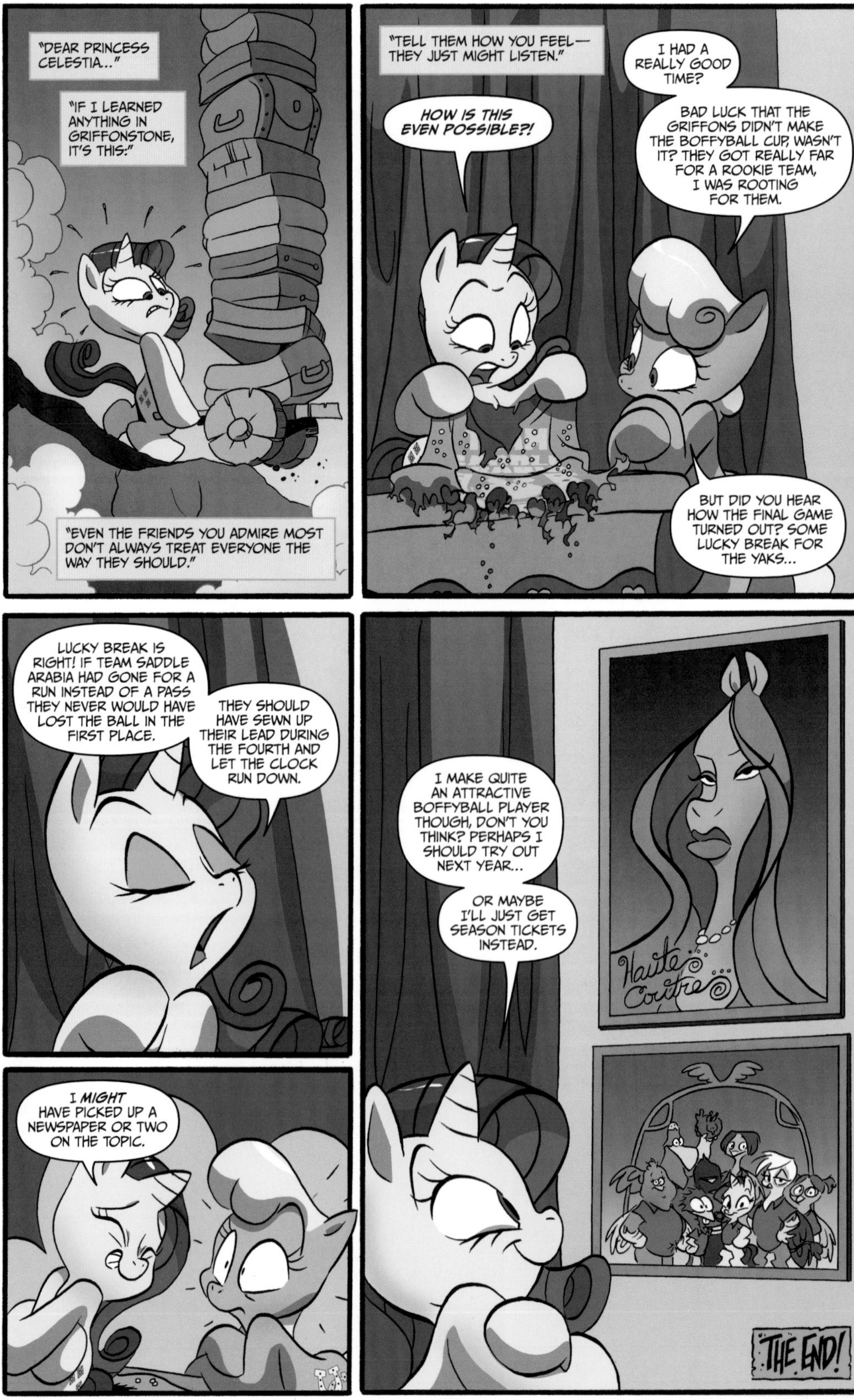
"DEAR PRINCESS CELESTIA..."
"IF I LEARNED ANYTHING IN GRIFFONSTONE, IT'S THIS:"
"EVEN THE FRIENDS YOU ADMIRE MOST DON'T ALWAYS TREAT EVERYONE THE WAY THEY SHOULD."
"TELL THEM HOW YOU FEEL— THEY JUST MIGHT LISTEN."
I HAD A REALLY GOOD TIME?
HOW IS THIS EVEN POSSIBLE?!
BAD LUCK THAT THE GRIFFONS DIDN'T MAKE THE BOFFYBALL CUP, WASN'T IT? THEY GOT REALLY FAR FOR A ROOKIE TEAM, I WAS ROOTING FOR THEM.
BUT DID YOU HEAR HOW THE FINAL GAME TURNED OUT? SOME LUCKY BREAK FOR THE YAKS...
LUCKY BREAK IS RIGHT! IF TEAM SADDLE ARABIA HAD GONE FOR A RUN INSTEAD OF A PASS THEY NEVER WOULD HAVE LOST THE BALL IN THE FIRST PLACE.
THEY SHOULD HAVE SEWN UP THEIR LEAD DURING THE FOURTH AND LET THE CLOCK RUN DOWN.
I *MIGHT* HAVE PICKED UP A NEWSPAPER OR TWO ON THE TOPIC.
I MAKE QUITE AN ATTRACTIVE BOFFYBALL PLAYER THOUGH, DON'T YOU THINK? PERHAPS I SHOULD TRY OUT NEXT YEAR...
OR MAYBE I'LL JUST GET SEASON TICKETS INSTEAD.
Haute Coutre
THE END!

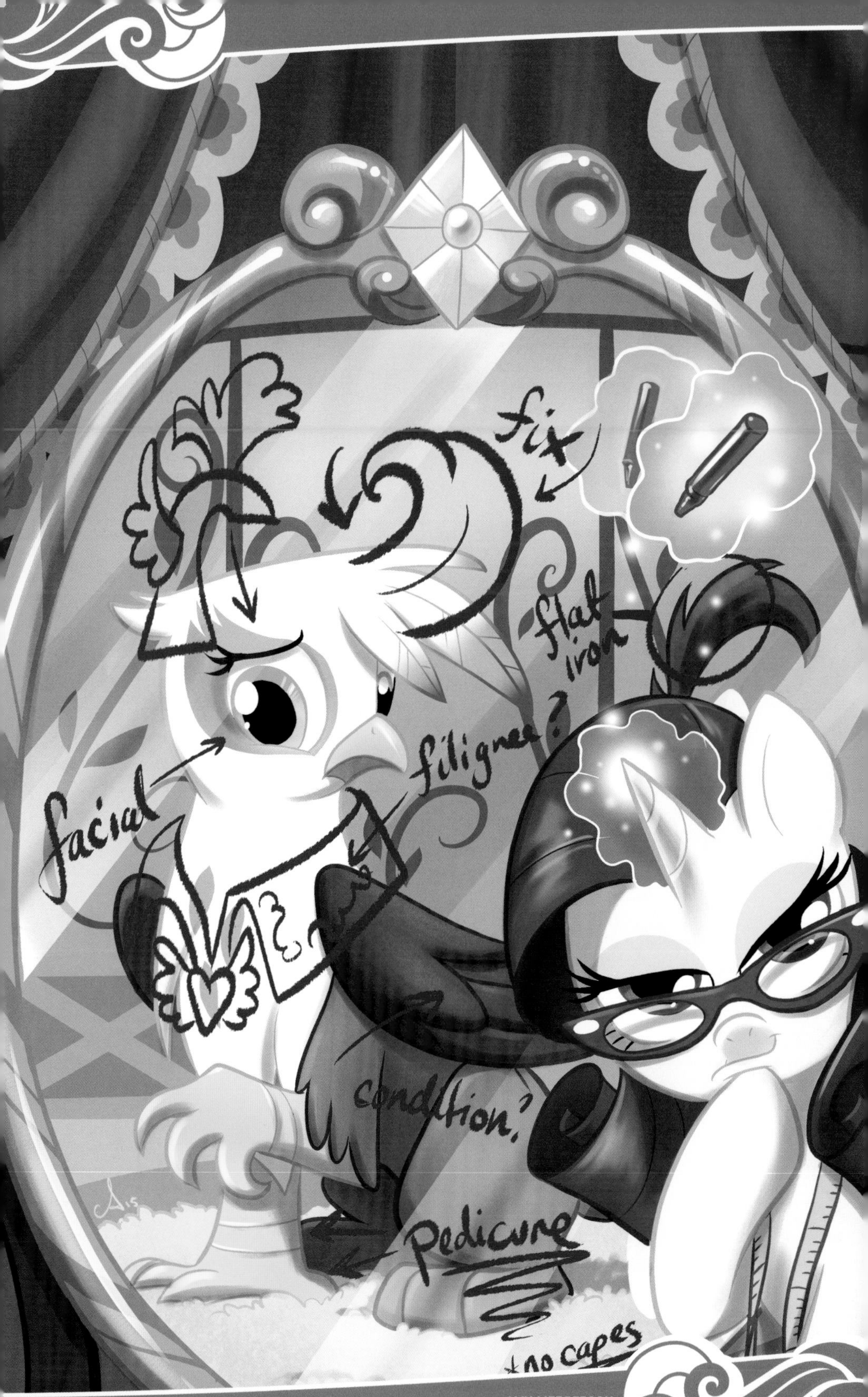
fix
flat iron
filigree?
facial
condition?
pedicure
*no capes

art by AMY MEBBERSON

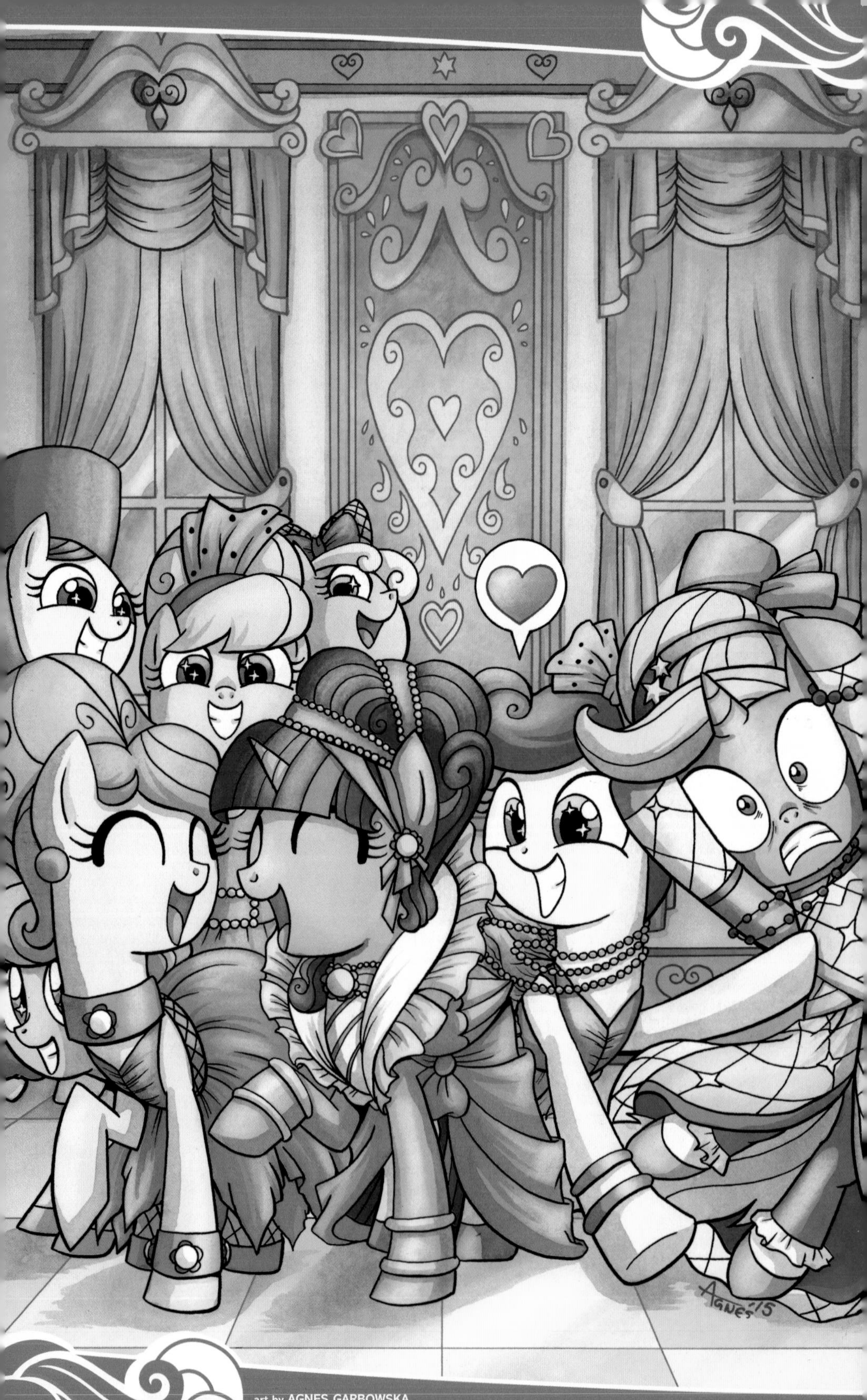
Agnes '15

art by AGNES GARBOWSKA

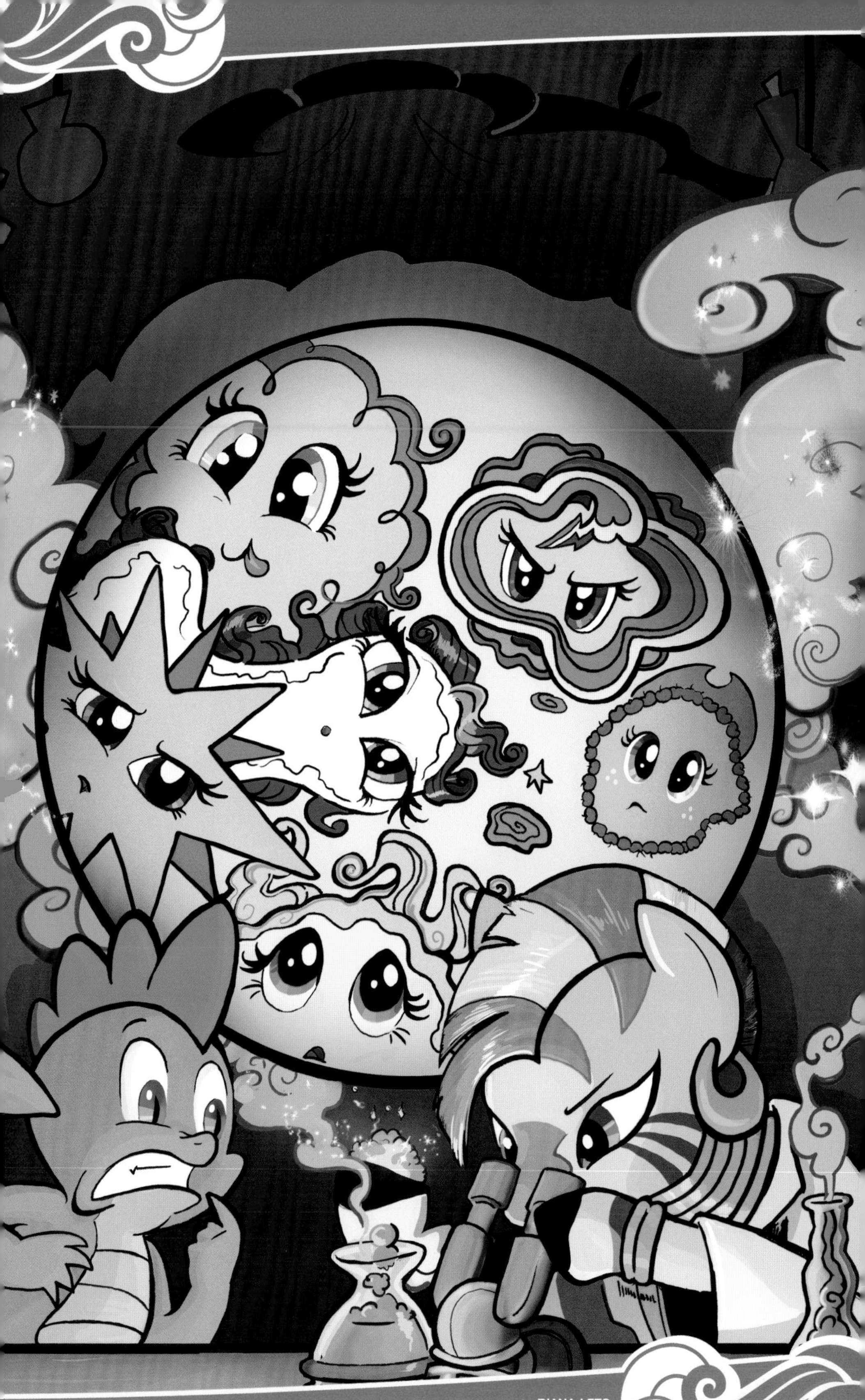
art by DIANA LETO

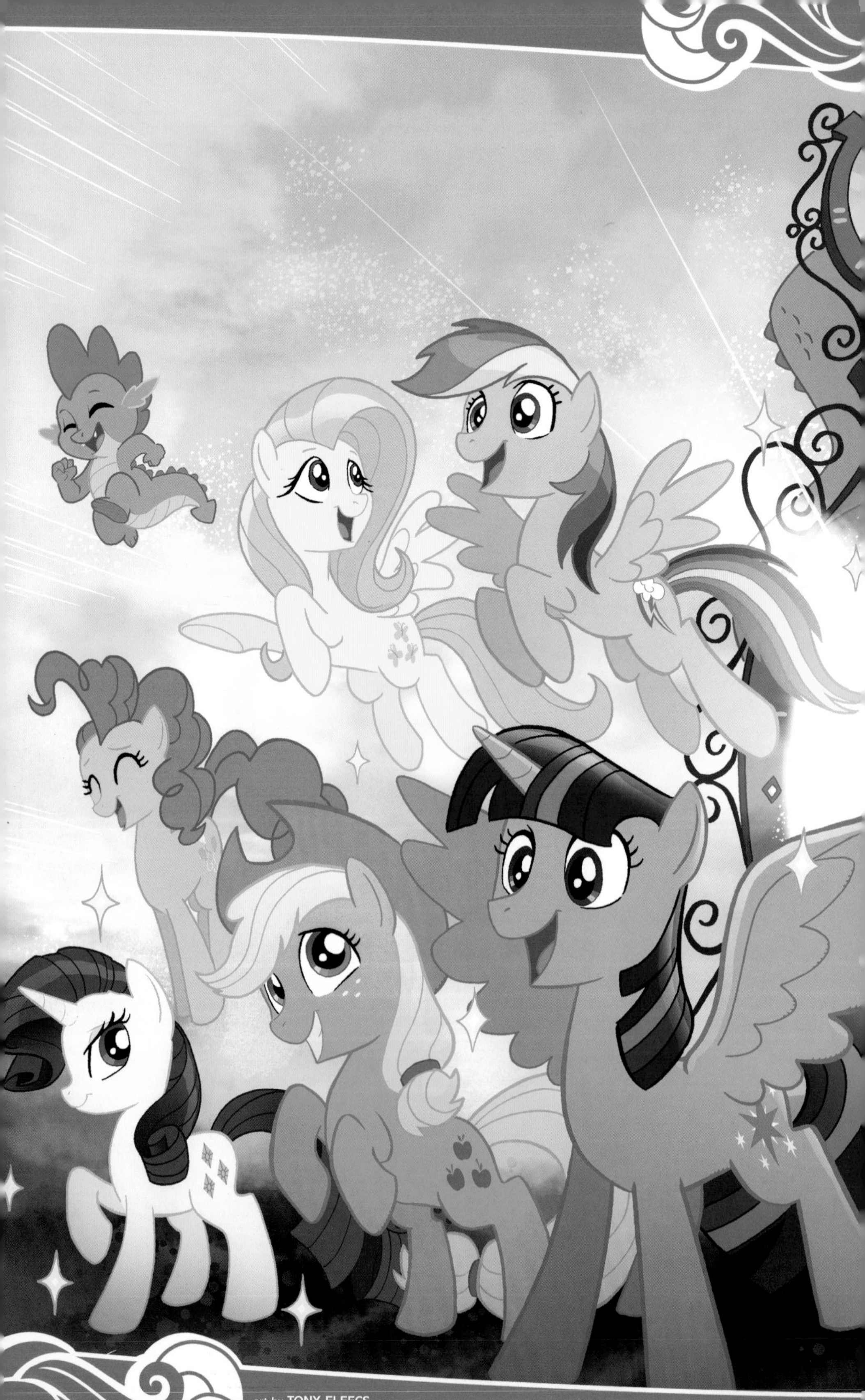

art by TONY FLEECS

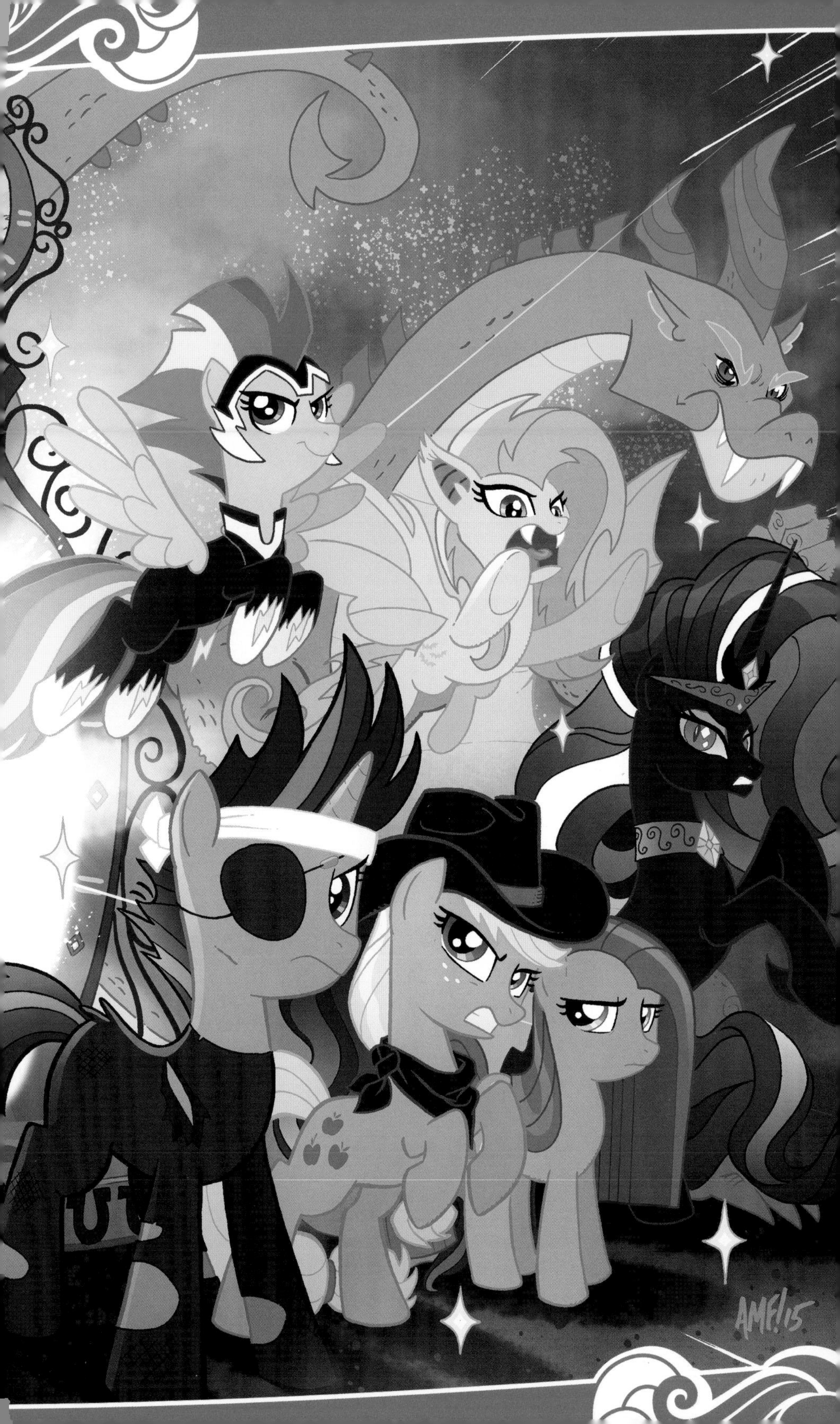
AMF!15

THE ONGOING ADVENTURES OF EVERYONE'S FAVORITE PONIES!

PONIES UNITE IN THIS TEAM-UP SERIES!

My Little Pony:
Friendship is Magic, Vol. 1
TPB • $17.99 • 978-1613776056

My Little Pony:
Friendship is Magic, Vol. 2
TPB • $17.99 • 978-1613777602

My Little Pony:
Friends Forever, Vol. 1
TPB • $17.99 • 978-1613779811

My Little Pony:
Friends Forever, Vol. 2
TPB • $17.99 • 978-163140159

SPECIALLY SELECTED TALES TO TAKE WITH YOU ON THE GO!

GET THE WHOLE STORY WITH THE MY LITTLE PONY OMNIBUS!

My Little Pony:
Adventures in Friendship, Vol. 1
TPB • $9.99 • 978-1631401893

My Little Pony:
Adventures in Friendship, Vol. 2
TPB • $9.99 • 978-1631402258

My Little Pony:
Omnibus, Vol. 1
TPB • $24.99 • 978-1631401404

My Little Pony:
Omnibus, Vol. 2
TPB • $24.99 • 978-1631404040

 WWW.IDWPUBLISHING.COM

ON SALE NOW